THE
flamingo
ANTHOLOGY
OF
NEW ZEALAND
**SHORT
STORIES**

THE
flamingo
ANTHOLOGY
OF
NEW ZEALAND
SHORT
STORIES

Edited by

MICHAEL MORRISSEY

Flamingo

An imprint of HarperCollins*Publishers*

Flamingo
An imprint of HarperCollinsPublishers

First published 2000
Reprinted 2000

HarperCollinsPublishers (New Zealand) Limited
P.O. Box 1, Auckland

ISBN 1 86950 335 X

Designed and typeset by Chris O'Brien
Printed by Griffin Press, South Australia on 80 gsm Ensobelle

Contents

Introduction

Unlike most anthologies, which either assay an historical overview or cast a selective net over the contemporary, this anthology is both historic *and* contemporary. With certain key figures it includes several rather than one story. Thus the reader is given more than the customary one item by which to respond to a writer's oeuvre.

This selection begins with Katherine Mansfield and ends with Emily Perkins. Both women published their first short story collection at a young age — Mansfield at 23 and Perkins at 26.

More than seventy years after her death, Mansfield's work remains as fresh and evocative as ever. Both poetic and realistic, her best stories have the power and intensity of the most vivid dream while remaining firmly rooted in life. In 'A Dill Pickle' the dance of memory, desire and feelings between a man and a woman, who re-meet after six years, echoes the contemporary cry of 'Get an Alpha Male Who's Willing to Commit'; clearly, the unnamed and nameless man in this brilliant story — despite wild promises and flattery — is unable to commit to anything, even to paying for untouched cream.

Mansfield's work is like a corridor of mirrors set at different angles. As you walk through you catch several reflections of yourself; move onward, and another set of impressions unfolds. Her stories swarm with detail but they are the minutiae beloved of an observant eye, not the details noted by social realists who want to know which company someone works for and what wage — sorry, salary — they draw. The absence of newspaper-style facts means that the interplay of feelings is richer and the overall effect one of multi-layered possibilities which allow of the most contemporary of readings. This is why Mansfield will remain a great writer (though a miniaturist) and, indeed, why she is the *only* New Zealand writer listed in Harold Bloom's Western Canon. (Allen Curnow should also have been included but as we have so often heard, that is another story, one that not even Bloom counted on.)

A frequent central figure in a Mansfield story is an upper or upper middle class woman disturbed by a death or other social intrusion. And as 'The Garden Party' reveals, such an event can be a crosser of social boundaries, an arrow between the classes so rigidly divided in Mansfield's time. But it is an arrow that only grazes and does not penetrate its target. The worlds remain separate; the Mansfieldian heroine accepts, albeit for a moment reluctantly, her class enclosure.

And possibly this is at once the saddest and most devastating criticism of all.

Looked at another way, the Mansfieldian heroine is a breathy almost excessively feminine character whose youthful high spirits are brought down by the cruel crush of events, the random accidents of life which — though small beer by male standards — present an almost intolerable male harshness when abraded against such a sensitive feminine spirit.

The abundantly textured Euro-atmosphere of Mansfield is stripped bare by a Neo-American laconicism — influenced by such authors as Sherwood Anderson, Ernest Hemingway and arguably John Steinbeck — in Sargeson's stories. Here the world is masculine and women can seem like an intrusion into mateship, a silhouette, never coloured in, of a deeper male bond that has nothing to do with homosexuality.

Much has now been made of the homoerotic subtext in some of Sargeson's stories but it is very much a *sub*text. No homosexual relations occur. In Sartrean terms (the concept has not dated) the protagonists ought to be allowed the dignity of their choice to be covert and not overt. Despite the expert rummaging exegesis now perpetrated on his stories they remain, in their flinty understated way, as subtle as Mansfield's. The milkman who comes to collect his money from the poor washerwoman in 'A Piece of Yellow Soap', the murderer and murderee in 'A Great Day' and the hunky hole-digging Jack of 'The Hole that Jack Dug' hide as much or more than they give away. For those accustomed to the usual understatement of Sargeson 'An Affair of the Heart' is a powerfully moving story that does not shrink from pity and pathos.

The influence of Sargeson extended over his contemporaries such as Roderick Finlayson, David Ballantyne, A.P. Gaskell and John Reece Cole. Later writers like Peter Hooper, Vincent O'Sullivan and Owen Marshall all paid their dues. The latter two in particular who were always its most sophisticated exemplars moved on to break with the Sargeson tradition. Apart from these 'name' writers, the Sargeson mantle fell on many other lesser-known writers both published and unpublished, so that its ambience — the emotional understatement, empathy for the underprivileged, a laconic give-nothing-away narrator, and what Lawrence Jones has called vernacular realism — dominated New Zealand prose fiction to an extraordinary degree. That dominance, waning by the seventies, eased further with his death and has now passed.

Though friendly with Sargeson, Duggan did not emulate the master but looked beyond our shores to Joyce for his inspiration. The cautious conventions of the time meant that Duggan's more openly sensual characters could never have their lovemaking graphically described; though Buster and Fanny in 'Along Rideout Road Last Summer' do manage to achieve being 'ballocky in the umber light'. Duggan's tendency to a rhetorical excess not unlike some of the purple passages of Malcolm Lowry is controlled and given the charming lilt of an Irish voice successfully grafted onto a New Zealand vernacular — or is it the other way around? In 'The Departure' Duggan shows how understatement — in counterpoint to his normal baroque style — is also within his powers.

It is possible to project Frame's work along a graph of loneliness. Loneliness can be just a woman who has attracted no partner or even friend, the human condition at large or the state preceding true madness which Frame has not merely visited but lived in probably most of her life. Arguably, the lonelier you are the closer you are to madness and conversely, to be mad is to be supremely lonely. Of course, and this is only a smart epigram, it is not that simple, as the so-called schizophrenic, depressed and manic-depressive (politically correct parlance for the latter, is now bipolar disorder) — to name only the Big Three — *know* in every pore of their being even if they cannot express it. Frame and American poets such as Lowell, Schwartz, Sexton (suicide)

Berryman (suicide) Plath (suicide) show the pathway of the bipolar writer is harrowing and hazardous. They have brought back messages from the dark but sometimes merry caverns of despair that the 'normally' mad cannot express. That Frame is still *alive* shows extraordinary inner tenacity, a perseverance I believe made only possible by writing itself, regardless of its quality though that has always been high and on occasions touched greatness. It is *writing*, not drugs, that has saved Frame.

In 'An Incident in Mid-Ocean', the text is mercilessly direct: 'Miss Abson was so lonely'; advertisements on the TV screen intuit Miss Abson's inner self; she is seeing a psychiatrist. In 'How Can I Get in Touch with Persia?' the derangement of the central character is more candidly displayed. 'The Bath' returns us to the bleak loneliness and helplessness of old age. Sometimes the poet predominates in Frame's work, but in this latter story it is reined in by the prosaic sombreness of Mrs Harraway's isolation and frailty. For those who tell us with a solemn flag-waving note in their voice that all is political, Frame's work is a poignant reminder that the inner world of human beings has no political agendas.

Much of Shadbolt's fiction, both short and long, is concerned with the ascertaining or affirmation of national identity. His characters are often self-conscious colonials refuting their own colonialism, either by paradoxically taking the very voyage that might confirm it (home to Mother England), or making roots in the far-flung land of Aotearoa. 'River, Girl and Onion' is probably the most sophisticated of Shadbolt's treatments on this theme, achieving an international cross cultural current by making Lila Russian-born and her companions variously, a 'true' ie fourth generation New Zealander and from Venezuela and Hungary. The epigrams are witty — 'In New Zealand even the bourgeoisie is petit bourgeois', and the conclusion satisfyingly open-ended.

With a deceptively easeful casualness, Stead has become our leading metafictionalist. Most of his fiction has absorbed a self conscious knowingness about the fiction-making process and Stead, like Nietzsche, must surely believe genius has light feet which is why his prose dances with such deceptive lightness. Instinctively, rather than theoretically, Stead is a Bloomian in practice: creation first, theory second.

'Class, Race, Gender: a Post-Colonial Yarn' engages us early on thus — '. . . It will perhaps serve a disarming purpose and make what I have to record seem less serious than it is, or than it ought to be, if I begin by explaining that this is a story told by Bertie to Billy, who told it to me.' If this were not metafictional chicanery enough the next sentence reads: 'More recently Bertie told me the story himself, so I've heard it twice and have had the chance to ask questions and fill gaps that remained after first hearing.'

Stead's frequent device of narrative remove dates back to the oft anthologised 'A Fitting Tribute', which began, 'I don't ask you to believe me when I say I knew Julian Harp, but I ask you to give me a hearing because in every detail the story I'm going to tell is gospel true.' The text is a well spun yarn that affirms what the initial tease playfully denies. Of course in plain language without the arcana of Stead's borderline eighteenth-century prose it is what the person in the street calls gossip. Gossip is oral story telling done around the dinner table as opposed to yarn-spinning around the camp fire or legends told in a darkened cave.

In other words these two *yarns*, though separated by thirty years, carry the same double coding — they mock contemporary theory while at the same time deploying it; and they demonstrate the Bloomian thesis that creation in the final analysis ('at the end of the day' in contemporary political parlance) must be given superior status ('valorised') above critical theory.

'Class, Race, Gender' et al packs it all in but the class difference seems the keenest part of the gap between Bertie and bright-eyed Shelley.

Haley's anti-heroes are bewildered Europeans who might have stumbled off the set of a play by Arthur Adamov. They may have taken too many drugs or simply arrived in a strange terrain to which they have no map. Memory will disorient rather than reassure. In 'Dutch Mosquito', Karl closes his eyes and finds himself on a membrane made up of coloured dots or hurtling along a hallucinatory road. Reality seems to casually offer sex which quickly becomes violence. Haley's worlds are unsettling, absurd. The running European (to borrow the title of one of Haley's early plays) is displaced, alienated, confused by memory, desire and random violence. He is geographically neurotic. He inhabits shards of memory, which may form a fractal but never quite make a mosaic. The missing pieces are in the reader's mind.

The bulk of O'Sullivan's earlier stories were residually influenced by Sargeson, as evidenced by their preference for demotic speech and their frequent use of working class individuals as central characters. In his most recent work, he has moved to the groves of academe, a shift indicated in the punning title 'Putting Bob Down'. In a daring scenario that must titillate the male psyche, two women argue over their shared relationship with the deceased. O'Sullivan's gift for florid but illuminating metaphor, which he has tended to reserve for his poetry, here enjoys a colourful spree: 'To carry metaphor in one's emotional arsenal is to carry a thin stick that snaps open to a gorgeous fan.'

Much of Grace's work is concerned with the value Maori place on land. The land *is* home, is central to being Maori. And as with all ethnic as opposed to urban displaced (or recently arrived) peoples it is a habitation tenemented by the spirits of bygone ancestors. Never bare but occupied. Hence the old man's anger and frustration in 'Journey'. 'The Lamp' is a delightful cameo of children's literal re-interpretation of the Catholic belief that the lit candle in a church indicates God's real presence. Grace's quiet simple tales have a haunting fable-like quality.

Kidman's 'Dry Rot' presents us with a marriage that is dying inexorably by slow degrees. As the chilling title informs us the marriage of Margaret and Edward Turner is like a tree kept upright by an outer husk only. Within, the marrow of the marriage is white-anted, dead, whereas in ironic contrast outside the 'sparkling rages' of Rotorua's neon burn. There is a sequence in which Edward dives 'deep and quick' to punish Margaret until curiously she eventually responds; this is followed by his declaration of love. Poignantly, his face becomes unrecognisable, forming a cold reversal of the romantic hope that at that vulnerable moment their love might somehow rekindle. I suspect that many New Zealand marriages end in speechless death and not with the dark pyrotechnics of incest and violent beatings.

The steadfast social realism of Kidman's stories belies their subtle strengths. Unlike say Mansfield's heroines (who we must suspect do not work) we always know how Kidman's characters make their way in the world. With their overt moralising and their love of background fact Kidman's stories can be directly linked to the great nineteenth century realists.

The small towns frequently visited by Kidman are the customary canvas of Marshall's protagonists. Marshall has spent most of his adult life in places like Timaru, Oamaru and Blenheim. Though humorous English travel writer Mark Lawson listed Timaru among the ten most boring places on earth, Marshall continues to quarry his finely wrought stories from such South Island towns. He has explored childhood and adolescence many times and none better than in 'The Paper Parcel', a paradigm example of the miniature tragi-comedy that the short story can fruitfully explore, an incident that could never sustain a novel but which tellingly encapsulates the resilient optimism of youth. If Timaru has been mistakenly dismissed as boredom personified then, in 'A View Of Our Country', the small metropoles of the upper South Island are viewed more colourfully by the international traveller Simon Palliser. Seddon is like the Ivory Coast, Ward reminds him of Spain, the seaward Kaikouras evoke Switzerland, Kaikoura itself suggests British Columbia, and the Waimakariri River brings to mind the Okavango River of Botswana. It's a Haley geographic re-mix without the Haleyian fever of disorientation.

In 'The Rule of Jenny Pen' New Zealand gothic finds its truest and most ghastly manifestation — as opposed to the playful mock-gothic of Ronald Hugh Morrieson. The litany of bullying tyranny slowly accretes to a point beyond moral discomfort to one approaching horror.

What makes Marshall's achievement unique is the controlled manner in which he blends a meticulously detailed social realism with a lyric diction — a literary methodology which recalls John Updike and other contemporary American authors.

While they may lack the poetry of Marshall's best work, McCauley's stories have a tenacious humanity that avoids an overly simple morality. Though contemporary feminist voices have successfully reversed earlier moral condemnation of the sex worker and tended to shift moral opprobrium to the 'exploiting' male client, 'Mia Culpa' evokes understanding and pity for Warren in his desperate quest for a new partner — as well as for Mia. The condemning remarks of Cheryl seem (at least to this reader) only possible for those who do not have the inner view afforded by McCauley's acute analysis.

A cultured European sensibility is manifest in all of Smither's elegant prose. Borges is a possible influence on her rich mosaic of references. (They are both learned bibliophiles after all.)

The bedazzle of bookish knowledge in 'The Mathematics of Jane Austen' is typical of her oeuvre. A witty insouciance and a refined irony lurk between the lines ready to ambush us. Beneath the layers of veneer — as thick as a good read — lies the humanity of her characters struggling to live.

Gender wars are the given theme of much of Keith's work. The difficult zone of masochism is seldom visited by New Zealand authors, and it is a daring inversion to have it as the basis for sexual molestation, rather than its more customary cousin, sadism — or in broader modern guise — power over women through violent means. 'Dancing in the Dark' — a title that might suggest either Marshall or Lloyd Jones — successfully recreates the bitter-sweet yearning of adolescence.

Both of Witi Ihimaera's stories demarcate Maori from Pakeha by contrasting the worlds of wealth and poverty that each inhabits. In this direct dichotomy Ihimaera reflects the same divide that occurred in Sargeson plus the ethnic differences. In 'The House with Sugarbag Windows' Watene has crossed over to the Pakeha world of affluence and privilege but retains an affectionate, a necessary, tie with the privation of his childhood.

Shonagh Koea's fiction often portrays socially isolated women being the object of dubious or unwelcome male advances. In 'The Dancing Master' though Mrs Bradford is married, within her marriage she is impliedly isolated and dissatisfied. The persistent Thorstensen releases her from wallflowerdom by waltzing her around the room, but this declaration is tellingly made while 'drawing on the tablecloth with a fork, little runnels that lead to nowhere, and wearing Thorstensen's secrets like jewels' — an ending which deploys a phrasing and a subtlety comparable to Mansfield.

Peter Wells is our most dedicated celebrant of the sensual. In story after story, his warm rapturous prose exalts the ecstasies of fleshly union. But this heaven has its accompanying hells and purgatories — the as yet incurable disease AIDS, the let-down lover, the relationship that cannot progress or is doomed to dissipate. Like Alan Hollinghurst, whom he admires and emulates, Wells does not consider that he is

16

writing 'gay' fiction, however homoerotic the imagery may be.

In several loosely linked stories we observe the relationship of Perrin and Eric. The first story included here captures the moment when the fatal disease is first detected and the brave reaction: 'It can't be allowed to win, *it won't, we won't let it*'. 'A Casual Kind of Incest' gives an ironic yet affectionate view of mother and son and amusingly debunks a family myth.

The haunting fables of John Cranna have a compaction and density that suggest myths recorded from a proximate and bleak future.

The war, which has disrupted and rubbleised civilisation, is obliquely referred to — 'They said Australia was caught in the exchanges.' 'Archaeology' is not science fiction — technology is irrelevant — but the world is a different place. Chris, the narrator, and Chris's mother are like Robinson Crusoes marooned on an isle that is as large and desolate as the remains of a ruined planet. The reconstructed bones of the moa we may read as an emblem of what humanity may become. Cranna's story has a slightly dated feel because it must have been written just prior to glasnost and the crumbling of the Soviet empire, the end of the cold war. No matter — its mythic fable qualities will assure its survival.

Possibly to a greater extent than any other contemporary writer, Lloyd Jones's easy-to-read narrative style masks an enormous though relaxed sophistication. 'This Place We Call Home' — the title could be from the *Reader's Digest* — is ironic. We are well into the story before the gender of the narrator is casually revealed. History and palaeontology — moa bones (again) and Maori land claims (again) — surface in 'This Place We Call Home'. Even more so since Ihimaera's early stories and Jones' '80s work, Maori land claims have increasingly become the main event within our political arena. Jones' story explores the sadness of a sick man baffled by protest, the futile gesture with which he tries to nail down and preserve the past. 'Me, Clark and Wilder' may perturb those unaware of the packaging of fiction for the American market, which is contrasted with the traditional lone writer determined to keep on writing even though it is about 'characters he will not talk about or admit into the light of day.' Thankfully, Jones has let in the sunlight.

No other short story writer of our time (ie the '90s) has made such an arresting debut as Emily Perkins. Variously 'experimental', ie fragmentary, and traditional in her narrative methods, she has a breezily readable and confident style that helps divert any doubts as to the deeper qualities of her work. 'Barking' with its aggressively hectoring adolescent first person voice could be compared to Holden Caulfield in J.D.Salinger's celebrated *Catcher in the Rye*.

Salinger:

> If you really want to hear about it, the first thing you'll probably want to know is where I was born, and what my lousy childhood was like, and how my parents were occupied and all before they had me, and all that David Copperfield kind of crap, but I don't feel like going into it. In the first place that stuff bores me, and in the second place, my parents would have two haemorrhages apiece if I told anything pretty personal about them.

Perkins:

> So I'm in my drama class, right? And I think like I want to be this very cool actor-type, Brando or James Dean or something — and I could have been too, you know, I really could. But the stupid dumb fuck drama class I'm taking is some idiot thing run by idiots and we spend all this time looking for our centres or relaxing or rubbing each other. It's pretty disgusting I'm telling you.

Who can resist such persuasively personal voices? I certainly cannot. And nor can many other readers. Notice how American-sounding are Perkins' inflections and vocabulary.

Thus in a broad generalisation we can see many New Zealand short story writers falling into two camps — the Europhiles (Mansfield, Frame, Duggan, Stead, Haley, Smither, Koea) who tend to the baroque and the metafictional and the Neo-Americans (Sargeson, Marshall, Keith, Jones, Perkins) who give us the heartfelt voices of adolescence or certain resonances and echoes which sound American rather than English. Through Sargeson also come the third group (only subtly different from the second by being less openly American), the social realists like Shadbolt, O'Sullivan, McCauley and Kidman and — with allowance for ethnic variations, and a softer, even at times sentimental, tone — Grace and Ihimaera. Of course Marshall and Jones are also social realists though of a more subtle kind.

I would categorise my own work as Neo-American (influenced by Vonnegut and Doctorow among others) with occasional seduction by Europhilia.

That leaves Cranna, magic realist and Kafka-esque fabulist and Wells, the lyric sensualist, uncamped.

Unlike my '80s anthology, *The New Fiction*, which assembled postmodernists exclusively, this anthology almost excludes them. For postmodern short fiction in this country has eased back from the highwater mark of the '80s. Whether ultimately desirable or not, the 'mainstream' with its incumbent realism of one mode or another — which this selection embodies — still tends to dominate our literary landscape.

Michael Morrissey
Auckland, 1999

A Dill Pickle

KATHERINE MANSFIELD

And then, after six years, she saw him again. He was seated at one of those little bamboo tables decorated with a Japanese vase of paper daffodils. There was a tall plate of fruit in front of him, and very carefully, in a way she recognised immediately as his 'special' way, he was peeling an orange.

He must have felt that shock of recognition in her, for he looked up and met her eyes. Incredible! He didn't know her! She smiled; he frowned. She came towards him. He closed his eyes an instant, but opening them his face lit up as though he had struck a match in a dark room. He laid down the orange and pushed back his chair, and she took her little warm hand out of her muff and gave it to him.

'Vera!' he exclaimed. 'How strange. Really, for a moment I didn't know you. Won't you sit down? You've had lunch? Won't you have some coffee?'

She hesitated, but of course she meant to.

'Yes, I'd like some coffee.' And she sat down opposite him.

'You've changed. You've changed very much,' he said, staring at her with that eager, lighted look. 'You look so well. I've never seen you look so well before.'

'Really?' She raised her veil and unbuttoned her high fur collar. 'I don't feel very well. I can't bear this weather, you know.'

'Ah, no. You hate the cold . . .'

'Loathe it.' She shuddered. 'And the worst of it is that the older one grows . . .'

He interrupted her. 'Excuse me,' and tapped on the table for the waitress. 'Please bring some coffee and cream.' To her: 'You are sure you won't eat anything? Some fruit, perhaps. The fruit here is very good.'

'No, thanks. Nothing.'

'Then that's settled.' And smiling just a hint too broadly he took up the orange again. 'You were saying — the older one grows —'

'The colder,' she laughed. But she was thinking how well she remembered that trick of his — the trick of interrupting her — and how it used to exasperate her six years ago. She used to feel then as though he, quite suddenly, in the middle of what she was saying, put his hand over her lips, turned from her, attended to something different, and then took his hand away, and with just the same slightly too broad smile, gave her his attention again . . . Now we are ready. That is settled.

'The colder!' He echoed her words, laughing too. 'Ah, ah. You still say the same things. And there is another thing about you that is not changed at all — your beautiful voice — your beautiful way of speaking.' Now he was very grave; he leaned towards her, and she smelled the warm, stinging scent of the orange peel. 'You have only to say one word and I would know your voice among all other voices. I don't know what it is — I've often wondered — that makes your voice such a — haunting memory . . . Do you remember that first afternoon we spent together at Kew Gardens? You were so surprised because I did not know the names of any flowers. I am still just as ignorant for all your telling me. But whenever it is very fine and warm, and I see some bright colours — it's awfully strange — I hear your voice saying: "Geranium, marigold and verbena." And I feel those three words are all I recall of some forgotten, heavenly language . . . You remember that afternoon?'

'Oh, yes, very well.' She drew a long, soft breath, as though the paper daffodils between them were almost too sweet to bear. Yet, what had remained in her mind of that particular afternoon was an absurd scene over the tea-table. A great many people taking tea in a Chinese pagoda, and he behaving like a maniac about the wasps — waving them away, flapping at them with his straw hat, serious and infuriated out of all proportion to the occasion. How delighted the sniggering tea drinkers had been. And how she had suffered.

But now, as he spoke, that memory faded. His was the truer. Yes, it had been a wonderful afternoon, full of geranium and marigold and verbena, and — warm sunshine. Her thoughts lingered over the last two words as though she sang them.

In the warmth, as it were, another memory unfolded. She saw herself sitting on a lawn. He lay beside her, and suddenly, after a long silence, he rolled over and put his head in her lap.

'I wish,' he said, in a low, troubled voice, 'I wish that I had taken poison and were about to die — here now!'

At that moment a little girl in a white dress, holding a long, dripping white lily, dodged from behind a bush, stared at them, and dodged back again. But he did not see. She leaned over him.

'Ah, why do you say that? I could not say that.'

But he gave a kind of soft moan, and taking her hand he held it to his cheek.

'Because I know I am going to love you too much — far too much. And I shall suffer so terribly, Vera, because you never, never will love me.'

He was certainly far better looking now than he had been then. He had lost all that dreamy vagueness and indecision. Now he had the air of a man who has found his place in life, and fills it with a confidence and an assurance which was, to say the least, impressive. He must have made money, too. His clothes were admirable, and at that moment he pulled a Russian cigarette-case out of his pocket.

'Won't you smoke?'

'Yes, I will.' She hovered over them. 'They look very good.'

'I think they are. I get them made for me by a little man in St. James's Street. I don't smoke very much. I'm not like you — but when I do, they must be delicious, very fresh cigarettes. Smoking isn't a habit with me; it's a luxury — like perfume. Are you still so fond of perfumes? Ah, when I was in Russia . . .'

She broke in: 'You've really been to Russia?'

'Oh yes. I was there for over a year. Have you forgotten how we used to talk of going there?'

'No, I've not forgotten.'

He gave a strange half-laugh and leaned back in his chair. 'Isn't it curious. I have really carried out all those journeys that we planned. Yes, I have been to all those places that we talked of, and stayed in them long enough to — as you used to say — "air oneself" in them. In fact, I have spent the last three years of my life travelling all the time. Spain, Corsica, Siberia, Russia, Egypt. The only country left is China, and I mean to go there, too, when the war is over.'

As he spoke, so lightly, tapping the end of his cigarette against the ash-tray, she felt the strange beast that had slumbered so long within her bosom stir, stretch itself, yawn, prick up its ears, and suddenly bound to its feet, and fix its longing, hungry stare upon those far-away places. But all she said was, smiling gently: 'How I envy you.'

He accepted that. 'It has been,' he said, 'very wonderful — especially Russia. Russia was all that we had imagined, and far, far more. I even spent some days on a river boat on the Volga. Do you remember that boatman's song that you used to play?'

'Yes.' It began to play in her mind as she spoke.

'Do you ever play it now?'

'No, I've no piano.'

He was amazed at that. 'But what has become of your beautiful piano?'

She made a little grimace. 'Sold. Ages ago.'

'But you were so fond of music,' he wondered.

'I've no time for it now,' said she.

He let it go at that. 'That river life,' he went on, 'is something quite special. After a day or two you cannot realise that you have ever known another. And it is not necessary to know the language — the life of the boat creates a bond between you and the people that's more than sufficient. You eat with them, pass the day with them, and in the evening there is that endless singing.'

She shivered, hearing the boatman's song break out again loud and tragic, and seeing the boat floating on the darkening river with melancholy trees on either side . . . 'Yes, I should like that,' said she, stroking her muff.

'You'd like almost everything about Russian life,' he said warmly. 'It's so informal, so impulsive, so free without question. And then the peasants are so splendid. They are such human beings — yes, that is it. Even the man who drives your carriage has — has some real part in what is happening. I remember the evening a party of us, two friends of mine and the wife of one of them, went for a picnic by the Black

Sea. We took supper and champagne and ate and drank on the grass. And while we were eating the coachman came up. "Have a dill pickle," he said. He wanted to share with us. That seemed to me so right, so — you know what I mean?'

And she seemed at that moment to be sitting on the grass beside the mysteriously Black Sea, black as velvet, and rippling against the banks in silent, velvet waves. She saw the carriage drawn up to one side of the road, and the little group on the grass, their faces and hands white in the moonlight. She saw the pale dress of the woman outspread and her folded parasol, lying on the grass like a huge pearl crochet-hook. Apart from them, with his supper in a cloth on his knees, sat the coachman. 'Have a dill pickle,' said he, and although she was not certain what a dill pickle was, she saw the greenish glass jar with a red chilli like a parrot's beak glimmering through. She sucked in her cheeks; the dill pickle was terribly sour . . .

'Yes, I know perfectly what you mean,' she said.

In the pause that followed they looked at each other. In the past when they had looked at each other like that they had felt such a boundless understanding between them that their souls had, as it were, put their arms round each other and dropped into the same sea, content to be drowned, like mournful lovers. But now, the surprising thing was that it was he who held back. He who said:

'What a marvellous listener you are. When you look at me with those wild eyes I feel that I could tell you things that I would never breathe to another human being.'

Was there just a hint of mockery in his voice or was it her fancy? She could not be sure.

'Before I met you,' he said, 'I had never spoken of myself to anybody. How well I remember one night, the night that I brought you the little Christmas tree, telling you all about my childhood. And of how I was so miserable that I ran away and lived under a cart in our yard for two days without being discovered. And you listened, and your eyes shone, and I felt that you had even made the little Christmas tree listen too, as in a fairy story.'

But of that evening she had remembered a little pot of caviare. It had cost seven and sixpence. He could not get over it. Think of it — a tiny jar like that costing seven and sixpence. While she ate it he watched her, delighted and shocked.

'No, really, that is eating money. You could not get seven shillings into a little pot that size. Only think of the profit they must make . . .' And he had begun some immensely complicated calculations . . . But now good-bye to the caviare. The Christmas tree was on the table, and the little boy lay under the cart with his head pillowed on the yard dog.

'The dog was called Bosun,' she cried delightedly.

But he did not follow. 'Which dog? Had you a dog? I don't remember a dog at all.'

'No, no. I mean the yard dog when you were a little boy.' He laughed and snapped the cigarette-case to.

'Was he? Do you know I had forgotten that. It seems such ages ago. I cannot believe that it is only six years. After I had recognised you today — I had to take such a leap — I had to take a leap over my whole life to get back to that time. I was such a kid then.' He drummed on the table. 'I've often thought how I must have bored you. And now I understand so perfectly why you wrote to me as you did — although at the time that letter nearly finished my life. I found it again the other day, and I couldn't help laughing as I read it. It was so clever — such a true picture of me.' He glanced up. 'You're not going?'

She had buttoned her collar again and drawn down her veil.

'Yes, I am afraid I must,' she said, and managed a smile. Now she knew that he had been mocking.

'Ah no, please,' he pleaded. 'Don't go just for a moment,' and he caught up one of her gloves from the table and clutched at it as if that would hold her. 'I see so few people to talk to nowadays, that I have turned into a sort of barbarian,' he said. 'Have I said something to hurt you?'

'Not a bit,' she lied. But as she watched him draw her glove through his fingers, gently, gently, her anger really did die down, and besides, at the moment he looked more like himself of six years ago . . .

'What I really wanted then,' he said softly, 'was to be a sort of carpet — to make myself into a sort of carpet for you to walk on so that you need not be hurt by the sharp stones and the mud that you hated so. It was nothing more positive than that — nothing more selfish. Only I did desire, eventually, to turn into a magic carpet and carry you away to all those lands you longed to see.'

As he spoke she lifted her head as though she drank something; the strange beast in her bosom began to purr . . .

'I felt that you were more lonely than anybody else in the world,' he went on, 'and yet, perhaps, that you were the only person in the world who was really, truly alive. Born out of your time,' he murmured, stroking the glove, 'fated.'

Ah, God! What had she done! How had she dared to throw away her happiness like this. This was the only man who had ever understood her. Was it too late? Could it be too late? *She* was that glove that he held in his fingers . . .

'And then the fact that you had no friends and never had made friends with people. How I understood that, for neither had I. Is it just the same now?'

'Yes,' she breathed. 'Just the same. I am as alone as ever.'

'So am I,' he laughed gently, 'just the same.'

Suddenly with a quick gesture he handed her back the glove and scraped his chair on the floor. 'But what seemed to me so mysterious then is perfectly plain to me now. And to you, too, of course . . . It simply was that we were such egoists, so self-engrossed, so wrapped up in ourselves that we hadn't a corner in our hearts for anybody else. Do you know,' he cried, naïve and hearty, and dreadfully like another side of that old self again, 'I began studying a Mind System when I was in Russia, and I found that we were not peculiar at all. It's quite a well-known form of . . .'

She had gone. He sat there, thunder-struck, astounded beyond words . . . And then he asked the waitress for his bill.

'But the cream has not been touched,' he said. 'Please do not charge me for it.'

Bliss

KATHERINE MANSFIELD

Although Bertha Young was thirty she still had moments like this when she wanted to run instead of walk, to take dancing steps on and off the pavement, to bowl a hoop, to throw something up in the air and catch it again, or to stand still and laugh at — nothing — at nothing, simply.

What can you do if you are thirty and, turning the corner of your own street, you are overcome, suddenly, by a feeling of bliss — absolute bliss! — as though you'd suddenly swallowed a bright piece of that late afternoon sun and it burned in your bosom, sending out a little shower of sparks into every particle, into every finger and toe? . . .

Oh, is there no way you can express it without being 'drunk and disorderly'? How idiotic civilisation is! Why be given a body if you have to keep it shut up in a case like a rare, rare fiddle?

'No, that about the fiddle is not quite what I mean,' she thought, running up the steps and feeling in her bag for the key — she'd forgotten it, as usual — and rattling the letter-box. 'It's not what I mean, because — Thank you, Mary' — she went into the hall. 'Is nurse back?'

'Yes, M'm.'

'And has the fruit come?'

'Yes, M'm. Everything's come.'

'Bring the fruit up to the dining-room, will you? I'll arrange it before I go upstairs.'

It was dusky in the dining-room and quite chilly. But all the same Bertha threw off her coat; she could not bear the tight clasp of it another moment, and the cold air fell on her arms.

But in her bosom there was still that bright glowing place — that shower of little sparks coming from it. It was almost unbearable. She hardly dared to breathe for fear of fanning it higher, and yet she breathed deeply, deeply. She hardly dared to look into the cold mirror — but she did look, and it gave her back a woman, radiant, with smiling, trembling lips, with big, dark eyes and an air of listening, waiting for something . . . divine to happen . . . that she knew must happen . . . infallibly.

Mary brought in the fruit on a tray and with it a glass bowl, and a blue dish, very lovely, with a strange sheen on it as though it had been dipped in milk.

'Shall I turn on the light, M'm?'

'No, thank you. I can see quite well.'

There were tangerines and apples stained with strawberry pink. Some yellow pears, smooth as silk, some white grapes covered with a silver bloom and a big cluster of purple ones. These last she had bought to tone in with the new dining-room carpet. Yes, that did sound rather far-fetched and absurd, but it was really why she had bought them. She had thought in the shop: 'I must have some purple ones to bring the carpet up to the table.' And it had seemed quite sense at the time.

When she had finished with them and had made two pyramids of these bright round shapes, she stood away from the table to get the effect — and it really was most curious. For the dark table seemed to melt into the dusky light and the glass dish and the blue bowl to float in the air. This, of course, in her present mood, was so incredibly beautiful . . . She began to laugh.

'No, no. I'm getting hysterical.' And she seized her bag and coat and ran upstairs to the nursery.

Nurse sat at a low table giving Little B her supper after her bath. The baby had on a white flannel gown and a blue woollen jacket, and her dark, fine hair was brushed up into a funny little peak. She looked up when she saw her mother and began to jump.

'Now, my lovey, eat it up like a good girl,' said nurse, setting her lips in a way that Bertha knew, and that meant she had come into the nursery at another wrong moment.

'Has she been good, Nanny?'

'She's been a little sweet all the afternoon,' whispered Nanny. 'We went to the park and I sat down on a chair and took her out of the pram and a big dog came along and put its head on my knee and she clutched its ear, tugged it. Oh, you should have seen her.'

Bertha wanted to ask if it wasn't rather dangerous to let her clutch at a strange dog's ear. But she did not dare to. She stood watching them, her hands by her side, like the poor little girl in front of the rich little girl with the doll.

The baby looked up at her again, stared, and then smiled so charmingly that Bertha couldn't help crying:

'Oh, Nanny, do let me finish giving her her supper while you put the bath things away.'

'Well, M'm, she oughtn't to be changed hands while she's eating,' said Nanny, still whispering. 'It unsettles her; it's very likely to upset her.'

How absurd it was. Why have a baby if it has to be kept — not in a case like a rare, rare fiddle — but in another woman's arms?

'Oh, I must!' said she.

Very offended, Nanny handed her over.

'Now, don't excite her after her supper. You know you do, M'm. And I have such a time with her after!'

Thank heaven! Nanny went out of the room with the bath towels.

'Now I've got you to myself, my little precious,' said Bertha, as the baby leaned against her.

She ate delightfully, holding up her lips for the spoon and then waving her hands. Sometimes she wouldn't let the spoon go; and sometimes, just as Bertha had filled it, she waved it away to the four winds.

When the soup was finished Bertha turned round to the fire.

'You're nice — you're very nice!' said she, kissing her warm baby. 'I'm fond of you. I like you.'

And, indeed, she loved Little B so much — her neck as she bent forward, her exquisite toes as they shone transparent in the firelight — that all her feeling of bliss came back again, and again she didn't know how to express it — what to do with it.

'You're wanted on the telephone,' said Nanny, coming back in triumph and seizing *her* Little B.

*

Down she flew. It was Harry.

'Oh, is that you, Ber? Look here. I'll be late. I'll take a taxi and come along as quickly as I can, but get dinner put back ten minutes — will you? All right?'

'Yes, perfectly. Oh, Harry!'

'Yes?'

What had she to say? She'd nothing to say. She only wanted to get in touch with him for a moment. She couldn't absurdly cry: 'Hasn't it been a divine day!'

'What is it?' rapped out the little voice.

'Nothing. *Entendu*,' said Bertha, and hung up the receiver, thinking how much more than idiotic civilisation was.

They had people coming to dinner. The Norman Knights — a very sound couple — he was about to start a theatre, and she was awfully keen on interior decoration, a young man, Eddie Warren, who had just published a little book of poems and whom everybody was asking to dine, and a 'find' of Bertha's called Pearl Fulton. What Miss Fulton did, Bertha didn't know. They had met at the club and Bertha had fallen in love with her, as she always did fall in love with beautiful women who had something strange about them.

The provoking thing was that, though they had been about together and met a number of times and really talked, Bertha couldn't make her out. Up to a certain point Miss Fulton was rarely, wonderfully frank, but the certain point was there, and beyond that she would not go.

Was there anything beyond it? Harry said 'No.' Voted her dullish, and 'cold like all blonde women, with a touch, perhaps, of anaemia of the brain.' But Bertha wouldn't agree with him; not yet, at any rate.

'No, the way she has of sitting with her head a little on one side, and smiling, has something behind it, Harry, and I must find out what that something is.'

'Most likely it's a good stomach,' answered Harry.

He made a point of catching Bertha's heels with replies of that kind . . . 'liver frozen, my dear girl,' or 'pure flatulence,' or 'kidney disease,' . . . and so on. For some strange reason Bertha liked this, and almost admired it in him very much.

She went into the drawing-room and lighted the fire; then, picking up the cushions, one by one, that Mary had disposed so carefully, she threw them back on to the chairs and the couches. That made all the difference; the room came alive at once. As she was about to throw the last one she surprised herself by suddenly hugging it to her, passionately, passionately. But it did not put out the fire in her bosom. Oh, on the contrary!

The windows of the drawing-room opened on to a balcony overlooking the garden. At the far end, against the wall, there was a tall, slender pear tree in fullest, richest bloom; it stood perfect, as though becalmed against the jade-green sky. Bertha couldn't help feeling, even from this distance, that it had not a single bud or a faded petal. Down below, in the garden beds, the red and yellow tulips, heavy with flowers, seemed to lean upon the dusk. A grey cat, dragging its belly, crept across the lawn, and a black one, its shadow, trailed after. The sight of them, so intent and so quick, gave Bertha a curious shiver.

'What creepy things cats are!' she stammered, and she turned away from the window and began walking up and down . . .

How strong the jonquils smelled in the warm room. Too strong? Oh, no. And yet, as though overcome, she flung down on a couch and pressed her hands to her eyes.

'I'm too happy — too happy!' she murmured.

And she seemed to see on her eyelids the lovely pear tree with its wide open blossoms as a symbol of her own life.

Really — really — she had everything. She was young. Harry and she were as much in love as ever, and they got on together splendidly and were really good pals. She had an adorable baby. They didn't have to worry about money. They had this absolutely satisfactory house and garden. And friends — modern, thrilling friends, writers and painters and poets or people keen on social questions — just the kind of friends they wanted. And then there were books, and there was music, and she had found a wonderful little dressmaker, and they were going abroad in the summer, and their new cook made the most superb omelettes . . .

'I'm absurd. Absurd!' She sat up; but she felt quite dizzy, quite drunk. It must have been the spring.

Yes, it was the spring. Now she was so tired she could not drag herself upstairs to dress.

*

A white dress, a string of jade beads, green shoes and stockings. It wasn't intentional. She had thought of this scheme hours before she stood at the drawing-room window.

Her petals rustled softly into the hall, and she kissed Mrs Norman Knight, who was taking off the most amusing orange coat with a procession of black monkeys round the hem and up the fronts.

' . . . Why! Why! Why is the middle-class so stodgy — so utterly without a sense of humour! My dear, it's only by a fluke that I am here at all — Norman being the protective fluke. For my darling monkeys so upset the train that it rose to a man and simply ate me with its eyes. Didn't laugh — wasn't amused — that I should have loved. No, just stared — and bored me through and through.'

'But the cream of it was,' said Norman, pressing a large tortoise-shell-rimmed monocle into his eye, 'you don't mind me telling this, Face, do you?' (In their home and among their friends they called each other Face and Mug.) 'The cream of it was when she, being full fed, turned to the woman beside her and said: "Haven't you ever seen a monkey before?" '

'Oh yes!' Mrs. Norman Knight joined in the laughter. 'Wasn't that too absolutely creamy?'

And a funnier thing still was that now her coat was off she did look like a very intelligent monkey — who had even made that yellow silk dress out of scraped banana skins. And her amber ear-rings: they were like little dangling nuts.

'This is a sad, sad fall!' said Mug, pausing in front of Little B's perambulator. 'When the perambulator comes into the hall —' and he waved the rest of the quotation away.

The bell rang. It was lean, pale Eddie Warren (as usual) in a state of acute distress.

'It *is* the right house, *isn't* it?' he pleaded.

'Oh, I think so — I hope so,' said Bertha brightly.

'I have had such a *dreadful* experience with a taxi-man; he was *most* sinister. I couldn't get him to *stop*. The *more* I knocked and called the *faster* he went. And *in* the moonlight this *bizarre* figure with the *flattened* head *crouching* over the *lit-tle* wheel . . .'

He shuddered, taking off an immense white silk scarf. Bertha noticed that his socks were white, too — most charming.

'But how dreadful!' she cried.

'Yes, it really was,' said Eddie, following her into the drawing-room. 'I saw myself *driving* through Eternity in a *timeless* taxi.'

He knew the Norman Knights. In fact, he was going to write a play for N. K. when the theatre scheme came off.

'Well, Warren, how's the play?' said Norman Knight, dropping his monocle and giving his eye a moment in which to rise to the surface before it was screwed down again.

And Mrs. Norman Knight: 'Oh, Mr. Warren, what happy socks!'

'I *am* so glad you like them,' said he, staring at his feet. 'They seem to have got so *much* whiter since the moon rose.' And he turned his lean sorrowful young face to Bertha. 'There *is* a moon, you know.'

She wanted to cry: 'I am sure there is — often — often!'

He really was a most attractive person. But so was Face, crouched before the fire in her banana skins, and so was Mug, smoking a cigarette and saying as he flicked the ash: 'Why doth the bridegroom tarry?'

'There he is, now.'

Bang went the front door open and shut. Harry shouted: 'Hullo, you people. Down in five minutes.' And they heard him swarm up the stairs. Bertha couldn't help smiling; she knew how he loved doing things at high pressure. What, after all, did an extra five minutes matter? But he would pretend to himself that they mattered beyond measure. And then he would make a great point of coming into the drawing-room, extravagantly cool and collected.

Harry had such a zest for life. Oh, how she appreciated it in him. And his passion for fighting — for seeking in everything that came up against him another test of his power and of his courage — that, too, she understood. Even when it made him just occasionally, to other people, who didn't know him well, a little ridiculous perhaps . . . For there were moments when he rushed into battle where no battle was . . . She talked and laughed and positively forgot until he had come in (just as she had imagined) that Pearl Fulton had not turned up.

'I wonder if Miss Fulton has forgotten?'

'I expect so,' said Harry. 'Is she on the 'phone?'

'Ah! There's a taxi now.' And Bertha smiled with that little air of proprietorship that she always assumed while her women finds were new and mysterious. 'She lives in taxis.'

'She'll run to fat if she does,' said Harry coolly, ringing the bell for dinner. 'Frightful danger for blonde women.'

'Harry — don't,' warned Bertha, laughing up at him.

Came another tiny moment, while they waited, laughing and talking, just a trifle too much at their ease, a trifle too unaware. And then Miss Fulton, all in silver, with a silver fillet binding her pale blonde hair, came in smiling, her head a little on one side.

'Am I late?'

'No, not at all,' said Bertha. 'Come along.' And she took her arm and they moved into the dining-room.

What was there in the touch of that cool arm that could fan — fan — start blazing — blazing — the fire of bliss that Bertha did not know what to do with?

Miss Fulton did not look at her; but then she seldom did look at people directly. Her heavy eyelids lay upon her eyes and the strange half-smile came and went upon her lips as though she lived by listening rather than seeing. But Bertha knew, suddenly, as if the longest, most intimate look had passed between them — as if they had said to each other: 'You, too?' — that Pearl Fulton, stirring the beautiful red soup in the grey plate, was feeling just what she was feeling.

And the others? Face and Mug, Eddie and Harry, their spoons rising and falling — dabbing their lips with their napkins, crumbling bread, fiddling with the forks and glasses and talking.

'I met her at the Alpha show — the weirdest little person. She'd not only cut off her hair, but she seemed to have taken a dreadfully good snip off her legs and arms and her neck and her poor little nose as well.'

'Isn't she very *liée* with Michael Oat?'

'The man who wrote *Love in False Teeth*?'

'He wants to write a play for me. One act. One man. Decides to commit suicide. Gives all the reasons why he should and why he shouldn't. And just as he has made up his mind either to do it or not to do it — curtain. Not half a bad idea.'

'What's he going to call it — "Stomach Trouble"?'

'I *think* I've come across the *same* idea in a lit-tle French review, *quite* unknown in England.'

No, they didn't share it. They were dears — dears — and she loved having them there, at her table, and giving them delicious food and wine. In fact, she longed to tell them how delightful they were, and what a decorative group they made, how they seemed to set one another off and how they reminded her of a play by Tchekof!

Harry was enjoying his dinner. It was part of his — well, not his nature, exactly, and certainly not his pose — his — something or other — to talk about food and to glory in his 'shameless passion for the white flesh of the lobster' and 'the green of pistachio ices — green and cold like the eyelids of Egyptian dancers.'

When he looked up at her and said: 'Bertha, this is a very admirable *soufflé*!' she almost could have wept with child-like pleasure.

Oh, why did she feel so tender towards the whole world to-night? Everything was good — was right. All that happened seemed to fill again her brimming cup of bliss.

And still, in the back of her mind, there was the pear tree. It would be silver now, in the light of poor dear Eddie's moon, silver as Miss Fulton, who sat there turning a tangerine in her slender fingers that were so pale a light seemed to come from them.

What she simply couldn't make out — what was miraculous — was how she should have guessed Miss Fulton's mood so exactly and so instantly. For she never doubted for a moment that she was right, and yet what had she to go on? Less than nothing.

'I believe this does happen very, very rarely between women. Never between men,' thought Bertha. 'But while I am making the coffee in the drawing-room perhaps she will "give a sign".'

What she meant by that she did not know, and what would happen after that she could not imagine.

While she thought like this she saw herself talking and laughing. She had to talk because of her desire to laugh.

'I must laugh or die.'

But when she noticed Face's funny little habit of tucking something down the front of her bodice — as if she kept a tiny, secret hoard of nuts there, too — Bertha had to dig her nails into her hands — so as not to laugh too much.

It was over at last. And: 'Come and see my new coffee machine,' said Bertha.

'We only have a new coffee machine once a fortnight,' said Harry. Face took her arm this time; Miss Fulton bent her head and followed after.

The fire had died down in the drawing-room to a red, flickering 'nest of baby phoenixes,' said Face.

'Don't turn up the light for a moment. It is so lovely.' And down she crouched by the fire again. She was always cold . . . 'without her little red flannel jacket, of course,' thought Bertha.

At that moment Miss Fulton 'gave the sign.'

'Have you a garden?' said the cool, sleepy voice.

This was so exquisite on her part that all Bertha could do was to obey. She crossed the room, pulled the curtains apart, and opened those long windows.

'There!' she breathed.

And the two women stood side by side looking at the slender, flowering tree. Although it was so still it seemed, like the flame of a candle, to stretch up, to point, to quiver in the bright air, to grow taller and taller as they gazed — almost to touch the rim of the round, silver moon.

How long did they stand there? Both, as it were, caught in that circle of unearthly light, understanding each other perfectly, creatures of another world, and wondering what they were to do in this one with all this blissful treasure that burned in their bosoms and dropped, in silver flowers, from their hair and hands?

For ever — for a moment? And did Miss Fulton murmur: 'Yes. Just *that*.' Or did Bertha dream it?

Then the light was snapped on and Face made the coffee and Harry said: 'My dear Mrs Knight, don't ask me about my baby. I never see her. I shan't feel the slightest interest in her until she has a lover,' and Mug took his eye out of the conservatory for a moment and then put it under glass again and Eddie Warren drank his coffee and set down the cup with a face of anguish as though he had drunk and seen the spider.

'What I want to do is to give the young men a show. I believe London is simply teeming with first-chop, unwritten plays. What I want to say to 'em is: "Here's the theatre. Fire ahead." '

'You know, my dear, I am going to decorate a room for the Jacob

Nathans. Oh, I am so tempted to do a fried-fish scheme, with the backs of the chairs shaped like frying-pans and lovely chip potatoes embroidered all over the curtains.'

'The trouble with our young writing men is that they are still too romantic. You can't put out to sea without being seasick and wanting a basin. Well, why won't they have the courage of those basins?'

'A *dreadful* poem about a *girl* who was *violated* by a beggar *without* a nose in a lit-tle wood . . .'

Miss Fulton sank into the lowest, deepest chair and Harry handed round the cigarettes.

From the way he stood in front of her shaking the silver box and saying abruptly: 'Egyptian? Turkish? Virginian? They're all mixed up,' Bertha realised that she not only bored him; he really disliked her. And she decided from the way Miss Fulton said: 'No, thank you, I won't smoke,' that she felt it, too, and was hurt.

'Oh, Harry, don't dislike her. You are quite wrong about her. She's wonderful, wonderful. And, besides, how can you feel so differently about someone who means so much to me. I shall try to tell you when we are in bed to-night what has been happening. What she and I have shared.'

At those last words something strange and almost terrifying darted into Bertha's mind. And this something blind and smiling whispered to her: 'Soon these people will go. The house will be quiet — quiet. The lights will be out. And you and he will be alone together in the dark room — the warm bed . . .'

She jumped up from her chair and ran over to the piano.

'What a pity someone does not play!' she cried. 'What a pity some-body does not play.'

For the first time in her life Bertha Young desired her husband.

Oh, she'd loved him — she'd been in love with him, of course, in every other way, but just not in that way. And equally, of course, she'd understood that he was different. They'd discussed it so often. It had worried her dreadfully at first to find that she was so cold, but after a time it had not seemed to matter. They were so frank with each other — such good pals. That was the best of being modern.

But now — ardently! ardently! The word ached in her ardent body!

Was this what that feeling of bliss had been leading up to? But then, then —

'My dear,' said Mrs. Norman Knight, 'you know our shame. We are the victims of time and train. We live in Hampstead. It's been so nice.'

'I'll come with you into the hall,' said Bertha. 'I loved having you. But you must not miss the last train. That's so awful, isn't it?'

'Have a whisky, Knight, before you go?' called Harry.

'No, thanks, old chap.'

Bertha squeezed his hand for that as she shook it.

'Good night, good-bye,' she cried from the top step, feeling that this self of hers was taking leave of them for ever.

When she got back into the drawing-room the others were on the move.

' . . . Then you can come part of the way in my taxi.'

'I shall be *so* thankful *not* to have to face *another* drive *alone* after my *dreadful* experience.'

'You can get a taxi at the rank just at the end of the street. You won't have to walk more than a few yards.'

'That's a comfort. I'll go and put on my coat.'

Miss Fulton moved towards the hall and Bertha was following when Harry almost pushed past.

'Let me help you.'

Bertha knew that he was repenting his rudeness — she let him go. What a boy he was in some ways — so impulsive — so — simple.

And Eddie and she were left by the fire.

'I *wonder* if you have seen Bilks' *new* poem called *Table d' Hôte*,' said Eddie softly. 'It's *so* wonderful. In the last Anthology. Have you got a copy? I'd *so* like to *show* it to you. It begins with an *incredibly* beautiful line: "Why Must it Always be Tomato Soup?" '

'Yes,' said Bertha. And she moved noiselessly to a table opposite the drawing-room door and Eddie glided noiselessly after her. She picked up the little book and gave it to him; they had not made a sound.

While he looked it up she turned her head towards the hall. And she saw . . . Harry with Miss Fulton's coat in his arms and Miss Fulton with her back turned to him and her head bent. He tossed the coat away, put his hands on her shoulders and turned her violently to him. His lips said: 'I adore you,' and Miss Fulton laid her moonbeam fingers on his cheeks and smiled her sleepy smile. Harry's nostrils quivered; his lips curled back in a hideous grin while he whispered: 'To-morrow,' and with her eyelids Miss Fulton said: 'Yes.'

'Here it is,' said Eddie. ' "Why Must it Always be Tomato Soup?" It's so *deeply* true, don't you feel? Tomato soup is so *dreadfully* eternal.'

'If you prefer,' said Harry's voice, very loud, from the hall, 'I can 'phone you a cab to come to the door.'

'Oh, no. It's not necessary,' said Miss Fulton, and she came up to Bertha and gave her the slender fingers to hold.

'Good-bye. Thank you so much.'

'Good-bye,' said Bertha.

Miss Fulton held her hand a moment longer.

'Your lovely pear tree!' she murmured.

And then she was gone, with Eddie following, like the black cat following the grey cat.

'I'll shut up shop,' said Harry, extravagantly cool and collected.

'Your lovely pear tree — pear tree — pear tree!'

Bertha simply ran over to the long windows.

'Oh, what is going to happen now?' she cried.

But the pear tree was as lovely as ever and as full of flower and as still.

The Garden Party

KATHERINE MANSFIELD

And after all the weather was ideal. They could not have had a more perfect day for a garden-party if they had ordered it. Windless, warm, the sky without a cloud. Only the blue was veiled with a haze of light gold, as it is sometimes in early summer. The gardener had been up since dawn, mowing the lawns and sweeping them, until the grass and the dark flat rosettes where the daisy plants had been seemed to shine. As for the roses, you could not help feeling they understood that roses are the only flowers that impress people at garden-parties; the only flowers that everybody is certain of knowing. Hundreds, yes, literally hundreds, had come out in a single night; the green bushes bowed down as though they had been visited by archangels.

Breakfast was not yet over before the men came to put up the marquee.

'Where do you want the marquee put, mother?'

'My dear child, it's no use asking me. I'm determined to leave everything to you children this year. Forget I am your mother. Treat me as an honoured guest.'

But Meg could not possibly go and supervise the men. She had washed her hair before breakfast, and she sat drinking her coffee in a green turban, with a dark wet curl stamped on each cheek. Jose, the butterfly, always came down in a silk petticoat and a kimono jacket.

'You'll have to go, Laura; you're the artistic one.'

Away Laura flew, still holding her piece of bread-and-butter. It's so delicious to have an excuse for eating out of doors and, besides, she loved having to arrange things; she always felt she could do it so much better than anybody else.

Four men in their shirt-sleeves stood grouped together on the garden path. They carried staves covered with rolls of canvas and they had big tool-bags slung on their backs. They looked impressive. Laura wished now that she was not holding that piece of bread-and-butter, but there was nowhere to put it and she couldn't possibly throw it away. She blushed and tried to look severe and even a little bit short-sighted as she came up to them.

'Good morning,' she said, copying her mother's voice. But that sounded so fearfully affected that she was ashamed, and stammered like a little girl, 'Oh — er — have you come — is it about the marquee?'

'That's right, miss,' said the tallest of the men, a lanky, freckled fellow, and he shifted his tool-bag, knocked back his straw hat and smiled down at her. 'That's about it.'

His smile was so easy, so friendly, that Laura recovered. What nice eyes he had, small, but such a dark blue! And now she looked at the others, they were smiling too. 'Cheer up, we won't bite,' their smile seemed to say. How very nice workmen were! And what a beautiful morning! She mustn't mention the morning; she must be business-like. The marquee.

'Well, what about the lily-lawn? Would that do?'

And she pointed to the lily-lawn with the hand that didn't hold the bread-and-butter. They turned, they stared in the direction. A little fat chap thrust out his underlip and the tall fellow frowned.

'I don't fancy it,' said he. 'Not conspicuous enough. You see, with a thing like a marquee' — and he turned to Laura in his easy way — 'you want to put it somewhere where it'll give you a bang slap in the eye, if you follow me.'

Laura's upbringing made her wonder for a moment whether it was quite respectful of a workman to talk to her of bangs slap in the eye. But she did quite follow him.

'A corner of the tennis-court,' she suggested. 'But the band's going to be in one corner.'

'H'm, going to have a band, are you?' said another of the workmen. He was pale. He had a haggard look as his dark eyes scanned the tennis-court. What was he thinking?

'Only a very small band,' said Laura gently. Perhaps he wouldn't mind so much if the band was quite small. But the tall fellow interrupted.

'Look here, miss, that's the place. Against those trees. Over there. That'll do fine.'

Against the karakas. Then the karaka trees would be hidden. And they were so lovely, with their broad, gleaming leaves, and their clusters of yellow fruit. They were like trees you imagined growing on a desert island, proud, solitary, lifting their leaves and fruits to the sun in a kind of silent splendour. Must they be hidden by a marquee?

They must. Already the men had shouldered their staves and were making for the place. Only the tall fellow was left. He bent down, pinched a sprig of lavender, put his thumb and forefinger to his nose and snuffed up the smell. When Laura saw that gesture she forgot all about the karakas in her wonder at him caring for things like that — caring for the smell of lavender. How many men that she knew would have done such a thing. Oh, how extraordinarily nice workmen were, she thought. Why couldn't she have workmen for friends rather than the silly boys she danced with and who came to Sunday night supper? She would get on much better with men like these.

It's all the fault, she decided, as the tall fellow drew something on the back of an envelope, something that was to be looped up or left to hang, of these absurd class distinctions. Well, for her part, she didn't feel them. Not a bit, not an atom . . . And now there came the chock-chock of wooden hammers. Someone whistled, someone sang out, 'Are you right there, matey?' 'Matey!' The friendliness of it, the — the — Just to prove how happy she was, just to show the tall fellow how at home she felt, and how she despised stupid conventions, Laura took a big bite of her bread-and-butter as she stared at the little drawing. She felt just like a work-girl.

'Laura, Laura, where are you? Telephone, Laura!' a voice cried from the house.

'Coming!' Away she skimmed, over the lawn, up the path, up the steps, across the veranda and into the porch. In the hall her father and Laurie were brushing their hats ready to go to the office.

'I say, Laura,' said Laurie very fast, 'you might just give a squiz at my coat before this afternoon. See if it wants pressing.'

'I will,' said she. Suddenly she couldn't stop herself. She ran at Laurie and gave him a small, quick squeeze. 'Oh, I do love parties, don't you?' gasped Laura.

'Ra-ther,' said Laurie's warm, boyish voice, and he squeezed his sister too and gave her a gentle push. 'Dash off to the telephone, old girl.'

The telephone. 'Yes, yes; oh yes. Kitty? Good morning, dear. Come to lunch? Do, dear. Delighted, of course. It will only be a very scratch meal — just the sandwich crusts and broken meringue-shells and what's left over. Yes, isn't it a perfect morning? Your white? Oh, I certainly should. One moment — hold the line. Mother's calling.' And Laura sat back. 'What, mother? Can't hear.'

Mrs. Sheridan's voice floated down the stairs. 'Tell her to wear that sweet hat she had on last Sunday.'

'Mother says you're to wear that *sweet* hat you had on last Sunday. Good. One o'clock. Bye-bye.'

Laura put back the receiver, flung her arms over her head, took a deep breath, stretched and let them fall. 'Huh,' she sighed, and the moment after the sigh she sat up quickly. She was still, listening. All the doors in the house seemed to be open. The house was alive with soft, quick steps and running voices. The green baize door that led to the kitchen regions swung open and shut with a muffled thud. And now there came a long, chuckling absurd sound. It was the heavy piano being moved on its stiff castors. But the air! If you stopped to notice, was the air always like this? Little faint winds were playing chase in at the tops of the windows, out at the doors. And there were two tiny spots of sun, one on the inkpot, one on a silver photograph frame, playing too. Darling little spots. Especially the one on the inkpot lid. It was quite warm. A warm little silver star. She could have kissed it.

The front door bell pealed and there sounded the rustle of Sadie's print skirt on the stairs. A man's voice murmured; Sadie answered, careless, 'I'm sure I don't know. Wait. I'll ask Mrs. Sheridan.'

'What is it, Sadie?' Laura came into the hall.

'It's the florist, Miss Laura.'

It was, indeed. There, just inside the door, stood a wide, shallow tray full of pots of pink lilies. No other kind. Nothing but lilies — canna lilies, big pink flowers, wide open, radiant, almost frighteningly

44

alive on bright crimson stems.

'Oh-oh, Sadie!' said Laura, and the sound was like a little moan. She crouched down as if to warm herself at that blaze of lilies; she felt they were in her fingers, on her lips, growing in her breast.

'It's some mistake,' she said faintly. 'Nobody ever ordered so many. Sadie, go and find mother.'

But at that moment Mrs. Sheridan joined them.

'It's quite right,' she said calmly. 'Yes, I ordered them. Aren't they lovely?' She pressed Laura's arm. 'I was passing the shop yesterday, and I saw them in the window. And I suddenly thought for once in my life I shall have enough canna lilies. The garden-party will be a good excuse.'

'But I thought you said you didn't mean to interfere,' said Laura. Sadie had gone. The florist's man was still outside at his van. She put her arm round her mother's neck and gently, very gently, she bit her mother's ear.

'My darling child, you wouldn't like a logical mother, would you? Don't do that. Here's the man.'

He carried more lilies still, another whole tray.

'Bank them up, just inside the door, on both sides of the porch, please,' said Mrs. Sheridan. 'Don't you agree, Laura?'

'Oh, I *do*, mother.'

In the drawing-room Meg, Jose and good little Hans had at last succeeded in moving the piano.

'Now, if we put this chesterfield against the wall and move everything out of the room except the chairs, don't you think?'

'Quite.'

'Hans, move these tables into the smoking-room, and bring a sweeper to take these marks off the carpet and — one moment, Hans —' Jose loved giving orders to the servants and they loved obeying her. She always made them feel they were taking part in some drama. 'Tell mother and Miss Laura to come here at once.'

'Very good, Miss Jose.'

She turned to Meg. 'I want to hear what the piano sounds like, just in case I'm asked to sing this afternoon. Let's try over "This Life is Weary."'

Pom! Ta-ta-ta *Tee*-ta! The piano burst out so passionately that Jose's

face changed. She clasped her hands. She looked mournfully and
enigmatically at her mother and Laura as they came in.

> This Life is *Wee*-ary,
> A Tear — a Sigh.
> A Love that *Chan*-ges,
>   This Life is *Wee*-ary,
> A Tear — a Sigh.
> A Love that *Chan*-ges,
> And then . . . Good-bye!

But at the word 'Good-bye,' and although the piano sounded more
desperate than ever, her face broke into a brilliant, dreadfully unsympathetic smile.

'Aren't I in good voice, mummy?' she beamed.

> This Life is *Wee*-ary,
> Hope comes to Die.
> A Dream — a *Wa*-kening.

But now Sadie interrupted them. 'What is it, Sadie?'

'If you please, M'm, cook says have you got the flags for the sandwiches?'

'The flags for the sandwiches, Sadie?' echoed Mrs. Sheridan dream-
ily. And the children knew by her face that she hadn't got them. 'Let
me see.' And she said to Sadie firmly, 'Tell cook I'll let her have them
in ten minutes.'

Sadie went.

'Now, Laura,' said her mother quickly, 'come with me into the
smoking-room. I've got the names somewhere on the back of an envelope. You'll have to write them out for me. Meg, go upstairs this
minute and take that wet thing off your head. Jose, run and finish
dressing this instant. Do you hear me, children, or shall I have to tell
your father when he comes home to-night? And — and, Jose, pacify
cook if you do go into the kitchen, will you? I'm terrified of her this
morning.'

The envelope was found at last behind the dining-room clock,
though how it had got there Mrs. Sheridan could not imagine.

'One of you children must have stolen it out of my bag, because I remember vividly — cream-cheese and lemon-curd. Have you done that?'

'Yes.'

'Egg and —' Mrs. Sheridan held the envelope away from her. 'It looks like mice. It can't be mice, can it?'

'Olive, pet,' said Laura, looking over her shoulder.

'Yes, of course, olive. What a horrible combination it sounds. Egg and olive.'

They were finished at last, and Laura took them off to the kitchen. She found Jose there pacifying the cook, who did not look at all terrifying.

'I have never seen such exquisite sandwiches,' said Jose's rapturous voice. 'How many kinds did you say there were, cook? Fifteen?'

'Fifteen, Miss Jose.'

'Well, cook, I congratulate you.'

Cook swept up crusts with the long sandwich knife, and smiled broadly.

'Godber's has come,' announced Sadie, issuing out of the pantry. She had seen the man pass the window.

That meant the cream puffs had come. Godber's were famous for their cream puffs. Nobody ever thought of making them at home.

'Bring them in and put them on the table, my girl,' ordered cook.

Sadie brought them in and went back to the door. Of course Laura and Jose were far too grown-up to really care about such things. All the same, they couldn't help agreeing that the puffs looked very attractive. Very. Cook began arranging them, shaking off the extra icing sugar.

'Don't they carry one back to all one's parties?' said Laura.

'I suppose they do,' said practical Jose, who never liked to be carried back. 'They look beautifully light and feathery, I must say.'

'Have one each, my dears,' said cook in her comfortable voice. 'Yer ma won't know.'

Oh, impossible. Fancy cream puffs so soon after breakfast. The very idea made one shudder. All the same, two minutes later Jose and Laura were licking their fingers with that absorbed inward look that only comes from whipped cream.

'Let's go into the garden, out by the back way,' suggested Laura. 'I want to see how the men are getting on with the marquee. They're such awfully nice men.'

But the back door was blocked by cook, Sadie, Godber's man and Hans.

Something had happened.

'Tuk-tuk-tuk,' clucked cook like an agitated hen. Sadie had her hand clapped to her cheek as though she had toothache. Han's face was screwed up in the effort to understand. Only Godber's man seemed to be enjoying himself; it was his story.

'What's the matter? What's happened?'

'There's been a horrible accident,' said cook. 'A man killed.'

'A man killed! Where? How? When?'

But Godber's man wasn't going to have his story snatched from under his very nose.

'Know those little cottages just below here, miss?' Know them? Of course she knew them. 'Well, there's a young chap living there, name of Scott, a carter. His horse shied at a traction-engine, corner of Hawke Street this morning, and he was thrown out on the back of his head. Killed.'

'Dead!' Laura stared at Godber's man.

'Dead when they picked him up,' said Godber's man with relish. 'They were taking the body home as I come up here.' And he said to the cook, 'He's left a wife and five little ones.'

'Jose, come here.' Laura caught hold of her sister's sleeve and dragged her through the kitchen to the other side of the green baize door. There she paused and leaned against it. 'Jose!' she said, horrified, 'however are we going to stop everything?'

'Stop everything, Laura!' cried Jose in astonishment. 'What do you mean?'

'Stop the garden-party, of course.' Why did Jose pretend?

But Jose was still more amazed. 'Stop the garden-party? My dear Laura, don't be so absurd. Of course we can't do anything of the kind. Nobody expects us to. Don't be so extravagant.'

'But we can't possibly have a garden-party with a man dead just outside the front gate.'

That really was extravagant, for the little cottages were in a lane to themselves at the very bottom of a steep rise that led up to the house.

A broad road ran between. True, they were far too near. They were the greatest possible eyesore and they had no right to be in that neighbourhood at all. They were little mean dwellings painted a chocolate brown. In the garden patches there was nothing but cabbage stalks, sick hens and tomato cans. The very smoke coming out of their chimneys was poverty-stricken. Little rags and shreds of smoke, so unlike the great silvery plumes that uncurled from the Sheridans' chimneys. Washerwomen lived in the lane and sweeps and a cobbler and a man whose house-front was studded all over with minute bird-cages. Children swarmed. When the Sheridans were little they were forbidden to set foot there because of the revolting language and of what they might catch. But since they were grown up Laura and Laurie on their prowls sometimes walked through. It was disgusting and sordid. They came out with a shudder. But still one must go everywhere; one must see everything. So through they went.

'And just think of what the band would sound like to that poor woman,' said Laura.

'Oh, Laura!' Jose began to be seriously annoyed. 'If you're going to stop a band playing every time someone has an accident, you'll lead a very strenuous life. I'm every bit as sorry about it as you. I feel just as sympathetic.' Her eyes hardened. She looked at her sister just as she used to when they were little and fighting together. 'You won't bring a drunken workman back to life by being sentimental,' she said softly.

'Drunk! Who said he was drunk?' Laura turned furiously on Jose. She said just as they had used to say on those occasions, 'I'm going straight up to tell mother.'

'Do, dear,' cooed Jose.

'Mother, can I come into your room?' Laura turned the big glass door-knob.

'Of course, child. Why, what's the matter? What's given you such a colour?' And Mrs. Sheridan turned round from her dressing-table. She was trying on a new hat.

'Mother, a man's been killed,' began Laura.

'*Not* in the garden?' interrupted her mother.

'No, no!'

'Oh, what a fright you gave me!' Mrs. Sheridan sighed with relief and took off the big hat and held it on her knees.

'But listen, mother,' said Laura. Breathless, half choking, she told the dreadful story. 'Of course, we can't have our party, can we?' she pleaded. 'The band and everybody arriving. They'd hear us, mother; they're nearly neighbours!'

To Laura's astonishment her mother behaved just like Jose; it was harder to bear because she seemed amused. She refused to take Laura seriously.

'But, my dear child, use your common sense. It's only by accident we've heard of it. If someone had died there normally — and I can't understand how they keep alive in those poky little holes — we should still be having our party, shouldn't we?'

Laura had to say 'yes' to that, but she felt it was all wrong. She sat down on her mother's sofa and pinched the cushion frill.

'Mother, isn't it really terribly heartless of us?' she asked.

'Darling!' Mrs. Sheridan got up and came over to her, carrying the hat. Before Laura could stop her she had popped it on. 'My child!' said her mother, 'the hat is yours. It's made for you. It's much too young for me. I have never seen you look such a picture. Look at yourself!' And she held up her hand-mirror.

'But, mother,' Laura began again. She couldn't look at herself; she turned aside.

This time Mrs. Sheridan lost patience just as Jose had done.

'You are being very absurd, Laura,' she said coldly. 'People like that don't expect sacrifices from us. And it's not very sympathetic to spoil everybody's enjoyment as you're doing now.'

'I don't understand,' said Laura, and she walked quickly out of the room into her own bedroom. There, quite by chance, the first thing she saw was this charming girl in the mirror, in her black hat trimmed with gold daisies and a long black velvet ribbon. Never had she imagined she could look like that. Is mother right? she thought. And now she hoped her mother was right. Am I being extravagant? Perhaps it was extravagant. Just for a moment she had another glimpse of that poor woman and those little children and the body being carried into the house. But it all seemed blurred, unreal, like a picture in the newspaper. I'll remember it again after the party's over, she decided. And somehow that seemed quite the best plan . . .

Lunch was over by half-past one. By half-past two they were all ready for the fray. The green-coated band had arrived and was established in a corner of the tennis-court.

'My dear!' trilled Kitty Maitland, 'aren't they too like frogs for words? You ought to have arranged them round the pond with the conductor in the middle on a leaf.'

Laurie arrived and hailed them on his way to dress. At the sight of him Laura remembered the accident again. She wanted to tell him. If Laurie agreed with the others, then it was bound to be all right. And she followed him into the hall.

'Laurie!'

'Hallo!' He was half-way upstairs, but when he turned round and saw Laura he suddenly puffed out his cheeks and goggled his eyes at her. 'My word, Laura! You do look stunning,' said Laurie. 'What an absolutely topping hat!'

Laura said faintly 'Is it?' and smiled up at Laurie and didn't tell him after all.

Soon after that people began coming in streams. The band struck up; the hired waiters ran from the house to the marquee. Wherever you looked there were couples strolling, bending to the flowers, greeting, moving on over the lawn. They were like bright birds that had alighted in the Sheridans' garden for this one afternoon, on their way to — where? Ah, what happiness it is to be with people who all are happy, to press hands, press cheeks, smile into eyes.

'Darling Laura, how well you look!'

'What a becoming hat, child!'

'Laura, you look quite Spanish. I've never seen you look so striking.'

And Laura, glowing, answered softly, 'Have you had tea? Won't you have an ice? The passion-fruit ices really are rather special.' She ran to her father and begged him: 'Daddy darling, can't the band have something to drink?'

And the perfect afternoon slowly ripened, slowly faded, slowly its petals closed.

'Never a more delightful garden-party . . .' 'The greatest success . . .' 'Quite the most . . .'

Laura helped her mother with the good-byes. They stood side by side in the porch till it was all over.

'All over, all over, thank heaven,' said Mrs. Sheridan. 'Round up the others, Laura. Let's go and have some fresh coffee. I'm exhausted. Yes, it's been very successful. But oh, these parties, these parties! Why will you children insist on giving parties!' And they all of them sat down in the deserted marquee.

'Have a sandwich, daddy dear. I wrote the flag.'

'Thanks.' Mr. Sheridan took a bite and the sandwich was gone. He took another. 'I suppose you didn't hear of a beastly accident that happened to-day?' he said.

'My dear,' said Mrs. Sheridan, holding up her hand, 'we did. It nearly ruined the party. Laura insisted we should put it off.'

'Oh, mother!' Laura didn't want to be teased about it.

'It was a horrible affair all the same,' said Mr. Sheridan. 'The chap was married too. Lived just below in the lane, and leaves a wife and half a dozen kiddies, so they say.'

An awkward little silence fell. Mrs. Sheridan fidgeted with her cup. Really, it was very tactless of father . . .

Suddenly she looked up. There on the table were all those sandwiches, cakes, puffs, all uneaten, all going to be wasted. She had one of her brilliant ideas.

'I know,' she said. 'Let's make up a basket. Let's send that poor creature some of this perfectly good food. At any rate, it will be the greatest treat for the children. Don't you agree? And she's sure to have neighbours calling in and so on. What a point to have it all ready prepared. Laura!' She jumped up. 'Get me the big basket out of the stairs cupboard.'

'But, mother, do you really think it's a good idea?' said Laura.

Again, how curious, she seemed to be different from them all. To take scraps from their party. Would the poor woman really like that?

'Of course! What's the matter with you to-day? An hour or two ago you were insisting on us being sympathetic.'

Oh well! Laura ran for the basket. It was filled, it was now heaped by her mother.

'Take it yourself, darling,' said she. 'Run down just as you are. No, wait, take the arum lilies too. People of that class are so impressed by arum lilies.'

'The stems will ruin her lace frock,' said practical Jose.

So they would. Just in time. 'Only the basket, then. And, Laura!' — her mother followed her out of the marquee — 'don't on any account —'

'What mother?'

No, better not put such ideas into the child's head! 'Nothing! Run along.'

It was just growing dusky as Laura shut their garden gates. A big dog ran by like a shadow. The road gleamed white, and down below in the hollow the little cottages were in deep shade. How quiet it seemed after the afternoon. Here she was going down the hill to somewhere where a man lay dead, and she couldn't realise it. Why couldn't she? She stopped a minute. And it seemed to her that kisses, voices, tinkling spoons, laughter, the smell of crushed grass was somehow inside her. She had no room for anything else. How strange! She looked up at the pale sky, and all she thought was, 'Yes, it was the most successful party.'

Now the broad road was crossed. The lane began, smoky and dark. Women in shawls and men's tweed caps hurried by. Men hung over the palings; the children played in the doorways. A low hum came from the mean little cottages. In some of them there was a flicker of light, and a shadow, crab-like, moved across the window. Laura bent her head and hurried on. She wished now she had put on a coat. How her frock shone! And the big hat with the velvet streamer — if only it was another hat! Were the people looking at her? They must be. It was a mistake to have come; she knew all along it was a mistake. Should she go back even now?

No, too late. This was the house. It must be. A dark knot of people stood outside. Beside the gate an old, old woman with a crutch sat in a chair, watching. She had her feet on a newspaper. The voices stopped as Laura drew near. The group parted. It was as though she was expected, as though they had known she was coming here.

Laura was terribly nervous. Tossing the velvet ribbon over her shoulder, she said to a woman standing by, 'Is this Mrs. Scott's house?' and the woman, smiling queerly, said, 'It is, my lass.'

Oh, to be away from this! She actually said, 'Help me, God,' as she walked up the tiny path and knocked. To be away from those staring eyes, or to be covered up in anything, one of those women's shawls even. I'll just leave the basket and go, she decided. I shan't even wait for it to be emptied.

Then the door opened. A little woman in black showed in the gloom.

Laura said, 'Are you Mrs Scott?' But to her horror the woman answered, 'Walk in, please, miss,' and she was shut in the passage.

'No,' said Laura, 'I don't want to come in. I only want to leave this basket. Mother sent —'

The little woman in the gloomy passage seemed not to have heard her. 'Step this way, please, miss,' she said in an oily voice, and Laura followed her.

She found herself in a wretched little low kitchen, lighted by a smoky lamp. There was a woman sitting before the fire.

'Em,' said the little creature who had let her in. 'Em! It's a young lady.' She turned to Laura. She said meaningly, 'I'm 'er sister, miss. You'll excuse 'er, won't you?'

'Oh, but of course!' said Laura. 'Please, please don't disturb her. I — I only want to leave —'

But at that moment the woman at the fire turned round. Her face, puffed up, red, with swollen eyes and swollen lips, looked terrible. She seemed as though she couldn't understand why Laura was there. What did it mean? Why was this stranger standing in the kitchen with a basket? What was it all about? And the poor face puckered up again.

'All right, my dear,' said the other. 'I'll thenk the young lady.'

And again she began, 'You'll excuse her, miss, I'm sure,' and her face, swollen too, tried an oily smile.

Laura only wanted to get out, to get away. She was back in the passage. The door opened. She walked straight through into the bedroom, where the dead man was lying.

'You'd like a look at 'im, wouldn't you?' said Em's sister, and she brushed past Laura over to the bed. 'Don't be afraid, my lass' — and now her voice sounded fond and sly, and fondly she drew down the sheet — ''e looks a picture. There's nothing to show. Come along, my dear.'

Laura came.

There lay a young man, fast asleep — sleeping so soundly, so deeply, that he was far, far away from them both. Oh, so remote, so peaceful. He was dreaming. Never wake him up again. His head was sunk in the pillow, his eyes were closed; they were blind under the closed eyelids. He was given up to his dream. What did garden-parties and baskets and lace frocks matter to him? He was far from all those things. He was wonderful, beautiful. While they were laughing and while the band was playing, this marvel had come to the lane. Happy . . . happy . . . All is well, said that sleeping face. This is just as it should be. I am content.

But all the same you had to cry, and she couldn't go out of the room without saying something to him. Laura gave a loud childish sob.

'Forgive my hat,' she said.

And this time she didn't wait for Em's sister. She found her way out of the door, down the path past all those dark people. At the corner of the lane she met Laurie.

He stepped out of the shadow. 'Is that you, Laura?'

'Yes.'

'Mother was getting anxious. Was it all right?'

'Yes, quite. Oh, Laurie!' She took his arm, she pressed up against him.

'I say, you're not crying, are you?' asked her brother.

Laura shook her head. She was.

Laurie put his arm round her shoulder. 'Don't cry,' he said in his warm, loving voice. 'Was it awful?'

'No,' sobbed Laura. 'It was simply marvellous. But, Laurie —' She stopped, she looked at her brother. 'Isn't life,' she stammered, 'isn't life —' But what life was she couldn't explain. No matter. He quite understood.

'*Isn't* it, darling?' said Laurie.

A Great Day

FRANK SARGESON

It was beginning to get light when Ken knocked on the door of Fred's bach.

Are you up? he said.

Fred called out that he was, and in a moment he opened the door.

Just finished my breakfast, he said. We'd better get moving.

It didn't take long. The bach was right on the edge of the beach, and they got the dinghy on to Ken's back and he carried it down the beach, and Fred followed with the gear. Ken was big enough to make light work of the dinghy but it was all Fred could do to manage the gear. There wasn't much of him and he goddamned the gear every few yards he went.

The tide was well over half-way out, and the sea was absolutely flat without even a ripple breaking on the sand. Except for some seagulls that walked on the sand and made broad-arrow marks where they walked there wasn't a single thing moving. It was so still it wasn't natural. Except for the seagulls you'd have thought the world had died in the night.

Ken eased the dinghy off his shoulders and turned it the right way up, and Fred dropped the anchor and the oars on the sand, and heaved the sugar bag of fishing gear into the dinghy.

I wouldn't mind if I was a big hefty bloke like you, he said.

Well, Ken didn't say anything to that. He sat on the stern of the dinghy and rolled himself a cigarette, and Fred got busy and fixed the oars and rowlocks and tied on the anchor.

Come on, he said, we'll shove off. And with his trousers rolled up he went and tugged at the bow, and with Ken shoving at the stern the

56

dinghy began to float, so Fred hopped in and took the oars, and then Ken hopped in and they were off.

It's going to be a great day, Fred said.

It certainly looked like it. The sun was coming up behind the island they were heading for, and there wasn't a cloud in the sky.

We'll make for the same place as last time, Fred said. You tell me if I don't keep straight. And for a time he rowed hard without sending the dinghy along very fast. The trouble was his short legs, he couldn't get them properly braced against the stern seat. And Ken, busy rolling a supply of cigarettes, didn't watch out where he was going, so when Fred took a look ahead he was heading for the wrong end of the island.

Hey, he said, you take a turn and I'll tell you where to head for.

So they changed places and Ken pulled wonderfully well. For a time it was more a mental shock you got with each jerk of the dinghy. You realised how strong he was. He had only a shirt and a pair of shorts on, and his big body, hard with muscle, must have been over six feet long.

Gee, I wish I had your body, Fred said. It's no wonder the girls chase you. But look at the sort of joker I am.

Well, he wasn't much to look at. There was so little of him. And the old clothes he wore had belonged to someone considerably bigger than he was. And he had on an old hat that came down too far, and would have come down further if it hadn't bent his ears over and sat on them as if they were brackets.

How about a smoke? Fred said.

Sure. Sorry.

And to save him from leaving off rowing Fred reached over and took the tin out of his shirt pocket.

That's the curse of this sustenance, Fred said. A man's liable to be out of smokes before pay-day.

Yes, I suppose he is, Ken said.

It's rotten being out of work, Fred said. Thank the Lord I've got this dinghy. D'you know last year I made over thirty pounds out of fishing?

And how've you done this year?

Not so good. You're the first bloke I've had go out with me this year that hasn't wanted me to go shares. Gee, you're lucky to be able to go fishing for fun.

It's about time I landed a position, Ken said. I've had over a month's holiday.

Yes I know. But you've got money saved up, and it doesn't cost you anything to live when you can live with your auntie. How'd you like to live in that damn bach of mine and pay five bob a week rent? And another thing, you've got education.

It doesn't count for much these days. A man has to take any position he can get.

Yes, but if a man's been to one of those High Schools it makes him different. Not any better, mind you. I'm all for the working class because I'm a worker myself, but an educated bloke has the advantage over a bloke like me. The girls chase him just to mention one thing, specially if he happens to be a big he-man as well.

Ken didn't say anything to that. He just went on pulling, and he got Fred to stick a cigarette in his mouth and light it at the same time as he lit his own. And then Fred lolled back in his seat and watched him, and you could tell that about the only thing they had in common was that they both had cigarettes dangling out of their mouths.

Pull her round a bit with your left, Fred said. And there's no need to bust your boiler.

It's O.K., Ken said.

You've got the strength, Fred said.

I'm certainly no infant.

What good's a man's strength anyway? Say he goes and works in an office?

I hadn't thought of that.

Another thing, he gets old. Fancy you getting old and losing your strength. Wouldn't it be a shame?

Sure, Ken said. Why talk about it?

It sort of fascinates me. You'll die someday, and where'll that big frame of yours be then?

That's an easy one. Pushing up the daisies.

It might as well be now as anytime, mightn't it?

Good Lord, I don't see that.

A man'd forget for good. It'd be just the same as it is out here on a day like this. Only better.

Ken stopped rowing to throw away his cigarette.

My God, he said, you're a queer customer. Am I heading right?

Pull with your left, Fred said. But I'll give you a spell.

It's O.K., Ken said.

And he went on rowing and after a bit Fred emptied the lines out of the sugar bag and began cutting up the bait. And after a bit longer when they were about half-way over to the island he said they'd gone far enough, so Ken shipped his oars and threw the anchor overboard, and they got their lines ready and began to fish.

And by that time it was certainly turning out a great day. The sun was getting hot but there still wasn't any wind, and as the tide had just about stopped running out down the Gulf the dinghy hardly knew which way to pull on the anchor rope. They'd pulled out less than two miles from the shore, but with the sea as it was it might have been anything from none at all up to an infinite number. You couldn't hear a sound or see anything moving. It was another world. The houses on the shore didn't belong. Nor the people either.

Wouldn't you like to stay out here for good? Fred said.

Ring off, Ken said. I got a bite.

So did I, but it was only a nibble. Anyhow it's not a good day for fish. It wants to be cloudy.

So I've heard.

I've been thinking, Fred said, it's funny you never learnt to swim.

Oh I don't know. Up to now I've always lived in country towns.

Doesn't it make you feel a bit windy?

On a day like this! Anyhow, you couldn't swim that distance yourself.

Oh couldn't I! You'd be surprised . . . get a bite?

Yes I did.

Same here . . . you'll be settling down here, won't you, Ken?

It depends if I can get a position.

I suppose you'll go on living with your auntie.

That depends too. If I got a good position I might be thinking of getting married.

Gee, that'd be great, wouldn't it?

I got another bite, Ken said.

Same here. I reckon our lines are crossed.

So they pulled in their lines and they were crossed sure enough, but Ken had hooked the smallest snapper you ever saw.

He's no good, Fred said. And he worked the fish off the hook and held it in his hand. They're pretty little chaps, aren't they? he said. Look at his colours.

Let him go, Ken said.

Poor little beggar, Fred said. I bet he wonders what's struck him. He's trying to get his breath. Funny isn't it, when there's plenty of air about? It's like Douglas Credit.

Oh for God's sake, Ken said.

I bet in less than five minutes he forgets about how he was nearly suffocated, Fred said, and he threw the fish back. And it lay bewildered for a second on the surface, then it flipped its tail and was gone. It was comical in its way and they both laughed.

They always do that, Fred said. But don't you wish you could swim like him?

Ken didn't say anything to that and they put fresh bait on their hooks and tried again, but there were only nibbles. They could bring nothing to the surface.

I'll tell you what, Fred said, those nibbles might be old men snapper only they won't take a decent bite at bait like this.

And he explained that off the end of the island there was a reef where they could get plenty of big mussels. It would be just nice with the tide out as it was. The reef wouldn't be uncovered, it never was, but you could stand on it in water up to your knees and pull up the mussels. And if you cut the inside out of a big mussel you only had to hang it on your hook for an old man snapper to go for it with one big bite.

It's a fair way, Ken said.

It doesn't matter, Fred said. We've got oceans of time. And he climbed past Ken to pull up the anchor, and Ken pulled in the lines, and then Fred insisted on rowing and they started for the end of the island.

And by that time the tide had begun to run in up the Gulf and there was a light wind blowing up against the tide, so that the sea, almost without your noticing it, was showing signs of coming up a bit rough. And the queer thing was that with the movement the effect of another world was destroyed. You seemed a part of the real world of houses and people once more. Yet with the sea beginning to get choppy the land looked a long way off.

Going back, Ken said, we'll be pulling against the wind.

Yes, Fred said, but the tide'll be a help. Anyhow, what's it matter when a man's out with a big hefty bloke like you?

Nor did he seem to be in too much of a hurry to get to his reef. He kept resting on his oars to roll cigarettes, and when Ken said something about it he said they had oceans of time.

You're in no hurry to get back, he said, Mary'll keep.

Well, Ken didn't say anything to that.

Mary's a great kid, Fred said.

Sure, Ken said. Mary's one of the best.

I've known Mary for years, Fred said.

Yes, Ken said. So I've gathered.

I suppose you have. Up to a while ago Mary and I used to be great cobbers.

I'll give you a spell, Ken said.

But Fred said it was O.K.

Mary's got a bit of education too, he said. Only when her old man died the family was hard up so she had to go into service. It was lucky she got a good place at your auntie's. Gee, I've been round there and had tea sometimes when your auntie's been out, and oh boy is the tucker any good!

Look here, Ken said, at this rate we'll never get to that reef.

Oh yes we will, Fred said, and he pulled a bit harder. If only a man hadn't lost his job, he said.

I admit it must be tough, Ken said.

And then Fred stood up and took a look back at the shore.

I thought there might be somebody else coming out, he said, but there isn't. So thank God for that. And he said that he couldn't stand anybody hanging around when he was fishing. By the way, he said, I forgot to do this before. And he stuffed pieces of cotton-wool into his ears. If the spray gets in my ears it gives me the earache, he said.

Then he really did settle down to his rowing, and with the sea more or less following them it wasn't long before they were off the end of the island.

Nobody lived on the island. There were a few holiday baches but they were empty now that it was well on into the autumn. Nor from this end could you see any landing places, and with the wind blowing up more and more it wasn't too pleasant to watch the sea running up the rocks. And Fred had to spend a bit of time manoeuvring around before he found his reef.

It was several hundred yards out with deep water all round, and it seemed to be quite flat. If the sea had been calm it might have been covered to a depth of about a foot with the tide as it was. But with the sea chopping across it wasn't exactly an easy matter to stand there. At one moment the water was down past your knees, and the next moment you had to steady yourself while it came up round your thighs. And it was uncanny to stand there, because with the deep water all round you seemed to have discovered a way of standing up out in the sea.

Anyhow, Fred took off his coat and rolled up his sleeves and trousers as far as they'd go, and then he hopped out and got Ken to do the same and keep hold of the dinghy. Then he steadied himself and began dipping his hands down and pulling up mussels and throwing them back into the dinghy, and he worked at a mad pace as though he hadn't a moment to lose. It seemed only a minute or so before he was quite out of breath.

It's tough work, he said. You can see what a weak joker I am.

I'll give you a spell, Ken said, only keep hold of the boat.

Well, Fred held the dinghy, and by the way he was breathing and the look of his face you'd have thought he was going to die. But Ken had other matters to think about, he was steadying himself and dipping his hands down more than a yard away, and Fred managed to pull himself together and shove off the dinghy and hop in. And if you'd been sitting in the stern as he pulled away you'd have seen that he had his eyes shut. Nor did he open them except when he took a look ahead to see where he was going, and with the cotton-wool in his ears it was difficult for him to hear.

So for a long time he rowed like that against seas that were getting bigger and bigger, but about half-way back to the shore he took a spell. He changed over to the other side of the seat, so he didn't have to sit facing the island, and he just sat there keeping the dinghy straight on. Then when he felt that he had collected all his strength he stood up and capsized the dinghy. It took a bit of doing but he did it.

And after that, taking it easy, he started on his long swim for the shore.

A Piece of Yellow Soap

FRANK SARGESON

She is dead now, that woman who used to hold a great piece of yellow washing soap in her hand as she stood at her kitchen door. I was a milkman in those days. The woman owed a bill to the firm I worked for, and each Saturday I was expected to collect a sum that would pay for the week's milk, and pay something off the amount overdue. Well, I never collected anything at all. It was because of that piece of yellow soap.

I shall never forget those Saturday mornings. The woman had two advantages over me. She used to stand at the top of the steps and I used to stand at the bottom; and she always came out holding a piece of yellow soap. We used to argue. I would always start off by being very firm. Didn't my living depend on my getting money out of the people I served? But out of this woman I never got a penny. The more I argued the tighter the woman would curl her fingers on to the soap; and her fingers, just out of the washtub, were always bloodless and shrunken. I knew what they must have felt like to her. I didn't like getting my own fingers bloodless and shrunken. My eyes would get fixed on her fingers and the soap, and after a few minutes I would lose all power to look the woman in the face. I would mumble something to myself and take myself off.

I have often wondered whether the woman knew anything about the power her piece of yellow soap had over me, whether she used it as effectively on other tradesmen as she used it on me. I can't help feeling that she did know. Sometimes I used to pass her along the street, out of working hours. She acknowledged me only by staring at me, her eyes like pieces of rock.

She had a way too of feeling inside her handbag as she passed me, and I always had the queer feeling that she carried there a piece of soap. It was her talisman, powerful to work wonders, to create round her a circle through which the more desperate harshnesses of the world could never penetrate.

Well, she is dead now, that woman. If she has passed into Heaven I can't help wondering whether she passed in holding tight to a piece of yellow washing soap. I'm not sure that I believe in Heaven or God myself, but if God is a Person of Sensibility I don't doubt that when He looked at that piece of yellow washing soap He felt ashamed of Himself.

The Hole that Jack Dug

FRANK SARGESON

Jack had got a pretty considerable hole dug in the backyard before I knew anything about it. I went round one scorching hot Saturday afternoon, and Jack was in the hole with nothing on except his boots and his little tight pair of shorts. Jack is a big specimen of a bloke, he's very powerfully developed, and seeing he's worked in the quarry for years in just that rigout, he's browned a darker colour than you'd ever believe possible on a white man. And that afternoon he was sweating so much he had a shine on as well.

Hello Jack, I said, doing a spot of work?

And Jack leaned on his shovel and grinned up at me. The trouble with Jack's grin is that it shows too many teeth. It's easy to pick they're not the real thing, and I've always thought they somehow don't fit in with the rest of him. Also his eyes are sky-blue, and it almost scares you to see them staring out of all that sunburn. I don't say *they* don't fit in though. They always have a bit of a crazy look about them, and even though Jack is my closest cobber I will say that he'll do some crazy things.

Yes Tom, he said, I'm doing a job.

But it's hot work, I said.

I've said it was scorching hot and it was. We'd been having a good summer, the first one after the war broke out. You'd hear folks say what lovely days we were having, and you'd be somehow always telling yourself you just couldn't believe there was any war on, when everything round about you looked so fine and dandy. But anyhow, I was just going to ask Jack if he wanted a hand, when his missis opened the back door and asked if I'd go in and have a cup of tea.

No thanks, Mrs Parker, I said, I've only just had one.

She didn't ask Jack, but he said he could do with one, so we both went inside and his missis had several of her friends there. She always has stacks of friends, and most times you'll find them around. But I'm Jack's friend, about the only one he has that goes to the house. I first ran across Jack in camp during the last war, though I only got to be cobbers with him a fair while after, when we lived at the same boardinghouse and worked at the same job, shovelling cement. In those days he hadn't started to trot the sheila he eventually married, though later on when he did I heard all about it. It knocked Jack over properly. He was always telling me about how she was far too good for him, a girl with her brains and refinement. Before she came out from England she'd been a governess, and I remember how Jack said she'd read more than ten books by an author called Hugh Walpole. Anyhow Jack was knocked over properly, and I reckon she must have been too. Or why did she marry him? As for me, I reckon it was because she did have the brains to tell a real man when she saw one, and hook on to him when she got the chance. But all that must be well over twenty years ago now, and it's always a wonder to me the way Jack still thinks his missis is the greatest kid that ever was, even though she couldn't make it plainer than she does, without a word said, that she's changed her mind about him. Not that you can altogether blame her of course. Just about any man, I should say, would find it awfully trying to be a woman married to Jack. But for a cobber you couldn't pick on a finer bloke.

One thing Mrs Parker's always had against Jack is that he's stayed working in the quarry year after year, instead of trying to get himself a better job. Meaning by a better job one that brings in more pay, without it mattering if it's only senseless and stupid sort of work you have to do. Of course, Jack knows that to run the house, with the snooks growing up fast, his missis could have always done with considerably more money than he's able to let her have. He lets her have the lot any way, he never would smoke or drink or put money on a horse. But he isn't the sort that's got much show of ever being in the big money, and any case it would need to be pretty big, because his missis is always coming to light with some big ideas. Not to mention a car, one thing she's always on about is a refrigerator. It would save money in the long run is what she reckons, and maybe she's right, but it's always seemed too much of a hurdle to Jack.

Do you know dear, I heard him say once, when I was a little boy, and my mother opened the safe, and there was a blowfly buzzing about, it sometimes wouldn't even bother to fly inside.

And Mrs Parker said, What's a blowfly (or your mother for that matter) got to do with us having a refrigerator? And Jack went on grinning until she got cross and said, Well, why *wouldn't* it fly inside?

Because dear, Jack said, it knew it was no good flying inside.

And you could tell it annoyed his missis because she still couldn't work it out, but she wasn't going to let on by asking Jack to explain.

But I was telling about that Saturday afternoon when we went inside, and Jack had his cup of tea and I wouldn't have one.

Well, do sit down, Mrs Parker said to me, but I stayed standing. It sounds dirty I know, but I'd had years of experience behind me. I've only got a sort of polite interest in Jack's missis and those friends of hers. They're always talking about books and writers, but never any I know anything about. Henry Lawson now, that would be different. Though I've always remembered that name Hugh Walpole, and once I started one of his, I forget the name, but I never got past the first chapter. I only go there because I'm Jack's cobber, but Mrs Parker is a mighty good-looking woman, so I suppose she's always naturally expected everybody of the male sex to be more interested in her than in her old man. Everybody is anyhow, except me. But still she's never seemed satisfied. And with things that way I've usually always picked on fine weekends to go round and see Jack, because then the pair of us can work in the garden, and I don't have to listen to his missis all the time nipping at him. And times when it comes on wet I've usually shoved off, though sometimes we've gone and sat yarning on the camp stretcher in the little room off the back verandah where Jack sleeps. Jack mightn't have the brains that his missis has but he isn't dumb, and I've always liked to hear him talk. He's such a good-natured cuss, always wanting everything in the garden to be lovely for everybody that walks the earth, and he'll spout little pieces of poetry to show what he means. Years before the war broke out I was listening to him talking about the way things were going with the world, and saying what he thought was going to happen. After all, the pair of us had been in the last war, and I agreed when Jack said he could see it all coming again. And he had more to worry about than I had, because his eldest one was a colt. (I say was, because later on it was rotten to get the news from Italy about him.)

Anyhow, one reason I stayed standing when Mrs Parker asked me to sit down, was because I thought I'd get Jack back into the garden sooner if I didn't sit down. And although he grinned round at the company, looking awfully hairy and sweaty though not too naked on account of his dark colour, and even spouted one of his pieces of poetry (which his missis several times tried to interrupt), he was all the time gulping several cups of tea down hot, and I reckoned he had that hole he was digging on his mind, which as it turned out he had.

That hole!

It was right up against the wash-house wall, and we went out and looked at it, and Jack said it would take a lot of work but never mind. He said he hadn't thought about me giving him a hand, but never mind that either. We could widen it another four feet so the pair of us could work there together. And he went and got the spade, and I began by taking the turf off the extra four feet, while Jack got down below again with the shovel.

Now, I've known Jack a longer time than his missis has, so maybe that's the reason why I know it's never any good pestering him with straightout questions, because if you do you only get an answer back like the one I'd heard his missis get over the refrigerator. Only seeing Jack knows me pretty thoroughly, he'll probably make it a lot more difficult to work out than that one was. So if he wanted to dig a hole that was all right with me, and I thought if I just kept my mouth shut I'd find out in plenty of good time what he was digging it *for*. To begin with though, I don't know that I thought about it much at all. It was Jack's concern, and he didn't have to tell me.

But I admit it wasn't long before I began wondering. You see, when we finished up that Saturday afternoon Jack said we'd done a good job of work, but how about if I came round and we carried on one night during the week? And that was all right, I said for one night I could cut out taking a few bob off the lads that were learning to play billiards along at the room, and I'd make it Wednesday. And Wednesday after work I had my wash but didn't change out of my working clothes, and after dinner I got on my bike and went round to Jack's place and found him hard at it. Also it was easy to tell this wasn't the only night he'd been working because already by now it was a whopping great hole he was working in. Anyhow we had our usual yarn, then the pair of us got to work and kept on until it was too dark to see any more. And just about then Jack's missis came round the corner of the wash-house.

Whatever are you two boys doing? she wanted to know.

We've been working Mrs Parker, I said.

Yes, she said, but what are you digging that hole for?

You see dear, Jack said, some people say they don't like work, but what would we ever have if we didn't work? And now the war's on we've all got to do our share. Think of the soldier-boys. Fighting's hard work, and Tom and me want to do our bit as well.

But before he'd finished Mrs Parker had gone inside again. I was putting my bicycle clips on my trousers, but Jack was still down the hole, and he asked if I'd mind handing him down a box with a candle and matches that I'd see in the wash-house. I watched while he lit up and fixed the box so the light shone where he wanted to work. And for a few minutes I stayed watching, the shovel going in deep each time under his weight, the candle-light showing up the hollows and curves made by his big muscles, and the sweat making him look as if he was all covered with oil. I left him to it, but said I'd be round again Saturday afternoon, and going home I thought perhaps it was a septic tank he was putting in. Or was it an asparagus bed? Or was he going to set a grape vine. It was evidently going to be a proper job any way, whatever it was.

Well. The job went on for weeks. As far as I could make out Jack must have come home and worked at it every night until late. He didn't like taking time off to shift away the spoil from the edge, so that was the job I took on, and I must have shifted tons of the stuff down to the bottom of the garden in the wheelbarrow. Nor would Jack let me go down the hole any more, he said it was too dangerous, and it certainly looked like it. Because once he'd got down deep he started to under-cut in all directions, particularly on the wash-house side, which seemed pretty crazy to me. Once he struck rock, so brought some gelly home from the quarry and plugged a bit in and set it off, and it brought a lot of earth down on the wash-house side. Then he had to get to work and

69

spend a lot of time rigging up props in case the blocks that were holding the wash-house up came through. I was hanged if I could get a line on what it was all about, and it was beginning to get me worried. His missis didn't ask any more questions, not while I was there anyhow, but I noticed she was getting round with a worried look, and I'd never felt that way before but I did feel a bit sorry for her then. About the only ones that got a kick out of the business were Jack's youngest snooks. The gelly he set off had been a real bit of fun for them, and they and their cobbers were always hanging around in the hope of another explosion. One that would finish off the wash-house, no doubt. Another thing was that for several weeks Jack hadn't done a tap of work in the garden, and one afternoon when Mrs Parker came out with cups of tea for us, she said he must be losing his eyesight if he couldn't see there was plenty just crying out to be done.

Yes dear, Jack said, in that good-natured sort of loving tone he always uses to her. Things being what they are between them, I can understand how it must make her want to knock him over the head. Yes dear, he said, but just now there are other things for Tom and me to do.

He was sitting on the edge of the hole, and after the strain of a long bout of shovelling his chest was going like a big pair of bellows worked by machinery. The day was another scorcher but blowy as well, and the dust had stuck to him, and run and caked, and stuck again, until about all you could see that was actually him was those eyes of his. And the bloodshot white and pure blue staring out of all that was something you almost couldn't bear to look at.

Yes dear, he repeated, we have other things to do.

And it was just then that half a dozen planes flying down quite low happened to suddenly come over. And of course we all of us stared up at them.

You see dear, Jack went on saying, though you could hardly hear him for the noise of the planes. You see dear, he said, we have more important things to do than those boys flying up there. Or at any rate, he went on, just as important.

But since we were watching the planes we didn't pay much attention to him. And it wasn't until they were nearly out of sight that I realized he'd disappeared down the hole again. You could tell he was there all right. The shovelfuls of spoil were coming flying up over the edge at a tremendous rate. And it was only afterwards, thinking it over, that I remembered what he'd been saying.

Well. This is the end of my yarn about Jack and the hole he dug. Next time I went round he was filling it in again, and he'd already got a fair bit done. All he said was that if he didn't go ahead and get his winter garden in he'd be having the family short of vegetables. And his missis had told him he'd got to do something about the hole because it was dangerous when there were kids about. So I took over wheeling the stuff up from the bottom of the garden, and Jack rammed it back in so tight that by the time he was up to ground level again there was practically nothing left over.

I must end up with a joke though. It was only a few summers later we had the Jap scare, and Jack earned a considerable amount of money digging shelters for people who were wanting them put in in a hurry, and weren't so particular how much they paid to get the work done. His missis appreciated the extra money, but she was always on to him to dig one for the family. All her friends agreed it was scandalous, the callous way he didn't seem to care if his own wife and children were all blown to bits!

As for me, I'm ready to stick up for Jack any time. Though I don't say his missis is making a mistake when she says that some day he'll end up in the lunatic asylum.

An Affair of the Heart

FRANK SARGESON

At Christmastime our family always went to the beach. In those days there weren't the roads along the Gulf that there are now, so father would get a carrier to take our luggage down to the launch steps. And as my brother and I would always ride on the cart, that was the real beginning of our holidays.

It was a little bay a good distance out of the harbour that we'd go to, and of course the launch trip would be even more exciting than the ride on the carrier's cart. We'd always scare mother beforehand by telling her it was sure to be rough. Each year we rented the same bach and we'd stay right until our school holidays were up. All except father who used to have only a few days' holiday at Christmas. He'd give my brother and me a lecture about behaving ourselves and not giving mother any trouble, then he'd go back home. Of course we'd spend nearly all our time on the beach, and mother'd have no more trouble with us than most mothers are quite used to having.

Well, it's all a long time ago. It's hard now to understand why the things that we occupied our time over should have given us so much happiness. But they did. As I'll tell you, I was back in that bay not long ago, and for all that I'm well on in years I was innocent enough to think that to be there again would be to experience something of that same happiness. Of course I didn't experience anything of the kind. And because I didn't I had some reflections instead that gave me the very reverse of happiness. But this is by the way. I haven't set out to philosophize. I've set out to tell you about a woman who lived in a bach not far beyond that bay of ours, and who, an old woman now, lives there to this day.

As you can understand, we children didn't spend all our time on our own little beach. When the tide was out we'd go for walks round the rocks, and sometimes we'd get mother to go with us. My brother and I would be one on each side of her, holding her hands, dragging her this way and that. We'd show her the wonders we'd found, some place where there were sea-eggs underneath a ledge, or a pool where the sea-anemones grew thick.

It was one of these times when we had mother with us that we walked further round the rocks than we had ever been before. We came to a place where there was a fair-sized beach, and there, down near low-water mark, was the woman I've spoken about. She was digging for pipis, and her children were all round her scratching the sand up too. Every now and then they'd pick up handfuls of pipis and run over near their mother, and drop the pipis into a flax kit.

Well, we went over to look. We liked pipis ourselves, but there weren't many on our own beach. The woman hardly took any notice of us, and we could have laughed at the way she was dressed. She had on a man's old hat and coat, and the children were sketches too. There were four of them, three girls and a boy; and the boy, besides being the smallest and skinniest, looked the worst of all because he was so badly in need of a hair-cut.

The woman asked mother if she'd like some pipis to take home. She said she sold pipis and mussels. They made good soup, she said. Mother didn't buy any but she said she would some other day, so the woman slung the kit on her shoulder, and off she went towards a tumble-down bach that stood a little way back from the beach. The children ran about all round her, and the sight made you think of a hen that was out with her chickens.

Of course going back round the rocks we talked about the woman and her children. I remember we poked a bit of fun at the way they were dressed, and we wondered why the woman wanted to sell us pipis and mussels when we could have easily got some for ourselves.

Perhaps they're poor, mother said.

That made us leave off poking fun. We didn't know what it was to be poor. Father had only his wages, and sometimes when we complained about not getting enough money to spend, he asked what we thought would happen to us if he got the sack. We took it as a joke. But this time there was something in what mother said that made us feel a little frightened.

Well, later on my brother and I made lots of excursions as far as that beach, and gradually we got to know the woman and her children, and saw inside their bach. We'd go home in great excitement to tell mother the things we'd found out. The woman was Mrs Crawley. She lived there all the year round, and the children had miles to walk to school. They didn't have any father, and Mrs Crawley collected pipis and mussels and sold them, and as there were lots of pine trees along the cliffs she gathered pine cones into sugar bags and sold them too. Another way she had of getting money was to pick up the kauri gum that you found among the sea-weed at high-tide mark, and sell that. But it was little enough she got all told. There was a road not very far back from the beach, and about once a week she'd collect there the things she had to sell, and a man who ran a cream lorry would give her a lift into town. And the money she got she'd spend on things like flour and sugar, and clothes that she bought in second-hand shops. Mostly, though, all there was to eat was the soup from the pipis and mussels, and vegetables out of the garden. There was a sandy bit of garden close by the bach. It was ringed round with tea-tree brush to keep out the wind, and Mrs Crawley grew kumaras and tomatoes, drumhead cabbages and runner beans. But most of the runner beans she'd let go to seed, and shell for the winter.

It was all very interesting and romantic to me and my brother. We were always down in the dumps when our holidays were over. We'd have liked to camp at our bach all the year round, so we thought the young Crawleys were luckier than we were. Certainly they were poor, and lived in a tumble-down bach with sacking nailed on to the walls to keep the wind out, and slept on heaps of fern sewn into sacking. But we couldn't see anything wrong with that. We'd have done it ourselves any day. But we could see that mother was upset over the things we used to tell her.

Such things shouldn't be, she'd say. She'd never come to visit the Crawleys, but she was always giving us something or other that we didn't need in our bach to take round to them. But Mrs Crawley never liked taking the things that mother sent. She'd rather be independent, she said. And she told us there were busybodies in the world who'd do people harm if they could.

One thing we noticed right from the start. It was that Mrs Crawley's boy Joe was her favourite. One time mother gave us a big piece of Christmas cake to take round, and the children didn't happen to be about when we got there, so Mrs Crawley put the cake away in a tin. Later on my brother let the cat out of the bag. He asked one of the girls how she liked the cake. Well, she didn't know anything about it, but you could tell by the way Joe looked that he did. Mrs Crawley spoilt him, sure enough. She'd bring him back little things from town when she never brought anything back for the girls. He didn't have to do as much work as any of the girls either, and his mother was always saying, Come here Joe, and let me nurse you. It made us feel a bit uncomfortable. In our family we never showed our feelings much.

Well, year after year we took the launch to our bay, and we always looked forward to seeing the Crawleys. The children shot up the same as we did. The food they had kept them growing at any rate. And when Joe was a lanky boy of fifteen his mother was spoiling him worse than ever. She'd let him off work more and more, even though she never left off working herself for a second. And she was looking old and worn out by that time. Her back was getting bent with so much digging and picking up pine cones, and her face looked old and tired too. Her teeth were gone and her mouth was sucked in. It made her chin stick out until you thought of the toe of a boot. But it was queer the way she never looked old when Joe was there. Her face seemed to go young again, and she never took her eyes off him. He was nothing much to look at we thought, but although my brother and I never spoke about it we both somehow understood how she felt about him. Every day she spent digging in her garden or digging up pipis, pulling up mussels from the reefs or picking up pine cones; and compared to our mother she didn't seem to have much of a life. But it was all for Joe, and so long as she had Joe what did it matter? She never told us that, but we knew all the same. I don't know how much my brother understood about it, because as I've said we never said anything to each other. But I felt a little bit frightened. It was perhaps the first time I understood what deep things there could be in life. It was easy to see how mad over Joe Mrs Crawley was, and evidently when you went mad over a person like that you didn't take much account of their being nothing much to look at. And perhaps I felt frightened because there was a feeling in me that going mad over a person in that way could turn out to be quite a terrible thing.

Anyhow, the next thing was our family left off going to the bay. My brother and I were old enough to go away camping somewhere with our cobbers, and father and mother were sick of the bother of going down to the bay. It certainly made us a bit sorry to think that we wouldn't be seeing the Crawleys that summer, but I don't think we lost much sleep over it. I remember that we talked about sending them a letter. But it never got beyond talk.

What I'm going to tell you about happened last Christmas. It was twenty odd years since I'd been in the bay and I happened to be passing near.

I may as well tell you that I've not been what people call a success in life. Unlike my brother who's a successful business man, with a wife and a car and a few other ties that successful men have, I've never been able to settle down. Perhaps the way I'd seen the Crawleys live had an upsetting influence on me. It's always seemed a bit comic to me to see people stay in one place all their lives and work at one job. I like meeting different people and tackling all sorts of jobs, and if I've saved up a few pounds it's always come natural to me to throw up my job and travel about a bit. It gets you nowhere, as people say, and it's a sore point with my mother and father who've just about ceased to own me. But there are lots of compensations.

Well, last Christmas Day I was heading up North after a job I'd heard was going on a fruit-farm, and as I was short of money at the time I was hoofing it. I got the idea that I'd turn off the road and have a look at the bay. I did, and had a good look. But it was a mistake. As I've said the kick that I got was the opposite to what I was expecting, and I came away in a hurry. It's my belief that only the very toughest sort of people should ever go back to places where they've been happy.

Then I thought of the Crawleys. I couldn't believe it possible they'd be living on their beach still, but I felt like having a look. (You can see why I've never been a success in life. I never learn from my mistakes, even when I've just made them.)

I found that the place on the road where Mrs Crawley used to wait for a lift into town had been made into a bus terminus, and there was a little shelter shed and a store. All the way down to the beach baches had been built, and lots of young people were about in shorts. And I really got the shock of my life when I saw the Crawleys' bach still standing there; but there it was, and except for a fresh coat of Stockholm tar it didn't look any different.

Mrs Crawley was in the garden. I hardly recognised her. She'd shrivelled up to nothing, and she was fixed in such a bend that above the waist she walked parallel to the ground. Her mouth had been sucked right inside her head, so her chin stuck out like the toe of a boot more than ever. Naturally she didn't know me, I had to shout to make her hear, and her eyes were bad too. When I'd told her I was Freddy Coleman, and she'd remembered who Freddy Coleman was, she ran her hands over my face as though to help her know whether or not I was telling the truth.

Fancy you coming, she said, and after I'd admired the garden and asked her how many times she'd put up a fresh ring of tea-tree brush, she asked me inside.

The bach was much the same. The sacking was still nailed up over the places where the wind came in, but only two of the fern beds were left. One was Mrs Crawley's and the other was Joe's, and both were made up. The table was set too, but covered over with tea-towels. I didn't know what to say. It was all too much for me. Mrs Crawley sat and watched me, her head stuck forward, and I didn't know where to look.

It's a good job you came early, she said. If you'd come late you'd have given me a turn.

Oh, I said.

Yes, she said. He always comes late. Not till the last bus.

Oh, I said, I suppose you mean Joe.

Yes, Joe, she said. He never comes until the last bus.

I asked her what had become of the girls, but she took no notice. She went on talking about Joe and I couldn't follow her, so I got up to leave. She offered me a cup of tea, but I said no thank you. I wanted to get away.

You've got Joe's Christmas dinner ready for him, I said, and I touched the table.

Yes, she said, I've got him everything that he likes. And she took

77

away the tea-towels. It was some spread. Ham, fruit, cake, nuts, everything that you can think of for Christmas. It was a shock after the old days. Joe was evidently making good money, and I felt a bit envious of him.

He'll enjoy that, I said. What line's he in, by the way?

He'll come, she said. I've got him everything that he likes. He'll come.

It was hopeless, so I went.

Then, walking back to the road I didn't feel quite so bad. It all came back to me about how fond of Joe Mrs Crawley had been. She hadn't lost him at anyrate. I thought of the bach all tidied up, and the Christmas spread, and it put me in quite a glow. I hadn't made a success of my life, and the world was in a mess, but here was something you could admire and feel thankful for. Mrs Crawley still had her Joe. And I couldn't help wondering what sort of a fellow Joe Crawley had turned out.

Well, when I was back on the road again a bus hadn't long come in, and the driver was eating a sandwich. So I went up to him.

Good-day, I said. Can you tell me what sort of a fellow Joe Crawley is?

Joe Crawley, he said, I've never seen him.

Oh, I said. Been driving out here long?

He told me about five years, so I jerked my thumb over towards the beach.

Do you know Mrs Crawley? I asked him.

Do I what! he said. She's sat in that shed waiting for the last bus every night that I can remember.

He told me all he knew. Long ago, people said, Joe would come several times a year, then he'd come just at Christmas. When he did come it would be always on the last bus, and he'd be off again first thing in the morning. But for years now he hadn't come at all. No one knew for sure what he used to do. There were yarns about him being a bookmaker, some said he'd gone to gaol, others that he'd cleared off to America. As for the girls they'd married and got scattered, though one was supposed to write now and then. Anyhow, wet or fine, summer or winter, Mrs Crawley never missed a night sitting in that shelter shed waiting to see if Joe'd turn up on the last bus. She still collected pine cones to sell, and would drag the bags for miles; and several times, pulling up mussels out on the reefs she'd been knocked over by the sea, and nearly drowned. Of course she got the pension, but people said she saved every penny of it and lived on the smell of an oil-rag. And whenever she did buy anything she always explained that she was buying it for Joe.

Well, I heard him out. Then I took to the road. I felt small. All the affairs of the heart that I had had in my life, and all that I had seen in other people, seemed petty and mean compared to this one of Mrs Crawley's. I looked at the smart young people about in their shorts with a sort of contempt. I thought of Mrs Crawley waiting down there in the bach with her wonderful Christmas spread, the bach swept out and tidied, and Joe's bed with clean sheets on all made up ready and waiting. And I thought of her all those years digging in the garden, digging for pipis, pulling up mussels and picking up cones, bending her body until it couldn't be straightened out again, until she looked like a new sort of human being. All for Joe. For Joe who'd never been anything much to look at, and who, if he was alive now, stayed away while his mother sat night after night waiting for him in a bus shelter shed. Though, mind you, I didn't feel like blaming Joe. I knew how he'd been spoilt, and I remembered how as a boy I'd sort of understood the way Mrs Crawley felt towards him might turn out to be quite a terrible thing. And sure enough, it had. But I never understood until last Christmas Day, when I was walking northwards to a job on a fruit-farm, how anything in the world that was such a terrible thing, could at the same time be so beautiful.

The Departure

MAURICE DUGGAN

Mr Lenihan walked slowly up the long concrete path which he had laid with his own hands; walked with his hands folded behind him. A loose heel-plate on his shoe rang as he walked. He looked from side to side. The garden plants extended in precise rows, puny and unflourishing, and behind them the rusted iron drum in which he burned the garden weeds smoked into the still air, the dark pall hanging. Mr Lenihan paused: he was dressed in grey flannels, uncreased, and a blazer in which each bold stripe warred with the next. He was, he thought, taking a last look round. He would leave next morning.

'Taking a last look round, Paddy?' Billy Price said, leaning over the garden fence where, from his side, convolvulus snaked through between the boards.

Mr Lenihan, who had never liked the man, who had never grown used to being called Paddy by the likes of him, said merely that he supposed you might call it that, and walked on with his shoe still ringing, towards the empty whitewashed fowl run and the line of fattening coops, built too with his own hands; towards the trellis of scarlet runner-beans, red flowers in the green leaves; towards the revolving clothes line around which the concrete path neatly turned. Billy Price, faced only with that departing back, incongruously gay, pulled a clown's face, watched a moment and went away.

The garden was drained of moisture and shade: the white-washed sheds glared: the heat struck trembling up from the path. Mr Lenihan crossed slowly between rows of dwarf peas in whose flowers bees worked, their drumming heavy in the heat: he noted with a little pleasure the perfection of tidiness. He liked to leave a place in good order. He left the path and crossed the red dusty weedless earth to a patch of grass that lay against the far fence. He looked at the sunflowers taped in their hot pride against the hot fence: the great yellow faces were averted. He stopped by the swing, built when the children were younger: he shook a cigarette out of a packet, lit it, and threw the match over the fence. The frame of the swing cast a short shadow, like a gallows: he looked up. ('Do push harder,' the children cried. 'We can see the sea.' But he had never seen the sea, not like that, not from up there where it showed, a corner of blue rag out where the earth ended, glimpsed and gone until rising it was caught again and again, upended or so it must have seemed, over the red and green hot roofs.)

A last look round. The passion-fruit vine with its fantastic flowers hid him from the house. He walked to the painted seat on which a few petals lay and sat down under the vine. He heard a bird knocking a snail on the path: he heard a telephone ringing. It rang and rang: the air was lifeless: the sound shrilled out urgent and premonitory. He drew on his cigarette and the smoke wound through the leaves. The telephone stopped ringing: he waited.

'Mr Lenihan. Mr Lenihan, telephone.' It was the housemaid, Doris, calling from the door. Mr Lenihan did not answer and sat very still. It wouldn't be anyone he wanted to talk to, he was sure of that. Doris's heels knocked over the concrete yard, and that too he had laid with his own hands. He watched her walk up the concrete path and look about her. The bird flew off with the hammered snail in its beak.

'Mr Lenihan.'

He was hidden; and it amused him to watch her. She scratched her arm and pushed back a straggling rope of hair. Hot and bothered, Mr Lenihan thought, lusting lightly over her naked calves and the small breasts neatly tenting her blouse. He would have liked to make some sign, to entice her into this dark shade.

'He's not here, Grace,' Doris called, and Mr Lenihan's irritation flared to match the hot, airless day.

Why did Grace do it? Why let the girl address her like that? He remembered an earlier housekeeper, the elderly Mrs Byrne: she'd never have been capable of an impertinence like that. He'd speak to the girl himself. 'You will oblige me by not referring to my wife by her Christian name, young woman.' Pompous, Mr Lenihan thought. Much better

take her and give her a shake; she's not more than seventeen, a mere
youngster. He'd take a pleasure in shaking her. He'd have liked to
hear her calling him Paddy. He grimaced: men who'd worked with
him in the firm for twenty years didn't call him that. Billy Price and
Doris would make a good pair. Mr Lenihan smiled at this prospect.
Then suddenly he was struck with another thought: it was here, on
this seat or was it a chair, his first wife had sat, watching him work in
the garden, soon after they were married and before she turned queer
and locked herself away. Well, God, you can rely on it, Mr Lenihan
thought. Grace wouldn't come at a trick like that. Not Grace; not likely.
But there was little consolation in that observation and Mr Lenihan,
thinking of his present marriage, stirred unhappily. It wasn't worth
going into, not in this heat. Even supposing he had made a mistake,
there was nothing could be done about it. Make the best of it, he told
himself; and it seemed for the moment like wise advice.

It would have been strange to him to discover, as in the next moment he came near to discovering, that peace or pleasure or ease lay,
not in the wilting tiny garden or along the concrete path laid with his
own hands, not where he so actively pursued it, but here in idleness
under the dark and secret vine with its flowers and setting fruit. He
crushed a leaf between his fingers: the vine had been planted haphazard by hands no one remembered and it rioted richly, untended, over
a rotting trellis he could not repair without destroying the vine.

Mr Lenihan surveyed it all in one reasoning stare — lifeless. Some
of the cabbages should have been cut long ago; the carrots should
have been dug. This was what he had made out of the wilderness and
it didn't seem anything to be proud of. It had been filled with rock
when he first came — the children unborn and his wife not yet turned
inwards upon that apparently unendurable spectacle of her private
and, to Mr Lenihan, unsuspected self — and he'd pushed through
the briar and the fennel, taking it as a challenge. The rankness and
neglect had been beaten back: he'd blasted out the rock and split it
piece by piece with a stone-hammer and those rocks lay now in great
enduring foundation supporting merely the passage of so many uneasy feet — Doris, Grace, himself, the kids. Mr Lenihan actually
groaned. Something had gone wrong. Wouldn't it, otherwise, have
been harder to leave?

He had no intention, at the moment, of adding up that sum of years, the time he had spent here. It was enough that he should keep up the pretence of believing that what the family was now advancing to — a country store in a featureless plain — was a change of some significance. (He couldn't remember when he'd felt so depressed.)

'I'll be glad to be shut of it,' Mr Lenihan said, and was surprised to hear his voice. He'd spoken aloud. The small spirit of the place continued to mock him from its bastion under the path. He knew, without the need of words to describe it, that the whole place, trim, weedless, barren, might have been just the mirror of his own personality, the pattern of a temperament from which some essential secret had been withheld. The wilting green was evidence enough; and he knew from experience how painful it was to him to plant anything that varied even by an inch from the lines he set out.

His cigarette had gone out: he turned it in his fingers and the grey-black ash fell to the grass. A breeze stirred in the vine. In the one patch of shade in the whole hot, naked garden he sat, feeling chilled and old and stale. The promise he had made to himself, one day to retire to a place with a few acres for a cow, a garden, poultry — a promise to escape — was unbelievable now. Mightn't it all turn out like this? Make the best of it; that seemed the depth of his wisdom now. Where then had it all gone wrong? He didn't know. But somehow the promised oasis was not; the desert swept in; and only his sense of quiet defeat was left to mark the place where date-palm and spring-water, a balm, had been intended. He had wanted to make something that would last; but it seemed a monstrous irony that his monument should be a concrete path.

The dapple of shadow over the lawn, under the leaves, danced at such a thought. Wound in with the writhing vine he caught a moment of satisfaction as the petals shaken by the summer breeze drifted down across his face.

Grace Lenihan, his second wife, came into the garden in slippers and dressing-gown: as each foot struck the path her ample flesh shuddered, her cheeks trembled. Her head was bound in a blue scarf, over rows of curling pins: the colour on her cheeks and lips, put there carelessly before a mirror kinder to her than this hot, noon eye, scaled slightly in the sun. She looked without interest over the parading rows of vegetables, up at the gallowed swing, across the lawn at the turning sunflowers. She did not see her husband: the passion vine hid him.

'Hot, Grace,' Bill Price said, over the fence.

'Hallo, Billy. Seen my old man?'

Mr Lenihan winced and gauntly smiled in the shadow where, gaudy and incongruous, his blazer showed all stripes. He leaned back secretly into the cool leaves.

'Earlier on I saw him,' Billy Price said. 'Taking a last look round, so he said. When do you leave?'

'Me? Oh not for ages,' Grace said. 'I'm in no hurry, heaven knows. Paddy's the one in a rush. He's going ahead tomorrow to be there when the things arrive. The boy goes down with the furniture. Margaret will come with me: we'll take our time.'

'What's the name of this place you're going to then?' Billy Price said.

Grace simulated a huge boredom. 'I haven't an idea,' she said. 'Somewhere back in the scrub-country: you can bet your boots on that. A post-office, a pub and a couple of scratching dogs: you know the sort of place. Oh God!' She seemed genuinely dismayed.

'The wife and I thought you might like a farewell drink,' Billy Price said.

'Paddy doesn't,' Grace said. 'He's practically teetotal. Imagine me married to a man like that, will you?'

'Doesn't know what he's missing,' Billy Price said. 'Do him a world of good. Still, I never noticed that you minded.'

'Why should I?' Grace said, scenting criticism. 'There's no harm in it. Have your fun while you're fit for it, that's my motto.'

'That's the girl,' Billy Price said. 'We'll fix it up. Isn't it hot though, and summer only started. Paddy's cabbages are taking a beating. Here: hold on a minute.'

His head, younger and richer in hair than Paddy Lenihan's, ducked energetically out of sight. Grace Lenihan leaned over the fence plucking unthinkingly at the sappy stems choked between the boards. Billy Price bobbed into view again holding a large and solid cabbage with lumps of moist dark earth clinging to its roots: he wrenched off the stalk and threw it forward over the fence where it lay, fertile and startling among the lifeless rows. Mr Lenihan saw them smile.

'There you are, Grace,' Billy said. 'Knocks Paddy right out of the picture.'

'I shouldn't, you know,' Grace said. 'Paddy's always carrying on about his stuff going to seed.'

'Ah well,' Billy Price said, and he leaned over the fence as far as he was able, bringing his face very close to Grace Lenihan. 'Pop it in the pot: he needn't know. I don't tell tales. What the eye don't see . . .' and his eye, bold and unrebuffed, roved up and down.

'I don't know about that,' Grace said.

'Don't forget you're coming over for a drink. Bring your sister, why don't you?'

'Sylvia? Yes, I might. I'll let you know. Thanks for the cabbage.' Grace held the huge crown nestled on her generous breast. Billy Price, leaning forward, touched the cool leaves.

'It's a beauty,' he said. 'Though I say it who shouldn't.'

Grace Lenihan turned smiling towards the house: from under her scarf the curling-pins, half covered, flashed like a diadem of steel. She pushed her carmine fingers into the cabbage, fastidiously withdrew a slug and dropped it, alive, on her husband's garden. She wiped her fingers on her gown where they left a silver smear. Mr Lenihan, lost still in the shade, watched her thud and vibrate down the path; heard her slippers slapping across the concrete when he could no longer see her.

'Doris,' Grace called. 'I say, Doris.'

Mr Lenihan stirred, a bald and frowning satyr among the leaves. He stood up: his striped coat struck gaudily into the sun: he crossed the garden and walked steel-shod and ringing up the path. The abandoned stalk, lush and violated, bled from its own heavy earth into the dust, mocking the sorry garden with the tale of the crown it had borne. Mr Lenihan bent stoutly down, seized the stalk so that its sap ran in his fingers and threw it back, hard and high, over the fence. Of all the impertinence, he thought. I shouldn't at all mind if it hit Mr Bloody Price in the eye.

Nothing happened: Billy Price was rocking gently in an old sacking hammock. The cold base of a foaming beer bottle stood on his naked chest.

*

Mr Lenihan faced the screen door; through it he saw the other side of the passion vine, and the concrete yard, out past the tunnel of porch and pergola. He stood before his family at the table. He whipped the carving knife over the sharpening steel and tried the knife-edge gently with his thumb. The guard on the steel was raised: he might have been some portly hero, or villain, armed with a poignard, thrust on to the stage to play out, clownishly, some melodrama of blood and revenge. The Sunday roast lay dark brown and pungent before him like pastoral tribute, hemmed with a circle of baked potatoes. Grace Lenihan presented her florid face to her husband from the other end of the table, over the dishes of vegetables, peas and cabbage and carrots, and the boat of dark gravy. Her back was to the sunlit vine. Margaret and Harry, children of Mr Lenihan's earlier marriage, and fasting from early Mass, sat still in their impatience. They faced across to Sylvia, Grace's sister, and the empty chair which would be Doris's when she came in from the kitchen. The table was an awkward shape, an elongated oval, bought because it would endure, because it was oak, at some auction of old furniture. It would last them out, Mr Lenihan frequently remarked; and the children wondered that he seemed to have so little understanding of how well wood will burn.

Margaret sniffed at the meaty air: she could taste still the senna-tea which Grace made her take each Sunday after Mass. It toned up the blood, Grace had been told, and she stood over Margaret as if waiting some miraculous flash and fire. It purged; it washed down, its bitterness only partly disguised with the liquorice Grace added to it, over the faint taste, as Margaret imagined it, of the unleavened and consecrated wafer. Margaret was not entirely sure that Grace's intention was quite free of blasphemy. The liquorice blackened her teeth; and what, she wondered, might it not do to that soul which she had been instructed to think of as floating pale and small somewhere inside her, borne like a white toy boat on that purging tide, a moment only safe and unstained.

Mr Lenihan squinted along the blade of the knife, took up the carving fork and plunged it into the meat: the juice bled out. He began to carve, putting an exact amount on each plate and stabbing out the potatoes. Sylvia passed the plates to her sister. Mr Lenihan, fierce and paternal, a just dispenser of the stuff of life, named the plates as they were taken up. The meat's rich odour struck up into the hot room.

'Yours, Mrs Lenihan,' Mr Lenihan said. 'Something from the outside. Yours, Sylvia; and Doris.' He looked up. 'Give the girl a shout, someone. And Grace,' he said, abandoning his little act of formality; 'what about something to drink on our last day. It's a farewell dinner in its way, a sort of midday last supper. Don't we have beer or something?'

'I don't see the need for blasphemy,' Grace said. 'And you know you don't like beer.'

'Come now,' Mr Lenihan said, grotesque and shrewd and red in the face. 'You must tell that to Billy Price.'

Grace turned to her sister a practised stare of incomprehension, innocence and doubt: her look suggested a fear for her husband's sanity, a long-suffering tolerance of his quirks of mind. What, her look demanded, could he possibly be talking about?

'Harry, and Margaret,' Mr Lenihan said. 'Aren't you starving?'

'What about yourself?' Grace said. 'Another minute or two won't kill them.'

'I'm coming to myself,' Mr Lenihan said. 'A bit near the bone for the old man.'

'Paddy, you're being silly,' Grace said.

'What about the beer?' Mr Lenihan said.

'Doris,' Grace called. 'I say, Doris.'

'What?' Doris said through the half-opened door.

'Bring a couple of bottles of beer when you come.'

'Beer?' Doris said. 'We are going gay.'

Mr Lenihan paused: the knife-point descended. He looked at the vacant door, at his wife, at her sister. He sat down. 'You see what I mean?' he said. 'I think we will have to let the girl go. I can't say I held her much of a gain in the first place. After our other housekeeper, I mean — Mrs Byrne.'

Grace flared. 'That old rabbit,' she said explosively. 'She'd too much to say for herself: you agreed at the time. Anyway, there has to be someone to help. What's the girl done now? You needn't be so touchy. She knows we don't drink beer, usually, so why shouldn't she be surprised? I'm surprised myself.'

'It isn't her province,' Mr Lenihan said, 'to make remarks. We have enough of that in the family without bringing in outsiders. Leave it now,' he said sharply to his wife's look. 'We won't discuss it now.'

'Does anyone need salt?' Sylvia said, offering the heavy cruet.

The plates went round. Grace had a moustache of fine sweat on her upper lip. Margaret and Harry bent over their food: they could feel their father's bitter anger, could see the heavy blood in their step-mother's face. One wrong word, one incautious glance, could involve them also. They ate with care, sitting in silence and rarely raising their eyes from their plates.

'Do sit up,' Grace said. 'You'll have a hump in your backs, next thing. Margaret, get your hair out of your dinner.'

Doris came into the room: she put the beer on the table without speaking and sat down and began to eat. Mr Lenihan reached forward to the beer.

'An opener, Harry,' Mr Lenihan said, giving Doris a stare of re-proof.

'Sideboard,' Doris said, chewing. 'Left hand drawer.'

'There,' Mr Lenihan said, and the bottles hissed. 'Pass your glasses. Ladies first.'

'You're not giving the kids beer?' Grace said. 'What next?'

'They'll maybe like it better than senna-tea,' Mr Lenihan said. 'Here's to us. One happy family. Here's to the wilds. Life in the backblocks,' he said, looking at his wife.

Margaret dipped into her glass and came up with a half-circle of froth above her mouth. 'It's very bitter,' she said.

'It always is,' Harry said.

'A fat lot you know about it,' Grace said. 'Get on with your meal.'

'Grace,' Mr Lenihan said. 'A little more cabbage, if I may.'

'Is it from the garden?' Sylvia said. 'It's very good. No,' she said to her sister's quick stare. 'No more for me thanks.'

Under the table Margaret and Harry touched. A fly went tirelessly up and down the window pane: the temperature in the hot room rose. Outside, the sun, descending into afternoon, blazed down. The family ate in a silence that was heavy and sour. Doris rose, collected the plates and went into the kitchen. A smell of cabbage and cooling fat came through the door.

'The meat,' Grace said. 'Take it, Margaret, if everyone's had enough.

Don't always wait to be told. There's a pudding.'

'I'm sorry,' Margaret said.

'Come back for the rest,' Grace said. 'Don't try to carry everything at once.'

'I don't see how people can just go on and on drinking beer,' Mr Lenihan said. 'And yet they do. Billy Price, for instance: the man soaks it up like a sponge. One glass bloats me. How does he do it?'

'There you go,' Grace said. 'I told you you didn't like it. But don't mind us if we enjoy ours. It's like an oven in here.'

Sylvia pushed back her chair and crossed the room to open a window. She stood before it looking out on to the hedge by the house and over the hedge to the next-door house and the road. The breeze was blowing in from the mangroves in the bay: the arch of sky between the houses was empty of cloud.

She would be glad when they had gone. The Lenihans wearied her. The bitter drumming, an undertone of constant anger and resentment lay under every movement or word in this house. And the effort to keep to her neutrality, never to take sides whatever her perception of the injustice or untruth, wearied her too. Paddy and Grace had been shouting at one another in their bedroom before the meal; about some conversation he'd overheard in the garden. 'A wicked snooper,' Grace had called him. Sylvia would be glad when they had gone. She wondered a moment at the monstrosity of the desire and the improbability of the agreement that had led to this unsuitable match. Paddy's wife had died; and there were the kids: Grace was quick to seize any chance of getting out of the necessity of having to support herself. But such an analysis hardly seemed enough to Sylvia, to justify their having undertaken this life of bitterness and reproach which could promise no possible coincidence of mood or pleasure. Poor kids, she said to herself, looking at the empty sky. She turned back to the table: she didn't, she realised, feel at all well. She didn't at all want her glass of beer; but to have left it would have meant facing Grace's charge of siding with Paddy.

'I suppose you managed better in Ireland,' Grace was saying. 'There are drunkards enough there, from all I've heard.'

'What have you heard?' Mr Lenihan contemptuously questioned. 'But no matter. In the old country I didn't drink. All I'm saying is that it's a poor look out for a man when his habits control him. That's the reason I'm in favour of prohibition.'

'Listen to him,' Grace said. 'Have you ever heard such nonsense from a grown man. A bit of company occasionally, instead of your old garden all the time wouldn't do you any harm. A picture show or a drink, where's the harm in that?'

'Dad,' Harry said.

'Wait a moment, son,' Mr Lenihan said. 'I don't care much for the films,' he said to his wife. 'Now a walk in the evening — you know I like that. I need a bit of fresh air after being inside all day.'

'Oh, a walk,' Grace said in the tones of one who having asked for strong drink is offered tea. 'Isn't that exciting? With all the old things just out to peer in everyone else's windows and mind anyone's business but their own. Really, Paddy, you're getting old.'

'Dad,' Harry said.

'What is it?' Mr Lenihan said.

'Can I go for a swim? And can Margaret?'

'No,' Grace said. 'You can't. You've enough of swimming. There's packing to be done. Don't pester your father,' she added, grotesquely.

'I'll give you a hand with the packing, Grace,' Sylvia said. 'They might be better out of the way.'

'It's well to be some people,' Grace said.

'They're young,' Mr Lenihan said. 'As long as you'll promise not to go in the water for an hour,' he said to Harry.

'We could all take an hour off,' Sylvia said, smiling as if at the enormity of the dereliction she was proposing. 'The packers aren't coming until tomorrow, are they?'

'An hour off,' Grace said. 'A lifetime would be more like it.'

It drew from her husband a grim look which she easily met.

'Off you go, then,' Mr Lenihan said to the children. He drank the remainder of his beer, grimacing. 'Sylvia,' he said. 'What will you do? Have you found a place for yourself?'

'I'll stay until Grace goes,' Sylvia said. 'After that I have a room in town, until I find something better.'

'We'll miss you,' Mr Lenihan said. 'Here, give me your glass.'

Sylvia watched hopelessly as her glass was filled.

'The way you sound,' Grace said, 'you'd think we were going right out of civilisation altogether.'

'And isn't that what you were saying, a moment or so back?' Mr Lenihan said. 'Though there are some who'd claim we've never been it it; civilisation, I mean.'

'It'll be as dead as mutton,' Grace said. 'I don't need to be warned about that.'

'It'll be lively enough,' Mr Lenihan said. 'You'll have the children to occupy you; and a new house to get in order. It's a risk to take, starting a new business with old ones folding up all round you. It'll keep us busy. There won't be time for anything else for a year or two.'

'Sylvia is coming for a weekend, when we are settled,' Grace said. The defiance in her voice was, they all recognised, for the threat he had offered her in the form of house and children. 'She'll make a break for me,' Grace vaguely added.

'Maybe Paddy would give me a job,' Sylvia mildly joked. 'Selling stuff to farmers' wives, perhaps. Though I should warn you I hardly know silk from cotton.'

'Ah, come,' Mr Lenihan said. 'You'd be priceless.'

'The kids got off without their pudding,' Grace said as Doris came into the room, bearing on a grey plate a steamed pudding like a severed breast. 'Aren't they devils?'

Sylvia raised her glass in front of her face and looked at Paddy and Grace through the brown liquor. The bright hot room darkened and became remote and still. In her childhood there had been a coloured panel in a door which gave her, as she raised herself to peer, just this sense of being huge, and outside everything.

'Doris,' Mr Lenihan said. 'You're being very quiet.'

'I was miles away,' Doris said.

'Well, we'll all be that soon enough,' Mr Lenihan said.

And to Sylvia it seemed, his remark, to bring to an end not only the long, unenjoyable and ill-tempered meal, but a term of sentence too, as though, beyond that brown room and beyond that vine which, turning, she now saw flickering with light, lay . . .

'What?' Sylvia said aloud. 'I wasn't listening, I'm afraid. What was it?'

'Nothing,' Mr Lenihan said. 'I was only saying that I shan't be sorry, after all, to turn my back on it.'

Along Rideout Road
that Summer

MAURICE DUGGAN

I'd walked the length of Rideout Road the night before, following the noise of the river in the darkness, tumbling over ruts and stones, my progress, if you'd call it that, challenged by farmers' dogs and observed by the faintly luminous eyes of wandering stock, steers, cows, stud-bulls or milk-white unicorns or, better, a full quartet of apocalyptic horses browsing the marge. In time and darkness I found Puti Hohepa's farmhouse and lugged my fibre suitcase up to the verandah, after nearly breaking my leg in a cattlestop. A journey fruitful of one decision — to flog a torch from somewhere. And of course I didn't. And now my feet hurt; but it was daylight and, from memory, I'd say I was almost happy. Almost. Fortunately I am endowed both by nature and later conditioning with a highly developed sense of the absurd; knowing that you can imagine the pleasure I took in this abrupt translation from shop-counter to tractor seat, from town pavements to back-country farm, with all those miles of river-bottom darkness to mark the transition. In fact, and unfortunately there have to be some facts, even fictional ones, I'd removed myself a mere dozen miles from the parental home. In darkness, as I've said, and with a certain stealth. I didn't consult dad about it, and, needless to say, I didn't tell mum. The moment wasn't propitious; dad was asleep with the *Financial Gazette* threatening to suffocate him and mum was off somewhere moving, as she so often did, that this meeting make public its whole-hearted support for the introduction of flogging and public castration for all sex offenders and hanging, drawing and quartering, for almost everyone else, and as for delinquents (my boy!) . . . Well, put yourself in my shoes, there's no need to go on. Yes, almost happy, though my feet were so tender I winced every time I tripped the clutch.

Almost happy, shouting Kubla Khan, a bookish lad, from the seat of the clattering old Ferguson tractor, doing a steady five miles an hour in a cloud of seagulls, getting to the bit about the damsel with the dulcimer and looking up to see the reputedly wild Hohepa girl perched on the gate, feet hooked in the bars, ribbons fluttering from her ukulele. A perfect moment of recognition, daring rider, in spite of the belch of carbon monoxide from the tin-can exhaust up front on the bonnet. Don't, however, misunderstand me: I'd not have you think we are here embarked on the trashy clamour of boy meeting girl. No, the problem, you are to understand, was one of connexion. How connect the dulcimer with the ukulele, if you follow. For a boy of my bents this problem of how to cope with the shock of the recognition of a certain discrepancy between the real and the written was rather like watching mum with a shoehorn wedging nines into sevens and suffering merry hell. I'm not blaming old STC for everything, of course. After all, some other imports went wild too; and I've spent too long at the handle of a mattock, a critical function, not to know that. The stench of the exhaust, that's to say, held no redolence of that old hophead's pipe. Let us then be clear and don't for a moment, gentlemen, imagine that I venture the gross unfairness, the patent absurdity, the rank injustice (your turn) of blaming him for spoiling the pasture or fouling the native air. It's just that there was this problem in my mind, this profound, cultural problem affecting dramatically the very nature of my inheritance, nines into sevens in this lovely smiling land. His was the genius as his was the expression which the vast educational brouhaha invited me to praise and emulate, tranquillizers ingested in maturity, the voice of the ring-dove, look up though your feet be in the clay. And read on.

Of course I understood immediately that these were not matters I was destined to debate with Fanny Hohepa. Frankly, I could see that she didn't give a damn; it was part of her attraction. She thought I was singing. She smiled and waved, I waved and smiled, turned, ploughed back through gull-white and coffee loam and fell into a train of thought not entirely free of Fanny and her instrument, pausing to wonder, now and then, what might be the symptoms, the early symptoms, of carbon monoxide poisoning. Drowsiness? Check. Dilation of the pupils? Can't check. Extra cutaneous sensation? My feet. Trembling hands? Vibrato. Down and back, down and back, turning again, Dick and his Ferguson, Fanny from her perch seeming to gather about her the background of green paternal acres, fold on fold. I bore down upon her in all the eager erubescence of youth, with my hair slicked back. She trembled, wavered, fragmented and re-formed in the pungent vapour through which I viewed her. (Oh, for an open-air job, eh mate?) She plucked, very picture in jeans and summer shirt of youth and suspicion, and seemed to sing. I couldn't of course hear a note. Behind me the dog-leg furrows and the bright ploughshares. Certainly she looked at her ease and, even through the gassed-up atmosphere between us, too deliciously substantial to be creature down on a visit from Mount Abora. I was glad I'd combed my hair. Back, down and back. Considering the size of the paddock this could have gone on for a week. I promptly admitted to myself that her present position, disposition or posture, involving as it did some provocative tautness of cloth, suited me right down to the ground. I mean to hell with the idea of having her stand knee-deep in the thistle thwanging her dulcimer and plaintively chir-ruping about a pipedream mountain. In fact she was natively engaged in expressing the most profound distillations of her local experience, the gleanings of a life lived in rich contact with a richly understood and native environment: A Slow Boat To China, if memory serves. While I, racked and shaken, composed words for the plaque which would one day stand here to commemorate our deep rapport: *Here played the black lady her dulcimer. Here wept she full miseries. Here rode the knight Fergus' son to her deliverance. Here put he about her ebon and naked shoulders his courtly garment of leather, black, full curiously emblazoned — Hell's Angel.*

When she looked as though my looking were about to make her leave I stopped the machine and pulled out the old tobacco and rolled a smoke, holding the steering wheel in my teeth, though on a good day I could roll with one hand, twist and lick, draw, shoot the head off a pin at a mile and a half, spin, blow down the barrel before you could say :

Gooday. How are yuh?

All right.

I'm Buster O'Leary.

I'm Fanny Hohepa.

Yair, I know.

It's hot.

It's hot right enough.

You can have a swim when you're through.

Mightn't be a bad idea at that.

Over there by the trees.

Yair, I seen it. Like, why don't you join me, eh?

I might.

Go on, you'd love it.

I might.

Goodoh then, see yuh.

A genuine crumpy conversation if ever I heard one, darkly reflective of the Socratic method, rich with echoes of the Kantian imperative, its universal mate, summoning sharply to the minds of each the history of the first trystings of all immortal lovers, the tragic and tangled tale, indeed, of all star-crossed moonings, mum and dad, mister and missus unotoo and all. Enough? I should bloody well hope so.

Of course nothing came of it. Romantic love was surely the invention of a wedded onanist with seven kids. And I don't mean dad. Nothing? Really and truly nothing? Well, I treasure the under-statement; though why I should take such pleasure in maligning the ploughing summer white on loam, river flats, the frivolous ribbons and all the strumming, why I don't know. Xanadu and the jazzy furrows, the wall-eyed bitch packing the cows through the yardgate, the smell of river water . . . Why go on? So few variations to an old, old story. No. But on the jolting tractor I received that extra jolt I mentioned and am actually now making rather too much of, gentlemen: relate Fanny Hohepa and her uke to that mountain thrush singing her black mountain blues.

But of course now, in our decent years, we know such clay questions long broken open or we wouldn't be here, old and somewhat sour, wading up to our battered thighs (forgive me, madam) at the confluence of the great waters, paddling in perfect confidence in the double debouchment of universal river and regional stream, the shallow fast fan of water spreading over the delta, Abyssinia come to Egypt in the rain . . . ah, my country! I speak of cultural problems, in riddles

and literary puddles, perform this act of divination with my own en-
trails: Fanny's dark delta; the nubile and Nubian sheila with her
portable piano anticipating the transistor-set; all gathered into single
demesne, O'Leary's orchard. Even this wooden bowl, plucked from
the flood, lost from the hand of some anonymous herdsman as he
stopped to cup a drink at the river's source. Ah, Buster. Ah, Buster.
Buster. Ah, darling. Darling! Love. You recognise it? Could you strum
to that? Suppose you gag a little at the sugar coating, it's the same old
fundamental toffee, underneath.

No mere cheap cyn...sm intended. She took me down to her
darkling avid as any college girl for the fruits and sweets of my flowering talents, taking me as I wasn't but might hope one day to be, honest,
simple and broke to the wide. The half-baked verbosity and the con-
ceit she must have ignored, or how else could she have borne me? It
pains me, gentlemen, to confess that she was too good for me by far.
Far. Anything so spontaneous and natural could be guaranteed to be
beyond me: granted, I mean, my impeccable upbringing under the
white-hot lash of respectability, take that, security, take that, hypocrisy,
take that, cant, take that where, does it seem curious?, mum did all the
beating flushed pink in ecstasy and righteousness, and that and that
and THAT. Darling! How then could I deem Fanny's conduct proper
when I carried such weals and scars, top-marks in the lesson on the
wickedness of following the heart. Fortunately such a question would
not have occurred to Fanny: she was remarkably free from queries of
any kind. She would walk past the Home Furnishing Emporium without a glance.

She is too good for you.

It was said clearly enough, offered without threat and as just comment, while I was bent double stripping old Daisy or Pride of the Plains
or Rose of Sharon after the cups came off. I stopped what I was doing,
looked sideways until I could see the tops of his gumboots, gazed on
Marathon, and then turned back, dried off all four tits and let the cow
out into the race where, taking the legrope with her, she squittered off
wild in the eyes.

She is too good for you.

So I looked at him and he looked back. I lost that game of stare-you-down, too. He walked off. Not a warning, not even a reproach, just something it was as well I should know if I was to have the responsibility of acting in full knowledge — and who the hell wants that? And two stalls down Fanny spanked a cow out through the flaps and looked at me, and giggled. The summer thickened and blazed.

The first response on the part of my parents was silence; which can only be thought of as response in a very general sense. I could say, indeed I will say, stony silence; after all they were my parents. But I knew the silence wouldn't last long. I was an only child (darling, you never guessed?) and that load of woodchopping, lawnmowing, hedgeclipping, dishwashing, carwashing, errandrunning, gardenchoring and the rest of it was going to hit them like a folding mortgage pretty soon. I'd like to have been there, to have seen the lank grass grown beyond window height and the uncut hedges shutting out the sun: perpetual night and perpetual mould on Rose Street West. After a few weeks the notes and letters began. The whole gamut, gentlemen, from sweet and sickly to downright abusive. Mostly in mum's masculine hand. A unique set of documents reeking of blood and tripes. I treasured every word, reading between the lines the record of an undying, all-sacrificing love, weeping tears for the idyllic childhood they could not in grief venture to touch upon, the care lavished, the love squandered upon me. The darlings. Of course I didn't reply. I didn't even wave when they drove past Fanny and me as we were breasting out of the scrub back on to the main road, dishevelled and, yes, almost happy in the daze of summer and Sunday afternoon. I didn't wave. I grinned as brazenly as I could manage with a jaw full of hard boiled egg and took Fanny's arm, brazen, her shirt only casually resumed, while they went by like burnished doom.

Fanny's reaction to all this? An expression of indifference, a downcurving of that bright and wilful mouth, a flirt of her head. So much fuss over so many fossilised ideas, if I may so translate her expression which was, in fact, gentlemen, somewhat more direct and not in any sense exhibiting what mum would have called a due respect for elders and betters. Pouf! Not contempt, no; not disagreement; simply an impatience with what she, Fanny, deemed the irrelevance of so many many words for so light and tumbling a matter. And, for the season at least, I shared the mood, her demon lover in glossy brilliantine.

But as the days ran down the showdown came nearer and finally the stage was set. Low-keyed and sombre notes in the sunlight the four of us variously disposed on the unpainted Hohepa verandah, Hohepa and O'Leary, the male seniors, and Hohepa and O'Leary, junior representatives, male seventeen, female ready to swear, you understand, that she was sixteen, turning.

Upon the statement that Fanny was too good for me my pappy didn't comment. No one asked him to: no one faced him with the opinion. Wise reticence, mere oversight or a sense of the shrieking irrelevance of such a statement, I don't know. Maori girls, Maori farms, Maori housing: you'd only to hear my father put tongue to any or all of that to know where he stood, solid for intolerance, mac, but solid. Of course, gentlemen, it was phrased differently on his lips, gradual absorption, hmm, perhaps, after, say, a phase of disinfecting. A pillar of our decent, law-abiding community, masonic in his methodism, brother, total abstainer, rotarian and non-smoker, addicted to long volleys of handball, I mean pocket billiards cue and all. Mere nervousness, of course, a subconscious habit. Mum would cough and glance down and dad would spring to attention hands behind his back. Such moments of tender rapport are sweet to return to, memories any child might treasure. Then he'd forget again. Straight, mate, there were days, especially Sundays, when mum would be hacking away like an advanced case of t.b. Well, you can picture it, there on the verandah. With the finely turned Fanny under his morose eye, you know how it is, hemline hiked and this and that visible from odd angles, he made a straight break of two hundred without one miscue, Daddy! I came in for a couple of remand home stares myself, bread and water and solitary and take that writ on his eyeballs in backhand black while his mouth served out its lying old hohums and there's no reason why matters shouldn't be resolved amicably, etc, black hanging-cap snug over his tonsure and tongue moistening his droopy lip, ready, set, drop. And Puti Hohepa leaving him to it. A dignified dark prince on his ruined acres, old man Hohepa, gravely attending to dad's mumbled slush, winning hands down just by being there and saying nothing, nothing, while Fanny with her fatal incapacity for standing upright unsupported for more than fifteen seconds, we all had a disease of the spine that year, pouted at me as though it were all my fault over the back of the chair (sic). All my fault being just the pater's monologue, the remarkably imprecise grip of his subject with consequent proliferation of the bromides so typical of all his ilk of elk, all the diversely identical representatives of decency, caution and the colour bar. Of course daddy didn't there and then refer to race, colour creed or uno who. Indeed he firmly believed he believed, if I may recapitulate, gentlemen, that this blessed land was free from such taint, a unique social experiment, two races living happily side by side, respecting each others etc and etc. As a banker he knew the value of discretion, though what was home if not a place to hang up your reticence along with your hat and get stuck into all the hate that was inside you, in the name of justice? Daddy Hohepa said nothing, expressed nothing, may even have been unconscious of the great destinies being played out on his sunlit verandah, or of what fundamental principles of democracy and the freedom of the individual were being here so brilliantly exercised; may have been, in fact, indifferent to daddy's free granting tautologies now, of the need for circumspection in all matters of national moment, all such questions as what shall be done for our dark brothers and sisters, outside the jails? I hope so. After a few minutes Hohepa rangatira trod the boards thoughtfully and with the slowness of a winter bather lowered himself into a pool of sunlight on the wide steps, there to lift his face broad and grave in full dominion of his inheritance and even, perhaps, so little did his expression reveal of his inward reflection, full consciousness of his dispossessions.

What, you may ask, was my daddy saying? Somewhere among the circumlocutions, these habits are catching among the words and sentiments designed to express his grave ponderings on the state of the nation and so elicit from his auditors (not me, I wasn't listening) admission, tacit though it may be, of his tutored opinion, there was centred the suggestion that old man Hohepa and daughter were holding me against my will, ensnaring me with flesh and farm. He had difficulty in getting it out in plain words; some lingering cowardice, perhaps. Which was why daddy Hohepa missed it, perhaps. Or did the view command all his attention?

Rideout Mountain far and purple in the afternoon sun; the jersey cows beginning to move, intermittent and indirect, towards the shed; the dog jangling its chain as it scratched; Fanny falling in slow movement across the end of the old cane lounge chair to lie, an interesting composition of curves and angles, with the air of a junior and rural odalisque. Me? I stood straight, of course, rigid, thumbs along the seams of my jeans, hair at the regulation distance two inches above the right eye, heels together and bare feet at ten to two, or ten past ten, belly flat and chest inflated, chin in, heart out. I mean, can you see me, mac? Dad's grave-suit so richly absorbed the sun that he was forced to retreat into the shadows where his crafty jailer's look was decently camouflaged, blending white with purple blotched with silver wall. Not a bad heart, surely?

As his audience we each displayed differing emotions. Fanny, boredom that visibly bordered on sleep: Puti Hohepa, an inattention expressed in his long examination of the natural scene: Buster O'Leary, a sense of complete bewilderment over what it was the old man thought he could achieve by his harangue and, further, a failure to grasp the relevance of it all for the Hohepas. My reaction, let me say, was mixed with irritation at certain of father's habits. (Described.) With his pockets filled with small change he sounded like the original gypsy orchestra, cymbals and all. I actually tried mum's old trick of the glance and the cough. No luck. And he went on talking, at me now, going so wide of the mark, for example, as to mention some inconceivable, undocumented and undemonstrated condition, some truly monstrous condition, called your-mother's-love. Plain evidence of his distress, I took it to be, this obscenity uttered in mixed company. I turned my head the better to hear, when it came, the squelchy explosion of his heart. And I rolled a smoke and threw Fanny the packet. It landed neatly on her stomach. She sat up and made herself a smoke then crossed to her old man and, perching beside him in the brilliant pool of light, fire of skin and gleam of hair bronze and blue-black, neatly extracted from his pocket his battered flint lighter. She snorted smoke and passed the leaf to her old man.

Some things, gentlemen, still amaze. To my dying day I have treasured that scene and all its rich implications. In a situation so pregnant of difficulties, in the midst of a debate so fraught with undertones, an exchange (quiet there, at the back) so bitterly fulsome on the one hand and so reserved on the other. I ask you to take special note of this observance of the ritual of the makings, remembering, for the fullest savouring of the nuance, my father's abstention. As those brown fingers moved on the white cylinder, or cone, I was moved almost, to tears, almost, by this companionable and wordless recognition of our common human frailty, father and dark child in silent communion and I too, in some manner not to be explained because inexplicable, sharing their hearts. I mean the insanity, pal. Puti Hohepa and his lass in sunlight on the steps, smoking together, untroubled, natural and patient; and me and daddy glaring at each other in the shades like a couple of evangelists at cross pitch. Love, thy silver coatings and castings. And thy neighbours! So I went and sat by Fanny and put an arm through hers.

The sun gathered me up, warmed and consoled; the bitter view assumed deeper purples and darker rose; a long way off a shield flashed, the sun striking silver from a water trough. At that moment I didn't care what mad armies marched in my father's voice nor what the clarion was he was trying so strenuously to sound. I didn't care that the fire in his heart was fed by such rank fuel, skeezing envy, malice, revenge, hate and parental power. I sat and smoked and was warm; and the girl's calm flank was against me, her arm through mine. Nothing was so natural as to turn through the little distance between us and kiss her smoky mouth. Ah yes, I could feel, I confess, through my shoulder blades as it were and the back of my head, the crazed rapacity and outrage of my daddy's Irish stare, the blackness and the cold glitter of knives. (Father!) While Puti Hohepa sat on as though turned to glowing stone by the golden light, faced outward to the violet mystery of the natural hour, monumentally content and still.

You will have seen it, known it, guessed that there was between this wild, loamy daughter and me, sunburnt scion of an ignorant, insensitive, puritan and therefore prurient, Irishman (I can't stop) no more than a summer's dalliance, a season's thoughtless sweetness, a boy and a girl and the makings.

In your wisdom, gentlemen, you will doubtless have sensed that something is lacking in this lullaby, some element missing for the articulation of this ranting tale. Right. The key to daddy's impassioned outburst, no less. Not lost in this verbose review, but so far unstated. Point is he'd come to seek his little son (someone must have been dying because he'd never have come for the opposite reason) and, not being one to baulk at closed doors and drawn shades, wait for it, he'd walked straight in on what he'd always somewhat feverishly imagined and hoped he feared. Fanny took it calmly: I was, naturally, more agitated. Both of us ballocky in the umber light, of course. Still, even though he stayed only long enough to let his eyes adjust and his straining mind take in this historic disposition of flesh, those mantis angles in which for all our horror we must posit our conceivings, it wasn't the greeting he'd expected. It wasn't quite the same, either, between Fanny and me, after he'd backed out, somewhat huffily, on to the verandah. Ah, filthy beasts! He must have been roaring some such expression as that inside his head because his eyeballs were rattling, the very picture of a broken doll, and his face was liver-coloured. I felt sorry for him, for a second, easing backward from the love-starred couch and the moving lovers with his heel hooked through the loop of Fanny's bra, kicking it free like a football hero punting for touch, his dream of reconciliation in ruins.

It wasn't the same. Some rhythms are slow to re-form. And once the old man actually made the sanctuary of the verandah he just had to bawl his loudest for old man Hohepa, Mr Ho-he-pa, Mr Ho-he-pa. It got us into our clothes anyway, Fanny giggling and getting a sneezing fit at the same time, bending forward into the hoof-marked brassiere and blasting off every ten seconds like a burst air hose until I quite lost count on the one-for-sorrow two-for-joy scale and crammed myself sulkily into my jocks.

Meantime dad's labouring to explain certain natural facts and common occurrences to Puti Hohepa, just as though he'd made an original discovery; as perhaps he had considering what he probably thought of as natural. Puti Hohepa listened, I thought that ominous, then silently deprecated, in a single slow movement of his hand, the wholly inappropriate expression of shock and rage, all the sizzle of my daddy's oratory.

Thus the tableau. We did the only possible thing, ignored him and let him run down, get it off his chest, come to his five battered senses, if he had so many, and get his breath. Brother, how he spilled darkness and sin upon that floor, wilting collar and boiling eyes, the sweat running from his face and, Fanny, shameless, languorous and drowsy, provoking him to further flights. She was young, gentlemen: I have not concealed it. She was too young to have had time to accumulate the history he ascribed to her. She was too tender to endure for long the muscular lash of his tongue and the rake of his eyes. She went over to her dad, as heretofore described, and when my sweet sire, orator general to the dying afternoon, had made his pitch about matters observed and inferences drawn, I went to join her. I sat with my back to him. All our backs were to him, including his own. He emptied himself of wrath and for a moment, a wild and wonderful moment, I thought he was going to join us, bathers in the pool of sun. But no.

Silence. Light lovely and fannygold over the pasture; shreds of mist by the river deepening to rose. My father's hard leather soles rattled harshly on the bare boards like rim-shots. The mad figure of him went black as bug out over the lawn, out over the loamy furrows where the tongue of ploughed field invaded the home paddock, all my doing, spurning in his violence anything less than this direct and abrupt charge towards the waiting car. Fanny's hand touched my arm again and for a moment I was caught in a passion of sympathy for him, something as solid as grief and love, an impossible pairing of devotion and despair. The landscape flooded with sadness as I watched the scuttling, black, ignominious figure hurdling the fresh earth, the waving arms, seemingly scattering broadcast the white and shying gulls, his head bobbing on his shoulders, as he narrowed into distance.

I wished, gentlemen, with a fervour foreign to my young life, that it had been in company other than that of Puti Hohepa and his brat that we had made our necessary parting. I wished we had been alone. I did not want to see him diminished, made ridiculous and pathetic among strangers, while I so brashly joined the mockers. (Were they mocking?) Impossible notions; for what was there to offer and how could he receive? Nothing. I stroked Fanny's arm. Old man Hohepa got up and unchained the dog and went off to get the cows in. He didn't speak; maybe the chocolate old bastard was dumb, eh? In a minute I would have to go down and start the engine and put the separator together. I stayed to stare at Fanny, thinking of undone things in a naughty world. She giggled, thinking, for all I know, of the same, or of nothing. Love, thy sunny trystings and nocturnal daggers. For the first time I admitted my irritation at that girlish, hic-coughing, tenor giggle. But we touched, held, got up and with our arms linked went down the long paddock through the infestation of buttercup, our feet bruising stalk and flower. Suddenly all I wanted and at whatever price was to be able, sometime, somewhere, to make it up to my primitive, violent, ignorant and crazy old man. And I knew I never would. Ah, what a bloody fool. And then the next thing I wanted, a thing far more feasible, was to be back in that room with its shade and smell of hay-dust and warm flesh, taking up the classic story just where we'd been so rudely forced to discontinue it. Old man Hohepa was bellowing at the dog; the cows rocked up through the paddock gate and into the yard: the air smelled of night. I stopped; and holding Fanny's arm suggested we might run back. Her eyes went wide: she giggled and broke away and I stood there and watched her flying down the paddock, bare feet and a flouncing skirt, her hair shaken loose.

Next afternoon I finished ploughing the river paddock, the nature of Puti Hohepa's husbandry as much a mystery as ever, and ran the old Ferguson into the lean-to shelter behind the cow shed. It was far too late for ploughing: the upper paddocks were hard and dry. But Puti hoped to get a crop of late lettuce off the river flat; just in time, no doubt, for a glutted market, brown rot, wilt and total failure of the heart. He'd have to harrow it first, too; and on his own. Anyway, none of my worry. I walked into the shed. Fanny and her daddy were deep in conversation. She was leaning against the flank of a cow, a picture of rustic grace, a rural study of charmed solemnity. Christ knows what they were saying to each other. For one thing they were speaking in their own language: for another I couldn't hear anything, even that, above the blather and splatter of the bloody cows and the racket of the single cylinder diesel, brand-name Onan out of Edinburgh so help me. They looked up. I grabbed a stool and got on with it, head down to the bore of it all. I'd have preferred to be up on the tractor, poisoning myself straight out, bellowing this and that and the other looney thing to the cynical gulls. Ah, my mountain princess of the golden chords, something was changing. I stripped on, sullenly: I hoped it was me.

*

We were silent through dinner: we were always silent, through all meals. It made a change from home where all hell lay between soup and sweet, everyone taking advantage of the twenty minutes of enforced attendance to shoot the bile, bicker and accuse, rant and wrangle through the grey disgusting mutton and the two veg. Fanny never chattered much and less than ever in the presence of her pappy: giggled maybe but never said much. Then out of the blue father Hohepa opened up. Buster, you should make peace with your father. I considered it. I tried to touch Fanny's foot under the table and I considered it. A boy shouldn't hate his father: a boy should respect his father. I thought about that too. Then I asked should fathers hate their sons; but I knew the answer. Puti Hohepa didn't say anything, just sat blowing into his tea, looking at his reputedly wild daughter who might have been a beauty for all I could tell, content to be delivered of the truth and so fulfilled. You should do this: a boy shouldn't do that — tune into that, mac. And me thinking proscription and prescription differently ordered in this farm world of crummy acres. I mean I thought I'd left all that crap behind the night I stumbled along Rideout Road following, maybe, the river Alph. I thought old man Hohepa, having been silent for so long, would know better than to pull, of a sudden, all those generalisations with which for seventeen years I'd been beaten dizzy — but not so dizzy as not to be able to look back of the billboards and see the stack of rotting bibles. Gentlemen, I was, even noticeably, subdued. Puti Hohepa clearly didn't intend to add anything more just then. I was too tired to make him an answer. I think I was too tired even for hate; and what better indication of the extent of my exhaustion than that? It had been a long summer; how long I was only beginning to discover. It was cold in the kitchen. Puti Hohepa got up. From the doorway, huge and merging into the night, he spoke again: You must make up your own mind. He went away, leaving behind him the vibration of a gentle sagacity, tolerance, a sense of duty (mine, as usual) pondered over and pronounced upon. The bastard. You must make up your own mind. And for the first time you did that mum had hysterics and dad popped his gut. About what? Made up my mind about what? My black daddy? Fanny? Myself? Life? A country career and agricultural hell? Death? Money? Fornication? (I'd always liked that.) What the hell was he trying to say? What doing but abdicating the soiled throne at the first challenge? Did he think fathers shouldn't hate their sons, or could help it, or would if they could? Am I clear? No matter. He didn't have one of the four he'd sired at home so what the hell sort of story was he trying to peddle? Father with the soft centre. You should, you shouldn't, make up your own mind. Mac, my head was going round. But it was brilliant, I conceded, when I'd given it a bit of thought. My livid daddy himself would have applauded the perfect ambiguity. What a bunch: they keep a dog on a chain for years and years and then let it free on some purely personal impulse and when it goes wild and chases its tail round and round, pissing here and sniffing there in an ecstasy of liberty, a freedom for which it has been denied all training, they shoot it down because it won't come running when they hold up the leash and whistle. (I didn't think you'd go that way, son.) Well, my own green liberty didn't look like so much at that moment; for the first time I got an inkling that life was going to be simply a matter of out of one jail and into another. Oh, they had a lot in common, her dad and mine. I sat there, mildly stupefied, drinking my tea. Then I looked up at Fanny; or, rather, down on Fanny. I've never known such a collapsible sheila in my life. She was stretched on the kitchen couch, every vertebra having turned to juice in the last minute and a half. I thought maybe she'd have the answer, some comment to offer on the state of disunion. Hell. I was the very last person to let my brew go cold while I pondered the nuance of the incomprehensible, picked at the dubious unsubtlety of thought of a man thirty years my senior who had never, until then, said more than ten words to me. She is too good for you: only six words after all and soon forgotten. Better, yes, if he'd stayed mum, leaving me to deduce from his silence whatever I could, Abora Mountain and the milk of paradise, consent in things natural and a willingness to let simple matters take their simple course.

I was wrong: Fanny offered no interpretation of her father's thought. Exegesis to his cryptic utterance was the one thing she couldn't supply. She lay with her feet up on the end of the couch, brown thighs charmingly bared, mouth open and eyes closed in balmy sleep, displaying in this posture various things but mainly her large unconcern not only for this tragedy of filial responsibility and the parental role but, too, for the diurnal problem of the numerous kitchen articles, pots, pans, plates, the lot. I gazed on her, frowning on her bloom of sleep, the slow inhalation and exhalation accompanied by a gentle flare of nostril, and considered the strength and weakness of our attachment. Helpmeet she was not, thus to leave her lover to his dark ponderings and the chores.

Puti Hohepa sat on the verandah in the dark, hacking over his bowl of shag. One by one, over my second cup of tea, I assessed my feelings, balanced all my futures in the palm of my hand. I crossed to Fanny, crouched beside her, kissed her. I felt embarrassed and, gentlemen, foolish. Her eyes opened wide; then they shut and she turned over.

The dishes engaged my attention not at all, except to remind me, here we go, of my father in apron and rubber gloves at the sink, pearl-diving while mum was off somewhere at a lynching. Poor bastard. Mum had the natural squeeze for the world; they should have changed places. (It's for your own good! Ah, the joyous peal of that as the razor strop came whistling down like tartar's blade.) I joined daddy Hohepa on the verandah. For a moment we shared the crescent moon and the smell of earth damp under dew, Rideout Mountain massed to the west.

I've finished the river paddock.

Yes.

The tractor's going to need a de-coke before long.

Yes.

I guess that about cuts it out.

Yes.

I may as well shoot through.

Buster, is Fanny pregnant?

I don't know. She hasn't said anything to me so I suppose she can't be.

You are going home?

No. Not home. There's work down south. I'd like to have a look down there.

There's work going here if you want it. But you have made up your mind?

I suppose I may as well shoot through.

Yes.

After milking tomorrow if that's okay with you.

Yes.

He hacked on over his pipe. Yes, yes, yes, yes, yes is Fanny pregnant? What if I'd said yes? I didn't know one way or the other. I only hoped, and left the rest to her. Maybe he'd ask her; and what if she said yes? What then, eh Buster? Maybe I should have said why don't you ask her. A demonstrative, volatile, loquacious old person: a tangible symbol of impartiality, reason unclouded by emotion, his eyes frank in the murk of night and his pipe going bright, dim, bright as he calmly considered the lovely flank of the moon. I was hoping she wasn't, after all. Hoping; it gets to be a habit, a bad habit that does you no good, stunts your growth, sends you insane and makes you, demonstrably, blind. Hope, for Fanny Hohepa.

Later, along the riverbank, Fanny and I groped, gentlemen, for the lost rapport and the parking sign. We were separated by just a little more than an arm's reach. I made note then of the natural scene. Dark water, certainly; dark lush grass underfoot; dark girl; the drifting smell of loam in the night: grant me again as much. Then, by one of those fortuitous accidents not infrequent in our national prosings, our hands met, held, fell away. Darkness. My feet stumbling by the river and my heart going like a tango. Blood pulsed upon blood, undenied and unyoked, as we busied ourselves tenderly at our ancient greetings and farewells. And in the end, beginning my sentence with a happy conjunction, I held her indistinct, dark head. We stayed so for a minute, together and parting as always, with me tumbling down upon her the mute dilemma my mind then pretended to resolve and she offering no restraint, no argument better than the dark oblivion of her face.

Unrecorded the words between us: there can't have been more than six, anyway it was our fated number. None referred to my departure or to the future or to maculate conceptions. Yet her last touch spoke volumes. (Unsubsidised, gentlemen, without dedication or preamble.) River-damp softened her hair: her skin smelled of soap: Pan pricking forward to drink at the stream, crushing fennel, exquisitely stooping, bending . . .

And, later again, silent, groping, we ascended in sequence to the paternal porch.

Buster?

Yair?

Goodnight, Buster.

'Night, Fanny. Be seein' yuh.

. . .

Fourteen minute specks of radioactive phosphorus brightened by weak starlight pricked out the hour: one.

In the end I left old STC in the tractor tool box along with the spanner that wouldn't fit any nut I'd ever tried it on and the grease gun without grease and the last letter from mum, hot as radium. I didn't wait for milking. I was packed and gone at the first trembling of light. It was cold along the river-bottom, cold and still. Eels rose to feed: the water was like pewter; old pewter. I felt sick, abandoned, full of self-pity. Everything washed through me, the light, the cold, a sense of what lay behind me and might not lie before, a feeling of exhaustion when I thought of home, a feeling of despair when I thought of Fanny still curled in sleep. Dark. She hadn't giggled: so what? I changed my fibre suitcase to the other hand and trudged along Rideout Road. The light increased; quail with tufted crests crossed the road: I began to feel better. I sat on the suitcase and rolled a smoke. Then the sun caught a high scarp of Rideout Mountain and began to finger down slow and gold. I was so full of relief, suddenly, that I grabbed my bag and ran. Impetuous. I was lucky not to break my ankle. White gulls, loam flesh, dark water, damsel and dome; where would it take you? Where was there to go, anyway? It just didn't matter; that was the point. I stopped worrying that minute and sat by the cream stand out on the main road. After a while a truck stopped to my thumb and I got in. If I'd waited for the cream truck I'd have had to face old brownstone Hohepa and I wasn't very eager for that. I'd had a fill of piety, of various brands. And I was paid up to date.

I looked back. Rideout Mountain and the peak of ochre red roof, Maori red. That's all it was. I wondered what Fanny and her pappy might be saying at this moment, across the clothes-hanger rumps of cows. The rush of relief went through me again. I looked at the gloomy bastard driving: he had a cigarette stuck to his lip like a growth. I felt almost happy. Almost. I might have hugged him as he drove his hearse through the tail-end of summer.

An Incident in Mid-Ocean

Janet Frame

In early spring when the days had just given up swallowing themselves at both ends like snakes and had started to display morning and evening lengths of pink light and poison-patterns of cloud, Miss Dolly Abson of Twenty-three Ivanhoe Road S.E.4. took part in an incident which aroused unpleasant comment and rumour in the neighbourhood.

She kissed, long and passionately, a little boy, Maurice Cooke, aged eight, who was coming through the school gate at ten past four in the afternoon. Many people noticed her action. They observed her flushed and nervous demeanour. They knew she was not even related to the child.

'Miss Abson gave me a long long kiss,' little Maurice said when he arrived home. 'Outside the school gates. She wouldn't let me go.'

Maurice's father who was a policeman listened intently. Miss Abson rented a room in his sister-in-law's house. He had heard that she possessed a 'mental history,' that she was receiving treatment from a psychiatrist at the local hospital. It was just as well, he thought, to look into the matter, to warn Maurice; one never knew; in spite of the modern outlook certain people should not be at large; harmless beginnings . . .

Miss Abson lived alone in a room on the second floor. She did not go out to work because contact with people worried and frightened her and she found it necessary always to build tall fires around her camp to ward off the beasts of prey which nevertheless surrounded her, their eyes gleaming through the woven darkness of the forest leaves.

Her hands were gnarled with digging moats and destroying bridges.

110

Arrows which were aimed at her window were deflected by the un-yielding glass and sometimes re-entered the hearts of those who had shot them.

Miss Abson had no friends. Her only recreations were walking to and from the shops and once a week, on an adventurously long journey which included three sets of traffic lights and one Ring Road, visiting the main local Library where she crept timidly from Sociology to Literature and History, hiding herself behind the tall shelves. Only rarely did she go to the Museums, for one time an officious attendant had taken her umbrella, her coat and handbag, and she had stayed the whole afternoon, terrified and stranded, in the shelter of the History of the Horse.

Therefore she chose to remain most of the time in her room. Her most frequent visits were to her psychiatrist at the hospital not far away. For these visits to him she wore her best clothes, her twin-set and terylene skirt, and changed her underwear. She touched her lips with Pond's Natural Lipstick and rubbed in the hollow of her throat, be-hind her ears, and on her wrists, next to her pulse, a tiny dab of cream perfume, Lily of the Valley. She brushed her hair with Trill which came in a tube and contained 'a replacement of natural oils.' Her psychia-trist sat in a room which had two chairs, a desk, a couch, and pot plants arranged along the window sill. He said, 'Good morning. How are you, Miss Abson?'

Miss Abson was so lonely. Once when she looked out of her win-dow she saw a little brown dog scratching at the garden. The little brown dog glanced up at her and winked boldly. Miss Abson felt her blood flowing warmly round and round the mulberry bush.

And then, at the beginning of a new term, little Maurice Cooke started school. Miss Abson had seen him at times visiting his aunt, and she had spoken to him and smiled at him. Once, when he called at the house and his aunt was out, Miss Abson brought him up to her room and gave him two foreign stamps with pictures of birds on them. They were birds with red feet standing in a swamp, and a bright blue bird flying in a bright blue sky with the sun like a cherry hanging in the corner and the tall gold grass growing from the earth beneath. They were beautiful foreign stamps. Miss Abson had placed them in a spe-cial position on her mantelpiece so that she might look at them whenever she felt lonely, but this day when she had invited Maurice to her room she was overwhelmed by a desire to shower him with gifts. So she gave him her chief treasure of the moment, the beautiful foreign stamps. He clutched them in his hot grubby fingers. He walked backward and forward in the room, trying out the carpet, and then he said abruptly 'I'd better go back to school. There's the second bell.'

Regretfully Miss Abson showed him downstairs and out the front door.

'Good-by, Maurice.'

'Good-by, Miss Abson.'

Then, returning to her room, Miss Abson noticed the torn pieces of foreign stamps lying on the carpet. Maurice had torn them while he was walking up and down. Miss Abson tried to stifle her feeling of betrayal and dismay.

He's only a little boy, she thought. I didn't really expect him to appreciate their beauty and value.

Yet her feeling of dismay persisted. Why hadn't he kept the foreign stamps, to love and treasure them?

Later in the week Miss Abson's landlady mentioned that if at any time Maurice rang the doorbell in the lunch hour would Miss Abson please let him in for a few minutes as he was afraid to go to the lavatory at school where the door would not shut and the big boys prowled around after the little boys?

Miss Abson promised to open the door to Maurice.

One lunch hour when she had eaten her cheese on toast and was drinking her coffee and had just started to bite into the Fruitie Bun (threepence halfpenny at the Whip-It Bakery in Ivanhoe Road) the doorbell rang and there was Maurice panting and nearly in tears and with mud all over his legs.

'Miss Abson, I fell in the mud, and there's a big boy after me. He hit me at dinnertime and to pay him back I stirred his custard with my fork and now he's after me.'

'Oh dear,' Miss Abson said. 'Do come in. You know where to clean yourself. You can stay with me until it's time to go back to school.'

Then, glancing round in case eavesdroppers were near, she whispered, 'If you want to go . . . you know . . . somewhere . . . you can.'

Maurice came in and cleaned himself (leaving black shoe polish

112

over his aunt's downstairs carpet) and Miss Abson took him upstairs to her room. What can I give him? she wondered. I should always have something here, ready for when he calls.

She rummaged in an old packet of letters and found a gay post-card from the United States, a relic of Ed Porlock who had been her pen friend in Ohio but who had stopped writing to her, he never said why.

'Here,' she said to Maurice. 'Here's a postcard. With stamps on it, too.'

Then she remembered, with a cry of joy which made Maurice stare at her in bewilderment, that there was a picture card, the Bushy-Tailed Galaco, from the packet of tea. She gave this card to Maurice. I must buy cornflakes in future, she thought excitedly. Cornflakes, and rice bubbles, and all those foods they advertise on television, all the foods with the gifts enclosed in the packets.

Miss Abson had watched advertisements on television. The small set in her room had been supplied by her landlord when in consultation with his wife who suspected that Miss Abson suffered from 'mental trouble' they had decided that a television set would be company for her.

'She needs company,' they said.

But after watching a few programmes Miss Abson had grown tired of television. It made too many demands on space and time; it interfered with thinking, and people on the screen were always smiling with false smiles which said, I know what you are up to, there in your bedroom, Miss Abson; also the characters flitted back and forth so dizzily, with shots ringing out; and the ladies had microphones in their bosoms, and their dresses were covered with scales, like mermaids; and the advertisements with their gift vouchers and giant double-sealed packs were so confusing . . .

Maurice thanked Miss Abson for the postcard from the United States, and having forgotten about the big boy who was after him and into whose custard he had poked his fork, he went happily back to school. Miss Abson gave him an apple to eat on the way, a rosy juicy apple.

A few days later Maurice brought two of his friends with him in the lunch hour, and Miss Abson invited them all to her room. Oh dear, what had she to give them? Ah! Hadn't she bought a Free Offer tube of toothpaste with a magnifying glass attached? Oh, where was it? And where was the tiny magnet which had taken her fancy in Woolworth's and which she had slipped into her bag when no one was looking? She could find neither the magnifying glass nor the magnet. Her face was flushed with the excitement of looking, lifting up papers, delving in corners, trying to remember, but it was no use, she could not find the gifts.

Then Maurice came up to her. 'We've got something for you,' he said. 'We got it in a penny surprise packet.'

He held up a tiny plastic skeleton.

Miss Abson was delighted. 'Oh,' she gasped. 'How clever! How kind! Don't you want it for yourselves?'

'We've got plenty,' Maurice said, like a millionaire. 'You have it.'

Thanking him, Miss Abson took the skeleton. And when Maurice and his friends had gone she propped the tiny white skeleton on her mantelpiece, as her latest treasure.

'Why,' she said, 'even its ribs are showing, and all the bones. How clever! Now if Maurice were to grow up to be a doctor he could be studying anatomy even now, identifying and counting the bones in this tiny skeleton! What if he decides to become a doctor? A psychiatrist perhaps!'

Miss Abson felt excitement surging through her. All kinds of plans tumbled through her head, whirling like washing in a washing machine.

And what if he grows up to be a scientist? Oh, Miss Abson thought, I wonder if my National Assistance grant is enough to buy one of those small microscopes so that Maurice can use it when he calls in the lunch hour? I wonder does he collect stamps? What books does he read? What toys does he play with? He owns a scooter — yes, I have seen him on Saturday mornings with his red scooter — or, perhaps, what about buying him a telescope? An astronomer! A member of the Royal Society!

Miss Abson grew quite dizzy planning Maurice's future, there were so many opportunities for him. When he came to the house now she questioned him closely about his school work and was disappointed when he showed no interest.

'He will grow to it,' she said to herself. 'There is all the time in the world for him. I wonder will he be a psychiatrist and sit in a room with pot plants along the window sill?'

And that afternoon she put on her best clothes as usual and went to visit her psychiatrist who sat aloof in his white coat and murmured, 'Yes, I see, I understand how you feel.'

Sometimes she longed to break her psychiatrist into pieces, like a biscuit, and see the icing in between; or to startle him so that his true self rose like a cloud of bees from the secret hive. She did not tell him about Maurice, how she was carefully planning his future, and how she felt so grieved when he did not seem to be aware of the plans being made for him, and was spending valuable time merely playing with his new bicycle and his set of toy trains.

Miss Abson now divided her life between her psychiatrist and Maurice. She thought continually about them both, and dreamed of them, but one night in her dreams when she gave her psychiatrist a tiny magnifying glass marked FOREIGN VALUABLE he stamped his black-polished shoe on it and smashed it to pieces, and Miss Abson woke up crying.

One day Maurice fell on the pavement outside and bruised his knee. Miss Abson's face went white with shock. She bandaged his wound and insisted that he lie down on her bed. Pleased at the attention, he lay on the bed, crushing the clean counterpane which the landlady supplied, by tradition, for the springtime and summertime; a floral cotton, with roses. Only the day before the landlady had exchanged the sombre maroon cover for the bright cotton, with the remark, 'Spring is on the way, doesn't it make you feel different? You'll want to get out and about more these spring days, won't you, Miss Abson?'

The landlady was troubled that Miss Abson stayed in her room and did not 'mix.'

One day when Miss Abson was saying good-by to Maurice at the door he requested, 'Kiss Me!'

Startled, Miss Abson laughed nervously, and did not kiss him but pressed him to her affectionately, then said a hurried breathless good-by. I wonder, she thought, did he notice my embarrassment? It was a simple request on his part. I hope I didn't make him think that kissing is something . . . strange. I hope I didn't seem too embarrassed.

Miss Abson was not used to kisses. She was overtaken with sudden gaiety. She went up to her room and opened the windows top and bottom to let in the spring air. She stayed by the window. She did not try to escape. The sun's penetration included her. She blushed and laughed and then, suddenly, an awful thought came to her.

What if Maurice goes home and says, innocently, 'Miss Abson kissed me today?' Won't they think there is something strange? I must keep away from the child. I definitely must keep away from the child.

A heavy depression came over her. She closed the windows. And the next day she stayed in bed with a cold, and the lodger who lived on the third floor went to the chemist's for her and returned with a bottle of medicine and a packet of tablets. The medicine was bright pink, such a pretty colour; it cheered Miss Abson considerably to take medicine which was such a gay colour. She measured for herself the required dose, punctually and carefully, and took the tablets four times during the day, in water, after food.

Near the end of the week when she had recovered a little, she got up and dressed, and rearranged her room, moving the bed to the opposite wall and the bookshelves to the corner near the window. The rearrangement pleased and soothed her. She felt happy again. The day was warm and fine with a fresh breeze blowing.

So she decided to take a walk. She walked up the road near the school, and it just happened that as she passed the gates there was Maurice on his way home.

'Miss Abson!' he shouted, running up to her. She felt excited at this public acknowledgment of herself.

'Kiss me,' Maurice pleaded, when he reached her. Now if I refuse, Miss Abson thought, it may seem strange. She laughed nervously.

'No, I'll blow you a kiss,' she said, putting her flattened hand primly to her mouth.

'No. Kiss me.'

So suddenly she leaned forward and kissed him, then took him in her arms and pressed herself to him, clutching him desperately as if he were her tiny rescuer in the middle of a lonely ocean. And that was when quite a crowd gathered to observe Miss Abson.

'Carrying on like that in the street, too, and she's no relation to him,' someone remarked.

Miss Abson still visits her psychiatrist. He still wears his white coat, and nods his head and murmurs, I see, I understand, I know how you feel. And when Miss Abson returns from the hospital she takes off her best clothes and her best shoes and puts on her old ones again, and sits in her chair by the window, looking at the people, and the dogs, and the cats balancing along the brick walls, and the cars passing.

And each day the waves lap against Miss Abson's world and the tide rises higher, over the floor and the baseboard and the table top and the television set and the mantelpiece where the two new foreign stamps lie unclaimed. They have pictures of birds on them, a swamp bird with red legs and a bright blue bird flying through a bright blue sky with the sun hanging like a cherry in the corner and the grass tall and gold growing beneath from the earth.

And soon all is submerged in the tide, and drowned.

A Sense of Proportion

JANET FRAME

The sun's hair stood on end. The sky accommodated all visiting darkness and light. Leaves were glossy green, gold, brown, dried, dead and bleached in drifts beneath the trees. Snow fell in all seasons, white hyphens dropping evenly, linking syllables of sky and earth. Flowers bloomed forever, spinning their petal-spokes like golden wheels, sucking the sun like whirlpools. Black-polished, brick-dusted, spotted ladybirds big as airplanes with pleated wings like sky-wide curtains parting, flew home to flame and cinders.

Houses had painted roofs of red and yellow with tall chimneys emitting scribbles of pale blue smoke. All houses had gardens around them, paths with parallel sides enclosing pebbles; gates were five-barred, with children swinging from them. The children wore red stockings. They had ribbons tied in their hair. Their eyes were round and blue, their eyebrows were arched, their lips were rosy. Their hands displayed five fingers for all to see, their feet pointed the same way, left or right, in gaudy shoes with high heels. The ocean was filled with sailing boats, the sky was filled with rainbows, suns, scalloped clouds.

Coats had many buttons, intricate collars with lace edges. The bricks of houses were carefully outlined. Front doors had four panels and a knocker in its exact position.

Winds were visible, fat men or witches with puffed cheeks in the four corners of the sky. The trees leaned with their skirts up over their heads.

The streets were full of painted rubber balls divided carefully into bright colours.

Men wore hats placed firmly upon their heads.

Dogs walked, their tails like masts in the air.

Cats had mile-long whiskers like rays of the sun. They sat, their tails curled about them, containing them. Their ears were pricked, forever listening.

The moon, like the sun, had a face, a smile, eyes, teeth. The moon journeyed on a cloud convoyed by elaborately five-pointed stars.

There was no distance or shade in our infant drawing. Everything loomed close to the eye; rainbows in the heavens could be clutched as securely as the few blades of bright green grass (the colour of strong lemonade) growing symmetrically in the lower right-hand corner of the picture.

Some years passed during which we learned to draw and paint from a small tin of Reeve's Water Colours: Chinese White, Gamboge Tint, Indigo, Yellow Ochre (which I pronounced and believed to be *Yellow Ogre*), Burnt Sienna: the names gave excitement, pain, wonder. We were shown how to paint a sunset in the exact gradations of colour, to make a blue water-colour sky, a scientific rainbow (Read Over Your Greek Book In Verse) receding into the distance. The teacher placed an apple and a pear in a glass bowl upon the table. We drew them, making careful shading, painstakingly colouring the autumn tints of the apple.

We did not paint the worm inside it.

We drew vases of flowers, autumn scenes, furniture which existed merely to cast a perfect shadow to be portrayed by a B.B. pencil. The Art lessons were long and tedious. I could never get my shadow or my distance correct. My rainbows and paths would not recede, and my furniture, my boats at anchor, my buildings stood flat upon the page, all in a total clamour of foreground.

'You must draw things,' said Miss Collins the Art Teacher, 'as they seem. Notice the way the path narrows as it approaches the foothills.'

'But it is the same breadth all the way!'

'No,' Miss Collins insisted. 'You must learn to draw these tricks of the eye. You must learn to think in terms of them.'

I never learned to draw tricks of the eye. My paint refused to wash in the correct proportion when I was trying to fill the paper sky with sunrises, sunsets, and rainbows. My garden spades were without strength or shape; their shadows stayed unowned, apart, incredible, more like stray tatters shed from a profusion of dark remnants of objects. My vases had no depth, and their flowers withered in their laborious journey from the table to the page of my scholastic Drawing Book Number Three.

The classroom was dusty and hot and there was the soft buzz of talking, and people walking to and fro getting fresh water and washing brushes; and Miss Collins touring the aisles, giving gentle but insistent advice about colours and shadows. Her hair was in plaits, wound close to her head. In moments of calm or boredom the fact or fancy rippled about the classroom, lapping at our curiosity, Miss Collins wears a wig. Once, long ago, in the days of the Spartans and Athenians, someone had observed Miss Collins in the act of removing her wig.

'She is quite bald,' the rumour went.

Like so many of the other teachers Miss Collins lived with her mother in a little house, a woven spider's nest with the leaves and rain closing in, just at the edge of town. She cherished a reputation as a local painter and at most exhibitions you could see her poplar trees, tussock scenes, mountains, lakes, all in faded colours, with sometimes in the corner, or looking out of the window of a decayed farmhouse, the tiny fierce black lines that were the shape of people.

Every term she gave us examinations which were days of flurry and anxiety when we filed into the Art Room and took our places at the bare desks and gazed with respectful awe at the incongruous display on the table — fruit, a vase of flowers, perhaps a kettle or similar utensil whose shape would strain our ability to 'match sides.' And for the next forty minutes our attention would be fixed upon the clutter of objects, the submissive Still Life which yet huddled powerfully before us, preying upon us with its overlapping corners and sides and deceptive shadows.

How I envied Leila Smith! Leila Smith could draw perfect kettles, rainbows, cupboards. Her pictures always showed the exact number of strokes of rain, when rain fell, the snowflakes when the scene required them. By instinct Leila Smith *knew*. On those days when the gods attended the classroom, penetrating the dust-layered windows hung with knotted cords so complicated that a special Window Monitor was needed to operate them, and the window sills ranged with dead flowers and beans in water — when the gods walked up and down the aisles at our Art Examination they showed extra care for Leila Smith, they guided her hand across the page. When they passed my desk, alas, they vindictively jogged my elbow. Miss Collins despaired of ever teaching me.

'How's your drawing?' my father would say, who had spent the winter evenings painting in oils from a tiny cigarette card the ship that carried him to the First World War. His sisters painted as well; their work hung in the passage — roses, dogs, clouded ladies, and one storm at sea.

'I can't draw,' I said. 'I can't paint.'

Miss Collins readily agreed with me. 'Your perspective and proportion are well below average. Your shading is poor.'

The obsession with shading fascinated me. All things, even kettles and fire shovels, stood under the sun complete and unique with their shadows, fighting to preserve them. It was an act of charity for us to draw the shadow with as much love (frustration, despair) as we gave to drawing the shape itself. In the world of Miss Collins, morning and evening were perpetual, with the shadows spread beautifully alongside each object, their contours matching perfectly, a mirror image of the body. Why was it that in my world the sun stood everlastingly at noon; objects were stripped of their shadows, forced to stand in brilliant light, alone?

In the end Miss Collins gave up trying to teach me to draw and paint. She spent her time giving hints to Leila Smith. Oh how wonderful were Leila's flowers and fire shovels, garden spades and kettles!

Sometimes Miss Collins would ask us to paint things 'out of our head.'

It showed, she said, whether we had any imagination.

I had no imagination. My poverty could not even provide shadows or proportionate rainbows. The paths in my head stayed the same width right to the foothills and over the mountains which were no obstacles to vision, as mountains are agreed to be; they were transparent mountains, and there was the path, the same width as before, annihilating distance, at last disappearing only at the boundary of the picture.

Distance did not cloud the outline of objects; trees were not blurred; you could count the leaves upon the trees, even on the slopes of the mountain you could count the pine needles hanging in their green brushes.

Yes, it was true; I had no sense of proportion.

When I last saw Miss Collins she had been taken to the hospital after a stroke, and was lying quietly in the hospital bed. She was dying. The torment of the unshaded world lay before her, the sun in her sky stood resolutely at noon, her life was out of proportion, there was no distance, the foreground blazed with looming and light.

She closed her eyes and died.

Her life, in its spider's web, had absorbed her. She had been aided, comforted, made less lonely, by acknowledging and yielding to a trick of the eye. How does one learn to accept that trick and its blessings before it is too late, before the shadows are razed and the sun stands pitiless at perpetual noon?

How Can I Get in Touch with Persia?

Janet Frame

Early in his life he grew mistrustful of messages borne to him by word of mouth or letter. He became concerned with invisible communications and the sly cryptic evidence of them in telephone wires, radio aerials, valves and switches, and, lately, the four hundred and five invisible lines of a television picture. Electricity fascinated him. When his parents talked of the 'old days' of gas lamps in the street and candles burning with their leaf-shaped flame at the foot of the stairs, he felt a special pride in the fact that he had always known electricity, the power of turning the switch and invading the room with probes of light or condemning it to darkness. When his mother plugged in the electric iron he used to rub his finger along the bottom of the iron, collecting the evidence, the mystical vibrations, tracing them along the cord to the unobtrusive three-pin plug above the baseboard, just inside the door. The repeated warnings BE CAREFUL OF ELECTRICITY, THE INVISIBLE KILLER, only increased its fascination. He became preoccupied even in sleep and dreaming with its mystery. He longed to seek out the reality of it, to put his hand into the dark and touch it.

He constructed his first transmitting and receiving set. He was filled with wonder and love at the variety of messages in the air. Sometimes messages came to him even while he was walking in the street or at work. While other boys of his age sought the company of girl friends and found their escape and pleasure in clubs, gangs, the telly, the dance hall, the cinema, he derived his entertainment and solace from the workbench in his tiny room on the top floor of the house where he had an increasing supply of electrical gadgets, wires, plugs, and his transmitting and receiving set. Often he would stay into the early hours

123

of the morning, tapping in code and talking to people in the distant countries which could only be located on the map by searching the index and then carefully trapping the area between its bonds of latitude and longitude. Every country was trapped in this way. Not one could hide or fake death in order to escape notice, such was the ruthlessness of the map of the world.

But all things were ruthless, all men and their instruments.

And what of Death?

He used to sit in the dark, sometimes not attending the signals on his wireless, considering the problem of death and the means of solving it with his one ally — Electricity. Then he would switch on the B.B.C. and laugh when the late-night clergyman entreated him to Lift Up Your Hearts For God Dwells on High, Come Unto Him All Ye that Labour and Are Heavy-laden and He Will Give You Rest.

Well, he was not heavy-laden, anyway. He was selected to receive special messages. The sound waves eddied about him, touching his skin, the palms of his hands, caressing him, even underneath his clothing; he throbbed with messages.

He worked as a packer in a Mail-Order Firm at Brixton. He applied for that job after the episode of the sea holiday when the family doctor had said that he needed rest, he had been growing too fast, and now that he was in his early twenties he should be leading a 'more normal' life.

Sometimes he stayed in bed all day.

'You great lout,' his father said. 'When I was your age . . .'

That was when he was working at the self-service store, on the adding machine, for he was interested in numbers and sympathetic to machines. Then for a while he stayed at home while the doctor persisted in telling him to get to the seaside.

But who would supply the money? He grew tired of hearing of the seaside.

For three days and nights without ceasing he communicated with foreign places. He called it his seaside holiday. It refreshed him. Besides, he had a plan in mind. It would astonish the world, it would show everybody. He slept with wires round his wrists to collect and store messages which came while he slept, for it would take much time and study to complete his plan, there was not a moment to be lost because the life expectation of every human being had lengthened and branched out at the edge with poisonous blossoms, wire flowers lit by concealed bulbs which flashed their urgency, red, gold, and dark green.

It troubled him that when he applied for the job at Brixton he was asked to sign a form stating that he was willing to be searched every evening before he left the factory. Why should he say that he was willing to be searched when he was not willing to be searched? What were they trying to seize from him? He was grateful that his messages, the receiving waves, were invisible, and his heart was learning to beat in Morse code, so as to transmit secret answers, and not a soul at the Mail-Order Firm knew of his secret preoccupations or of his growing power and alliance with electricity.

'Get out and about,' his father said, 'instead of tinkering and talking to Persia.'

So he went one night to the wrestling, and although he listened carefully to the names of the holds — Full Nelson, Drop Kick, Toe Hold, Body Scissors — and tried to grasp the special significance of them when applied to his secret plans, the spectacle of wrestling did not interest him. He had gone there only to please his mother when she said, 'Yes, do as your father says, have an evening out, to the stock-car racing or somewhere.'

His heart had beaten fast with dread when she said, 'or somewhere,' for the expression was so vague that he knew she was trying to convey a special meaning, perhaps a warning. Had she intercepted a message intended for him?

Sometimes when he came home at night he found that his father had gone down to the pub and he was alone with his mother. He enjoyed these evenings. He sat in his father's chair by the stove and watched his mother bending and twisting the wire to make the frames of the lamp shades which she afterward fleshed with stiff material, like parchment, painting flowers and scenes and faces upon it. Making lamp shades was her hobby. She had orders from so many people that she could hardly keep up with the demand. Some she gave away, others she sold; it depended. As he sat there watching and talking to her, telling her about the latest messages from Persia, and about his job in the Mail-Order Firm, he would at times be overcome by a haunting fear at the sight of his mother's face and the used look of her skin, as if someone in the Mail-Order Firm had charge of her, stamping wrinkled destinations upon her face in a crude impersonal way, as if she had changed into one of those dull-coloured envelopes which are issued by the Post Office with the instructions, RE-USE, ATTACH FLAP AND RE-USE TO ASSIST ECONOMY DRIVE. What did it mean? He would try to forget his fear. He would renew the conversation, giving detailed accounts of his day at work, but when the silences came his mind would be occupied with the problem of destinations, areas of land and their ownership, human mortgages, electricity; chiefly electricity.

When his father returned from the pub, he would stop talking to his mother and get up from his father's chair, and go quickly to his room, close the door carefully, lock it, draw the curtains, and sit at his workbench considering the wonderful prospects of electricity. Once, he heard rumours that his enemies were closing in upon him but he suppressed his immediate panic and smiled with scorn — was not electricity his lifelong ally?

But I need to catch up, he thought, with urgency. I should have studied it from the very beginning. In the medical world it is a miracle. I should have gone on and been a doctor.

Gone on? Where? To Persia?

Splutter, peep-peep, dot-dot-dot.

That was the language which he had learned and which he could now understand more easily than the language of people, of his mother and father. He could hear their murmurs to each other on the stairs, a rustling sound, like a straw broom sweeping debris or other messages of a hard substance, metal or stone, being shaken to extract them from the bottle in which they had drifted thousands of miles across the ocean.

He turned from listening to them and switched on his receiver.

Splutter, peep-peep, dot-dot-dot.

He felt lonely. The language infuriated him suddenly. He switched off and sat on his bed and listened to the B.B.C. Any Questions? Does the Team think? Will the Panel tell me?

'Go on,' he said, and lay down on his narrow bed and closed his eyes.

It happened that there was an epidemic of flu in the district. Everybody seemed to be catching it. Some of the workers at the Mail-Order

Firm were taken ill, and were sent home, and calling on their doctor on the way home they were put on the panel and given prescriptions for fancy nose sprays, bottles of medicine, boxes of pills.

First his father had flu and recovered.

He knew that he would be immune from it as he needed all his strength for the important work which was to decide his destiny. He realized that he could not be spared from his nightly conversations with far countries, and from the time-devouring problems of electricity.

The flu avoided him, and arrived at his mother. Quite surprisingly she talked in her sleep one night and his father called him, saying stupidly, 'Mum's talking in her sleep. She's delirious. We'll get the doctor.'

He did not approve of his father's suggestion. He was seized with jealousy which raged in him, making his face turn a violent red and his heart thud and throb against his chest. Why was his father not consulting him, instead of a doctor?

His jealousy subsided, his face paled; his heart was heavy with disappointment. No one knew of his secret qualifications; he would have to take action, prove himself; human lives were in the balance, the entire human race depended upon him. It was time; he would act; how?

The doctor came, after four hours. And by morning his mother was dead.

When he heard the news he went to his room and tuned in to Persia.

His mother was dead. Her unfinished lamp shades lay upon the table, beside the useless twists of copper wire. Her face was at last franked and cancelled with free death. Or so the world believed. He could not understand, he could not think clearly. He stayed all that night and the night before the funeral, leaning over his transmitting and receiving set, trying to interpret thc new signals which had found thcir way amongst the splutter, peep-peep, dot-dot-dot.

The day of the funeral was as sunny as Bank Holiday, and the ride to the cemetery had a festive air about it, with the hearse speeding along so that his mother might keep her last appointment.

But his mother disliked appointments; she had never kept them;

and this was not her last, oh no, oh no. He burst out laughing in the back of the car.

'It takes people in different ways,' his father said.

'We all need a good cry,' said his aunt from Liverpool.

And when he saw them lowering his mother's coffin into the grave he still did not cry, and after the funeral he went straight home and got in touch with Persia.

He was talking to Persia, and trying to understand the complexities of the strange new code when he conceived his plan. When his father, as had been arranged, went north to Liverpool to stay with the aunt, he would be alone in the house. That was his opportunity.

Two days later he hired a Self-Drive car. He drove in the evening to his mother's grave, dug up her coffin, opened it, removed his mother's body which he wrapped in a blanket and laid gently in the back of the car.

He kissed his mother. He began to cry. 'Don't worry,' he said. 'I've never believed it. Even when they wanted to search me to take my life away from me, I've never believed it. All the messages have proved it is not true. There is no death, now that I have solved the mystery. You did not guess, did you, that I had solved the mystery, all this time in my room with the copper wire and switches and a few strips of aluminium? I'm going to bring you back to life. You can't die, not any more; besides, the people are waiting for their lamp shades to protect them from the light, all up and down the street they are waiting for their lamp shades, and soon you'll be making them, and I'll be sitting by the stove, watching you, talking to you.'

He drove the car home, and carried his mother to her room, and laid her on his bed. Far into the night he worked to attach the wires and switches to her body. She lay with gold and silver insect-scaffolding over her; like Gulliver wired to earth by the little people.

'She is regaining her strength,' he said confidently, distributing wires, locating switches, placing a light bulb on her breast.

At half-past three in the morning he made a cup of tea on the gas ring in the corner of his room. He offered the tea to his mother, first taking a few sips to test whether it was too strong or too sweet as she did not fancy it that way. She did not move. She did not even raise her head to drink the tea. He switched on the electric current. A slight shock trembled through his fingers and along his arm as he touched the network of wires, but still his mother did not move. He drank the tea himself. Then he kissed the cold gray face; there was a blue tinge under the skin, like deep water. He crumbled a piece of Rich Tea Biscuit over the mouth in the hope that her tongue would dart forth, like a lizard's tongue, and seize it. But there was still no movement. He rechecked the wires and the switches. His face was dazed and pale; his cheekbones felt massive, seized by a clamp; his mouth was dry.

'She is regaining her strength,' he repeated.

He sighed. He found another blanket, and lay beside his mother on the narrow bed. 'When I count twenty,' he said to himself, 'she will come alive.'

He counted twenty; she was not breathing.

'If I hear a motor bike while I am counting fifteen, and if the edge of the curtain moves during the following fifteen and the light from the street lamp outside shines in a slit upon the wallpaper, then she will be alive. He counted fifteen, listening anxiously for the motor bike, and opening his eyes to observe the patch of wallpaper where the street lamp would shine.

He heard a motor bike. A wind blew the edge of the curtain, letting in the light. But nothing persuaded his mother to wake.

'It takes time,' he said, his heart heavy with the humiliation of needing to include motor bikes, numbers, street lamps, in his perfect plan, to rely on ordinary visible objects when the secret world of electricity was under his command, as his agent and slave.

He drew another blanket over him and slept. He lay there for two days, never entirely losing his faith in the power of the electricity, but relying more and more upon chance happenings, shadows, noises, radios in the next house, to influence his mother, to compel her to wake. But the motor bikes, the lorries, cars, roared up and down the street; shadows formed and dissolved and the light made patterns on the wallpaper; and his mother stayed dead. From time to time he still switched the current on and off in the hope of reviving her.

It only needs time, he thought. A season, a spring or summer.

His head felt unearthed, ancient, like the skull of a mammoth. Drums beat in the sky; his skin was too tight, it would not fit.

At three o'clock the next afternoon when the man from the

Self-Drive Hire Company called, knocked, and got no answer, when neighbours saw the accumulating milk bottles outside the door and the paper boy found his papers not collected, when the world, as it does in a feat of intensely interested arithmetic, put two and two together, the police were called. They forced an entry to the house. They searched. When they came to his room they found his mother lying on the bed, laced with wires and switches. He was leaning over the transmitting set in the corner of the room. Tears were streaming down his face. He was trying to get in touch with Persia.

The Bath

JANET FRAME

On Friday afternoon she bought cut flowers — daffodils, anemones, a few twigs of a red-leaved shrub, wrapped in mauve waxed paper, for Saturday was the seventeenth anniversary of her husband's death and she planned to visit his grave, as she did each year, to weed it and put fresh flowers in the two jam jars standing one on each side of the tombstone. Her visit this year occupied her thoughts more than usual. She had bought the flowers to force herself to make the journey that each year became more hazardous, from the walk to the bus stop, the change of buses at the Octagon, to the bitterness of the winds blowing from the open sea across almost unsheltered rows of tombstones; and the tiredness that overcame her when it was time to return home when she longed to find a place beside the graves, in the soft grass, and fall asleep.

That evening she filled the coal bucket, stoked the fire. Her movements were slow and arduous, her back and shoulder gave her so much pain. She cooked her tea — liver and bacon — set up knife and fork on the teatowel she used as a tablecloth, turned up the volume of the polished red radio to listen to the Weather Report and the News, ate her tea, washed her dishes, then sat drowsing in the rocking chair by the fire, waiting for the water to get hot enough for a bath. Visits to the cemetery, the doctor, and to relatives, to stay, always demanded a bath. When she was sure that the water was hot enough (and her tea had been digested) she ventured from the kitchen through the cold passageway to the colder bathroom. She paused in the doorway to get used to the chill of the air then she walked slowly, feeling with each step the pain in her back, across to the bath, and though she knew

131

that she was gradually losing the power in her hands she managed to wrench on the stiff cold and hot taps and half-fill the bath with warm water. How wasteful, she thought, that with the kitchen fire always burning during the past month of frost, and the water almost always hot, getting in and out of a bath had become such an effort that it was not possible to bath every night or even every week!

She found a big towel, laid it ready over a chair, arranged the chair so that should difficulty arise as it had last time she bathed she would have some way of rescuing herself; then with her nightclothes warming on a page of newspaper inside the coal oven and her dressing-gown across the chair to be put on the instant she stepped from the bath, she undressed and pausing first to get her breath and clinging tightly to the slippery yellow-stained rim that now seemed more like the edge of a cliff with a deep drop below into the sea, slowly and painfully she climbed into the bath.

I'll put on my nightie the instant I get out, she thought. The instant she got out indeed! She knew it would be more than a matter of instants yet she tried to think of it calmly, without dread, telling herself that when the time came she would be very careful, taking the process step by step, surprising her bad back and shoulder and her powerless wrists into performing feats they might usually rebel against, but the key to controlling them would be the surprise, the slow stealing up on them. With care, with thought . . .

Sitting upright, not daring to lean back or lie down, she soaped herself, washing away the dirt of the past fortnight, seeing with satisfaction how it drifted about on the water as a sign that she was clean again. Then when her washing was completed she found herself looking for excuses not to try yet to climb out. Those old woman's finger nails, cracked and dry, where germs could lodge, would need to be scrubbed again; the skin of her heels, too, growing so hard that her feet might have been turning to stone; behind her ears where a thread of dirt lay in the rim; after all, she did not often have the luxury of a bath, did she? How warm it was! She drowsed a moment. If only she could fall asleep then wake to find herself in her nightdress in bed for the night! Slowly she rewashed her body, and when she knew she could no longer deceive herself into thinking she was not clean she reluctantly replaced the soap, brush and flannel in the groove at the side of the bath, feeling as she loosened her grip on them that all strength and support were ebbing from her. Quickly she seized the nail-brush again, but its magic had been used and was gone; it would not adopt the role she tried to urge upon it. The flannel too, and the soap, were frail flotsam to cling to in the hope of being borne to safety.

She was alone now. For a few minutes she sat swilling the water against her skin, perhaps as a means of buoying up her courage. Then resolutely she pulled out the plug, sat feeling the tide swirl and scrape at her skin and flesh, trying to draw her down, down into the earth; then the bathwater was gone in a soapy gurgle and she was naked and shivering and had not yet made the attempt to get out of the bath.

How slippery the surface had become! In future she would not clean it with kerosene, she would use the paste cleaner that, left on overnight, gave the enamel rough patches that could be gripped with the skin.

She leaned forward, feeling the pain in her back and shoulder. She grasped the rim of the bath but her fingers slithered from it almost at once. She would not panic, she told herself; she would try gradually, carefully, to get out. Again she leaned forward; again her grip loosened as if iron hands had deliberately uncurled her stiffened blue fingers from their trembling hold. Her heart began to beat faster, her breath came more quickly, her mouth was dry. She moistened her lips. If I shout for help, she thought, no one will hear me. No one in the world will hear me. No one will know I'm in the bath and can't get out.

She listened. She could hear only the drip-drip of the cold water tap of the wash-basin, and a corresponding whisper and gurgle of her heart, as if it were beating under water. All else was silent. Where were the people, the traffic? Then she had a strange feeling of being under the earth, of a throbbing in her head like wheels going over the earth above her.

Then she told herself sternly that she must have no nonsense, that she had really not tried to get out of the bath. She had forgotten the strong solid chair and the grip she could get on it. If she made the effort quickly she could first take hold on both sides of the bath, pull herself up, then transfer her hold to the chair and thus pull herself out.

She tried to do this; she just failed to make the final effort. Pale now, gasping for breath, she sank back into the bath. She began to call out but as she had predicted there was no answer. No one had heard her, no one in the houses or the street or Dunedin or the world knew that she was imprisoned. Loneliness welled in her. If John were here, she thought, if we were sharing our old age, helping each other, this would never have happened. She made another effort to get out. Again she failed. Faintness overcoming her she closed her eyes, trying to rest, then recovering and trying again and failing, she panicked and began to cry and strike the sides of the bath; it made a hollow sound like a wild drum-beat.

Then she stopped striking with her fists; she struggled again to get out; and for over half an hour she stayed alternately struggling and resting until at last she did succeed in climbing out and making her escape into the kitchen. She thought, I'll never take another bath in this house or anywhere. I never want to see that bath again. This is the end or the beginning of it. In future a district nurse will have to come to attend me. Submitting to that will be the first humiliation. There will be others, and others.

In bed at last she lay exhausted and lonely thinking that perhaps it might be better for her to die at once. The slow progression of diffi-culties was a kind of torture. There were her shoes that had to be made specially in a special shape or she could not walk. There were the times she had to call in a neighbour to fetch a pot of jam from the top shelf of her cupboard when it had been only a year ago that she herself had made the jam and put it on the shelf. Sometimes a niece came to fill the coal-bucket or mow the lawn. Every week there was the washing to be hung on the line — this required a special technique for she could not raise her arms without at the same time finding some support in the dizziness that overcame her. She remembered with a sense of the world narrowing and growing darker, like a tunnel, the incredulous almost despising look on the face of her niece when in answer to the comment 'How beautiful the clouds are in Dunedin! These big billowing white and grey clouds — don't you think, Auntie?' she had said, her disappointment at the misery of things putting a sharpness in her voice, 'I never look at the clouds!'

She wondered how long ago it was since she had been able to look up at the sky without reeling with dizziness. Now she did not dare look up. There was enough to attend to down and around — the cracks and hollows in the footpath, the patches of frost and ice and the potholes in the roads; the approaching cars and motorcycles; and now, after all the outside menaces, the inner menace of her own body. She had to be guardian now over her arms and legs, force them to do as she wanted when how easily and dutifully they had walked, moved and grasped, in the old days! They were the enemy now. It had been her body that showed treachery when she tried to get out of the bath. If she ever wanted to bath again — how strange it seemed! — she would have to ask another human being to help her to guard and control her own body. Was this so fearful? she wondered. Even if it were not, it seemed so.

She thought of the frost slowly hardening outside on the fences, roofs, windows and streets. She thought again of the terror of not being able to escape from the bath. She remembered her dead husband and the flowers she had bought to put on his grave. Then thinking again of the frost, its whiteness, white like a new bath of the anemones and daffodils and the twigs of the red-leaved shrub, of John dead seventeen years, she fell asleep while outside, within two hours, the frost began to melt with the warmth of a sudden wind blowing from the north, and the night grew warm, like a spring night, and in the morning the light came early, the sky was pale blue, the same warm wind as gentle as a mere breath, was blowing, and a narcissus had burst its bud in the front garden.

In all her years of visiting the cemetery she had never known the wind so mild. On an arm of the peninsula exposed to the winds from two stretches of sea, the cemetery had always been a place to crouch shivering in overcoat and scarf while the flowers were set on the grave and the narrow garden cleared of weeds. Today, everything was different. After all the frosts of the past month there was no trace of chill in the air. The mildness and warmth were scarcely to be believed. The sea lay, violet-coloured, hush-hushing, turning and heaving, not breaking into foamy waves; it was one sinuous ripple from shore to horizon and its sound was the muted sound of distant forests of peace.

Picking up the rusted garden fork that she knew lay always in the grass of the next grave, long neglected, she set to work to clear away the twitch and other weeds, exposing the first bunch of dark blue

135

primroses with yellow centres, a clump of autumn lilies, and the shoots, six inches high, of daffodils. Then removing the green-slimed jam jars from their grooves on each side of the tombstone she walked slowly, stiff from her crouching, to the ever-dripping tap at the end of the lawn path where, filling the jars with pebbles and water she rattled them up and down to try to clean them of slime. Then she ran the sparkling ice-cold water into the jars and balancing them carefully one in each hand she walked back to the grave where she shook the daffodils, anemones, red leaves from their waxed paper and dividing them put half in one jar, half in the other. The dark blue of the anemones swelled with a sea-colour as their heads rested against the red leaves. The daffodils were short-stemmed with big ragged rather than delicate trumpets — the type for blowing; and their scent was strong.

Finally, remembering the winds that raged from the sea she stuffed small pieces of the screwed-up waxed paper into the top of each jar so the flowers would not be carried away by the wind. Then with a feeling of satisfaction — I look after my husband's grave after seventeen years. The tombstone is not cracked or blown over, the garden has not sunk into a pool of clay. I look after my husband's grave — she began to walk away, between the rows of graves, noting which were and were not cared for. Her Father and Mother had been buried here. She stood now before their grave. It was a roomy grave made in the days when there was space for the dead and for the dead with money, like her parents, extra space should they need it. Their tombstone was elaborate though the writing was now faded; in death they kept the elaborate station of their life. There were no flowers on the grave, only the feathery sea-grass soft to the touch, lit with gold in the sun. There was no sound but the sound of the sea and the one row of fir trees on the brow of the hill. She felt the peace inside her; the nightmare of the evening before seemed far away, seemed not to have happened; the senseless terrifying struggle to get out of a bath!

She sat on the concrete edge of her parents' grave. She did not want to go home. She felt content to sit here quietly with the warm soft wind flowing around her and the sigh of the sea rising to mingle with the sighing of the firs and the whisper of the thin gold grass. She was grateful for the money, the time and the forethought that had made her parent's grave so much bigger than the others near by. Her husband, cremated, had been allowed only a narrow eighteen inches by two feet, room only for the flecked grey tombstone In Memory of My Husband John Edward Harraway died August 6th 1948, and the narrow garden of spring flowers, whereas her parents' grave was so wide, and its concrete wall was a foot high; it was, in death, the equivalent of a quarter-acre section before there were too many people in the world. Why when the world was wider and wider was there no space left?

Or was the world narrower?

She did not know; she could not think; she knew only that she did not want to go home, she wanted to sit here on the edge of the grave, never catching any more buses, crossing streets, walking on icy footpaths, turning mattresses, trying to reach jam from the top shelf of the cupboard, filling coal buckets, getting in and out of the bath. Only to get in somewhere and stay in; to get out and stay out; to stay now, always, in one place.

Ten minutes later she was waiting at the bus stop; anxiously studying the destination of each bus as it passed, clutching her money since concession tickets were not allowed in the weekend, thinking of the cup of tea she would make when she got home, of her evening meal — the remainder of the liver and bacon, of her nephew in Christchurch who was coming with his wife and children for the school holidays, of her niece in the home expecting her third baby. Cars and buses surged by, horns tooted, a plane droned, near and far, near and far, children cried out, dogs barked; the sea, in competition, made a harsher sound as if its waves were now breaking in foam.

For a moment, confused after the peace of the cemetery, she shut her eyes, trying to recapture the image of her husband's grave, now bright with spring flowers, and her parents' grave, wide, spacious, with room should the dead desire it to turn and sigh and move in dreams as if the two slept together in a big soft grass double-bed.

She waited, trying to capture the image of peace. She saw only her husband's grave, made narrower, the spring garden whittled to a thin strip; then it vanished and she was left with the image of the bathroom, of the narrow confining bath grass-yellow as old baths are, not frost-white, waiting, waiting for one moment of inattention, weakness, pain, to claim her for ever.

River, Girl and Onion

MAURICE SHADBOLT

For Jenny Bojilova

1

That Saturday began badly for Lila.

That Saturday began with the bird. Or, to be exact, without the bird.

The bird was a yellow-green canary which sang from a square wire cage in the courtyard below her window. It was an old courtyard, unevenly paved, with three walls where plaster peeled from bleached brick. At the open end, facing the street, there was an iron railing and a flight of stone steps descending to a dark cellar. Above was a predictably smoky patch of London sky. Five battered garbage cans stood there; and there also, in mild and middling weather, the caged canary sang. Rain would see the old spinster owner of the bird hastening to make safe her pet: the cage would be withdrawn, a window would close, and thin lace would curtain the canary within a dim, drawing-room world. Of that Lila could see little: a cabinet stocked with fragile china, a corner of faded carpet, and two potted plants. Her only contact with that melancholy world was when she flung her window wide on a sunlit morning to hear the canary's song. At that hour Lila preferred joy to melancholy.

In this circumstance, in this receptive mood, Lila one sunny spring noon discovered the absence of the bird. She was alarmed and horrified. For there was the courtyard, painted pale gold, without a song, without a bird; and the spinster's window was fast. Lila shivered in her thin nightdress and distractedly drew a thick woollen dressing-gown over her shoulders.

It seemed a symptom of some tragedy: the bird had escaped and flown; the bird was dead; the spinster was dead; or both, the woman

138

and the pet, were dead. These seemed to Lila the limit of possibilities; but as an omen in Lila's life the event seemed to have unlimited possibilities. Not even the news, which she heard later in the day, that the spinster had merely taken her annual holiday with a sister in Devon, and had given the bird into care of a neighbour, rescued Lila from her intuition of impending disaster. It did, however, jolt her into the realization that she was thinking in Russian; and had, in fact, since she had risen to the songless courtyard, been thinking in Russian. The thoughts coming so darkly had demanded the language. For once, however, she made no effort to revert to English; moodily she tidied her small room and drew the curtains on the afternoon.

When Cecil arrived at five, he found her dramatically arranged upon the bed in a darkened room. This did not surprise him: he was used to what she called her peasant moods. He was used also to dramatic arrangements of her body, and darkened rooms. He shook off his duffle-coat and sat silently on the end of her bed. He lit two cigarettes and handed one to Lila. '*Spaseebo bolshoi,*' she murmured.

'*Pazhahlsta,*' he returned and fell silent, since he had already reached the limit of his Russian. His eyes became accustomed to the dark. She was dressed simply; she wore a loose roll-neck black sweater and her long legs were sheathed in tight slacks. One leg was crooked delicately, while the other cut a straight black line down the pale bedcover. At the head of the bed was an effective arrangement of arms. The pillow was awry, and her head rested crosswise on it; her face was an oval pale and withdrawn in darkly fanning hair. He admired the complete picture and wondered if he should make love to her. He rejected this idea on grounds of expediency, since it was plain that a bout of love-making, however minor in dimension, would delay them over-long in the room; and they had to meet Paul at seven. And it was clear that he would have difficulty getting Lila there on time anyway.

2

Lila was considering Cecil not as a lover; but as an adviser in the matter of love. The fact that Cecil served fitfully as a lover only enhanced his value as an adviser.

Her friendship with Cecil had not been of long duration. They
met on a long sea voyage, from New Zealand to Southampton. Lila
had lived in that country since infancy; Cecil was a fourth generation
New Zealander. His well-connected family included prosperous
pastoralists, hard-drinking clerics and unprincipled politicians; its less
distinguished side numbered a saint or two. Cecil was of the less distinguished side.

All this Lila learned from Cecil, a vague young man with rumpled
clothes and woolly hair, on the long haul up the Pacific to the Panama
canal. Her relationship with the islands they were leaving was far less
complex. She had simply been taken there as a child after spending
her first years in Europe. She had, she once calculated, been conceived
in Warsaw, seen out most of gestation in Leipzig, been born in Paris,
and then shipped to the Pacific before war or revolution again over-
took her family. Life in New Zealand had a schizophrenic quality; she
was always a traveller in a limbo between languages.

The world of her native language was one of wistful evenings at the
family fireside, and of bleak old people at Orthodox services praying
for the deliverance of Holy Russia; the world of her adopted language
was confusingly casual. Though her parents might hold aloof from
this world, there was after a while no question but that they must surrender their daughter to this new country.

That was reason for distress; at times cause enough for them to
speak of a return to Europe, where there would be a proper respect
for traditional values. Sometimes events, the end of the war or the
death of Stalin, brought hope and fresh despair. Lila was even more
cause for anguish. When she began university, they were happy; when
she dropped out they were unhappy. When she announced that her
current boy friend was secretary of the university Communist Party,
they were unnerved. And when at last she took an interest in drama,
their feelings were mixed; they reasoned that it was good that their
daughter should find something to enliven her, but their relief was
tainted with a long-held suspicion of the theatre, and the fear that
their daughter might mix with loose women and homosexuals. They
were fortunately not able to see the ease with which their daughter
mixed with these people. Rejoicing in her apparent success, they were
even able to conceal their squeamishness when she appeared in the

Saroyan play as a prostitute, and in a Sartre play as a lesbian; her mother, in fact, conceded that in the latter play she would never have known her little girl, her *malenkaya dyevotchka*.

Actually it was no longer adequate to call Lila even a *bolshoya dyevotchka*. At the unlikely height for a Russian girl of six feet and half an inch (the climate, her parents explained) she had the appearance of a mature woman. Certainly she was afflicted with the discontents of womanhood. Even her parents now seemed to agree that a girl of her age should find the other sex a major preoccupation; indeed they began to seem eager that life should soon bestow the twin blessings of marriage and childbirth upon her. Two boys from the White Russian community became regular visitors, though never at Lila's invitation, to the house; they seemed anxious to co-operate in bestowing bless-ings. They might have been less anxious had they known, when one or other of them visited the house on a Sunday afternoon, that Lila had the night before drunk whisky and gone to bed with a neurotic but rather brilliant young artist who threw the whisky bottles out of his attic window and sometimes said obscene things to Lila. These polite young men had arrived on the scene altogether too late; their only hope, had they known it, was that Lila might one day tire of having obscene things said to her. Not that she was fond of hearing these things, or of the artist; it was just that he gave an impression of being human. Also she was not anxious to become the recipient of twin blessings.

Already it seemed to her that she squandered far too much of her dramatic energy upon life. She abandoned the artist and won a schol-arship to study in London; and one rainy autumn day found herself waving farewell to her tearful parents from the deck of a ship.

She met Cecil at meal-times; they were at the same table. He was lost and moody among all the strange people; since she was the only one who seemed prepared to listen to him, he followed her about the ship. His sombre face waited for her whenever she came up on deck or turned away from a game. She supposed him brilliant, since he talked about life. After some time, however, it emerged that his regret was that he knew so little about life. 'All the twenty-four years of my life I have been sitting in classrooms and lecture-rooms having things told me,' he explained. 'Nobody gave me a chance to know things.' He had finished university with honours in philosophy; now he was going to Paris. He might study; he might write. Paris seemed the place for a good many things. Two difficulties which he discounted as minor were that he had no money, and spoke no French. But he was confident. 'I read once, in a magazine,' he said, 'about a man who went around the world with twenty pounds and one language.'

After a while he thought fit to say, 'I hope, Lila, you do not think I am pursuing you from some concealed physical motive. My motive is purely intellectual.' Lila was relieved. Presently, however, she felt distinctly dowdy and unattractive; she also began to feel self-conscious and silly. She powdered her nose frequently, studied her clothes carefully, and ensured her head was at the right tilt for a pleasing silhouette when she spoke to him on the deck at night.

At length, the night after Pitcairn, he kissed her, more by accident than design. And the night after Curaçao, where they drank iced beer on a cool white terrace overlooking the sea, there was an incident under a lifeboat on the upper deck. Nevertheless, the voyage between Pitcairn and Curaçao had been a slow one.

After the incident Cecil felt obliged to propose marriage. Lila suggested Cecil have more experience before marriage. 'I am thinking of it only for your sake,' she explained. She added that she believed their affair very Lawrentian; for Cecil's benefit, however, she was unable to specify what she meant since her artist friend, from whom she had acquired the word, had used it in undiscriminating fashion. 'No doubt, Cecil,' she said, 'you will in time understand what I mean. With experience.'

They were in London three days together. After they discovered Piccadilly Circus small and grubby, St. Paul's pigeon-spattered, and the Thames marvellous, Cecil left for Paris. Two weeks later, when Lila called at New Zealand House for her mail, she found an urgent note from Cecil which informed her that he was back in London. 'I am desperate,' the note concluded.

Hoping to save him from suicide, Lila took a taxi to the cheap Bloomsbury hotel where he was staying temporarily. He had no patience with her message that tomorrow the birds would sing. 'It was terrible,' he said. His money dwindling, he was forced to sleep on boulevard benches and slowly nibble long loaves of bread to outwit hunger. He was friendless and alone and twice, while he was sleeping outdoors, it had rained. There had been experiences. Once an incomprehensible gendarme seemed about to arrest him. Another time, in hope that he might glimpse someone famous or perhaps hear English spoken, he recklessly spent sixty francs on a small coffee at the Café de Flore and fell into conversation with a nice young American who bought him two glasses of beer and talked about Gide. Cecil had not stopped running until he found the staid old buildings of London walling him in again, and people speaking a substantially understandable language. He was about to cable a friend for money to return to New Zealand.

Since Lila was at that time lonely in London, disliking her drama school, her fellow students, her landlady and the weather, and most of all the fact that she went alone to the theatre, she was glad to see Cecil and tried to persuade him to stay. After two expensive weeks of coffee, beer, meals and double theatre tickets, she eventually persuaded him; and forgot to be lonely.

After Cecil took a job at eight pounds a week caring for rabbits and guinea pigs in a hospital laboratory, and could pay for his own theatre tickets, Lila suddenly found him a liability. For she met a personable young man at the drama school who seemed more interested in her than in other personable young men, and who took her to cocktails before and after the theatre; consequently she wanted to see less of Cecil.

On lonely Sundays, however, when Cecil trudged bleak streets and tired of looking at the paintings in the galleries, he ended his wandering by knocking at Lila's door. In time Lila began to find this irritating. She suggested Cecil should make other friends in London. 'I am thinking of it only for your sake,' she explained. Cecil tried hard to make friends. At the hospital, though, where he was ordered about by crabby nurses and severe doctors graded in a baffling hierarchy, he only had time to make friends with the cockney boy who swept the floors. This cockney boy, who had a pimply face and a sweet nature, had never heard of Kant or Hegel and privately thought Cecil bloody queer. He took Cecil rock'n'rolling at the Palais. Though Cecil escaped with only bruises and abrasions of a minor nature, the evening was sufficiently alarming for the boy not to take Cecil again.

Cecil persevered in his quest for friends. But not until a Sunday when Lila was away, weekending in Somerset with her young man, did he find any. That afternoon, at Speakers' Corner, he found two. He was afterwards grateful to Lila, for had she not so often reminded him of his duty to himself to make friends, he would obviously not have spoken to the two young men with strange accents who seemed to enjoy arguments.

They were students, these two, and shared a room in Gower Street. Jose was from Venezuela and Paul was from Hungary. Jose had been a wanderer ever since he had gone into exile after leading a student strike in Caracas; he had studied in Mexico City, Berlin and Paris. Paul had been in London since late 1956; he also had been some kind of student leader. Both spoke English of an erratic variety. They had only really been speaking it since they had come to England and had evolved a strangely private idiom. Certainly they confused Cecil. They confused him even more with their arguments. Cecil could contribute little since he had so far failed to meet up with the finer points of Marxism.

Jose was handsome, his skin richly coloured by Indian and Negro blood; he had a neat moustache, brilliant teeth, and astonishingly vivid eyes. He wore bright check shirts and a leather jacket. Cecil could imagine a pistol tucked carelessly in Jose's belt; in fact, Jose's personality so much appealed to him that he immediately stopped writing a rather long and complicated story about a young man who looked after rabbits and guinea pigs, and began writing another about a young Latin American revolutionary with wicked eyes. Cecil worked on this story for some months while at the same time, under the guidance of Jose and Paul, studying internal contradictions and dialectical leaps. His difficulty with the story was that he could find no end. He ignored those who advised him that it was no longer necessary for short stories to have ends. Cecil preferred to fly in the face of literary fashion. 'It is cheating to have no ending,' he said.

Paul was a contrast. His face was thick and heavy; he smiled rarely, and dressed darkly. He suffered prolonged moods of depression; and, so Jose once told Cecil, often cried out in his sleep.

Paul's father, a socialist veteran and ally of Bela Kun in 1919, had after the second world war been prominent in the new Hungarian government until arrested and shot as a fascist Titoist-Trotskyist and

144

imperialist agent. Paul, a student activist, was asked to denounce his father; since he declined to do so, he was expelled from university and went to work in a factory. He was there four years until, after his father's corpse was rehabilitated, he was readmitted to university. When trouble in Hungary began he had spoken with some authority about the nature of the government. He was not able to speak with much clarity about what happened after the tanks blasted into Budapest. His last clear memory was of participating in a radio broadcast before some of his remaining friends, fearing for his safety, pushed him into a fast car headed for the border.

He was tumbled about from bed to bed, place to place; people kept trying to make him say things he didn't want to say. He wanted to say different things, but when he said different things, no one seemed to be listening. Naturally, because of his father's name, a large number of journalists wanted to talk to him. He should have been a gift for any journalist; instead of a gift, he was a problem. For example, when asked to outline his disillusionment with Communism, he unreasonably persisted in saying he was still a Communist, and that Rakosi, Krushchev, Stalin and the rest were not Communists at all; and the journalists fiddled, talked among themselves, and lit cigarettes. In the end, then, he began to say nothing and the journalists lost interest. When he reached London he met Jose, with whom he had corresponded since Jose visited Budapest for a youth festival. He was ill for a while, and Jose looked after him. Jose would listen to what he wanted to say. Jose could sometimes even make Paul smile.

Jose entertained Paul by persuading him to laugh at the English. Jose once said he hoped Cecil didn't mind them laughing at the English. 'You are English colonial, no?' he said.

'Please do not worry,' Cecil said. 'I feel my inherited English blood must have undergone some change under the South Pacific sun. It is probably something dialectical. For I have no longer anything in common with this tribe of strange castes and rituals. I am not an Englishman of the colonial variety. I am a Polynesian of the pale-skinned variety.'

'You are an angry young man, yes?' said Paul.

'No,' said Cecil. 'I am an unhappy young man.'

Lila, while Cecil dutifully developed new friendships, had begun to give herself to twilights of the soul, and wandered at dusk through streets and parks. Her young man had left her for a baronet's daughter who would one day inherit a fine estate and several large companies. Lila could have competed against this girl, who was actually a silly creature, but she could not compete against the fine estate and large companies. She was also disillusioned with the theatre. Her height made her unfit for consideration in any serious dramatic role. Plainly a woman with such difficult statistics could only hope, at best, to play comedy. Also she objected to the methods of tuition at the school. These seemed more concerned with displaying flesh than revealing the soul. She deduced that the school was more a slave-market than a school for the theatre. Lonely and depressed, she resented the fact that Cecil no longer came to see her. 'He is mean and disloyal,' she told herself sulkily, 'after all I have done for him. But I have my pride. I will not seek him out.'

They met again by accident in a book shop in the Charing Cross Road. Lila was reading a life of Stanislavsky, and Cecil a novel well reviewed in the Sunday papers. Cecil often did this. After a study of the Sunday papers he selected the novel most favourably reviewed and read it on Sunday afternoons all the way down the Charing Cross Road. He read an average of forty pages in each shop; then moved on to the next.

On that afternoon, when he met Lila, he ignored his cool reception and took her to an espresso bar where he gave her a long and detailed appraisal of the contemporary literary scene and assailed a prominent new writer. 'He ignores the role of the cash nexus,' he said. Lila, with the memory of the baronet's daughter still fresh, was inclined to agree with Cecil's view of the cash nexus but, preserving her frigid front, did not say. Instead she burst into tears. This blunted the point Cecil was making about the definitive nature of the Hungarian revolution.

Cecil was embarrassed. When they left the espresso bar he perceived the most obvious way of ridding himself of his embarrassment. 'I will take you home,' he said. Lila sprinkled fresh tears on the busy footpath. 'You are only trying to dispose of me,' she claimed. Lila wanted not to be disposed of; but to be loved. 'I have a suggestion to make,' Cecil said finally. Lila was by this time relieved to know Cecil was capable of making any suggestion whatsoever. 'I will take you to meet two good friends of mine,' he said. 'The company may do you good.'

They ate that night in a little Italian restaurant just off the Tottenham Court Road. This became a habit; every Saturday the four met to eat in the same place. Afterwards they walked Soho or went to a Thames-side pub. Sometimes, though rarely, their number was increased by a stray Latin American, Hungarian or New Zealander. One feature of their group, however, was that there was never an Englishman. They all regretted this. 'Maybe,' said Paul, 'we should better know England if we knew just one Englishman.' Lila said she knew an Englishman once and didn't like him anyway; but Lila was prejudiced. Each week they exchanged stories gathered from observation of the native population of London. For example, Lila once reported, 'Today I saw a bowler-hat kissing a girl.' This story, however, was disbelieved.

Lila departed stormily from her drama school. It was the result of a tutor describing Russian character so that the students might better involve themselves in a Chekhov play. Lila quarrelled with this description as superficial, and indeed stupid; but the tutor countered with the remark that Lila could scarcely profess to know a great deal about Russian character since she had never lived in Russia. Lila, who felt the truth of this keenly, was dismayed and angry. 'If I am not a Russian,' she demanded, 'then what am I?' 'Very probably,' replied the tutor coolly, before proceeding with evaluation of the Russian character, 'you are a New Zealander.' Lila walked out of the class. 'I am a woman without a country,' she told them sadly the following Saturday. 'I am a lonely voyager on a strange sea.'

'We are all voyagers,' Paul observed. 'All lonely voyagers on strange seas. Even,' he added significantly, 'even Cecil.' This was to reassure Cecil and include him in their company since, though Cecil was the only one of them who felt free to return to his own country, he still lacked money to do so.

'What can I do?' Lila appealed. 'Where will it end?' She tried to get work in repertory; she finished working as a waitress. She received a large number of tips and propositions from the customers she served. Lila took the tips and ignored the propositions; they nevertheless disturbed her. 'I am sliding down,' she declared. 'I shall be on the street in a few weeks.' However, Jose, Paul and Cecil promised to save her; they would, they said, keep her as collective mistress. Lila did not think this idea amusing. 'Where will it end?' she said.

One Sunday afternoon she walked with Jose through Kensington Gardens; afterwards they passed along the street which held the Soviet embassy. Up and down the street small children played, jabbering in Russian; their parents promenaded and gossiped in the sunlight. Lila was excited; she had never heard so many talking Russian around her before. She began to shiver. 'I feel queer,' she said. 'Quickly, I must sit down.' Jose was alarmed and attentive. 'Have you one ache in the head?' he said uncertainly. No, said Lila. It was not a headache. 'It is nothing,' she added. 'It will go away soon.'

It did not go away soon. Some days later Lila returned to the street and talked to the cultural attaché at the embassy about going to Russia and working in the Soviet theatre. The attaché discussed socialist realism. This upset Lila. 'I am an unsocially realist person,' she said the following Saturday. 'There is no place for me.'

Lila, who was a head taller than chunky Jose, had fallen in love with him. This presented difficulty. Lila liked to give the impression of being a loose woman. She gave a good impression of being a loose woman. Also she liked to leave the impression of being in love with everyone; in this she was successful too. That was the difficulty. For when she told Jose she loved him, Jose presumed she told Cecil and Paul the same thing; and felt no urgent or personal concern.

Lila on principle disapproved of revolution. Yet she managed to listen without protest when Jose announced, in a fit of frustration, that instead of studying philosophy, it would be far better if he learned to use a tommy-gun. Lila soothed him; and he told her about his father, a colonel in the Venezuelan army who, since late adolescence, had had a pouched pistol swinging against his thigh. When a disagreement with the current dictator sent him into exile in Mexico, his father, without his pistol for the first time in twenty years, felt naked, and constantly slapped his unadorned thigh in bewilderment. He stayed indoors, fearful of open streets in daylight and dark streets at night. With such a father it was not surprising that Jose should have begun life a pacifist. But now he was convinced pacifism was useless. 'I have dead pacifist friends,' he said, to clinch his argument. 'Maybe,' he added presently, 'I am no right to say the tommy-gun is superior to philosophy. Combining the tommy-gun and philosophy is one big problem.'

Lila was alarmed when Jose spoke of returning to Venezuela. 'What will become of you?' she cried. Jose answered the question coolly. 'Maybe for me only more exile,' he said. 'I think I will no be dead. They make dead only big men. I am one little man.' Lila was not reassured. When she said 'What will become of you?' she meant 'What will become of me?' Jose appeared to think revolution risky enough without marriage too. Lila displayed affection for Paul and Cecil in hope of making Jose jealous; since Jose had not minded this situation at the beginning he saw no reason why he should dislike it now. It was also less demanding.

Lila became despondent. To console her, Jose read her Lorca as they lay in her room, or sat in the pale sunshine among the falling autumn leaves. Lila listened with impatience; she liked the sound of Spanish, she explained, but she couldn't understand the words. Jose bought her a book of English translations and she followed him through the *Romancero Gitano*. 'Is beautiful, no?' said Jose. 'I like much the poem of the gypsy and the woman who was no a maiden.' 'It was a very ephemeral affair,' said Lila. 'Russians do not have ephemeral affairs. They love with the soul.' Jose was silent and thoughtful.

'Jose, darling,' Lila said, 'why don't you take me away somewhere?'

'I will take you to Brighton,' Jose said. Jose had heard of the English custom of weekends at Brighton. But Lila really wanted to be taken to Paris. When they went to Paris Lila found herself miserable; Jose insisted on visiting all his exile friends and discussing, in rapid Spanish, the political situation up and down the Americas while Lila sat dismayed in corners of crowded, smoky little Latin Quarter rooms. Jose's friends all seemed to find Lila, and her height, very amusing; she became tired of hearing them refer to her, when they talked to Jose, as *su amiga alta* and *su amiga loca*. 'I wish we had gone to Brighton,' Lila said after three days. Jose concluded that she was impossible to please.

Paul and Cecil saw each other often. Paul was still unhappy about people trying to make him say things he didn't want to say. One friend of his had gone back to Hungary safely by saying all the things they wanted said there; another had made himself prosperous, writing and lecturing in America, saying what they wanted said there. Both had written him letters. One called him a traitorous counter-revolutionary; the other called him a traitorous stooge. 'I want only to be left alone,' Paul said.

Cecil was persevering with literature. He had found no end for the story about a character like Jose; and returned to his story about the young man who looked after rabbits and guinea pigs in a hospital. After some deliberation he attached an end to his story; it showed the young man being taken to a mental hospital and, in his cell, proclaiming himself a guinea pig. Cecil thought this story ironic and symbolic of the human condition. He read the story to Paul. He explained that the young man in the story had only a passing resemblance to his own character. Paul said he understood perfectly; but suggested the end of the story sounded contrived. Cecil began writing a new, rather bitter story about a Hungarian.

On New Year's Eve Jose and Paul gave a party. Their room had been conscientiously tidied: coloured streamers tangled from their ceiling: the table was set with wine and beer, bright paper hats, salt biscuits and potato crisps. When they arrived, Lila received flowers and kisses, and Cecil a large glass of beer. They sang away the time before midnight. The landlady came upstairs to complain about the noise. Jose, with Latin charm, pacified her and sent her downstairs with a gin and tonic.

At midnight, wearing their bright party hats, they stood holding hands in the centre of the room. Cecil and Lila taught Jose and Paul to sing *Auld Lang Syne*. After midnight, separate again, Jose revealed he was returning to Venezuela. Since everyone had been drinking, and everyone spoke frequently of returning home, only Paul, who knew already, took the announcement seriously at first. But when Jose went on to explain that he had received a letter from Caracas which told him a movement was afoot against the regime, and which urged him to return as soon as he could, Lila, who wanted to hear no more, rose to her feet with a stricken face. 'This room is stuffy,' she said. 'I want to open a window.' Jose said he hoped to get a post lecturing at Caracas university; it would be a good cover for clandestine political activity. 'Even with the window open,' Lila said, 'this room is still stuffy. Why don't we got for a walk?' The other three, drowsy with drink and chilled by the rush of frosty air into the room, were not enthusiastic. When Lila became insistent they pulled on their coats and followed her down into the street.

At Piccadilly the crowds were thinning in the cold evening, leaving the Circus webbed with streamers and strewn with confetti. There was a man being sick on the footpath; another asking passers-by if they were Irish.

By the time they found coffee in a dimmed Soho, they were miserable. 'In New Zealand,' Cecil said, 'it is summer. After midnight we go swimming.' Paul said he was going to bed. 'That,' said Cecil, 'is the most sensible idea I have heard for a full hour.'

Jose took Lila home. When they were alone together, walking lifeless streets, Lila said, 'It is terrible. The new year is two hours old already.' Jose was silent. 'When are you going?' she said finally. He was not sure. 'But soon,' he added. She took his arm tightly. 'Will you remember me?' she said. Yes, he would remember her; and Paul, and Cecil. But her particularly? Yes, her particularly. 'How could I forget?' Jose sighed. And — who knew? — maybe after the revolution she would come to Venezuela, he said; she, and Paul, and Cecil.

But Lila only said, 'Wouldn't it be a wonderful thing if we could just go on walking like this, arm in arm, on and on, for ever?' Jose, who thought the night too cold to enjoy walking, failed to embrace the notion with conviction.

At the airport, the morning he left, there were gifts and tears. They would all, he said, have to visit Venezuela soon. Jose embraced all three dispassionately and strutted jauntily across the tarmac to the waiting aircraft. '*Salud!*' he cried before a door sealed him from sight. A hand waved at a window and the aircraft rose up into a cloudless sky. Lila, in the restaurant, said she wouldn't have coffee. 'I want English tea,' she said. 'Very weak, with milk and sugar.' The next morning, opening her newspaper, she read about tanks racketing through the streets of Caracas.

3

'It is getting late,' Cecil said. To verify this he rose from the bed, crossed the room, and peeled back the curtains to reveal the darkening courtyard.

'Of course,' said Lila. 'It is always late.'

Cecil let the curtains fall with a swish. The courtyard depressed him. He turned to Lila; and discovered she depressed him too. 'We shall keep Paul waiting,' he said.

'We are always waiting,' Lila said. 'In our different ways. All of us are waiting.'

'Lila,' said Cecil gravely, resuming his place on the edge of the bed, 'you generalize too much from particulars.' He paused and sighed. 'But I know,' he added, 'that you are miserable just now. I mean about Jose and everything.'

'It is more than eight weeks,' Lila said. She meant since she, Paul and Cecil had received postcards which showed Caracas in colour, and told them Jose had arrived. 'And I have written sixteen letters, and there is still no answer. After all, he can't be busy now, can he? The revolution was over almost as soon as he arrived.'

'Perhaps,' said Cecil, 'they are consolidating. And preparing against the counter-revolution. Who knows?'

'God knows,' Lila said firmly. 'He could have sent another post-card at least. Don't sixteen letters deserve something?'

Cecil allowed that they did; and shrugged. Presently he took Lila's long slender hand and rested it gently on his palm, as if measuring it for weight and size. He spoke carefully. 'You must bear in mind, Lila, that Jose may have a girl friend, or a fiancée, or even a wife, in Venezuela.'

'Impossible,' Lila said with vigour. 'He hasn't been there for years.'

'Nevertheless,' Cecil said, shrugging again, 'such things are not unknown.' He was content to leave it at that. He meant, however, no cruelty; he wanted Lila to become herself again. She was playing her present role with too much verve.

'I want to ask your advice,' she said at last. 'Do you think I should go to Venezuela? There are planes flying all week, and I have almost enough money. It is perfectly safe now there is no revolution.'

'I think it would be unwise,' Cecil said. 'To say the least. Apart from all the more obvious reasons, if you spent all your money flying to Venezuela, you would have none left to pay your fare back to New Zealand.'

Lila abruptly withdrew her hand from Cecil. 'Who said I was going back to New Zealand? I didn't.'

'I was coming to that,' Cecil said quietly.

'Anyway,' Lila continued, 'why New Zealand? The world is my country.'

'No one has said that seriously since Thomas Paine,' Cecil observed. 'He also said mankind was his religion. But that is, of course, beside the point.'

'You annoy me,' Lila said. 'How can I go back? To go back would be to admit the world has defeated me.'

'See it as a tactical movement to the rear,' Cecil suggested.

'I don't understand why you should talk about New Zealand.'

'I was coming to that,' Cecil repeated patiently.

'Then I wish you would come to it. And stop — what is it? — beating about the bush.'

Cecil took Lila's hand again. 'Lila, why don't you come back to New Zealand with me?'

'Is this another proposal?'

'You might consider it one.'

'Very well. You astonish me, Cecil. But I have just one question to ask: how can you possibly expect to keep me in the manner to which I am accustomed?'

Cecil made a thoughtful survey of the room, the meagre collection of belongings within it. 'It should not be too difficult,' he said.

'How can you understand?' she cried. 'How could you possibly understand?' She pointed an accusing finger at him. 'You are a materialist. So you can think only in material terms.'

Cecil felt helpless.

'And when,' Lila continued, 'I asked if you could keep me in the manner to which I am accustomed, it would not occur to you that I meant in a manner quite other than material: that I meant in the manner of inner life.'

'I am aware,' said Cecil, 'of your spiritual inclination.'

'Do you seriously expect me, Cecil, to surrender my rich inner life to become the wife of a New Zealand petit bourgeois?'

'On the contrary,' Cecil said indignantly. 'My background is working-class. My father is a truck-driver and very proletarian. I am not petit bourgeois.'

'In New Zealand even the bourgeoisie is petit bourgeois,' Lila said, rising from the bed. 'Now, shall we go?'

They met Paul a little after seven in the restaurant. His face was no more grave than usual; but he was strangely quiet during the meal. When coffee came he revealed the cause. He had a letter from Venezuela.

'Why,' Lila protested, 'haven't I got one?'

Probably because, Paul said, she had not taken the precaution of writing her return address on the back of her letters. In any case, the letter had not been from Jose, and was written in Spanish. Since Paul knew little Spanish, he had been forced that morning to go out and purchase a Spanish-English dictionary and a grammar. He had spent the rest of the day preparing a translation.

'Well?' Lila said.

The letter was from Jose's wife. It appeared that Jose and some other students had been involved in a skirmish with militia during the closing stage of the uprising; because they were poorly armed, most of the students, including Jose, had been killed. The concluding part of the letter expressed some moral and religious sentiments which were idiomatic in expression and too difficult for Paul to translate.

After a time Paul suggested they walk. Lila, confessing a headache, agreed. Cecil, saying nothing at all, followed them out of the steamy restaurant into the cool night.

They wandered in no direction, through bright streets and dark, streets crowded and streets empty, until a late hour found them on the embankment. Nearby was a pub; noise came to them faintly. Lila watched the river and shivered. Lights criss-crossed the dark water.

'We shall be philosophical,' Lila said.

'Yes,' Cecil said.

'We shall,' Lila said, 'smoke cigarettes and look out upon the river. If we wish to be philosophical, we may reflect on how life is like a river, lazily twisting and sharply plunging, a river of many currents interwoven. If the image is too tired and outworn, forgive me. It is convenient and near at hand. Sometimes good images are hard to find. We have not yet learned to package them in plastic and put them into deep-freeze so that they may be purchased fresh and ready-made — though that day too may come. However,' she finished, shivering again, 'I think we could find a better place to spend the evening.'

Cecil and Paul watched Lila with curiosity. It occurred to Cecil, as they began walking again, that he had an end for at least one story.

Presently they found more coffee. It was in a gloomy little cave of a place with shiny espresso machine, juke-box jazz, and bare wooden tales. At the next table a number of bearded young men swarmed about a girl with long yellow hair, black sweater and corduroy slacks; the girl's face, while not particularly pretty, had a very serene expression. There was a perfect stillness in the way she sat at the centre of the bubbling young men.

'What are you watching her for?' Lila asked Cecil. 'Am I not so interesting?'

'I was thinking,' he said. 'There, if you still want one, is your image. But I will not elaborate.'

'Nonsense,' Lila said. 'You want to make it glamorous suddenly. Young men flirting with a fair muse. But there is nothing glamorous. Life is about as glamorous as an onion. Peel it down, skin after skin, and what have you got in the end? Nothing. Only tears. Only the tears.'

'You are being very brave,' Paul said, reaching for her hand.

'We are all being brave,' Lila said. 'Or trying to be. And who knows? Perhaps we are.'

After a long silence, they all at once began to talk. Paul thought that, after all, he might return to Hungary soon. Perhaps he could escape having to say anything; perhaps not. Perhaps he could escape prison; perhaps not. 'There is no longer profit in running away,' he said. 'Countries are much like suits of clothes. I think it is better to wear only the dirty suit of one's own country than to keep covering it with the dirty suits of other countries. Eventually one could suffocate in such dirt.' He shrugged, turned his empty palms upwards, and smiled sadly.

It was late. The music had subsided, and the girl with yellow hair had left with one of the bearded young men. Cecil talked about returning to New Zealand, where life was less intemperate. Lila also confessed that her ambitions were now on the modest side.

When the shop closed, they went into the night and found a slender moon risen. A peace had descended on the city, the murky river, the old buildings.

Cecil was telling Paul that in New Zealand there were no revolutions. 'Sometimes,' he added, 'I think that is a good thing, and sometimes I think it is a bad thing.'

Lila took their arms and fell into step between them.

'And sometimes,' she said, 'you don't know what you are saying.'

Class, Race, Gender: a Post-Colonial Yarn

C. K. STEAD

It will perhaps serve a disarming purpose and make what I have to record seem less serious than it is, or than it ought to be, if I begin by explaining that this is a story told by Bertie to Billy, who told it to me. More recently Bertie told me the story himself, so I've heard it twice and have had the chance to ask questions and fill gaps that remained after the first hearing.

I got to know Bertie and Billy a long time ago when we were all students in England. Bertie was, and indeed is and will always be even when he's dead, an Englishman. His fuller, though not entire (there are several intermediate ones) name is Herbert Lawson-Grieve. Friends and family called him Bertie, and so, although we, Billy and I, found it absurd, adding to the general feeling that he was less a real person than a character out of P.G Wodehouse, Bertie is what we called him.

Billy is South African. His full name is Villiers de Groot Graaf which among our group became Bill Goat Gruff — Billy for short. Billy and Bertie were friends before I knew them. They were at Oxford together, at the same College, Merton, Billy studying ('reading', as they say in England) engineering, Bertie law. Like Bertie, Billy had money, lots of it, which came from what he called 'a family in diamonds'.

I was a graduate student on a scholarship from New Zealand, writing a thesis which I hoped might be published as a book. But it was our passion for sport that brought us together — that, and a particular kind of boyish temperament. ('Chappish', I think it would be called these days, with, of course, deep disapproval.) There was a lot of beer drinking, a lot of horsing about, a lot of talk about 'girls'. We loved Western movies and practised shootouts in the parks. I think we were

156

quite serious students, but we were having a good time.

There was another student of that time I should mention because he has provided my title — or the first half of it: Peter Mapplethwaite from Scunthorpe. I've once or twice glanced at a map looking for Scunthorpe and not succeeded in finding it, but the way Pete pronounced it, and the word itself, suggested slums, coal mines, sunless skies and rickets — the part of England which those of us who were (shallow and ignorant, no doubt) visitors skirted around on our way to the lakes or the moors, to North Wales or to Scotland.

Mapplethwaite was a Marxist and a man of the people. Peoplethwaite, Bertie called him; and then Marplethorpe, Pepperpot, Maxiwank, Whistlestop, Cuttlefish — anything at all but his real name. Pete could be good company. Billy and I imitated his accent and he imitated ours. He knew me as the New Zillander who liked igg sendwiches; and Billy as the Seth Ufrican who didn't want to talk about bleck prytest.

Pete had absolutely no sense of tune, but he sang dialect songs — I suppose they were from his region — in a flat ugly-funny voice. Some of these took the form of dialogues, one of which went, as I remember,

> 'Where's tha bin, lud?'
> ''awkeen paypers.'
> ''o for?'
> 'Meyuncle Benjamin.'
> 'Wha's 'e gin thee?'
> 'Skinny ole 'et'ny.'
> 'Silly ole blawk
> 'e ought ta dee.'

I tried to make Pete part of the group but it was no use. It didn't matter too much that he sometimes wanted to lecture Billy about the situation of the 'blecks'. There were a few occasions when Billy hung his head in helpless shame, and then flared up in angry Boer pride; but mostly he could cope with it. But it was the two Englishmen, Pete and Bertie, who couldn't mix. It wasn't even that there was great animosity between them. It seemed more like embarrassment.

Once I asked Bertie was it a problem for him that Mapplethwaite was a Marxist. Lord no, he said; that was no problem at all. Lots of chaps from school (he always spoke of 'school' as if the word meant to me exactly what it meant to him) had been Lefties. I waited for him to go on and for a moment he seemed flummoxed. Then he lowered his voice and said that for him personally the problem was Mapplethwaites's feet.

I thought at first that this was some kind of joke, but it wasn't. We'd all been at a party in north Oxford when Pete had vomited and passed out cold — so 'cold' we thought he was dead. We'd got him on to a bed and someone had taken off his shoes and socks.

'He had such nasty long white monkey-feet,' Bertie said, almost in awe; 'and the soles — did you notice? — they were *black*.'

Those feet, and Bertie's reaction to them, belonged in something peculiarly and impenetrably English, and I gave up my efforts towards an accommodation. I didn't want to seem a busybody on someone else's turf. But I've gone on seeing Pete on my visits to England, calling on him at the north London Polytechnic where he lectures on what's called Culture and Gender Studies, and going for a drink with him at his local.

Over the years Pete has been a Moscow communist, then a Peking communist, his faith coming to rest finally, when Mao died and the Gang of Four were arrested, on the régime in Albania. Later again, when the Berlin Wall came down and piece by piece the whole communist empire fell apart, I expected to find him depressed and defeated, but he wasn't. On my last visit he seemed more relaxed and confident than he'd been for years. Communism was pure now, pure theory; it hadn't yet, he explained, been put into practice — not anywhere. All those attempts at it had been corrupt and imperfect. Communism lay somewhere up ahead, the great future which all the world's peoples would enjoy when at last they came to their senses and realized the evils of capitalism. Meanwhile all serious 'analysis' (his favourite word) of anything and everything came down to three words: class, race and gender.

That's why Peter Mapplethwaite figures in my account: because if I told him this story (something I can't imagine I would want to do) he would say that it illustrates perfectly the justness of the intellectual framework which has ruled his life; whereas to me it illustrates (if it illustrates anything) just the opposite — that life is subtler and more complex than the theories men construct to explain it.

I've also continued to see Bertie — much more of him than of Pete — and so has Billy. But Billy's visits to England and mine have never coincided; and it wasn't until he came to New Zealand, accompanying the Springboks on their first post-Apartheid tour, that we were able to get together again. Our talk was of rugby, of the new South Africa (which made him proud, but nervous too), and of the old days when we'd been students in England. Bertie's name came up often, and we were sorry he wasn't there — but we knew he would be watching the test matches on television; and I had an amusing and, as Pete would have said, culturally insensitive fax from him when a South African forward bit the All Blacks captain's ear and was caught by the cameras.

'Anent ear-eating,' Bertie's message ran. 'Why the fuss? When in Rome, n'est ce pas?'

What did he mean? What could he have meant except that cannibalism was a local tradition, wasn't it — so why not?

From time to time Billy and I have each tried to persuade Bertie to visit us at home. His answer to Billy has always been that he would come 'when South Africa has a black President'. Since none of us believed this would happen in our lifetime, it was his way of saying he would never come. To my invitations he always replied (adopting what he thought was my accent), 'Tow far, moite. Thenks — oi'd love tow. But tow far.'

Bertie, of course, speaks that tortured, alternatively clipped, squeezed, swallowed and diphthongised English which signals, even (and perhaps especially) to those who mock it, impeccable social credentials; and it is one of the jokes we share, and revert to often, that his second mother-in-law, who was French, could always understand my outlander's English but had the greatest difficulty making sense of his.

Bertie has lived most of his adult life in a beautiful house with a beautiful walled garden in the town of Marlow on the Thames. He inherited the place from a maiden great-aunt when he was still a young man; and for many years he commuted all the way in to London where he worked as a solicitor specialising in marine insurance which he liked to tell us was properly called 'bottomry'. After his third marriage Bertie gave up the City firm in which he'd risen to become a partner, and opened a small office of his own in his home town. He's there still, prosperous and apparently content, with a wife so young he some-times jokingly introduced her as 'My wife and child'.

Bertie's house is full of sporting prints and cricketing photographs. Along the hallways and up the stairs you can see the rugby and cricket teams — school, university, business and local — he has played for. There's a cabinet of sporting trophies, and pictures of two or three racehorses. I've noticed too that he's something of a Narcissus. There are several painted portraits of him around the house; and a rather grand gold-framed mirror in his dining room, placed where, when conversation around the table begins to run into the sand, he can pass the time staring at himself.

In the seventies Bertie let his hair grow rather long, with side-burns, and that's the look he has tended to stick with; and as the hair has thinned and gone grey-streaked, and fashions have changed, it has left him looking less than the dashing and fashionable fellow he once was. But he's tall (six foot two or three), strongly built, still handsome, still full of charm and energy and generosity. Bertie does things in style; and to be met by him at the station with flowers and champagne, as if you were a visiting foreign dignitary, is to experience a sort of expansiveness which none of us where I come from would be capable of, even if the wish and the impulse towards it should happen to stir.

It was when Billy was on one of his visits to England that Bertie told him the story about his involvement with the Cockney woman whose name was Thelma Button, but who was known to her workmates as Thelly, or sometimes Shell. During Billy's Springbok-accompanying visit to New Zealand he passed the story on to me. ('You're a writer, Carlo,' he said; 'you can disguise it can't you?') And so, on my most recent visit to England, when I recognised during a late night drink-ing session with Bertie that we were on the borders, so to speak, of this same narrative territory, I prompted, listened, questioned, remem-bered, reconstructed. Here is what I learned.

Bertie was, as he put it, 'between marriages at the time' — de-pressed, bored, restless. This was in the last of his years working for the big impersonal City firm he'd been with for almost twenty years. His second wife, Françoise, had left him, not for another man, nor for any reason except that she'd grown to hate living in England. One day, with the help of the mother-in-law who couldn't understand Bertie's conversation, she packed her things and, with their child, returned to Paris.

'It was a fearsome blow to the pride,' Bertie said. 'Nothing like that had ever happened to me before. So of course the old mind went blank for a time and I came to consciousness a few months later realising I was drinking too much, eating fast fodder, not getting any exercise, becoming fat, ratty and inefficient. It was bad. All bad. That was when I started thinking about Shell.'

She served lunches in a popular place where lawyers often went for a quick bite when they weren't entertaining clients. She was small, well-shaped, bright-eyed, pretty, good-humoured, with the broadest of London accents, and she and Bertie had hit it off right from their first encounter. She teased him; he responded. Their exchanges were always (as he put it) 'remorselessly joky', but with an undertone of flirtation. But what really attracted him was her hair. It was shiny brown, wiry and curly, and despite her best efforts to keep it neat it sprang out from her head as if it had a life of its own. It was the kind of hair, he said, that you want desperately to touch.

Bertie never thought about this woman except when she was there in front of him, serving him salad or cottage pie. She was a very minor character in his life, one of thousands with walk-on parts. The idea that she might be more, or other, never occurred to him. When she disappeared from the lunch place and went to work somewhere else he didn't notice that she was gone.

Then one day he met her in the street. He was used to seeing her in a white smock and apron, and if it hadn't been for that head of hair he might not have recognised her. She told him she had a new job, with hours that suited her better because she started early and was finished in time to pick up the kids (she had two, Jack and Jill) from school. Also she had every Wednesday afternoon free.

And then, taking him by surprise, she said if he was ever passing on a Wednesday afternoon he ought to drop in for a cuppa.

'It was the boldness of the thing,' Bertie said. 'You couldn't be mistaken about it. She just looked me in the eye, grinned wickedly, and said it. And then she wrote her address on a piece of paper and pushed it into my hand. I must have looked flabbergasted, but that only made her laugh. She said, "Come on Mister, don't look so

161

frightened. Hasn't a pretty girl ever invited you to tea before?" And she walked off and left me there.'

Shortly after that Francoise, his lovely French wife, left him. There were those months of dereliction, and the realisation that he must take himself in hand, re-order his life, discipline himself. But it shouldn't, he told himself, be all hard work. There must be some fun, some entertainments, some good times. Clearing the pockets of a jacket and trousers one day, readying things for the dry cleaner, he found the slip of paper with Thelma Button's address, and remembered that invitation with its suggestion of a good deal more than tea.

So an affair (if that's the word for such an arrangement) started. Thelma, or Shelley as he was soon calling her, lived in a block of flats just off Clerkenwell Road near to Gray's Inn, only twenty minutes walk, or five by taxi, from Bertie's office which was close to the Barbican. His secretary learned to keep the hours from one to 3.30 clear on a Wednesday and he spent them in bed with Shelley; and even many years after what was to be their last dreadful encounter, Bertie couldn't speak of the first weeks and months of that association without a certain brightening of the eye and a lift in the voice.

The flat, on the second floor of a dingy red-brick apartment block, was drab and cramped, but it had a balcony looking inward to a shady courtyard with a single tree. They used to make love, then lie in bed looking out into the upper branches of the tree, talking, exchanging stories, dozing, until they'd recovered sufficiently to do it again, after which they would shower together and return to their separate lives.

Their talk was full of teasing and banter, but with a rich undertone of affection. He told her about the people in his office; she talked about Jack and Jill, family, neighbours. Because he called her Shelley he told her about the poet who had once lived in his town of Marlow, writing revolutionary poems while his wife Mary wrote *Frankenstein*. A week or so later she had *Frankenstein* beside her bed. She'd found it in a bookshop, bought it and read it. He asked what she thought of it.

''orrible,' she said. 'Did you like it Bertie?'

He had to admit he'd never read it.

Once he bought her a gold chain, knowing — or thinking — that she would have to hide it from her husband. But she made him help her put it on, saying she would never take it off.

'What about Arthur?' he asked. She said she would say she'd found it in the street.

Bertie seldom asked about Arthur, preferred not to hear or think about him; but now and then she would speak of him. He was a guard at the British Museum; and though she always said he was 'harmless', that was the best she could say of him. All day he sat in a chair watching over ancient vases and statues, and in the evening he sat watching television, especially football which didn't interest her in the least. His back was bad. He never had anything to say. Sometimes Shelley would tell him about something she'd read or seen and he would say, 'That's very interesteen, Thel.' That's what he'd said when she told him the story of Frankenstein. 'Interesteen.' She seemed to find Arthur's pronunciation of the word unforgivable. It drove her mad. It excused her infidelity.

As Bertie explained it to me, it was some time before he began to understand what kind of a woman Thelma Button was and why she'd made him this, as it had seemed, outrageously frank offer of herself. She was not at all what he'd supposed — either 'wild', desperate, a beaten wife, or even attracted to him by his patrician looks and manner. Shelley was not inexperienced; but her life had been on the whole sober and orderly, constrained by modest beginnings, low income, early marriage, and two children born within a year of one another.

As for Bertie's attractions: she knew perfectly well that he was of a certain 'class'; but to her such men had always seemed faintly comic — not to be taken seriously. It was almost an obstacle to her liking him; just as her 'class' — the fact that she referred to her husband as 'Arfur', complained that her children came home 'filfy' from school, talked about someone having 'nuffing in 'is 'ead', or said she'd heard this or that 'on good aufori'y', had made her seem to Bertie quite beyond the pale. No. Bertie's attractiveness to her had been something else, something she herself found mysterious and inexplicable. All she could say about it was that it had something to do with his voice and his eyes and his laugh. And also, once she got to know him better, his smell. But almost from the first exchange between them she'd felt she was falling in love with him.

This was a fact which only slowly became clear to Bertie. He found it flattering, disconcerting, unintelligible, reassuring — both welcome and unwelcome; for while it made for great sex, and helped restore the confidence which a much-loved wife's departure had undermined, it also added a burden of responsibility and of guilt. Increasingly as he got to know Thelma Button, Bertie felt affection and gratitude. Her talk was lively and witty. Her generosity was boundless. Her body was lovely and her hair magical. He began to think of her as his secret garden. But to fall in love, even a little, with someone who had things 'on good aufori'y' was quite beyond him.

'Not possible,' he said when I asked him. 'Simply out of the question. Sometimes, you know, I'd try to imagine taking her to things — to dinner parties, Lord's, Wimbledon, Covent Garden. I'd try, Carlo. It was . . . ' He looked at me with an expression that appealed for understanding, for absolution. 'It was unthinkable.'

So he decided he must stop seeing her. If she'd been able to take their affair as he did, as an adventure, a diversion, an unlooked for luxury, a secret bonus Life had handed out with no strings or complications, there would have been no problem. But he could see that every visit made the love she felt for him, and which he couldn't think of matching, more powerful, more all-consuming.

She, of course, soon recognised that the depth of her feeling troubled him, and she tried to conceal it or make light of it. But there were moments when she would say, 'I'd die for you, Bertie,' or even (and much worse), 'I'd let you kill me if you wanted to. I'd love you for it.' He would be struck with a sense of awe and helplessness then, and with the wish to escape. To have evoked great love could only be good for his wounded ego; on the other hand, to find himself unable to return it inevitably reduced the beneficial effect. Herbert Lawson-Grieve's secret garden had begun to have about it the feel of a cage.

But still the decision that he must end their affair wasn't translated into action. He would think of it as he left her flat, resolving that this would be the last. By the following Monday the resolve would be gone. By Wednesday he would hardly be able to complete his morning's work for thinking of what the afternoon was to bring. But now, because he was in two minds about Shelley, a sort of ambiguity had begun to creep into his feelings about what he did with her in bed. He enjoyed — enjoyed enormously — and yet did not enjoy. He marvelled, and was half-repelled. Sometimes he felt like a circus animal required to do ever-more remarkable tricks. Shelley was the trainer and her whip was true love.

The break didn't come until he was sent to New York on business for the firm. It wasn't a city he enjoyed and he would normally have asked them to send someone else. This time he accepted the task willingly, and even made it last longer than was necessary. By the time he got back to London he felt the Shelley habit had been broken.

But now came phone calls from her; and when these were blocked by his secretary, there was a postcard. It was of a large pink breast painted to look like a winking pig, the nipple its snout. On the back she had written, 'Here's my knocker, Berty luv. Where's yours?'

This, coming to him in the office, giggled over by the secretaries, was outrageous — but of course she meant it to be. Bertie was angry, but he was also ashamed. He had tried to end the affair because she loved him too much, and that seemed to him the honourable thing to do; but it had not been honourable — it had been cowardly and wrong — to try to end it by simply absenting himself without a word. He must go and (as he put it) 'face the music'.

The 'music', however, when it came on the following Wednesday was not a simple and catchy tune. At first, when he tried to tell her they must call it off, she reproached him — something she hadn't done before; then she wept, shouted, told him she would always love him, threatened suicide, insulted him. He found it painful, and the pain focused especially on one fact — that she appeared to have dressed herself up for the encounter, and that the clothes seemed to him in the worst possible taste.

As Bertie explained it to me, he has no exact memory for women's clothes, often doesn't remember colours, or remembers them incorrectly — yet at the same time he always takes away a generalised, and in some ways quite precise, impression. Shelley, as he remembered her that day, was wearing a yellow dress of some kind of stiff material, with a short skirt, and around her head, over that rebellious but briefly tamed hair, a band of the same colour.

'There seemed to be little bows and frills everywhere,' he said. 'I may be exaggerating, but it seemed to me she only needed a tray of sweets and ices and she could have gone to a fancy dress ball as an old-fashioned cinema usherette.'

He had never, he told me, felt so fond of her, nor so self-reproachful and so determined to protect her. He couldn't give her what she wanted — he could not; and so the only thing for it was to remove himself. That's what he tried to explain, while she argued, wept, threatened, pleaded.

At last however, when he was on the point of exhaustion, despair and rage, she changed tack — seemed to accept that he was going, and that he wouldn't be back. Before he went, however, she would like, she said, to show him her 'new friend'. She went to the drawer beside her bed and took something out. He thought it must be a photograph, but what she held up to him was a plastic vibrator. Bertie knew what it was, but only because there had once been an Anne Summers sex shop in Tottenham Court Road and from time to time he'd looked in as he went by and had seen such things, all manner of phallic shapes and sizes, in shelves in long rows.

She held it out for him to touch, but he drew back from it. She pressed a little switch and it began to buzz. She put one foot on the bed and he saw that she was wearing no underclothes. She ran the plastic head of the buzzing phallus through her pubic hair, which grew as coarse and curly as the hair on her head. And then, while he watched, slowly, very slowly, she pushed it into herself.

'My mouth went suddenly dry,' Bertie said, 'and I knew it — I was done for. I said, "I'm going Shelley" and she said — putting her head back, you know, as though she was really enjoying it — "You're not going nowhere, my Ber'ie." She was right of course. I felt as if I was going towards the door but I wasn't. She was like a magnet. It was like being dragged bodily, against your will.'

He'd been looking down into his drink as he told me this, and I remember how he looked up now, appealing for a friend's compassion. 'You have to understand Carlo, I was hungry for it. I'd been all those weeks in New York, and there'd been nothing. Nothing but the occasional hand-job.'

'So,' I said, when he fell silent. 'What did you do?'

It was a silly question. 'What do you think I did?' he replied. 'I took it out and put mine in. We did it dressed, half-dressed, undressed. We did it up against the wall, on the floor, in the bed. We did it standing, sitting, lying. I didn't care any more. Fuck it, I thought. Life's too

difficult. Let's enjoy ourselves. And that's what we did. Three o'clock
came around, 3.30 — I didn't care. I was busy. I was fucking. I was
happy. I was being myself for a change and I was enjoying it.'

So the afternoon passed. And it occurred to him afterwards that
she must all along have been confident of success, because she'd arranged for Jack and Jill to go to a friend's place for supper. They fucked
and they talked, and talked and fucked, and finally they slept . . .

Bertie was woken by her shaking him, staring down at him. 'Wake
up,' she was saying. 'Jesus Christ. Ber'ie, wake fucking *up*. It's *'im!* It's
Arfur!'

Then she was out of bed and across the room to the hallway. He
heard her snib the Yale lock. There was a conversation going on in the
corridor — Arthur talking to a neighbour. In a moment he would try
and open his own door with the key, and find he couldn't.

Back in the bedroom Shelley was gathering up her things. She
hissed at Bertie to get dressed. ''e'll go downstairs to the caretaker to
report there's something wrong with the lock. Then you scarpa. Go
down the other stairs. I'll pretend I snibbed it by mistake.'

She vanished into the bathroom. And now from the front door
came the scraping of Arthur's key as he tried to turn it in the lock.
Bertie dragged on his underpants and trousers, wrestled with his shirt
which he found had lost a button in the earlier, equally violent, struggle to get it off.

Arthur's voice came through the door. 'Thel? You in there Thelma?'
He rattled the door handle. 'Thel?'

And then the key was withdrawn, the voice muttered to itself, footsteps receded down the corridor.

Now, Bertie thought — now was his chance to escape. He would
get out and would never come back. He thought of setting off, running, carrying his shoes. But no, the idea was ridiculous. Some sort of
dignity had to be preserved.

He was sitting on the bed's edge dragging on his socks when he
heard a new sound, a scraping and scrambling. The balcony out there
was shared with the flat next door. Arthur had gone through the flat
of the neighbour he'd been talking to in the corridor. Now, from
the balcony, he was scrambling up over a closed window to an open
fanlight.

From where Bertie sat he could see, across the hallway and through another door, a pair of long black trousered legs pushing, sliding, hanging, dropping.

There was a thump as two feet hit the sitting room floor. Shelley's voice quavered from the bathroom. 'That you, Arfur?'

Bertie put his head down and dragged at his shoes. He tugged at the laces. Footsteps approached. At that moment, he told me, he felt a desperate calm. The blow would come down on the back of his head, on his neck — he had no doubt of that. He wouldn't defend himself; couldn't. He would die; but it wasn't fear he felt — it was embarrassment. It was shame.

Two large black shiny guard's shoes arrived and planted themselves opposite the two brown shoes into which Bertie's feet were still refusing to fit. He persisted, dragging the laces wide apart.

'One has to do something while waiting to die,' Bertie said. 'I remember wondering would the blow hurt, or would I pass instantly and painlessly into another world of floating shapes saying things like, "Hullo, dear. I'm your mother." '

But there was no blow. Nothing was said. There was only the heavy breathing of a wronged husband who had just climbed through a fanlight.

'I raised my eyes slowly.' (Bertie was acting it out for me now — bending forward, twisting his head around to look up at the occupant of those shiny shoes.) 'There was the line of the trousers. When I got to the thighs I saw the hands, hanging at his sides. They were coffee coloured, with sickly palms. I raised my eyes further and there was a coffee face to match. My first thought was, "Why the fuck did she never tell me he was black?" '

The dark mask looking down at him showed no violence. That ought to have been a relief; but violence would have been simpler. It would have given him something to do.

He tried to read Arthur's face. There was anxiety in the eyes; and around the mouth something like contempt.

'This is a dreadful business,' Bertie managed to say. 'I'm really most frightfully sorry.'

He stood, picking his jacket up from the floor. That uncovered the vibrator. They both, he and black Arthur, looked down at it lying there like a severed penis.

Bertie said he'd better go.

Shelley had been right — Arthur wasn't a talker; but his silence at this moment seemed strangely powerful and impressive.

Bertie moved out into the hall. His walk was unsteady. At the bathroom door he stopped and called to Shelley that he was going.

The bolt slid back and she appeared in a dressing gown. Behind her he could see the yellow dress trampled on the wet tiled floor. She nodded to him, glanced at Arthur.

Bertie moved to the front door — only a step or two in those cramped quarters. He unsnibbed the lock, opened the door, and felt a moment of relief.

But was it right to leave without another word? He turned. Shelley had come out of the bathroom. Arthur out of the bedroom, and they were standing side by side, 'like two piano keys,' Bertie said, 'the ebony and the ivory. They made a handsome couple.'

To Arthur Bertie said, 'You won't hurt her.' He meant it to be something midway between a question and an instruction.

Arthur said, 'Out.' That was the beginning and the end of his talk.

Shelley looked at Bertie reassuringly. She was quite safe seemed to be the message. So he went, closing the door gently behind him.

Out in the street he was assailed all over again by embarrassment. He turned west, away from his office, crossed Gray's Inn Road, walked along to Southampton Row. In Kingsway there was a men's clothes shop that had always , as long as he could remember, announced that it was having a Closing Down Sale. He went in and chose himself an unpleasant business shirt that had a faint green tinge to it. It would replace the one with the tear and the hanging button.

He also thought of it as a penance. Handing over his credit card he asked the young woman did she have any with hair linings.

'So-rree?' she quacked at him. He didn't repeat it.

It was raining now. He took a taxi back to the office. The secretaries had gone. He sat at his desk looking out at the rain drifting past the ugly looming towers of the Barbican. He thought of Françoise and a few tears sprang into his eyes — a mixture of anger and regret. He thought of Arthur's shiny black shoes and winced. He heard the partner in the next office getting ready to leave. He went to her door. Her name was Coral Strand. They'd worked together for years, knew one another well.

'That's a nasty shirt, Herbert,' she said at once. 'It's not the one you had on this morning.'

He never got used to the fact that women noticed clothing so precisely. 'The other one,' he said, 'got torn off my back by a woman desperate to have me.'

Coral smiled wearily. 'Of course.' It was a tired old joke. How odd, Bertie thought, that it should be true.

'Do I seem to you an absurd person?' he asked.

'No,' she said, 'not especially.' She snapped her case shut. It was a signal that she had little time for talk, and certainly none for what he had once overheard her call 'a therapy session with our Bert'. Deluded by her name, which still suggested to him a tropical paradise, Bertie had long ago, and very briefly, imagined he and Coral Strand might become lovers. Inwardly he now thought of her as the Head Girl.

'Not especially,' he repeated. It was hardly reassuring.

'About average,' she said, easing him into the corridor and closing the door. 'We're all a bit absurd sometimes, aren't we? See you tomorrow Bertie.'

He didn't go back to Marlow that night but spent it at his club. He has taken me there sometimes for lunch or dinner and I can report that it seemed a dreadful place where faded lackeys served tasteless food to dead men in suits. Bertie, however, finds some kind of ancient comfort in brown leather and panelled walls, and comfort was what he needed.

Next morning he went first, not to his office, but to the British Museum. After a lot of aimless wandering through the halls and galleries he found Arthur dozing on a chair in a corner among ancient clay burial urns. Bertie roused him with a sharp cough and said his piece: that he was very disturbed at what had happened. That it had not been as bad as it must have seemed (this in an attempt to allow for any story Shelley might have concocted) but that he wanted to apologise sincerely. That it had been his fault entirely, not Thelma's. That it would never happen again.

Arthur didn't get up. He listened, staring with blood-shot eyes at a large broken urn. When the little speech was over he asked, 'You got fifty quid?'

Bertie was taken by surprise. For just a moment it seemed a wonderful relief, the possibility of doing something, paying something, by way of recompense, of absolution.

Yes, he said, he had fifty, certainly. He had more . . .

All the while scrabbling to get his wallet out, to get it open . . .

He held out a fistful of notes. Here were at least fifty pounds, probably seventy. He didn't count, and there hadn't been a moment to reflect on what Arthur's request might signify.

Arthur beckoned him closer. Bertie leaned down over him, holding the money.

'Now stick it up your arse,' Arthur said, 'and fuck off outa here.'

Out in the street he seemed to have lost control of his legs. He ambled uncertainly in the direction of the City, still holding the fistful of notes, looking for a passing taxi showing a light and then, when one came along, not hailing it. He saw a florist's shop, went in and put the money on the counter. What he wanted, he explained, was as many flowers as this would buy sent at once, this morning, to . . . And he gave her name and address.

'And for the card, Sir,' the florist said.

Ah yes, the card. He took it and after a moment wrote on it, 'To Shelley from Keats. Love you for ever.'

For the duration of the brief moment it took to write it, Bertie said, and for perhaps thirty seconds afterwards, he felt it was true.

I didn't quite believe — or was it just that I didn't want to believe? — that that was the end of the story.

'Just for thirty seconds?' I said. 'No more?'

He met my eye for a moment, shrugged, and looked down at the table between our comfortable chairs. 'Let's refill these glasses,' he said.

Dutch Mosquito

RUSSELL HALEY

There was one mosquito in his room and it was a large one to judge by its sound which was so high pitched as to be almost inaudible to human ears. But *he* could hear it. More penetrating in its single note than the massed chorus which in Queensland had hovered nightly outside his sleeping net in the house at Flying Fish Point.

Karl was working late in his room in Middelburg. The Provinciale Bibliotheek was long since closed for the evening but Karl already had enough data to begin the first draft of his article on the Delta Plan. He reached out and tuned his transistor to Radio Caroline. Karl had long ago learned to work with a moderate level of background noise. If the radio were not turned on while concentrating then the chances were that you would begin to listen to the sound of your own breathing or the blood moving through the arteries near the ears.

But the noise of the insect was different from low-volume music. He could hear it now even above the slurred flute sounds of Jethro Tull.

At Flying Fish Point Connie and he slept in a single bed. It was too hot even for a sheet and during the night their naked bodies pressed against the protective net. In the mornings they showered together in the little cubicle down under the house. There were times, out of the rainy season, when they had to conserve water which came, not from the mains, but from the big galvanised iron tank at the side of the house. The tank was a breeding ground for mosquitoes.

The dark sheen of her skin with the raised bumps of insect bites on her arse where she had been bitten through the net.

'Do me here Karl — in the shower.' Connie could never use the

172

straightforward word. It was always 'do'.

'If you finish your work quickly we can do it.'

Sometimes in the monsoon season they would hear the coconuts falling from the trees into the sand — their unfenced garden which ran right down to the beach. The nuts fell with a sinister hollow sound like heads striking against concrete . . . or the way in which Jane had cracked sea-eggs on that holiday up beyond Kaitaia. They too had broken like brittle skulls. He had never been able to eat the contents — the organic brainlike slime. Nor, in Queensland, had he ever touched the liquid from the coconut except when Connie used it in the sauce of a curry. But to drink the grey cold liquid from a glass as she did . . . it was there again above his head . . . not seeing any target but trying to judge by sound Karl jumped from his chair and clapped his hands together. He looked at his palms for the hoped-for sight of the dead insect. There was nothing. Except for a freckle on the ball of his right thumb which he'd never noticed before.

In Macquarie Fields, where he had no net (nor anyone like Connie), the mosquitoes had been so burdened with his blood that they were suicidally slow. The old Italian who owned the house where Karl lived showed him how to watch for an insect landing on his bare arms. He would allow them to insert the proboscis and then tense the muscle, drawing the skin tighter so that the insect was trapped. As slowly as you liked you could slap the creature into oblivion. The trick always seemed to work when Luigi demonstrated it but Karl never had any success.

Connie was a great believer in mosquito coils. Before they went to bed she used to pad across the bare wooden floor of the room and crouch to light the coil of a joss-like chemical. She was always careful to place the little tin triangle on which the coil stood in a saucer, so that the residual ash was collected. Her favourite coils were Tiger Brand and Karl always suspected that it was the picture she really liked rather than the acrid smell of the burning coil. Then she would run back across the room and scramble under the net with Karl and then they tucked the net carefully under the mattress and sat up together, the net touching their hair, while they made sure there were no mosquitoes trapped with them inside their net.

Because the bed was so small Connie used to lie on top of him. When she raised herself her damp skin pulled against his.

'You like me to do you don't you?' Connie was the only woman he'd had who liked to talk once he was moving inside her. And it was a curious embarrassment to Karl.

'Yes, I like it.'

This position seemed to alter her physiology completely. When he lay over her she was a long dark tunnel into which he could drive until he disappeared, until *he* was no longer there, just an infinite regression of self until he was nothing but a tiny point of light in the darkness. But with her moving on him, her thin flesh over him, it was as though there were a wall or ledge of firmness against which he butted. And his self was like a star flaring in the dark with sharp spikes of light, brittle and fragmenting. And unintentionally he would hurt her with the force of his driving and it was like a soft pain for her, winding somehow, like blows against a bruise. Then, with his hands hard against her buttocks he would try to stop her moving but his fingertips would feel the slide of his own flesh into her and he'd be lost again, a burning ache until it peaked like a thin jet of flame and he came, against the wall, the ledge. Almost always before her and when she knew she spoke in a torrent, as though her words could hold him hard and erect until she could come.

Outside in the street someone was driving a motorised bicycle, a *bromfiets*, up and down. Karl opened his window and looked below. A boy, or perhaps a girl, he couldn't really tell, was trying to drive the bicycle in a figure-eight turn. But the street was too narrow and when the bicycle stopped moving the engine note rose until it sounded as though the whole machine would shake to pieces. And yet whoever it was down there was trying, obsessively, to perform the feat. Karl shut his window again and drew the curtains but he could not close out the irritating sound.

He began to prepare coffee on the small gas ring in the corner of his room. Lately he had been buying more food to supplement his meals. Not that Madame Brun was niggardly with the breakfasts she made. But no matter how large a meal Karl ordered in the cafés in town, by late evening he was hungry again. While the water for his coffee was coming to the boil he spread a slice of Ryvita with quark, a local preparation which tasted like a combination of yoghurt with cottage cheese. He realised suddenly that the noise from the figure-of-eight cyclist was no longer there. Yet he hadn't noticed when it had ceased.

Karl spooned damp yellow sugar into his coffee and balanced his cup on the arm of his chair while he rolled a cigarette. He nipped off the stray ends of tobacco and dropped them back into the blue packet. He drew deeply on the cigarette and immediately felt light-headed. He drank some coffee and closed his eyes.

Karl lapsed for a moment into nothingness, or rather a kind of undifferentiated awareness. Millions of red, blue, green, violet pin-points. His skin and frame no longer bounded him. He was on the inside of an ever-expanding membrane made up of these infinite numbers of coloured dots. Then a flat road seemed to stretch out before him. He was driving through a totally featureless landscape except that it was a priority road because signs now appeared — orange diamonds on a white background. Karl opened his eyes — his room appeared to shudder back into being. But he was still moving silently forward with a steady accelerative thrust in the armchair, driving forward along a hallucinatory road. An intersection on his right and a huge semi-trailer pulling out in front of him. He could see the crusted mud on the underside of the chassis of the trailer. He went into it. Fully. Silently. And his consciousness diffused out into coloured fragments again.

It was like a waking nightmare. He was moving again on the same road. The truck pulling out again. He aimed between the wheels of the trailer. It was lower than his car. He ducked. Above him the roof tore away. He was spinning down the road on the far side of the truck — fragments of glass and torn metal all round him. But he was beyond, out, through it.

Sitting in his room in Koepoortstraat Karl knew that he had somehow to break this moment, because it wasn't a moment, a point in time, at all. It was a continuum. He did not know how he had got in. It was like a dream of being out above space on a high wire. One had to deliberately manipulate the dream. Invent a parachute. Jump and float to safety.

He stood up and went to his wardrobe and found a pair of soft-soled shoes. He put his tobacco, papers, matches in his pocket and made sure he had money. Karl let himself out of the *pension* silently, leaving the door on the latch. It was very nearly midnight. The cold struck through his clothing.

Even in a small town like this there must be a café still open.

175

Karl found one, The Black Rider, after a walk of ten minutes. There was a noisy crowd inside and Karl stood at the bar trying to get served. A jukebox was playing loudly and two couples were dancing. He tried to order a beer but the man behind the bar seemed not to notice him.

Karl was standing next to a woman in a green dress. She was perched on a bar-stool.

'Een bier alstublieft,' Karl said again. The woman turned to him.

'You are German?'

'No, English — New Zealand.'

The woman reached out grinning and pinched the lobe of his ear painfully.

'You will have to shout if you want a drink. Everyone wants to be served at the same time. Give me your money.'

Karl handed her the five-guilder note. The woman was served in a moment, with two beers Karl noted, but he was relieved rather than annoyed. He nodded his thanks and carried his glass over to an empty table. There was a burst of laughter from the bar.

Perhaps it was only because most people in the bar were drunk and Karl was sober but he could sense a tension, something edged and discordant, in the café. A middle-aged man kept trying to break in on one of the couples, moving into the space between them and then jigging back awkwardly. He couldn't dance as they danced. He dangled his arms and hopped from one foot to the other.

Karl glanced round the bar. A man sat alone, hunched, with a grotesque mask pushed up onto his forehead so that he could drink. The mask was that of a skull with dayglo green eye-sockets.

Karl drank half his beer and then looked up when he realised that the woman who had obtained his drink was standing at his side.

'Will you dance Englishman — it is Carnival you know?' She turned her head back towards the bar and shouted something in a raucous voice which Karl could not understand.

'All right,' he said, 'but I'm not very good.'

They moved out onto the narrow strip of floor and Karl began to dance, very self-consciously, keeping a distance between the woman and himself.

'Come here,' she said abruptly, in mock anger, and grabbed Karl. She moved herself against him. Karl tried to steer her towards the

176

rear of the dance floor so that they could not be seen quite so easily from the bar. His only intention was to avoid the gaze of the woman's friends.

'Ah — so,' the woman said and began to grind herself against him. Her movements were so strong and deliberate that Karl could feel the coarse rasping of her jutting pubic arch against him.

She was ten years older than him at least and she smelled of perfume and beer and sweat. In spite of this, perhaps *because* of this if he were honest, he felt himself stiffen against her. The woman was almost wrestling with him.

'You get excited,' she spoke close to his ear.

The music ended and Karl muttered an excuse to go back to his table. The woman joined her friends at the bar and Karl heard them laughing again. He tried to look at them without appearing to be paying any attention. But he saw that a man had swung round on his seat to face away from the bar. He looked at Karl directly. He wasn't laughing.

In a glance Karl saw that he was a big man, balding, with large hands. The man wore a heavy signet ring which was half-buried in the flesh of his finger.

Karl finished his beer with one swallow and rose to leave. As he passed the people at the bar the man dropped off his seat and his shoulder caught Karl so that he almost lost his balance.

'I'm sorry,' Karl said, though he knew that the big man had deliberately nudged him. The man stared at him angrily.

'You want violence?' he said.

'No I don't. I apologise for knocking into you.' Karl heard his own voice as though someone else had spoken. It was light and high.

The woman put her hand on the man's arm.

'Leave him alone Hans — he's an Englishman.'

Karl wondered how her statement could calm him down — the fact that she emphasised that he was English, seemed not only incorrect but absurd.

The man shook his head slowly and Karl realised that he was far more drunk than he had first appeared to be.

'That's good because . . .' The man whistled through his teeth and swung his foot out towards Karl's crutch. It was a demonstration rather than an intended blow and Karl had moved quickly out of range.

Another record suddenly blared out from the jukebox and the woman pulled the man towards her and began to dance with him in amongst the crowd near the bar. The man, who now seemed to have forgotten Karl completely, dug his hands into the flesh of the woman's buttocks and he raised her off her feet, bending backwards as he did so, so that she was forced even harder against him.

Outside, Karl ran down a side street. Not because he was afraid he might be followed but more to try to relieve an overwhelming internal pressure.

When he reached his *pension* he did not go inside. He got into his car and switched on the ignition. The engine turned over slowly. He pulled the choke right out and then tried again. The motor caught, spluttered, and then settled down to a steady beat.

Karl drove through town till he made a left turn at the railway station and then out towards Bergen-op-Zoom. He had been driving at seventy-five along the highway for fifteen minutes before he realised he had not fastened his safety-belt nor turned on the headlights.

He drove home at forty, headlights full on, watching all the way for intersections out from which articulated trucks might suddenly glide.

Karl woke at 4 am from a deep sleep. He imagined himself and Connie swimming in the warm waters of Etty Bay and then he slipped, was under, seeing her naked body from below and he could *breathe*. Karl lay on the bottom of the sea, on the sand, watching as sea-snakes glided through the water, stirring the sand with their fluted tails.

He drew in draught after draught of the warm water and then she slowly settled down onto him in absolute silence. Her hair hung for moments above him before it too descended, closing over his face, bringing total darkness.

Putting Bob Down

VINCENT O'SULLIVAN

It is usually assumed that if a man has two mistresses or two wives, then they must be physically quite contrary types. Perhaps literature has corrupted that part of our thinking irretrievably. There is always the 'dark she, fair she', as the gloomiest of English poets once wrote. Or what we drew from those books we were reared on. Walter Scott. Nathaniel Hawthorne. There is a blonde girl who embodies the domestic virtues, who wears a plaid shawl, looks after an aged father, and gazes at the hero with eyes so blue that ice floating in the coldest fjords is not to be compared. Truly. And there is a raven-haired woman who speaks directly from the blood. She is Mediterranean, and behind her we see the temples of forgotten faiths, a rage for existence which that blonde girl knows nothing of. She carries phials in her pocket, while the Anglo-Saxon angel has merely an address book in her reticule. Which is introductory to this simple fact: when Bob Roberts died, there were two women at his graveside. They were almost identical.

Helene, whose name had always enchanted him, said as they walked away from the dark gaping hole, 'We all get finally I suppose what we most deserve.'

The other woman was called Frith. She hated her name intensely because of that mucky story about the bird. She said, 'If only we did.'

Metaphor is something that Helene hates more than anything on earth. A plate is a plate. A fish is a fish. A plate can never be a fish, even if it is shaped with fins and painted with scales, and signed Picasso in the corner. Because there is always the irrefutable test. Give a hungry man a plate painted like a fish.

Frith does not think like that at all. To carry metaphor in one's emotional arsenal is to carry a thin stick that snaps open to a gorgeous fan. There is a semicircle of wonder as close as the palm of one's hand. Japan, as she once explained it to Bob, sits waiting in Dabtoe. There is holocaust in every match that is struck correctly.

At the graveside both women stepped forward simultaneously, to take a handful of clammy yellow earth. One had removed her glove while the other had kept hers on. The better dressed of the women reached out her right hand to the trowel which the undertaker offered them. The other woman took her handful from the left. Frith thinking of a cake offered on a cakeslice. Helene looking only at the clogged crumbs of earth.

When Helene threw that clutch of dirt into the grave, onto the polished wood and the freshly engraved metal plate, she knew quite absolutely she tossed dust to dust. So did Frith. But she was thinking how she knew beyond any disbelief in resurrection or anything else, that she was throwing eternity onto dear dead Bob. That all of us, walking or sleeping, wear bodies which are indeed the merest tip of the past, the arrowhead that shall then lie round for a million years. She thought, I am throwing the dust of today onto the ash of stars.

Bob had said to them separately, 'You cannot expect me to choose between you. You just can't.'

Each of them had said in her own way, which in fact was very similar, 'We're not cannibals, love. We don't believe for a minute that one has to devour the loved one.' Helene had spelled it out. 'Isn't that what we've been fighting against for millennia. That old *mine, mine* nonsense?' Frith put it like this. She said, 'If we could only think of sex as an aesthetic experience too, as well as a mere tingling of nerves.' (In her mind she saw the telephone exchange her mother worked at while she herself was a child. And on some days too many bells ringing in that small town for one operator to cope with. Until mummy's hands finally across her ears with the room ringing about her and the lights flashing on the switchboard and simply not enough hands for too many wires. With mummy crying *oh shit oh dear*.) What Frith in fact was saying: 'If you won a painting I mean. You don't turn it to the wall if someone else enjoys it too.'

At the graveside she wore a plain grey suit and Helene a black frock with a cut-away matching jacket. From not very far away they might have been sisters, one of them clearly richer than the other. They had both taken a taxi to the cemetery. Neither thought it important which of them had known the corpse the longer time.

Even now, if it came to the push, Bob would not have known what woman he preferred. Thank God though there had never been anything sneaky about the liaisons. He had told Helene quite openly. He had said, 'I don't consider myself a particularly randy sort of man but there's something I'd better tell you.' It was almost as if she had expected him to say it. She had stroked his hair as she leaned across him. He had thought, I'm buggered if I'd have taken the same thing from her. But another time when he had forgotten an appointment with her, Helene threw things at him when he next came into the house.

Frith was so much milder. Yet she wore exotic underthings and said the strongest words when her breath caught and her hands fluttered across his rump.

A point to be made here is that it's not at all the same thing as looking through a doorway, although it's easy enough for writers to imagine that it is, when the figures pull back from the sunlit and lovely oblong which is the top of a grave. To imagine it is like friends going from a room. As a matter of fact the legs are absurdly out of proportion to begin with. They are positive pillars. The heads too such disproportionate bumps above the big swinging handbags, the hands the women held together in their dark gloves rather like the mitts of boxers touching as they prance in their corners. Then when they drop those handfuls of dirt. Honestly, the way the clods came pouring in you'd think they had it in for you.

'I'm only a journo,' Bob used to tell them. 'Only run of the mill in the least elevated of callings.'

'It must be so marvellous to use words at all,' Frith said. 'With that freedom, I mean. That control. All I ever do, day after day, is hear children recite their grammar. Hear them conjugate, decline, fumble with sentences they will never know how to use. Languages!' she sighed. 'Those complicated and dreary ladders. Where do they expect them to reach?'

She liked it when he nuzzled close against her, ran his hand down her stomach and left it lying there. 'A man is like the *Zeitwort*, do you understand that? The verb. Women are so many nouns.'

When both of them stood back from the long bright space hanging there above him, he thought how lovely a patch of pure blue could seem.

The women turned away and walked for perhaps a minute in silence. Then Helene was saying to Frith, 'In the six funerals I've been to in this cemetery this is the first one it hasn't rained.'

They were cutting across the rows of the buried towards the road. A champion billiard-player's monument with its slate table, its marble cue, struck them as too absurd. 'God knows what Bradman will have. A whole oval made from brass.' They touched each other's arms in amusement. 'Imagine what Bob would think, us talking like this!' They remembered how he believed that women knew nothing about sport.

As it happened, he thought a great deal. He thought of Helene's knee on the side of his bed, her preparing to throw herself across him like the great Jim Pike across Phar Lap himself, and his telling her, 'You are lovelier than anything I know.' And her playfully putting her hand across his mouth so that he bit at that fleshy part just down from her little finger. Her saying to him. 'Never say *than*. Never say *like* or *as*. Do you hear?' Pressing with her strong knees against his sides. And his saying quite seriously, so that she roared with laughter, 'There's not a love poem I bet you in the whole of literature for that part of a woman's body. That little soft bit there on the side of your hand.' Helene would even laugh sometimes in the middle of their loving. With Frith there was either no talk at all, or those words she would never think of using anywhere else.

The first time he had ever seen them together. At an art opening he had to write up for his paper because the critic was down with the mumps. He was terrified at the thought of speaking to both of them at the same time. He leaned close to Frith as he came in and saw her by the table with the catalogues. 'There's an awful lot of people I have to nod to tonight. Or the paper does rather. Know what I mean?' He brought her a glass of wine and looked at some pictures with her. She knew the names of all of them without referring to her catalogue.

Helene said out very loudly, 'This is the most boring exhibition I have ever seen.' He had been shocked. He looked at the famous black figures against their ochrous background, the flashes of gums and flowers like gunshot in the violence of the light. She said, 'Introduce me to her anyway. She can't be worse than this.'

They had reminded him of a Moore exhibition as they peered down at him a few minutes ago. Their heads so small and distant, mere tufts on pyramids of flesh.

Helene, he had sometimes thought, liked to be with him so that she could *hone*. On anything. On politics or race or people they knew. 'Private money makes it so easy,' he would say to her. 'I could sneer at half the price.' She sat with her legs tucked under her, her glass of wine reflecting like a great coin. Folded on her knee was the paper with his column. 'What would you do if you actually had to *look* at something? Come into the open without your clichés? Your little images? Run like a nigger flushed from the cane-brakes, I wouldn't be surprised.' Her teeth when she teased him like that! So white and even and gleaming. She enraged him. And then so deliberately looking at her watch, declaring that her husband already had left his office, was stroking this very moment life into his Bentley. But the excitement never really wore off, because there was one lesson he learned very early. To root above one's station is the first step to the stars.

It is surprising how little it shocks one to hear that a friend is dead. It would surprise one more at times to hear that he had won a fortune or written a book or even that he had remarried. Death, when the chips are down, is a very ordinary thing to come to terms with. No sooner has one heard it than there are those meetings with other friends, the ceremonies that nudge it so easily, so gently, away from the warm place where we stand ourselves. To buy a hat, for example. How much of grief can be absorbed in that. To buy, as indeed Frith did, new black underwear for the funeral. Appreciating her own dark joke as she tried it on at home, for a moment there Bob was alive again, watching her from the bed, assuring her she was a bit of all right, bloody oath she was! That other time twenty years ago when she had surprised him with what she wore beneath her dress. The day she had opened the book that he gave her at the end of their first summer. In the tiled vestibule of the Seacliff Hotel! The dark pines on that space of lawn across the street, a solitary girl walking there in a white frock. *Munch!* Bob had said when he looked at her. One of his dreadful artistic puns. Just before he gave her the brown-paper wrapped present and told her to open it in the car. 'I'll open it now!' she had said, and they were tussling, fooling about, people giving them the oddest looks as they passed at the foot of the big staircase. She tore the brown paper and saw that marvellous gilded face. The thick black lines on the eyelids. The cheekbones of pure gold. All because she had said once, *wouldn't you love to go to Egypt?*

After the women withdrew, there were minutes in that oblong of brilliant light when almost nothing happened. A palm frond waved across bottom left. A flight of longnecked birds that could have flown from a Russian movie flicked over very high up. Then a man sat there briefly with his feet dangling down as though he sat on a wharf, and smoked a cigarette. When he stood up again he hitched his belt and shouted across to another bloke to move his arse. And the earth started to rain in. Bob tried to remember something. Yes! That quick flowing across of girths and bellybands as ground-level cameras caught the jumpers at Beecher's Brook. The clods flying out from the impacting hooves. The clods now pouring down and the blades of the shovels flashing above there like aircraft in low flight.

And by Christ to hear them now you'd think they had been cobbers from way back.

Helene said, 'You must have known him as long as I did?'

'I suppose I must have,' Frith said. 'At least as.'

Helene said, 'Did he mention me much?'

'You know what men are,' Frith said.

Helene asked again, 'Did he ever mention me?'

'Only to denigrate,' Frith said. 'To say he was chained to a cunt the way men used to be tied to benches in galleys.'

Helene said, 'Whenever he mentioned you it was like he spoke of a disease.'

Bob enjoyed their saying that. He thought how even here you could write your own column. But the women refused his script. They did not squabble as he had hoped. What Frith said in fact was this: 'He lied to both of us, of course.'

'He was a liar all right,' Helene said. 'And he wasn't even that bright, either.'

But there are ways the dead unsettle the living. There are casual remarks made long ago in the warm rooms of the flesh which become weapons in neatly-cuffed and buried hands. Bob thought, it is the least I can do for them now.

'Metaphor is shit,' Helene had said to him once, putting down his paper. His livelihood and his skill dismissed just like that. He had told her you have to be well off to say that. Only the rich were content to be exactly where they were. All very well for her with her fat books of philosophy she could read all day, her picture of Bertrand Russell like a boiled chook on her desk.

'If it wasn't for imagery life would be one long walk along a gutter.' That to Frith. Her blue pencil in her hand, saying that to be able to put 9 out of 10 on a schoolgirl's work was indeed *délice*, *10* out of *10* was *jouissance*. They had a silly game in which she came to bed only after a pupil had scored the top mark. While Bob lay thinking then as now, that for a heavy smoker life indeed could be worse than keeping a gutter eye out for what his old man had called derbs. 'For every ten drowned butts there is one that lies there dry enough to light.' Not every father has that much wisdom to give a son.

He thought very hard about cigarettes, and the room where the women were talking.

In the large quiet room above the park Helene saw the walls flare sharply at her, then return to their tasteful white. It frightened her because she knew there had been no alteration in the light. She said to Frith, 'What were you thinking just now?'

Her dead lover's anterior and it seems always concurrent mistress said, 'I was thinking how life is like a rainbow when we come to think of it.' Strangely, for a moment there Frith had felt as though she bent back on space, her head and heels drawn towards each other, the ether as the poets call it so sparkling about her. *Arc-en-ciel — c'est moi.* Her eyelashes had seemed like the spokes of an iridescent wheel. She wondered if Bob was trying to get through to her. While Helene, because she was the cleverer of the two, thought: if that dead bastard is coming at this one . . . Talk of things like telepathy made her want to throw up. I am a single and finite mind, she told herself. I am not a bloody button in some cosmic jukebox.

From her chair on the other side of the comfortable lounge, Frith watched how her friend's hands met and laced and moved in the silvery light, the point of her cigarette so alive across there, so brilliant.

Alive, she thought. As the dusk rinsed and dipped in the long low mirror that ran the length of the far wall.

He had quite expected the first night to pass slowly. The light coming up across the surrounding rows made him think of arriving at Kennedy airport in New York, one morning when it was very early, on a dawn flight from the West. Manhattan's blocks, its tall secular angels above their strips of narrow street, had made him think it was like a cemetery.

He thought, given time I suppose I shall remember everything. I shall get bored I suppose with this outlook as I have with every other until I remember this one is for keeps. And oddly, that quite comforted him. There would be the chance at last to find one experience that was inexhaustible. He would want to remember precisely what this sensation was like, the first light breaking of the first day. To recall it would be to continue it, to extend it and to know how this day differed from the second. And through memory living those two days as the third was added, and so on. The hundredth. The ten thousandth. To discriminate each moment, as he had liked to quote when he was a student, 'on that day of frost and sun' or whatever it was. Six crosses ranged to the right, then. A stone child dropping a stone rose. Those bloody Italian inscriptions he could never read! Then the college tower far over there beyond the fence, across petrol stench and the trees. There were some positions as he knew that had a damned sight less than this to pass the time. And in the distance there a corner of a building with the dawn smearing its upper windows behind which, had one turned directly about and walked through the lounge with its morbid mirror and its Aubusson birds, one would come to a passageway as they called it when he was a child in which a fumed oak stand protruded antlers for one's hat and a painted Victorian can waited for the winter months to receive one's umbrella, past which one proceeded clothed as a rule or dishevelled at times or on some few occasions starkers towards a bedroom where a woman now lay looking at the light which broke not only there for her but across a city, and given time, a country; a dawn into which she might walk from her own front steps with their small ornamental lions and along an empty street to the locked iron gates which suppose were opened, she might then pass through and walk on between and beneath the elaborately cut stones and the marble figures, the religious confectionery which made her think if not of the bread of life at least the cake of eternity, and so come to the mound where the flowers already wilted although some of them this time yesterday had not been cut, their binding ribbons straggling damp, the handwritten consolations already dribbled ink. From a point equidistant, say, that mound of the grave, the shape of the bed in this greyish light, were not so fancifully unalike. Only Helene tugging her covers close, hoping for further sleep before she had to rise and take her bath and dress. At which moment, Frith: that quite as loved but much less wealthy woman lay thinking of how at Père Lachaise she had stood at the graves of so many famous, of Oscar of Abelard of Alphonsine Plessais Chopin Daudet it could have been of Colette too so she heard later but had missed her at the time. *The grave's a sad and lonely place*, who said? It is a bed it is a bed, she thought. I am running out of what-it's-likes!

When the women met at the Jewish cake-shop at St Kilda Helene said the moment her gloves were removed and lay like something skilfully skinned beside her, 'That old sod's been on my mind practically non-stop all week.' Stabbing the golden arse of a *pêche* concoction. 'Don't tell me he hasn't been on yours?'

'My mind becomes blank whenever I try to think of him.'

'I wake,' Helene said, 'in the early hours and my mind's as full of nonsense as that glass counter there of European gut-rot.'

'You go over the past?' Frith said. She peeled the paper from the *torte* she had chosen.

'Sometimes I remember the past like it's the present.' Both women noticed the unexpected word that established itself in Helen's sentence.

Frith's cheek bulged horribly as in children's caricatures of toothache. She swallowed the wad of sweetness away. 'I used to dream for a bit but now it's pure bareness. *Le néant*.'

Helene said, 'Every morning when I do get round to walking all I smell is earth.' She laughed. 'I'm starting to think like you!'

Bob remembered a cake shaped like a ship with white frosted lines of rigging at a Sea Scout Christmas Party in 1948. He thought of four meringues that sounded like a gravel path when he crunched them and he had wolfed them down one after the other at the wedding of a cousin who wore a military uniform. He recalled in no particular order seedcake with aunts on Sunday afternoons kisscakes with his mother measling down icing-sugar from a flour-mill lamingtons soggy as a rained out oval *Kuchentorten* and *Schlagsahnetorten* during his time abroad. Those aerated squares of pure dryness Frith dipped in her tea while she went on about Proust. He could think of every cake he had ever eaten. No two had been alike. No mouthful was identical with a following or preceding mouthful.

'I'm so sick of this already.' Helene slapped her tiny fork down on her plate. One cheek of her *pêche* remained untouched.

Frith dabbed at her lips with a paper napkin.

Back with their brandies they began to talk of God.

Helene said that when she was a child there had been a crucifix on her grandmother's wall. Two narrow strips of black wood and a grey contorted figure like a deep-freeze lizard.

Frith said she could still sing hymns quite seriously. At weddings or funerals for example. She never gave it a thought between times, mind.

Helene said she would have shot priests if she had been a Spaniard in the old days. 'I see those bastards in black I want to reach for my branding irons.' Which was not really so strong an image and certainly not a metaphor, when used by a woman who was a grazier's wife.

Bob used to joke that in any case a Christian was only a lapsed atheist. He had known so many anti-clerical jokes that he couldn't keep up with invitations to speak at Catholic men's dinners.

But Frith had perched on him once, *in flagrante*, and quoted some lines of John Donne about tuning his instrument here at the door. He had turned on her and told her not to be so bloody disrespectful.

The two women now sat in the lounge and looked over the massed trees to the black iron fence and its acres of remembrance.

'You do wonder though what becomes of one. Gauguin's great painting, *Who are we?* Etcetera. Cliché that it is.'

Helene reached irritably for her cigarettes. 'Anything worth saying is a cliché.'

'Aquinas, wasn't it, thought that you couldn't use any predicate at all of God? That any statement at all was pure tautology?'

'He fucking would,' Helene said. She had hated the Angelic Doctor since her childhood, when she heard that story about a semicircle

188

being cut in the refectory table for his bulk to sit down to meals.

The women sat in silence for several minutes. Then Frith said, 'If He is there, it makes every moment so infinitely of value.' She was sightly embarrassed that she had said it.

'If he isn't of course,' Helene said, 'every moment must be more valuable still.'

'What?' Frith sounded surprised.

'Because there is only a straight line and not a circle. There is no redeeming time, I mean. Each act stands as itself forever.'

Bob thought, 'What if you're both wrong, you smart bitches?'

A picnic in the You-Yangs. The only time he had been with them both together, apart from that art show. A busload of them during a weekend seminar on 'Responsibilities of the Press'. Frith there because she believed such questions mattered, Helene — although she would not even know the word — because she was by nature a groupie. For opera. For *The Tree of Man* during its first year out. For existentialism in its time and then for Vietnam. Only a rich woman could have afforded to care for so much. So at least Bob thought while he sat behind them in the bus, listening to an academic who had been on the same panel with him that morning. He watched the heads of his mistresses sway and bounce.

That outcrop of ancient rocks gave him the creeps. He detested people who used words like numinous, or a few years later spoke of 'the vibes'. He looked at the group about him. Thirty minutes standing in prehistory, as they liked to think, then haring back to the free piss at the cocktail party. The thought of those great grey boulders, the sudden abutments and leaps of rock, depressed him enough to make him consider staying on the bus. Which of course a good journo would never do, because he would not seem one of the team. So he walked with the sociologist who he suspected could not have written a convincing cheque, while the two women he slept with followed some distance behind. Frith said, looking up at the pure blue that hazed off towards the city, 'It's like being inside a jewel on a day like this.' Helene told her she had read how you saw further at this time of year than at any other. 'You can see a candle burning at night three miles away.' That in fact was no more true than the bit about the jewel.

Someone in the group had snapped photographs as they walked

189

along. Eighteen years later Helene handed a print across the coffee table to her recent good friend. She said, 'Remember that afternoon do you?' Bob was some little way ahead. He was turned in profile, laughing. He looked young and happy. The collar of his sports jacket, so typically, was turned up at the back. In the distance far beyond him was the thin strip of the Geelong road. A woman's head was blurred beside him, but her hair was dark and long. Frith took her glasses from her purse. 'Which one of us is that — next to Bob there?'

Helene gave that laugh which sounded so butch Bob used to tell her it reminded him of rugby changing sheds. 'I'm damned if I remember,' she said. Her quieter friend began to laugh as well. The photograph fell as it passed back between them. 'Easy on it,' Frith said. 'One of us is being dropped.' That struck them both as very funny. Helene rubbed at her eyes as though smoke was stinging them.

The women went on to speak of something else, then something else again. It may have been a week later or a month. The two furthest crosses, and the rose-dropping child, were no longer clear in any case. The lawnmower that sometimes charged past like those bloody speedboats that used to irritate him so much the summer when he and Helene lay on that perfect beach on the Tasman Peninsula, that didn't seem to bother him too much at all. He was beginning to forget the names of horses, and football players, and the meals he had once eaten. He was not quite sure any more if *Mille feuilles à la crème* was a cake or a sprinter.

They were leaving the expensive restaurant where Helene had taken Frith to lunch. The afternoon was late as they passed the proprietor who swung back the door for them. They could see the gold tooth near the back of his head. If they wished to sit on with another coffee, he was assuring them, until five, five-thirty, what did it matter? They were not customers, but friends. Frith thought how that would sound so epigrammatic in Latin. While Helene leaned forward in front of her. She heard her friend's face scrape against the man's. She thought how the dangling palm there above the two embracing humans was like a great green hoof. *I hear an army charging*, she thought. What nonsense comes into one's mind!

Helene stood in the street with her car keys fretting in her glove, looking to right and to left.

'You left it up near Parliament,' Frith offered. 'Didn't you?'

'Of course,' Helene said, 'near that little lane where the press boys play about.' Old darling Bob! she thought.

Frith felt her eyes prickle suddenly with tears. Very aware, even now in the diminishing light and the sated aftermath of food and drink and her friend's expensive brooch not turned merely but *flashing* at her, aware of the lovely drifting of the past through the present's glint and whirl, knowing there was something on the tip of her tongue, in the back of her mind, an image just dissolved: with Helene turning as they walked up the slope to the sticks of traffic lights playing their brightness against the massive building, turning and saying with a smile. 'Do you realise we went a whole meal and never mentioned him?' People were walking between them, separating them, allowing them again to come together.

'Remember this same light that time the same at where was it, do you?'

'Dreamed it,' Helene said.

A man saying 'sorry' as he nudged against them.

'Wit then,' Frith laughing, knowing she was a trifle drunk. 'Would you believe I can't get my mouth round his name?'

'Wittgenstein?' They had talked about him at lunch.

'He sounds like a capital.'

'A brand of cigars.'

'*Prestige ist eine Zigarre namens Wittgenstein.*'

'Stop it!'

Oh their voices high, high and happy, happy and so thin and distant. Voices remotely clapping can one say that? Impacting anyhow softly. Like gloves say meeting hush so softly above there in the greying distance that first far day that afternoon, the praying over, the hands of the women palming like a singer's is it, her hands clasping under the notes, the most silent clapping?

On the pedestrian crossing Frith remembering, 'Was it Wittgenstein said can to dream have a present tense?'

Journey

PATRICIA GRACE

He was an old man going on a journey, but not really so old, only they made him old buttoning up his coat for him and giving him money. Seventy-one that's all. Not a journey, not what you would really call a journey — he had to go in and see those people about his land. Again. But he liked the word Journey even though you didn't quite say it. It wasn't a word for saying only for saving up in your head, and that way you could enjoy it. Even an old man like him, but not what you would call properly old.

The coat was good and warm. It was second-hand from the jumble and it was good and warm. Could have ghosts in it but who cares, warm that's the main thing. If some Pakeha died in it that's too bad because he wasn't scared of the Pakeha kehuas anyway. The pakeha kehuas they couldn't do anything, it was only like having a sheet over your head and going woo-oo at someone in the lavatory . . .

He better go to the lavatory because he didn't trust town lavatories, people spewed there and wrote rude words. Last time he got something stuck on his shoe. Funny people those town people.

Taxi.

It's coming, Uncle.

Taxi, Uncle.

They think he's deaf. And old. Putting more money in his pocket and wishing his coat needed buttoning, telling him it's windy and cold. Never mind, he was off. Off on his journey, he could get round town good on his own, good as gold.

Out early today, old man.

Business, young fulla.

Early bird catches the early worm.

It'll be a sorry worm, young fulla, a sorry worm.

Like that is it?

Like that.

You could sit back and enjoy the old taxi smells of split upholstery and cigarette, and of something else that could have been the young fulla's hair oil or his b.o. It was good. Good. Same old taxi same old stinks. Same old shop over there, but he wouldn't be calling in today, no. And tomorrow they'd want to know why. No, today he was going on a journey, which was a good word. Today he was going further afield, and there was a word no one knew he had. A good wind today but he had a warm coat and didn't need anyone fussing.

Same old butcher and same old fruit shop, doing all right these days not like before. Same old Post Office where you went to get your pension money, but he always sent Minnie down to get his because he couldn't stand these old-age people. These old-age people got on his nerves. Yes, the same old place, same old shops and roads, and everything cracking up a bit. Same old taxi. Same old young fulla.

How's the wife?

Still growling, old man.

What about the kids?

Costing me money.

Send them out to work, that's the story.

I think you're right, you might have something there old man. Well here we are, early. Still another half-hour to wait for the train.

Best to be early. Business.

Guess you're right.

What's the sting?

Ninety-five it is.

Pull out a fistful and give the young fulla full eyes. Get yourself out on to the footpath and shove the door, give it a good hard slam. Pick me up later, young fulla, ten past five. Might as well make a day of it, look round town and buy a few things.

Don't forget, ten past five.

Right you are, old man, five ten.

People had been peeing in the subway, the dirty dogs. In the old days all you needed to do to get on to the station was to step over the train tracks, there weren't any piss holes like this to go through, it wasn't safe. Coming up the steps on to this to go through, it wasn't safe. Coming up the steps on to the platform he could feel the quick huffs of his breathing and that annoyed him, he wanted to swipe at the huffs with his hand. Steam engines went out years ago.

Good sight though, seeing the big engines come bellowing through the cutting and pull in squealing, everything was covered in soot for miles those days.

New man in the ticket office, looked as though he still had his pyjamas on under his outfit. Miserable looking fulla and not at all impressed by the ten-dollar note handed through to him. A man feels like a screwball yelling through that little hole in the glass and then trying to pick up the change that sourpuss has scattered all over the place. Feels like giving sourpuss the fingers, yes. Yes he knows all about those things, he's not deaf and blind yet, not by a long shot.

Ah warmth. A cold wait on the platform but the carriages had the heaters on, they were warm even though they stank. And he had the front half of the first carriage all to himself. Good idea getting away early. And right up front where you could see everything. Good idea coming on his own, he didn't want anyone fussing round looking after his ticket, seeing if he's warm and saying things twice. Doing his talking for him, made him sick. Made him sick them trying to walk slow so they could keep up with him. Yes he could see everything. Not many fishing boats gone out this morning and the sea's turning over rough and heavy — Tamatea that's why. That's something they don't know all these young people, not even those fishermen walking about on their decks over there. Tamatea a Ngana, Tamatea Aio, Tamatea Whakapau — when you get the winds — but who'd believe you these days. They'd rather stare at their weather on television and talk about a this and a that coming over because there's nothing else to believe in.

Now this strip here, it's not really land at all, it's where we used to get our pipis, any time or tide. But they pushed a hill down over it and shot the railway line across to make more room for cars. The train driver knows it's not really land and he is speeding up over this strip. So fast you wait for the nose dive over the edge into the sea, especially when you're up front like this, looking. Well, too bad. Not to worry, he's nearly old anyway and just about done his dash, so why to worry if they nose dive over the edge into the sea. Funny people putting their trains across the sea. Funny people making land and putting pictures and stories about it in the papers as though it's something spectacular, it's a word you can use if you get it just right and he could surprise a few people if he wanted to. Yet other times they go on as though land is just a nothing. Trouble is he let them do his talking for him. If he'd gone in on his own last time and left those fusspots at home he'd have got somewhere. Wouldn't need to be going in there today to tell them all what's what.

Lost the sea now and coming into a cold crowd. This is where you get swamped, but he didn't mind, it was good to see them all get in out of the wind glad to be warm. Some of his whanaungas lived here but he couldn't see any of them today. Good job, too, he didn't want them hanging round wondering where he was off to on his own. Nosing into his business. Some of the old railway houses still there but apart from that everything new, houses, buildings, roads. You'd never know now where the old roads had been, and they'd filled a piece of the harbour up too to make more ground. A short row of sooty houses that got new paint once in a while, a railway shelter and a lunatic asylum and that was all. Only you didn't call it that these days, he'd think of the right words in a minute.

There now, the train was full and he had a couple of kids sitting by him wearing plastic clothes, they were gog-eyed stretching their necks to see. One of them had a snotty nose and a wheeze.

On further it's the same — houses, houses — but people have to have houses. Two or three farms once, on the cold hills, and a rough road going through. By car along the old road you'd always see a pair of them at the end of the drive waving with their hats jammed over their ears. Fat one and a skinny one. Psychiatric hospital, those were the words to use these days, yes, don't sound so bad. People have to have houses and the two or three farmers were dead now probably. Maybe didn't live to see it all. Maybe died rich.

The two kids stood swaying as they entered the first tunnel, their eyes stood out watching for the tunnel's mouth, waiting to pass out through the great mouth of the tunnel. And probably the whole of life was like that, sitting in the dark watching and waiting. Sometimes it happened and you came out into the light, but mostly it only happened in tunnels. Like now.

And between the tunnels they were slicing the hills away with big machines. Great-looking hills too, and not an easy job cutting them away, it took Pakeha determination to do that. Funny people these Pakehas, had to chop up everything. Couldn't talk to a hill or a tree these people, couldn't give the trees or the hills a name and make them special and leave them. Couldn't go round, only through. Couldn't give life, only death. But people had to have houses, and ways of getting from one place to another. And anyway, who was right up there helping the Pakeha to get rid of things — the Maori of course, riding those big machines. Swooping round and back, up and down all over the place. Great tools the Maori man had for his carving these days, tools for his new whakairo, but there you are, a man had to eat. People had to have houses, had to eat, had to get from here to there — anyone knew that. He wishes the two kids would stop crackling, their mothers dressed them in rubbish clothes, that's why they had colds.

Then the rain'll come and the cut will bleed for miles and the valleys will drown in blood, but the Pakeha will find a way of mopping it all up no trouble. Could find a few bones amongst that lot too. That's what you get when you dig up the ground, bones.

Now the next tunnel, dark again. Had to make sure the windows were all shut up in the old days or you got a face full of soot.

And then coming out of the second tunnel that's when you really had to hold your breath, that's when you really had to hand it to the Pakeha, because there was a sight. Buildings miles high, streets and steel and concrete and asphalt settled all round the great-looking curve that was the harbour. Water with ships on it, and roadways threading up and round the hills to layer on layer of houses, even in the highest and steepest places. He was filled with admiration. Filled with Admiration, which was another word he enjoyed even though it wasn't really a word for saying, but yes he was filled right to the top — it made him tired taking it all in. The kids too, they'd stopped crackling and were quite still, their eyes full to exploding.

The snotty one reminded him of George, he had pop eyes and he sat quiet, not talking. The door would open slowly and the eyes would come round and he would say, I ran away again, Uncle. That's all. That's all for a whole week or more until his mother came to get him and take him back. Never spoke, never wanted anything. Today if he had time he would look out for George.

Railway station much the same as ever, same old platforms and not much cleaner than the soot days. Same old stalls and looked like the same people in them. Underground part is new. Same cafeteria, same food most likely, and the spot where they found the murdered man no different from any other spot. Always crowded in the old days especially during the hard times. People came there in the hard times to do their starving. They didn't want to drop dead while they were on their own most probably. Rather all starve together.

Same old statue of Kupe with his woman and his priest, and they've got the name of the canoe spelt wrong, his old eyes aren't as blind as all that. Same old floor made of little coloured pieces and blocked into patterns with metal strips, he used to like it but now he can just walk on it. Big pillars round the doorway holding everything in place, no doubt about it you had to hand it to the Pakeha.

Their family hadn't starved, their old man had seen to that. Their old man had put all the land down in garden, all of it, and in the weekends they took what they didn't use round by horse and cart. Sometimes got paid, sometimes swapped for something, mostly got nothing but why to worry. Yes, great-looking veges they had those days, turnips as big as pumpkins, cabbages you could hardly carry, big tomatoes, lettuces, potatoes, everything. Even now the ground gave you good things. They had to stay home from school for the planting and picking, usually for the weeding and hoeing as well. Never went to school much those days but why to worry.

Early, but he could take his time, knows his way round this place as good as gold. Yes, he's walked all over these places that used to be under the sea and he's ridden all up and down them in trams too. This bit of sea has been land for a long time now. And he's been in all the pubs and been drunk in all of them, he might go to the pub later and spend some of his money. Or he could go to the continuous pictures but he didn't think they had them any more. Still, he might celebrate a little on his own later, he knew his way round this place without anyone interfering. Didn't need anyone doing his talking, and messing things up with all their letters and what not. Pigeons, he didn't like pigeons, they'd learned to behave like people, eat your feet off if you give them half a chance.

And up there past the cenotaph, that's where they'd bulldozed all the bones and put in the new motorway. Resited, he still remembered the newspaper word, all in together. Your leg bone, my arm bone, someone else's bunch of teeth and fingers, someone else's head, funny people. Glad he didn't have any of this whanaungas underground in that place. And they had put all the headstones in a heap somewhere promising to set them up again *tastefully* — he remembered — didn't matter who was underneath. Bet there weren't any Maoris driving those bulldozers. Well, why to worry, it's not his concern, none of his whanaungas up there anyway.

Good those old trams, but he didn't trust these crazy buses, he'd rather walk. Besides, he's nice and early and there's nothing wrong with his legs. Yes, he knows this place like his own big toe, and by Jove he's got a few things to say to those people and he wasn't forgetting. He'd tell them, yes.

The railway station was a place for waiting. People waited there in the old days when times were hard, had a free wash and did their starving there. He waited because it was too early to go home, his right foot was sore. And he could watch out for George, the others had often seen George here waiting about. He and George might go and have a cup of tea and some kai.

He agreed. Of course he agreed. People had to have houses. Not only that, people had to have other things — work, and ways of getting from place to place, and comforts. People needed more now than they did in his young days, he understood completely. Sir. Kept calling him sir, and the way he said it didn't sound so well, but it was difficult to be sure at first. After a while you knew, you couldn't help knowing. He didn't want any kai, he felt sick. His foot hurt.

Station getting crowded and a voice announcing platforms. After all these years he still didn't know where the voice came from but it was the same voice, and anyway the trains could go without him, it was too soon. People.

Queuing for tickets and hurrying towards the platforms, or coming this way and disappearing out through the double doors, or into the subway or the lavatory or the cafeteria. He was too tired to go to the lavatory and anyway he didn't like . . . Some in no hurry at all. Waiting. You'd think it was starvation times. Couldn't see anyone he knew.

I know I know. People have to have houses, I understand and it's what I want.

Well it's not so simple, sir.

It's simple. I can explain. There's only the old place on the land and it needs bringing down now. My brother and sister and I talked about it years back. We wrote letters . . .

Yes yes, but it's not as simple as you think.

But now they're both dead and it's all shared — there are my brother's children, my sister's children, and me. It doesn't matter about me because I'm on the way out, but before I go I want it all done.

As I say, it's no easy matter, all considered.

Subdivision. It's what we want.

There'll be no more subdivision, sir, in the area.

Subdivision. My brother has four sons and two daughters, my sister has five sons. Eleven sections so they can build their houses. I want it all seen to before . . .

You must understand, sir, that it's no easy matter, the area has become what we call a development area, and I've explained all this before, there'll be no more subdivision.

Development means houses, and it means other things too, I understand that. But houses, it's what we have in mind.

And even supposing, sir, that subdivision were possible, which it isn't, I wonder if you fully comprehend what would be involved in such an undertaking.

I fully comprehend . . .

Surveying, kerbing and channelling and formation of adequate access, adequate rights of ways. The initial outlay . . .

I've got money, my brother and sister left it for the purpose. And my own, my niece won't use any of my money, it's all there. We've got the money.

However that's another matter, I was merely pointing out that it's not always all plain sailing.

All we want is to get it divided up so they can have a small piece each to build on . . .

As I say, the area, the whole area, has been set aside for development. All in the future of course but we must look ahead, it is necessary to be far-sighted in these concerns.

Houses, each on a small section of land, it's what my niece was trying to explain . . .

You see there's more to development than housing. We have to plan for roading and commerce, we have to set aside areas for educational and recreational facilities. We've got to think of industry, transportation . . .

But still people need houses. My nieces and nephews have waited for years.

They'd be given equivalent land or monetary compensation of course.

But where was the sense in that, there was no equal land. If it's your stamping ground and you have your ties there, then there's no land equal, surely that wasn't hard to understand. More and more people coming in to wait and the plastic kids had arrived. They pulled away from their mother and went for a small run, crackling. He wished he knew their names and hoped they would come and sit down by him, but no, their mother was striding, turning them towards a platform because they were getting a train home. Nothing to say for a week or more and never wanted anything except sitting squeezed beside him in the armchair after tea until he fell asleep. Carry him to bed, get in beside him later, then one day his mother would come. It was too early for him to go home even though he needed a pee.

There's no sense in it, don't you see? That's their stamping ground and when you've got your ties there's no equal land. It's what my niece and nephew were trying to explain the last time, and in the letters . . .

Well, sir, I shouldn't really do this, but if it will help clarify the position I could show you what has been drawn up. Of course it's all in the future and not really your worry . . .

Yes yes, I'll be dead but that's not . . .

I'll get the plans.

And it's true he'll be dead, it's true he's getting old, but not true if anyone thinks his eyes have had it, because he can see good enough. His eyes are still good enough to look all over the paper and see his land there, and to see that his land has been shaded in and had 'Off

Street Parking' printed on it.

He can see good close up and he can see good far off, and that's George over the other side standing with some mates. He can tell George anywhere no matter what sort of get-up he's wearing. George would turn and see him soon.

But you can't, that's only a piece of paper and it can be changed, you can change it. People have to live and to have things. People need houses and shops but that's only paper, it can be changed.

It's all been very carefully mapped out. By experts. Areas have been selected according to suitability and convenience. And the aesthetic aspects have been carefully considered . . .

Everything grows, turnips the size of pumpkins, cabbages you can hardly carry, potatoes, tomatoes . . . Back here where you've got your houses, it's all rock, land going to waste there . . .

You would all receive equivalent sites . . .

Resited . . .

As I say, on equivalent land . . .

There's no land equal . . .

Listen, sir, it's difficult but we've got to have some understanding of things. Don't we?

Yes yes, I want you to understand, that's why I came. This here, it's only paper and you can change it. There's room for all the things you've got on your paper, and room for what we want too, we want only what we've got already, it's what we've been trying to say.

Sir, we can't always have exactly what we want . . .

All around here where you've marked residential it's all rock, what's wrong with that for shops and cars. And there'll be people and houses. Some of the people can be us, and some of the houses can be ours.

Sure, sure. But not exactly where you want them. And anyway, sir, there's no advantage do you think in you people all living in the same area?

It's what we want, we want nothing more than what is ours already.

It does things to your land value.

He was an old man but he wanted very much to lean over the desk and swing a heavy punch.

No sense being scattered everywhere when what we want . . .

It immediately brings down the value of your land . . .

. . . is to stay put on what is left of what has been ours since before we were born. Have a small piece each, a small garden, my brother and sister and I discussed it years ago.

Straight away the value of your land goes down.

Wanted to swing a heavy punch but he's too old for it. He kicked the desk instead. Hard. And the veneer cracked and splintered. Funny how quiet it had become.

You ought to be run in, old man, do you hear.

Cripes, look what the old blighter's gone and done. Look at Paul's desk.

He must be whacky.

He can't do that, Paul, get the boss along to sort him out.

Get him run in.

Get out, old man, do you hear.

Yes he could hear, he wasn't deaf, not by a long shot. A bit of trouble getting his foot back out of the hole, but there, he was going, and not limping either, he'd see about this lot later. Going, not limping and not going to die either. It looked as though their six eyes might fall out and roll on the floor.

There's no sense, no sense in anything, but what use telling that to George when George already knew, sitting beside him wordless. What use telling George you go empty handed and leave nothing behind, when George had always been empty handed, had never wanted anything except to have nothing.

How are you, son?

All right, Uncle. Nothing else to say. Only sitting until it was late enough to go.

Going, not limping, and not going to die either.

There you are, old man, get your feet in under that heater. Got her all warmed up for you.

Yes, young fulla, that's the story.

The weather's not so good.

Not the best.

How was your day, all told?

All right.

It's all those hard footpaths, and all the walking that gives people sore feet, that's what makes your legs tired.

There's a lot of walking about in that place.

You didn't use the buses?

Never use the buses.

But you got your business done?

All done. Nothing left to do.

That's good then, isn't it?

How's your day been, young fulla?

A proper circus.

Must be this weather.

It's the weather, always the same in this weather.

This is your last trip for the day, is it?

A couple of trains to meet after tea and then I finish.

Home to have a look at the telly.

For a while, but there's an early job in the morning . . .

Drop me off at the bottom, young fulla. I'm in no hurry. Get off home to your wife and kids.

No, no, there's a bad wind out there, we'll get you to your door. Right to your door, you've done your walking for the day. Besides I always enjoy the sight of your garden, you must have green fingers, old man.

It keeps me bent over but it gives us plenty. When you come for Minnie on Tuesday I'll have a couple of cabbages and a few swedes for you.

Great, really great, I'm no gardener myself.

Almost too dark to see.

Never mind. I had a good look this morning, you've got it all laid out neat as a pin. Neat as a pin, old man.

And here we are.

One step away from your front door.

You can get off home for tea.

You're all right, old man?

Right as rain, young fulla, couldn't be better.

I'll get along then.

Tuesday.

Now he could get in and close the door behind him and walk

without limping to the lavatory because he badly needs a pee. And when he came out of the bathroom they were watching him, they were stoking up the fire and putting things on the table. They were looking at his face.

Seated at the table they were trying not to look at his face, they were trying to talk about unimportant things, there was a bad wind today and it's going to be a rough night.

Tamatea Whakapau.

It must have been cold in town.

Heaters were on in the train.

And the train, was it on time?

Right on the minute.

What about the one coming home?

Had to wait a while for the one coming home.

At the railway station, you waited at the railway station?

And I saw George.

George, how's George?

George is all right, he's just the same.

Maisie said he's joined up with a gang and he doesn't wash. She said he's got a big war sign on his jacket and won't go to work.

They get themselves into trouble, she said, and they all go round dirty.

George is no different, he's just the same.

They were quiet then, wondering if he would say anything else, then after a while they knew he wouldn't.

But later that evening as though to put an end to some silent discussion that they may have been having he told them it wasn't safe and they weren't to put him in the ground. When I go you're not to put me in the ground, do you hear. He was an old man and his foot was giving him hell, and he was shouting at them while they sat hurting. Burn me up, I tell you, it's not safe in the ground, you'll know all about it if you put me in the ground. Do you hear?

Some other time, we'll talk about it.

Some other time is now and it's all said. When I go, burn me up, no one's going to mess with me when I'm gone.

He turned into his bedroom and shut the door. He sat on the edge of his bed for a long time looking at the palms of his hands.

The Lamp

PATRICIA GRACE

There was a red lamp in church with a lit wick floating in oil that showed that God was home. God was everywhere but especially in church were the lamp burned. The lamp sat in a shiny gold basket that hung from a beam by three golden chains.

The playground was empty and the other kids had gone by the time Jeanie and Mereana had finished sweeping the classroom floor for Sister. Sister told them to go straight home, but they thought they would make their visit first, as they did on most afternoons after school.

Sister had instructed all the children that they should visit God in the church so that they would become holy. Visits got their sins forgiven — and all the marks and stains they had on their souls from fighting, forgetting, spitting, swearing, lying, being lazy, talking, laughing, playing with privates, bad manners, bad spelling and having bad companions could be cleaned off if you visited enough, and if you confessed. Your soul was a glowing white ball made of light that was inside your body seated at the base of your stomach. You had to keep it clean.

As well as visits you could store up prayers, genuflections, masses, offerings, blessings, communions, good thoughts and good deeds. If you had collected enough by the time you died you could get a good place in heaven, like a block of sky saved for you, and also it lessened the time that you needed to spend in purgatory getting your sins burned away.

The two girls crossed the playground, went up the church steps and into the porch. It was a little square porch and a good place to play Witchy in the Corner if there were enough of you, and if there was time.

But there were other things to do. They went first of all to shake the poorbox to see if it rattled. It did. There was something inside but it wasn't money. Jeanie slotted in a milk top she had saved, and Mereana found a leaf to put in. Then they went to finger the little books that told about sin and prayer, sacraments, saints, the rosary, families, the Trinity, the missions, commandments, catechism and the Far East. The books were full of big words and the girls tried to read some of them. Some of the books had pictures of holy people with sad faces and eyes looking up to heaven.

After that Mereana tried on a lady's coat that had been left hanging on a hook, but she looked silly. Jeanie tried it on and she looked silly too. It made them laugh.

Well it was all right to laugh in the porch as long as there were no telltales watching, but you didn't laugh in the church. They stretched and twisted their faces to stop themselves from laughing because it was time they went in. They clapped their hands over their mouths and turned their backs on each other, but that didn't work. Laughing wasn't much to do with faces and mouths, or backs. It came from inside somewhere. It came from way down in your stomach, filled up your chest, then exploded out of your face.

And it made you cry. They went over to the books again and found sad pictures of the saints and martyrs to look at, but that didn't help either. It seemed to make them laugh and cry all the more, which was something they would have to be sorry about later and confess. They went out of the porch and leaned over the stair-rail laughing and laughing until the laughter was all gone. Then they went back into the porch with their lips pressed together, and stood in the doorway that led into the church.

They peered into the gloom of the church looking out for Mr Ticklekiss with his mops and brooms. If there were other girls around, like at lunchtimes when there were lots of them, and when there was noise and shouting outside, it was quite funny when Mr Ticklekiss came sneaking up to tickle and kiss them. They'd get up and run along the kneelers and dive under the pews. Their lips would come unstuck and they'd giggle and squeal with Mr Ticklekiss coming after them. Then suddenly Mr Ticklekiss would open a door and disappear. They'd go out later and they'd see him clearing the gutters or weeding the paths. He wouldn't look at them or speak.

But sometimes, like now, with no noise and no people, it was scary, because Mr Ticklekiss was like his mops and brooms. He had no footsteps, and he came out of the church walls or from out of the posts of the church with no noise. He was tall and spooky, and his long, pale hands flapped at the ends of his sleeves as though they had been just sewn there, the way that dolls' hands sometimes were.

Mereana and Jeanie looked into all the corners of the church. They looked at all the posts and hiding places of the church and along all the pews. There was no one — not even Bird Lady, who came every morning and afternoon on her bike with her shawl fluttering and flapping behind her. In church she would kneel in the front pew, as still as one of the statues, with her shawl pulled closely about her.

There was just the quiet, dark church with the statues looking down, and the Stations of the Cross, which were nothing but square shadows high on the walls. There was the terrible gaping loft where the choir sang for high mass on Sundays, and there was the little red glow that was the lamp, which showed that God was home.

The girls reached for the holy water, signed themselves with it and went in. They kept their lips jammed together so that no sound would escape.

They genuflected and went up to kiss the big toe of the crucified Jesus, the toe worn and shiny from being kissed thousands of times. The crucified Jesus had big square-headed nails in his hands and feet, in nail holes surrounded by pink blood. There was more pink blood on his forehead beneath the crown of thorns, and pink drops coming from the spear hole in his side. Mereana and Jeanie really felt sorry for Jesus. He gave every drop of his blood to make them good but they were bad all the same. They looked at each other with sad faces, making sure they kept their mouths shut tight.

Then they knelt to pray the 'Our Father', 'Hail Mary' and 'Glory Be'. They said acts of contrition and kept kneeling even though their knees hurt. Now that their eyes had adjusted to the light they could see the wall pictures which made up the Stations of the Cross. It really wasn't fair about poor Jesus in the garden sweating out his pink blood, then being sold, and whipped and laughed at, and having all his clothes torn away. After that he was made to carry the big cross all the way to Calvary.

But if they prayed hard enough, and did good deeds, then Jesus might think it was worth it. It was like helping him. If they could be really good then they were being like the man Simon, who helped Jesus when he fell. Or they were like Veronica, who went up to Jesus and wiped his face with a towel. Then Jesus put his face on the towel like a photo. If they prayed hard, and were good, and had sore knees, and if they kept their lips shut tight and pressed the palms of their hands together, then Jesus might be able to look down and see it was worth it as he sat up there in his chair beside his father with a new crown on his head. He might smile.

Just then, while they were kneeling and praying, one of the Sisters came in carrying an unlit candle and a window pole. She put the candle down, reached up and hooked the window pole into the ring underneath the basket and pulled the lamp down.

The girls watched as she took out the red glass bowl with the light in it, then put it down on the communion rail where she would put in more of the oil and change the wick. But before she blew the flame out she lit the candle, so that while the lamp was out there was the flame of the candle to show that God was everpresent in the church. It was called perpetual light.

Then when Sister had relit the lamp she picked up the gold basket and the candle and went out. The girls knew that she would be out in the sacristy cleaning the gold basket with Brasso, rubbing to make it shine.

But just now, there was the little glowing lamp sitting on the communion rail, right down low where they could see.

They nodded to each other and stood, moving quietly along the kneeler, out of the pew and up to the rail. They stared and stared at the little flame that showed God's everpresence. They squatted, and peered up through the red glass at the dancing flame. It was difficult to keep their lips tight together.

They stood up again and Jeanie leaned over and blew, very gently, on the flame. It danced and shimmered. Mereana blew too, softly, and the wick began to sail gently in the oil, carrying its little fire.

Jeanie and Mereana looked at each other for a moment, then they both leaned over the little lamp and blew hard, together. And suddenly the flame was gone.

Gone. They grabbed hold of each other and shut their eyes, waiting for the high roof to crack and fall, waiting for the walls to come smacking down. They held on to each other, waiting, listening. God was gone, and now the Devil could come leaping down out of the choir loft and throw them in fires. They clung together for a long time in the silence, then after a while they opened their eyes. Then they ran.

They ran clattering down the aisle, through the porch, down the steps and across the playground. And Mereana, who thought she might get left behind, grabbed the back of Jeanie's tunic and yelled 'Wait!'

They ran out of the gate and down the street, with Mereana yelling 'Wait!' and Jeanie yelling 'Let go, let go!'

At the crossing they stopped, breathing hard, and they stared into each other's wide-open, round eyes. Then they ran again, across the road and along the footpath, dodging in and out amongst the shoppers until they came to the street where they both lived. They stopped there and leaned against a fence, picking grass which they held against their sides to take away stitch.

'We both did it,' Jeanie said, just to make sure.

'Yes.'

Then they sat without speaking, knowing that their souls had shrivelled inside their bodies, that they'd killed God and let the Devil loose to come grabbing them by the ankles and tossing them into everlasting fire.

They waited. After a long time they knew it was late. Lights were going on in houses.

It was *really* late and they were both going to get hidings, good hidings. For a while they talked about the hidings they were going to get. They didn't care because they deserved it. They wouldn't cry. Tomorrow, in the morning, they'd tell each other how many hits. They'd tell if they cried or didn't.

They began to run along the street that they both lived in, pushing open their gates, running along their paths.

'Count.'

'Don't forget to count.'
'And we'll tell each other.'
'In the morning.'
'We'll tell.'
'Tell.'
'Don't forget.'
'In the morning.'
'Tomorrow in the morning.'

It Used to be Green Once

PATRICIA GRACE

We were all ashamed of our mother. Our mother always did things to shame us. Like putting red darns in our clothes, and cutting up old swimming togs and making two — girl's togs from the top half for my sister, and boy's togs from the bottom half for my brother. Peti and Raana both cried when Mum made them take the togs to school. Peti sat down on the road by our gate and yelled out she wasn't going to school. She wasn't going swimming. I didn't blame my sister because the togs were thirty-eight chest and Peti was only ten.

But Mum knew how to get her up off the road. She yelled loudly, 'Get up off that road, my girl. There's nothing wrong with those togs. I didn't have any togs when I was a kid and I had to swim in my nothings. Get up off your backside and get to school.' Mum's got a loud voice and she knew how to shame us. We all dragged Peti up off the road before our mates came along and heard Mum. We pushed Peti into the school bus so Mum wouldn't come yelling up the drive.

We never minded our holey fruit at first. Dad used to pick up the cases of over-ripe apples or pears from town that he got cheap. Mum would dig out the rotten bits, and then give them to us to take for play-lunch. We didn't notice much at first, not until Reweti from down the road yelled out to us one morning, 'Hey you fullas, who shot your pears?' We didn't have anywhere to hide our lunch because we weren't allowed school bags until we got to high school. Mum said she wasn't buying fourteen school bags. When we went to high school we could have shoes too. The whole lot of us gave Reweti a good hiding after school.

However, this story is mainly about the car, and about Mum and how she shamed us all the time. The shame of rainbow darns and

211

cut-up togs and holey fruit was nothing to what we suffered because of the car. Uncle Raz gave us the car because he couldn't fix it up any more, and he'd been fined because he lived in Auckland. He gave the car to Dad so we could drive our cream cans up to the road instead of pushing them up by wheelbarrow.

It didn't matter about the car not having brakes because the drive from our cowshed goes down in a dip then up to the gate. Put the car in its first gear, run it down from the shed, pick up a bit of speed, up the other side, turn it round by the cream stand so that it's pointing down the drive again, foot off the accelerator and slam on the hand-brake. Dad pegged a board there to make sure it stopped. Then when we'd lifted the cans out on to the stand he'd back up a little and slide off down the drive — with all of us throwing ourselves in over the sides as if it were a dinghy that had just been pushed out into the sea.

The car had been red once because you could still see some patches of red paint here and there. And it used to have a top too, that you could put down or up. Our uncle told us that when he gave it to Dad. We were all proud about the car having had a top once. Some of the younger kids skited to their mates about our convertible and its top that went up and down. But that was before our mother started shaming us by driving the car to the shop.

We growled at Mum and we cried but it made no difference. 'You kids always howl when I tell you to get our shopping,' she said.

'We'll get it, Mum. We won't cry.'

'We won't cry, Mum. We'll carry the sack of potatoes.'

'And the flour.'

'And the bag of sugar.'

'And the rolled oats.'

'And the tin of treacle.'

'We'll do the shopping, Mum.'

But Mum would say, 'Never mind, I'll do it myself.' And after that she wouldn't listen any more.

How we hated Wednesdays. We always tried to be sick on Wednesdays, or to miss the bus. But Mum would be up early yelling at us to get out of bed. If we didn't get up when we were told she'd drag us out and pull down our pyjama pants and set our bums on the cold lino. Mum was cruel to us.

Whoever was helping with the milking had to be back quickly from the shed for breakfast, and we'd all have to rush through our kai and get to school. Wednesday was Mum's day for shopping.

As soon as she had everything tidy she'd change into her good purple dress that she'd made from a Japanese bedspread, pull on her floppy-brimmed blue sunhat and her slippers and galoshes, and go out and start up the car.

We tried everything to stop her shaming us all.

'You've got no licence, Mum.'

'What do I want a licence for? I can drive, can't I? I don't need the proof.'

'You got no warrant.'

'Warrant? What's a warrant?'

'The traffic man'll get you, Mum.'

'That rat. He won't come near me after what he did to my niece. I'll hit him right over his smart head with a bag of riwais and I'll hit him somewhere else as well.' We could never win an argument with Mum.

Off she'd go on a Wednesday morning, and once out on the road she'd start tooting the horn. This didn't sound like a horn at all but more like a flock of ducks coming in for a feed. The reason for the horn was to let all her mates and relations along the way know she was coming. And as she passed each one's house, if they wanted anything they'd have to run out and call it out loud. Mum couldn't stop because of not having any brakes. 'E Kiri,' each would call. 'Mauria mai he riwai,' if they wanted spuds; 'Mauria mai he paraoa,' if they wanted bread. 'Mauria mai he tarau, penei te kaita,' hand spread to show the size of the pants they wanted Mum to get. She would call out to each one and wave to them to show she'd understood. And when she neared the store she'd switch the motor off, run into the kerbing and pull on the handbrake. I don't know how she remembered all the things she had to buy — I only know that by the time she'd finished, every space in that car was filled and it was a squeeze for her to get into the driver's seat. But she had everything there, all ready to throw out on the way back.

As soon as she'd left the store she'd begin hooting again, to let the whole district know she was on her way. Everybody would be out on the road to get their shopping thrown at them, or just to watch our mother go chuffing past. We always hid if we heard her coming.

The first time Mum's car and the school bus met was when they were both approaching a one-way bridge from opposite directions. We had to ask the driver to stop and give way to Mum because she had no brakes. We were all ashamed. But everyone soon got to know Mum and her car and they always stopped whenever they saw her coming. And you know, Mum never ever had an accident in her car, except for once when she threw a side of mutton out to Uncle Peta and it knocked him over and broke his leg.

After a while we started walking home from school on Wednesdays to give Mum a good chance of getting home before us, and so we wouldn't be in the bus when it had to stop and let her past. The boys didn't like having to walk home but we girls didn't mind because Mr Hadley walked home too. He was a new teacher at our school and he stayed not far from where we lived. We girls thought he was really neat.

But one day, it had to happen. When I heard the honking and tooting behind me I wished that a hole would appear in the ground and that I would fall in it and disappear for ever. As Mum came near she started smiling and waving and yelling her head off. 'Anyone wants a ride,' she yelled, 'they'll have to run and jump in.'

We all turned our heads the other way and hoped Mr Hadley wouldn't notice the car with our mother in it, and her yelling and tooting, and the brim of her hat jumping up and down. But instead, Mr Hadley took off after the car and leapt in over the back seat on top of the shopping. Oh the shame.

But then one day something happened that changed everything. We arrived home to find Dad in his best clothes, walking round and grinning, and not doing anything like getting the cows in, or mending a gate, or digging a drain. We said, 'What are you laughing at, Dad?' 'What are you dressed up for? Hey Mum, what's the matter with Dad?'

'Your dad's a rich man,' she said. 'Your dad, he's just won fifty thousand dollars in a lottery.'

At first we couldn't believe it. We couldn't believe it. Then we all began running round and laughing and yelling and hugging Mum and Dad. 'We can have shoes and bags,' we said. 'New clothes and swimming togs, and proper apples and pears.' Then do you know what

Dad said? Dad said, 'Mum can have a new car.' This really astounded and amazed us. We went numb with excitement for five minutes then began hooting and shouting again, and knocking Mum over.

'A new car!'

'A new car?'

'Get us a Packard, Mum.'

'Or a De Soto. Yes, yes.'

Get this, get that . . .

Well, Mum bought a big shiny green Chevrolet, and Dad got a new cowshed with everything modernised and water gushing everywhere. We all got our new clothes — shoes, bags, togs — and we even started taking posh lunches to school. Sandwiches cut in triangles, bottles of cordial, crisp apples and pears, and yellow bananas.

And somehow all of us kids changed. We started acting like we were somebody instead of ordinary like before. We used to whine to Dad for money to spend and he'd always give it to us. Every week we'd nag Mum into taking us to the pictures, or if she was tired we'd go ourselves by taxi. We got flash bedspreads and a piano and we really thought we were neat.

As for the old car — we made Dad take it to the dump. We never wanted to see it again. We all cheered when he took it away, except for Mum. Mum stayed inside where she couldn't watch, but we all stood outside and cheered.

We all changed, as though we were really somebody, but there was one thing I noticed. Mum didn't change at all, and neither did Dad. Mum had a new car all right, and a couple of new dresses, and a new pair of galoshes to put over her slippers. And Dad had a new modern milking shed and a tractor and some other gadgets for the farm. But Mum and Dad didn't change. They were the same as always.

Mum still went shopping every Wednesday. But instead of having to do all the shopping herself she was able to take all her friends and relations with her. She had to start out earlier so she'd have time to pick everyone up on the way. How angry we used to be when Mum went past with her same old sunhat and her heap of friends and relations, and them all waving and calling out to us.

Mum sometimes forgot that the new car had brakes, especially when she was approaching the old bridge and we were coming the opposite way in the school bus. She would start tooting and the bus would have to pull over and let her through. That's when all our aunties and uncles and friends would start waving and calling out. But some of them couldn't wave because they were too squashed by people and shopping, they'd just yell. How shaming.

There were always ropes everywhere over Mum's new car holding bags of things and shovel handles to the roof and sides. The boot was always hanging open because it was too full to close — things used to drop out on to the road all the time. And the new car — it used to be green once, because if you look closely you can still see some patches of green paint here and there.

Dry Rot

FIONA KIDMAN

'We'll be at the motel soon,' said Edward Turner.

'Yes,' agreed his wife.

'Will you be glad?'

'I expect so. I'm getting tired,' she replied. Though, as always, she didn't look it.

They had floated into the town on a cushion of neon light. The signs along the double-laned street were just beginning their sparkling rages, as evening approached. Even so, it seemed early for them to come on, the summer light still being clear. But Rotorua was like that, so they'd heard. Edward remembered reading what a specially imported man of letters, dropping in on New Zealand to revitalise the country's groaning cultural image, had written about the town, upon safe return to his own native shores. What had he said of it? 'The sulphurous New Zealand Las Vegas, a shrieking nightmare of one-night-stand motels — yet the locals had been thoroughly contaminated by the insouciance of the itinerant population and surely it was the country's fun capital.' Funny how things stuck in one's mind. And presumably the lights must appear early so that no one trundling up the boulevard could misunderstand that the purpose of this place was fun.

Edward looked at Margaret sitting beside him, arching her throat as her head swivelled from side to side taking in the new hotels, the built-up area where once there had been an airport, clear spaces where there used to be trees. Her eyes had a strange set to them somewhere between memory and anticipation. A look he had seen on her face before, and one that somehow always surprised him. Sometimes it had been in their bed. Once it had been when their last child was conceived.

217

They already had two and he had thought it enough. She had turned to him, the look on her face muted into intangibles under the reading light, and told him that she wanted the child, it was the right time, would he give her the child that night. He'd said, and he remembered that quite clearly too, 'Are you sure we can afford it?' even though he knew more about their finances than she did. He'd said it because really he was too tired to perform well, and the thought of conceiving a child just like that, there and then to order, seemed to demand a special effort, which had made desire as elusive as God, whom he had fallen out with long ago. And because the look had started to fade and he believed he loved her, he'd said yes, and had ordered for himself an erection, in order that she have her delight and her child, with the spontaneity she had willed for herself.

Not that he expected it. It can't happen, he had thought. I am not creating life. Life is energy and I am tired. But she was right, holding her belly close and snug afterwards, knowing and smiling that night — and angry with herself weeks later on account of her foolish and regrettable inclinations.

Now she was thirty-nine, and the child was ten.

Other times, he had seen her face, which was evenly proportioned, not beautiful, but so regular that it had a quality of impeccability which intrigued men, yet earned their respect, and was admired by women; and it would be set the same. He would wonder what was to come and it would turn out that she had a special curry on, or successfully imitated a restaurant meal; or then again, it was a new cosmetic.

Memory and anticipation. Why remember? he would think. The past, their past didn't add up to a great deal, if you stopped and counted. And yet in retrospect it was always worth indulging. Strange. Possibly more comfortable to consider because it was over, than was the future with which one was still required to contend.

So here she was with her face in that strange set again, only this time he had been expecting it, because she had willed this journey, and so help them both, enough had gone between them these past few months for him to hope that her will would carry them through. For even the comfort of the past had gone.

Their car was wide and luxurious. She had sat all afternoon on the journey from Wellington with her easy posture, fitting neatly behind her seat belt, hands clasped lightly in her lap, and they had discussed nothing but the cancellation of the milk and papers, and the passing countryside — the extraordinary growth of Turangi, the beautiful houses in Taupo, the speed at which one could travel from Wairakei to Rotorua.

Edward reached over and picked up Margaret's hand. 'It's changed,' he said.

Of course it's changed. It was 1954. The smell was the same, but it's twenty years ago. Twenty years since we came on the bus, you still in the dark suit with the gangster-type lapels, and still self-consciously but proudly wearing the confetti in your trouser cuffs. And me, with dress at mid-calf and hat brim over my eye. We looked different. It was a dingy little town, even though it was high summer and the carnival was on at the lake-front. Why shouldn't it have changed its clothes too? Of course you would say 'It's changed.' Poor Edward. What can you say? What do I leave you to say? I'm remembering though, and you know it. And I'm excited too, which you also know, because you've known me so long, blast you. So it's crazy to come here and try and talk ourselves back to the beginning of things. It's so crazy it's worth a try though. Edward, don't you see that? Try and see it. No, that's not fair on you Edward. I know you're trying, or we wouldn't be here. My thought mike. That's what it is. I guess it would worry you to know I had a thought mike. If you knew what that was. Sandra explained it to me. It's what actors go on to when they're doing radio plays, and it's supposed to be old hat for people to talk to themselves — they're not supposed to do it in real life, and seeing there's no way of conveying the insides of their minds which explains their motivations, they go on to a thought mike, and then the insides of their brains are exposed. An interesting idea. Anatomically, the enlarged and greatly modified part of the nervous system contained in the cranium of vertebrates. What shit I talk to myself. But out loud? It's only with you Edward, that thought is impossible to convey. You, a living breathing, hearing receptacle for words; that's when I switch on the thought mike.

'Yes,' said Margaret. 'The place has changed.'

Then the town itself burgeoned around them, glisteningly new. He sensed that she was disappointed in spite of herself, in spite of the fact that she was probably talking herself into believing that the place should have changed.

'Oh Edward, there's the old Grand Hotel, do stop,' Margaret cried. As he slowed down, she said with obvious pleasure, 'At least that hasn't changed.'

'And there's the lake ahead. It looks the same under the pollution.'

'That's not fair Edward. You could make a sunset sound like a treatise on the environment.'

'You can't escape it, can you?'

'That's pragmatic.'

'Not as much as you think. Seen enough? We can go in tomorrow.'

'Perhaps we should have stayed here after all.'

'I thought we agreed that wasn't sensible,' said Edward.

He knew he was right too, not that this was quite the time to make something of it. The time of crisis was upon them and they had come to it, hating it and frightened, shying away, for a long time trying to deny that it had come. But when it had, and there seemed no way back, she — who had seemed finally to accept it more than he did, was more compliant about the details, concerned more for him it seemed than herself who in some obscure way she believed would 'manage all right' — had suddenly suggested that they should take this trip back to Rotorua where they had spent their honeymoon, in the summer twenty years before.

Perhaps they could start again, recall the beginnings, revive the promises. Others had, why not them? That's what she had said to him on Christmas night, while the children were doing the dishes. They were at home. Anna, the honeymoon baby who had just finished her first year at teachers' college; Mike with still a couple of years to go at school, who was spending his Christmas on a farm, and of course Jenny the child. Even though normally they were all still living at home it had been different that night, because they didn't often take it for granted these days that home together was the best place to be, usually they bickered or wanted to be in different places. Even a room could be — well, polluted to use his word, if one walked through it at a time when it displeased another member of the family.

But Christmas, ah! That was different, and he had known wryly that, for him, sentimentality about the festival was definitely part of the ageing process. He had flicked on the television to watch the Queen, waiting for the familiar words about 'my family' and 'the great family of the Commonwealth' and whether she'd said them this year or not he couldn't remember, because tears had stupidly prickled behind his eyelids, and yet he didn't even stand up for the Queen at the pictures any more.

Margaret had asked him to delay separation proceedings till after the school holidays, because of Jenny, and he'd agreed, for they intended to be so sensible about it, and had gone out of their way to avoid letting the children know what was happening, keeping their quarrels till midnight when everyone was asleep, meeting for lunch like strangers, courteously and moderately-voiced in coffee bars or discreet pubs, to discuss their differences. With the result that Jenny was as irritable as if they had been throwing the breakfast dishes at each other. They couldn't see why, but they agreed that she must be very affected, so it must be got through as decently and efficiently as possible, but no traumatic school holidays thank you; no summer that would stand out for her as the year of the terrible time, the bad time, when dad went away. It would just be like a bad patch at school, indistinguishable from other bad patches.

Yet, having decided all this, still Margaret had turned to him, in the quiet light of their sitting-room, relaxing in the beautiful furniture which he had designed specially and uniquely for them in his furniture factory, and suggested this trip.

'Don't get carried away by my Christmas spirit,' he had said sharply. 'I've had too much booze.'

'It's not that,' Margaret had said, 'I wasn't going to ask you tonight but it seemed to make sense to say it now. We could go up to Rotorua by ourselves. Anna can look after Jenny. If there were just the two of us we might be able to see things more clearly — say things when we feel like it instead of waiting till the coast is clear. You know what I mean?'

He knew. 'It makes sense,' he had said, rolling the idea around experimentally with the words. It did, too, because there were so few positive reasons for them not living together. Like lots of couples they knew. Nothing you could stand off and blame each other for. A kind of gathering incompatibility, the sour, sad leftovers of fun that once was. The drift. Continental drift certainly. Great land masses inexplicably moving in impassable seas. Like his furniture, which was beautiful and relaxed. Everything so relevant, full of measurement and exactitude, and yet emotion. That was at the heart of things of course. You couldn't translate positives like timber and cloth into beauty without emotions, and Margaret never saw that. She was so much emotion, so that she saw herself as all the feelings and tenderness and excesses, extracting the pearl from the oyster. If she could understand the pain that went into the pearl. Well — he felt misunderstood it was true, but of course in their decent fashion he wasn't blaming her, because he didn't understand either. They'd tried to talk about it, face it, but in the end it was an accumulation of mistakes stemming from the same sense of difference.

So pointless the difference, that she was right — it was worth trying for; her idea of a trip made sense.

'Do you think Rotorua would be the best place?' he'd asked her on Christmas night. 'It won't be the same you know.'

'No, I know,' she'd agreed. 'But we can identify at least, and we needn't expect it to be exactly the same.'

'If it doesn't work mightn't you be more disappointed than in another place?'

'Oh forget it,' she'd snapped then, testing his defeat.

'No, I won't,' he told her, short with determination, now that she had challenged him.

'Will we stay at the Grand?'

'Oh no, a motel.'

'That's great. Meals — '

'Don't be silly. You can eat out whenever and wherever you like, you know that.'

'Then why not the Grand?'

'Identify, you said. Okay let's. But, for Christ's sake, don't let's wallow in it. Would you like the same room, the same bed, the same sheets with the same virginal blood sloshed around?'

Her nose had flared white round the nostrils. 'You have had too much to drink. And keep your voice down. The children — '

'Yes. The children.' He remembered how angry he'd been with the children when she said that. Quite unreasonably. Or was it?

'I don't suppose you remember them banging on the wall in the Grand that night. We finished up making love at midday so they wouldn't hear next door.'

She laughed at that. 'We were going to call Anna Siesta, weren't we?'

They had locked fingers with some mutual comfort.

'I swear our kids take watches round the clock nowadays. There's always one of them up.'

'Yes, I know.'

'I'd like us to be on our own.' Meaning that he'd like to know her sexually, in total privacy and without haste, as they hadn't experienced it in years.

'In a motel. Like adulterers.'

'If you like. Actually peace and quiet was what I'd had in mind, but if the other idea appeals, use it. We might have to get used to it yet.'

'Adultery? You mean you'd — '

'Spread it around when we split up? I'm not planning to take vows, are you?'

And that night, too, she'd turned the strange look on him.

Oh Margaret, Margaret, what are we doing, alone in a foreign country, speaking different tongues, and yet having no one else except each other for support? Margaret, smooth and brown, mahogany hair, skin palest teak, changing reflecting polished eyes. Margaret, you are like the good things I like to shape and hew, mould and glorify, but I would never use you. Not meaning to.

So they had come here. Maybe to please him which was good. She wanted him to know that she had tried. He must believe for her sake that she was trying.

They turned the corner further down the road to where the motel stood facing the lake and the carnival.

Clowns and carnivals, ferris wheels and octopuses. So like us, so like us. Edward. Funny faces over sad hearts, sideshows and the world turning over beneath us, flailing arms on immovable objects. If I were to reach out and touch you now that's how it would feel. Our bodies unmoving, with limbs reaching and circling and maybe connecting, with reaction as temporarily uplifting as the flying tentacles of the mechanical octopus. The sinking.

What did we do at the carnival? I forget. Except that we took pictures of ourselves in a do-it-yourself photograph box and kept them. I have them still. I have held them, full of hope like the people who took them, finding it harder to recognise those kids of the fifties. People of our time. We are travelling back to find them. Maybe, if we take care, and look here and there at the waterfront, and through the carnival, if we walk the frenzied summer street, if we linger by the sulphur cauldrons, we will come upon them unawares; long-lost friends whose photos we have kept these twenty years past. What a reunion we will have.

'The carnival's as noisy as ever,' remarked Edward. 'I hope it doesn't keep us awake tonight.'

'Did you bring your pills?' Margaret asked.

'Of course. What about yours?'

'I think — damn, I can't remember. I hope I put them in.'

'So do I,' said Edward irritably. 'For God's sake, we'll never get a doctor here to prescribe for something like that.'

'I can take some of yours.'

'You know they don't agree with you. Well, are we going to get out?'

They entered the motel. Edward booked them in, and they went to their unit. It was hygienic and stainless steel, simon-pure and white, very white indeed, the concrete blocks painted like a detergent advertisement. But cool. Margaret ran her fingers along the channels between the blocks and suddenly laid her forehead against them, as Edward put the cases down. He watched her in silence, as she absorbed the coolness through her skin. She looked up and smiled at him, as if the sensation had soaked right through her brain, distilling the heat, whatever feverishness ran through her mind.

'It's quite nice isn't it?'

'Comfortable.'

She noticed his eyes flicking over the chrome-framed furniture.

'Not your thing — ours,' she corrected herself, because it was nonsense to deny that their taste in appearances agreed.

'Just as well maybe — impersonal.'

'Yes. Very good for finding strangers.'

'What?'

'Nothing! — What about dinner?'

'There's a restaurant along the street. Quite good, the chap in the office said.'

'Oh marvellous. I'll just freshen up and we'll go. I'm hungry, aren't you?'

'Yes. Yes I am.'

They were beautifully polite. All so smooth, thought Edward and wondered if the smoothness was the habit, the barrier they had each built around themselves. The courtesy, the excessive care not to quarrel in front of the children, the civil agreement that they could be good friends providing they lived apart, considering their common taste, and muted sympathy which never verged on preoccupation with each other's interests.

As they walked along the street to the restaurant, he looked across the lake. The evening had fallen quickly towards real darkness and the contours of the lake and hill were barely discernible. On Mokoia Island, in the centre of the lake, lights had been lit so that the bulk of land was suspended above the plate-glass stretch of water, lying so still it would surely break if the wind moved. Like them, he thought, dwelling on their relationship. It was like them, yet individually each would see it differently. The compass had many points of anger and dislike. He would view that lake with a distasteful eye on its pollution, knowing that beneath the glass surface lay poison.

While she would look at the glass and think of a clear window through which one might accidentally walk and come out on the other side, bleeding and scarred.

Either way, one was damaged.

She became easily impatient of his compulsive fascination with shape, content, matter, yet she liked the results. This he could never understand. Back in the days when enterprise could make or break you for life, and there was an automatic distinction between the man of imagination and the hewers of wood, he had astounded people by being both, and succeeding in business enterprise as well. He had become apprenticed as a cabinet-maker, and when that was finished, he had gone to work in the forests. Throwing away a good trade his family said. In the forest he had learned about wood, its variety and gradations, its feel and its colour. He'd earned a lot of money there too, and after going bush for a year, had enough to travel. He headed straight for Sweden and Denmark. Drifting, they said. Back he came and into the forests again for a year. Still young, but they said he didn't know what he was after.

He knew exactly and had done all along. Stocked up again financially from bush work, he was ready. That's when he started building furniture on his own; furniture different from what New Zealanders knew then, based on Scandinavian lines. The pattern started to fall into place; everything had served its purpose and although the first year was hard, he was prospering before his critics had had time to draw breath. Design, environment, texture; no wonder it was his passion. Too engrossed, no time to be a human being, was the next criticism. Which he promptly disproved, having waited for the time when humanity would be enjoyable. Was he cold then? Calculating?

Impossible, because there were times when the waiting and the long learning process had been so hard. The time was just right when he met Margaret, who was mobile and gay, not beautiful, but symmetrical and richly coloured — and also somewhat tired of the football crowd she had cheered for every Saturday, in between weeks at the dental clinic where she worked. Afterwards, she would call that the grey period of her life, yet he was not sure that this was strictly true. He believed that, as with himself, the time was right. She was to flower and develop, to control her erratic directions. Since then, though, the control had become tight, the spontaneity lost. Aesthetically she fitted well, but he was never sure of her emotionally.

She had never returned to her old career, though she wanted to work. In Wellington, after Jenny had gone to school she looked after a small antique shop in the mornings when nobody in their right senses bought antiques, till the proprietor came in and took over at lunchtime. He had caught her often, carefully dusting faded paintings and Sheridan chairs, and wondered if it was a reaction against him; care for the shapes of lost centuries, but then she would surprise him with the rare purchase of a piece supremely beautiful, perhaps jade or ivory, maybe a plate, which was of extraordinary excellence and complemented his furniture and designs more imaginatively than he could have done himself.

After dinner they returned to the motel and she unpacked.

'D'you want any help?' he asked her.

'Not a thing.' She flipped on the button of the small television for him and he concentrated on the soap opera in front of him till he felt bubbles coming out of his ears.

Margaret was walking around in her brassiere and panties, hair gleaming darkly through the white nylon.

They had been to *Hair* that year. She loved it and he hated it. After the show she had stood in the sitting-room and lifted her hands ecstatically above her head, feet planted apart, the stance adopted by the cast in the nude scene.

'That was beautiful, so beautiful,' she had said.

'I'll guarantee they all cut and dyed them the same shape,' he had replied, his head throbbing with the pain of the noise.

'What?'

'The pubic hair. They were all the same. I'll bet yours and mine wouldn't look the same shape.'

'Shall we look?' she'd invited him, but he had gone to bed with nothing further on his mind than sleeping off the effects of the evening before he met an overseas buyer the following morning.

Now her breasts were swelling about the line of the brassiere and he remembered that her period would be due in a week, and realised that this was why she had insisted on this date for the holiday, when it would have been more convenient for him a few days later.

'I love you,' he said quietly, testing the words carefully above the television.

'What?'

He switched the noise off.

'Get into bed, dear.'

'Yes all right. I'm ready for it.'

'Tired?'

'Exhausted. I'll get my nightie.'

'Don't, please don't.' He was slipping his clothes off fast.

She turned her face away, as if it were a perfectly natural part of unhooking her brassiere, but it was just a shade too fast. He saw she was vexed.

He put out the light, and to punish her, dived deep and quick. She fought him momentarily, then it came right. He relaxed their tempo as she answered him. Outside, the carnival cried, a plaintive candy-floss note, and strobe meandered to their window, jabbing holes in the dark.

He rolled over so that her breasts hung over him, enveloped his face. 'I love you', he said, harsh and violent. She came, and he rolled them back, not losing the connection, so that he was above her again, and perilously close to the end, which he didn't want, needing for his own vanity for her to enjoy him more. The strange yet familiar noise in the back of her throat which declared her pleasure, drew him on and closer. He reached up and switched on the light, hoping that the sight of them in motion would help keep the descent at bay. Her eyes widened at the sight of his face.

'Edward,' she said in a kind of startled wonder, as if his face was so unrecognisable that it shocked her. 'Edward.'

He let go, draining, and it felt as if his life was slipping out of him, and it was entirely without meaning. He watched his convulsing body, as if at a spectator sport, looked coldly and dispassionately at the place where they were jointed, withdrawing slowly and all the time looking into her face, too, as if she were a stranger.

Her face was lying against his hand and he felt it hot with her tears.

'Edward, I'm sorry,' she whispered.

'It's all right,' he said tiredly, for they were both bewildered, already losing sight of what had gone wrong.

Edward lay down, with a weariness so profound that he still felt as if he was hovering on the edge of death and it didn't matter. The French had an expression for woman's orgasm which translated as 'the little death'. Was it of no account for a man? Sex and death, they were very close. Perhaps that was what it was, he thought — his dull, sleepy brain, losing control of the exact memory of how her face had looked. Perhaps she thought you were dead, and she woke up and found herself screwing with you. It would frighten her. He should understand. He put his hand out on hers, and together they fell asleep.

In the morning it was bright and the day promised heat. They were careful and polite and they put thought into their day. They treated each other with great kindness for the next two days, sightseeing in moderation, asking with concern when either thought that the other might be tired or bored. They 'did' Whaka again, and the Rainbow Springs, soaked in a hot pool when their feet swelled, and deliberately did not play remembers. They shopped for the children, and one night they made love again, but with infinite respect and care for each other.

— *Edward I am looking for a couple of people, don't you know. I've got a photo of them back at home, but I don't need it, I'd recognise them at once. I'm sure they're here, but I feel as if I've been searching for years and I simply cannot locate them. How long will I go on looking for them? I am growing tired.*

They walked through the carnival each evening. On the third night, Margaret persuaded Edward that they should spend some money there, just for the hell of it. He had had enough of the noise of the dodgems which were at the town end of the carnival ground, and after their first night in the motel had resorted to sleeping tablets again. They bought toffee apples and she suggested that they go on the ferris wheel, but he cried off, as they had had wine with their meal, so they went on the ghost train instead, and both came out suitably unsmiling, though it was dreariness and not fear that prompted their reaction.

As they walked back, one of the sideshows attracted Margaret. A row of widely-grinning faces moved mechanically from side to side.

'Shall we look?' she asked.

'Let's get back,' he said shortly, and threw his toffee apple into a rubbish tin. 'God, those are filthy things.'

He walked ahead as Margaret lingered by the huge-mouthed faces. A young man from the booth shouted at her. He had longish blond hair sticking damply round his neck in the heat, and a pale face which looked as if it slept much by day. He hitched down his skinny-rib sweater over narrow hips and held out a handful of coloured balls. Margaret walked back to him. Another young man came out and leaned on his friend's shoulder. This one was different. Though he had the same night-owl look about him, he had dark hair close-cropped but stylish, coming to a widow's peak on his forehead, above over-bright blackish eyes. Almost gypsy, specially imported to take on tour round carnivals; indolent, a trifle fat, but yes, definitely stylish.

Edward could see that, as he turned to wait for Margaret and saw that she was bantering with them. He watched her, feeling so remote and strange that he had to lean against a telegraph pole, while the dark one came out and put his arm around her, and held her hand to help her aim the ball at the gaping faces.

Mouth open, relaxed, Margaret dropped the first ball; then the second. The third time she shrieked as the ball evidently found the favoured number.

The fair one looked at the dark one who hesitated slightly, then nodded. A large doll was pushed into her arms. Edward could see that some sort of argument was developing and although Margaret was still laughing and excited, she was looking round worriedly too, and trying to push the doll back to the men.

Edward shouldered his way through the crowd to where they stood.

'Oh Edward,' Margaret cried. 'Where on earth did you get to? Look, this is so silly. These two men let me have a go just for the fun of it — I wouldn't buy a turn because I can't do these things — well, you know me, and now — it's so stupid, I've won, well not won, because I can't — I mean I hit the number for this doll, which is quite the most expensive prize on the stand — but if I haven't paid for my turn I can't possibly take it, can I?'

'No, I don't think you can.'

'Luck of the game, mister,' said the dark one, leaning against his counter and inspecting his fingernails. 'We take our chances round here, same as the lady does if she pays her money. I don't mind giving it to her.' The eyes darted over Margaret.

'Nearly time to close down,' said the blond. 'Haven't got all night, mister. Not to spend round here anyway.' He and his mate smiled knowingly at each other.

'I'll pay you for my wife's use of your facilities then,' said Edward.

'Oh, come on now, that's a laugh. A bit of an insult, really. You paying off a spot of our good nature with thirty cents,' said the dark man.

'Do you want the doll?' said Edward sharply to Margaret. 'I'll pay for it.'

'No — '

'Oh, come on. Thought you said a minute ago you had a little girl. Didn't she say she had a little girl, Ted?'

'That's what she said, Jeff,' said the nail-picker.

'Well, seeing you've related your life history to Ted and Jeff, you should be able to sort things out with them,' Edward said, and ploughed back into the crowd.

His hands were shaking when he opened the motel door. He put the electric jug on to make tea, and sat down to wait, then got up again. There was work in the pocket of one of the suitcases which she didn't know he had brought with them. The papers covered with designs were lying neat and uncreased in their envelope. He drew them out and laid them on the table. The jug was boiling, so he made the tea and set out two cups. As he heard her footsteps outside, he turned to the work on the table. The door opened and she stood there looking at him and taking in the designs on the table.

The whiteness of the room had an explosive quality, as if they were inside a giant tennis ball turned inside out, and it might suddenly swell and burst. The centre light above him held pale, atonal whiteness that he had not noticed before. A blazing white coming down to meet his white paper, so that they fused into stabbing shafts of no-colour. His head was aching intolerably.

Defiantly Margaret walked in and placed the doll on top of the designs.

'I took it,' she said.

'So I see,' he said, without lifting his head, and placed the doll to one side, so that he could sketch a detail on to the work. 'There's a cup of tea made.'

'I won't bother thanks,' she replied. 'I'm off to bed.'

The doll leered at him as he heard her undressing and turning the covers back. Only children smash dolls, he thought. Or poke their eyes out with pencils. Or bicker over their ownership. The bed creaked as Margaret got in.

After a while he took his pills and joined her. They slept back to back.

In the morning they avoided each other's eyes, but Margaret wrapped the doll up in a piece of newspaper and stuffed it in the bin outside.

'You didn't have to do that,' he said.

'I know I didn't. I chose to.'

'As you chose to take it. You could at least give it back to them if you don't want it.'

'I don't care what happens to the doll,' she said.

He saw that she had dressed as soon as she got out of bed, a fact which had eluded him till then, because of the way they were refusing to look at each other.

'I'm going out for a bit,' said Margaret briefly.

'Yes,' he said, having expected this. 'It might be best. Where will you go?'

'Just around.'

'Will I meet you back here at lunch-time?'

She calculated. 'Say dinner-time. It'd be better. I'm sure it would be better.' Starting to waver, and needing to convince herself, she added, 'If you're sure it's all right?'

'It's fine,' he replied, studying the newspaper that the motel people left on his doorstep. It was an Auckland paper, instead of the Wellington one, such as he was used to studying on the train each morning from Khandallah, and its unfamiliarity was as difficult as a map of a strange town. He felt doubly inclined this morning to disagree with its contents. Perversely he gave it all his attention. Margaret lingered at the door, waiting for him to look up. When he didn't she let herself out without speaking.

As soon as she had left he changed out of his pyjamas, putting on linen slacks, a cotton-knit sweater and, after some consideration, the pair of roman sandals Anna had given him for Christmas. His toes looked long and strange, curling down like blue-white claws, and he found them oddly disturbing, like a part of his body he hadn't really seen before. It felt as obscene walking abroad in the day with those skeletal appendages sticking out as if his fly was undone. Nervously he checked that it wasn't.

The day stretched out before him in idleness and solitude, yet he didn't mind as much as he had expected to. The car was there for him to use if he wanted to, and he realised guiltily that he should have suggested to Margaret that she take it, but consoled himself that the situation wasn't so bad that she wouldn't have taken it if she had really wanted it.

The blue-green light over the lake was diffusing into heat haze with the rising summer morning. It drew Edward, magnet-like, and he wandered along the street and down the short road violently edged with magenta petunias, past the rheumatism hospital, till he reached the water's edge.

Willows festooned a boatshed, swans floated past, trailing silk. As he approached, they shattered the calm, climbing out of the water and surrounding him to make sibilant crosspatch noises, stretching and craning their necks at him as they looked for food. Their presence was black and menacing to Edward. A girl-child, too young to be unattended by the lake, ambled up amongst them. She clapped her hands and laughed, and immediately the swans transferred their attention to her. Some of them were larger than her and one, the largest, stretched its wings like enormous fans, an avenging, crazy angel, reaching up and above the girl, with its neck in a downward curve and beak wide open.

'Get out of it, go away,' Edward screamed. He jumped and stamped till the swans retreated, then when they had gone back into the water, he turned upon the child with fury. 'What are you doing here? Go away, go home, you stupid child.'

The child, who had been unafraid till then, looked at his contorted face and turned to run.

Edward subsided on the steps cut in the wall along the lake front. Cold sweat made him shiver in the heat.

The water lapped at his feet, smelling and full of junk, orange peel and paper. The swans sailed serenely past, ignoring him now. He thought they looked like evil lake apparitions, so magnificently beautiful yet maybe poisonous, an apotheosis of the evil within the lake. Memory raking in mythology, he could only think of Excalibur, which did not fit, and no arms rose from the lake, and no sword shone above the water, yet the death of Arthur did not seem so inappropriate. Something was dying here, something would die, and he wondered, twisting his nostrils against the stench, if it might be the death of his own soul, if indeed he had one. He and Jesus Christ being so offhand with each other, he failed to see how he could find out.

He thought of Margaret and wondered what she was doing and thinking. Sure to be thinking, but he wouldn't know what till it was cut and tailored to fit her needs. His fault that.

The lake wasn't really ugly, he reflected. It was beautiful if one used eyes and emotional senses, and not just reason and rational senses. He thought of Sweden where he had been very happy.

Sweden. Maybe that was where he had gone wrong. But he really had been so happy. Stockholm had opened her arms and embraced him. Everything there was clean, beautiful, well-defined. There, he had learnt the value of form and design. Sweden had become for him the idyllic symbol of his existence, the substitute for holiness.

In the early fifties there were so few causes. So neutral. Yes, that was what he was. One of the neutral generation. The great patriotism of the war was behind the young. Be glad you're alive, so glad that you didn't have to go. It's all been done for you, and you're lucky, lucky that 'they' did it for you, that you were too young. Exist, make good. Be worthy.

Born too late for that holocaust, too early for the great dreams, the mighty ideals of today's young. No Vietnams, no demonstrations, nor even a golden time to discover oneself, as they did today. Not even time to ride waves on a surfboard, to jump in old cars and gather the countryside under the spinning wheels of jalopies. Too early for Elvis and rock even, though thinking back he knew Margaret hadn't been. That era had happened when the babies were little, and they had gone one night to find out what it was all about, inspired perhaps by truck-loads of rock'n'roll kids dancing in jamborees and marathons, grey and ill from lack of sleep as they were paraded through towns, still dancing, towards another record; or maybe just by the hordes of glue-haired youths who lounged the streets in imitation of the Pelvis. They had gone to *Love Me Tender*, and it wasn't what they expected at all. Or rather, he was unimpressed as he had expected to be, and Margaret had cried which was a surprise for both of them, when the chubby-kid-made-good from somewhere outback of an America they had never seen, clasped his microphone, a forerunner of all the phallic mike-fondlers to come, and sobbed his plea deep inside it, to 'love him tender'. Edward and Margaret never spoke of it.

After, he knew she read Kerouac, but she never discussed it with him, and in time these matters faded.

Sweden. Yes, in a neutral world he had asked for an ideal, and it had given him just that. In the end, it had even made him a rich man, which was more than one could expect of most of the Holy Grails the kids searched for now.

Sweden. He had never shared it with her, the woman Margaret. She knew what it meant to him of course, and asked to be let in, to share the secret places that inhabited his mind. Take me to Sweden she had once asked him, but he refused, saying too quickly, and re-vealing anger, that such a trip was only practicable if it were in the line of business and he had no need to go. She didn't ask him again.

Sometimes though, she would ask him to go to Swedish films with her. Films were one of her things, she had a good mind for them, drily assessing their worth to her in a clever quick way and was unshaken if the most erudite critics disagreed with her. Nearly always he refused to go. To see Sweden like that was to look through a window at a familiar landscape he could not touch, populated by people he didn't know.

One night Margaret had gone to *Elvira Madigan* and when she came in from it, he could see she had been crying.

'It must have been a tear-jerker,' he'd said.

'I suppose it was, though it hardly touched me. It was just — too pretty,' she had replied.

'Then why are you crying?'

'Because I was by myself,' she had replied, 'and I'd looked forward to it a great deal, but it was generally a disappointment. The funny thing was that it had some subtleties which surprised me, delighted me really, because just when I was least expecting them, and thinking, well, this really is too much, something would happen. There was this part where the girl sold a painting of herself for the price of a meal. It had been painted, so she said, by a dwarf in a Paris café, and we saw for a moment the initials on the canvas. They were TL and I thought, what a marvellous understated subtle thing, that's Toulouse-Lautrec, of course, and I caught my breath, forgetting the man next to me wasn't you, and said 'Did you see that?' No one else had seen it, you could tell by the way they didn't move or murmur, only I had seen it, and I thought how clever, I must share that with Edward. Only it wasn't you and I apologised to the man, but he must have thought I was a tart because he got up and moved away.'

A few days later — it had been a couple of years ago — she had asked him for the first time, if he would consider a separation.

So he had tried to go to the films with her once or twice after that. The last Swedish one had been a Bergman. It was *The Touch*. Margaret would say, afterwards, that the story lacked finesse, but Edward identified with the woman's obsession for cleanliness, and when the man, the foreigner, knelt before Bibi Anderssen and kissed her breasts, he had thought, yes, that is me, and she is Sweden.

Afterwards, in order to disguise how they felt, the argued academically over whether 'the touch' referred to sexuality, or the hereditary muscular dystrophy which the foreigner carried and had probably impregnated in his mistress.

On that night, after Anna came in, later than them, and had gone to bed, Edward agreed with Margaret that he would consider a separation.

He rose stiffly from his position on the steps. He knew he would be badly sunburned from this exposure.

So he went round to the jetty. The launch had left for Mokoia Island earlier in the morning. Children rode tawdry coloured runabouts out into the lake, and the boats appeared to break down frequently so that a man would have to go racing after them in another craft to tow them in. The water shook and frothed with this steady movement.

Edward glanced down to the other side of the jetty, attracted by shouts. A girl was swimming there. Seal-like, her head appeared from the water, blue-black and glistening. She was Maori, with eyes surprisingly grey in her warm-bright face. All over she laughed, he saw, as her body rose. She had jumped into the water with her clothes on, and a bright orange shirt clung to her, showing her breasts free and casual, nipples alive and unfettered. Jeans below.

If I had a camera I would take a photo click, click, click, Edward reflected. But they would never show what I can see, which is total beauty, gloriously carnal.

Carnal knowledge? Of whom? Of myself, of whom she is part. I know myself to look at her.

Between her legs two boys, or maybe men — men-children — dived, grabbing her, pulling her deep into the water and themselves, and all rising, laughing and laughing.

Incredible anguish swept through him, that he was not in the water with them, and he knew quite surely, that if he were to leap into the water, she would receive his presence, and offer herself casually into his arms because he had dared to join her in the water.

The papers, the peel, the green–fingered slime-cast week swirled around him in his mind's eye, and he hesitated. One of the boys with her sunk his teeth into her thigh, his hand clasping her crotch.

She would let me, she would let me, Edward thought. So long as she was in the water.

The water no longer seemed evil; she had collected the good and the beautiful, captured the colour and the light, the amazing skywater complexity of the day, and blended them into something different.

The other boy in the water covered her nipple with his mouth; her head pivoted back, her mouth opened catching pleasure and throwing it laughingly back at the bystanders.

Then, like an eel, she had twisted out of the grasp of her lovers and was out of the water in a flash, out upon dry land.

It was too late, Edward stood on the wharf, his feet melding into it, his body wooden with disbelief.

The girl raced away across the grass toward the carnival, the boys in hot pursuit.

He walked on around the lake front, bitter and angry. The vile lake had thrown up beauty and he had been too frightened that the water might soil him.

So he came to the village of Ohinemutu, and the church surrounded by graves built above the ground inside of it, because of the sulphuric pools below. The church had been rebuilt since he had last been there, and was not as comfortably ethnic in its styles as it had once been. He remembered that he and Margaret had been there on the honeymoon, and that it had been very traditionally Maori, but now there were great sand-blasted windows. It was spectacular and thoughtful though, he had to admit to himself, particularly the window looking on to the lake depicting Jesus Christ walking on the waters. For once he felt a sympathy towards Jesus. He had been afraid to get His feet wet too. Maybe they identified.

An old, old Maori man was showing people around. So old that his skull gleamed behind his skin, a hollow waxy head, issuing forth slurred speech and garbled instructions. A woman tourist spoke to a companion in French.

Without a change in his patter, the old man gave her the information she required in her own language. The group fell silent.

'Where did you learn French?' asked another tourist.

'In Flanders,' said the guide simply, and his eyes seemed to recede even further into his head. The French woman held out her hand, and he took it, vaguely bowing to her. The time to shepherd the visitors from religion to culture had arrived and the guide shambled out of the church towards a small building where a man was carving wood.

Duty was apparently done at this point, for a bus driver took up his station, languidly protecting his charges before they climbed back into the bus, and the guide shuffled off down the road which led past the lake.

Edward followed a few paces behind. He was curious to see where the man went. A meeting-house stood to his left amongst a conglomeration of decrepit but inhabited shacks and shiny new image-maker houses. A tangi was in process and Edward thought with disappointment that the man would go in. Apparently his respects had been paid, or the matter did not concern him, although that seemed unlikely, but at any rate, he kept going.

Edward fell in step beside him. 'Tangi?' he asked, though it was obvious.

Out of the skull, the lips moved tiredly. 'A little fella. The lake.' He nodded towards it. 'Just out here in the raupeka.'

'Drowned in the lake?'

'Yes. Oh, many go. Many have gone.'

'It's a bad lake,' said Edward.

The other stopped to reflect. 'I was born across there on Mokoia. It hasn't killed me.'

They continued a little further on, and stopped together at an old house with a lean-to verandah. A row of plastic fly-screen strips hung across the door.

'My place. Do you wish to come in?'

Edward acquiesced.

Inside it was coolly dark after the glare outside, plain and cheap with deal chairs and a wooden table, and old-fashioned heavy arm chairs covered in ragged moquette. On the floor a young man sat, bent intently over wood that he was carving. He glanced up and nodded at Edward.

'Sit down.'

'Thank you,' said Edward.

'Henare, my mokopuna,' said the old man. 'My grandson.'

Slice and chisel, the wood slivered away as the younger man deftly shaped his material. Edward sensed that here was something different.

'He's good,' he said, to the grandfather.

'Yes,' said his companion. 'You see my hands?' He held out gnarled, knotted fingers. 'They won't work for me any more. So few know how

238

to carve the true way. He is learning. So few are prepared to learn from the old any more. He learns. He is a good boy.'

'Will he sell it?' asked Edward

The grandfather shrugged. 'Who knows? It is not of such great value. The skill to do it is.'

'I'd like to buy it,' Edward said.

Henare spoke. 'It won't be finished today. You can buy others at the village.'

'I don't want those,' said Edward. 'I — don't buy carvings as a rule. I care for skills — they are my — true values.'

'To have true values, one must love, the skill comes from the loving. Loving what is done, and what it is done for,' said Henare.

Tenderness shone between him and the old man.

'Will it be finished tomorrow?' said Edward urgently.

Henare nodded.

'Then — if I come back — will you keep it for me? I don't mind what I pay.'

'It'll be here, friend,' said Henare. 'There'll be no charge.'

'Oh but I must — '

Henare had risen to his feet, and for Edward the interview was over. 'You'll come back then?' Henare said. 'Late in the day. Then it'll be finished.'

'Yes, I'll come.'

As he walked back, the day was unaccountably bluer and sky and lake coincided in an impermeable horizon fractured only by light.

Margaret had traipsed through town all day. At first she had thought of taking a bus sightseeing, or even a bus that would take her some place out in the country, but she wasn't ready yet to sit it out on her own. Besides it would have been a renegging, a turning-back. Decisions had been made, now all that remained was the choice of time.

It was punishing in the city, and after a few turns, monotonous. One just kept walking round in squares, and always landed back in the one, broad, main drag, as Anna and Mike would have called it. 'Musak' blared along the streets and in nearly every shop she entered. There were few bookshops in which to seek quiet, and it took a long time to find an antique shop. The dress shops were good she had to admit, and on the strength of it bought a brightly striped blazer in colours she had nothing to match.

Finally, in mid-afternoon, her aching feet forced her to find a place to sit. She recalled a coffee-shop in a complex built around a fountain. As she entered the arcade she saw a toyshop and looked for something to take home to Jenny. A large bride doll grinned toothily at her and she remembered the doll she had thrown away in the morning. Jenny was too big for dolls anyway. She glared at the doll's smirk in disgust. The big sell. The wonderful white wedding; the big con set to organ music. It had been the year of the great cardboard fix. The year of 'the wedding' when women in her street — and God knows, it was supposed to be a classy neighbourhood at that — sat glued to their television sets clutching cardboard photos of Elsie Tanner, so that they could get 'really close' to the events on the screen.

She went on in and ordered coffee at the coffee-shop.

And how am I any better? I, who have come back to this provincial hick town dossed out in tourist colours, to re-glimpse what I thought was happiness. Maybe there are people here who are alive, in the truly living sense, and happy, but I can't find them. I remember wide streets, and they are still wide, but in those days they were nearly empty, now they are overflowing. I am here to recapture time past, but time has gone by here, too, and I blame the place. What were we then? Children of a time they are now recalling with nostalgia. Where our parents were the young of the thirties, we now glory in, or sorrow over, or regret, the fifties. They're doing it all over, the films, the books, the weeklies: they are turning us back to that time of our youth. Funny if Edward was thinking that too. Not that I'd ever know, or would I? Important point — we're not likely to tell each other, we just keep on guessing what the other's thinking now.

They even fetched out dear old Tennessee Ernie Ford this year — or did he just wander in — I forget — and he pontificated — in the fifties the ground was ploughed the crops were sown — and the clods broken. That's what he said. And God I believe him. What a child of the medium I am really. I came back to find it, and I'm surprised because it's gone. Except, maybe, in a dirty pile of carnival tents.

'Hi kitten,' said a voice. She looked up. The two men who had given her the doll were standing beside her. Margaret drew herself together, and returned their boldness with a long, cool look.

The dark one, whom she remembered as Ted, stared right back, his gaze unflickering.

'Nice, isn't she Ted?' said Jeff.

Ted stared. Margaret felt herself staring to burn.

'You fancy her, don't you?' said Jeff.

She got to her feet. 'If you don't mind — '

They both swung back from her.

'Oh we don't mind,' said Ted. He smiled, lips breaking over white teeth. 'If you feel like a drink, we're there any evening for the next week. Just pop in.'

'Thank you,' she said, retreating and not looking back.

When they saw each other again, Edward told her about the girl in the lake and the old man and the carver, but it was the girl she seemed to be interested in. 'How did she make you feel?' she asked.

'How do you mean?'

'Sexy?'

'No, for God's sake. Clean — '

'Clean?'

'Yes. I felt — no, not just her — everything in a different light. I felt, really felt — quite a lot.' She looked at him curiously.

In bed that night, they made love again.

He was careful not to put on the light, but he found her moving strangely under him. There was a violent urgency in her. Her finger-nails raked his back, sweat slid between them. 'Oh Christ, oh fuck, come on,' she cried in his ear. He did, nearly losing her as she strained fighting for something, he didn't know what it was. After, as they lay in the dark, apart, she said wonderingly, 'Is that you Edward?'

He wondered who she had been with in his arms.

She went out again the next day. He had thought of asking her to go home, but she was obviously not ready to go, and the carving he had ordered lent him a sense of unfinished business in the town. Tonight he must really insist that they pack and go the following day.

He waited all day, the stark motel room bearing down on him. All day she didn't return, and he began to fret. As evening approached he knew that if he was to have the carving he must go for it then.

The heat of the day had waned suddenly and chillingly, and the cloud had descended. This sharp drop in temperature had affected the steam in the hot pools at Ohinemutu. The steam swirled and twined around him; dense, fireless smoke, catching in his lungs.

At the house, Henare met him on the verandah. The carving was wrapped in a piece of newspaper. The young man pulled the paper back, so that Edward could see the carving. He caught his breath.

'That's magnificent,' he said. 'I've never held — let alone owned — a carving as good as that.'

'It's better than you'll get around town,' said the carver matter-of-factly.

'I know. Where's your grandfather? I'm going tomorrow so I'd like to say goodbye to him and thank him for letting me come here.'

Again Henare's voice was matter-of-fact, but his eyes travelled beyond Edward, to the lake. 'He's not so well tonight. He's lying down. But he asked me to say goodbye. He liked meeting you.'

Edward glanced at him. 'I can't — ' he muttered awkwardly, holding out the parcel.

Henare looked at his hands. 'I have the skill,' he said. He turned to go in. 'I can't leave him for long.'

'Thank you, thank you,' Edward said, and walked back into the steam. Tears were tugging behind his eyelids. He brushed his face with the back of his hand; it was damp from the mist around him. The lake was almost level with his feet. A car came round too fast so that he almost had to jump into the water. Ahead of him the church loomed up, and he thought of the stained-glass window.

'I am frightened, very frightened. I don't know why.' And then, 'But I'll be all right. I must be.'

And he was. As he passed the church and headed back to town the mist cleared. In his hand he clasped the carving. He unwrapped it and stuffed the paper in a tin. He had come through.

What had they said to him? The true values are in the loving. No, the skill is not enough. Sweden fell away from him like something long gone. He'd sacrificed so much, clinging to things which no longer mattered, too sparing with his love for that which was closest and needed him. There was life and truth and vigour in him to rediscover the world. With Margaret. He'd kept her at arm's length for nearly half a lifetime, hers anyway, enclosed in his own private capsule of vision, without allowing her a glimpse, shutting her out.

He hurried on towards the motel. Near the jetty he saw the girl who had swum in the lake the day before. His heart lifted. The final freedom, to look upon this girl, this wild-water creature. He would follow her and look upon her as a last release.

Margaret had walked past the rheumatism hospital. Its doors facing the lake led out to verandahs where twisted children sat in wheelchairs. Their limbs were grotesque and she wondered if they were in pain. It hurt her deeply to look at them.

I am a cripple. I am a cripple. I have had my legs and arms cut off, and soon there will be nothing left. It's so bloody and brutal. I must strike back while there is still time.

She walked as far as it was possible to go, and came to what was probably swamp in the winter. The area was covered with branches of fallen trees, bleached white and skeletal.

And there are the bones, the white twisted limbs; filaments of dead flesh. Gnarled children's bodies and massacres. Pain and division. Pale light gleaming dull through this tortuous, agonised web. Finally . . . finally . . . I have found what I came to find in the place. Limb upon limb upon limb and I will cast my last . . . useful . . . sane . . . living . . . flesh . . . out amongst dead limbs . . . and what it left . . . will walk . . . a hollow shell among other shells which breathe and talk . . . and move . . . and no longer . . . feel. For they are dead limbs. And there will be no turning back. And I will be alone . . . which is not a new thing . . . but it must in the end, be acknowledged . . . for what it is.

Margaret returned slowly past the hospital, the boatshed, past the swans, and as she approached, she saw Edward far off, coming from the opposite direction.

A girl had been playing ball near the water with some youths. As she watched her, Margaret realized from the way Edward had described her, that she must be the same girl he had seen in the lake. Intuition flashed. Earth mother, bitch goddess, it didn't matter. The knowledge was quick and sure. The time was chosen.

Very quickly, almost running, Margaret doubled back and along behind the carnival. She was out of breath when she reached the dodgem's side, but the manoeuvre had enabled her to come into the carnival by the far entrance. It had only taken a few minutes. Cautiously she edged along the far side to the candyfloss stall, so that she could watch Edward approach.

He was closing in on the girl when she broke away from the boys and ran with the ball towards the fairground. As Margaret had expected, he swung away from the lake and towards the carnival.

Her breath was back to normal. Deliberately and without hurry, she walked to the booth with the great heads swivelling their watermelon-coloured mouths backwards and forwards. Jeff was lounging in front of the tent, a cigarette slung loosely on his lip. Lazily he picked his frame together and called over his shoulder. In a minute Ted appeared in the doorway, bare to the waist, a towel draped over his shoulder.

He smiled. 'I was expecting you,' he said.

'Come for your drink, have you?' said Jeff.

'If it's still offering,' said Margaret.

'I reckon it is,' replied Ted.

'Concession rate day to old-age pensioners,' Margaret said acidly, as a last tribute to herself.

Ted placed his hand on her shoulder, and through her blouse she could feel his bare flesh, and she smelled him too.

'They can come if they like darling, but not while you're around,' he murmured against her ear.

A strange feeling, that was not altogether strange, because she knew that it had often made Edward behave differently to her, was coming, crawling through her, making her turn to glimpse her husband who was wending his way towards her through the carnival jungle, and back at the new man, with his arm about her. She looked at Edward, and he looked at her; then she went into the tent, as the fair youth screamed mocking promises at the passers-by.

*

And Edward had seen her look. The old set look, somewhere between memory and anticipation.

With the sudden clarity which comes just before the weariness that descends and obliterates all coherent thought, a long-obscure problem resolved itself. She did not ask me to this town to make me think she tried, he thought. She asked me here to comfort me. To let me think that I had tried, to comfort me into thinking that it was not my fault, but hers. The last maternal act.

The girl from the lake had gone. Margaret had gone.

In his hand was a wooden object which he had acquired too late to be of the value it might have been. Night was falling, in a chill summerless wind. The blank had fallen.

He made his way back to the motel room, where the white walls expanded and contracted like billowing, moving planes against his tired brain. He sat and waited for the end of his marriage to begin.

The Paper Parcel

OWEN MARSHALL

For a long time I thought everybody could see the future in the way I could myself: an expectation based upon desire. The dream logic of the mind. Even though events were often very different, it was the reality I blamed and not the vision. The reality failed to match the vision which was the first and greater view. The actual encroached, but expectation drew off, and set up again upon the high ground of the future.

I remember asking Dusty Rhodes what he thought being in a submarine was like. I dunno he said, I dunno do I, until I've been in one. What a way to live. He didn't know any better. He was spared any disillusion at least. No matter how many times it happened I felt a sense of loss and betrayal when things proved other than I had seen them. Not different only, but also less in fitness and in unity.

Like the fancy dress ball for instance. I was twelve when the senior classes had a fancy dress ball to end the year. It was a strict convention that you had to have a partner in advance. Anyone not paired off would hold his hand in fire rather than turn up that night. As far as I knew I had only three attributes to attract the opposite sex. I was the second fastest runner in the school, I was top in maths, and I had blue eyes. Dusty Rhodes was fastest boy. I never beat him, although sometimes I dreamt I might. I became accustomed to despair and his greasy hair in front of me as we ran race after race. Dusty drowned in the Wairau the next year; by the berth of the coaster which used to come over from Wellington and up the river. For years I had a guilt that I might have wished it. I was second fastest in the school to Dusty. I used to boast to the others that my legs just went that fast without any effort from the rest of me. To enhance this I had the habit of looking sideways as I ran, as if to see the cars on the road to the bridge, and escape the boredom of my automatic legs. Being top of maths was the second thing, and quite beyond my control. I was always top and never had an explanation for it. I was fearful I would lose the trick of it. And the blue eyes. There were only four boys with blue eyes in the class, and Fiona McCartney told Bodger that she liked blue eyes best. The class had been singing beautiful, beautiful brown eyes, and Bodger asked her which she preferred. Fiona McCartney blushed and said blue eyes, and the other girls giggled. I didn't forget that. I was beginning to store up points of knowledge about girls. Fiona McCartney was the oracle about such things at that school.

So those were the advantages I had going for me, and I exploited them to the full in the weeks before the fancy dress dance. I never ran so often or so fast; I was closer to first and further from third than ever before. I turned my head to the side with casual indifference and the old legs went with a will. I took to answering more maths questions in class, and fluked most of them right, and I used to widen my eyes when I was close to girls so that the blue of them would be more conspicuous.

Fiona McCartney passed a message to me saying she wanted to see me by the canteen at playtime, and when she came we went over by the sycamores and railing. She put one hand on the railing and swung her right foot in an arc on the grass. She glanced at her friends by the canteen and considered she had set a good scene. I widened my eyes at her, and held my breath without realizing it. She told me that she wouldn't be going to the dance with me. I hadn't asked her, but she knew she was every boy's choice and was letting me down gently. As I was the second fastest and so on she realized my expectations. I felt dizzy then remembered to breathe out again. She said I'd have no trouble getting someone to go with. The girls had been talking, she said. She said the girls had been talking, and she put the tip of her tongue between her teeth and smiled. I smiled back and widened my eyes, as if I were aware of what girls said.

It made me more anxious though, Fiona saying that, especially when we started having dancing practices. I wondered which of the girls had partners arranged already, for I wanted to avoid the humiliation of asking them. Kelly Howick saved me the trouble. At the third practice she said to me that I wasn't much of a dancer and was I going to the fancy dress night. I said that I thought that I probably would. Casually I said it, and looked to the side as if I were running. I widened my eyes too; which wasn't much good when I was looking away. Are you listening, she said. In the past I'd thought about Kelly mainly as the girl most likely to keep me from fluking top in maths. She was top in most things. She had definite breasts though, and was pretty. Only a certain matter-of-fact manner prevented her from being more like Fiona McCartney. It came to me that she was willing to be my partner. Only later did it also occur to me that she and her friends had made the decision without my presence being required. I will be your partner if you like, she said. She didn't need an answer. She seemed pleased for me. She smiled at me, and at her friends, as we moved awkwardly to the dancing instructions of Bodger and Miss Erikson.

I'd had my share of success in life, but in that school hall I felt for the first time the heady stuff of sexual preferment. Kelly Howick had sought me out. I looked with contempt upon the others in the hall. Dusty Rhodes who could only run fast, and Bodger with the sweat stains on his shirt. For the first time I perceived myself in the mirror of the feminine eye; I was filled with casual arrogance and power. I was aware of a new dimension to life. My head kept nodding indolently as we danced, and my shoulders shrugging in some instinctive male response.

The knowledge of sexual magnetism was a novelty. I felt I should be able to tap it for other purposes. The day after the dancing practice I raced Dusty again. I felt the new power within me and was resolved to express it in my running also. I would bury him. In fact it made not an inch of difference. I still had to run behind Dusty, his hair bobbing. And he didn't even have a partner to the dance. It was a shock to discover that the power generated by sexual preferment was not directly transferable to athletic performance.

In my mind I was quite sure how the fancy dress dance would be. Sure, I had been let down somewhat in the past by the failure of events to conform with my directions, but I wasn't responsible for that. I saw Kelly and myself always in the centre of the hall; always in the better light, and somehow slightly larger than our classmates. I would dance, or stand quietly and attract the attention of other girls because of my blue eyes and a certain calmness of manner. Kelly would be constantly asking my opinion, and I would be giving it with easy finality. Instead of the lucky spot waltz there would be quizzes on tables, or a sprint the length of the hall and back when Dusty happened to be outside.

Kelly Howick talked to me during practices. I made the adult discovery that some people are ugly. I'd had the foolish idea that there were no common standards of appearance. Now I began to realize otherwise. Collie Richardson for example, who told the best jokes in the school. He had a very small upper lip. It was like a little skirt, and his gums and teeth were always exposed beneath it. Once I realized he was ugly I never liked his jokes as much again.

At practices Kelly took over my instruction. She gave an individual repetition of what Bodger and Miss Erikson kept saying. You've not got much rhythm have you, she said. Me! Second fastest and with automatic legs. In other circumstances it would have irritated me, but in the complacency of preferment I let it pass. Certain things about girls have to be tolerated for the overall benefit.

I skidded on loose stones by the sycamores next day and put a long graze along my left forearm. Mrs Hamil put iodine on it and Kelly was quite concerned. It won't show on the night will it, she said. What are you going to wear anyway? What is your outfit like? Her saying that made my arm begin to throb. The blood seeped out into beads despite the iodine. I hadn't done anything about a costume. Getting a partner as the priority had obscured all other aspects of the dance. I asked my mother about it that night, and she said that's nice, a costume party is nice. Sure, we'll think of something. And my father made jokes for his own amusement about being cloaked in ignorance, or dressed in a little brief authority. I could tell they didn't have the right view of the ball at all; that they were thinking of it as some party, some kids' thing.

Tony Poole said his parents were hiring a full cowboy outfit with sheepskin chaps, bandanna and matched revolvers. Dusty's parents were pretty poor; I thought he wouldn't have much to wear even when he did arrange a partner. But he said his cousin had a Captain Marvel costume which had been professionally made. What is it you're going as, Kelly asked me again. I started questioning my mother once more. What was she going to do for me? Kelly was going as Bo Peep. What about my costume, I said to my mother. Oh, we'll rustle up something don't you worry, she said. But I did. The more casual and unperturbed she was, the more I worried.

Finally my mother said she thought I should go as a parcel. A parcel; Jesus. She remembered someone at the New Year's party as a parcel, and he was a great hit. It was a cheap costume too, she said. A parcel; Jesus. It was the originality of it that intrigued her, she said. Anyone could go as a policeman or a musketeer, people grew tired of seeing them. The parcel left only head and limbs out she said, and I could make up a giant stamp with crayons; and over my parcel body have stickers saying Fragile, London, This Side Up, Luxemburg, Handle With Care. The parcel was set to torpedo my night with Kelly Howick. Bo Peep Kelly with her beginning breasts and braided hair, and me as a brown paper parcel with a stamp done in crayon.

There was a sense of inevitability about the parcel. I tried to persuade my mother that I should go as something else. I said I wouldn't wear it, but the parcel became part of me before I ever saw it; something irrevocable and humiliating before I was even dressed in it.

The dance was supposed to start at eight. It said so on the printed sheet I brought home. Nobody arrives at a dance on time though, my mother said. She never realized how little adult convention applies to the young. It said eight o'clock on the sheet didn't it? Why would it say that if it didn't mean it? Nobody comes to a dance till later, my mother said. It's just how it's done. But I saw eight o'clock written. I knew everyone would be there. Anthony Poole in his cowboy outfit, and Kelly as Bo Peep.

On that Friday I didn't run well. Dusty beat me without hardly trying, and although I looked away as I ran, I was having a hard time to keep ahead of Ricky Ransumeen in third place. My automatic legs were being affected. I thought a good deal about that because it seemed unfair. When I was selected by Kelly, when desirability was conferred on me, although the power was great it hadn't made me any faster, as I told you. But on that last day as I turned my head in studied casualness, instead of the flowing leaves of the sycamores by the fence, I saw myself in a parcel costume with a crayon stamp. Just for a moment there in the stippled leaves and keeping pace with me was a *doppelgänger* in a parcel. I lacked rhythm as I ran; I lacked a full chest of air; my automatic legs made demands.

It wasn't until after tea that my mother even began the parcel. I had to wear my swimming togs so no clothes would show below the parcel. The brown paper strips were wrapped around me like nappies, and round and round my chest, and a hole cut for my head and arms. I was tied with twine and with a yellow ribbon in a bow at the front. Over my heart was stuck the crayoned stamp, huge and serrated. Other oblong stickers were plastered on with flour-and-water paste. This Side Up, Handle with Care, On Her Majesty's Service, Do Not Rattle. I was finally packed by eight o'clock, and set off on my bike for the school assembly hall. I tried to sit up straight on the seat so that the parcel wouldn't crinkle too much. The wrapping made noises as I rode, and the greasy blue and red head on the stamp grinned in the setting sun. I told myself that the parcel was really quite clever and would go down well. I could only half believe it, yet I never seriously thought about not going. The power of sexual preferment was enough to transform me; it would make difference distinction, and nonconformity audacity. To be with Kelly Howick would be sufficient to defeat the parcel.

They had started of course. I knew it. The sheet had said eight o'clock after all. The light from the hall spilled out into the soft summer evening. The noise of the band and the dancing slid out with the light, and echoed in the quad. Bodger patrolled the grounds, alert for vandalism or lust. Late, said Bodger. He looked at my costume and said no more. As I went in he was still there on the edge of the light and the noise, and with his blue evening as a backdrop. He had his hands behind his back, and he swayed forward on his toes. Hurry up then, said Bodger. I slipped in round the edge of the door, and worked my way over to the boys' side. Tony Poole had a curled stetson, sheepskin chaps, check shirt and six-guns with matching handles. He came back from seeing Fiona McCartney to her seat. Tommy was a fire chief with a crested helmet that glittered, and a hatchet at his belt. Dusty's Captain Marvel insignia was startling on his chest, and his cloak was cherry rich and heavy. And I was a parcel. A brown paper parcel with bare legs and sandshoes. A brown paper parcel which crinkled when I moved. A brown paper parcel with a stamp drawn up in red and blue. It wasn't right: not for the second fastest runner in the whole school, not for the top maths boy, and the one preferred by Kelly Howick. What the hell is that you're wearing, said Dusty. Wouldn't you like to know, I said.

I went over to claim Kelly when the music began for the next dance. It was a foxtrot. I had learnt both sorts of dance. A waltz was where you took one step to the side every now and again, and a quickstep was where you kept forging ahead. A foxtrot is just a slower quickstep. I'm a little late, I said, smiling and nodding. I found without meaning to that I was trying to compensate for being a parcel. Kelly's Bo Peep outfit suited her. The bodice with the crossed straps accentuated her breasts, and she had a curved crook. She looked fifteen at least. As we danced I knew that she was looking at the parcel. I heard myself laughing loudly at Captain Marvel who was fighting with a pirate, but Kelly kept looking at my costume. I was going to come as a pirate myself, I said, I had a better pirate outfit than that; a huge hat with skull and cross-bones, and an eye-patch. What, she said. I was going to come as a pirate, I said. I can't hear you for all the noise your brown paper makes, Kelly said. It wasn't so of course. The band was making more noise than the parcel. No, she was giving me the message. Even the way she danced with me was different from the other times. She had a dull expression on her face, as if she was doing me a favour by dancing. I tried whirling her around, the way Bodger and Miss Erikson had demonstrated. I nearly fell over, she said. It was a lesson for me in the transience of sexual preferment. It was apparently something that had to be taken advantage of immediately.

I was determined not to mention being a parcel. Not admitting it was some way of keeping the full force of its humiliation from me. I quite like Dusty's Captain Marvel suit, I told Kelly. A bit overdone, but I quite like it. I told Miss Erikson I'd help with supper, she said. It won't be worth you coming over for the next dance for I'll start helping her soon I think. Sure, sure I said, we must have the grub on time. The grub on time! I couldn't believe I was saying it. And afterwards I'll probably help with the washing up, Kelly said.

Flour-and-water paste isn't very successful when there's any movement. Some of the stickers were starting to work loose on the brown paper. This Way Up fell on the dance floor. Handle with Care came off and I tucked it under the twine. It worked down low on my waist, and Dusty and Ricky Ransumeen started pointing and laughing at its anatomical juxtaposition. I took Kelly back to her side of the hall after the dance. See you then, I said. She slipped amongst the other girls with a murmur. Who could blame her? As I went back over the floor I could see several of my labels lying there. Fragile, Via Antwerp, Airmail. Maybe someone would start collecting them and draw attention to them. The parcel was ceasing to be recognizable as such. Without stickers, wrinkled and lopsided after the dancing, it had lost what little illusion of costume it ever had. I was a kid wrapped in brown paper and wearing bathing togs and sandshoes. Ah, Jesus me. Only the stamp over my heart seemed firmly stuck. A mark of Cain in crayon that leered out on all the world, and would not release itself or me. I was beaten all right. I couldn't maintain any longer my vision of how the night should be. And the withdrawal of sexual preferment had weakened me; my esteem had eroded. I began to work my way towards the door; a paper parcel through the batmen, policemen, riverboat gamblers and Indian chiefs. Little Wade Stewart was a Pluto. He came to me with Fragile. Is this yours, he said kindly. Yes, what a dag isn't it, I said. I kept moving towards the door, and reached it as the lucky spot waltz was announced.

It felt good outside. The summer dusk, the distanced and impersonal buildings, the lucky spot music fading as I made my way to the bikesheds. Bodger loomed up. I got a bit of a nosebleed, I told him, but as I was by myself he wasn't interested. I rode out of the grounds, and the crinkle of the parcel and the lessening music conjoined down the quiet street. I allowed myself the indulgence of self-pity for a time. I was outside myself; I accompanied myself; I consoled myself, for the bland incomprehension of adults and the loss of sexual status. I felt I had been hard done by, that was the truth. Perhaps there would be a fire in the hall. I imagined the flames leaping from the walls, and the riverboat gambles and the fairy queens put to flight. Faster and faster I biked. I saw the fiery press of the blaze, the terror of my classmates, the impotence of Bodger and Miss Erikson. I stood up on the pedals in the soft, summer night and put on a sprint that would have carried me clear of any possible pursuit. Parcel my arse, I shouted, and louder, parcel my arse. I reckoned that I was about the fastest bike rider at that school. I reckoned that even Dusty Rhodes wouldn't be a patch on me at that. I felt the wind on my flight pushing the brown paper against me as I swept without a light down the blue streets.

There was a light in the living room when I reached home however. I put my bike away, and looked through the gap between curtain edge and window-side. My mother was listening to the radio and talking; my father was cleaning his shoes on a newspaper spread by his chair. I had to find some immediate focus for revenge, and they would serve as enemies. I crept into the kitchen and took a packet of my father's cigarettes from behind the clock, and struck a match to inspect the pantry cupboard. Mixed fruit pack, I chose; raisins, candied peel, sultanas, figs, cherries. I took the fruit pack and cigarettes to the woodshed. I sat on the pine slabs in the lean-to there, and ate the fruit mix and smoked my father's Pall Mall. I ripped off the stamp in crayon, and burnt holes in it. I flashed the glowing cigarette against the navy sky, writing Zorro in swift neon. I undid the twine and unwrapped the parcel, burying the pieces in the woodheap. Jesus, I said, so what? Who cares about the dance and being a paper parcel? I was still second fastest in the school wasn't I. Wasn't I! I sat in my togs and singlet, ate my dried fruit, and watched the smoke curl as shadows from my fingers. And next time it would be different. I could see so clearly the next year's dance; when I would be Napoleon and Fiona McCartney my Josephine. That's how it would be all right.

A View Of Our Country

OWEN MARSHALL

Simon Palliser had spoken to the Blenheim Rotary Club on his experiences as a noted traveller, and I agreed to drive him down to Christchurch so he could see something of the country on the way before flying out to Paris via Singapore. I was going on business anyway, and the President thought that I could do our scenery justice, so Palliser would have an impression of the place to take with him.

As we crossed the high bridge close to Seddon, Simon Palliser looked down to the blue, wild flowers and the pooled water. He asked me if I'd ever been to the Ivory Coast. 'I flew in to Abidjan,' he said. 'Some fifteen years or so I suppose after they got their independence from the French. The heat was killing, and after a few days I decided to move into the hinterland. I hired a car and drove to Yamoussoukro where the President had his palace. I'm telling you this because crossing that river reminded me of the crocodiles of Yamoussoukro. I drove 240 kilometres to get there, through Ouossou and Tomumodi, along a road more and more enclosed by jungle and the red soil the jungle fed on. But at Yamoussoukro itself the jungle had been cleared and a modern city built alongside the President's family village. Great plantations had been laid out too, of mangoes, pineapples and avocados. Down one side of the President's palace an artificial lake had been created and stocked with turtles, catfish and crocodiles. There had been no crocodiles in that district before, I was told.

'The crocodiles were fed late in the afternoon, and the hotel hired a driver from the Baoule tribe to take me to view them. The driver met me on the broad boulevard in front of the foyer entrance. He was a cheerful and talkative man with fair English. He began to tell me about his country as we walked to the carpark. It was a little cooler than the coast, and a mist gathered in the city of Yamoussoukro; at once such a modern place, yet the site of chiefly power for hundreds of years.

'There was a causeway across the lake to the palace gates lined with coconut palms and iron railings, and at the gate the Presidential Guard stood sentry. The crocodiles waited with their mouths agape, on a shelf of sand between the embankment and the lake, and the feeder came in a pick-up truck and took buckets of meat to feed them. He called lovingly in French as he threw pieces down to the crocodiles who seemed short-sighted and inefficient eaters. It began to rain heavily, and colours came up on the backs of the crocodiles, and more crocodiles and a few turtles came out of the lake. The mist crept closer and the rain dimpled the surface of the lake. The feeder then took a chicken from his truck, and swung it back and forth in the rain above the railings; all the time appealing in French to the crocodiles. Then he tossed the chicken into the air.

'The chicken gained courage from being free in the air and rain. It flapped stoutly and landed over the heads of the crocodiles and in the lake. As it landed a turtle surfaced, as if it had duplicated the flight beneath the water, and the chicken was seized. It was an auspicious thing to happen. The feeder was alarmed and angry; my Baoule driver was glum. The feeder climbed the fence and ran towards the water across the sand to frighten the turtle. Instead one of the largest crocodiles jumped forward like an ungainly rabbit and had the keeper's leg in his mouth. There were perhaps twenty or thirty people watching, and the feeling of all seemed not one of horror, or even active concern, but a deep hopelessness. The crocodile backed into the lake, giving several gulping changes of grip which drew the feeder more firmly to him. The feeder called out once in French, then was silent, and his long robe trailed behind him. One of the guards fired into the air, and the keeper's wide eyes were fixed on us, his audience, even as he disappeared.

'The rain dimpled the lake surface just the same; turtle and chicken, crocodile and man were gone, leaving us powerless in the wet. "Quickly come away with me now," my driver said. I was thinking that there had been no crocodiles at all at Yamoussoukro until the lake had been dug for the President's palace.'

256

It was a dry year in Marlborough. When we stopped a little past Ward for a thermos of tea, the hills were very brown and the heat confused their outlines. Palliser said it reminded him of Spain. 'Emotionally, Spain was a turning point for me,' he said. 'A woman I was very much in love with, left me to take up a United Nations job in the Mato Grosso, and I drifted south into Andalusia and was very drunk for several weeks. You know Andalusia I suppose? Of the several weeks I can remember nothing; a blank in my life, then I sobered up in the little town of Baeza in the hills above the Guadalquivir. I can feel the very evening; the air heavy with jasmine and orange blossom, the soil red as a heart. There were prickly pears at the roadside and within some of them the torreo bird had picked out small nests, and their heads watched at the entrances as I passed. My friend took me to the café to hear the gypsies sing the cante jondo, and all through it the more stolid locals sat at the back tables and continued with their dominoes. I didn't drink, and watched the gypsies under the influence of wine move from the plaintive cante jondo to a wild flamenco; all castanets and exclamation. In the midst of it a farmer brought in a lynx he had killed in his fields, and hung it from a beam by the door for his friends to admire, or to attract a buyer for the skin perhaps.

'As the gypsies danced and sang, as the domino players became steadily more absorbed in their own purpose, I sat with the scent of jasmine and orange blossom through the café door, and the Persian gleam of fur upon the lynx. It turned slowly on the cord, first one way then the other, as if its tufted ears still sought some magnetic north of freedom.'

The seaward Kaikouras crowd the main road to the ocean's edge south of the Clarence river and rise abruptly to over 3,000 metres. Simon Palliser had a love of mountains. 'Of course Switzerland has been something of a second home to me,' he said. 'Several times between expeditions I rested at Brunnen on the shores of Lake Luzern. Do you know it? A town of solid, unpretentious houses on a flat strip of land, while beyond it the steep, glaciated slopes descend into the lake like the sides of a fiord. I made a base at the guest-house of the Gotthardt's usually, and from my upstairs room I had a view of the small steamer berths, and the many trees of that part of the town. I remember on one of their election days taking the rack and pinion railway from Brunnen to Axenstein, a high resort with magnificent views across the lake. Because of the elections and the season there were few people travelling, and in my compartment only one other person; a Swedish woman, beautifully dressed, who spoke excellent German. She told me in a gentle, quite unselfconscious way that she had been travelling to overcome her grief at the recent death of her husband, and that her main difficulty was coping with the loss of sexual satisfaction brought about by the abrupt end of her marriage. She had found no opportunity for solace not repugnant to her she said, until seeing me who bore a singular resemblance to her husband.

'It was all so natural, so kind, so tinged with inevitability. We stood close in the corner of the rack and pinion carriage, with her lovely skirt folded up. Her tears were wet on my cheeks: perhaps I cried myself. She clasped her hands at the small of my back and pulled strongly. Past the blond hair fastened back from her smooth face, the lake seemed quite calm from such a height and pine forests rose up to the snow line on the mountains above the water. She murmured her husband's name through her tears, I recall. Have you travelled to Sweden? Sven is a common Christian name there.'

As we drove down the coast close to Kaikoura, Palliser thought he saw a seal on the rocky shore. He was interested because of the heavy swell also, and the scene reminded him of British Columbia. 'I had a temporary job in conservation there,' he said. 'I was camped in the magnificently unspoiled Pacific Rim National Park on Vancouver Island. My main task was checking on the sea lions which lived in groups on rocky islets off the coast. On the one day in three or four the swell allowed, I would circle the outcrops in the small boat provided, count the sea lions and record the colour of any tags recognised through the binoculars. Most days I couldn't go out, and I would walk through the stands of Sitka spruce which fringed the beaches, or I would push into the rain forest further inland. The garter snakes would sidle under salmonberry bushes as I approached, and in the cathedral quiet of the rain forest could be heard just the organ music echo of the great Pacific rollers breaking on the first American coast to obstruct them.

'It was cool rain forest, without many birds, and often difficult to walk through because of the swampy places and fallen trees. Ferns and mosses thrived on the decay, as did puff balls, stallion heads and frilled fungi which added the only vivid colours: visceral gleams of red, yellow and spotted black orange, powdered horns like those of a myriad snails sprouting electric blue from the cancerous side of a log.

'After storms I would walk the grey sand of the Pacific beach, see the heaped driftwood, whole trees sometimes, and piles of rotting sea-weed which were alive with jumpers. Some of the driftwood still had soil and stones in its roots and gum on its branches, other pieces had been fully digested by the sea and were worn and pale like old soap. On one morning I was amazed to see the vast horns of a caribou caught in the cleft of a tree close to the water line. The tips of the tines were four metres apart, and the antlers would make an arch that two men could march through without stooping. I couldn't dislodge it from the driftwood, and overnight everything was carried away again by the tide and the storm. So are opportunities lost and nothing can be done. I've often thought that the only explanation of such size is that the horns and skull that held them must have been a prehistoric find, carried down to the sea at last from Alaska or the Yukon where some great bull died ten thousand years ago.'

Simon Palliser slept for a while then, his head jogging on his shoulder, and woke when we were coming through Parnassus. I was going to explain the origin of the name for him when we saw a small girl and her doll waiting patiently for the rural delivery man on the grassy roadside by her farm mail box. 'She reminds me of a child I met once in Mexico,' said Palliser. 'On my way to Tierra del Fuego I stopped in Mexico and took the opportunity to visit the Mayan ruins at Chichen Itza. I drove out from Mérida after a meal of tamale with black beans. Rather than the pyramids and temples it was the sacred well of sacrifice that interested me. A huge, circular limestone opening, and twenty metres down sheer rock walls to water which is twenty metres deep again. Young men and virgins were sacrificed in full finery there; the remnant of the jutting altar can still be seen. Government divers have recently managed to recover gold masks and skulls from the mud.

'I had my lunch of chocolate and melon by the stones and shadow of the well's lip, and some Indian children squatted around me to beg a share. I could hear the murmur of the visitors and the more assured, single voices of the guides. I could see people clambering up the stepped side of the pyramid. I thought how this setting of absolute tyranny and religious death had become with time a picnic spot and oddity; the stones and pits denied the sacrifice which had given them their significance. When they had eaten my food the children left me, except for one small girl who calculated that I must have something hidden, or that I would tip her for the privilege of being rid of her. She sat by the rim of the well of sacrifice, and childlike twisted her fingers into the cracks of the wall while watching me intently. All in an instant her fingers drew out a ring of gold with blue amethyst centre, which had lain so long so close to all the people passing. While my mouth was still opening, she rolled the ring once in her fingers as a pebble, and still with her eyes fixed on mine, reached her thin hand over the rim of the well and dropped the jewel to the water and mud far below.

'She must have seen something in my face then that dismayed her, for she bounced up and skimmed away through the heat of Chichen Itza to join the other urchins. There was nothing I could do, you see; nothing that would bring back such a chance missed.'

I thought the Canterbury plains a good contrast to the landscape earlier in the day, and I told Palliser that the Waimakariri which was coming up, was one of our major rivers. 'For me,' he said, 'the river which has my soul is the Okavango, and I've seen both Niles, the Mekong, Mississippi, Rhine, Ganges, Amazon, Yangtze, Congo, Euphrates, the Don and the Orinoco. The Okavango flows away from the sea into the Kalahari; wonderful incongruity. In ancient times there was a huge lake over most of Botswana, but earthquakes altered the courses of the other rivers which fed it, and now only the Okavango continues spreading over 18,000 kilometres into a million channels and lagoons: the inland estuary of a once inland sea. The great Okavango flows into the sand, holds back the shimmering menace of the desert each year. It's one of the most beautiful and luxuriant places in the world, and protected from the worst of modern encroachment by the tsetse fly and sleeping sickness. I've been drawn back again and again, as perhaps you have yourself. On an early visit I was charged by a tusker while hunting zebra, and had to shoot. The authorities made me pay an excessive elephant license fee despite my protests that I had acted only in self-defence. The ivory was confiscated, although I kept the tail and later had an ebony stock fitted to it, making a fly swat.

'On that visit to the Okavango old Johannes de Wette was still alive, and living on one of the estuary islands in the south. He was 87 years old and his brother in law had captured Winston Churchill during the Boer War. De Wette was one of the true white hunters and we sat overlooking the papyrus beds, listening to the slap of catfish and myungobis, the ugly cries of the malibu stork, while he told me of the old days on the Okavango. They used to make hippo rafts to navigate the swamps by shooting four hippo in the head and sewing their mouths closed. After twelve hours the heat so blew their bellies up that they had the buoyancy of gigantic corks, and were used one at each corner of a log raft. De Wette and his comrades would drift through the channels raised up on hippo carcases as if on a dais. Among the Botswana in those days they were treated like royalty, and de Wette said that a bed of Botswana maidens was provided for the hunters — 18 or 20 girls, their bodies gleaming with fig oil, would lie with arms and legs intertwined to make a couch for the night. De Wette's seamed, Afrikaner face was impassive as he told me, but his deep eyes were wistful as we watched a magnificent white-necked fish eagle plummet from the sky into the deep channels of the Okavango.'

As we came into the quiet, spread suburbs of Christchurch, Palliser contrasted them with the intensity of Calcutta. He had come down from Tibet to convalesce he said, after suffering from frost-bite, and to avoid the tourist traps had found a room in the Ashin district of Calcutta. 'It's always been my object to take part in the real life of any place I find myself in,' he said. 'You will remember no doubt the typical stench that part of Calcutta has; the cooking fires, exhaust fumes, oil and dung, the smell of the river and of the cremation grounds further out. Part of that smell too is poverty and loss of dignity. All within sight of the domed Victorian Railway Terminus, memorial to the Raj, and not far from the *maidan* — the lungs of Calcutta.

'My room was made of tar paper and the sides of packing cases from the Bala engineering works. As I lay on my sleeping bag at night I could see stamped on the boards above the curtained doorway the words, Store Away From Boilers.

'My small-time landlord liked to entertain me by taking me to the bazaars in the evening, spurning the untouchables from our path with the hauteur of a man of property. Street after street where life went on; everything is done in the streets because there is no option. Past the pumps in the street for household water, past the stall holders and beggars, the people crouched in doorways, the goat boy selling milk as required from his animal's udder, the banana sellers, hooded rickshaws with their drivers squatted between the poles and resting. One night we saw a goldfish and ball-bearing eater outside a flower shop and a potter's. There are no ends to the way a man can be demeaned in search of a living. Up to ten goldfish and ball-bearings I saw him swallow, then sing for a while, then regurgitate them into a plastic bag of water, so that they swam again apparently unharmed. In the narrow alley at the side of the potter's shop were piles of clay and wood, shards of pottery, trays of small images of Kali set out to dry. The sideshow swallower may have noticed me watching with more interest than most of the passing crowd, or perhaps it was just as a European who gave him an American dollar that I received attention. He stood before me with a smooth, handsome face, and swallowed five ball-bearings the size of golf balls and in good English told me that he was a B.A. 'You are seeing what a person will be doing for sake of family,' he said. 'What we are brought to is a terrible thing.' Behind his personal misery was all the beauty of the flower shop; garlands of jasmine and marigolds from the red soil, roses even, and a few sacred lotus blooms set further back. The swallower became vehement at his plight; shouting to be heard above the transistors and bazaar noise. In his misery he forgot to maintain muscular control of the ball-bearings in his gut, and they must have moved down for suddenly he screamed with pain and fell back amongst the marigolds and jasmine. It drew more people and more interest than his former act, and all the watchers loudly gave advice as to the best way to cure him. The flower seller called loudest of all about the dying man. I asked my landlord what he was saying and was told the vendor demanded to know who would pay for the crushed jasmine and roses.'

I left Simon Palliser at his hotel by the Square. He was grateful he said to have had the opportunity to see something of the nature of the country here, and to spend time getting to know me. We could see the Cathedral quite clearly, and Palliser said as I left that it reminded him of a peculiar thing that happened while he was staying in Strasbourg some years before.

The Rule of Jenny Pen

OWEN MARSHALL

The heavy moonlight gave it all the appearance of quality linen, flattering the exposed walls of the Totara Eventide Home, and the lines of stainless steel trolleys and wheel chairs by the windows glinted like cutlery upon that linen. The moon was more forgiving than the sun, allowing a variety of interpretations for what it revealed. The shadowed places were soft feathered with blue and grey, like a pigeon's breast.

The only sound was Crealy pissing onto Matron's herb garden. The white cord of his striped pyjamas hung down one leg, and his bald head was made linen in the moonlight. 'Had enough?' Crealy asked the sage, basil and thyme. Residents were not supposed to come out and treat the Matron's herbs to such abuse. Crealy felt his life stir as ever at the defiance of rules. He could see the trim, summer lawn and the garden which paralleled the side path to the slope of the front grounds. The moonlight lay over it all as a linen snowfall.

Crealy had never before lived in a place so pleasant to the eye, or so well organised — and he hated it. Always a big man, he had never done anything with it; lacking the will, the resolution, the brains and the luck. At eighty-one and in Totara Home, he found that time had awarded him a superiority which he had been unable to earn any other way. He had given little; and lasted well.

Crealy's bladder was empty, so he put a large hand over his face to massage his cheeks, while he waited for an idea as to what to do next. Even in the moonlight the kidney spots on the backs of his hands showed clearly. He could think of nothing novel to do so decided to persecute Garfield. He went back through the staff door of the kitchen,

263

and bolted it carefully behind him. Before seeking out Garfield, Crealy wanted to be sure that Brisson was settled in the duty room. He went slowly through the kitchen and the dining room, through the corridors which were tunnels in the Totara of all their past lives.

Crealy stood in the shadow of the last doorway, and looked into the corridor which led past the duty room. He was like a bear which pauses instinctively at the edge of a forest clearing to assess possibilities of gain or loss. He walked slowly down the corridor of mottled, yellow lino, his breathing louder than the regular shuffle of his slippers. Before the duty room he slowed even further as a caution, but his breathing was as loud as ever. The door was ajar, and Crealy looked in to see Brisson at leisure.

The duty room had a sofa, a chair, a log book with a biro on a string, a coffee pot, a telephone, a typed copy of the fire drill on the wall. It had the worn, impersonal look common to all such rooms in institutions, whether hospitals or boarding schools, army depots or fire brigades. Brisson lay on the sofa, and held up a paperback as if shielding himself from the light. His head was round and firm like a well grown onion, and light brown with the sheen a good onion has too. He wore no socks, just yellow sneakers on his neat feet. Crealy was surprised yet again to see how young some people were. He'll lie there all night and do nothing, thought Crealy.

'Who's that huffing and puffing outside my door?' said Brisson without moving, and Crealy pushed the door and took a step into the doorway. 'Ah, so it's you, Mr Crealy,' said Brisson. He swung the book down and his legs onto the floor in one easy movement. 'Why are you wandering the baronial halls?'

In reply Crealy made a gesture with his large hands which seemed more resignation than explanation. Brisson was lazy, arrogant, shrewd — and young. He took in Crealy: the awkward size of him, the sourness of his worn, bald face, the striped pyjamas, and between them and slippers, Crealy's bare ankles with the veins swollen. Brisson gave a slight shiver of joy and horror at his amazing youth and Crealy's old age.

'Mrs Vennermann said you squeezed the blossom off her bedside flowers,' he said. Crealy itched his neck; his fingers sounded as if they worked on sand paper, and the grey stubble was clear in the light of the room. 'She said you pick on people. Is that right?'

'She took my Milo,' said Crealy. Brisson picked up the exercise book that served as the log for duty shifts.

'Shall I put that in here then? Shall I? Mr Crealy deprived of his Milo by Mrs Vennermann. For Christ's sake. And someone said that you have been making Mrs Halliday all flustered. Aye?'

'It's just all fuss,' said Crealy. He began to think how he could get back at Mrs Vennermann.

Brisson smiled at his own performance, looked at old Crealy, at the mottled lino like a puddle behind him, at the exercise book with the cover doodled upon and the biro on a string from it. He considered himself incongruous in such surroundings. He had such different things planned for himself. 'I won't have a bully on my shift, Mr Crealy. If I have to come down to the rooms then look out. And don't you or the others come up here bothering me.' Brisson hoped to be with Nurse McMillan. What time was it?

'I don't do anything,' said Crealy in his husky voice. 'It's Jenny Pen.'

'What's that?'

'Eh?' said Crealy.

'Go to bed,' said Brisson, and saw the old man turn back onto the puddle lino; heard the shuffle and breath of him as he went back to the rooms of the east wing. Brisson did an abrupt shoulder stand on the sofa to prove age not contagious, then relaxed again with his book and thoughts of Nurse McMillan.

When Crealy reached the room he shared with Garfield, Mortenson and Popanovich he was ready for a little action. Jenny Pen time. Jenny Pen was a hand puppet that Garfield's grand-daughter had made at intermediate school. Although christened Jenny Pencarrow it looked more like Punch, or the witch from Snow White, for its papier mâché nose and chin strove to complete a circle. Jenny Pen had a skirt of red velvet, and balanced all day on the left hand knob of Garfield's bed. At night, ah torment, she became the fasces of Nero's power, the cloven hoof, the dark knight's snouted emblem, the sign of Modu and Mahu, the dancing partner of a trivial Lucifer, a tender facsimile of things gone wrong.

265

Crealy lifted Jenny Pen from the bed end, and thrust his hand beneath the velvet skirt. He held her aloft, and turned her painted head until all the room had been held in her regard. Garfield began to cry; Mortenson turned the better side of his face aside, and wished his stroke had been more complete. Popanovich was just a shoulder beneath his blankets. Crealy walked Jenny Pen on her hands up Garfield's chest, and she seemed of her own volition to rap Garfield's face. 'Who rules?' said Crealy.

'Jenny Pen,' said Garfield. Garfield had played seventeen games for Wellington as fullback, and later been general manager for Hentlings. It was all too far away to offer any protection.

'Lick her arse then,' said Crealy hoarsely, and Garfield did, and felt Crealy's hand on his tongue. 'You're on Jenny Pen's side, aren't you?' said Crealy.

'Yes.' Garfield's voice barely quivered, although the tears ran down his cheeks. He could scarcely conceive the life he was forced to lead: his soul peeped out from a body which had betrayed him in the end.

Crealy's eyes glittered, and he looked about to share his triumph with others. 'What about you, Judge; want to do a little kissing?' Mortenson gave his half smile.

'It's difficult for me,' he said slowly.

'Bloody difficult with only half of everything working.' Crealy walked over to the last bed, and shook Popanovich's shoulder. There was no reaction. 'What sort of a name is that for a New Zealander,' he said. 'Bloody Popanovich!' He banged his knee into Popanovich's back, but there was no defence of the name. It put Crealy in an ill humour again, and he went back to Garfield with Jenny Pen. He began to go through Garfield's locker. 'It's share and share alike here, Garbunkle.'

'Communism has the greatest attraction to those with the least,' said Mortenson in his slurred voice, knowing Crealy was not bright enough to follow.

'Shut up,' said Crealy. He placed a bag of barley sugars and a box of shortbread biscuits on top of Garfield's locker. 'Is that all you use-less bugger,' he said. He looked at Garfield for a time, letting Jenny Pen rest on the covers, almost basking in the knowledge shared between them of Garfield's weakness and his strength. And even more, the mutual knowledge of Garfield's former strength and superiority,

Garfield's achievements and complacency, now worthless currency before Crealy who had achieved nothing except the accidental husbandry of physical strength into old age.

'What else have you got hidden after all them visitors?' Crealy slid his free hand slowly under Garfield's pillow, and withdrew it empty. 'Come on now you bugger,' he said.

'Just leave me alone.'

'Make Jenny Pen sing a song,' said Mortenson. Sometimes Crealy would have Jenny Pen sing 'Knick Knack Paddy Wack Give A Dog A Bone', or 'Knees Up Mother Brown'. It was an awful sound, but better than the beatings.

Crealy listened a while, to make sure that no one was coming who could take Garfield's part, then he pulled the near side of the mattress up and found a packet of figs. 'That's more like it,' he said. He sat on the bed as if he were a friend of Garfield. 'You selfish old bugger,' he said mildly. 'How many figs do you reckon there are here?'

Garfield didn't answer, and Crealy took hold of his near ear and shook his head by means of it until Garfield cried out. 'Don't you start calling out, or you'll get more,' said Crealy. He opened the packet and began to eat. 'For every one you're going to get a hurry up,' he said, and gave Garfield one right away.

So it began. Popanovich remained in hibernation beneath his blankets, Mortenson watched, but tried to keep the true side of his face as expressionless as the other, even though his good leg was rigid. Garfield covered his ears, and Crealy ate the figs, hitting Garfield's face with each new mouthful. 'Figs make you shit, Garfield old son,' he said, 'but I'll make you shit without them. That's rich isn't it. I said that's rich isn't it, Judge?'

'Exactly,' said Mortenson carefully. What time was it? He tried to remember some of the letters of Cicero he had been reading.

The one light from Garfield's locker cast a swooping shadow each time Crealy leant forward solicitously to hit Garfield, and when Crealy held Jenny Pen up in triumph she was manifest as a montrous Viking prow upon the wall. Mortenson had to accept the realisation that there were underworlds which he had been able until recently to ignore; now he was part of one, suffering and observing, powerless through reduced capacity and fear.

When he saw a little, shining blood beneath Garfield's nose he could contain his opposition no longer. Yet stress undid his recent progress and Stefan Albee Mortenson, barrister, solicitor, notary public could produce before the court of Jenny Pen, only. 'Creal youb narlous narl stapp awus nee.'

'Careful, Judge. I don't need your squark. I might come across and give you more than just this feathering Garfield's enjoying. I'll do the side of you not already dead, you pinstripe squirt.'

Mortenson had nothing more to say, and Garfield sat with his chin on his chest as if in a trance. 'Had enough?' Crealy asked him. 'You're gutless the lot of you.' Crealy was bored with his immediate subjects, and with Jenny Pen still on his hand as his familiar he went to wander the night corridors of the Home. No conversation began in the room he left. Popanovich feigned the sleep of death, Garfield remained slumped in his bed and Mortenson had no way of travelling the distance between them to offer comfort.

Mrs Munro knew nothing of Totara's netherworld. She had her own room in the separate block before the cottages, and the sun was laid on the polish of several pieces of her own furniture which had accompanied her. Mrs Munro could never understand those who complained of time dragging. She herself delighted in time to spare for all those indulgences a busy life had denied her; all those intellectual and emotional considerations that the slog of a seven-day dairy had prevented her from enjoying. She wore the track suit which she had insisted on for a Christmas present. She liked the comfort, the lack of constriction, the zippers at ankle and chest which made it easy to get off. She liked the two bright blue stripes and the motif of crossed racquets, even though she had never played sport.

Despite something of a problem with head nodding, and a hip operation on the way, Mrs Munro was quietly proud that although she was an old woman, she was not a fat, old woman. She didn't complain about the food, and she drew more large-print library books in a week than anyone else in the Home. She rejoiced in an hour to wile away over a cup of tea, or in writing to Bessie Hambinder, or in putting drops in her ear, or measuring her room with the tape from the sewing basket. Miss Hails from the main block did visit too often it was true, and her repetitions tended to start Mrs Munro's head nodding, but there was always the bedding store-room as a sanctuary, and Mrs Munro had built a little dug-out in the blanket piles where she could rest in her track suit after lunch until Miss Hails had given up looking for her, and gone visiting elsewhere.

For the present though she counted the spots of a ladybird on her window sill, and watched sour, old Crealy smoking on a bench by the secure recreation area. Crealy was not compulsive viewing, and when Mrs Munro finished her computations concerning the ladybird she decided she would begin her next romance of the British Raj.

Crealy's cigarette was the last in the packet he had stolen from Popanovich, who was sleeping again. The days were not as enjoyable as the nights for Crealy, because he was too much under the eye of authority, and the spirit of his fellows was not as easily daunted when the sun shone. He wondered if Mrs Halliday was by the goldfish pond, but couldn't see her, and so he went back indoors to check Mortenson's locker before lunch. In the main corridor he came across Mrs Joyce, who had her blood changed quite regularly at the clinic. Her fore-arms and elbows seemed forever to have the yellows, purples and blues of ageing bruises. Mrs Joyce had made binoculars of her hands and stood with them pressed to the glass doors, staring out. 'What's out there?' she asked Crealy.

'Herbs and spices, sycamores and young people. And bloody work.'

'I can't see it,' said Mrs Joyce.

'You've gone daft in there.' Crealy rapped on her head with his knuckles, but she kept peering out into the sunshine through the tunnels of her fingers.

'Let me join Jesus,' she said. Crealy looked down at her pink scalp beneath the white hair. Because there was no resistance whatsoever that she could make, because she was not even aware of his malice, Crealy couldn't be bothered hurting her.

'Dozy old tart.'

'Let me come to thee sweet Jesus,' said Mrs Joyce. Crealy had a chuckle at that, and at how Mrs Joyce was peering through her hands and the glass, although everything outside was perfectly clear to him.

Matron Frew heard the chuckle from the office, and it reminded her that she wanted words with Crealy. She first of all took Mrs Joyce's arm in hers, and walked with her down to the dayroom. She was back before Crealy could quite disappear from sight down the corridor however, and she told him with some bluntness of the indirect complaints she'd been receiving, particularly from staff who had noticed Crealy pestering Mrs Halliday and Mr Garfield.

'Mark my words,' said Matron Frew. 'I will be watching, and also I'm making mention of things in my report to the board this month. You show an unwillingness at times to be a reasonable member of our community.'

As she spoke Crealy hung his head, but not from meekness or contrition. He was counting the number of useable butts in the sandbox by the office door, and when he had done that he imagined himself in the mild, summer night standing over Matron's herb garden, and pissing on the chives, parsley, mint, fennel and thyme. A lifetime in the indifferent, hostile or contemptuous regard of others had rendered Crealy immune to all three. He recognised no value or interest other than his own.

On Wednesday evenings Matron Frew turned off the television in the east wing lounge and organised communal singing. It was not compulsory as such, but absence meant no chocolate biscuits at the supper which followed. As a professionally trained person, matron knew that a variety of stimulus for the elderly was important.

The committed, the egotistical and the hard of hearing stood close around the piano, the infirm or less enthusiastic were rims at a greater distance. Golden oldies they sang, to Matron's accompaniment. 'The Kerry Pipers', 'Auld Lang Syne', 'The Biggest Aspidistra In The World', 'On Top Of Old Smokey'.

Matron had begun her career as a physiotherapist and it showed in her playing: the keys kneaded like a string of vertebrae; each tune well gone over and the kinks removed. 'Waltzing Matilda', 'Home On The Range', 'The White Cliffs Of Dover', 'Some Enchanted Evening', 'Polly Wolly Doodle'. Matron Frew allowed her charges to respond in their own way and order, but she always had Nurse Glenn or Nurse McMillan guide Mr Oliphant to the uncarpeted area by the door because the pathos of any Irish tune made him incontinent.

A refrain, particularly with high notes, would sometimes trigger

Miss Hails' weakness and she would begin the incessant repetition of a word. It happened sure enough during 'Riding Down From Bangor', and for several minutes Miss Hail sang only 'May'. Crealy was present not just for the chocolate biscuits, but because it gave him perverse satisfaction after the Matron's rebuke, to exercise intimidation almost under her gaze.

He stood on Mrs Dellow's toe during 'Annie Laurie', and stared into her face, daring her to respond. Her thin voice assumed even greater vibrato and her eyes misted. Crealy then leant in comradeship over blind Mr Lewin and sprayed saliva into his face as 'Christopher Robin Went Down With Alice'.

When the chocolate biscuits came at last, Crealy kept himself between them and George Oliphant until they were all gone, then he said, 'Now isn't that a bugger, George, they seem all gone.'

'Silver Threads Among The Gold', they sang, and 'Swing Low Sweet Chariot'. 'Home, home, home, home, home, home,' Miss Hails continued, until Matron Frew told her to suck her thumb until the cycle was broken. 'Knees Up Mother Brown' Crealy liked, but because it was his favourite the others found no pleasure in joining in.

Mortenson enjoyed the association the songs bore, even if not the singing itself. He preferred to be at some remove from the piano and his fellows, for then he could imagine other company and past days: his mouth would twitch and his good hand move to the melodies. 'Some Enchanted Evening' — he would sing it with Deborah as they drove back from ski-ing, ready for court work during the week. He hadn't realised then, that all roads led to this. 'Roo, roo, roo, roo, roo,' began Miss Hails.

Before midnight, aware of an odd, sighing wind around the Home, Crealy made a patrol of his domain; only his harsh breathing and shuffle gave him away. In his own room everything was as it should be — Garfield was weeping, Popanovich sleeping, and Mortenson in his snores fell every few minutes into a choking death rattle which woke him briefly, then he slept and it all began again.

Further down the corridor Mrs Doone was talking to herself as she strung up non-existent Christmas decorations. Every night was Christmas Eve for Mrs Doone, and the wonder and *frisson* of it were freshly felt night after night. 'Compliments of the season, Mr Ah — ah,' she said as Crealy slippered by. Around the corner, Crealy paused outside the room Mrs Oliffe and Miss Hails shared. Miss Hails was doing her thing of course; for almost an hour she had been repeating the sound tee, while Mrs Oliffe was trying to find nineteen across which was Breton Gaelic for divine harbinger.

'Oh, stop going tee, tee, tee, tee,' Mrs Oliffe said, but the simple satisfaction of it set her off also, and she joined in. Outside, Crealy could hear them in unison, tee, tee, tee. He found his own head nodding and his mouth formed the sound. One night it might spread through all of Totara, and capture them in a transport of repetitious senility.

Crealy put his hand to his face to stop himself. He looked carefully down the corridor. 'Mad old tarts,' he said. He considered opening their door and frightening them into silence, but the chances of being caught up in their chant and left nodding with them indefinitely was too great. He went on, still with one hand on his face. Tee, tee, tee, tee, faded behind him.

Outside the Matron's office were chairs for visitors, and a varnished box with a sand tray in it for smokers amongst the visitors. Crealy was able to find several butts worth using again, before he noticed Mrs Joyce standing by the main doors once more. 'Jesus loves me this I know,' she said. She had two overcoats on, and stood with her hand on the catch of the locked door. 'I'm going home,' she said. 'I've been here nearly a fortnight and they are expecting me back now.'

'You've been here for years,' said Crealy.

'Oh no, just a fortnight, and I need to be at home for every special occasion. We've always been a very close family you see.' Crealy went through her double set of pockets as she talked, but all he could find was a small book of stamps. 'They may well send a car for me,' she said. They both looked through the glass doors for a moment, but there was only empty wind and moonlight: no car parked on the linen of the drive.

'You can go home this way,' said Crealy, taking Mrs Joyce by the lapel and leading her towards the kitchens.

'Has the car come then?' she said, and 'God will provide, you know. Even Solomon in all his glory.' Crealy led her through the dining room laid for breakfast, and the kitchens, where worn, steel surfaces glinted like new bone. He unbolted the service door and set Mrs Joyce in the gap. 'There you are then,' he said. 'The main drive's just around the corner.'

'It's a clear path to home, thank Jesus.' The blue second coat would barely fit over the first, and pulled her arms back like the flippers of a penguin. Rather like a penguin she began walking, struck her head on a pruned plum branch, and reeled past the herb garden.

'What's your name again?' said Crealy, but Mrs Joyce didn't answer, and still unsteady from the blow made the best pace she could around the side path. She had the scent of freedom; she had a promise of home.

Crealy waited until Mrs Joyce was well gone and there was no sound of pursuit or return, then he went out himself and stood in the summer night, sniffing the aromatic air of Matron Frew's herb garden. He hung out his cock, and waited patiently for his prostate to relax its grip so that he could enjoy the physical relief and pleasurable malice of watering the herbs. He had both in good time, then he stood under the sycamore by the old garages and had one of the visitor's cigarette ends, after nipping off the filter.

The sycamore creaked and murmured in the night breeze which blew out from the land to the sea. Despite the ache in his joints, Crealy enjoyed being by himself there beneath the branches, and higher the summer sky, for he knew that he had always been unloved. Even though old age at Totara had given him a mirror image power and significance while always before he had been subjugated, he liked still to be alone, to have no sources of action or response other than himself. So he stood beneath the sycamore, and enjoyed his cigarette ends guardedly, shading the glow with a palm, and looking out to the better lit parts of the grounds. 'No bastard can see me,' he said. 'No bastard knows I'm here.'

Even a summer's night grows cold for old bones, and Crealy came in and bolted the door behind him. 'Had enough?' he had asked the mint and parsley as he went by them. He inspected Mrs Joyce's stamps in the dim light. He wanted to search her room, but had forgotten her name. Crealy had never been an intellectual, and at eighty-one he found it difficult to move and think at the same time. So he remained stopped in the semi-light between kitchen and dining room, and he tried to remember what he had been going to do before he met Mrs Joyce.

He went into the pantry beyond the stainless steel moonlight of the kitchen, and lifted out a large tin of golden syrup. He took a thick crust from the toast drawer and with his fingers as a ladle spread golden syrup on it. The syrup lay dark in the tin, but silver in glints as it twined from his fingers.

Crealy replaced the tin, and stood with the bread and syrup in his clean hand, sucking his other fingers. He looked into the shadowed dining room: the identical tables, evenly spaced, and an oblong of light across them from the corridor. The golden syrup was rich and energy giving. Crealy began to wonder if Mrs Halliday was having one of her spells in the Home. He stood in the kitchen doorway as a Neanderthal at the entrance to his cave. The syrup made a silver necklace to the floor. Crealy couldn't remember: couldn't remember at all.

'Bugger me,' he said at last. He was unable to come up with anything, so he stopped thinking, allowed the motor-sensory centres priority again, and moved into the lino tubes which were the Totara corridors.

At the duty room, Crealy decided to check on Brisson in case he was doing the unexpected thing and actually making a round. There was no key for the duty room door, but when Crealy pushed lightly against it, he found that Brisson had set the end of the sofa hard to it. Then he heard voices. Nurse McMillan talked as she and Brisson made love, but her topic was dissatisfaction with conditions of service, not romance. Lovemaking altered the normal rhythm of her words so that odd, accentuated syllables were driven out of her. 'GOD we've all thought OF handing in our resignNATIONS,' she said.

'There's nothing in all the world to match it,' Brisson said.

The palm of one of Crealy's large hands still rested on the door, though he pressed no more. He listened to a tune which mocked him, and his arthritis drove him on, shuffling and disgruntled; missing out as usual. Mrs Doone had finished putting up her Christmas decorations for the night, and the corridor was as bare as when she first began. Even Miss Hails was silent, but as Crealy passed Mr Lewin's room he heard a talking clock. 'It is twelve o'clock, midnight,' said the talking clock. Like a fox at a burrow entrance, Crealy stood before the door, but the clock didn't speak again, and blind Mr Lewin who must have activated it made no sound either.

As he neared his own room Crealy could hear Mortenson's stricken breathing, and remembered with sudden vividness a time more than thirty years ago when he had been a cleaner at the Nazareth Hall and Mortenson had been president of a group that banqueted there. Crealy had looked out from the serving hatch, waiting to begin clearing up, and S.A. Mortenson CBE, barrister, solicitor, notary public, city councillor and party chairman, had been standing at the top table; standing in his dinner jacket to give an erudite speech which was buoyed up constantly by delighted applause and laughter from the other tables. The recollection had such strength that Crealy felt again the flat ache of his own inconsequence, but it passed and he was aware of the cream Totara walls again, and the struggle Mortenson had to breathe.

Crealy laid Popanovich's open bottle of lemonade on the bed so that it would wet the sleeping man's feet, and plucked Jenny Pen from Garfield's bed end and held her briefly aloft. 'Wake up, Judge,' he said, and took Mortenson's nose between Jenny Pen's hands.

Mortenson's good side woke with horror. What time was it? 'Let's have poetry tonight,' said Crealy. He made himself comfortable on the bed with his room-mate. 'And I want to see you enjoying it, Judge; getting into the swing of it,' he said.

And where the silk-shoed lovers ran
with dust of diamonds in their hair,
he opens now his silent wing

began Mortenson indistinctly.

Crealy put one of Jenny Pen's fingers into the slack side of Mortenson's mouth and pulled it into the image of a smile. 'Let's not be half-hearted about this. Try something else,' said Crealy. Mortenson wished to disregard the setting his sense made for him, and the only escape was through the words. He did his best with a bit of 'The Herne's Egg'.

Strong sinew and soft flesh
Are foliage round the shaft
Before the arrowsmith
Has stripped it, and I pray
That I, all foliage gone,
May shoot into my joy.

'Eh?' said Crealy. He tired quickly of poetry, even when seasoned with humiliation. 'Had enough,' he said. His thoughts turned to Garfield. There were hours to go, years maybe, before it would be day again.

Blind Mr Lewin was guided by Mrs Munro to the sunroom in the east wing the next afternoon. Mr Lewin loved the warmth, and found that he could sleep easily during the day in full sunlight. Mrs Munro kindly led him down, and Lewin could feel the warmth even as they approached the end of the corridor. Mrs Munro's head nodded companionably as she pulled a cane chair close to the large window; so close that Lewin was able to put out his hands and feel the glass while sitting comfortably. And she gave him his talking clock to cradle so that he would not be anxious about his meals. Mr Lewin thanked her, and listened to the departing footsteps.

He had never seen the sunroom, and instead of the meek, faded place that it was, looking out over the crocodile paving and lawns in front of the cottages, he imagined it cantilevered high into the sun's eye and with only the yellow, benevolent furnace of the sun to be seen from the window. Lewin had known far worse times.

While Mr Lewin slept, Crealy elsewhere watched Mrs Halliday. Mrs Halliday was only in her sixties, but subject to Huntington's chorea in recurring spells during which she often came into the Totara Home to relieve her family. Crealy always took a considerable interest in her visits, for her breasts were large, she still had firm flesh, and caught at the right moment she could be used without much recollection of it.

Towards the end of the long afternoon she was at her most confused, and Crealy watched from outside the television lounge until he saw her talking to herself and constantly folding and unfolding her cardigan. He went in and firmly led her along the trail of mottled lino to the sunroom, which visitors or clergymen sometimes used to have their talks. 'Has the family come? Has Elaine?' said Mrs Halliday. Crealy was quite pleased to see blind Lewin there, close to the window, for he could pass as a chaperone at a distance, but not act as one on the spot. Crealy sat Mrs Halliday with her back to the window.

'Your family are coming soon,' he said, and opened the front of her dress.

'Is that you, Mrs Munro?' asked Lewin.

'Shut up,' said Crealy.

'The family you say,' said Mrs Halliday. She allowed Crealy to unclip her bra at the back, and he scooped out her breasts so they made two full fish heads in the flounce of her dress.

Lewin was still groggy from his sleep, but he didn't wish to seem discourteous. 'Where would we be without families,' he said gallantly, and fingered his talking clock for reassurance. Crealy stroked Mrs Halliday's breasts, and clumsily rolled her nipples between thumb and forefinger so that she pursed her lips and put her hands on his wrists.

'You need to get changed for your family,' said Crealy absently.

'What time is it then?' asked Mrs Halliday. Lewin pressed his clock. 'The time is 4.42 pm,' it said.

Crealy took another minute of satisfaction in the sun, then refilled Mrs Halliday's bra, and with some difficulty fastened it across her back. Matron Frew might come looking for her soon. 'Stay here and talk to Lewin,' he said.

'Am I changed for my family?'

'Good enough,' said Crealy.

'Who is that?' said Lewin, turning an ear rather than an eye for better comprehension.

'Jenny Pen rules,' said Crealy as he left.

The impartial sun which Mr Lewin enjoyed, shone on Mortenson who sat in his wheel chair on a landscaped hillock which looked over the SRA — the safe recreation area. Within it the bewildered or fretful, the complacent and serene could be left in security. Only the staff could manage the latch. Crealy called it the zoo, but it was pleasant enough, more like a kindergarten. There were seats with foam cushions for thin flesh, and raised garden plots which keen Totarans could work on without stooping or kneeling.

The SRA was overlooked by the wide windows of the dining room on one side, but to the north side there was a view across the grass and gardens towards the cottages and the spires of the great world. Mortenson could see the goldfish pond in the zoo, and George Oliphant dolefully shaking the back of his trousers because he was in trouble again.

The Matron and Dr Sullivan stopped beside Mortenson on their round, but finished their conversation before greeting him. 'I've no idea how Mrs Joyce managed to leave the block in the first place,' said Matron.

'It can't be helped.'

'It's a puzzle though.'

'I haven't told her family the actual circumstances of the death: to minimise the trauma you see. And how are you, Mr Mortenson?'

'Mr Mortenson is brighter every day,' replied Matron. Mortenson gave his half smile. He could see the exquisite glow on the sunlit tulips, feel the sun's good will on his faithful side, and hear Miss Hails practising her word for the day. The word was Nell, or perhaps Knell; how was anyone to know but her.

'Nell, nell, nell, nell,' said Miss Hails. Like a prayer wheel she gave a benediction over all the zoo, the lawn, the cottages, the totality of Totara and beyond. 'Nell, nell, nell, nell, knell.'

'Well, nice talking to you,' said Dr Sullivan, and they went on their way. Mortenson felt an itching tic begin at the corner of his eye. In all that ground of apparent pleasure he wondered what Crealy was up to. What time was it? It came to Mortenson that his karma had been assessed; that from the best of lives he was in a spiral descent of reincarnation from which he would emerge perhaps a six-spot ladybird, as counted by Mrs Munro, and would clamp the stem beneath the wine glow of the sunlit tulip blooms.

What time was it? Dr Sullivan and Matron were tyring to wake Popanovich. 'It's always the same. Ah, well, he seems healthy enough and sleep can't hurt him.' Dr Sullivan smiled at the other three in the end room, while Matron moved Popanovich in the bed. The doctor was not a dour person; he believed in good spirits and optimism. He looked about for something that would provide an occasion for light-heartedness and rapport.

Matron sensed that the mood had abruptly changed, though at first she didn't see that behind her Dr Sullivan had taken Jenny Pen from Garfield's bed and mounted her on his hand. Garfield began to shiver, and put his hands out, palms uppermost, as if to play patter-cake. Crealy hung his head to one side like an old dog, while the whites of his eyes showed as he kept things in his view. Mortenson felt a sweat break out on his good thigh beneath the rug, and his smile was slow to form and slow to fade. He smiled as a Christian might smile who catches the Devil out walking in the daytime.

'What a good life we lead at Totara,' said Dr Sullivan in falsetto for Jenny Pen, and he jiggled her to emphasise his humour. The only responses were those of Matron Frew's crepe soles on the lino, and at a distance Miss Hails saying her catechism for the day. It drifted to them down the corridor.

'Mi, mi, mi, mi, mi, mi.'

'Perhaps puppeteer isn't my calling,' said Dr Sullivan. He was disappointed by his reception and withdrew into professionalism. Matron knew how to keep that patter going.

Crealy's arthritis was giving him gyppo again. To appease it he walked the maze of corridors, and watched from window after window the sunshowers above the grounds. Dramatic clouds were towed across the sky, and when they met the sun they were lit with red and orange embers which glowed and shifted into the deep perspectives. From the dining room Crealy saw a travelling shower fracture the surface of the zoo pond, so that the goldfish lost their shape, and became just carrots in the shallow weeds.

On his second circuit Crealy noticed that Nurse McMillan had left the office, and that the morning's mail lay partly sorted on the counter. He eased in, and his stiff hands found envelopes addressed to Mortenson, to Oliphant and Garfield. He pocketed them, and was cheered by the petty malice even though he couldn't see Mrs Halliday in the TV room as he went past. For the life of him he could not remember when he last had a personal letter. Garfield on the other hand received far too much kind attention from outside, and Crealy decided to give him a hard time until the weather improved. He began to search for Garfield, but George Oliphant saw him checking the TV room, and afterwards went to the window which could be seen by Mortenson and gave a warning by semaphore, which Mortenson passed on to Garfield.

Garfield began his slow but urgent escape down the corridors of hours towards the bedding store-room. The door there had a plunger and cylinder to draw it closed without slamming. To Garfield the mechanism seemed to take an eternity to work, and the cylinder hissed as his view of the corridor and bathrooms narrowed. Garfield sat in semi-darkness, content with the little light entering from a glass strip above the door.

The broad shelves had stacks of sheets and pillowcases, and on the floor were piled blankets which rose like wool bales. Garfield sat on a half-bale to wait it out. He didn't trouble himself with the metaphysics of his situation: what he had come to. The former Wellington fullback and general manager for Hentlings sat grinding his teeth in the bedding store-room of Totara Eventide Home, and listening to the perpetual echoing orchestration which his tinnitus inflicted on him.

Crealy found him there.

It was nearly four. The showers had become less frequent, and a rainbow stood clearly behind the cottages, fading up towards the sun. Yet Mortenson couldn't concentrate on his history of Rome; he felt a helpless consideration for Garfield, and a fear of Crealy. He knew that where there are no lions then hyenas rule.

His chair was very low-geared, and despite the busy noise of its motor, Mortenson moved only slowly along the corridors towards the bedding room. At alternate windows the day's strange weather was displayed as sunlit promise, then skirts of rain from fiery clouds, then blue sky once again. The door took all the thrust his chair could manage, and sank closed behind him so that the failing light and hiss half hid Crealy's torture of his friend.

'Hello, Judge,' said Crealy. Once he found that Mortenson had come alone, he was pleased. He had become almost bored with Garfield. Yet an advantage can be gained or lost quite unexpectedly and with such an absence of drama that it is easy to miss the significance. Crealy moved to get a better leverage, overbalanced on the soft surface and fell backwards just a couple of feet into the comfortable crevasse fashioned by Mrs Munro between the banded blankets. His old arms and legs moved silently in the shadows, as if he were a beetle on his back there. He was too stiff to turn easily.

Mortenson took a pillow with his better arm and pushed it across Crealy's face.

'Come on,' he said to Garfield. It was more a delaying tactic at first, with neither of them having much hope of success; even Crealy gave a sort of grin whenever he managed to free his face, as if he recognised his temporary difficulty, but would soon pay them back all right.

But the more Garfield and Mortenson pushed, and the more Crealy twisted, the deeper his shoulders sank between the blankets. He began to pant and jerk; the others saw a chance indeed and their lips drew back in the dark and they pressed for all their lives. Crealy's big arms and legs fell in harmless thuds against the embracing blankets. Mortenson felt strength and justice in his good arm even though it trembled with exertion, and Garfield was on his knees to use his body weight upon the pillow.

'Had enough. Had enough, Crealy old son,' he kept whispering. The competitive urge in Garfield revived one last time. Crealy's arms and legs moved less, but his body bucked.

'Now let us play Othello,' slurred Mortenson.

'Had enough,' sobbed Garfield.

For a good time after Crealy was still, they continued to hold the pillow over his face. Accustomed to such full tyranny as his, they could hardly believe that they had beaten him so completely. Even when they heard his sphincter muscles relax, and had the smell of him, they held the pillow down. 'Had enough?' said Garfield tenderly.

'Put the pillow back,' said Mortenson finally, and he wiped the tears from Garfield's face. They didn't look again at Dave Crealy, who was a big, stupid man lying well down amongst piles of blankets. Garfield opened the door a little, and when he saw that there was no one outside he held it back for Mortenson's chair, and the snake hissed behind them in the dark.

As they went home they met Mrs Munro guiding Mr Lewin to the sunroom. Mrs Munro delighted in being useful, and was thinking also of a nice cup of tea. 'There's a rainbow,' she said, nodding. Mortenson and Garfield could see its thick, childish bands behind the cottages; at the same time the sun was strong enough to cast shadows from the benches in the grounds. Who knows what Lewin saw, but he could hear with them the piping of Miss Hails at a distance.

'Na, na, na, na, na, na, na, na.' Mr Lewin pushed the button on his clock.

'The time is 4.19 pm,' the clock said.

Mia Culpa

SUE MCCAULEY

After Elaine died — that's how he chose to think of it, to others she might be alive and working in Lambton Quay, but to Warren she was dead. The grieving process, that way, was easier. Cheryl had told him this was so. Not that she had first-hand experience of either kind of grief, except for her mother's death, and that's not at all the same; you expect to lose parents. But Warren had pictured Elaine in a coffin of pale wood, wearing the peach-coloured dress she'd bought last summer from Kimberleys. Then he had pictured himself dropping white rose petals that tumbled in slow motion past clay walls to land among the lilies which lay on the lid of the pale wood coffin. Then he drank his way through a third of a bottle of Napoleon brandy. And Cheryl was right — mourning was quite a pleasurable kind of grief compared with the other kind.

But almost ever since that day he buried Elaine, Warren had been on the lookout for someone to replace her. He didn't mean to be, he didn't want to be; he would have liked to reach out and cover the eyes of that part of him that was always peering around in hope and longing.

Wherever he went — wine bars, car park buildings, the supermarket, social gatherings — that humiliating part of him was on the alert. Many other people, he'd discovered, were watching in just the same way. Women and men, some of them even while they were sitting or walking with someone who appeared to be their partner. When Warren and Elaine were together he'd never looked around in that way. Had Elaine?

Sometimes his eyes would connect with the eyes of one of those watching women and he'd feel a small tingling jolt as if he'd laid one finger on a low-volt electric wire, even though not one of those women was what he was looking for. He didn't know what that was, exactly, but he gathered that the watchful part of him would recognise such a woman the moment he saw her.

Perhaps he just wanted another Elaine? Only one that would stay. Was that just a natural part of the grieving process, or proof that Warren was stupid?

He wanted someone his own age or a bit younger. Elaine was three years younger than him, which seemed just about right. Yet they looked so sharp, these young women, all steely and cutting edged. *Just out for themselves*, he thought, censoring Elaine from the equation so as not to think ill of the dead.

Even at work, where there was no one worth watching, Warren had caught himself glancing too often and too long at Cheryl who was, at thirty-two, only a little older than him. Cheryl wasn't the sharp-edged kind, but she was married with children. When her children grew up, would she go off and leave her Jim? You never could tell what was going on in a woman's mind.

When Elaine . . . departed, all three women in Warren's office had begun looking at him in a new and unfriendly way. That's how it felt, as if he had suddenly become the stuff of stranger danger. It made no sense. He was the same person as he'd been the week before, and the week before that. Was it his silent grief they despised? Or was it because, after seven whole years, Elaine had thrown him aside like a worn-out tracksuit? Alignment — was that what he'd seen in their evasive eyes? *She must have had a reason.*

Robert, too, had become uncomfortable in Warren's presence, juggling pity and embarrassment as if they were hot coals. As he passed the desk where Warren hunched, arms clasped across his broken heart, Robert would toss down band-aid phrases: *more fish in the sea . . . play the field . . . fancy free . . . I should be so lucky.*

'So why,' snapped Margaret, who'd overheard the last, 'do you stay with Nan?'

'You've got me there,' said Robert.

Fish swim on Warren's screen when he leaves it in idle mode. There may not, he thinks, be that many left in the sea — not any more. You only have to watch them unloading crateloads from the big joint-venture fishing boats down at the wharf to wonder how many are left out there to breed. There might be more fish, already, on computer screens than in the world's oceans.

As for the other kind — the ones in public places who see him looking but pretend not to, and the others who look right back — even if they were just what he wanted, they would still be strangers.

He and Elaine had been at school together. They hadn't been friends, but at least they knew each other so that when they met again at Gareth's wedding they had a reason for talking.

'How did you and Jim meet?' Warren asks Cheryl.

'In the Barrington Mall,' said Cheryl. 'Me and my mate, Margie, used to hang out every Thursday night in the Barrington Mall. Pathetic, eh?' And she laughs.

'Arnie came to fix my washing machine,' says Margaret. Warren has heard it before. Margaret widowed with three small children; Arnie stepping through the door in his overalls. For five days she'd been doing the washing in the bath, stomping it like grapes, wringing by hand and it was winter.

'I found Ron on the Heaphy Track,' says Colleen drily. 'Should've left him there.' The others smile in sympathy.

'Pushed him over a cliff, more like,' says Margaret. Ron is an office legend. Ten years of marriage and Colleen walked out, now can't imagine why she stuck it so long. Last year Ron was in the paper, convicted for false pretences. Not what you'd expect from a tramping man. Colleen lives alone, goes mountain climbing in her holidays with her friend Rita. Ron, she says, cured her of men.

Warren gets asthma from walking, is too old to hang around malls and never meets anyone new at this desk-bound job.

But now he remembers the man in the TV ad, the one who has been trying to get a woman for at least a year now. A perfectly presentable man, which just goes to show how hard it can be. The man in the ad had advertised. Well, he would, naturally. All the same, if *he* could, why shouldn't Warren?

At home Warren drags out Saturday's paper from the garage and reads the personal columns. He remembers how Elaine used to spread the paper on the floor and read crouched in sphinx position. Sometimes even the small ads. The weirder ones she'd read aloud for Warren. *Athletic man seeks bi woman and partner for fun times.* They would giggle over the bizarreness of some people and Elaine's tongue would come out and lick along her bottom lip. If she stayed there reading for long enough she would sometimes leave the paper to come and sit astride him, sliding her tongue into his mouth.

Now Warren tries to remember if the two of them had laughed at the lonely ads or just the kinky ones. There are quite a lot of lonely ads — *Sincere rural gent seeks kind non-smoking woman* — but they are almost all from men. The exceptions are from a *fun-loving, roly-poly woman* and the *woman seeking sexy times*. Warren feels embarrassed on behalf of them both. A little desperately he scans the print for the word *relationship*, which has such a solid ring. *Love*, he's discovered, even *partner* cannot be trusted to mean what you might suppose. What about *soulmate?*

Looking for a soulmate. Don't be shy. Join our singles club.

She sounded nice, the woman who answered. 'Just don't expect miracles on your first evening.'

Warren marked the night on his kitchen calendar. This was in August. The singles club met every two weeks in members' homes. That first time, Warren was struck by two things: the number of people who said to him, 'We're all in the same boat' (sailing above all those fish?) and the way people kept their eyes to themselves, as though just having come along was all the availability they could manage.

There was no one who looked absolutely right, but there were two or three who might turn out to be if he knew them better.

In September Warren asked Karen, a solo mother, out to dinner. The slant of Karen's lips reminded him of Elaine. He watched those lips as she ate, as she talked.

Two nights later they went to a pub to hear the Warratahs. Karen joined in the line dances and Warren watched and knew for sure that she wasn't what he wanted.

He couldn't possibly tell her so.

'See you at the club on Tuesday, then,' she said, getting into her Mini.

'Yes,' said Warren. 'See you Tuesday.'

Which meant he couldn't go to the singles club anymore.

By October, spring had seeped into Warren's veins, filling him with restless impatience. The prospect of spending any more evenings alone in the flat watching television became unbearable. He thought about moving in with others — young single people who knew how to live on their own, and would have friends and friends-of-friends who came to visit. He began going out every night, driving around the streets. It was as if, without this sense of motion, he might cease to exist. Sometimes he would drive out to one of the beaches and sit for a time watching couples or the people walking their dogs. (Should he get a dog? At least for the meantime?) Other nights he would simply drive around the city, including Manchester Street, where the hookers paraded. Tried to imagine himself pulling up on the kerb alongside one, but he wasn't the type.

At least not until the night when he noticed her. *Recognised* her, in fact, as the woman that hopefully peering part of him had been looking for. Surely she couldn't be one of them? Such a pretty woman, showing lots of leg, but otherwise properly dressed. None of that tacky thigh-boots-and-suspenders stuff. This one looked nice. And not a bit like Elaine.

All that was just an impression from the far side of the road. When Warren drove back, more slowly, on the other side, she was even lovelier than he had thought. He must stop the car, wind down the passenger window; that's how it was done.

But what if she didn't come over to talk to him? What if she did? And how much money would he need?

What if she was just a student or a barmaid, waiting for her friend?

Warren drove around the corner and parked. Sat for a moment, giving her time to meet her friend, to walk away, to climb into a stranger's car. Then he got out and walked around the corner into the chill easterly wind. She was still there. She gave him a wide-open smile.

'Nice night,' he said.

'Is it?' She shivered, but gave him another smile, just as dazzlingly friendly as the first.

It gave him the courage to ask.

'Are you, you know . . . available?'

'Very much so.' Another smile.

'Ah . . . how much . . . ?'

'Depends on what you're after.'

Love, he thought. That's what I'm after. But he couldn't say that. What should he say?

'Basic,' she said, 'is sixty dollars for half an hour. Cash.'

'Right,' said Warren numbly. He realised he'd expected her to cost more, to cost so much that it was out of the question. Then he could've just gone home to bed and thought about her.

'There's a cash machine just down the road. It takes most cards.'

She pointed helpfully. The bank was a couple of hundred metres away. Westpac, Warren's bank. She saw his hesitation.

'Do you have a card?'

He nodded. A card, luckily, with overdraft facilities. 'But shouldn't we . . .?' He wasn't sure what he was trying to say.

'You go and get the money first.' Her tone of voice said, *There's a good boy*. Firm and kindly. 'Better get a bit more in case you want to do extra things.' Then, as if she was reading his mind. 'I'll still be here, it's a quiet night.'

He almost ran, glancing back a couple of times to make sure she was still waiting. While he was at the machine a car drove past him then slowed right down at her corner. He stood watching the car while the machine dealt out his banknotes, but the driver had only slowed before turning. She saw Warren looking and waved out as if he and she were old friends.

She took him, that first time, along the street and up a back stair-way to a small room. In the corridor they met an older woman with aquamarine eyeshadow and prominent teeth. The two women gave each other a hug, and the older one smiled toothily at Warren and said, 'Don't worry. You're among friends here. Mia is just a lovely person.'

'That's your name? Mia?'

She nodded, wriggling fingers at her departing friend.

'I've never met anyone called Mia,' he said. 'I only know the film star, the one that was with Woody Allen.'

'Everyone says that,' she told him, unlocking a door.

Inside the room Mia took charge. She was years younger than him yet she seemed so confident, so at ease. Like the mother Warren wished he'd had: smiling, coaxing, admiring, praising. She didn't get many men as young and attractive as Warren. He was a nice person, she could tell that the moment she met him. Nice people were even rarer than young and attractive ones.

She felt so wonderful beneath his fingers, her mouth was so warm, her skin so silky, half an hour was nowhere near enough; and there were other things she was planning to show him. Luckily he'd got another eighty dollars just in case.

He walked with her back to the corner. 'Can I see you again?'

'Of course,' she said. 'I'm here Thursday, Friday, Saturday and Sunday nights.'

That hadn't been quite what he meant. There was something special between them — she'd almost said so.

It became Thursdays and Sundays. She had other regular customers, but they weren't as special as him. Only he got a ten-dollar discount, that's what she said. She wasn't used to men who treated her as nicely as he did, with so much respect.

To prove just how nice he was, Warren sometimes used the half-hour to take her to one of the nicer bars just for a drink and a talk. What with the price of the drinks on top of her fee it worked out pretty expensive, but he liked so much the attentive way she listened, leaning towards him, and her deep gurgle of a laugh. And he liked the way other men looked at them, the slightly hostile, envious glances he caught but pretended not to notice.

By mid-November she was taking him to her place instead of that bleak little room in the massage parlour. She rented an inner-city apartment (it was far too up-market to be called a *flat*) and her furniture was new and expensive, straight out of Ballantyne's or McKenzie and Willis. She liked nice things, she had impeccable taste. Warren would have hated for her to see his flat, especially now he'd sold the rimu coffee table and the video player and the settee. He didn't resent having sold them, though they'd fetched much less than he'd hoped; furniture was a small price to pay for the way he floated, blissful and buoyant, through the hours around and between Thursday and Sunday nights.

In early December Warren took out a bank loan. He said he needed to replace his car. The lie slid from his lips with surprising ease, but then it wasn't a bad kind of lie; banks wanted to lend you money and didn't really care what it was for. But a Mia-fund would have been a little hard to explain and even harder to justify, so why bother trying? Even to himself.

He had no choice, that was the bottom line; he had no choice.

At work they had seen the change in him and guessed at the cause. They probed — Margaret, Cheryl and Colleen — but he told them nothing, just sat there nursing his grin. They teased him, then, with speculation and innuendos which Warren ignored. His silence felt like a powerful thing; he sensed the women's renewed acceptance of him.

No, more than that, their *approval.*

'I shall,' he told them, 'neither confirm nor deny.'

They chorused a little squeal of delight.

The Christmas social was coming up. A Friday night. He asked Mia if she would go with him.

She bit her lovely bottom lip. 'How long would we be there?'

'Three hours? Maybe, four?'

'A pity it's on a work night,' she sighed. 'At this peak time of year. Four hours on the job and I'd take home five hundred.'

'Three hours,' said Warren, 'and I'll be paying you, of course.'

Mia smiled at him. 'Let's say two hundred and seventy — on a special Warren Christmas discount.'

'Are you sure?' He didn't want to be costing her money.

When she nodded, he kissed her on the corner of her mouth.

'Thank you, my love-erly Mia.'

She was waiting outside her apartment building, dressed just right. Classy, but in an understated way.

'How do you want me to be?' she asked him in the car.

The question surprised him.

'Just yourself,' he said. 'And I'm your boyfriend. Which is true be-cause that's how I think of myself.'

'You're so sweet.' She leant across and kissed him on the cheek. 'And my name? What's my name?'

'Mia, of course.'

'What if one of my other customers is there?'

Warren felt his jaw drop. Why hadn't he thought of that? But he knew why — he'd censored out any thoughts of what she did for a living and who she might do it with. He'd chosen to regard her as an astute and successful businesswoman, which was how she seemed to see herself.

'Don't worry,' she soothed. 'It's hardly likely. This is a big city.'

Warren felt his shoulder muscles ungripping.

'That's right. Besides, you'll just be meeting us lot from accounts. We all stick pretty much to our own little group at these Christmas dos.'

They were all there before him, which was how he'd intended it to be. He watched their faces as they noticed him walking across the room with Mia's hand tucked inside his. Saw Colleen nudge Cheryl, who leant across Jim to alert Margaret, whose mouth fell open then composed itself and leant to whisper in Arnie's ear, while Cheryl was pointing and grinning for Robert's benefit and Nan was looking in confusion from one gaping or smirking face to another.

Robert's expression was the best of all. *Gobsmacked*, that was the only word for it.

Warren sat Mia down beside the carafe of white wine and introduced her clockwise around the table.

'Mia,' they said. 'M-i-a ? Like thingee the film star?'

Jim poured her a glass of wine which she had barely brought to her lips before their more probing questions began. Warren realised with a lurch of his stomach that he hadn't really thought this thing through. Just be yourself, he'd said!

He needn't have worried; a few minutes of listening assured him of that. Mia answered all their questions so convincingly, and with such an endearing trace of diffidence, that Warren felt himself falling in love all over again with his new, shy yet down-to-earth young woman who had come to the city from Geraldine to train as a social worker.

Was some of it true? How much?

'Well!' muttered Margaret, smothering the cheese platter as she pressed her bulk across the table. 'Where on earth did you manage to find *her*?'

'Ah,' Warren pretended to flick an almost invisible something from the surface of his beer, stalling for time. 'Well, actually you should ask her — she tells it much better than me. Excuse me sweetheart,' he said to Mia, who was telling Cheryl about her three student flatmates, 'but Margaret wants to know how we met.'

He gave her a smile that felt a little desperate but which the others would surely interpret as fond and intimately significant.

'Where did we meet?' Mia looked at their now expectant faces. 'It was so corny,' she said, 'such a cliché, you wouldn't believe.' She flashed a smile at Warren then took a large mouthful of wine. Her face took on a remembering look.

'It was quite late at night,' she said, 'and my car had broken down. Well, it wasn't actually my car, it was my flatmate's, and it was a heap of junk. But this night I'd had to borrow it . . .'

Warren sat there entranced, seeing it all happening the way she described it, nodding his head, *Yes, yes, that's right . . .*

It was some time later that he noticed how quickly she emptied her glass and how often and willingly Jim, who sat on the other side, re-filled it. Mia's laugh, by that time, had become rather loud and very frequent. It began on a high note and slid away, getting thinner and thinner like an anteater's tail. Warren could see from Robert's watch (he had pawned his own the month before) that he still had forty minutes of Mia's company to go. He thought they might sneak off early, back to her place — the others would understand (nudge, nudge, wink, wink). Compared with Mia, his colleagues and their partners seemed exceedingly dull and inconsequential. He wondered at himself for not having noticed this colourlessness before.

He was about to whisper to Mia that they would leave soon when she asked directions to the ladies and heaved herself out of her chair. Rather unsteadily, she set off. Should Warren go with her? No, better not to draw attention, he would just pretend he hadn't noticed.

But Colleen had. 'Is she all right?'

This wasn't directed at anyone in particular and Nan was at that moment telling Warren about the difference between the Japanese maple and the more common variety. Warren knew nothing about maples and didn't wish to, but they saved him from having to consider Mia's wavering progress across the room.

Just as Colleen got up to follow Mia, Robert rescued Warren from his horticultural wife and took him to the bar, where the senior staff and a few spendthrift juniors were buying scotch on the rocks and brandy and dry, in preference to the free wine and low-alcohol beer the company had provided.

Robert had been thinking about his future; had Warren?

Warren shook his head in instant, though perplexing, guilt. Ought he to have been thinking about Robert's future? Why?

'Well you should,' said Robert.

At the end of next year he planned to retire and take things easy. They'd have to advertise, naturally, for his replacement, but a personal recommendation from Robert would carry much weight.

'If you get my drift,' said Robert, placing a brandy and dry ginger ale in Warren's hand.

'But . . .' Warren stared down at his glass, moved it about so the ice cubes tinkled. 'But . . . seniority? All of them are older than me, and Colleen's been there almost forever.'

'Warren, Warren, seniority . . . all that nonsense went out the window years ago. We all know that. Your colleagues are fine women but as figures of authority? What management will be looking for is a bit of get-up-and-go, plus some experience. Can't promise, of course, but you'd have every chance.'

Mia, thought Warren. It was because of her. In his whole life no one had ever before seen him as a get-up-and-goer.

'Just keep it to yourself,' said Robert, patting Warren's shoulder. 'Drink up and we'll have another. Cheers.'

'Yes,' said Warren. 'Thank you. Happy Christmas.'

HOD! Would Mia maybe consider marrying a head of department? Even if she wouldn't, at least he'd be able to pay back his bank loan and replace his settee and coffee table.

When Robert and Warren returned to the table, Mia was there, hunched forward in her chair with her head clutched in her hands. Warren had never before noticed how fragile and young her shoulders and upper arms looked. He saw this even before he became aware of the faces of those around her. The way they were looking at him.

'What is it?' said Robert.

But their eyes stayed on Warren, who was standing there almost in the the middle of a very large room feeling cornered, back up against a wall and unable to move. In a strange sort of way — precognition? — this situation felt very familiar.

Cheryl was the first to speak.

'We know!' she said. 'She told us.'

'We never,' said Margaret, 'thought you would stoop so low.'

'She's a prostitute,' Nan explained to Robert. 'It's true. He hired her for the evening. He's one of her regular customers.' She laid each word out fastidiously in a surgically gloved voice.

They all looked at Robert for his reaction, but nothing showed.

'Nineteen!' hissed Margaret. 'Our Vicki's age. Just a child.'

From Mia's hidden face came a small sound that might have been a sob.

Arnie pushed back his chair and stood up. He straightened his shoulders and pushed out his chest, his eyes on Warren. 'So what have you got to say for yourself?'

'I . . .' What was there to say? What did they want him to say?

'Mia. Mia?'

She raised her head just a fraction. Warren took a step towards her but, as he did, Margaret lunged sideways and dragged Mia protectively into her arms.

'Come on,' she ordered Arnie. 'We're taking the poor kid home to a decent bed. Some loving care — that's what she needs.'

Mia flopped like a rag doll between Margaret and Arnie as they arranged her into a transportable shape.

Jim went with them to open the doors. Warren watched until they were all out of sight.

'She got drunk awfully fast,' he said, thinking aloud.

'Who wouldn't?' Cheryl was draining the carafe of red into her glass.

'No,' said Colleen. 'It's the pills do that.'

'What pills?' Warren and Cheryl both together, but no *snap*, no linking of little fingers.

'The pills,' said Colleen, looking at no one, 'that she was taking so that she could endure all the stuff men made her do.'

'Without throwing up.' Cheryl threw out a grin that Colleen caught and tossed to Nan.

Now Robert sighed loudly and shook his head at Warren in the manner of a bull that may or may not intend to charge. Even his eyes now looked small and glinting and bull-like.

'It's an offence for the woman but not for the man,' Colleen announced. She turned to Warren. 'So you can't be arrested, you'll be pleased to know.'

'Men can do no wrong.' Halfway through a sarcastic rolling of the eyes, Cheryl remembered Robert and gave him an anxious glance. But Robert was too busy staring at Warren while pretending not to.

'I never knew Mia was taking pills.' Did that sound like some kind of pathetic plea for sympathy?

'Alison,' said Colleen. 'Her name is Alison. Mia is just a made-up name.'

Telling him, *That's how much you knew about her.* Nan giving a little smile and nodding her endorsement. Robert still glowering.

'I suppose,' Warren muttered, 'you'd all like me to resign?'

No one spoke. Snatches of conversation drifted in from the surrounding tables. Jim, rejoining them, picked up on their silence and almost tip-toed the last few steps. Warren felt a prickling at the back of his eyes. *Please don't let me cry.*

'So what do you have to say for yourself?' Nan, stepping in to save him from their cruel silence, sounded almost kindly.

Warren took a deep breath.

'It's not like that. It's not. You see, I love her.'

That silence again. Again the buzz and fragments of distant conversations.

'That's not love,' said Cheryl, and now Warren noticed that her voice was slurred. 'It's screwing. Sex and love are not the same thing, though men still haven't figured that out.'

'You don't even know her,' said Robert wearily. 'How can you love someone if you don't even know them?'

'If you don't *respect* them,' said Nan, and threw her husband an indecipherable look.

'I did resp—'

'No, you didn't,' said Colleen, 'or you wouldn't have taken advantage.'

Warren just wanted to sit down. The danger of tears was past, a small relief. *Alison,* he was thinking. *Alison!* The name didn't fit her at all. He could dislike an Alison.

'She did all right,' he said suddenly. 'I've spent a packet on her. You ought to see the way she lives. She earns more than all of us put together.'

Again they were all looking at him in that way, and now he remembered. Primary school playground; same faces, same feeling of bewildered fear.

'No wonder Elaine left you,' said Cheryl. 'No bloody wonder.'

The Mathematics of Jane Austen

ELIZABETH SMITHER

Jane Austen must have been very fond of the number 2. Have you ever noticed it? Two proposals by Darcy; two good sisters (and three foolish ones); two ill-mannered matriarchs, Mrs Bennet and Lady Catherine de Bourgh; two unsuitable suitors, Mr Collins and George Wickham. Two attempts to reside at Netherfield; two friends, Darcy and Bingley; two attempted elopements, Lydia and Georgiana Darcy. Oh there are countless others. Jane Austen even admitted it was unlikely a man would propose a second time. Two brothers-in-law: Darcy and Wickham. Everything has a pair, a shadow in psychoanalytic terms. Miss de Bourgh (sickly) and Georgiana (sickly but saved). Even Elizabeth is caught between the twin scales of Jane (universal benevolence) and Charlotte Lucas (everyone has her price).

A variation of these thoughts — and a new example of two-ness: the marriages of the Gardiners (soundly based) and the Bennets (short-lived lust) — occurred to Irene Fisher as she crossed the quad between Direct Marketing and Zoology where a trailorload of dead white chickens were parked. But could she work it into a suitable proposal, one that would impress her supervisor, crusty and conservative Professor Mordaunt, who practically regarded Jane Austen as his own child?

No she would not mention it at today's meeting: she would listen and nod, act the acolyte, because this is what Professor Mordaunt preferred. She would be as self-effacing as Jane faced with visitors.

'Just *Pride and Prejudice*,' Irene says to Professor Mordaunt. 'I just want to use *Pride and Prejudice*.'

'And when did you come to this decision?' Professor Mordaunt asks. His face is deeply marked and some of the lines are fatigue.

'Over the last month,' Irene replies, thinking it best not to say while she was crossing the quad.

'You will severely limit yourself, you realise that,' Professor Mordaunt says, not raising his eyes from Irene's face, as if he attempts to solicit a blush. 'You are abandoning the altogether more ferocious *Sense and Sensibility, Emma* with its delightful female jealousy, *Persuasion*, I need not go on.'

'I realise *P&P* has been thoroughly analysed in the past.'

'And by those — excuse me, dear lady — more esteemed than Miss Irene Fisher. Scholars of impeccable credentials.'

Irene flinches a little at this and the professor looks as if he has scored a hit. But having reduced her — for such is his mechanism — he instantly relents.

'There, there,' he says patting her hand. '*P&P* is my favourite as well, in spite of the charms to the aged of *Emma*. I'll be your batman, if you like.'

'I should like it a good deal,' Irene replies, thinking if her thesis can get through this minefield it will be marked elsewhere.

'Well then,' says Professor Mordaunt, sinking into his cavernous old chair with grubby cushions. 'We need a detailed outline.'

No, thinks Irene, rising finally, we need those cushions washed. She can see Cassandra bustling about, saying to Jane, 'I'll just do the cushion covers if you'll make a suet pudding.'

Irene slips into the university library and goes to the section of the occult. It is a small section: numerology, palmistry, witchcraft. Some of the tomes on witchcraft are impressively dense, as if lending an air of respectability. Irene takes down a book called *The Key to the Universe* and makes some notes. *The number 2 is the symbol of Duality. It is the number of Differentiation, the 'fall into matter'. By the Pythagorians it was called audacity.* Of this only *audacity* pleases, though Irene considers Jane Austen greatly concerned with financial security. But surely first impressions, pride or prejudice, count for more? If they are unresolved there will be no Pemberley, no phaeton with a nice little pair of ponies to go round the park. She is simply a real writer, Irene muses, as her own pen scratches away at the nonsensical vague mysticism. *The Number*

2 is, therefore, the Number of Contrasts and the 'pairs of opposites', good and evil, truth and error, day and night, heat and cold, health and sickness, pleasure and pain, joy and sorrow, male and female, etc., and because of this it is called by some 'the beginning of evil'.

Irene skims some comments on Adam and Eve and alights on *2 representing the marriage made in heaven. But before such a marriage can be consummated on all planes it must be confirmed on earth according to the legal requirements of the country in which the ones so united dwell.* Is this the beginning manoeuvre of Mr Darcy's letter, to size up the respective statuses: Elizabeth's mother and father against the Gardiners; Lydia, Mary, Kitty against the counterweight of Elizabeth and Jane?

Irene buys a carton of orange juice and a sandwich sealed in a little plastic container like a tomb, and goes to sit under a beech tree in the park. Perhaps, a small voice of reason suggests, two-ness is nothing more than the unquenchable optimism of a spinster, a free-ranging romanticism above an unvaried existence. Large parts of Jane's life were ordered and even the occasional cataclysmic move ironed out. A spinster may well be more optimistic than a married woman. Yet how does Jane understand so well the tremor caused by a letter, a sighting, a stiff visit ending in bows? What a young heart leaps inside Elizabeth Bennet and how truly decent is Fitzwilliam Darcy.

Irene is usually home by 3.30 p.m. in time for Ben's return from school. Sue, Ben's mother, with whom Irene boards, assures her this is not necessary, that Ben will fling his satchel on the floor and find his way to the fridge. But Irene, since she has decided to have no children of her own, endeavours to greet Ben. Sometimes, like *The Simpsons*, they arrive at the driveway together.

Sue works in broadcasting, as a research assistant to a famous female broadcaster. Her days are an endless adrenalin rush of bringing details together, soothing interviewees, soothing the star, sweet-talking at the height of panic. Sue drinks too much coffee, as does the star. When she gets home around 6 p.m. she falls into an oversized chair and kicks off her shoes. Irene pours two large gin and tonics. Sometimes she provides a shoulder massage.

'So, how did you get on with the professor?' Sue asks, after a big gulp of g&t.

'So-so,' says Irene, nibbling on an olive. 'I think he'd prefer the full canon instead of just *P&P*.'

'And what about your theory, did you discuss that?'

'No, I chickened out. It needs development. I can't very well go to him with a book on numerology.'

'Numerology? That's something we might use on the programme. Particularly if we could find a scandal attached to it. Or am I thinking of Scientology?'

They eat lasagne and salad and Ben takes his ice cream and peaches into the den to watch the *X-Files*.

Irene hesitates to mention two-ness to Sue but then she reflects Ben is their two-ness — Ben and Fleet the red setter that Irene walks each night while Ben and Sue have time together. Fleet is part of Sue's marriage settlement: once they lived on a lifestyle block. Still, Fleet has adapted well enough to city life, lolloping by her side as they stride through the suburbs; it is her chance to walk fast and Fleet's to slow down. They can let him run only at weekends when they go to the beach or drive into the country.

Two is also the number of friendship, Irene reflects, as Fleet trots beside her. She thinks of Elizabeth Bennet crossing field after field in an English drizzle to comfort her deliberately drenched Jane. Surely her petticoat, trailing in the mud, is a sign of passion. Passion not yet fixed on its proper object, but perhaps passion must first be illustrated in an unconscious manner. Mr Darcy is required to witness the petticoat and draw his own conclusions. Then Irene thinks of another perambulating two-ness: Elizabeth and Caroline Bingley walking in the great room after dinner, to display themselves to Mr Darcy. Has Jane Austen turned every coin over for this purpose? Was she a player of heads or tails?

If Jane Austen permitted in her novels an undue use of the second chance — 'undue' as compared to its prevalence in real life — is it simply a plot device which she found effective or does it represent a more profoundly held belief, a personal philosophy or wish? This thesis will concentrate on her best known novel, Pride and Prejudice, *published in 1813 and originally titled* First Impressions, *but examples of second chance abound in all her works and may be readily discovered by the reader.*

Did Jane Austen herself wish for a second chance, a return of suitor? But Irene will not say that. However, she will say something about romanticism. She writes *Romanticism* on a fresh page in her exercise book and then a question: *Is Romanticism an essential element in the notion of a second chance?*

'I want ten examples,' Professor Mordaunt says to her when they meet and Irene finally introduces her theory. She is careful to keep her voice lowered and measured, for Professor Mordaunt likes feminine girls, smart girls with brains whom he can encourage. He likes to feel he has made them smarter than men. It is very warm in Professor Mordaunt's room and the air outside is heavy and still. In the quad below Irene can see students walking singly and in pairs and a couple embracing under a tree.

'Take care whether you mean duality, the twice-repeated event or simply a closure into which you read something that is not there.'

When Irene looks surprised at his acquiescence, a sly smile spreads over his face.

'Get along then. What are you waiting for?'

Irene is almost inclined to bow like Elizabeth beginning a set at the Netherfield ball.

The ball at Netherfield (two balls) is the first item on Irene's list. She will explain that her examples are not in any order of significance, nor are they to be equally regarded. An insult at a ball is not to be placed alongside a second proposal.

1. Two balls at Netherfield. The refusal to dance by Mr Darcy, then the seeking (unsuccessfully) of Elizabeth's hand.
2. Mr Darcy's two proposals.
3. Mr Darcy's pivotal letter explicating two problem areas: Jane and Wickham.
4. Two exemplars of foolishness: Mrs Bennet and Lady Catherine de Bourgh.
5. Elizabeth makes two journeys (both involving Darcy), to the Collinses (Hertfordshire) and Pemberley (Derbyshire). Jane Austen never travels without a purpose.

There is something haphazard about these entries and Irene feels dissatisfied. Didn't Jane Bennet also make two journeys? The one where she is surrounded by the Gardiner children and the second to Gracechurch Street? Suddenly the world seems full of purposeful carriage journeys. Irene herself feels a great need to stretch her legs. Besides, five examples is enough for one afternoon. She closes her door, clatters (sound of hooves?) down the stone stairway and emerges in the rose garden.

That evening when she walks Fleet, Ben comes with her. He wants to ask her something, and the dusk and the anonymous streets are a good place to ask. If only Irene wouldn't keep pointing out things: the way some colours stand out as if they are waiting for darkness or how Fleet only goes ahead a certain distance before he looks back.

'Some kids at school think you and Mum are lesbos,' Ben says finally, as they pause to cross Eden Avenue.

'Lesbians,' Irene corrects. Not one of Jane Austen's worries. 'No, darling,' she says, putting an arm around the thin shoulders. 'It's natural people should think that, but we are just good friends. We went to school together, about the age you are now. Then when you were born and the marriage broke up, your mother needed a boarder. I was just back from overseas, so I came to stay. We thought you might like two mothers. Don't you?'

'Most of the time. Yes. But they don't understand at school.'

'I expect some of their parents are secret cross-dressers, or drag queens, or into child pornography, or fantasise about sleeping with sheep. Or wear false hair or have their noses straightened or their bums tucked. Ignore them, Ben. Just say to them, 'Are you sure about your own set-up? My mothers could take a lie detector test any day'.'

'Thanks, Irene.'

'Call me Number Two Mother.'

'Race you home.'

Jane and Cassandra. So close. The original two. Undoubtedly Cassandra is the model for Jane. A sweetness fine and ungrained. Unyielding in its hope of Bingley. Jane Bennet is practically a cosmologist, imagining the globe as an ever-evolving kindness. Whereas Jane Austen, alias

Elizabeth, perhaps wrote down and thereby dispersed those observations that allowed her to remain a loving sister and aunt. How therapeutic it might have been to make a suet pudding in the kitchen. How far from the materialism that underpins marriage. *The number two is the foundation of marriage, the reunion of 2 expressions in 1 soul. Any couple looking upon marriage in this light would naturally recognise their duty to the community as to themselves.*

Still there is another week to go before her next meeting with Professor Mordaunt. Examples of two-ness will come to her as she walks in the park. There is no example of two dirty petticoats, but everything turns on its obverse. Perhaps Lizzie Bennet's toilette is exceedingly scrupulous thereafter. Did she think while she was crossing stiles and fields . . . *I never could be so happy as you. Till I have your disposition, your goodness, I never can have your happiness.* Or did she simply drift and ruminate, as active minds often do, subsumed in nature?

Sue is making beefburgers when Irene gets home. It is Thursday night, Ben's night for ordering dinner. He writes his order at the beginning of each week on the kitchen whiteboard so it can be included in the weekly shopping. Lately Sue and Irene have been taking him with them, under protest, to calculate the cost of what he eats. He carries a pocket calculator and hesitates between two sizes of Coke. Sue swears she's not trying to make him feel guilty, like Elinor Dashwood over meat.

'The second step,' Sue argues, 'is to teach him to cook what he buys, carefully, and without waste.' So tonight Ben is setting the burgers in a non-stick pan with a little olive oil, a sprinkle of salt and a few twists of pepper from the giant grinder that sits, like a household god, on the bench. The buns are toasting under the grill and being watched like a hawk; the lettuce, tomatoes, cheese slices and ketchup stand ready. The ketchup glows like a military uniform at Meryton. The necessary colour contrast of militiamen, Irene thinks, as some of the ketchup runs down her chin. She holds the bun tightly with her fingers, like holding down a bonnet, made over, and tied with ribbons.

Later Irene and Sue lounge in easy chairs with mugs of coffee. Elizabeth Bennet always uses courage as a spur to speech, so Irene asks Sue if she has ever been proposed to twice.

'By the same man? Never.'

'Did you ever turn anyone down in no uncertain terms and then receive a second offer?'

'Never. What is this? Forty questions?'

'No, I'm thinking of Mr Darcy and Elizabeth Bennet. "*Let me thank you again and again, for that generous compassion which induced you to take so much trouble, and bear so many mortifications . . .*" All so he could propose a second time.'

'Extraordinary, I should say. A clear case of being besotted. Perhaps a coup de foudre?'

'No, because he refused to dance. He thought her average, her figure average at first. It was only when she spoke and he saw the connection of a lively mind to lively language.'

'And everyone else was so dull a suitor must come back for more? Not very like real life, is it? I thought I was always pretty animated on a first date. Then or never.'

'Listen to this,' Irene interjects, pulling a crumpled page from her pocket. '"*The number 2 is sacred to all female deities, such as Rhea, Isis, Vishnu, the Virgin Mary, as it represents the Mother-force separated from the Father and ever-seeking the union that it may bring forth. It represents all the productive forces in nature, including nature-sounds, voice and speech; for it is through sound that creation is brought forth.*" '

'Writing is a form of sound. Perhaps Jane Austen's life was too orderly. Was she a gardener by any chance?'

'A sort of scientist of language? Professor Mordaunt would like that. Or a mathematician. I'm sure she was good at budgeting.'

'That reminds me. Will you do the shopping next week?'

Walking under the trees in Albert Park, Irene wishes now she had included Elinor and Marianne. Two sisters and two suitors; the spectacular second chance, though different for females, of Anne Elliot and Captain Wentworth. Suddenly it occurs to Irene that the pairs are not perfect at first and adjustments have to be made. Elizabeth (free speech and spirit) must learn sound reasoning and an equably applied imagination to lower Wickham and raise Darcy. This is how the novel moves. Two-ness, adjustment, one-ness. Irene sits under an oak as old as the tree at Lambton and boldly adds to her list:

6. Two examples of male foolishness: Mr Bennet (detachment) and Mr Collins (pedantry). Whereas Mr Gardiner combines sense and action.

7. Mrs Bennet's character and marriage echoed by Lydia Bennet's marriage to Wickham. Two examples of infatuation yielding to indifference. Genetic?

8. Two courses at dinner. Fish? Fowl?

9. Wickham has two career options: church and army.

10. Both Darcy and Elizabeth have a greatly loved sister: Georgiana and Jane.

But these will not do. Professor Mordaunt will get his teeth into 'two courses for dinner'. You might as well say Kitty trims two bonnets. Or Wickham joins two regiments or rejects two livings. Twice Mr Gardiner visits Pemberley, the second time to fish. Perhaps two and not one trout rise on his perambulation. Then Irene thinks of what she had read of Cassandra's life after Jane died, how withdrawn and private it became, a life of living bereavement. And how Jane, once at Chawton, urgently sent for Cassandra as though engulfed in panic. The cause of the panic was an alteration in family fortunes, the reading of a will.

8. (writes Irene, removing two partridges or boiled fowls) The two themes of money and marriage.

Ben walks rapidly alongside a fence which is too high to jump. Behind him the footsteps, padded, nonchalant, like wolves which delicately advance upon a dead campfire. Ben has seen a film of wolves and their strange hesitancy, as if they bring a mere calling card, when the final advance begins. And last year Sue and Irene had taken him to see real wolves at the zoo. 'Like ladies in fur coats going to the opera,' Irene had laughed, pointing out the too thin legs, but Ben could not take his eyes off their pacing. Only the panthers seemed as restless.

The persecution of Ben had begun slowly enough. Sue and Irene had come to a Home and School evening and to parent interviews together. Ben had wished Irene wouldn't come but she insisted. Fleet had come too, for his night walk. Two women with a red setter between them, striding down the corridor.

The boy at the interview before him had become the ring leader. Soon Ben's lunch was being stolen, his sports gear went missing, a pocket was ripped off a blazer. A project with a relief model was doused with blue-black ink. The final stage was to stalk him. It could only lead to a beating.

But not tonight. Head down in his misery, brain willing his Nikes to move faster, a gradual accumulating speed that might leave his tormentors in his wake, Ben does not see a woman bearing down on him. She is full-busted, narrow-hipped, and has thin legs like a wolf.

'My goodness,' she cries as he slams into her. Then, 'Don't I know you? Haven't I seen you with Irene Fisher?'

I have forgotten Mary Bennet contrasted with Elizabeth Bennet at the pianoforte, Irene thinks as she sits in Professor Mordaunt's room, gazing out at the leaves of an oak tree. But such details will not convince. Professor Mordaunt's countenance is set in an expression so customary to it, a kind of sardonic disdain, a scholarly weariness, that it is impossible to imagine the younger fresh face that once lay beneath. Did he ever — for he was made a full professor very young — bound up the stairs to his room or welcome an importuning student with a show of enthusiasm? Does his condescension to women students date from some miraculous year in which their brains were definitively proved smaller?

'Two balls at Netherfield cannot equal two proposals by Darcy, nor can you prove that Jane Austen was deliberately replicating the elder Bennets' marriage in Lydia and Wickham's set-up. Wickham and Mr Bennet may share some disagreeable characteristics — their judgement of women, for instance — but Mr Bennet remains a gentleman, as Elizabeth is fond of pointing out. I always thought she was clutching at straws. And Mrs Bennet hardly attains the rank of Lady Catherine, whose knowledge of etiquette is profound.'

'Except in her remarks about the Bennets' west-facing sitting room and her trying to extract a denial from Elizabeth,' Irene wants to protest, but she knows it is wiser to remain silent. She thinks of Mary Bennet listening to Mr Collins and perceiving a majesty in the length of word.

'But,' says Professor Mordaunt, perceiving her downcast Mary Bennet face, 'there is enough in your notion to interest me, I think. Provided, and this is a big proviso, you start with the most obvious blocks of resemblance and don't allow yourself to become distracted with feminine fripperies like boiled fowls, two pianos or bonnets in a hat shop.'

'Still they might make an interesting codicil,' Irene offers, recovering something of the spirit of her heroine.

'Run along,' Professor Mordaunt growls, 'before I change my mind. Let me see an introduction in writing.'

'I think something's bothering Ben,' Sue says to Irene that evening as they are clearing away the supper dishes. 'Do you notice how silent he is lately?'

'He didn't want to go to school this morning. Said he had a stomach ache. Perhaps I was wrong to force him.'

'Tomorrow's Friday. Let's pick him up after school and take him to dinner and a movie.'

Before she sleeps Irene takes up *The Key to the Universe* and some more of the chapter on *The Number 2*.

Let 2 remind you that the great problem of humanity on this globe is the perfect blending and mastery of the positive and negative expressions of the Great Creative Force through its pairs of opposites, the sexes. Then she thinks of Jane Austen in the kitchen at Chawton, chopping suet into flour, pleased to be free of polarities: Elizabeth Bennet and Fitzwilliam Darcy, Elinor and Marianne Dashwood, Emma Woodhouse and Jane Fairfax. And yet she can never be quite free of her characters who keep her company as much as Cassandra does. It is her own nature she is describing: romantic and worldly, astute and playful, rising to speech like the plentiful trout in the ponds at Pemberley?

Ben's mistake has been in trying to explain he has two mothers. My mother is divorced and lives with a friend. It is a mistake to explain anything. Two mothers, no father, two lesbos, poor little sook. It doesn't matter that one mother works in broadcasting and the other is at university. That he sees about as much of them as two fathers, though they

306

make up for it at weekends. Anyway his mother is quite masculine, good at making decisions. What a rich road he has opened to his tormentors.

Unbeknown to him, the two mothers are now speeding towards him along Gillies Avenue. Irene is in her tracksuit, as she has just come from the gym; Sue on the other hand is heavily made up: she has had a tryout for television earlier in the afternoon. When the make-up girl hands her a tissue and pushes a pot of cold cream in her direction she decides to leave it on. 'I think I look quite glamorous, if you squint.' Sue is wearing a soft green suit over a black bustier, and very high heels which she kicks off while driving.

They come on the little group of flailing boys by a low stone wall.

'Ben,' shouts Irene, who has the better eyesight. 'Stop the car.'

Sue pulls up on a yellow line and the two women leap out. Sue is barefooted but she clutches one bright red shoe. Irene seizes the largest perpetrator in a head lock; Sue brings the pointed heel down on the base of the neck of another. Inspired by Professor Mordaunt's doubts about two-ness in Jane Austen, Irene lifts an insect-like boy straddling Ben under the armpits and throws him over the stone wall.

'Just don't say we're your mothers,' Sue says as they roar off to avoid an approaching parking warden.

'You're going to have two beautiful black eyes,' Irene remarks admiringly. 'Wear them with pride.'

Then she turns to Sue and murmurs, 'Nice one, Cassandra.'

The Mathematics of Jane Austen

The duality of forces, the two-ness, which occurs sufficiently often in Jane Austen's novels to warrant at least an interest, may be exemplified in Pride and Prejudice. *Other novels in the canon share the characteristic two-ness which is sometimes stated in a title:* Sense and Sensibility, *for example. But the two-ness seems to go deeper, postulating a view of the world in which opposing forces, moral, financial, social, attract a counter-poise, so that good strives against evil, probity against falsehood, infatuation against a longer-enduring love. Was Jane Austen a mathematician as much as Stephen Hawking is a cosmologist? Did she view the admittedly narrow world she inhabited as worked by levers?*

But this will not do. Irene takes up a red pencil and runs it through all the words that follow 'love'.

What's in a Name?

MICHAEL MORRISSEY

Once upon a time there were three sisters called Faith, Hope and Charity. So what's in a name? Not a lot it might appear. Faith was a sceptic, Hope was, well . . . hopeless and Charity was a loveless blonde. Inner assessments, spoken aloud in moments of anger though only to each other and never to the world which, let it be said, had succumbed to the nominal fallacy that a noun carried some ontological guarantee of what it delineated. To the world then, they were the . . . Three Virtues. Like the Andrews Sisters before them they formed a glamorous triplet, gorgeous to a fault. The public of the late nineties had tired of nose-candying guitarists and bisexual blondes with pointed breasts; they longed for some good old-fashioned decency as well as good singing. Even Sir Howard Morrison had to admit that they harmonised splendidly. The Virtues also made much bewitching capital out of their nude shoulder blades, gulls' wing eyebrows and full collagenless lips. As the Spice Girls faded, the sleeker, sophisticated and yet ultimately more wholesome Three Virtues flourished. They were forties, yes, but the forties put through a nineties postmodern remake. Beloved by poststructuralists and Mr and Mrs *Reader's Digest* Condensed Book alike, the Three Virtues had a meteoric rise. They seemed headed for the moon and the stars beyond and indeed they did go aloft when Japan set up a space station. Their witty harmonising in freefall in slinky but tasteful halter-top dresses and high heels became the image of the millennium. If the world was going to end then at least Virtue(s) would be preserved, punned a standup comedian. Of course the planet continued stubbornly to spin and with each revolution the Virtues' light gained wattage.

Their finest moment came when they were flown into an African trouble spot and fearlessly walked on their highly sensible high heels towards some approaching tanks. The world held its breath. The tanks stopped in their soldier-grinding tracks. A billion people ceased to exhale. The turrets of the tanks open. Grimy battle-weary faces emerge. In close up we see their hardness, their wickedness yielding to the Virtues. The soldiers embrace the spotless trio who naturally do not mind if a small amount of dust and oil besmirches their sexy dresses. The camera which has passed the lie detector test with flying colours since the moment of its concoction allows us to see a male tear working its way down a battle-hardened face and drop into the dust as harmlessly as a miniaturised hand grenade made of salt and water. It is the year 2000. The millennium has been reached. Peace has broken out. Humanity has been saved from its own evil.

But then the rumours started. The whole thing had been staged. The war was just a video. Those dead children lying face down in the mud were just actors and not even very well paid. Faith, Hope and Charity appeared on the world's screens, their customary night-time rictuses set in dignified daytime denial. Faith said they could polygraph her any time they liked and her palms would not sweat. Hope said the war had been real and the peace was just as real. Charity said little but cried a lot and as usual tears carried the day. The world believed. Virtue prevailed. The rumours died a quiet death though some said — another rumour no doubt — that the rumour-mongers had been paid a sum of money with as many digits as an international phone call to shut up.

A time capsule shot into outer space by a Sino-Russo-American rocketship carried the image of the Virtues beyond the solar system and ever onward to some patiently waiting and hopefully benign aliens who some said were already among us (and already fans of the Virtues). When a sceptic asked what if aliens had no ears, he was drowned out by cries of eager denial. The ancients had got it right — there was a Music of the Spheres and the Virtues were its songsters. Beyond the empyrean of the ionosphere, a re-imaged God closed Her eyes in celestial bliss.

After these dizzy heights a tour of Las Vegas was anti-climactic. Nevertheless, the Virtues insisted they were still human and not goddesses and what better way to prove their humanity than appearing under a cathedral of pulsating neon? Their smiles were still passports to a fame which had turned a divided world of 200 plus countries into a unified mosaic — a chameleon, cynics said, that could change to suit its environment, the flaw in this mordancy being it was the lizard with the swivelling eyeballs that was inducing the environment to change hue to suit itself.

It could not last but it did. The arms industry shrank, Islam and Christianity held hands. But the Virtues' apparently scandal-less lives were to be disrupted by an unexpected transmogrification. As the flawless trio jetted in from their triumphal Yankee tour, the eyes of families long since familiar with their homely yet tastefully sexy femininity were stunned to see the middle member of the trio — Hope — return from Las Vegas breastless and moustached, her voice lowered by half an octave.

Hope had become Hank.

'It never felt right being a woman,' baritoned Hank. 'I was a man trapped in a woman's body.' No matter how many times the inversion of this has been uttered ('I was a woman trapped in a man's body') the notion of Hope becoming Hank was too much to be readily accepted. An unshockable world had at last been shocked. A transgender war broke out with prominent spokespersons on both sides. Orthodox Jewry withdrew beneath its long kiss-curls and Islam and Christianity parted company. Catholicism was divided.

But Hank had some more surprises up *his* sleeve.

He converted to Rome and began training as a priest. He took to his new role with such fervour there could be no doubt of his vocation. In the urban wastelands of central America he would be espied working with the indigent. What Mother Teresa had done for the poor of Calcutta Father Hope now did for the underprivileged of Mexico City.

And what of the Virtues? As a duo they began to lose popularity. Their supreme success had depended on their being — like the Deity — three in one.

Hank rose quickly through the ranks of the clergy. Bishop, archbishop, cardinal — all in a few years. When the current Pope was killed in a plane crash but Father Hope (Father Hank in the chronically disrespectful tabloid press) was miraculously spared, it was clear the finger of God was luminously pointed in but one direction.

Pius the Thirteenth ascended the papal throne as the third millennium got under way. Contrary to expectation he was not a liberal pope. He disapproved of abortion, masturbation, divorce, women priests and homosexuality. However, he proved a strong advocate of the supreme theological virtues — Faith, Hope and Charity.

What's in a name? Everything it might appear.

Beethoven's Ears

MICHAEL MORRISSEY

When Ludwig van Beethoven died on 26 March 1827, his ears were amputated by the eminent anatomist Dr Joseph Wagner and placed in a jar filled with spirits of wine. Beethoven had slowly been going deaf since 1801 and Wagner wanted to examine his ears and try to ascertain the cause. In his autopsy report, Wagner noted that 'the external ear was large and irregularly formed, the scaphoid fossa, but more especially the concha, was very spacious and half as large again as usual'. He also noted that the great composer's liver had shrunk to half normal size and was of a 'leathery consistency beset with knots the size of a bean'; the spleen was double normal size and the excretory duct of the pancreas 'as wide as a goose quill'; the stomach was 'distended', and the body 'much emaciated'. In short, Beethoven was a mess.

However, on examining the brain, Wagner found its convolutions to be 'remarkably white' and 'very much deeper, wider and more numerous than ordinary'.

But to return to the ears. They sat in the spirits of wine-filled jar for several weeks, but before Wagner could complete the examination, the jar mysteriously disappeared. No one is quite sure what happened to the jar, but it is thought to have been illegally sold by Wagner's servant to an English doctor and smuggled across the English channel into the sceptred isle. Having been fruitlessly examined by the English doctor (the syphilitic cause of Beethoven's deafness then being unrecognised) the ears were returned to the jar and placed on display in his living-room for the curious scrutiny of dinner guests. In 1843 an urchin chimney sweep stole the jar and sold it to a pawnbroker who eventually persuaded a baronet from Kent that they were indeed Beethoven's ears.

When Phineas T. Barnum made his triumphal tour of Great Britain with Tom Thumb and the mother-daughter team who had won American hearts by playing Topsy and Little Eva in *Uncle Tom's Cabin*, the baronet offered the colourful American entrepreneur the ears for ten guineas. Barnum accepted the offer. So Beethoven's ears joined the Feejee Mermaid, Chang and Eng (the famous Siamese twins), Lionel the Lion Faced Man and General Tom Thumb, the world's most famous dwarf. When the general lifted one of the ears from the murky preserving fluid and placed it over one of his own diminutive organs and pretended to hear messages from beyond the grave both of the Fat Ladies would invariably shriek — to a duo of thigh-slapping delight from the Siamese twins.

The ears subsequently went underground (as it were) and were not seen or heard of again until the World Fair in St Louis of 1904. Soon after, they fell into the hands of the Great Tosca, a turn of the century hypnotist and mountebank, who claimed that 'the ears of the great German composer Beethoven had peculiar psychic properties'. They could, said the Great Tosca, hear a person's innermost thoughts. Tosca, a tall bearded man weighing eighteen stone, would stand blindfold on stage with the jar balanced delicately on his head, and reveal the embarrassingly private thoughts of his largely female audience. He would tell people what they had in their handbags, where they had been in the previous week, and what they had eaten for supper. These spectacular feats would produce thunderous applause and Tosca's assistant, a French girl from Marseilles, swears that on good nights 'the ears would undulate ever so slightly' in appreciation of this crude symphony of hand clapping.

But now the fate of Beethoven's ears takes a forked path. According to the European theory, the ears were sold to an eccentric, and unsuccessful composer called Erasmus Windhover. Windhover was the creator of several leadenly dull choral works and a large body of chamber music that had never been performed (though he would often hum these opuses aloud for the benefit of Beethoven's ears).

Six months later, Gustav Mahler received a visitor claiming to have in his possession the Tenth Symphony of Beethoven and would he care to conduct it? Mahler was sceptical but accepted the score and studied it closely. An hour later Mahler called Windhover back into his study. He said it was always a pleasure to meet a representative of the nation that had produced Purcell and Elgar. Then Mahler coughed and said that though the work did indeed appear to be in the style of Beethoven, the third movement was almost identical to the third movement of the *Eroica* and the concluding movement was very similar to the concluding movement of the Seventh. In short, the Tenth Symphony of Beethoven was a fake. Enraged, Windhover swore that he knew the symphony to be 'a true and original work of Beethoven', for had he not taken down every note, line by line under the dictation of the great composer himself? It was typical of Mahler, an Austrian, to be jealous of Beethoven, a German, etc., etc. Mahler bowed and said curtly, 'Good-day to you, Herr Windbreaker.'

Undeterred by Mahler's scepticism, Windhover returned to his pastoral retreat near Salisbury Plain, where he composed an eleventh Beethovenic symphony. Out-Mahlering Mahler, he called it the Symphony of the Ten Thousand. It called for two thousand musicians (502 first violins, 502 second violins, 240 violas, 240 cellos, 200 basses, 80 flutes, 80 oboes, 20 clarinets in E flat, 60 clarinets in B flat, 5 bass clarinets in B flat, 8 bassoons, 4 double bassoons, 27 horns, 10 trombones, 5 bass tubas, 6 harps, 3 celesta, 3 sets of tympani, 3 cymbals, 2 tambourines) and eight thousand singers. The local parish priest was 'deeply impressed' by Windhover's dedication to the craft of choral and orchestral music but inquired politely of Windhover how it was they could accommodate so many visitors in their village of three hundred? 'The Lord will provide,' Windhover replied. But the Lord, it seemed, was intent on turning a deaf ear to this posthumous masterpiece of Beethoven. When Windhover met with no interest in London musical circles, it is said he went to the famous circle of stones at Stonehenge and buried the ears under the largest stone. Some now claim that Beethoven's ears transformed Stonehenge into a gigantic listening device. Others maintain that the famous black magician, Aleister Crowley dug them up and hung them around his neck, deriving much of his horrible powers from having them so close to his villainous heart. It was rumoured that The Great Beast nailed the ears above the table near the door of his infamous Black Magick restaurant, where strong men were weeping into their daemonically hot curries. The ears, Crowley said, greatly enjoyed the peculiar atmosphere of sexual deca- dence and diabolic incantation, as well as the sound of strong men weeping. When Crowley died, the ears were cremated and co-mingled with his ashes and placed in an urn on top of the Rock of Cefalu, where they remain to this day.

The alternative or 'Colonial' theory is that the ears passed from the Barnum show to a theosophist, who gave them to Annie Besant. When Besant visited New Zealand in the nineteenth century, she be- stowed them upon the local branch of the Order of the Golden Dawn. After the First World War, they appeared once more on the shelf of a Mrs Eleanor Spencer, a Dunedin music teacher, who said 'they could always detect false notes'. It is said that they are in the possession of the most musical of Mrs Spencer's eighty-seven grandchildren, but, according to another account, they re-entered show business . . .

In 1905 the Fuller Brothers toured with Cleopatra, 'a fearless snake charmer'. Cleopatra, who caused 'strong men to experience a strange shuddering thrill' and women to 'shriek in horror' at her skilled han- dling of boa constrictors, anacondas and black snakes, swore that Beethoven's ears kept her from being bitten. When Cleopatra was ap- proached to donate Beethoven's ears to a time capsule, she agreed, even though parting with them was going to put her life in jeopardy. Where the time capsule is buried, no one knows, but it was rumoured to be secured under the Largest Wooden Building in the World. It is feared that, should the time capsule be excavated it will be as cor- roded by water as the time capsule retrieved from a well beneath the former District Court in Auckland.

There is even a post-Colonial theory concerning Beethoven's ears (especially espoused at the University of Auckland). According to its exponents, Beethoven's ears never existed or if they existed 'we as ex- Colonials have no need of them. We don't need European ears anymore; we have our own.'

It is uncertain, perhaps, whether Beethoven's ears still lie beneath Stonehenge or with Aleister Crowley's ashes or with one of Mrs Spen- cer's musical grandchildren or buried in a Wellington time capsule. It is certain, probably, that the ears will be in some way listening to

human endeavour through all eternity and that many of us will believe — and who can do otherwise? — that throughout the aeons to
pass they will listen to the sounds of new civilisations as well as their
collapse, which will be heard by those ever-alert organs as a strange,
exciting but somehow orderly music.

Hitler's French Letter

MICHAEL MORRISSEY

We broke in during the twilight hour of a long January evening. 'Wonder if there'll be any swastikas up,' murmured Frank. 'No Frank, she came here to forget the past — remember?' The interior of her house suggested someone who had lived in poverty. The dwelling had been gutted by fire and all that remained were a few old scraps of yellowing newspaper (*New Zealand Herald*, May 11, 1941) — which I casually noted was the day Hess had parachuted into Scotland in an attempt to talk England into a peaceful settlement — and the chaise longue. It sat near the fireplace at a rakish angle, a hint of recent disturbance.

What are we doing? Practising the time-honoured student art of poozling — the art and craft of removing discarded furniture and other objects from abandoned or vacant houses. Poozle booty can include wardrobes, tables, chairs, beds, mattresses, pots and pans, refrigerators, washing machines, knives, forks, pictures, boiling coppers and clothing. The rarest thing to be found would be money. You are more likely to meet a human being. Which is what we did. More or less. But let me return to the house.

The poozle house was a ramshackle two-storeyed wooden villa threatening to fall into a gully behind and beneath it; until recently, it was occupied by a woman in her eighties. Rumour, supported by the evidence of uncollected newspapers, had it that she had died, heirless. She had been an eccentric old woman, reputedly with a connection to the Third Reich.

The dairy owner, who knew most people's business, alleged she had been mistress to one of the higher ranking Nazis. Which one?

Hitler was spoken for. Himmler and Goebbels appeared asexual. Goering was an obvious choice, but she didn't look like the Goering type, which I imagined to be a beefy chested Brunnhilde in riding boots, wielding a hippopotamus whip. Herr Hess was my choice. An estrangement had occurred — that was the real cause of Hess's ill-fated flight to Great Britain. Our elderly but now deceased neighbour had betrayed her allegiance to Aryan civilisation and come to live and die in obscurity in far-flung New Zealand. So her chaise longue was obviously worth poozling. It might contain some revealing artifact from the Third Reich . . .

'Let's go,' I said to Frank. We picked up the chaise longue and carried it out. We had taken it but five yards when we saw her — the most beautiful young woman at university.

Her name was Claire Luxford-Smythe. She was rich, delicate — and beautiful. It's hard to conceive nowadays but in those times most young women were shapeless puddings who wore mum-knitted jump-ers and were destined (if not promptly married) for a career in typing, clothing assembly or nursing. Beauties were rare and stood out like mediaeval beacons during a Stygian (or should that be Styxian?) night. Frank had long made himself sick with longing over this beauty whose complexion suggested tuberculosis and poetic talent. She was so re-mote from my world I didn't even waste my emotional energies with longing, let alone infatuation. I'd always imagined she lived in Remuera, in a huge mansion set amid several rolling acres of flawlessly mani-cured garden, so when I saw her walking down Grafton Road we both realised at once she must live in the area and could be spoken to. The question was — what to say to the university's most sought-after beauty? Written any good essays lately?

Then Frank had an attack of genius. He put his end of the chaise longue down on the pavement — I quickly followed suit — and said to Claire Luxford-Smythe in a voice of seductively languid confidence, 'Care for a lift?'

To my amazement she smiled and put her hand on the side of the couch. Seemingly uneasy on her feet, she opened her mouth to speak and . . . dribbled. I noticed her eyes were rolled back and she was shaking. Then she collapsed. 'My God, what did you do to her?' I said to Frank.

'Can't you see she's having an epileptic fit? Quick — get her up on the couch!' He laid her rather long but elegant body along the chaise longue. 'Quick! Loosen her clothing!' I put my hand on the top button of her blouse.

'Leave her alone, you swine!' cried a shrill voice in my ear. Before I identify the utterer of these hostile words and their possible underpinning rationale, I would like to point out that both narrator and friend Frank were off their respective faces. They were, ladies and gentlemen, completely ripped. This chemical disarray gave them an edge — an edge without edges if you get my point. They were stoned, because prior to the poozling of Hess's mistress's chaise longue they had dropped in on Ivan, who was the best kind of genius, a vague genius.

'We seem to be having a dopeless moment,' was all the hint needed for Ivan to roll up a colossal joint — proof of social genius at least. We wound up whacked as Easter chooks during a Russian orthodox Lent (a saying of Ivan's) while he expounded a new theory about how all perception, particularly bourgeois perception, was a form of fascism — a tyranny of the senses whereby up is up and down is down. I half expected Ivan to fly up to the ceiling in defiance of the law of gravity, that species of oppression by avoirdupois.

It was Ivan's paranoid neighbour who yelled the accusation, but it was Ivan who came to the rescue at that instant by saying, 'They're in my play.' That was true, but he had forgotten to tell us of our involvement.

The play was a gigantic seven-part epic about the seven ages and sins of Man. Absurd, eh? It was at once apparent not only that the age from nought to ten was the age of Greed, ten to twenty the age of Envy, twenty to thirty the age of Lust, thirty to forty the age of Covetousness, forty to fifty the age of Anger, fifty to sixty the age of Pride, and sixty to seventy the age of Sloth, but also that, after three score and ten, your sinning days were over and all was sluggish virtue. It was also apparent that we were cast in the infantile age of Greed. Claire Luxford-Smythe, seven years old, had had too many lollies and collapsed into our pram. We were rolling her homewards. Ivan, it was clear, was attempting an ambitious fusion of myth and contemporary satire.

Now that our accuser had trundled back into the wooden slum

from where she had emerged like a moray eel, Ivan explained that we actually were invited to be in a drama in the basement of a house quite close by — the play was in the experimental stage, but was one that showed the evolution of Man and Woman through the depiction of mythic archetypes. Know Thine Archetype Shall Be the Whole of the Law! Claire Luxford-Smythe was a wise old woman in a trance and we were young princes who were to awaken the young woman that lay imprisoned in her withered old body. So it was that the recovering Claire, who was not quite herself after her fit, found herself coming to on stage in a dingy Grafton villa basement. She played the part of bewilderment very convincingly — the audience of eight cheered and clapped loudly.

During the play (Ivan's naughty idea) Claire was to suddenly discover, wedged into the crevice of the chaise longue (said to be Baudelaire's couch), a small packet of contraceptives which Frank identified as Hitler's French letter — still unused, fresh as the day it was first packaged in the sadly Jewish factory of its manufacture. Would it stand up to contemporary New Zealand usage? Would it stretch pound for pound, inch for inch, as much as a Newton urgent dispensary Featherlite Durex on a Saturday night when two tattooed hoons decided to give it a test run on Sharleen, the check-out girl? A question that a foolish man may ask and a wise person cannot answer. The fact is, while still recovering from her fit, Claire Luxford-Smythe — beautiful remote ethereal Claire — was clutching a prophylactic (unopened), identified by Third Reich authorities Frank, Ivan and your narrator, as Hitler's French letter.

A door burst open — it was easy for us to guess that someone had been listening at its hinge for some minutes. It was the same woman who had accused us of being born out of wedlock.

'I'm not dead!' the old woman declared. 'I went up north for a few days to visit my nephew — he's in an ironlung — and when I got back everything in my house had been moved out! Sold! Stolen! That's not Hitler's French letter; that was left by my immoral niece! That's not Baudelaire's couch, that's my chaise longue. I want it back now!' I looked at Frank. Claire Luxford-Smythe looked at both of us and . . . dribbled.

The audience of eight applauded loudly. Clearly, they thought the old woman's proprietorial speech was part of Ivan's play. It was an absurd situation and the play (if it was a play) was clearly Absurd. (Ionesco and Adamov were big at the time.)

Suddenly Claire Luxford-Smythe recovered from her fit and sat up. Yes, she did ask the perennial question of temporarily confused heroines in Victorian melodramas as recorded on black and white celluloid. ('Where am I?')

'You are in a play,' responded Ivan in bland European tones.

'Are you all right, dear? Did you faint?' The old woman had detected that Claire was not part of the plot. (Absurdist plays have no plot.) 'Would you like a cup of tea? The rest of you whippersnappers can get off my property.'

'We're not whippersnappers, we're performers,' Ivan said smoothly. 'Madame, you have stumbled upon an exciting development in avantgarde theatre.'

'In my house, you puppy.'

'Is this really your house?' asked Frank.

'I own most of the street, boy. And that's my chaise longue you pillaged.' For one stoned moment I thought she had said poozled — I certainly did not want elderly landladies appropriating our exclusive Grafton vocabulary.

'It appears we have made a grave error,' said Ivan. (Was the appalling pun intentional?) 'We thought you had entered the realm of spirit.'

'You're much sturdier than that, aren't you?' said Claire Luxford-Smythe, taking charge with teeth-dazzling confidence. Suddenly she had stopped being ethereal, though no less beautiful. At that moment I grasped a shattering truth — divine-looking girls were not merely mute goddesses but could possess strong character, precise intuition and the power of intelligent and hugely compelling speech. 'Now you two, return this couch at once,' she ordered (it did not seem like an order). 'You may be needing this,' she handed me the French letter, which I blushingly pocketed — I had yet to use such a device. 'Would Hitler have owned a French letter? — don't be ridiculous!' I felt dizzy with love for Claire Luxford-Smythe.

The audience of eight were somewhat bewildered by their basement Grafton Absurd theatre becoming a real life situation; in fact the reappearance of an apparently dead landlady was absurd (if not Absurd). They were all corduroyed, denimed and pleasingly hairy — the young women with unruly manes, the young men vigorously unshaven with an air of intellectual haughtiness. My kind of person.

The mysteriously undead landlady told us her life story. She was born in Estonia or Latvia, her father had been a White Russian and her mother, a gypsy contortionist and magician's assistant. Mother's speciality was being sawn in half. Her father had been smuggled out of Russia into Latvia while hiding in the box, curled up like a large moustached foetus. He became a spy for the Americans during the flapper era. When the Americans learnt the Russians had no military secrets of value (the 1920s, remember), they tried to corrupt the Soviets with a sinister drug injected into the bloodstream via the ear, called jazz. But Russian lugs were jazz-proof or so rimed with frost they could not hear the seductive wailing of saxophones: the plot failed. Meanwhile, her father taught her the tricks of the trade. She grew up in an atmosphere of polyglottry and espionage; speaking four languages fluently, she in turn became a spy for the British against the Germans. She had dined with Himmler and knew of the Final Solution, but the Allies (whom she told) took no action. (Had she met Hess?) When she arrived in the United States she was recruited as a double agent, smuggling out Russian nuclear secrets hidden in her double hollowed heeled shoes. In fact, she became a treble agent, passing American information back to the Russians. Sometimes she would have American intelligence in her right shoe and Russian data in her left. One day she got the shoes mixed up, but that didn't matter because she had much the same information in each shoe. During the winter of 1943 she was apprehended and 'questioned' by the Gestapo. 'First, they pulled out my fingernails, then my toenails. Both feet. But I told them nothing. You girls — imagine that you had on your most uncomfortable shoes, the ones that pinch the most. Multiply that pain by a hundred times and you get some idea of what it's like to have your toenails pulled out. And my torturer was so handsome. Had the circumstances been otherwise, I could have fallen in love with him. During my ordeal he played Strauss. I cannot hear a waltz now without having twinges in my little toe.'

One of the more leonine-looking girls had tears running down her cheeks. Yet there was more — much more. At the conclusion of this classic twentieth-century saga of woe, so far off the Richter scale of our Grafton experience and suffering, only one response was possible — a cup of tea. Shamefaced, we returned everything we had poozled. Our drama was no longer absurd (though totally Absurd).

I must have been wittier and more attractive than I imagined, because in a few years I discovered that I was married to Claire Luxford-Smythe (who wasn't rich). That stumps you, doesn't it? And that wonderful old woman gave us the chaise longue as a wedding gift. I have it (and Hitler's unopened French letter) still. And by the way, our donor landlady did not own any of the houses (though she had camped in one of them with her pile of newspapers), nor was she a spy; she was mad, and for a morning we were part of her magnificent delusions. This is the surprise ending. Absurd, isn't it?

Pleasuring Mr White

SHERIDAN KEITH

When Mr White divorced his first wife Mary, to marry his secretary, Irene, he was under the impression that Irene was cold and masterly, and would give him the sort of callous treatment he yearned for and felt he deserved. He liked the fact that she smoked, that she was indifferent to the toll upon her lungs, and his, that this constant smoking implied. That she never looked at him he interpreted to mean she considered him unworthy of notice, a judgement he concurred with.

You might have thought that a man like Mr White, with his weak chest, would have run a mile from a chain-smoker. In fact his relationship with her was an act of self-assertion, though like many acts of self-assertion, hopelessly misjudged.

Women had always annoyed him. His older sister had died a cot-death before he was born, deserting him prenatally, and focusing their mother's guilt into a remorseless beam of caring, directed exclusively at the twinned, pink organs of breathing that had failed so inexplicably within his sister's tiny rib-cage.

His chest had been a never-ending source of humiliation. He caught cold frequently and spent hours under draped towels inhaling Friars' Balsam. He had had to endure wearing coats, and pullovers, woollen singlets, scarves, Balaclavas, to the extent that he looked like a polar explorer and every physical effort felt encumbered, either by material restrictions, or the guilt engendered when he removed a single item of clothing. Not to mention the teasing. He was called 'Igloo' at school.

When he was ill his mother added to his burden by heaping abuse on his padded shoulders. It was all his fault, he must have allowed

324

himself to get cold, he hadn't wrapped up well enough, he must have played with someone who'd breathed germs onto him, he'd forgotten to rub Vicks on his chest, he'd played too vigorously and got overtired. Didn't he know he was the only thing in her life? How dare he worry her like this.

He would burrow to the bottom of the bed and cough as quietly as possible down where the blankets smelt of his toenails and muffled the sounds coming from his struggling lungs. He began to envy his deceased sister, who'd had the foresight to give in before wasting any energy on the battle.

His mother's wildest threat was that she would send him to live with her sister in Arizona, where the desert air would dry out his lungs. She was the town clerk of a small place called Eloy, and he had seen a picture of her wearing a gun holster, with impressive revolvers emerging. He had nightmares about wandering alone through landscapes of cacti and dry river beds, his lungs becoming crisp as seaweed baked in a heartless sun.

His first marriage as not an attempt to escape from his mother, he wasn't that brave, but he had hoped to ameliorate her influence. Mary got on well with his mother, learning her cues quickly, becoming a convincing understudy. The marriage drifted along indifferently. It was only when Irene entered his office, looking like Mrs Simpson, thin as a bony rat, wearing a tight dress in an evil shade of peacock blue, her hair hennaed, and exhaling clouds of smoke, that Mr White became aware of the requirements of destiny.

Unlike Mrs Simpson who had wanted to be Queen of England, but had been foiled, Irene didn't want anything, certainly not another woman's husband. Well, apart from keeping her job. She liked the money, she liked clothes, and shoes, and secretly, and in shame, she collected dolls.

In reality Irene was not what she seemed, or at least not what she seemed to Mr White. Her cigarette smoking, far from being a wilful assertion of pulmonary indifference, was a nervous requirement. What he interpreted as cold superiority was really a total lack of self-esteem. She never looked him in the eye, not, as he hoped, because she found him insignificant, but because she was too afraid to confirm what she feared, that he was looking at her.

And looking at her he was. He couldn't take his eyes off her pathetic ribcage, swathed in peacock crêpe de chine. He followed the complicated labyrinths of her hairstyle secured by thin metal grips into coils reminiscent of ear-muffs, and he wondered at her lips, and the lipstick thereon. Was it really purple? He couldn't wait to buy an ashtray to collect her cigarette stubs.

Irene was far too submissive to ask permission to smoke, and far too addicted to go without, so she smoked rather as if she was having a half-hearted stab at it, a throw-away style that made her look as if she were sampling rather than partaking, much as a wine taster might swirl the fluid about in the mouth and then spit it out. Her cigarettes were often only half smoked, but she would light up again immediately.

Mr White began to dream about Irene, dreams in which she blew perfect smoke rings for his erect penis to pass through. In another dream he begged her to have intercourse with him, but she said, slyly and enigmatically, 'Only when you can lie on your back and balance a Bible on your dick will I succumb.' He took this to mean that the sanctity of marriage was a requirement, though who knows what it might have signified.

In reality they were stiffly formal with each other, and it was not until the Christmas office party that Irene, aware of the awesome loneliness of the Christmas holidays stretching for weeks in front of her, and Mr White, structured by the office alcohol, achieved unity. He backed her into a wall, lifted her dress of emerald taffeta, and with a flurry of fingertips inserted his own small self beyond the gleaming difficulties of her underwear into the warm confines of her mysterious tunnel. As if she had been a steam train she let forth a cloud of smoke as Mr White sought to enclose her purple lips with his mouth, and achieve a double seal, which made him think of preserving jars.

Irene looked to one side, a glance Mr White took to speak of derision. The moment he withdrew she lit up a fag, and he was determined to marry her. He sent his wife away on a holiday (he worked for a travel agency and got cheap flights) and changed every lock on every door of the house. When she returned, poor Mary could no longer gain access. Crying bitterly she went into one of the neighbours, who had seen Irene and her suitcase move in. Needless to say, the neighbours never spoke to Irene, or to Mr White again, feeling a certain loyalty to the first wife.

Irene and Mr White eventually married, after Mr White's divorce, but he soon realised Irene was as keen to look after and cherish him as his mother and his first wife had been, and when he asked her to spit on him she did it, but without relish. Any other indignities he craved she utterly refused to cooperate with. No children were forthcoming and Mr White wouldn't undergo tests to ascertain whether he was in any way to blame. Irene's only act of self-assertion was to claim the small bedroom of their house as her play room, and within its locked interior she played with her dolls, dressing and undressing them, giving them rides on the rocking horse, tucking them up to sleep in their prams.

Mr White began a weapon collection. He was especially interested in Japanese swords, the very sight of which made most people feel ill. Irene gave up work in the hope that she would become pregnant but she didn't, and then she lost the courage to re-enter the work force. She bought a large parrot that stood in a cage in the kitchen, and kept a jar of sweets on the window sill so that the neighbourhood children would come and chat with her.

The years passed. Mr White's mother died, and he went out and bought a particularly ugly disembowelling sword to commemorate her passing. Irene's doll collection was worth a lot of money, and she sent a Steiff teddy bear to Christies where it sold for ten thousand pounds.

In his late forties Mr White was diagnosed as having inoperable lung cancer. Their relationship improved somewhat as Irene flung herself into the role of nurse/companion, and he transferred the guilt he normally felt when ill into accusations directed at her for making him a passive smoker. It was no longer his fault, and she agreed, accepting total responsibility and guilt for his condition, but still unable to give up her fags.

One day in spring when he was very ill he decided to walk in his garden. The sun was to blame. It lay on his shoulders with the warmth of a fine silk shawl, inviting the muscles to relax, allowing his rib-cage some respite from the incessant coughing of the last stages of the disease. It allowed him to hope he might be feeling a little better, well enough to venture into the garden to examine the fresh bright leaves that were also responding to its imperatives.

Chartreuse. He identified the colour of the tiny fragile leaves covering the Japanese Maple. The points of the five-fingered leaves were still directed downward, translucent with lush nutrient, shimmering in the sun. By mid summer they would be totally flat, and by autumn the leaves would be dry and brown and rolling back on themselves, before floating away with the wind.

He leant heavily on his silver-handled walking cane and looked gloomily into the ornamental goldfish pond. He poked at the lily pads with his stick, hoping to discover one of the fat goldfish underneath, but as time had passed, mutations had overwhelmed the original stock, so that now most of the fish were black, and almost impossible to see against the tangle of weeds and stalks. The goldfish pond was in the shade of his high house, and so he walked down, drawn by the sun, out of the shadow. The idea came to him that he would like to walk along the road, just to the corner where the steps came up from the road below, and from where he could see the airport. He hoped to see one of the 747s take off. An aeroplane, lifting from the runway, steadying itself, and then finding direction: it almost made him believe in the immortality of the soul.

On the street the light was brighter than he expected, and the southerly caught him by surprise. Surely there hadn't been any white caps on the waves when he'd looked at the harbour from his window? He staggered along the road, resting at each lamp-post, aware of his considerable frailty. He hadn't told Irene he was going for a walk. Perhaps he should have mentioned it to her as he had passed her in the kitchen, cleaning out the parrot's cage. But, he reminded himself, he hadn't known he was going for a walk then, so there was nothing to reproach himself with. When he got round the corner he'd sit down at the top of the steps and have a rest before the return journey.

He was disappointed to find there were no planes on the airport, neither on the runway that thrust itself like an ironing board into the harbour, nor waiting patiently beside the terminal building. The air shimmered above the tarmac. As he reached the top of the steps he began to cough. He staggered down two or three steps so that he could sit with something to support his back. His chest muscles were giving him the squeeze, forbidding him to take in any of the chill air that was blowing at him, happy to tantalise the skin on his hands, throw the oily strands of his grey hair into his eyes, and slip down the back of his neck. The air became as precious as a fortune, and he put his head down to his feet the better to grovel at it.

At the bottom of the steps, a long way down, a college girl was coming home from school. Two hundred, perhaps three hundred steps she had to climb. She was wearing a green pleated school uniform, carried a school bag and a hockey stick with her hockey boots tied to the stick by their laces. Inside the bag her exercise books are sullied by her uneaten sandwiches, with buttery circles appearing between the consistent blue ruled lines.

Mr White catches his breath at last, and watches the blonde bobbing hair of the schoolgirl as it progresses towards him. He is feeling immensely sorry for himself, wondering how, when he had done pretty much as he pleased, life had ultimately not been a pleasurable experience. Things were never what they seemed. Recently he had begun to wonder about his first wife, Mary, whom he had cast off so discourteously, and without just cause. Would his life have been happier if he had never dallied with Irene?

The schoolgirl walking up the steps is Amanda Livingstone who lives with her parents and brother in the house below Mr White's. She knows all about him: her mother was one of his first wife Mary's friends, one of the few who used to visit her in the mental hospital after she had her breakdown, after the divorce. Amanda knows all about Irene too, she was one of the neighbourhood children who would go and talk to her for a hand-out of sweets, on the pretext of talking to the parrot, and one day she even went inside and was taken to see the doll collection. Amanda thinks Irene is probably the loneliest woman in the world.

Amanda is feeling cross that she missed her bus stop and has had to walk up the steps. Normally she would have come up the zig-zag, which was easier. The steps were daunting even to a fit teenager. You went down the steps, especially if you were in a hurry, but you came up the zig-zag. It was like snakes and ladders.

And now there is the problem of Mr White, slumped at the top of the steps. She will have to walk past him. The idea comes to her that what she should really do would be to kick him down the steps, boot him as hard as she can, perhaps she could even say something like,

'Remember Mary? She cut her wrists you know, or maybe you didn't know? And Irene, what sort of a life have you given her?'

But as she gets closer, step by step, she sees how pathetic he looks. His face is yellow, sweating. He is panting like an old dog whose matted coat is heavy and hot. His hair looks unwashed. His crumpled stance allows no opportunity for Amanda to attack, he is already defeated.

So she intends to ignore him, to act as if he simply wasn't there.

As she reaches the step where his feet are tucked into the angle, she looks away from him. It takes her by surprise when he wraps his arms around her legs, and hugs them to him. She is out of breath and taken aback, her stride is interrupted, and for a moment she thinks she will fall on to her knees, and ladder her brown regulation stockings. He tries to pull her legs into his body, and puts his cheek against the left calf. He says, 'Mary, sit down a while, I want to explain . . .'

Amanda is enraged. She wrestles her legs free by kicking into his chest. She is shocked at how much anger she feels. As she twists her body out of his reach her hockey stick swings round, and the boots bang into his face.

'You disgust me,' she says, without a backward glance, and walks quietly away.

After some time Mr White manages to drag himself home, where Irene, relieved to see him again, undresses him and puts him to bed. She takes off his coat, his pullover, the shirt, the singlet, the trousers, the longjohns, the underpants, and averts her face in order to blow her cigarette smoke away from him. He is feeling happier, she can see that. He is not quite so annoyed by her dressing and undressing of him, as if he were a doll. He has in fact become doll-like, quite malleable, no longer bristling and attempting to do things for himself that she is quite happy to do for him. She pushes his arms into his pyjama jacket, buttons it up firmly. She pulls the pyjama pants up his withered legs, pulling him forward off the bed to bring the seat under the weight of his buttocks. She ties the cord securely and swings his legs around under the blankets.

His head sinks back into the pillows, and there is serenity in his expression. He is thinking of the schoolgirl's gloriously shaming words, her painful kick to his heart, and the slam of her mud-encrusted hockey boots as they smashed into his face. He has fallen in love with her. He worships her, such unexpected, wholehearted abuse. He will hear her angry words ringing in his ears until he breathes no more. 'You disgust me,' she had said, 'You disgust me,' he says it quietly to himself, under his breath, while he feels his face for any trace the hockey boots may have left. 'You disgust me.' He repeats it again. Yes, it was far more than he had hoped for, or deserved.

Dancing in the Dark

SHERIDAN KEITH

That there was a river rolling past, outside in the night, seemed perfectly appropriate, water under the bridge and all that, the river as the everlasting symbol of time passing. That the river was the Thames, the famous Thames, the one in London, added a certain gravity, spinning the thing halfway across the world. That the room was the River Room of the Connaught Hotel, no less, takes the woman, the man into a tier of society only the colonials could infiltrate so effortlessly, and, at that time, with such accents. That her hair was Vidal Sassooned, her slim body underwrapped by Mary Quant, and overwrapped by Laura Ashley (before she turned to wallpaper), hosed (now *there* language lets us down rather badly) by Christian Dior, shod by Bally of Switzerland, all indicates that the woman, Rosemary, thought she knew which way was up, in spite of coming from down under. The emerald that lit her engagement finger and transmitted shafts of verdant light, although smaller than the Ritz, would not have seemed ill at ease there. All this then, all this and a large ten-piece band polished brassily and about to blare, when across the crowded room, just as in the song, the enchanted evening song, she saw, there, over there where the potted palms fringed the dark window overlooking tethered barges whose navigation lights shone in the river water, black-tied, martinied, with his shoes shining, just as they had the night they had met at the teenage dance at the Karori Baptist Hall, was Max Palmer.

Ten years. Ten years later. Max Palmer, her very first boyfriend, making her eyes roll in their sockets when she was fifteen and still at school, though she was quite unaware she was doing it, rolling her eyes.

That was what he liked about her, he said, during one of their stilted, yet surprisingly personal, conversations.

'Nonsense,' she replied, 'I don't do anything like that. I don't roll my eyes.'

'You do, you know. Look, you're doing it now!'

She still denied it, though she supposed she must be doing something with her eyes to make them feel as if they were floating away, to make them change into two blue balloons that had just risen up into the blue sky so that she could no longer tell the difference between her eyes and the sky. Yet these balloons were somehow attached to his brown eyes, along mysterious silken strings, at the end of which they played, and were happy. Each fleck of light that darted from his brown eyes would send her eyes spinning, faster, and the spinning had a purpose, its purpose was to create a great whirlpool, a vortex that would drag his brown muddy eyes up from the earth, along the slippery threads, in order to bring his face so close to hers that she wanted to stop breathing. To let only the tiniest and most essential stream of breath flow out of her mouth so that nothing, not even a particle of air, would disturb the space between his face and hers.

(You're going too far, there is danger of over-inflation. Calm down now, you're getting carried away here.)

The tiresome details. She'd just sat School Cert. She was staying the weekend with her schoolfriend Tessa. In Karori. They'd spent the first half of the day ironing their dresses, and, more importantly, stiffening their petticoats. They used a solution of gelatine and sugar to impregnate the petticoat fabric. The iron turned brown and refused to move forward, in places the fabric even seemed to melt, leaving ridges of glistening brown curd. An aroma of toffee filled the room. But the petticoats were certainly stiff, 'stand-alone'.

For an hour they lay flat on their backs, lotion on their faces, balls of cotton wool soaked in witch-hazel covering their eyes, heavy and cold. It was like going blind. They wanted eyes in which the whites would be whiter than white, eyes that would gleam in the dark, eyes in which no tracery of red blood vessels would detract from their appeal. (You'd have thought they were already alcoholics.)

Rosemary and Tessa sat together at school, crammed into a double desk at the back. Tessa was cruel, and Rosemary sulked, it was an uneasy relationship, though not dull. It was Tessa who had insisted Rosemary bring her Pat Boone records, but when Rosemary did, in her usual contrary style all Tessa would play was Brahms. They talked about the agony it was, going to dances, how they would never go to another one if this wasn't any good, and how they planned to spend the entire night in the Ladies' if they weren't asked to dance within the first five minutes. And they pledged to each other that they would come home together, no matter who they met.

Then they washed their hair, using Tessa's mother's shampoo. (*Halo everybody, Halo, Halo is the shampoo that glorifies your hair* . . .) Rosemary sighed. She would be the one sitting out, she knew. Tessa was normal height for a start, she was blonde, that was always an advantage, and most important of all, she had breasts that stuck out, that boys wanted to get their hands on. Rosemary was a bean pole, with straight brown hair, totally lacking in any chest. Her mother cut her hair. Tessa's was cut by a hairdresser, her mother put it into heated rollers, it came out all bouncy, like yellow snakes dancing on her head. They tried with Rosemary's, but it seemed to make things worse.

'Why don't you get your hair cut properly?' asked Tessa. 'It's all uneven, it looks as if it's been chewed.'

'Does it?' Rosemary hadn't really noticed, she actually thought it was looking better than usual. 'I suppose it must need cutting.'

'Who do you go to? They must be hopeless.'

'Oh, just someone down the road.'

'You mean someone in a house, not a beauty salon?'

'No, a beauty salon.' She was getting all confused.

'You're lying,' said Tessa. 'I can tell. Your mother cuts it, doesn't she?'

'I don't know,' and really she didn't know, she felt so hot and confused.

'God, you're thick,' said Tessa.

'Well why do you go around with me then?' queried Rosemary.

'I really don't know,' said Tessa, testing her fingernail polish to see if it was dry. 'You're just so thick at times.'

Rosemary was right. At the dance Tessa was whirled away, out into space, by a young man who looked seriously older than all the boys waiting nervously down their end of the room. He had to be in his twenties, maybe he was even thirty? What was he doing there? Rosemary sat on the girls' bench and pretended not to care, there was no way she could get to the sanctuary of the Ladies', it was down the other end, and the floor was crowded. There always seemed to be more girls than boys, that was the way of dances, of the world probably. But then, as she was despairing, or beginning to despair, she noticed a tall, good-looking boy walking along the edge of the floor, coming down towards her. No good getting hopeful, there were at least six girls still sitting on the bench. She looked at the floor. He was probably going to ask the girl sitting on her right. She kept her eyes cast down, and then, there were his black shiny round-toed shoes right in front of her black patent leather pumps. He positioned them with precision, as if he were a soldier, his shoes almost, but not quite touching her shoes, and he was asking her to dance. Asking her. He was asking her to dance, and so she stood up, very gingerly, because that was always the hard part, because she was so tall, and when she stood up it was as if she was growing and growing at that very moment, and she couldn't stop herself from going on growing, and usually she ended up taller than the boy who'd asked her to dance. She could always see from their faces how pissed off they were, and they'd look angry the whole time they pushed her around the dance floor. But this boy kept on being taller, even when she got to her full height, even not bending her knees. Immediately she saw his lovely brown eyes, they were so dark, and she wanted to dive straight into them, there and then.

(So now, ten years later, those feet, those polished shoes, well probably not the same shoes exactly, that might be stretching it, the same shininess is what I'm getting at, are standing over there by the potted palms, and one of those hands, certainly the same hands, that took hers a little nervously as they began to dance, is holding a martini, recognisable from the speared olive and the open-shaped glass, while his other hand rests casually — nervously? — within the pocket of his Moss Bros dinner jacket trousers, and the elbow nudges the window pane, below which the Thames flows, and will still be flowing today.)

They danced together, and were no great shakes as dancers, but that didn't seem to matter because you stood front to front when you danced, and that was where the great mystery took place, front to front.

And he would step forward and she would step backward, for this was the foxtrot and men still led women. And led them astray. Rosemary always had difficulty going backwards. At school during the gym lessons that turned into ballroom dancing she inevitably ended up as the man. This young man held her pleasantly, with her leading arm not too high, and his other arm somewhere around her back. She'd never danced with anyone before who made it feel so right. Usually boys either held you so tight you could hardly breathe, so that you nearly fell over together if you got your feet wrong, or they held you miles away, as if they didn't really want to touch you anyway. But this boy (who you know to be Max Palmer) held her in a way that felt absolutely perfect.

After the dance finished he took her back to the girls' bench, deposited her, and wandered back to the boys' end of things ('territory' would be a better word). It was difficult to tell what impression she'd made, she rather feared that was the last she'd see of him, because he hadn't offered to buy her a coke.

Tessa spun up on the arm of her chap, and sat down. He went off to buy drinks.

'Golly, he's *fast*!' she said, and told Rosemary how he'd stuck his tongue into her ear, while they were dancing, in spite of the fathers who were supervising.

'I didn't know what it was for a moment,' she said, 'It was all wet and horrible.' But she looked extremely pleased with herself.

They called him 'Stirling' after that, for Stirling Moss, because he was so *fast*. Stirling arrived with cokes for them both, and Rosemary thought she really ought to be polite to him, in spite of the fact that he looked greasy and shifty, and so old! Thirty at least. Anyway, Tessa seemed to like him, she was blabbering away so that no one could get a word in.

Then the music began again, and it was 'take your partners' time and the agony began all over. Tessa and Stirling disappeared with a flurry of ankles and petticoats. Rosemary sucked the last dregs of coke again and again for something to do, and wondered if the lovely young man could possibly arrive for a repeat performance, or whether he'd already asked someone else this time around.

Suddenly he was there! Stretching out his arms for her all over again. It was amazing, marvellous. He said he liked her dress, and had she made it? He liked her dress! And she said, Yes, she'd made it, without even thinking, just because she wanted to say yes to everything he ever said, yes, yes, yes. Then she looked at her dress, and it was the pink one, with the black velvet bows down the front, and she hadn't made it at all. It was one of the very few dresses she had that was a bought one. He said he had a younger sister who tried to make herself clothes, but they always looked terrible, not nearly as nice as her dress.

And she was going to say, I do make most of my clothes but actually I didn't make this one, but what she said was, 'I do make most of my clothes,' and then she stopped, because she just didn't seem to be able to say more than a few words at a time when she was looking at him. And it sounded as if she was showing off, which she hadn't meant at all. Then he asked her what her name was, and she could hardly think.

What was her name? That was absolutely crazy, fancy not being able to think of her name! But then she remembered it was Rosemary, and she said, Rosemary, Rosemary Baker. He said he liked the name Rosemary, and he repeated, Rosemary Baker, and said, 'I'll have to remember that.'

He wanted to remember her name! It crossed her mind that this was the moment she ought to ask him what his name was, but somehow she couldn't get the words together. But then he said, 'My name's Max' (we know, we know), and he said a surname as well, but she could only think Max, only remember Max, only say to herself, Max, Max, Max. She said she liked the name Max, it sounded interesting. He told her he was a med student hoping to pass his Intermediate, and she confessed to having sat School Cert. He told her he was eighteen, and she said she was fifteen. Three years, an enormous three years between them.

(He has finished his martini, accepted another from a tray that has passed his elbow. He is talking in a group of other dinner-jacketed men. Canapés are being interpreted, consumed, crumbs falling onto black shiny lapels, white handkerchiefs daub at buttery lips.)

At the end of that dance she really had to go to the ladies', she was almost desperate, what with the Coca Cola, and all the excitement, but when she pushed through the door, there was a great queue for the solitary, fought over, loo, and a crowd of girls all peering into the one mirror over the washbasin. (So much for the amenities at the Karori Baptist Hall.) While she stood in the queue, squeezing her legs together with increasing firmness, and jigging up and down a little as that seemed to help, she took out the bi-valve powder compact her mother had given her and looked in the round mirror. She thought it was directed at her face, but all she could see was the part under her right arm where her pink dress exhibited a half moon of perspiration, while the other half moon shone from under the pink puff sleeve, together forming an almost complete circle. How could that be? She'd put on heaps of Tessa's mother's roll-on (Odorono) and it just hadn't worked at all.

Then Tessa turned up and said that Stirling had asked if he could see her home, and she'd said yes, so that meant Rosemary would have to find her own way back to Tessa's, in spite of their promise, the promise they'd made to go home together, no matter what. Tessa now said that Rosemary would spoil it all, if she tagged along. Rosemary knew there was no point in mentioning their agreement, Tessa had that look in her eye.

Finally it was her turn in the lavatory cubicle, and after she'd been to the loo, which was a heavenly relief, she tried to dry her armpits with some lavatory paper, and wondered whether she should stuff some up there, in her puff sleeves. But what if it fell out, that would be even worse than losing her petticoat, which had happened once when the elastic broke. How was she going to get home? She didn't even know the way back to Tessa's very well, she didn't live in Karori. Could she ask Max? No, you didn't ask boys, you waited for them to ask you.

Tessa really was the pits, thought Rosemary. That was absolutely typical. You couldn't rely on her for anything. She'd dump you the minute anyone more interesting came along. But she didn't have to worry about getting back to Tessa's because Max did ask to take her home, and he even knew the street where Tessa lived. They danced the last dance together, 'Love Letters in the Sand', and everyone sort of slowed up, and the lights were turned down, just for a few minutes, and the world seemed to fall into the centre, and not apart, and everyone became dreamy, and slow, and slower, and she was leaning on him, and her head was resting on his shoulder, and his hands were on the small of her back, and the feeling was better than any feeling ever had been. Then the lights came on, and it was good to be able to say to Tessa, 'I'm going home with Max, see you there.'

(Rosemary, standing on the other side of the crowded room, looks down at her emerald ring, and goes through a flurry of difficult emotions that are to do with her fiancé, and wonders again why he never seems to want to make love to her, and listens again to the story he told her of how, as a boy, when he was a choir boy at St Pauls — yes the real St Pauls, the one Christopher Wren designed, the one that lifted its dome out of the smoke of the Blitz — a beautiful boy, he said, the sort of beautiful boy men from the congregation would come up to after the service, and offer boxes of chocolates, five-pound notes if he would . . . But she hadn't wanted to hear any more. Maybe it will be different when they are married.)

So they set out, Max and Rosemary, walking along the night streets. It was after midnight, a few cars went past, it was very beautiful, stars in the southern sky, the Southern Cross, the Dipper, he pointed them out, in the summer warmth. He put his arm around her as they walked, and that felt lovely, and some of the time he held her hand, it was almost like holding onto a warm glove. But it was his skin. She kept thinking, my skin is next to his skin. The warmth was really surprising. It was much warmer than her mother's hand. Her mother still sometimes held her hand, although Rosemary hated it. She still grabbed hold of it when they were crossing roads, and sometimes just because she wanted to hold Rosemary's hand, because she was her little girl. Rosemary would take her hand away, as soon as she could, and her mother would complain, and say what a cold thing she was, and how in her family they liked showing affection and that she must take after her father, because he was cold. Her heart screwed up inside her when her mother held her hand, her mother's hands were scratchy, with fingernails that were as hard as elephants' tusks. They dug into her hand, and she wanted to get her own hand back, and she knew she wasn't cold. Holding Max's hand, she knew she wasn't cold.

Headlights of passing cars shone on them, illuminating his face, gilding her happiness. She didn't have to feel frightened in the dark streets, she was with someone, a man, part of a couple. She didn't know where Tessa had got to, she and Stirling were nowhere to be seen. They waited at one point for them to catch up, but as there was no sign they went on. At the top of Tessa's path they waited again. Max got out his tiny leather diary with the pencil down the spine, and wrote down her name and phone number, standing under the street light. How grown-up and sophisticated it seemed. Had she got her phone number right? She thought so. Perhaps he really would ring her up and ask her out!

Tessa still hadn't come, so after a while Rosemary said 'Goodnight'. There was a moment when they looked into each other's faces, but didn't quite kiss. Perhaps the street light was too bright. In a way it was better than a kiss, it was a sort of long, eye to eye embrace, without actually touching. It was a field of gravity, set up, waiting. Rosemary walked away, out of the zone, but knowing it was there, would stay there, go on existing between them.

(One of the hotel flunkeys approaches Max, with a note on a silver tray. He picks it up with the hand that was in the pocket and opens it, one-handed. He says something to one of his companions. He nods to the messenger, and follows him out. Surely he's not leaving? The evening is only beginning, the band haven't yet begun to make speech impossible, there would have been plenty of time. He'll be back, surely he'll be back. It must be a phone call.)

She found her way through the kitchen where Tessa's parents had left the light on, two glasses of milk and biscuits on the table, to the bedroom, Tessa's bedroom. She went to bed, stacking her petticoats in the corner. She couldn't sleep, her heart was racing, she kept thinking about Max, and saying the name, Max, Max, and seeing his brown eyes. Listening for Tessa to come in. Worrying about Tessa with the fast man. Drifting off. And just when she'd be about to go to sleep she'd sort of snap, her body would snap, as if she were falling out of bed. It was a horrible, new, feeling.

Then Tessa arrived and turned the light on. That was a relief.

'God he was *fast*. I'm never going out with him,' she said.

'Do you know, he tried to get me to take off my knickers. And when I wouldn't he made me put my hand on it . . .'

'On it? You mean, his thing?'

'Yes, he unzipped it, and shoved my hand in.'

340

'Really?'

'Yes. Then he took it right out, waved it around for all the world to see.'

'Shivers! What did you do?'

'I ran. Well, I'd had enough. I ran home, really fast, he couldn't keep up, and he had to put it back in again. I'm never going out with him.'

She sounded rather pleased all the same, drank her milk noisily and ate a biscuit. She didn't bother to take her clothes off, she just descended onto her bed, making a scrunching noise with her petticoats, and was soon fast asleep, giving little snorts from time to time. Rosemary lay awake all night. At least, that was what it felt like, with the music spinning in her head. Pat Boone singing 'On a day like today . . . We pass the time away . . . Writing love letters . . . in the sand.' His voice was sickly and sweet and deep and took her down, down those three first notes . . . on a day . . . down into deep, beautiful feelings.

When they got the photos of the dance Tessa looked at the one of Rosemary and Max and said, 'Hasn't he got thick lips? Did you give him a thick lip or something?' Was she jealous?

It made Rosemary cross. 'No he hasn't got thick lips, he's got great lips.'

'Have you kissed them then?'

'Yes, of course,' she lied.

'Well, what was it like, was he any good at kissing?'

'Yes, he was fine.'

'He's got a real moonface, hasn't he, a moonface. In fact he looks a bit like a pig.' She laughed.

'He doesn't look like a pig.' Rosemary was getting furious.

'He looks just like a pig. I'm going to call him Porky, that's a good name for him, Porky, what's his other name?'

'Palmer.'

'Porky Palmer, great!'

There wasn't a photo of Stirling and Tessa, they'd been outside snogging at the crucial moment.

'Has he rung you up then, asked you out?' Tessa wanted to know everything.

Rosemary held the photo to her breast and sighed melodramatically before taping it to the inside of her desk lid.

'No, not yet, but he's got my number. Anyway, I hope he doesn't ring. I probably wouldn't be allowed to go out anyway.'

'You just don't tell them. You've got such a cow of a mother, say you've got something on at school or say you're coming to my place. If Stirling asks me out, that's what I'm going to do, tell Mum I'm staying at your place.'

'But you said you wouldn't go out with him again, he was too *fast*.'

'No, I didn't say that. He wasn't all that *fast*.'

'You did, you really did, you said you wouldn't go out with him because he tried to get your knickers off.'

'Did I say that? No, he never. I must have made that up just to shock you.'

And Rosemary blew up, 'You're just a liar, you say whatever suits you at that moment. You say I'm stupid, you're the one who's stupid, you're a stupid bitch, and Max hasn't got a moonface, and he doesn't look like a pig, and don't call him Porky.'

And after that they didn't speak to each other for ages, even though they were sitting at the same desk.

Max, Max, you will ring me won't you, please Max . . .

Max, you haven't forgotten my number now have you? You wrote it down.

Max, what about ringing that nice girl you met at the dance.

Max, Max.

On Wednesday night, at exactly 7.30 pm, Max phoned Rosemary and asked her if she'd go with him to the pictures. *War and Peace* was on at the St. James.

(You know it all, you know the way Rosemary looked out of the side of her eyes to catch a glimpse of Max sitting next to her, how she had to shut her eyes to press the image down into her head and keep it there forever. Forever?)

(Forever, it seemed forever until he came back into the room, the River Room, Connaught Hotel, remember?)

*

She wouldn't let herself cry (we're back in the St James now), not when Count André lay, for all the world, dead on the field of battle, his eyes gazing up into the sky, clouds rolling, rolling, nor when Natasha refused Pierre's offer of marriage and he turned sadly away, knowing himself to be a bumbling idiot, so much sadness, but no, she wouldn't let herself cry, and if wet drops started falling out of her eyes it wasn't crying, it wasn't anything to do with her.

And when Max was accepted for med school which meant he would go away to another city and she wouldn't see him for months, only in the holidays, she wouldn't let herself cry. He said, 'I'll never forget you,' and he mentioned the bit about her rolling eyes that we came in with.

He promised to write, and he did. Two letters, the first, lonely and loving, the second, distant. He'd met someone down there, he was sorry.

It was inevitable, she told herself. Inevitable. He was down there, all those women students, inevitable. Nothing to be hurt about. She was still at school after all, another two years. It had been lovely, but it was inevitable. He was everything she could have wanted, and was no longer to have. Everything she could have wanted, that someone else was having. And she saw him holding someone else's hand, taking someone else to the pictures, taking someone into his bed? Would he do that? Was he doing that to some girl at that moment?

The look in her eyes became distant, as if they didn't want to see anything that was close by. She spent a lot of time by the window in her bedroom, just looking as far away as she could, looking at the hills in the distance, leaving her eyes over there, over on the hills, the hills that were as far as the eye could see. Perhaps if she sent her eyes away, into the distance, into the future, they might find him out there?

(Where is he? She can't see him. He'd come back in, she'd seen him come back in, then she glanced away, knowing he was back. Now where was he? She can't see him, not with the group he was with, no-where. She doesn't know yet, but the hand that held hers has put the martini glass back on the silver tray, said 'Goodnight' to his friends, and walked away.)

Eventually she had to know. She goes up to the group he was with, they're talking, don't like it when she interrupts.

'Max,' she says, 'Max Palmer, he was here a few minutes ago, I used to know him.'

'You mean Porky, Porky Palmer. Yes, pity he had to go, he'd only just got here. His wife's having a baby.'

She hadn't known that anyone else called him 'Porky'. It was like a stab. Several stabs. Married, a baby, in London. She looks out the window at the Thames, a greasy river. Across on the South Bank the Royal Festival Hall is all lit up. But the biggest stab is Tessa; for a moment it has brought back Tessa, when her hair was like golden snakes. He might not have known about her. At least she wouldn't have to tell him about her, he could well have asked. He might well have said, what happened to that friend of yours, what was her name, Tessa? Yes, Tessa. What happened to Tessa? And she'd have had to tell him.

She still found it hard to talk about Tessa. Her pretty curly hair went like a lifeless wig after the baby. Stirling married her, at least you could say that for him, he married her. She was sixteen, but he needn't have bothered, the baby was dead. She went sort of loopy afterwards, she got very fat. They'd been driving along the motorway, she and Stirling, except that his name was Ian, they didn't call him Stirling any more, he was Ian then, they were going somewhere, going to Taupo was it? She just opened her door and rolled out, into the traffic. At least that was his story, but who knows. Who knows? You never really knew with Tessa.

The brassy band starts up, 'Dancing in the Dark', and though the room is bright, too bright, the river outside is an ominous thread. That's what we are all doing, Rosemary thinks, dancing in the dark.

The Dancing Master

SHONAGH KOEA

Thorstensen came threading through the crowd just before half past ten, when the music started. By that time a stag's head the decorators had brought in wore festoons of hired bow ties, silk evening scarves, a top hat and Mrs Bradford's own black stockings. The evening had decayed away into a never-never land of chicken skeletons and dessert gateaux.

'Will you dance with me? Would you care to dance with me?' said Thorstensen. His outstretched hand across the table might have been sly or shy, she was not sure. 'Won't you dance with me?' said Thorstensen and the slim ovals of his gold cufflinks were as thin as the covering on a man's soul.

'Watch out for Thorstensen,' Bernard had said, but that was hours ago when they ran out their own front door to the waiting taxi, its peremptory hooting like a preliminary call to battle. Bernard had forgotten all that now and sat chin in hand as he idly ate some fruit salad, talking to Wevers about the next board meeting and complaining that the champagne tasted like creaming soda.

'You mean the alleged champagne,' said Wevers and tapped his hairy nose.

'Right,' said Bernard. 'The alleged champagne it is. I stand corrected.'

'You steer very well clear of Thorstensen, little lady,' Bernard had said earlier. 'Thorstensen's put the skids under more men than you've had hot dinners. Stay away from Thorstensen.' Thorstensen was the new company head.

The taxi hooted again as one of her high heels caught in the doormat.

'Blow old Thorstensen,' she said then. 'Who cares about old Thorstensen, anyway? Blow these shoes, blow the whole thing, Bernard. For two pins, Bernard, I'd stay at home, I'd be like old weasel-faced Madley's wife and send you off by yourself. Blow company parties,' and she tore the lacerated heel from the rope matting. 'Never mind about old Thorstensen. It's the dancing I'm terrified of, Bernard. At the school I went to you could only have dancing lessons if you had a partner and nobody ever asked me. What will I do, Bernard, if someone asks me to dance?'

'They won't,' said Bernard, tramping towards the far gatepost.

'Thanks,' she said. 'Thank you, Bernard. What a lovely evening I look forward to.'

'No need for sarcasm, my dear,' said Bernard and gave the address to the driver who looked at them in the rear vision mirror with hooded calculating eyes as they drove through sudden rain.

'I knew it rang a bell,' said the driver as he drew up under the office veranda. 'You've got that Thorstensen.' Eight floors of the company premises reared above them, the windows brilliantly lit for Thorstensen's gala evening. 'I've got you slotted now,' he said. 'I've read about your Thorstensen in the Sundays.' Thorstensen sounded like an illness.

'Excuse me,' said Thorstensen now and Bernard's small spoon remained suspended over the last slice of banana, 'I'm asking you to dance. Wouldn't you like to come and dance with me?' and he held out that inviting hand again.

Beside them the company engineer, dressed as a fusilier, plunged his hands down the neckline of somebody's wife, a thin girl with a sharp little face like a wedge of cheap sweet cake.

'I must thoroughly investigate how this superstructure is kept up,' he shouted and the sound of her laughter was wild and shrill as she threw her corsage of violets at the stag's head.

'I think the party's getting rough,' said Thorstensen. 'Won't you dance with me?'

Earlier, the empty foyer had an air of forgotten excitement as though crowds had already passed that way and while they waited for the lift she watched the taxi driver fill in his notebook outside. The silhouette of his humped figure held a peculiar and unintentional menace and his radio splattered through the night, words distorted so it seemed more like distant gunfire than messages about innocent journeys.

'It's not going to be a pleasant evening,' said Bernard. 'Lunches last week and a ball this week — I don't know how they expect me to find the time. We're late, and I'm not sure yellow's your colour.'

'Yellow and pink,' she said, 'and it's not and my shoe's nearly ruined as well.'

The lift bore them upwards and smelt faintly of cigars as though somebody, anxious to have a jolly evening for the entire time, had anticipated later pleasures.

They passed accounts and advertising on the first two floors, computer programming on the third and flashed past the wider hinterland of middle management on the upward journey. Beyond the serpentine lengths of executive corridors lay office suites with drinks cabinets and tweed sofas, oil paintings. There secretaries were called personal assistants and had secretaries of their own. They all nurtured bright-eyed young men under forty-three who did aerobics.

The lift spilled them out on the eighth floor, usually a staid boardroom, and they stepped forth into an instant baronial hall with plastic beams and flashing electric candle bulbs in the candelabras.

'Oh my God,' said Bernard, 'they've had the decorators in. Oh my God, it's fancy dress. I thought they were joking.'

'Thorsty won't be pleased with you,' said a fat man as he passed. 'Didn't you get the memo from the lovely Caroline? Thorsty said it was to be fancy costume. Thorsty said it was to be a Victorian evening with everyone joining in the spirit of the thing. Don't you like my dress kilt? It's Black Watch.'

'It would be,' said Bernard.

'Who was that man, Bernard?' she tugged at his arm. 'Who was that fat man?'

'That's Wevers,' said Bernard, 'and keep your voice down, Bridget. Wevers is a dangerous man. You watch out for Wevers. Wevers is the axe-man. Wevers fires the bullets.'

'Show me Thorstensen, Bernard. Which one is Thorstensen?'

'I can't see him.'

'Where would they have got those lovely dresses, Bernard?' There seemed to be a parade of crinolines.

'Hired them, or made them — how should I know.'

In a corner a woman with ringlets and a black lace dress sat on a man's knee and began to sing light opera, trilling on the high notes till her curls fell askew.

'Oh my God,' said Bernard, 'Mrs Bradford's well on the way.'

Mrs Bradford began another song, waving one hand in time to the waltz. Her ringlets tumbled further down and her rings flashed, massive diamonds in trios on the left hand and on her right a large ornate offering that might have been a signet ring, a man's ring. She tossed the hand that wore it with a careless insolence as though the ring were a reprimanding gift, even a legacy, from an admonishing father, worn now to acknowledge an influence that must be defied.

'Did Mrs Bradford's father die recently?' she asked.

'How should I know. I can't keep up with your questions. Who's Wevers and where's Thorstensen and where do people get their dresses and did Mrs Bradford's father die? How should I know?'

Dinner was a forgettable two hours, but soothed by meat and wine and cake, the crowd parted for a moment and Bernard suddenly said, 'There, there, look now — that's Thorstensen at the top table, in the middle beside the woman in red.'

For a moment she saw him clearly. One hand shaded his eyes as if the light were too bright or, she thought later, he was bored.

'But Bernard,' she said as the woman in red stood up, blocked that clear view of a thin dark face, 'he's quite a young man. Thorstensen's quite a young man. I always thought he was an old, old man with an ugly face. Why didn't anyone tell me Thorstensen was young? You never tell me anything.'

'How many times must I ask you?' Thorstensen had withdrawn his hand now. 'Won't you dance with me? Please, won't you come and dance with me?' The big clock beside the stag's head said twenty-eight minutes past a mis-aimed black sock. 'I think the party's getting rough,' said Thorstensen again as Mrs Bradford screamed. 'Please, for heaven's sake, won't you come and dance with me?'

'I can't,' she said. 'I can't dance. I've never learned. There are lots of other people who'd love to dance with you.'

'That's all fibs,' said Thorstensen. 'I think you're a fibber.'

Bernard stirred uneasily, put his spoon down.

'I suppose you've noticed we're not in costume,' he said, 'and I don't know if you've met my wife.'

'No,' said Thorstensen, 'and yes, I have now,' and he took her away through the crowd, holding her hand in an imprisoning grip, to where the orchestra was beginning to play. They wore red velvet coats and the music hung in the air, full-bodied and luxuriant, like the scent of peonies.

'You could dance with someone else,' she said and tried to pull her hand away. 'I can't dance, truly. I've been terrified all night.'

'Fibber,' said Thorstensen.

'No, really. At the school I went to you could only have dancing lessons if a boy asked you to be his partner and nobody ever asked me. Bernard never dances. Bernard never danced with me in his life.'

'I don't believe you,' said Thorstensen.

'Why couldn't you just have a cocktail party?' They were beside the dance floor now. 'That other man only ever gave cocktail parties or dinners. I can manage cocktail parties and dinners and lunches. I've caught up on everything except dancing. Why did you have to have dancing?'

'I like dancing,' said Thorstensen. 'I love dancing. I used to like dancing with my wife.'

'I wish,' she said, 'that you'd just given a dinner. That other man used to have things flown in for dinners — salmon and oysters and blueberries, things like that. Blueberries,' she said, 'are horrible. I re-member he had blueberries flown in once, when blueberries were new, and I saw them squashed all over the floor.'

'Did you, indeed,' said Thorstensen, and they glided away across the floor. 'I knew you could dance,' he said.

'I tripped over your toe.'

'No,' said Thorstensen, 'I tripped over yours, and you're a fibber.'

'I'm not,' she said, 'honestly. I was a very dull, common, ugly, grace-less girl and nobody ever bothered about me. It took me years to catch up.'

'Where was this?' He gave her a suspicious look then and when she told him the name of that small old town he straightened his arms, held her away so he could look at her again. 'I can't believe that. You're a terrible fibber,' and she skipped round the corner beside the grand piano, joyful that the old bitter life had left no mark, that it was not apparent it had been lived at all.

'I saw you at the lunch last week,' he said. 'Why did you have a hat on?'

'I saw you too. I thought you were that new traveller they've got. You know the one they all talk about, that one who's supposed to have been married to someone in a soap opera.'

'But why did you have a hat on?' So the traveller did not interest him, she thought.

'It was only an old black beret I wear in the rain. It was raining when I went to catch the bus into town. I don't have a car any more.' But would he be interested in that either?

'Why didn't you take it off?' he wanted to know. 'Nobody else had a hat on.'

'I know,' she said. 'That's why I left it on.'

'Ah,' said Thorstensen as if he understood and he swung her into a large clear space that seemed to have been left for them by the others. They left a clear space for Thorstensen, she noticed, as hens put a space between themselves and a predator.

'Do you see that man over there,' he said, 'that man with the yellow hair? That's Abrams. I hate Abrams. Abrams swindled me. He's dancing with his wife. Do you know his wife?'

'I know hardly anybody.'

'Wise,' said Thorstensen. 'Very wise. They're both awful. You wouldn't like Abrams.'

'He's very ugly,' she said. 'I wouldn't worry about him if I were you. All that money couldn't make him beautiful. Money can't buy beauty,' she said, 'or charm, can it?' and she looked up into his bright face as, laughing, he danced them off the floor into the old upper vestibule, decked for the evening as a garden room.

'Mind the step,' he said but she still tripped, laughing and looking up at bright brave Thorstensen. 'I knew you could dance,' he said. 'I knew you were a fibber. You're as light as a feather and your hands are so cool.'

'I'm terrified,' she said. 'That's why my hands are cold,' but he laughed and swung her round again.

'Fibber,' said Thorstensen. They seemed to hang in that conservatory with its silk flowers and artificial trellis like people on a swing.

'I love dancing,' he said. 'I used to dance when I was a grave-digger. I went to dancing lessons on Friday nights. I started off as a grave-digger, did you know that?' The worst thing was, he said, when the old bones were scattered, when one grave had to be dug on top of another.

'The first job I had was in a hospital kitchen,' she said, and they changed the dance then from a foxtrot to a quickstep as if to get away from the graveyard and her old sink.

'I like your cuffs,' she said. 'I like those double cuffs turned back like that.'

'They're French cuffs,' said Thorstensen. 'Have you ever read Hartigan? You'd enjoy Hartigan. Hartigan explores the relationship between work and luxury. French cuffs are my luxury and I can look at them while I work. Hartigan, you see? You must read Hartigan.'

'I will,' she said and as the music changed to a waltz he suddenly stood still in the middle of the floor like a lost boy. 'But this is a waltz,' he said. 'I've forgotten how to waltz.'

'Waltzing's easy.' She grasped his elbows and swung him lightly round. 'I'll teach you how to waltz. One two three, one two three.'

'I knew you could dance,' said Thorstensen. 'I knew you were a fibber.'

'All wallflowers know how to waltz, silly,' she told him. 'They learn how to waltz round their own kitchen tables, all alone.'

As they passed Abrams again Bernard called from beside a potted palm, 'I've got your coat. It's after eleven. The taxi's waiting.' A quick and greedy half an hour had passed already.

'He's a nice fellow, is he?' asked Thorstensen. 'Bernard?' Oh very nice, she told him, on a good day, at the right moment, when viewed with the light behind him.

'I see,' said Thorstensen and she thought he did.

As their taxi drew away from the kerb Thorstensen stepped from the shadows, tapped on a window.

'You don't mind, do you,' he said, 'if I hitch a ride? We could sing all the way home. I know the first hundred and four verses of "Eskimo Nell".'

They dropped him at the beginning of an oak avenue and she

351

watched him out of sight, the sound of his whistling sharp and clear on a westering wind.

'He seemed in an odd mood tonight,' said Bernard. 'What was he saying to you? I saw you talking. I saw you laughing.'

'He was only laughing about my hat, Bernard, my old black beret, that's all. He just asked if you were a nice fellow and I said you were, and I said why did he have to give a ball because I'm terrified of dancing. I said why couldn't he just give a cocktail party or a silly dinner like that other man. That's all, Bernard.'

'Oh my God.'

'Bernard, I do wish you wouldn't keep saying "Oh my God" all the time.'

Towards November that year, when the Christmas decorations were starting to be put up in the shops, receivership loomed after board-room infighting and two takeover bids by the multinationals. The company shares dropped overnight and Thorstensen's house in the avenue of oaks was found empty one day with its big front door swinging open in the breeze. At an entailed auction of the contents a big brass bed with Sèvres plaques fetched three times the estimated price and an antique dealer, of hitherto irreproachable reputation, had to be hustled out the back door to a waiting ambulance after behaving with marked peculiarity during the sale of the silver.

The gossip writers of the financial columns dug deep but found Thorstensen's sudden departure was worth only a paragraph or two. No one knew his friends or his foes.

'I hate Abrams,' he had told her, 'but I'm very fond of little McIndoe. I rely on McIndoe. I get very fond of people sometimes,' he said, 'do you?' and she said she did. 'I never let them know, though,' said Thorstensen. 'I hide it. I keep it a secret. Do you do that?' She nodded again.

He was called a workaholic, a self-actualisation man who studied under a guru whose name nobody knew. That very afternoon she ran straight to the library to find Hartigan.

'We'd have him on toast,' they said, 'if we knew where he came from, if we could just find out where he started off, if we could dig up some mud. Was he ever married?' they wanted to know.

That night she said to Bernard, 'Do you remember the night

Thorstensen hitched a ride in our taxi? If you ever told anyone about that, Bernard, I'll go, do you understand. Is that quite clear?'

The rumour surfaced then that the Mastertons' grandmother, on the trip of a lifetime, had seen Thorstensen walking through a shopping plaza in Vancouver. His name was reputed to be on the books of a worldwide executive employment agency. Somebody else said he had been glimpsed on a KLM flight from Singapore to New Delhi, in business class eating lobster off a tray. Later the same month a short paragraph appeared in some of the financial pages announcing he had gone to Burundi to work for the Aga Kahn.

'Would the Aga Khan be a nice man to work for?' she asked at the next company party. 'Would the Aga Khan be kind to him? Would it be pleasant living in Burundi? Would he like it there?'

'That's it in a nutshell,' said Wevers, tapped his hairy nose again and held out an oily hand. 'Put it here, lady.'

'What do you play off?' That would be someone at the other end of the table. 'What's your handicap? Whoops, Bernie old chum, we've lost your good lady. Not a golfer, is she?'

It was safe then to wander away, easy to find another table with a vacant seat or two, simple to sit talking to the flowers in the middle of the crowd.

'I liked Thorstensen,' she could say then. 'Thorstensen taught me how to dance. I was a wallflower all my life till Thorstensen asked me to dance. He made up for all the years when no one chose me. I loved him. You couldn't imagine how bright and brave he was,' she would say, drawing on the tablecloth with a fork, little runnels that led to nowhere, and wearing Thorstensen's secrets like jewels.

The House with Sugarbag Windows

WITI IHIMAERA

Watene couldn't help it. He burst out laughing.

He'd been standing at the curved bay window watching with wine-warmed eyes as the rain lashed across Kelburn. All of a sudden he'd felt cold and the thought had come to him:

— Better close the sugarbags so the rain doesn't come in.

He'd reached up to grab the sugarbags and the heavy drapes had surprised him. Not like sugarbags at all, not rough nor having the earth smell of kumara and kamokamo. Then he had looked at his hands — one was holding the drapes and the other was grasping, of all things, a delicate-stemmed wine glass.

And he'd laughed. After all, it was so amusing to remember those sugarbag windows, especially after all these years. Amusing? Once upon a time he would have used the words funny or hardcase.

Bemused, Watene let go of the drapes. Even the words he used had changed. Just like the sugarbag windows.

He remembered where he was. At Alan and Janet's place — a party for a mutual friend, Colin, who was going to Washington on a diplomatic posting.

— That was some laugh. What's the joke?

Alan. Standing there beside him, crystal decanter in hand.

— Aaah, Watene grinned. Just in time.

He held out his wine glass to be filled. Behind him he could hear the social chatter of other guests, muted to a tasteful murmur by the surrounding sound of quadraphonic Vivaldi. Circling through the strains of *l'Estro Armonico No 9*, the guests dipped and swayed and described elegant figures across the room as if engaged in some delicate

354

courtly dance. Their conversation was illumined with grace — baroque music always seemed to have such effect, unlike loud rock mixed with beer which brought out the brash and blatant in people. Here the tone was as smooth and as rich as the red wine and as polite as the music. As ingratiating too, and so deeply satisfying to Watene's palate he could almost believe he'd been born like this, standing here with wine glass in hand amid these people in this house in Kelburn.

He lifted his glass in salute to Alan.

— And now? Alan asked. The joke?

— It was nothing, Watene answered. It wasn't important. Just something I remembered.

— About what? Alan persisted.

Watene shrugged his shoulders. He looked round the room — wood panelling, old colonial furniture, expensive paintings in ornate frames, roses in a crystal vase, Persian carpet, circular stairway, glittering chandelier, latticed windows — and fingered the drapes. His eyes began to twinkle again.

— Oh, he answered hesitantly, I was just standing here and all of a sudden I remembered the house I was born in. It's raining outside, you see, and I thought I'd better draw the sugarbags across the window and . . .

— Sugarbags?

— To stop the rain from coming in and . . .

Watene hesitated. He looked at Alan. Smiling. Amused.

— I knew you wouldn't understand, Watene said. It was nothing. Nothing important.

— Hmmmn, Alan answered. It was certainly important enough to take you away from the party. Aren't you enjoying yourself? You're not bored are you?

— Oh no, Watene said.

— Thank God for that, Alan smiled. Well don't stand here by yourself for too long. It doesn't do my image as a host any good.

Watene nodded. He saw some new arrivals at the door and indicated them to Alan.

— Must look after my image, Alan sighed. I'll come back to you later. All right? In the meantime, Watene, circulate. Meet my friends. You should find much in common with them.

Watene watched as Alan left him, moving towards the arrivals, dispensing wine and greetings on the way. He began to envy Alan his gift, for it was a gift to be able to divert people and make them feel at home. Alan made it seem so simple too, that was his great achievement, socialising with ease and assurance as if he was accustomed to it. But after all this was his home, these were his people, he had been born to this life and to this style and was secure here whereas Watene . . . He turned to the window again. He sipped his wine thoughtfully and a gradual sense of satisfaction and pride began to well within him as he saw his reflection shimmering across the landscape. Kelburn on a wet winter afternoon. The epitome of colonial elegance set with grace and taste amid the green of native bush. Red brick and tile tilting with the waving fern. White plaster and wood panelling and windows paned with emeralds. Wide empty streets, concrete pathways and well-kept gardens. Select. Secure. Beautiful storeyed houses for upper-floor people. And here he was, for all the world to see, part of it.

With confidence he made to rejoin the party. He saw Colin waving to him across the room. He grinned back and took a step away from the window.

It happened again. The curtains. Sugarbags across the windows. Rain thrumming like heavy knuckles on the tin roof and splashing through the windows onto the dirt floor. Outside, within the rain-dark square of window, blurred by the rain, Mum and Dad hurrying home.

Startled, Watene looked round him. For a moment it seemed that he and the other guests were sipping wine and chatting in a large room lined with newspaper, treading expensive shoes across a dirt floor and exchanging greetings over a trestled table. A single oil lamp swayed from the exposed beams of the ceiling. Smoke billowed out of the open fire where huge black pots swung on wire hooks over burning wood. Apparently unaware of their surroundings, the guest gossiped on long benches or apple boxes and took cheese delicacies and olives from tin plates. The smoke did not seem to bother them as it curled with the wind through the room. The door was open and in the doorway, shaking the rain from themselves, were Mum and Dad, being ushered in by Alan.

— How are you, Watene?

Colin with his girlfriend, Francesca, clinging to him. The smoke cleared. The chandelier twinkled again. The scuff marks of the dirt floor resolved themselves into the curlicued patterns of the Persian carpet.

— Oh, hullo, Watene answered, distracted.

— We saw you coming over to us, Francesca said. But then you just stopped. So we decided to come to you.

She smiled but her eyes were sad at the prospect of Colin leaving her. The Vivaldi was not an accompaniment to joy but more like a pavane for steps measured with sorrow.

— I hope things go well for you, Watene said to Colin. How long will you be in Washington?

— Four years, Colin answered.

— A lifetime almost, Watene said. Things will have changed by the time you returned. We'll have changed. You'll have changed too.

Things will have changed. The echoes of the word sprang upon him. Although he continued to chat with Colin and Francesca, Watene began to feel those words resounding through his mind, nudging him persistently, plucking like pincers at his heart. Try as he might, he could not rid himself of them, shake them off, tell them begone. His body became a tuning fork softly humming and scattering the years with its vibrations.

As he stood there, wine glass in hand, listening to Colin, be began to remember his childhood and where it started. In that house. The one with the sugarbag windows.

That house. It stood in the middle of nowhere at the top of a dense-forested valley overlooking the river where his mother washed the clothes. He had been born there, during an early morning when the mist was steaming across the hills. In that solitary place, his eldest sister had delivered him. She'd been eleven at the time. Later, his father had buried the afterbirth in some secret place. Watene had been the fourth child and first son.

It was a small house. More like a tin shed. He had been a sickly child until his parents had taken him to see an old kuia well-known for her healing powers. In later years, Watene's mother had been reluctant to tell him about that visit except to say that the kuia had hooked her finger into Watene's mouth and pulled strings of hard phlegm from his tiny throat. Although he improved, his early years were filled with sickness. His mother had fed him by first chewing the food in her mouth and then pushing it with her tongue into his.

His first memory was of being carried down to the river on his mother's back and sitting and watching while she and his three sisters slapped clothes on the rocks and dipped them in the water. All the years they lived in that place of his birth he associated the river with the slap slap slap of clothes against stone and soap swirling in the currents. The family did not have a washing machine because they did not have electricity. Even if they did have electricity they would not have been able to afford a washing machine. Washing machines, like flush toilets, modern stoves, refrigerators, gas fires, electric lights and hot water cylinders belonged to the world beyond where the hills turned blue, where the occasionally-glimpsed DC3 pointed its droning flight as it descended from the drifting clouds.

Yet his father could joke at their poverty. When you're as far down as we are, he used to say, there's only one direction to go — up.

Up? Where was that? As a young boy, Watene had been mystified by his father's words. He and his sisters accepted the world as it was because it was the only world they knew. The concept of an up or down direction was puzzling; the world just *was*, the way they lived was, simply, the way they assumed things were supposed to be. After all, whenever they went into the village twelve miles away the people there lived exactly like themselves, didn't they? Yes, they did know of others who had more than they had — the local school teacher, the owner of the general store, the big farmers — but these weren't people. They were pakehas and their world was so distant, so remote, that the children could never comprehend their way of living as being normal. What was normal was what the children saw: the way their relations and friends lived, in houses just like their own. And in that world there was no up or down, no basis for comparison with their own lives. Everything was the same.

It wasn't until some years later, when Watene had started school, that he'd discovered where up was, what poor meant and how his kind of people were regarded.

Until he was three, Watene had slept in a small wooden cot in his parents' room. There were two bedrooms in that tin house: his parents and he slept in one, his three sisters slept in bunks in the other. They slept on mattresses stuffed with horsehair and their blankets were grey army blankets made smooth and soft by incessant washing. Then his mother had given birth to another child, the second son, and Watene had begun sleeping with his eldest sister in her bunk.

The only other room had been their kitchen, dining room and sitting room all in one. One entire wall was their fireplace providing them with both a cooking place and source of warmth during the cold winter. Wire hooks were strung along an iron beam running the length of the wall, and from the hooks dangled the black cooking pots. The fire was kept going morning till night, the smoke billowing grey through the tin-sheeted chimney. The smoke-baked earth was the floor. A wooden table, two benches and makeshift apple-box chairs, a meat safe and a cabinet were the only furniture in the room. In an attempt to make the room look more colourful his mother had pasted newspaper and pictures from magazines on the other walls. And, with the help of his sisters, she had made her curtains from sugarbags.

From the exposed rafters hung the oil lamp and fading decorations of some long ago Christmas. Dark-framed photographs of his parents and the children were propped above the doorways. The prized possession, a whalebone mere, lay on the window-sill. Beside it was the family's one book, the Maori Bible.

The life of the family was centred on that room. In it, Watene had learnt to crawl and then to walk. He'd watched as his mother woke every morning with the sun to nurse the glowing embers of the fireplace into flame and prepare the morning kai. He'd sat in its doorway with his sisters who bathed him and then themselves with water from an outside tank. He'd played on the floor while his sisters dressed for school after having done the morning duties — the milking, feeding the fowls, and the dish-washing in a tin tub by the outside tank. He'd farewelled them as they walked the six miles to the bottom of the valley where they would wait for the bus into the village. Sometimes, if he'd found work, his father would accompany them. If so, then Watene would attend to his brother during the long hours while his mother swept the floor with manuka brush, bottled fruit, salted meat, baked bread from flour and water, and did all those daily tasks in calm acceptance of their need to be done. Then it was down to the river to wash the clothes or across the fence to till the gardens, baby slung on her back and Watene ambling after her, until the sun was half way in its downward flight. Back from the river or gardens she would hasten with her children to stoke the fire, prepare the night's food, feed the baby at her breast and await the return of the rest of her family.

This had been the normal routine of her days, patterned with sweat and the dull throb of fatigue. Yet she did not feel any fury or rage against the way she lived. Sweat, fatigue, pain and sometimes hunger were to be borne because they were part of the only life she knew.

But in that life there had been laughter too and joy in her family. During the long winter nights, by firelight and the lamp's glow, she and her family would sit round the table and play cards or knuckle-bones with smooth stones from the river or just talk while her girls ironed their clothes, her husband carved wood with a pocketknife and her two sons chased each other across the floor. She was content enough. Her family had been her life. Her family and working for them.

His father, Watene supposed, had been what would now be called a 'seasonal worker', a rather glossy term to describe someone who worked when there was work to be had and who eked out his existence by tilling the soil. (When Watene had needed to fill in forms seeking financial help to get him through high school and university he'd been so embarrassed about the question of his father's occupation that he'd written: 'farmer'.)

The family lived on tribal land, a small patch of thin soil which lay on the periphery of the expanse his people had once held in common. The rich and fertile lowland now belonged to the pakeha.

Only remnants of the ancestral land, like pieces of broken biscuit, remained to his father and others like him. On this land his father and mother raised the subsistence crops — the kumara, corn, kamokamo — which composed their staple diet. They supplemented these with puha, mushrooms, wild blackberries and cabbage tree leaf stalks picked during their ranging over the hills. During fruit season, the children and their mother would work in the local orchards and bring home boxes of peaches, pears and apricots to be bottled for eating during the following year.

The river supplied eels and the hills wild pig. His mother raised hens and his eldest sister — until Watene was old enough to take her place — milked two cows morning and night.

The earth was good to them and kind but even she could not sustain them through all her seasons. Winter, when earth grew cold, was the leanest season of all, leaner still if Watene's father was too long without the paid work which would enable them to have mutton, sugar and other groceries most families took for granted. Then it was a matter of keeping warm, carrying on and waiting for the earth to grow young again.

But it was the way of things. The family lived in stoic acceptance, knowing that after winter summer always came. And with the summer would come work — shearing in a gang with others who, like themselves, had been waiting for the winds to warm.

In this manner they had lived. In that tin house on that piece of land in the middle of nowhere. From that place and life ruled by the seasons, Watene had one day departed with his sisters and walked down the valley to catch the bus into the village to begin school. For a while he had continued to accept life as his family lived it as the way life just was.

Then, when he was seven, Watene had brought home his school report. It had been a good report. He'd asked his mother to sign it for him. She told him he should wait until his father got home but Watene had not wanted to wait. He'd set his face with stubbornness and, angry, his mother had grabbed a pencil. Asking him where she should sign, she had stabbed an 'X' in the place. Then, although it was dark, she had gone out of the house towards the gardens to push at the earth under the thin moon.

With that single act, Watene had remembered his father's words. Yes, the only way for them was — up. He'd committed himself with anger to that climb. He'd fashioned for himself an image of the life he wanted. And he'd pursued it down that valley road leaving behind that house with the sugarbag windows.

Watene's fingers tightened on the wine glass.

And he'd finally caught up with the image and, although he did not like all about the person he'd become, he was at least true to the image.

He was back at the bay window again after having circulated among the people Alan had wanted him to meet and spoken to all those others with whom Alan averred he'd much in common. The hardcase thing about windows was that one could look out and fill the landscape with the figments of one's own imagination, colour it according to one's mood and animate it as one wished. *Hardcase?*

— I've been ordered to rescue you, a voice said beside him.

A reflection joined his in the window. A girl with small black eyes and magenta lips and the rain sweeping through her face. Pretty in the fashionable manner.

— From what? Watene asked.

The girl glanced at him, amused, and licked her wine glass with the tip of her tongue.

— Perhaps sugarbags? she said.

Watene's fingers tightened again. Alan must have mentioned it to her. No, Alan would never understand. Nor this girl.

She saw his discomfiture and smiled like a cat.

— Well you must admit it does sound rather curious, she continued. But then you're rather curious yourself. Alan has told me all about you. An honours degree and an important job in Treasury — I must say I am suitably impressed.

— I'm glad for you then, Watene answered somewhat puzzled at the cutting edge in the girls' tone.

— It's just that you're so unexpected, she said. But I imagine you come from a better background than most.

— I'm sorry to disappoint you, Watene tried to laugh.

— Oh dear. You mean you *are* a poor Maori boy who's made good?

Her tone was mocking. Watene remembered an encounter he'd had in a hotel a few weeks before. A girl, just like this girl, had witheringly accused him of being a middle-class Maori. He'd asked himself: what was wrong with that? He wanted what he'd never had. He visualised it in terms of a two-storey red brick house, money in the bank and two cars in the garage. Nothing was going to stop him from getting it.

— Yes, he answered the girl. But don't let that stop you putting me down.

— I won't, the girl answered.

— But I must warn you, Watene continued, that I've met your

curiosity and your kind before. Always wanting me to conform to your image of what a Maori is supposed to be. And when I don't conform then you look for convenient reasons, for surely there must be some explanation for my being such an — aberration?

The girl laughed. Her laughter was like an eel flicking its tail and eluding his grasp.

— Well it won't work, Watene said. Whether you like it or not I'm here to get exactly what you've always had, to compete with you at your own game.

— Oh dear, the girl said again. You sound just like one of us.

— I am, dear lady, Watene whispered as he kissed her lips. So there's no need for you to be curious about me, is there?

He made a low bow and walked away. He went to a table where a decanter of wine was sitting and poured wine into his glass. Then he stood there, listening to the hum around him.

— So you've met our Nicola, Alan grinned. Bitchy isn't she! Sometimes I wonder whether she is actually as naive as she appears to be.

— She just likes playing games, Watene answered. Why the hell did you tell her about the sugarbags?

— She was curious about you. It just slipped out. Look, what on earth is wrong with you today?

Watene shrugged his shoulders.

— I guess you could say that I've caught up with me, he answered.

— Oblique answers and nonsensical words, Alan sighed, are all it appears I'll be getting from you.

Other friends came to join them and talk. The Vivaldi was replaced by Mozart. Outside it began to get dark but inside the atmosphere remained gay under the glittering chandelier.

That house. His family had finally left it when Watene was nine years old. They had moved to a large coastal town where his father got a job on the wharf, loading and unloading cargo from ships that plied the coast. His sisters had married among their own kind while he, Watene, continued in his climb. His mother had died during his second year at university. The strange thing was that she'd always pined for that house in the valley and had always wanted to return.

But he could never return. In a way it would be like taking a step backward. And yet . . .

Watene smiled ruefully. In some respects, the girl he'd met in the pub had been right. He was middle-class. But he wasn't going to be middle-class forever, no. For the time being, maybe, but he hadn't finished yet.

— Come and join us, Watene!

He heard Colin calling him to where he and Francesca were playing some silly game. He nodded.

But that house hadn't finished with him yet and as it continued to nudge his memory he felt a sudden flood of affection for it. For nine years it had kept him, nurtured him and looked after him. No matter how far he went he would never forget it because it had been at the beginning of his life.

Anyway, it seemed that it would never let him forget.

He grinned and looked towards the windows. Sugarbags fluttering in the wind. Smoke billowing through the room.

— Yes, he whispered. I need you to remind me and to make me remember who I am. And I will need you more as I keep on climbing. Never leave me.

He joined Colin and Francesca. The wine burst within him and lifted his spirits.

— You're back with us are you? Colin asked.

— I suppose I am, he answered.

He lifted his wineglass in a secret toast and whispered the words to himself:

— To houses with sugarbag windows, he said.

The Kids Downstairs

WITI IHIMAERA

There was a top flat and a bottom flat, an upstairs and a downstairs, and Rangi and Susan went to view the top one — 'one dbl bdrm, unfurn, sep. ent, 5 mins to city, suitable m.c., $29 pw'.

— Is this really it? Susan asked as Rangi eased the car into the kerb outside the address given by the landlord.

'It' was an old dull-grey wooden house in a stretch of houses squashed like a concertina. The house itself looked the most squashed of all, appearing as if its builder had suddenly noticed a small sliver of space and decided to fill it in. That he'd managed the feat was to his credit but the appearance of the house was not. Its long narrow windows looked like an open mouth caught in the middle of a toothless yawn. There didn't seem to be any garden, the brick retaining wall in front of the house was cracked and the way up the concrete steps was blocked by an old discarded sofa.

— It might be better inside, Rangi suggested. It can't be any worse, surely, than the other flats we've been to look at.

The landlord was waiting at the top of the steps. He came down towards the car smiling in a rather desperate manner. However, it didn't seem as if he was so desperate after all when he saw Rangi. His mouth curved into a tight little purse and, when he spoke, he dispensed his words like bright silver coins he was reluctant to use.

— You *are* Mr and Mrs Johnson? he asked.

— Yes.

— And it *was* you who rang me, Mr Johnson?

— Yes, Rangi answered.

— Hmmmm. And you *did* say you were a civil servant and that your wife was a librarian?

— I did indeed.

— It's just that I didn't expect . . .

The landlord hesitated. Then a gleam of hope shone in his eyes.

— You *are* married, aren't you?

Susan showed him her wedding ring and engagement ring, dangling them with irritation before his peering face.

— Oh, the landlord said.

His eyebrows arched. He looked at the rings again and then at Rangi and Susan's car. The purse of his mouth opened wide.

— Well, he said. I suppose it's all right then. For you to see the flat I mean.

He led them up the steps, past the old sofa, unlocked the door to the top flat and accompanied them in.

For a moment Rangi and Susan just stood there in the hall.

— Yes, it is in a bit of a state, the landlord said. I haven't had time to tidy up after the last tenants left — owing me rent I might add. But a quick clean will work wonders. And once you've got your own furniture in, it will look just like your own home.

— Sorry? Susan asked.

— Well, it does have possibilities, the landlord answered lamely.

He stepped aside as Susan swept up the stairs away from the sight of mud-blue carpet, cartons of junk piled precariously atop one another and wallpaper patterned with mould. At the top of the stairs she stumbled on the landing. An empty beer bottle slowly bumped its way down the steps to the landlord's feet.

— Hmmn, Susan said.

The signs appeared ominous but the flat itself was, under the circumstances, surprisingly clean. Apparently the previous tenants had tidied it up to the landing and then pushed everything down the stairs to accumulate at the bottom. From all appearances the flat had once composed three upstairs bedrooms of the house and an upstairs bathroom. One of the bedrooms had been converted into a kitchen-dining room, another into a living room with sunporch, and the third had remained a double bedroom. With some satisfaction Rangi noticed that all the rooms were very large, the sunporch was a decided asset and the landing was big enough to be a room itself — Susan could have her piano there. He looked at Susan and saw the gleam in her eyes. Yes, the flat did indeed have 'possibilities'. Rangi and the landlord followed her as she clucked and hmmmned her way from room to room.

The walls had been painted Hideous Yellow except for those of the kitchen and sitting room which still retained their original brown and green striped wallpaper. The carpet was Regulation Green Felt covering the entire floor except for a large square of floorboards in the bedroom.

— The bed will cover that, the landlord said helpfully.

The refrigerator didn't work, clothes would have to be washed for 'fifty cents for each 12 lbs at the friendly local laundrette', there was no telephone, the tap over the bath leaked, the kitchen window couldn't open, parts of the sitting room ceiling were stained but . . .

— Hmmmn, Susan said.

She banged on the walls, stamped on the floorboards, tried the electric plugs, inspected the stove and concluded each act by emitting a loud sigh and shaking her head. The landlord was suitably impressed. Susan could be very impressive when she wanted to be. Then she nodded her head.

— We'll have to think it over, she said.

The landlord retreated to the landing while Rangi and she went into a huddle in the sunporch to weigh the pros and cons of the flat. It was too expensive for what it was but it wasn't really *that* bad if one considered how difficult good flats were to come by in Wellington. The sunporch had a good view, the kitchen was up to standard and the walls could, after all, be repainted. The carpet wouldn't look too awful once furniture was in its place and anyway they could always buy rugs to hide most of the green. Most important of all, they couldn't really stay with friends for too much longer, they needed to be settled before Rangi started work the next week and it would be good to live so close to the city so . . .

— If you're worried about the rent we could negotiate, the landlord interrupted.

Susan gave Rangi a keen look. She loved bargaining.

— How much is it? she asked.

— Twenty-nine dollars a week, plus two weeks rent in advance and a bond of fifty dollars, he answered.

— Make it twenty dollars a week plus two weeks in advance, no bond and we will wallpaper and repaint, Susan said.

— Twenty-seven dollars, one week in advance, no bond, I'll get rid of the junk downstairs.

— Twenty-three dollars. New fridge.

— Twenty-six. No bond.

— Twenty-four.

— Twenty-five fifty.

— Twenty-five.

— Done.

The landlord eyed Susan with respect.

— All right, she said. We'll take it.

— Are you quite sure? he asked.

He didn't seem at all sure himself.

— Yes.

— Well, that's it then isn't it, he answered. When will you be moving in?

— This Saturday perhaps? Rangi asked.

The landlord nodded. Rangi duly paid him a week's rent plus one week in advance and he gave Rangi the keys to the flat. Then he accompanied them down to their car.

— I'm sure you'll be very happy in the flat, he said as he shook hands and left.

Susan and Rangi watched him as he walked down the road.

— You drove him a bit hard, Rangi said. I think we're lucky to have gotten the place at all.

— Huh, Susan answered. *He's* the lucky one. He knows good tenants when he sees them. He's lucky he's got us in at all.

They stepped into the car. The house was still yawning.

— The first thing I'll have to do is make curtains, Susan said. And by the way, *his* attitude to you better improve!

The moved in the next weekend.

During their first week in the flat a series of events occurred which did not augur well for the future: the removal van which had brought their furniture from Gisborne broke down just outside the gate, Rangi gashed his hand while assembling the bed, the water pipes broke in the bathroom and a young girl was assaulted by an intruder who broke into a flat four houses up the street during daylight. Furthermore, the landlord had omitted to tell Susan and Rangi about the Australian guys who lived downstairs and the old alcoholic who slept in a bach at the back of the house.

The sofa still blocked the steps.

— Hmmmn, Susan said.

For the first few days, she and Rangi were too immersed in cleaning, decorating and moving into the flat to notice their surroundings. Susan scrubbed the kitchen floor and cupboards, vacuumed the carpet and wiped the walls; Rangi moved furniture into place and began painting the entrance hall. Every now and then, they would dart down to the corner of the street to buy odds and ends needed in the moving-in process — a hearth brush, screwdriver, mirror, rugs, Ajax, mop and, most important of all, flea powder.

— For your pet, sir? the chemist asked Rangi.

— No, for carpets and cupboards and . . .

The chemist backed away a couple of feet eyeing Rangi warily as if expecting fleas to pounce on him at any moment. Why he backed away was puzzling to Rangi because he had just felt a flea bite in the shop. The whole area in which they lived seemed infested with fleas just waiting for some juicy leg to come strolling past.

With the fleas came the flickering of doubt about their surroundings. During daytime the area seemed innocuous enough, rather quiet and appearing quite respectable. But from five o'clock onward, the street would be cluttered with parked cars and people walking to and from the big hotel at the corner and the area would suddenly become populated by strange apparitions.

Once, when Rangi was waiting to be served in the local grocery, he felt heavy breathing down his neck. He turned to find a huge Amazon in flaming dress and five o'clock shadow fluttering eyelashes at him.

— Hullo big boy, the thing breathed.

Then, one night while Susan was putting out the rubbish she saw something come grunting and clinking toward her. She took up a karate position and watched, amazed, as an old man lifted his hat to her, passed by, switched on the light in the bach and called:

— And now, sweet madam, I bid thee goodnight.

But the alcoholic was nothing compared to the Australian guys downstairs. Around eleven, there would be bangings and crashings and then gigglings, heavy breathing and creakings of bedsprings in the oldest rhythm of all. For the two weeks that the Australians remained, Rangi and Susan did not once see them or the girls they brought home.

Nor did they see much of the next tenants either — a family of European immigrants who cooked aromatic and exotic dishes, wore black clothes and swathed themselves in shyness. They stayed three weeks.

Then appeared a young girl who had taken the flat on behalf of herself and three friends. The friends never materialised and the girl left in rather undue haste, the reason for which was enigmatically indicated by a visiting policeman who said:

— We've been after her and her mates for some time now.

The whole area was a place for transients. They came, they stayed a while and then they left. The only evidence they had been there at all lay in the letterboxes where letters addressed to many different names accumulated. 'Not known at this address', Susan would write on the letters which arrived at their flat. 'Return to sender', 'Gone'.

One late night a young girl arrived looking for 'Barry'. I've got to find him, she said. I've got to. He used to stay here once. I've got to find him . . .

They came and they went, the transients. From the sunporch, Rangi and Susan would watch them come and go. Sometimes it seemed as if only they, the fleas, the wild cats that screamed at night, and the landlord who arrived every Saturday morning for the rent were permanent in that turning world. Despite the feelings of their friends who were horrified that they actually lived in that area, Susan and Rangi stayed on. Perhaps it wasn't a safe place but at least people really *lived* there and did not close themselves off behind curtains drenched blue with the light from television screens. And they, Rangi and Susan, had redecorated their flat according to their taste and were happy there. (Oh, the landlord whispered in awe at the furniture and art prints on the wall.) In that street of old concertina-d houses, in that flat overlooking the maze of neon-strung inner city streets, they were content enough.

And if they had ever felt lonely at not knowing their neighbours well enough or long enough, that loneliness was soon dispelled when, three months after they'd taken the flat, the kids moved in downstairs.

There were five of them and they were to sleep in what was supposed to be three bedrooms, though one was only the size of a large cupboard. One of the girls and her boyfriend slept in the double bedroom, the two other boys shared the second bedroom and the second girl had the cupboard. The flat had been vacant for two weeks and the first inkling Rangi had that the kids had moved in was when he came home from work to discover the old sofa had been moved from the steps.

— Where's it gone? he asked Susan. You mean to say the landlord has finally taken it to the tip?

— No, she said darkly. Some kids have taken the downstairs flat. Relations of yours no doubt.

— Oh? Rangi grinned.

— They arrived this afternoon. They can't have much furniture.

— Relations, huh? The landlord must be hard up for tenants. Never mind. At least it was good to have two weeks' peace and quiet.

A loud bang resonated through the floorboards. For a moment there was silence. Then loud music began to blare from a radio.

— Hmmmn, Susan said.

— Shall we go down and say hullo? Rangi asked.

The volume of the radio increased.

— Sorry? Susan shouted.

— Shall we go and introduce ourselves?

— Let them get settled in first! she screamed.

They began dinner to the Rolling Stones, had dessert through Osibisa and cleared the table to the accompaniment of Pink Floyd. Every now and then the radio would shatter with static as the station was changed and, by the time the dishes were ready to be washed, Susan's face had assumed that familiar look of irritation.

— For goodness sake, she shouted. How long is this going to keep up!

— Maybe they're having trouble getting settled! Rangi screamed back.

An hour and umpteen radio stations later, Susan had had enough.

— I'll settle them! she said.

She went to the record cabinet, took out Tchaikovsky's 1812 Overture, put it on the turntable, turned up the amplifier and *boom* — cannons began to roar, bells began to chime and the London Symphony Orchestra invaded the house. The floor quaked and the walls vibrated. Against such competition the sound of the radio downstairs dwindled into insignificance. After the recording had finished there was complete and utter silence. Susan smiled with satisfaction. Obviously the kids downstairs had gotten the message. But not for long, for suddenly the radio blared through the floorboards again. With a murderous glance Susan replayed the Tchaikovsky and, for a quarter of an hour, it seemed that upstairs and downstairs were battling for sound supremacy. Rangi had no doubt as to who would win — nothing, but nothing, could compete with Susan's stubbornness, Cambridge P40 Amplifier and R50 Loudspeakers. They were a winning combination, though perhaps an unfair one.

Half an hour later, just before the house was about to cave in, the kids downstairs acknowledged defeat. The radio bleated into silence.

— First round to us, Susan giggled as she and Rangi prepared for bed.

Rangi wasn't so sure when, at five the next morning, he and Susan were blasted out of their dreams by the downstairs radio again. Susan gave a roar of displeasure through the window. The radio was switched off and a chorus of chortles floated up to her.

— Morning, missus!

Susan had to grin to herself.

— Hmmmn, she said to Rangi as she nestled close to him. I think those kids have settled in now.

From that morning onwards the matter of the radio was settled. If ever it was too loud, Susan had only to play a few bars of her Tchaikovsky (the record later regarded by the kids as that 'awful cannon *thing*') to indicate it should be turned down or, better still, off.

The next afternoon when Rangi arrived home, Susan was not in the flat. At first he thought she was out doing the weekend shopping. Then there was a knock at the door. He looked down the stairs to see a mouth surrounded by bushy hair.

— Gidday brother, the mouth said.

— Kia ora, he answered.

— The name's Koro. Looking for your missus? She's down here with us.

— Oh? Rangi laughed. We were going to come down tonight to say hullo. She beat me to it!

He shook hands with Koro and followed him into the downstairs flat. Susan was in the kitchen on hands and knees helping two girls scrub the floor.

— Hullo darling, Susan said as she offered him her cheek to peck at.

The girls giggled to each other and put their hands over their mouths.

— These are Thelma and Rose, Susan continued. We've been shopping together and when we got back I thought I'd help them clean up their flat. It's in an awful state. Absolutely filthy.

Koro rolled his eyes as the girls giggled again.

— Hoi, he said to the one called Rose. Look at this dirty spot you missed!

He pointed to the place and Rose splashed water over him. Susan and the girls laughed as he put up his hands in mock defence and backed away through the door. Rangi followed him into the room where the old sofa was. The two other boys were there, one cleaning the windows and the other washing down the walls.

— Looks like you're busy, Rangi said to them.

— It's your missus, one of the boys answered.

— A real slave driver, the other boy groaned.

Rangi laughed. That Susan, she was running true to form. He winked at Koro who looked at him conspiratorially.

— You want a beer, brother?

He didn't wait for a reply. He picked a bottle from a crate near the sofa and wrenched the cap off with his teeth.

— Take a break, boys, he said to the others.

Rangi found a place on the floor. Koro introduced him to his mates Johnny-Mack and Sambo. They began talking. A few moments later, Susan came to the door with Thelma and Rose. She put her hands on her hips.

— Hmmmn, she said.

The two girls giggled again.

— Your missus is sure a hardcase, Johnny-Mack whispered.

The boys moved over. Susan and the girls joined them.

The kids had no furniture. They slept on mattresses on the floor but they had dreams of doing the flat up and making it look nice. At twenty, Koro was the eldest of the five kids and was regarded as their boss. He and Rose planned to get married some time but didn't seem to be in any hurry about it. Thelma was Rose's cousin — a small, dumpy girl who wore long loose dresses to hide her size. Johnny-Mack and Sambo were just mates. They had all previously rented a place near Aro Street.

— We got kicked out, Koro told Rangi. To make way for the motor-way, ay.

They had been looking for a flat for ages and felt themselves lucky to have gotten the one below Rangi and Susan.

— Rose rang up lots of places, Sambo said. She knows how to talk, ay Rose.

— Yeah, Rose continued. But when I was asked my name and I gave it I used to be told the flats had just been taken and it was all lies.

— Landlords don't like Maoris, Koro said.

— But that never happened to me, Rangi answered.

Koro looked at him apologetically.

— No offence, brother, but you got a pakeha name, he said. That makes a difference when you're hunting for a flat.

— It's so unfair, Susan interrupted.

— Not to worry, Koro laughed. At least we got us a place now.

The landlord was charging them thirty-five dollars a week in rent. They had paid him a bond of seventy dollars and two weeks rent in advance. They were broke now, but Thelma had a job in a sewing fac-tory (I make my own clothes, she said proudly), Rose was starting at Mister Chips down the road (Be able to bring home chicken and chips every night, ay) and Sambo worked in a bakery. Koro and Johnny-Mack didn't have any jobs — their last had finished a couple of weeks ago — but they hoped to find work soon on some construction site. Susan was aghast.

— You don't seem to have much money, she said.

— Enough for the rent, Koro answered.

— What about when the bills come in? she asked. The gas, the electricity, the food? And you've still got to buy beds and a table and some chairs for the sitting room.

— What's wrong with this? Johnny-Mack asked pointing at the old sofa. Thelma's going to sew a cover for it and it will look just like new.

Susan wasn't so sure.

— Yes, well . . . she began. Have you got a sewing machine, Thelma?

— Have to buy one, Thelma answered.

Susan looked at Rangi and shook her head.

— We'll be all right, Koro said.

— Yes, at least you've a radio, Susan hinted.

The kids laughed. Then Rose asked if Rangi and Susan would like to have a look at the rest of the flat. Susan found it depressing — even worse than their own upstairs flat before they had moved in. She listened as the two girls chatted excitedly about how they would decorate each room.

— Don't try to do too much at once, she cautioned. After all, you haven't much money.

— But we've already got some things we can use, Rose answered.

She showed Susan the posters, empty beer bottles, rose-framed mirror and cheap ornaments she was sure would transform the flat into a nice place.

— You just wait and see, Thelma nodded. Next time you come down here you won't recognise it.

— Hmmmn, Susan said.

Rangi looked at his watch. He indicated to Susan that perhaps they'd better leave the kids now. He invited them to come upstairs but they seemed embarrassed. Koro said he and the boys would go down to get some fish and chips for tea. Rose and Thelma were unsure whether they would go with the boys or not.

— Come and have a cup of coffee at least, Susan said to the girls.

They giggled. *Coffee.* Then they said okay, but they wouldn't stay too long. They followed Rangi and Susan upstairs where Rangi excused himself to change out of his clothes. From the bedroom he could hear Rose and Thelma whispering about the flat. He found them in the sitting room, looking at the prints on the walls, gingerly touching the expensive ornaments and treading carefully on the carpets. When Susan came in with the coffee on a tray they weren't quite sure how they should behave. They seated themselves and held their cups carefully in their laps.

— You've got a nice place, Rose said.

— Just as well we don't live up here, Thelma sighed. Too many things to break up here!

They sipped their coffee and stared around the room. Susan tried to put them at their ease for she could sense something about the flat had made them shy.

— We'll go now, they said when they had finished their coffee.

— All right, Susan answered. Is there anything I can lend you?

— We've got all we need, Rose said.

— If you do think of anything just ask, Susan told them. And come up any time.

The girls thanked her. They seemed to be in haste to leave. But as soon as they got to the door they were relaxed again.

— See you, they said.

Susan shut the door.

— That wasn't like you to offer to lend them things, Rangi said to her.

— What else could I do? she answered. They don't have *anything* down there. I hope they'll be all right.

— Well don't say I didn't warn you.

— But they didn't ask for anything, she answered.

— Not now perhaps, but . . .

— Oh, she grumbled.

She began walking up the stairs, then she paused on the landing.

— Is there something wrong with this place? she asked.

— No, of course not.

— Hmmmn. They didn't seem keen on it. Hope they come up again.

She began preparing dinner.

Although the two girls did come up now and then, they always seemed to prefer Rangi and Susan coming down to them.

Over the following month it seemed as if the kids would make out all night. Around five each morning, Susan and Rangi would hear Sambo moving in the flat downstairs and swearing about having to get to the bakery. Then at seven, they'd hear Thelma use the toilet and gallumph about on her heavy feet. (Such an ungainly girl, Susan used to think.) If Rose was on early shift at Mister Chips, she'd be awake too.

— Hurry up in there! Rose would yell at Thelma if she was taking too long in the lav.

By that time, Susan and Rangi would be getting ready for work too. They often met the two girls staggering out of the bottom flat.

— Boy, I hate getting up in the morning, Rose would moan.

She would cast a murderous glance at the curtained windows and shout:

— Koro! Johnny-Mack! You fullas better find a job today!

They never ever answered. And sometimes, when he returned home, Rangi would see Johnny-Mack sitting in the window strumming his guitar and singing along with the radio.

— No luck today? he would ask.

Johnny-Mack would just grin and keep on singing. He and Koro weren't lazy, really. Rangi often suspected that they couldn't get a job because they were just too scared to go and ask. He never really knew what they did during those long days — perhaps the girls gave them enough money to have a few games of snooker or a couple of jugs at the pub. Once, Rangi saw the lounging in the Cuba Mall. They were waiting for their mates, they said.

On a couple of occasions when Rangi had returned home he found the two boys sitting on the steps having a feed of kina. They'd been diving out near Petone and, alarmed, Rangi had warned them that the harbour was polluted.

— There were plenty other people out there, Koro said.

— The kina tastes all right, Johnny-Mack reassured Rangi.

— Not to worry, Koro laughed.

'Not to worry,' that was the kids' philosophy of life. When Rose and Thelma were running late for work they didn't really seem to care about it. If Sambo was too tired to go to work at the bakery he just stayed in bed without a second thought for his job. None of them really worried about anything at all.

They hired a television set, watched it avidly for a few nights and then tired of it. They dug a garden at the back, discussed what they would grow in it and then lost interest.

They bought tins of paint, intended to paint the whole flat and started on a wall but didn't even finish *that.*

— It was too much work, they said. We want to have a good time.

All the grand plans they had to make the flat look nice never materialised. And the borrowing began. Have you got a spare mattress, brother? Can you spare some pots? Some knives and forks? A blanket?

— I thought they were going to buy everything they needed, Susan said.

— I warned you, he answered.

The old sofa remained uncovered. Susan offered Thelma the use of her sewing machine when she found Thelma had actually bought some material.

— Doesn't matter, Thelma answered. I sew all day and I'm sick of sewing. And we're going out tonight anyway.

They were always going out, the kids. Three nights a week they would be at the movies and on Sunday nights they would go to the late night horror double feature.

— You want to come with us? they would ask Rangi and Susan. There's two Dracula movies on tonight.

— No, we'll stay home and have some peace and quiet, Rangi would joke.

— You and your missus are always staying at home, the kids would say. Don't you get bored?

Sometimes the kids would go to the pub. After the pub during weekends they would bring their mates back to their flat and have a party. Susan and Rangi soon discovered that the best way to spend their Saturday nights was *out.* That, or else accept the kids' invitation to join their party.

— You must be mellowing, Rangi said to Susan. You don't growl as much as you used to about noise!

— I like the kids, she answered. They're good kids. Anyway. I'll fix them tomorrow when they want to sleep in!

It became a standard joke after every party for Susan to play 'that awful cannon thing' the following morning.

— We give in, missus, the kids would yell.

Then Susan would take the record off. Only occasionally was she annoyed at the parties. There was at least the consolation of knowing that the next day the kids would be too busy sleeping to make any further noise.

Once, the landlord made a disparaging remark about them. Susan had been very short with him.

— If they're not good enough for your flat why did you rent it to them? she snapped before shutting the door in his face.

She liked them but she was also firm with them. She tried to help them because they were so careless about their lives. She got them bank accounts they never used, lent them books they never read and gave them advice they never took.

— It's all right, missus, they would say. Not to worry.

— Oh, they're so hopeless, she would tell Rangi.

He would smile at her. Susan never liked giving in.

— They're all right, he would answer. They're enjoying themselves aren't they?

Yes, they were enjoying themselves, the kids. Until, halfway through their second month in the downstairs flat.

It happened slowly. It was like watching a crack develop in cement that was never hard enough.

Rangi came home one day to find Sambo sitting outside in the sun with Koro and Johnny-Mack. They were all reading comics.

— Some people have all the luck, he said to them. You got off early today, Sambo?

Sambo shrugged his shoulders and flipped a page.

— He got his marching orders, Koro answered. Too many days off, ay Sambo!

Koro nudged Johnny-Mack and they laughed. Sambo grinned too. The three of them thought it was a great joke.

— I didn't like it there anyway, Sambo said. Too much flour. Made me look like a pakeha.

Rangi tried to laugh with the boys. Thoughtfully he left them and went upstairs.

— Hullo, darling, Susan greeted him.

He kissed her and put his arms around her.

— Sambo got the sack today.

— Hmmmn.

— And I don't think Koro and Johnny-Mack have found jobs yet.

— Huh. Those two never will. They've grown out of the habit of working.

— Yes, well it looks like only Thelma and Rose will be bringing in any money. And Thelma can't make that much at sewing.

— They'll have to cut down on their spending then, Susan answered. Or else the boys will have to find jobs. And quick.

But over the following three weeks the kids appeared to be doing neither — not cutting down on their spending nor the boys looking for jobs. They continued to go out to the movies and the pub and to have their parties during the weekend.

— Are you kids getting on all right? Rangi asked them at one of their parties.

— Yeah, Johnny-Mack answered.

— How's the money situation now?

— We're all right, Rose giggled. The landlord's brassed off though. We didn't pay him last week. We have to pay him seventy dollars next week. Hardcase!

Rangi sought out Koro among the partygoers.

— Look, Koro, he suggested. Why don't you cut down on the booze and use the money to pay the rent?

Koro looked at him, astonished.

— Brother, you must be joking!

He just didn't understand.

— But where are you going to get the money from? Rangi asked.

— The girls got enough. Not to worry, brother.

The next rent day the kids had indeed enough for the landlord. But after paying him they only had a few dollars left to see them through the week.

— Just enough to buy us some bread and butter, Sambo joked.

— And your bills? Susan asked.

— They can wait, Koro said. Come to think of it we can get our groceries on the tick at the corner shop. We need those coupla dollars to go out tonight!

Susan and Rangi eyed each other.

The kids managed to get through that week and the next but by the time the third week arrived they were beginning to stagger under the weight of their need to pay the rent and the gathering bills. As their situation worsened, the kids began to change too.

— Look Koro, Rangi said. You can't rely on the girls all the time. One of you boys has just got to get some work.

— Not to worry, Koro answered.

But Rangi could see that Koro *was* worried. The lack of money meant the kids couldn't afford to have as much fun as they used to. They were staying home more often, not having as many parties nor as many laughs. They hung around the flat, bored and picking on each other — until the girls' paydays when the money would flow and the beer crates would be bought in.

A few weeks later, they couldn't pay the rent again. Susan heard the landlord talking sharply to them and, after he had left, there was a knock at the door.

— Gidday, missus, Koro said. We're a bit broke this week. Can you loan us five dollars?

Susan nodded. She gave him the money. That night, the kids went to the pictures. Susan was absolutely livid.

— I thought he would buy food with the money, she told Rangi.

— He never said he would, Rangi answered.

— Yes. But. Oh, they're so hopeless.

That night, while they were in bed, Rangi and Susan were wakened by the sound of an argument downstairs. The participants seemed to be Thelma and Sambo. As Rangi listened, he heard the argument develop into a fight. Thelma screamed.

— You better go down there and see what's happening, Susan said.

Rangi put on his dressing-gown, walked down the stairs and knocked on the door of the downstairs flat. Johnny-Mack opened the door.

— This has got nothing to do with you, Johnny-Mack said.

The next morning, Thelma came upstairs. She had a black eye and a cut lip. She asked to use the telephone.

— I'm leaving, she said. They piss me off down there. Always asking me for money and I have nothing left for myself.

— Where will you go? Susan asked.

— My auntie lives at Taita, Thelma asked.

She telephoned for a taxi to take her to the station. Then she said to Susan:

— Will you come downstairs with me? They know I'm leaving. They might hit me again.

Susan nodded okay. She called Rangi and the three of them went down to the flat. They knocked on the door. There was no answer. They tried the handle. It was locked. Thelma began to cry.

— What on earth is wrong with them! Susan raged.

She banged on the door with her fists. Inside the radio started blaring.

The taxi arrived.

— You'd better come back next week to get your clothes, Rangi said to Thelma.

He gave her some money for the taxi. He and Susan kissed her goodbye. When they walked up the steps they saw the curtains in the bottom windows moving with shadows.

That night, the four kids remaining went to the pub. When they returned, they were really drunk. They turned on the radio and began banging on the walls and hitting the ceiling with a broom handle. Susan was saddened.

— They've never been like this before, she said. Why have they started now?

— Perhaps they blame us for Thelma's leaving, Rangi answered. Are you going to play your Tchaikovsky?

— No, she whispered. It used to be a joke before. Now I'm not so sure whether it is or not.

They didn't see much of Koro, Rose, Johnny-Mack or Sambo over the next few days. Then Thelma returned, got her clothes and left. Rangi and Susan watched as Rose hugged her goodbye while the boys kissed her. It seemed as if they had made up.

— I'll get our dinner ready, Susan said.

They sat down and ate in silence. Then there was a knock at the door. They ran downstairs. Koro, Rose, Johnny-Mack and Sambo were standing there. Embarrassed. Looking at the ground.

— Gidday, brother. Gidday, missus.

— Hullo, Koro.

— We've come to ask you down to our place for a coupla drinks. Now that Thelma's left, we've decided to split too.

— You're leaving?

— All of us. Tomorrow. We've come to say goodbye.

Susan took Rangi's hand. For a moment there was silence.

— We're sorry about the past few days, Koro continued. We been having some hassles lately.

— Forget it, Susan answered. We understand.

— You'll have a few drinks with us then? Rose asked.

— We'd be delighted, Susan said.

It was a small party. Just the top flat and the bottom flat together. The flat still looked the same as it had when the kids had moved in. The same mattresses on the floor, the same emptiness. Susan attempted to get drunk but never quite managed to. Johnny-Mack played the guitar. Sambo sang. And Rose cradled her head in Koro's arms.

Then Susan had a go at a hula, which was just ridiculous.

— You're trying too hard, Rangi grinned.

They cracked open the last bottle, drank it, and then just sat there.

— Well, time for bed, Rangi said.

— Let's stay a while longer, Susan answered.

— You'll get too maudlin, he told her.

The kids laughed.

— You've got a good missus there, brother, Koro said.

Rangi nodded.

— Does the landlord know you're leaving? he asked.

— No.

— Don't you think you ought to let him know?

— What for! Anyway, the rent we paid him in advance and the bond should cover what we owe him.

They had still not learnt anything, the kids. They were as careless as ever, as 'not to worry' as ever. The only way they knew of not worrying was to walk away from their problems and leave them behind — the bills, the responsibilities, everything — and start up somewhere else until the accumulation of worries compelled them to move on again.

Rangi sighed. He helped Susan to the door.

— Uh, brother, Koro hesitated. One more favour? Can you lend us a few dollars? All of us, we're broke.

Rangi gave him twenty-five dollars. He knew he would never see the money again.

— We'll say goodbye in the morning, he said.

— Yes, in the morning, Susan said sleepily. I'll miss you all, you know. Don't know why, though.

She leant on Koro's shoulder and, all of a sudden, they were all standing with their arms around each other — Susan, Koro, Rangi, Rose, Sambo and Johnny-Mack.

Susan and Rangi climbed the stairs to their flat. Rangi put her to bed. When they woke the next morning, the kids had already gone. Susan and Rangi went down to the bottom flat to collect the things that they had lent the kids. The mattress had cigarette burns in it, the pots were black and some of the cutlery was missing.

— What the hell, Susan said.

They locked the door and left the key in the lock.

The landlord arrived during the night a week later.

— We'd better go down and tell him about the kids, Susan said.

The landlord was furious when they told him the kids had left.

— I knew I shouldn't have let the flat to them, he fumed. I've a good mind to call the police in.

— Whatever for! Susan exclaimed.

— Just look at the place, look at it!

— It looks the same as when they took it, Susan huffed. And I should know because Î helped them scrub the floor.

— But they owe me two weeks' rent, he argued.

— They paid two weeks in advance, didn't they? Susan asked. And they paid a bond, didn't they? Surely that should make up the loss?

— That's not the point, the landlord said. They should have given me notice that they were leaving.

Rangi could see that Susan was losing her temper.

— Come on, he said to her. This isn't our problem.

Then he heard the landlord mumble to himself:

— This is the last time I'll ever let a place of mine to Maoris.

For a moment, Rangi couldn't believe his ears. He felt Susan stiffen.

— I'm sorry? she asked. What did you say?

— They're just a bad lot, the landlord continued. I'm better rid of them.

— Now wait a minute, Rangi said. I'm a Maori too, you know.

The landlord looked at him, astonished. His mouth fell open, his cheeks flushed and his eyelids began to beat fast like batwings.

— Oh, but you're *different*, he smiled. You're married to Mrs Johnson.

Rangi felt the rage rising inside him as he began to laugh.

Perrin and the
Fallen Angel

PETER WELLS

Who has not been a slut, has not been human.

Eric Westmore did not consider himself either a beauty or a gorgon. People did not run out of rooms gagging: but, on the other hand, not too many were driven to distraction by his glance. This did not preclude great explosions of attraction: yet such was Eric's nature, ironic, self-mocking — or was it merely self-doubting — that he always put these frissons down to poor eyesight or a case of mistaken identity, which would almost inevitably catch up with him sooner or later.

He sat now in the brackish quiet of the Alexandra Hotel. It was 10 April 1986.

The Alex was a charmingly Edwardian hostelry on the outside, a wedding-cake of plaster arranged, tastefully, to snare passers-by on two back streets: it looked like the tiara, Eric always thought, of a minor Scottish peeress. It was the last week of it being a gay, or indeed any kind of pub. It was going to be demolished. All over the city, in a speculative frenzy driven by the stock-market, Edwardian and Victorian Auckland was being reduced to dust.

Even now, as Eric sat in the dullard moments of the quarter-hour before noon, demolition drills were attacking the air in nearby streets, a dull repetitive sound, drill to a toothache.

Yet it was a beautiful day, he said to himself, inclined to feel mellow (he was, after all, in the opening stages of, as he himself said, *a romance*, putting just the right ironic emphasis on what some might call a love affair and others might call a fuck). It was a superb day in early autumn: the crispness of winter had begun to lie like an essence over the lingering heat of summer. As if to symbolise his content, just as

Eric walked down the street towards the pub, a yacht had serenely passed across the gap between two buildings, tightrope walker on his line of bliss.

Yet.

Eric, on the cusp of 38, aware that the tidal shifts of time were now beginning to run against him in a way that no amount of gym nor artful haircuts could entirely alter, knew there always had to be a *yet*, a determinant in his bliss.

The *yet* he was thinking of now, as he sat in the pub gazing thoughtfully at a block of sun on the carpet — 'like winter butter set out on a white porcelain dish,' he memorised for his column — was the phone call from Perrin that morning.

The phone had gone off at 7.30, aggressive as an alarm.

Matthew was still in the shower while Eric was standing in front of the stove, staring mindlessly at the milk he was scalding for *caffe lattè*.

Perrin's voice cut through his groggy sleepiness. 'Can we meet to-day?'

'Today?' said Eric, who was still adjusting the sensuality of the night before to the demands of prosaic daylight.

'*Yes, today,*' said Perrin without any of his customary humour. He sounded pissed off — or was it sour?

Did he suspect already, Eric wondered, about Matthew?

Matthew, as if an apparition appearing on cue, walked into the kitchen stark naked. Eric admired his body — which, of course, he was meant to do: his freedom, his flanks, his beautiful tassel-like cock. Matthew did a small coquettish whirl then sat down, forgetting Eric completely, and, picking up the morning's newspaper, began to study his horoscope.

'As soon as possible,' said Perrin's voice, again, in Eric's ear.

Eric had taken his eyes away from Matthew, unwillingly, and cast his mind ahead to his day. He thought of how much more work he had to do to get his daily food column readable. Then there was his guerrilla raid on an unsuspecting new restaurant, the one specialising in New Zealand game products.

'What about after six?' Eric suggested, looking tentatively at Matthew.

Matthew was, instead, investigating his pubic hairs with a mono-maniacal scrutiny.

'*No. Earlier.*' Perrin was being relentlessly persistent.

'You could meet me at that new place — Faringays. I've got to *cruelle* it.'

Perrin and he always called Eric's reviews 'to *cruelle de ville*' it.

A pause.

Perrin's response was definitive. '*I don't feel like food.*'

Silence again as, in the background, Eric heard someone say good morning to Perrin and Perrin, crisply adjusting his tone to genial busy executive, batted back the greeting. Perrin said then, close to the phone: 'I want to see you, Eric.'

'*I need to see you baby,*' he said in one long breath of confession.

Oh no, sweetheart, you haven't been seeing Sweet Sixteen *again*, Eric was about to whiplash back. Sweet Sixteen was a troublesome, if nubilely splendid, Niue Islander Perrin was being relentlessly pursued by. But something about Perrin's tone told him it was not going to be their usual enjoyable slanging match, in which mutual insult and hilarious parody mounted up until Perrin, almost inevitably, managed to cap Eric off with a flourish of obscene absurdity. Perhaps it was too early in the morning.

Or perhaps, Eric thought more reasonably, Perrin had a hangover. Or was it just that super-melodramatic flu which was casting Perrin into increasingly sombre moods: what Eric lightly dubbed his 'dame aux camellias' complex.

'*Please,*' said Perrin, who was not one to beg.

Eric had quickly succumbed. They would meet at the Alex a few minutes before 12. They would go on from there to somewhere 'quiet'.

Just as he put the receiver down, in that second before Perrin clicked off, Eric had an insane urge to put the phone back up to his ear, to listen harder, deeper, more faithfully to the textures of Perrin's silences, the underground music of his tone. But Eric was running late. His deadline for his food column was leering, the phone was already shrilling and then, of course, he had had hardly any sleep after his night with Matthew.

Matthew.

It was true, a good seven-eighths of his mind was given over to, willingly occupied by, thoughts of this young man who had suddenly, accidentally — impetuously — entered his life. Even as Eric now sat waiting at the Alex, 11 minutes before noon on that April day in 1986, he closed his eyes for a second, to reconnect with that world which still swirled, fragrantly as the scents of sex, through his consciousness.

Obligingly — or was it obediently? — he was wafted up to serene and great height, as if he were in a glider which could not, would not, ever meet with catastrophe. And far below him he saw the body of Matthew, a vast landscape which stretched from horizon to horizon: a country he was beginning to be familiar with, his favourite destinations — Matthew's mouth, between his legs, his smooth buttocks like peeled grapes. Was it folly for a writer on food to conceptualise his new lover in terms of fruit, of vegetables? (His cock a courgette left on the vine too long and grown tautly too large, the pillows of his chest a perfectly ripe pawpaw he loved to lick and gnaw on, the cleft of his arsehole, well, not to be too ridiculous, moistly pink as perfectly cured Christmas ham. He could go on, his Matthew, his banquet, his feast.)

Perhaps this objectification, Eric lectured himself as he sat there, was simply defensive. It was part of his emotional defensiveness that he tried to picture Matthew in terms of appetite, keeping clear of that minefield, that scarred battleground of the emotions called love. Oh keep me clear of that, sighed Eric, seasoned trooper of the wars of the heart.

With a conscious effort — but also with a pang of regret that he must leave such a perfumed landscape, one with its own laws, its own hegemony over his unconscious — he tried to focus on the exact present.

He dallied with his glass of tonic, looking for a moment at the bubbles. Then a faint smile of anticipation softened his face. He longed for Perrin to arrive, so he could gently, as if accidentally, spill the treasure of his new romance before Perrin's eyes.

He had been seeing Matthew for over three weeks and, though Perrin and he, old friends, well, *ancient* friends, touched base at least once a week, he had carefully screened the event from Perrin, until the romance, affair, the series of fucks — whatever it was — had some stable *emotional* basis.

Perrin, meanwhile, had noticed nothing: neither Eric's soaring spirits, nor his pleasurable languor, not even, on the one occasion he had managed to coax Perrin down to the pool, the expressive lovebites on the back of Eric's neck.

Perrin was inclined to be myopic anyway. His battles at the Equal Opportunities Commission, where he was a pugnacious lawyer, at times occupied all his fields of vision: when he wasn't, that is, pursuing remarkable pieces of Clarice Cliff, or unusually sensual young men whom he unearthed from unlikely situations, like post offices in small towns or half-empty laundromats — any of those situations which require a selective perception, tempered by endurance and fired by an almost fanatical flare of desire, and desirability. Or was it an unfillable capacity to be approved of, to be loved?

Perhaps that was why Eric wanted to torment Perrin, just slightly, at this moment. Perrin always had such spectacular success sexually (with, of course, its attendant moments of tedium, like courses of penicillin) that Eric felt drab and frowsy beside him. Eric always felt, in this situation, that his own desirability was diminished, a point he was not beyond getting petty about.

So now he carefully, and with a sense of epicurean enjoyment, selected his poisoned shafts. 'He (Matthew) is 23 (young), a student of architecture (a brain). He plays basketball (good body). And he's cute (rampant sexually).'

Eric toyed with the various ways he could casually, without undue emphasis, introduce this new persona to his and Perrin's life. Eric knew Perrin would want particulars: he would realise, as soon as Eric had introduced Matthew to him verbally, that it was merely a prelude to him meeting Matthew himself. Eric always regarded it as part of his lovers' educational process that they should meet someone as civilised, as exquisitely nuanced, as Perrin. Many a callow youth had learnt a correct table-setting in his presence.

Perrin would, perhaps, have him and Matthew round for one of his delightful casual, perfectly produced Thai meals. Other friends would be there. They would range over politics, personalities, fashion, food. In this way Matthew would enter a mutual zone of friendship, that *terra cognita* Eric had relied on ever since he had discovered it, tremblingly, in a state of hilarious ignorance, in what he now called, with sardonic quotation marks around it, *his youth*.

He looked around appreciatively. It was in a pub like this, Victorian, slightly seedy, scented with all the beers supped by many forgotten drinkers — to drown what sorrows, evoke what dreams, nobody could any longer say — that he and Perrin had first met.

It had been Eric's first venture into a gay pub.

In a mood of determination which had about it the air of a suicide mission, Eric had bid farewell to his old self in his bedroom mirror and set out, one Friday night (15 May 1969, his old, deplorable diaries told him — marked with a significant X). He had presented himself, white-faced, at the bar. As far as he could see, there were only men there, apart from one extraordinary woman who appeared to be the hostess. She was dressed, head to foot, in a glittering black mumu, her most pronounced feature a suntan so intense it appeared less her skin than a form of basted flesh on which pieces of gold were placed, ornamentally, to great advantage. This theme was carried into her mouth where her teeth were bedizened in a similar precious metal. Overall she escaped, by a mere hair's-breadth, being spectacularly gaudy.

Eric went straight to the bar and asked for something he took to be a typically sophisticated 'gay' drink. 'A Negroni please.'

The barman had looked at him, was about to ask how old he was. Then something in Eric's face — his desperation, perhaps — made him hesitate and then, speaking almost *sotto voce* — say, 'Wait a sec.' He turned to serve two men who hung on each other's shoulders and, both casting conspicuous looks at Eric yet making him feel as if he wasn't quite there, continued to address each other in fluted tones.

Both men wore what Eric took to be a club uniform: white shoes, beige crimplene slacks and hair which appeared to be both subtly teased and unsubtly lacquered. Their faces, variously wrinkled, were glaucous with moisturiser. 'Two double gin and tonics, love,' one of them asked the barman, in tones not quite so orchestral.

His companion smiled tentatively at Eric, and Eric felt his face crack a little as he smiled back. His heart was beating so hard he felt sure they could hear it.

The men departed, and the barman casually came back. 'Do you know how to make a Negroni,' he asked quietly, without any suggestion of aggression or even undue attention in his voice.

Eric flushed. He did. His throat was dry when he started speaking: he coughed up air over sandpaper.

The barman waited. Eric nodded. 'Yes,' he said, and told him.

While the man proceeded to make it, Eric said to him: 'I looked it up.' Then he said: 'I like reading recipes.' As he said this, he felt a swoon overtake him, a flush begin to rise up his face.

The barman had turned to look over his shoulder at him, not so much sharply but as if to check out the ingenuousness of the remark. Seeing Eric's discomfort he slid the drink towards him, and shaking his head when Eric offered payment, solemnly withdrew.

Eric realised something nice had happened to him.

Safely in possession of something to hold, something to do, Eric slid his tongue into his drink experimentally. As soon as the alcohol hit his tongue, he had to try hard not to let his face react. It did not taste as he imagined the recipe would. Nevertheless, having obtained the drink in such special circumstances, he could hardly go back and ask for something else.

He must enjoy himself: that terrible imperative. He looked around the room to see who was looking at him. No one. It was extraordinary.

He looked around again, in panic. Nobody was taking the slightest bit of notice of him.

It was at this moment — this lacuna in his life — that Perrin McDougal walked in the door.

At this stage, before he had settled sublimely into his looks, wearing them with all the assurance of a bespoke jacket on carefully muscular shoulders, Perrin appeared a diffident, indifferent-looking youth. He was thin, high-nosed, dressed dramatically, head to toe, in black. He paused under a light, as if for dramatic effect, then threw his long amethyst scarf over his shoulder with a defiant emphasis.

This caused a momentary hush — almost of awe at someone contravening 'taste' so much. Then at the back a voice was heard to say something — thankfully, Eric thought, indistinct (it sounded like 'drama queen') — then there were guffaws or collapsed lungs of laughter.

Perrin, holding his profile in a distinctly Oscar Wilde manner (the young Oscar Wilde), as if he did not hear, obtained a drink and went into speedy exile — a miscalculation of effects? — by a wall.

Inevitably, it seemed, because they were the two people on their own, so spectacularly isolated, their eyes located each other. It was like radar — radar of the dispossessed.

It was Perrin who finally made the move across the room to him. Sidling up, he looked at Eric for a moment, radiant with silence.

Eric, panicking — was this his first pick-up? — said, with a dry voice, 'There's quite a crowd here tonight, isn't there?'

His new companion turned on him an eye from which satirical emphasis was not entirely absent. 'I *hate* crowds,' Perrin pronounced.

'Why . . . why do you wear black?' Eric asked, racking his brain for clever, unusual things to say.

'I'm in mourning for the world, of course,' Perrin said superbly.

Eric, who was not *au fait* with Edith Sitwell's autobiography, believed he found himself in the presence of acerbic genius. 'Are you from out-of-town?' he asked, looking into Perrin's thin face, pimples just visible by his nose.

Perrin seemed uncomfortable, even nervous. Nevertheless, so convinced was he of his superiority that he looked Eric up and down, then said drily: 'The unpleasant fact of the matter is, I come from a Rue Morgue called Hamilton.'

Eric's eyes widened. 'That has a lake, doesn't it?'

'In which,' said Perrin, who spoke as if always between parentheses 'the unhappy citizenry are driven to throw themselves, for their *divertissement.*'

Eric laughed, and Perrin congratulated him on his appreciation of wit, with a surprisingly shy, even tentative, smile. Then he turned to the room, sighing slightly.

'You see before you . . . a refugee. In fact, I clean dishes at the Hungry Horse.'

Eric saw that Perrin was by no means as self-assured as the turn of his scarf, the cut of his phrase. With this discovery, he felt himself to have attained a similar, happy refugee status.

A long, not unfriendly silence fell in which both did an inventory of the room, frequently and nervously sipping their drinks.

Eric was soon surprised to find his glass was empty: not a drop could be seduced from its shimmery viscous surface. Perrin's glass was similarly empty.

They both looked down at the diminution of their hopes and, as if in musical concert, sighed heavily together.

It was clear that, having created grand effects, neither had a penny.

'What were you drinking?' Perrin asked.

Eric, tentatively, told him. Perrin was thoughtfully silent (later he would admit he had never heard of the drink). 'I only ever drink Fallen Angels,' he said, with a high tilt to his nose which Eric read as instant glamour.

From that day on he would always think of Perrin — who later came to detest the drink as oversweet, the epitome of his early lack of sophistication, his suburban pretensions — as synonymous with that first occasion, when they had both tremblingly met and Perrin's mode of identification was, along with Edith Sitwell, a long amethyst scarf, a sense of the early Oscar Wilde, and a drink called Fallen Angel.

Later that night they left the pub, as if accidentally, together.

They walked to the bus stop still talking and each, on the point of saying goodbye, speedily allowed the other to understand that he could be found at the pub the following Friday.

Neither confessed it was his very first visit.

Now, sitting in the Alex so many years later, more mature, filled out into his body in a way which made him feel he knew himself, Eric glanced around the bar. The men there all knew they were men: the few women's names bandied about were always used, as it were in quotation marks, knowingly camp. The barman, fleshily muscular, with a tightly trimmed moustache, looked for all the world like a rudimentary Tom of Finland sketch requiring a few master strokes for sublime completion.

This world of the Alex now was light years away from that hotel, so long ago, in which Eric had nervously awaited his second meeting with Perrin.

That night Eric had allowed himself a small glass of beer. He was determined to keep sober. While he waited, anonymously, the crowd had swiftly grown. It was late summer and there was that lax, overexcited air of sensuality — of louche possibilities — in the air.

Eric relaxed his body against the wall.

'Everything OK here, darlink?' a voice said to the side of him.

Eric turned. Pushing through the crowd towards him, like a beaver, was a small man with waved pale blue hair and what looked like make-up on his face — or was it simply moisturiser? As he got nearer he closed his pink, slightly unguent lips together, cupid-fashion, and then laughed, revealing teeth which looked older than he was.

'Darlink! hold *onto* your funwig,' this man murmured to him, a mite melodramatically. His whole face was animated by a pleasantly puckish charm.

'Oh?' said Eric, not knowing quite how to reply. He broke out laughing.

Now, 'Call me Fay,' the little man said, pausing as if for breath. 'After the late great Fay Wray,' he murmured then, looking around the room in small darts and flicks, poisoned pricks of looks. 'We call her late,' whispered Fay, 'because she never comes on time! Famous for it!'

He looked around sharply, no longer smiling. 'Excuse me, dear, a dreadful clutch of old hags awaits,' declared Fay in a conspiratorial whisper, during which Eric felt his backside pinched, not unpleasurably — as if the man called Fay were a merchant and he was only taking a prudent feel of the fabric. Fay indicated with his head four men standing together, bodies turned, almost on display, to the constituents of the bar: 'We call them Boil, Toil, Struggle and Poke.'

'Ciao,' he called then, melting back into the throng. Eric imagined the departing remark was a Chinese codeword.

At this point Perrin appeared beside him, unwinding himself out of his long purple scarf, sweating and bad-tempered. He had missed his bus and had to hitch a lift, he said. He intimated it had not been a pleasant adventure. When his lift found out the nature of the pub, he had turned threatening. Perrin had opened the door while the car was still moving and run, he said with superb dramatic emphasis, 'for my very life'.

But he still had in his hands a gift for Eric: a 'borrowed' library copy of Edith Sitwell's autobiography. 'The beginning of your *aesthetic* education, my dear,' he said expansively.

Eric bought a round of Fallen Angels, nonchalantly, as if this were an everyday drink for both. They drank these perhaps too quickly. Then Perrin bought a round.

By this time the room, as crowded as an audience at a boxing ring, had taken on a certain hectic tone: at any moment, it seemed, the bell would ping, the lights would lower, the main match would start. Obligingly, the bells began to shrill, urgent as the flutter of blood coursing through Eric's wrists.

Fay suddenly popped up beside him, almost with a suggestion of old-time vaudeville magic (later he found out that Fay had trained in Sydney as a show dancer before breaking his hip and ending up as a waiter). As the tidal swill of men swirled him past, Fay called out, 'Do you want to come to a party?'

'Oh,' said Eric, thinking.

'*Yes*,' said Perrin quickly, '*I* would.'

Everyone was spectacularly drunk. People were walking about, banging into walls. A middle-aged man, unwatched by most, was doing an impromptu, slightly wobbly strip on a chair. 'Oh, *trust* Fanny,' someone was saying acidly. 'One *whiff* of alcohol, and *off* come her easies.' Another fanatically serious man circulated through the crowd, wearing someone's mother's best ming-blue bri-nylon suit.

Eric and Perrin stood together in a crowded kitchen. Fay was surrounded by people, as if he were a great courtesan holding court.

'And yes, they put me on the overnight from Wellington,' Fay was saying, ' *"escorted"* onto it by two large beasts. *Irish detectives.* They put me on and said, "Don't be in too much of a hurry to come back." Just to remind me they punched me. In turns.' There was silence. 'And then, after that, they said, "We've got some mates up in Auckland *waiting for you when you get in.* Just to make sure you don't cause any trouble up there, like." '

Fay left a brief, eloquent pause. 'So here I am, a poor helpless wretch,' he resumed, raising his eyes heavenward, in roguish imitation of a wilting Mary Pickford. He lisped softly, and with extraordinarily convincing pathos, 'Just doing the best that I can.' A particularly wicked look passed over his face.

Fay then rose with great dignity, the dignity of an Empress Eugenie receiving the news of the fall of the Third Empire, the death of her only son. He turned and, in a spectacular wavering motion, as if tilting to follow the impulse of his feet, he listed towards the door, finding it open almost by accident, so that, faintly surprised, even vaguely non-plussed, the man called Fay disappeared into the halloo-ing night.

Eric and Perrin had to walk home, as the buses had long since stopped. They walked through suburbs of spectacular silence. To entertain themselves each told the other a little about himself.

By the time they had parted — the first car was going to work — they had exchanged the same information: in order to cure them of their homosexuality, Perrin had had shock treatment, Eric aversion therapy.

They looked at each other, slowly smiling, in the diminishing night. It had not worked.

Outside, in the street, there was a sudden crumbling sound, as a tidal wave of masonry came crashing down. In a few seconds, all that was left was a cloud, a hideous perfume, a perforation of memory almost.

The entire structure of the Alex had shuddered in that moment, as if in apprehension. Outside the windows, the air became frail with grit.

Pneumatic drills took up their sound again, a drumroll at once curiously undramatic yet relentless.

At that moment, as if blown in by the gust of energy from the latest demolition, a figure arrived, tentatively, and hovered by the door. The light was behind him yet Eric could see, immediately, the newcomer was not Perrin.

The man moved slowly out of the dust-filled sunlight, feeling his way, almost by toe, towards the bar. Eric felt a quiet claw of shock. The man was dressed with a certain hectic vivacity: his once-tight jeans were now winched in, painfully; over what was clearly a skeletal stomach, a belt with studs glinted with the eyes of a snake which had long ago lost its fury. And the man's face, gauntly handsome, haggard indeed, with deep heavy lines running from nose to chin, was shining with sweat, pale, white: he had not shaved, thus accentuating his dramatic pallor.

For one dreadful moment, Eric imagined he could remember the man: that is, he could recall a finer, fitter, indeed quite handsome man who seemed, now, like a distant, more healthy brother. *That* stranger — not *this* one, surely — had exchanged a few looks with Eric in the bar many years go. Then *that* man, with his image of health and vigour, of whom this frail, too-old young man was a *doppelgänger*, had disappeared. He was rumoured to be in NY. He was either a waiter, according to one story, or, in the version preferred — because more apocryphal — he was the lover of someone very rich, very powerful and, to the public at least, very heterosexual.

Now this man had returned home and the sum of his voyage was making his way from the door to the bar in the Alex.

The occupants of the pub had grown briefly silent: then a series of falsely animated conversations broke out, like sweat on a forehead.

The newcomer reached a barstool but, suddenly relaxing his body against it, as if he had reached the end of what had become a too long and arduous mission, he misjudged its height so that, like a building collapsing sideways, his whole body began to topple down towards the carpet. At this moment, all pretence was abandoned.

The man beside him, a comfortable pool of flesh, who propped up the bar from the minute it opened, getting slowly sozzled as the day went on, reached out an automatic arm, as if he had a spare limb set aside for the safety of drunks and others similarly incapacitated. Holding the falling man arrested for a moment, he got to his feet and, as if the other were a doll now, or a giddy child, plonked him down four-square on the seat and held him secure.

At this the skeletal brother of the once-handsome man, once so much in command, the accruer of so many ardent looks, let out a wild laugh, its hilarity mocking everyone there in the gay pub, in its last days before being demolished. It was as if this man, so near his own end, clairvoyantly sensed that this place where so much life had gone on — where, indeed, rudimentary yet important transactions of a civi-lisation, a small branch of culture, had taken place — would be rendered faithlessly, by some dark law of anarchy, into a hole in the ground, an essential nothingness which might become, if it were lucky, the tarmac of a carpark.

Eric threw the last drops of his tonic back. Where *was* Perrin, why was he late when he had been so bloody melodramatic on the phone in the morning? And what was so bloody pressing?

Eric's contemplative eye, as if a needle within a compass of anxiety, returned to the man at the bar.

He was talking with an eerie, rambling gusto, telling the story of his travels. Eric could see from the faces of the listeners that they did not know whether to believe what he was saying, or believe something more profound, less acceptable.

Eric looked away quickly. He stared longingly out the door. The sun was still there, but it was gauzy with the dust of departing buildings. A huge demolition truck roared along the street, splicing everything abruptly into shadow.

He looked back into the room, quickly. He did not want to think of *that*.

He was prepared, of course, he used condoms, had studied the arcane codes of safe sex. (Come on him not into him, as the explicit ones said.) Yet, to Eric at that moment, the disease was still a foreign war, happening, thankfully still, *over there*, a distant place from which occasional returned soldiers, like this one, emerged in the locals' midst, gnarled, bearing tales of defeat greater than anyone could possibly imagine. And to a certain extent it was unimaginable: this savage hewing down of men who had just climbed out of the darkness, emerging into light.

What the bloody hell was keeping Perrin? Suddenly Eric had an almost hysterical desire to flee the pub. He wanted to be outside, to be near the harbour or on top of one of the volcanoes where he could look down at the city, make some sense of his life. What was Matthew but a diversion; he was fooling himself by saying he wasn't falling in love. Of course he fell in love every time. What the fuck do you expect from someone who grew up with the fateful tunes of *South Pacific?* 'Somewhere across a crowded room . . .'

The drills suddenly swerved into closeness. Eric caught his own face in a mirror opposite: he was surprisingly, even insistently, physically *there* for someone who, at that moment, felt a peculiar see-saw of elation dipping down into black depression. He and Perrin had talked in the early days of having tests because, as Perrin had said, 'Let's face it, darling, we've both been utter sluts in our time . . . but then,' he had added thoughtfully, lifting his eyes up and looking towards a far distant point, as if he were delivering the eulogy for a generation, 'who has not been a slut has not been human.'

Eric had laughed.

Now he tried, with an almost fanatical need, to think of Matthew. He tried to conjure up in his mind those images of their love-making which acted, almost, as a way of banishing his anxieties. He began to wish, almost desperately, that Matthew was there with him, so that he might just casually brush by, knocking his body into Matthew's as if to recall what was real — against what could only be feared.

Yet at this moment, when he most needed him, Matthew refused to appear by osmosis.

It was now eight minutes past 12, on 10 April 1986.

At that moment, as if exactly timed to an acme of pleasurable late-ness, Eric saw another figure arrive at the door.

At first, because of the light behind him, Eric couldn't tell whether it was Perrin. It was certainly Perrin's height, and approximate weight, but the person's body language was so different: slumped back, not pushing forward, standing there on the mat as if momentarily dazed, as if emerging out of a long black moment of introspection — thought — peregrination — a limning of the harsh white noon light, chalky almost, plashing and pouring down the side of, yes, it was Perrin's face.

He was still at the door, as if breaking off from some thought which possessed him. It was in his eyes as they searched the few people in the room, and the room went momentarily quiet *again* before, in quick shock waves, conversation took up, sealing over the startled apprehen-sion that already, like an almost imperceptible drumroll, the words *again* and *again* and *again* were making themselves heard, explosions from the distant war landing closer and closer to that spot so that it was finally unavoidable that one day soon, or was it even now, a direct hit would be made and the whole culture, if it were not to be wiped out, would have to go underground again — disperse, change its na-ture — or else *fight.*

As if in the wake of this apprehension — or was it the beginnings of comprehension? — Perrin began to move slowly towards Eric. Each fraction of a centimetre closer he got, it was like a realisation being brought personally, without words, from Perrin to Eric, from Eric to Perrin, from Perrin to Eric.

Eric wanted to rise to his feet, he wanted to open his arms wide and put Perrin within them and hug him forever, till he could recover, get all right. The words were already forming in his mind, angry and furious: we will fight this bloody thing, it can't be allowed to win, *it won't, we won't let it.*

Yet already Perrin had raised his face to Eric's, as if he wished to intimate to him that he could sustain no thought, so deafened was he by the vast explosion which had, the day before, in a quiet doctor's room, blown away everything he believed in and held dear to his life.

So it was, in the pub, in the last weeks before its demolition, before the farewell party which everyone confidently expected to be halcyon, Perrin did what he would never have done, really, or only when completely drunk: he put his hand out and Eric, as if by accident, caught it.

Together, they began to hold on.

A Casual Kind of Incest

PETER WELLS

May you be the last of your line to perish
—Scots curse

'Slower! What are you trying to do? *Kill me?*' Elsa Elsworthy, née Wolfe, raised her heavily beringed hands before her as a mask.

Bonnington wondered if, in fact, he was.

He felt a familiar brush of irritation. He wondered if he was doing the right thing. As always with his mother, there was a tangled skein of emotions. He had wanted to give her a day out. He was feeling guilty because he hadn't been able to see her in well over a month. But the simple truth was he felt dread at being in her company, as if all time had evaporated and they were back again as they had been when he was an only child, before he knew any better; when he believed her to be the most knowledgeable person in the world, source of all his intelligence.

'I can never work out,' his mother began. Her tone had the air of a pronouncement, one in which was expressed all her assuredness of being a Wolfe; that is to say, someone who knew their place in the world. Not a great and noble place, it is true. If you had searched the annals of New Zealand history you would find no knights, no honourables, not even a mere city councillor. But the Wolfes, as was her wont to say to her Mah Jong partners, the Wolfes were the life-blood of the nation, energetic people who through their own shrewdness had risen to a certain point so that now, in the closing years of the twentieth century, she, Elsa Bonnington Wolfe, great-grand-daughter of the lowlands Wolfe who had landed at Nelson 'without so much as a groat in his pocket', as he picturesquely said ('lost in the Napoleonic wars' she added grandly, when Bonnington began trying to piece together the puzzle of his family) — now Elsa was in the happy position of being a rentier living in fear of one thing only: the demise of her capital preceding her own death.

Mother and son were off to Taupo to meet their mutual kinswoman. Ethel Groudge, née Wolfe, unhappily divorced, had added purpose to her life by becoming the Wolfe family archivist.

'I can't for the life of me work out,' Elsa took up again, in a tone which said she perfectly well could, 'why you, *a doctor!*' her voice never failed to make a genuflection before the word, 'why you, a doctor, should take it upon yourself to drive such a dreadful, a truly awful heap!' She glanced about its contents, gym shoes, old magazines of quite suspicious provenance, a musty towel.

'It's as if you're ashamed of *what* you are, *who* you are!'

She left this last statement lingering in the air. It was her idea of sensitive comment, of allowing an idea to float. She who was famous for her bluntness, her inability, some would say, to confabulate or lie. Or as others might have it, those unfortunate enough to fall under her glance (when for example a certain woman was found embezzling petty cash from the Ladies Tennis Club Fund), her opinions had all the delicacy of a branding iron on tender flesh.

Bonnington sighed a little. He felt proud of her that, at seventy-six, she was still so alert and dynamic. Yet he felt a deeper shame that he, aged forty, was still paying court to her, listening to her silly homilies when all he longed to do was shout out: *I am a grown man, a doctor who daily faces issues of life and death.* He thought of his own rooms (now it was he who was in control) and the men to whom he had to say they had come into contact with the virus. He thought of their reactions, watching their world suddenly immolate: from a stunned silence, to a rage of unseemly rapturousness, on towards an almost breath-taking casualness.

Yet here he was with an old woman, his own mother, the woman who had given him birth, his whole existence, and she was so casually spendthrift with life, careless with death. Where was the fairness in that? Who made this weird and unjust imbalance? He longed sometimes to shout this out to his mother. But, and he had to be careful here, he could not be too harsh to such an elderly woman, someone hesitating, herself, before the precipice of death. Yet at the same time this very

sense of imminent end hastened him to make his terms, be honest —
ask that they look at each other at these last moments, face to face.

Instead they sat staring ahead, the landscape streaming across the
windscreen and flowing either side of them: landscape of his childhood, irredeemably changed now. Horse studs which had gone
bankrupt, farms over-mortgaged; small signs almost hidden, like old
feelings, deep within the erosion of a landscape.

He eased the window down. He needed fresh air.

'Don't Bonny, please,' his mother instantly said, shielding what
remained of her hair. 'I've just had it set.'

Unwillingly Bonnington made a compromise gesture: closing the
window so it didn't affect his mother's frail carapace, yet leaving it
open just enough so he didn't feel he was suffocating. He had begun
to sweat. He changed his position on the seat, hunching over the wheel.
The violence of his feelings, familiar to him from any number of occasions when he had gone out with his mother, still surprised him. Almost
imperceptibly, his foot pressed down on the accelerator.

'Your father and I — ' she looked at Bonnington momentarily, as if
daring him to notice her lapse in tone. But then they were safely alone,
where any small sin could be forgiven. 'Your father and I stayed with
Ethel's parents when your father returned from the War. Of course,'
she sighed here, inspecting the pattern on her tweed skirt thoughtfully, 'I never realised growing up that our side of the family had so
much *more* than hers. I never knew,' she almost whispered this, butting
up pattern to pleat then pulling them swiftly apart, 'that Ethel's father
was a problem drinker.'

Bonnington longed to say: you mean he was an alcoholic? You mean
he made Ethel's life a living hell? He longed to be so deplorably spe-
cific, if only to wound and bruise his mother's soft and suffocating
camouflages. But, on the other hand, he did not want to hurt her. He
loved her.

He could smell her beside him now, her familiar flesh smell com-
pounded with that of the fresh scones she had baked for the journey,
her parsimonious dabs of perfume behind ear and on wrist. He was
aware of the water in her eyes, the blood running through her body. It
was in this sense of her that lay his insensate beginning, and also knowledge of her end.

'Bonny, are you *listening* to me?' she now said querulously, turning in her seat with a certain stiffness to take a good look at him.

She observed his profile for a moment with mixed feelings of power-lessness and deeply familial pride. He had exactly the same brand of Ronald Colman looks her husband had had, the ones she had suc-cumbed to and, of course, lived to regret. Looking at her son now, as she had done ever since that dreadful night over twenty-five years ago, when he had 'spoken to her' — made *his* truth clear — Elsa searched his face and body for signs that other people might be able to read only too clearly: that she had bred, as she said in the first instance, 'God forgive me: a queer!'

Time had softened this to a hesitant, unwilling, yet finally accepted nod, a descent as much as an acceptance of the changed world still in molten motion. 'What you and your friends like to call — I don't know why when it isn't at all — *gay*.' The last murmured, or savoured in her mouth, like an unaccustomed swear word, one of the famously Anglo-Saxon expletives exiled forever from her too genteel lips.

It was still a mystery to her how she, relentlessly normal, as she said to herself, down to the bottom of her stockinged feet, could have pro-duced an only child who turned out to be, well, *abnormal* in this way. Yet, and here she had to say very quickly to her friends who shared knowing looks among themselves, she could hardly have had a more attentive child. Even her friends had to admit, grudgingly, Bonnington was that thing known as 'a good son'. Whether this would save him, or incinerate him, only time would tell. She let out a child-like sigh. Her fingers returned, trying to make sense of the tartan of her skirt.

Landscape whirred past at an increasing pace. Small towns where betting shops and the pub were the focuses of activity; empty windows by which knots of children huddled round the inspiration of a glue-bag. Then more remorseless green.

She gazed at it meditatively: that soft hysterical green of over-pro-duction, a memory almost of those days when New Zealand had been rich. Now she felt only the monotony of a single idea carried to a mel-ancholy conclusion. She shifted her view, microscopically, till she saw, on a distant incline, a marae.

'*This*,' she pronounced cryptically, even amused as she indicated with a flick of her head the cyclorama beyond the glass, 'was where our ancestor Angus Guy Wolfe disappeared. He was eaten by the Maoris. You know,' she added, as if quoting. 'The Maori Wars.'

'The Land Wars,' he corrected her, his tone a trifle flat, as if worn down by repeated usage. Bonnington had heard this story a thousand times: from his early childhood, when it had thrilled him with its air of being a *Boys' Own* instalment of a radio drama, through to the present, of adult disillusion, when he could question and note carefully the small differences in her telling.

'What exactly happened, do you think?' he now casually laid the trap at her feet.

His mother was fossicking in her purse. She took out a barley sugar, unwrapped it, began to suck thoughtfully. This was followed — horrors! — by her getting another one out for him and unwrapping it, offering it to him replete on its own little cellophane napkin.

'Well —' she said, taking up her story. She relaxed. The claustrophobia of hills and river faded away. She had glimpsed the satisfaction of a far horizon. A small smile softened her features.

'He was a colonel in the army and — I don't quite know how — he became separated from his men.' Her tone indicated to Bonnington's expert ears the beginning of artifice. 'Then he was found by the Maoris who captured him and — *ate him.*' It was all quite simple in Elsa's world.

'Were his bones found?' Bonnington kept his eyes ahead, white lines leaping almost hypnotically towards him.

He felt his mother turn and glance at him, thoughtfully.

'No,' she murmured, her tongue gently suggesting to the barley sugar it had better begin to dissolve. (Better to dissolve than break apart.)

'Well, how did they know he was actually eaten?' It was Bonnington's turn to glance at his mother.

There was a moment of silence in which he heard, suddenly, her jaws break into the crystalline sugar. She had done this unconsciously, an indication perhaps of the pressure he was bringing to bear on her.

Very distantly, as if uninterested, he murmured: 'You said he was a colonel?'

Suspecting an ambush, Elsa moved uneasily in her seat and applied herself to the particularities of the land. They were passing the black-humped hill where Maori kings were buried. A spectacularly bleak and barren piece of landscape, she always thought. With that killer bend coming up for the unsuspecting Pakeha.

'I can't quite recall,' she murmured, as if she had lost interest in that line of thought. 'Ask Ethel. She's made it her life's aim to find out all that sort of tommyrot.'

'It's just that I know,' his tone of voice was ominously even. 'Maori only ate people of great mana. It wasn't so much cannibalism as a talismanic act: consuming the person's wairua.'

Unthinkingly, his foot had sunk down on the floor. He wanted speed, he wanted to move out of that safe middle distance, to arrive at his conclusions. But as if resisting now, or sensing to what cruel destination he might be taking her, his mother became almost childishly fretful. She even let out a small moan.

'Please don't speed Bonny. *Please.*' She almost whispered this.

'I don't mean to.' His foot pressed further down on the accelerator.

'Bonnington. *Did* you hear what I said?' She spoke in a voice which echoed out of his childhood: Mother as authority. It still had the power to make him sit up, then get angry at his own reaction.

'I've been driving, Elsa, since I was sixteen and I've never had an accident.'

They swept past a poignant home-made cross.

'There's always a first time.'

He shot a look at her.

'You just have to trust me, Mum.'

'*Mother!*' she amended furiously, as if he sought, this late in the day, to change the rules of the game. 'How many times . . .'

'Do I have to tell you!' he added, shadow to the body of her thought. He couldn't help it. He was laughing.

His mother, gripping her purse to her tightly, turned to look at him then looked back ahead. Road leapt towards her, a nauseating sprint.

'You may laugh.'

He balanced his fingers delicately round the steering wheel. The car began to curve round a corner. Yet as they finished what felt like the last careless curl of the bend, the car continued on, as if it had a mind of its own. Wheels lost contact with road surface. Outside, pine tree, clay bank, tarmac blended into a frieze.

The car rocked to a stop facing the opposing lane of traffic.

At that moment — it had the dramatic appearance of a demon in a Noh play, rising up through the floor — a stock truck began roaring down towards them, horn blaring. Bonnington did not know what to do. While he hesitated, or rather his indecision became his decision, the truck recklessly swerved out in a wide arc, taking to the wrong side of the road. A calf's face, frozen mid-cry, flashed by. Within a second a swill of excrement, steaming, lay on the road where they might have died.

Bonnington sat still in momentary shock. Then he grabbed the steering wheel, reversed the car back into its proper lane and they began, with surreal sedateness, to drive again. Neither he nor his mother said anything.

When she continued to remain silent — he had reached a point when he might even have welcomed an 'I told you so' — he glanced towards her. As if still stunned by what had almost happened, she was staring ahead. Aware of time, aware of circumstance, aware of the diminishing space between two irreversible points, he sought to re-establish some warmth. As the truck had hurtled past, she had moved briefly into some unknowable space, some area of infinite aloneness, one he could not specify but felt, perhaps, might be something like an apprehension of a final separation between him — the last of the Wolfes — and the woman who had given him his life.

'Now you know, Bonny, don't you,' Elsa murmured when they drew up outside cousin Ethel's house — a one-time bach now serving as permanent residence. 'Don't believe everything she tells you.' Bonnington watched his mother go through the ancient rite of her maquillage: a fresh mouth painted on, several fluffings of pastel-scented powder, adjustments to her coiffure. Presentable again, she turned to face him. 'She's got it in for us because her father never really amounted to much. Whereas of course, your grandfather . . .'

She left the last discreetly silent, an implied eulogy as she rewound her lipstick. Both of them assumed the bland faces of those who feel they may possibly be watched. They exited the car and proceeded up a narrow path of home-mixed concrete. If they were Maori, perhaps this was the moment when a silvern sprinkle of karanga might break out, summoning the spirits to help them: this would be followed by the pressing of temple to temple, as if to reach in each other's eyes the shadow of the spirit of their ancestors.

Instead, together, a mother and her son, the last of the Wolfes, moved up the slender concrete path to the front door. The door chimes rang up and down the scales: shadow of Big Ben.

Ethel, when she opened the door, was a middle-aged woman his mother might have characterised as 'lacking in self-respect'. She had a face from which make-up was signally absent. Worse — and this was unforgivably bizarre, Bonnington could see his mother thinking as she shrewdly took in the socio-economic indices of her niece's apparel — she wore a slightly soiled tracksuit, as if this occasion, relatives visiting, was lacking in social significance.

But a sudden transformation, one of those characteristic acts of vivacity, or self-invention by which his mother never ceased to surprise him, seemed to have overtaken Elsa. She was suddenly a good old girl, the 'mad old bag' as she sometimes called herself, full of colonial spirit, ready to enjoy the moment on whatever terms, in whatever company she found herself. She leant forward, her face wreathed in smiles and claimed her niece's wrist.

'Good heavens, Ethel. I remember when you fitted on a trike!' Her hand was clasped tightly round Ethel's slightly rotund wrist. It was if she, or memory, did not want to let go.

Ethel showed that slight queasiness all family members feel when they come face to face with the custodial nature of memory. Then she stood aside.

'Enter the surgery,' she said, a curious smile on her lips. 'Do.'

'I've only got teabags,' she called out through an open door after she had led them into the lounge, then abandoned them. Although it was a warm day, there was not a window open. Elsa moved quickly towards a sepia photograph of the family boot factory. 'I've laid the family tree out on the kitchen table,' Ethel called out. 'It's the result of a lifetime's skulduggery.'

She brought back a pot of tea and a plate of round wine biscuits which she placed carefully down on a glass-topped coffee table surgically stripped of all other ornament. More to Bonnington than his mother, she said, 'They call me the Detective down at the local library.'

She laughed. 'Once I get hold of a fact, I never let it go.'

'We were talking on the way down,' Bonnington decided to open up the enigma of their family's past, 'about Angus.' His mother shot him a look of reproach. 'The Man the Maoris Ate.'

'Oh that old acorn,' Ethel cried gaily. 'You were brought up on that too!'

In Elsa's eyes she suddenly took on the emetic qualities of a nurse slipping on rubber gloves.

'It's a fascinating case of the way in which truths get distorted. Half a mo. I'll get the facts.' She went away and fossicked in a shoe box.

Bonnington exchanged with his mother a coolly charged look which hovered like a question mark — a taiaha over a word called *facts*.

His mother broke the silence by reaching across, as if impulsively, to take a biscuit.

'You don't bake, dear,' she said with genial irony to Ethel. 'You don't have the time, I expect.'

Ethel, however, was deaf to such subversive texts. A look of concentration had fallen across her face. 'Ah,' she said at last. 'Found you, you little monster! Don't think you can get away from me!'

She held in her hand a pale blue document of shiny governmental provenance. Its dense black script had the force of legality — of unexpected and uninspected clauses which, later in life, could wreck havoc.

'I got this from the Imperial War Office,' Ethel said airily, waving the document as if to dry its ink. 'This —' she paused for rhetorical effect, putting some dated spectacles on, which immediately enlarged her eyes to a slightly gorgon prominence, '— took me more than six months to locate.'

Elsa looked at her niece, her face betraying no emotion as her hand, almost with a ventriloquism of its own, relayed the biscuit to her mouth. She began, soundlessly as possible, munching. Bonnington listened to the little mouse-like mastications of his mother's teeth — still her own! — while she delicately reduced the fibre of the biscuit to pulp.

'Basically this report establishes that he wasn't captured at all. He went AWOL. The night before a battle.'

'It's their way of saying,' Ethel looked up, first at Bonnington, then, more lingeringly, at his mother, '— he deserted.'

There was the profound silence of a dying fall as Elsa's cup came to rest, in protest, bone chine to bone china, Royal Aynsley, Made in England.

'Well, I *certainly* never heard that,' Elsa Bonnington Wolfe said, as if loudly asserting her innocence.

'It was a good move, as it turned out,' Ethel said cheerfully. 'Heck of a lot of limeys got wiped out.' She let out a belly laugh.

Bonnington reached over, with an artful dissemblance of casualness, to snatch the document.

'He was a corporal, not a colonel!' he said a shade too brightly, waving the page at Ethel.

'His wife applied for charity relief,' Ethel continued. 'Thirteen kids. Husband scramarooed. In the next census she's listed as a laundress.'

Bonnington could not look at his mother. He was afraid she could read, wounded as she was by these *unspeakable* disclosures, a note of triumph in his eyes.

'In those days,' Ethel continued placidly, 'there was no dole of course. The women who moved round with regiments were often prostitutes. Even if they were called something else.' She shrugged philosophically.

Elsa Bonnington Wolfe stared at her niece intently, face a mask.

'But what about the lowlands?' she demanded. 'My father told me how his grandfather arrived in Nelson without so much . . .'

' . . . as a groat,' finished Ethel. 'Oral history,' she said in a dismissive tone.

He felt rather than heard the sharp intake of his mother's breath.

'I can't get back far beyond the Wolfe who came out here. There was a lot of unemployment at the time. People went wherever they thought they could find something to eat. They might have come from anywhere. I've a parish record of the birthdate of our ancestor who came out here. Before that, nothing. We may never know.'

There was a sudden and vertiginous silence, as if Bonnington and his mother were staring at a deep dark hole down which all the Wolfes were bit by bit disappearing; that black hole of the past, of want, of crime, of poverty — the dark borders of anarchy which surrounded them now, threatening . . . His mother appeared to be listening to some sound, apparently internal. Was it a pebble she had cast down the well, surreptitiously, as if to test there was ever an end? She was caught up instead in a soundless blizzard: a vacuum of emptiness so powerful it might pull them all in. Shakily she pushed her cup away from her. A light veil of sweat covered her brow, beading her powder.

'Perhaps,' he said, fearing it might even be too much for her, 'we might take a turn round the garden?'

'I . . .' his mother struggled to her feet, a look of distress on her face. They both stared up at her.

An unmistakable sound of flatulence came from beneath Elsa's pleated tartan skirt.

'Ethel. The loo! Where?'

Sentinel against awful consequence, her niece pointed.

Her hand over the back of her skirt, genteel to the very end, mimicking sorrow, apology, yet with an acceptance of life's little ironies, Bonnington's mother retreated.

'It's those *bally* biscuits,' Elsa shot out by way of accusation. She had not finished the battle with her niece yet. 'Bought biscuits have *never* agreed with me.'

Outside, in the sharp air of the central plateau, Bonnington and his cousin walked and looked at her rows of staked-up dahlias. Bonnington suppressed his instant thought (and this, he mused, was where the rot of family snobbery never ended), that the dahlias were, every one of them, 'common', their colouring 'technicolour diarrhoea', 'vile'.

'How is the old girl really?' Ethel asked him in accomplice tones. 'Problems with the old plumbing?'

He felt now a protective sense for his mother: this woman who had fought for him to realise himself, to be as he was now, independent, well off; someone who even wanted to face the truth. The intricacy of her truths, her fictions, had helped him to understand life. He did not want to destroy. He wanted only, perhaps, to build a stronger boat. The world was afloed; her sort — his sort? — were sinking. It was a time of swim or drown.

'She's not so bad for her age,' he said carefully. And he left a small pause, as if describing not so much something which was of dubious ancestry as possessing a positive form of knowledge: a kind of carving, perhaps, which was dying out in the world, yet whose very rarity raised its value. She was, in her own small way, remarkable. He did not quite know why, but felt himself tremulously near to tears: of humility, or humiliation, he did not know.

'I'd better go and see if the poor old thing is OK,' his cousin said.

'Oh no,' Bonnington was alarmed. 'She'd much rather be left on her own. She'll make a comeback when she's good and ready.'

He dropped his mother back at her townhouse, in a poorer street, a 'better' suburb where she still lived alone, still proud, still independent. He put down by her feet the wicker basket in which the now empty thermos stood, sentinel beside the immemorially old biscuit tin which had held legions of home-made biscuits.

He turned to go. She hesitated for a moment.

Inside the house was dark and cool and she looked about her distractedly, as if she didn't quite know where she was.

'You alright, Mum?' he murmured.

She looked at him then, her son, Bonnington Wolfe, the last in the line.

'Bonnington,' she sighed. She passed a hand over her face.

'What, Mum?' He returned her gaze.

'It doesn't matter, does it?' she said doubtfully. '*We* know who we are, don't we, Bonny?'

He was uncertain what she was asking of him.

She smiled hesitantly.

'It's how we treat each other, isn't it?' she said then, as if she had thought of it on the journey back home. 'It's what we *do* to each other. That's what's finally important.'

For a moment there were traces of doubt on her face. He was clever, her son, he had a medical degree. But what did he know? What could he know? She smiled at him briefly, softly; then, the world held in suspension between two points, she leant forward slowly and gave him a farewell kiss.

Archaeology

JOHN CRANNA

We lived that summer of the war in a house that looked down over a dry valley to the low blue wall of the Tasman Sea. Between the house and the sea was a riverbed in which the stones gleamed like polished skulls in the sun, and beyond the riverbed, a grove of apricot trees, and when in the late morning the wind came down from the hills behind the house, the trees would stir quietly as though touched by the ghosts of the gold-diggers who a century before had left the valley. Apart from the apricot trees there was little in the valley but tussock grass and the occasional ruined shack with its iron roof adrift and moving cautiously with the wind.

We lived there, he and I, with his mother, who in the mornings sat among the skulls in the riverbed weeping, and in the afternoons crept silently through the cool rooms of the house in search of insects. The house had stood now for a very long time, and along the side facing down the valley to the sea was a wooden verandah from which the white paint peeled and flaked with the sun and the wind. In the evenings we sat on the veranda and watched the dusk settle into the Tasman, and imagined, a thousand miles beyond, the red disc of the sun hanging low over the Australian deserts. We talked on these evenings of the war, of which we knew almost nothing, and discussed our theories about how it might have begun, about whether the exchanges had stopped, but we had no hard facts on which to base our theories, there had been no travellers on the coast road for months, and our small plastic radio had for some time now given us no news.

During the day we worked on the ground beside the house, extending the small garden to several times its previous size and

414

constructing an irrigation channel to bring water from a stream in the nearby hills. The channel enabled us to grow a number of vegetables in the barren soil of the valley, and had been put together from the remains of a sluice run we had found in one of the gold workings in the hills. On the day of its completion we held a small ceremony, for which Chris's mother dressed in her best clothes and made a short, incomprehensible speech, but when the clear water of the stream started on its new course between the timbers of the channel she began to weep and we had to cancel the rest of our little ceremony and return to the house. She lived between two rooms at the back of the house, every few days moving her possessions from one to the other, so that one of the rooms was always quite empty, the floor-boards dusty and bare and the drapes removed from the windows. When I asked Chris about this he shrugged and grinned in his nervous way, Maybe she gets bored in one room, he said, unembarrassed by the madness of his mother. He was seventeen, older than I was, and little taller, we had been friends now for a long time, and when our fathers were taken by the navy because they were fishermen and the war seemed inevitable, I had come to stay with him on the coast. Each day we went to the beach and took shellfish from the pale yellow sand for the evening meal, varying our method of preparation from night to night to avoid tiring of our constant diet of food from the sea. Afterwards, on the veranda, we listened to the radio, aware of the need to conserve the batteries, but there was nothing to be heard except the uninterrupted buzz of static, as though the waveband was being jammed by unseen electrical storms beyond the horizon. I watched the sea at dusk, searching for the flicker of distant lightning, but nothing disturbed the dissolving line of sea and sky.

The lack of news did not appear to worry Chris, he was concerned more with day-to-day matters, such as the condition of the water channel and his plan to build a boat so that we might catch larger fish offshore. We sat on the verandah one evening and he spoke about the boat in his quiet, sure voice. He had found some sound planks and a few pit-props in a working up the valley, he said, and he would carve the props into ribs and fashion a clinker hull from the planks. When I sat and listened to Chris talk in this way, I found it hard to believe that our time in the house was anything but a long holiday, and although I had not yet made the connection between the war and the behaviour of his mother, I felt sometimes that her strange ways were all that prevented this from becoming a permanent delusion. Earlier we had heard her moving with her insect jar through the distant rooms of the house, and now she appeared beside us on the veranda, holding the top down rigidly on the jar, as though afraid that its contents might escape. Two grey moths lay on their backs in the bottom. Chris looked at her solemnly, Are you sure they're dead, Mum? he said. His mother examined the fragile shapes through the glass, holding the jar up to the lamp overhead, then abruptly disappeared down the steps into the dark. We heard her making her way to the riverbed, where each night she buried her catch on the bank above the smooth white stones.

When I could no longer hear the sound of her steps I said, What will she do when there are no insects left to catch? and Chris grinned, Maybe we can persuade her to come to the beach with her jar and catch fish instead. His mother had lost interest in the ordinary things of life, she did not have it in her to help with finding food or with cooking, and when, on Sunday mornings, I took her down to the beach to wash, she resisted me strongly, not so much from fear of the sea, but rather because she held something against it. When eventually I got her to the beach, she stood stiffly in the shallows while I scrubbed her with sand, she said nothing, but it was plain that she hated the seawater on her body. The ocean that month was a glassy green, there had been no storms and the debris along the beach had remained undisturbed now for as long as I could recall. When I sat with my line in the sand, I could close my eyes and conjure in my mind the exact pattern of debris along the tide-line, from the scattering of bone-white pumice to the position of the last desiccated twig. They were long, empty afternoons, with just the burning sky and the flat green sea, afternoons spent locked into a trance that would be broken only by the jerk of the line around my wrist — and then I was alert, touched by a startling invisible life, a life I could never believe existed until the nylon was taut and running, sending back its message of terror from the swarming bed of the sea.

And the sky to the west did not change, I watched it as I fished, neutrally and without expectation, and at the end of the day I took the fish back up to the house to fry on the iron stove in the kitchen, and we sat at the table and ate and joked with Chris's mother. Sometimes she smiled and we would pretend that she understood our jokes, but we knew that in reality she smiled because of some unimaginable event in the other distant world that she inhabited. She had begun to look thinner and more pale of late, so that we pressed food upon her, we gave her the largest portions of fish, but she would often leave her food unfinished and no amount of urging would persuade her to eat any more.

One afternoon Chris and I went up the valley to the gold workings to search out wood for the boat he was planning. A century before, the upper valley had been well populated with men looking for gold, and above the stream bed we came upon a collection of derelict huts and their complicated arrangement of wooden parapets and sluices. We worked on a sluice run until we could free its boards with ease, digging to loosen the framework from the earth. Then Chris stopped and stood up, he held in his hand a long tapered bone from which he shook the remaining traces of soil. What's this? Leaning forward, he pointed the bone at my chest, he was frowning heavily, You are condemned to take this boat we build, and sail in her to the west for all eternity, he said, and I said, Don't joke, what kind of animal is it anyway?

We scraped at the earth at the base of the frame and came upon other bones, they were laid out in a pattern that twisted in under the frame posts, and after a while Chris said, I think it's a man. Maybe the miners buried people alive under their buildings for luck, like the Melanesians. But the skeleton was too large to be human, the bones of the legs were exceptionally long, and as we uncovered more of it, we could see that the creature had a thin, curved neck like a swan, but much longer and more powerful. Then I said, It's a moa. We both stopped digging and sat back from the skeleton. We shouldn't move it, I said, and Chris said, But who is there to show it to? We sat and looked at the bones for a while, a little afraid, aware that the great bird had remained undisturbed for a thousand years. Then Chris said that we should collect the bones and take them to the house, where we could piece the skeleton together again, it would be safer there, though safer against what, he did not say. That evening we sat on the verandah and tried to remember what we knew about the great flightless birds that had ruled the country before man arrived from the north and hunted them into oblivion. We argued about their size and colouring, and finally agreed that they had been as high as twelve feet, with powerful, scaly legs and a plumage of deepest blue. Chris was certain that they were predators, able to catch their victims through their great speed across the ground, but I was sure that they did not kill, that they were stately birds who were able to live quietly among the rich grassland of the time.

In the days that followed, we laid out the bones in a shed beside the house and began to fit them together. I had made a sketch of how they lay and Chris had glued a piece of paper to each bone and numbered it according to my drawing, the way we imagined scientists did. Because the skeleton had been twisted where it lay in the earth, our attempt to arrange it in its true shape was based partly on how we imagined the bird must once have looked. We worked on the moa late into the evenings, the two of us crouched in the shed under an oil lamp with the bones scattered around us, arranging, adjusting, fitting and matching the pieces we had taken from the earth, until we were light-headed with the effort of it, and still the great bird lay stubbornly misshapen on the floor, less clear now in its form than when we had uncovered it first at the head of the valley. We had been working on the bird now for more than a week, and we sat defeated in front of the skeleton, looking down at the bones, which showed ashen white in the dull light from the lamp. Are you sure you didn't make a mistake with the numbering? I said. Chris stared at me for a moment without speaking, then turned back to the bird, and I wished that I had said nothing. We went up to the house and switched on the radio. That evening the static seemed a little more subdued than usual, and as Chris carefully turned the dial, I thought I caught the fragment of a human voice. I grasped his arm, Turn it back. We found the spot almost immediately, and for the first time in many months a broadcast filtered out of the night, a voice that was infinitely fragile, as though exhausted by continual battle against the static that choked the waveband. We could catch only occasional words and could make no sense of them, until without warning a clear phrase emerged, '. . . windsheer across the equator . . . cloud projected south . . .' before the voice faded and was submerged once more in the relentless surf of static. Chris looked up and shrugged, Just a weather report, he said. We discussed the static and what might be causing it, but as on previous occasions we could think of no explanation that sounded at all convincing and eventually we lapsed into silence. Chris's mother sat bent forward beside us, the insect jar on the table next to her unfinished meal. Chris said, Aren't you hunting tonight, Mum? It pained him to see her like this, hunched forward as though paralysed, he preferred her to be occupied with her inexplicable rituals of capture and burial, he felt responsible for her when she was still. His mother made no response, she was watching the night outside in the particular intent way she did from time to time, and I knew that she would remain like this until after we had gone to bed.

Next day the weather changed, and for the first time since the beginning of summer a haloed sun shone through high cloud. At the beach, where I sat fishing in the sand, the colours were bleached from the land and a dull wind blew in off the sea. I sat all afternoon without a bite on the line, day-dreaming of a port in the north where the days, the weeks and the months had been marked out by the coming and going of a rusted trawler in which men shouted and joked, and where the catch was tumbled still living onto a quay that smelled of bilges and diesel. Towards evening the shoals had moved offshore and I wound in my line, as the onshore wind strengthened and whipped the tussock on the dunes behind the beach. By the time I reached the house the wind was funnelling up the valley to lift dust from the hills beyond and slamming the door to the skeleton shed. Chris was in the kitchen preparing sea-eggs and had filled a huge bowl with their translucent pulp. I looked at the bowl and he laughed at my expression, Have you seen Mum? he said. I shook my head and turned away from the bowl of pulp to the window. You left the shed door open, I said. Chris started up from the table, That must have been her.

We went to the shed and pulled open the door against the wind, inside the skeleton lay inert in the dust, the great neck curved towards us, as though straining towards the light. We had kept the discovery of the creature from his mother, not knowing quite why, and now for an insane moment I thought, She's found it and pieced it together for us, and then I saw that the creature was the same as we'd left it the day before, misshapen and incomplete. Chris bent down to examine the skeleton, then looked around the shed. Some of it's gone, he said. One of the long bones that made up the legs of the bird had been removed, and although we searched the shed and went through the pile of bones that we had failed to fit into place, we could find nothing. Then distantly, from down the valley, came the sound of his mother's voice. At first we could not place it as we hurried towards the sea, and then we saw her, a slight figure standing beyond the apricot trees, the great leg bone of the moa clenched in her hand, screaming her incomprehensible accusations at the Tasman Sea as the wind blew in out of the chaotic dusk.

The wind blew steady and warm all night without a break, and in the morning it was still high when I went to check on the irrigation channel, which was vulnerable to wind where it crossed a gully as a raised bridge. Chris could remember nothing like it on the coast, it came now from the west at a constant speed, so dry that it wilted the crops and cracked the mud in the riverbed. The water in the irrigation channel had slowed to a trickle, as though the wind had sought out the stream that supplied it and dried it off at its source. Since her discovery of the skeleton, Chris's mother had taken refuge in her room, and she would not come out, even for meals. She lay on her side in a corner, her knees drawn up to her chin and her eyes fixed on a wall, oblivious to the food that we left for her on the floor beside her mattress. She held in her hand the moa bone, which she would not let go of, and she gripped it so tightly that I could see the sinews in her forearm stand out beneath the skin. We tried to get her to eat, but she would not hear us, instead she moved closer to the wall, holding the bone against her breasts, as though afraid we would take it from her. We worked silently on the skeleton now, for several days the steady wind threw up so much dust that work outside was impossible, we spent all our time in the shed with the bird, shuffling the remaining bones through an endless series of patterns that made no sense, we did not talk, somehow we could no longer think of very much that we wanted to say to each other.

And then the wind dropped and on the same day we had a visitor. She came along the coast track in the late afternoon, she was about our own age, and her hair was cropped very short on her head. We had seen no one in months, and we watched in surprise as she came up to the verandah and threw her bag on the steps. She looked dirty and tired. Do you have any water? she said. Later we sat together around the table and ate, and she told us that she had been travelling for five days up the coast, and in that time she had seen no one at all. She had come across a number of deserted houses, the occupants it seemed had gone inland to the mountains, though she did not know why. After telling us this she was silent, and we watched her eat the sweet potatoes and shellfish we had cooked. She ate awkwardly, her jaw moved at a slight angle to her head, as though her jaw-bone had once been broken. It was clear that she was very hungry so we did not ask her more questions, we let her eat undisturbed. When she had finished the meal she looked up and spoke: In the south they said that Australia was caught in the exchanges. There was a silence, I looked at Chris, then indicated the transistor radio. Could that be causing the static? She picked up the radio, listened to a burst of static, then placed it back on the table and shrugged. I dunno, she said, then, Where can I sleep? I put a mattress in the room next to Chris's mother and left the girl to her exhaustion. Chris and I sat up late that night arguing about our visitor and what she had told us. Chris was inclined not to take her news seriously, he said that she did not look very trustworthy, and that the word of a total stranger should be treated with caution. But what if she's right? I said. Chris got up tiredly from the table, You think too much, he said, and went in to bed. Next morning, before the others were up, I walked down to the beach to look at the horizon. The morning was still and quiet beneath a burnt-out sun, and to the west a haze covered the sea. Nothing showed in that western sky, it was as blank as it had been all summer, an empty gateway to the continent a thousand miles beyond, and after a time I went back up to the house for breakfast.

I found Chris in his mother's room, crouching by her mattress, a plate of cold toast beside him on the floor. He was speaking to her in a new, urgent voice. You've got to eat, Mum, you'll get ill if you don't. She did not even look at him, she remained with her face to the wall, the bone still gripped firmly in her fist. He tried again. We have a visitor, she's from the south. If you come and have some breakfast, you can meet her. His mother pulled her knees into her body and huddled closer to the wall. Chris got up and we went out into the kitchen where the girl was finishing her breakfast. She glanced up as we came in and continued eating, carefully cleaning the last scrap of food from the plate. Who was that? she said without interest. My mother. She's ill, said Chris. The girl looked suddenly uneasy. What's she got? There was a long pause, and then I said, She seems to have lost her appetite. The girl said she planned to continue up the coast that day, she did not want to speak of her eventual destination, and in the afternoon she went off up the coast path with a wave, and did not look back. Later we found our last cheese and a tin of honey missing, and Chris said, What did I tell you?

We worried about his mother now, it had been three days since she had eaten, she lay frail and thin on her mattress and her eyes were dark holes in a white face. I put the insect jar beside her on the floor and sat with her that evening, a lamp by the open window to attract the night insects, hoping that this might help her to rediscover her old obsessions. When she slept, her breathing came in shallow gasps, as though she did not trust the air to enter her lungs when she was not awake. I dozed in a wooden chair beside her mattress, half listening to the ocean and dreaming of the creature that once walked its ancient shore. The bird was very clear now in my dreams, its curved beak and bulbous, searching eyes, and in those eyes was an intelligence that spoke to me out of the past, there was some knowledge there that I strained towards but could not grasp, and in the moment that I felt I might understand, a subtle shift in the rasping breath of the sleeper propelled me awake, my palms moist with sweat and my heart pounding in my chest.

The keel of the boat we were planning lay in the garden, but the enthusiasm I felt for the project was gone, and I only half believed now that the craft would ever be completed. We disagreed over the way in which the hull should be fixed to the ribs, we seemed now to be opposed on the smallest of issues. I told Chris that the method he proposed was dangerously fragile and the fixings might part in a heavy sea, but he insisted that as the originator of the plan to build the boat he had the final word in matters of design. I had not seen him like this before, the old diffidence was gone and had been replaced by a hardness that was quite new. The house, which had seemed so large when I arrived in the spring, now seemed small and cramped, we could no longer escape each other there, and I spent more time away on long walks in the hills and along the beach. We continued to leave food for his mother but mechanically now, without much hope, for she had lost all contact with the outside, and I knew that only some change within the sealed world of her madness would free her to eat. She would not even let us wash her and gradually the odour of her body crept through the house until it was so sharp that it took away the breath, like a thin strong hand at the throat.

Often on my walks I would find myself at a place I recognised as being miles from the valley, without being conscious of how I had arrived there. One afternoon I found myself above the sluice run where we had discovered the moa. I sat on the step of the shack and stared at the mound of earth still fresh beside the hole we had dug. It seemed an age since we had found the skeleton, but in reality it had been only a few weeks. And then I was on my feet. Of course, how stupid we had been. Some of the bones were still in the ground! I was in the trench, scrabbling with my hands at its sides and sifting through the loose earth in the bottom, each pebble a lost fragment of the bird, I was certain that a few more inches would reveal the vital bones we had missed. Eventually I sat back against the side of the trench and examined my hands. I had driven a wood splinter into my palm and my nails were torn and bleeding. There was nothing in the trench, not even the smallest shard of bone, and as I sat there beneath the sluice run I thought suddenly how foolish we had been to remove the creature from the dry earth of the gold-field where it had lain undisturbed for so long.

When I returned to the house Chris was standing at the door to his mother's room. He was half turned away from me and did not move when I came in. What is it? I said. He turned as if to speak, his face drained of colour, but in the end he said nothing. I went to the door and looked into the dim room. The insect jar lay shattered on the floor, and with one of the pieces his mother had carefully cut both her wrists. The blood had dried to a crust that spread out on the floor before her in a crisp red sheet, and although she sat upright in her chair and looked across the room at us with round, interested eyes, it was clear that she was quite dead. She was dressed in her best clothes, the one she had last worn at the ceremony we held to open the irrigation channel, and as I stood there in my shock, I thought, At least she looks like someone's mother again now. Later that afternoon we combed her hair and pinned it back the way she had once worn it, then we cut her fingernails, which had become ragged and bitten. When we finished we took her down to the river bank and buried her beside the smooth white stones, she was very light and either of us could have carried her there alone. The moa bone was still clasped in her hand and I suggested that as a mark of respect for her last obsession we should bury it with her, but in the end we could not bear to do it, to sacrifice in this way such an important piece of the bird, and before we lowered her into the trench we had dug in the flinty soil, Chris gently prised her fingers loose from the bone.

Somehow our work on the moa now became something over which we had lost control. We were drawn each day to the shed as surely as we were drawn each day to the sea for our food, there was some larger imperative involved that we did not even try to talk about, but which was as real as our daily routines of survival. We did not seem to be any closer to a solution, but we knew now that there was no question of not finishing what we had begun. Sometimes, after hours of work, we would find that we had entered a cul-de-sac we had left some weeks before, we were repeating our mistakes, and it was at these times that our task seemed most hopeless. We blamed each other for these errors, though little was openly said. Each of us now saw the other as an obstacle to progress on the bird, and often we would work for hours without a word passing between us, locked into the bitter isolation that our work had brought us. Chris had developed a rash that began on his back and spread to his neck, his face and his arms, until his upper body was covered with raised weals. I said that we should eat separately in case it was contagious, and that I should work in the skeleton hut alone, but he maintained that the rash was caused by the dry wind, which blew in off the sea every few days.

I was dreaming every night now, harsh vivid dreams that were more real than the days themselves. I dreamt of a beach from which the ocean has withdrawn so that the seabed is exposed to the horizon, a naked plain of sand on which stranded creatures struggle for breath in shallow pools. And I dreamt of a harbour where a young girl with close-cropped hair sits beneath a yellow canary in a cage.

She is absorbed in her task, which is to cut with a pair of scissors a perfect circle from the sheet of paper she holds in her hand, and as it is completed, the circle becomes a disc that glows first red, then whitens to an incandescent heat, until it burns itself into the retina of my dreaming eye.

Parts of the irrigation channel had begun to collapse and we could no longer find the energy to repair the damage. The early summer had become a distant time with no connection to the present, the projects we had planned seemed to be little more than futile exercises that had diverted us from the more important business we were now engaged in. Everything was sacrificed to the creature, to the hut where the dry scrape of bone on bone, the scuffle of some emerging pattern on the dirt floor and the magnified whisper of our own breathing were the sounds that marked out the boundaries of our waking hours. By now our stocks of food were running down, we had no more sugar or flour, and although Chris talked vaguely of an expedition down the coast to one of the abandoned houses the girl had seen, I knew we would never go. At the beach, the shoals seemed to have moved away from the land, and on some days I caught nothing at all. Then one morning I found that the tide had marooned a huge swarm of jellyfish on the beach and in the shallows, and for three days fishing became impossible. They were a type I had seen occasionally in the nets of trawlers that had been fishing in the tropics, their bodies a pale mauve flecked with pink, and I wondered how they came to be many hundreds of miles south of their home waters. After a few days they began to rot, and the wind blew the stench up the valley so there was no escaping it, it hung there in the house as it had once before, and I woke up that night with the sweat cold on my body, certain that Chris's mother was back with us, that she lay with her bone and her rasping breath on the floor of the room next door.

For three days we survived on rice and a little dried fruit, and on the fourth day the stench from the beach was so great that I did not even bother to check whether fishing was possible. Instead I sat on the veranda and repaired my floats. Chris came up from the shed and watched me for a time. Then he said quietly, Are you going to the beach? We had not spoken that day, and I shook my head without looking up from my work. He watched me for a while longer, then

425

went over to my fishing tackle and began loading it into its sack. What are you doing? He threw the sack over his shoulder and started towards the beach, down the slope to the riverbed, picking his way among the stones, an arm extended for balance. I got up and leant against the veranda rail, a point of hot metal seemed to press up against my ribs and my vision blurred a little so that I had difficulty in following him as he continued down the valley. Then I was down the steps and after him, slipping and scrabbling in the riverbed, I could hear myself shouting, but what I heard made no sense to me. By the time I reached the beach he was wading out through the shallows with the line in his hand, the jellyfish a grey carpet that folded in behind him. I ran into the sea and felt the creatures cling suddenly to my legs, they had been dead for days but now they came alive in opposition to me. I struggled towards Chris, he glancing back over his shoulder, then turning and wading on towards the outer edge of the bobbing carpet. The creatures disintegrated as I forced my way among them, I was up to my waist in a soup of jelly and tangled filaments, I was getting no closer to Chris, but my blind anger drove me on through the stench that rose choking around me and through the insects that hung in clouds over the grey sea. There was no escaping the insects, they bit my neck and arms and lodged in my ears and in my nostrils, I was inhaling them, spitting their bitter taste from my tongue and wiping them clear of my stinging eyes. And then suddenly I was free of the swirling bank of insects and wading into open water.

Chris stood motionless a few yards ahead of me, gazing out to sea, and as I made my way towards him he let go of the line he was carrying so that it spun away into the clear water, the skein of invisible nylon unravelling as it sank. We stood there very still, up to our waists in water, and looked at our new horizon, a horizon across which stretched a shimmering band of palest green. It lay in a continuous arc that appeared to touch the coast to the north and south, but this was an illusion brought on by the scale of the thing, and by the curve of the horizon, and I knew that it must still be far out to sea. Despite its distance I could see that it had an internal life of its own, it was illuminated from within by a flickering that appeared to be due to electrical storms and which disturbed its surface like the movements of eels beneath the surface of a pond. The beauty of the thing took the breath away, we stood there hypnotised for a long time, watching its imperceptible progress across the face of the ocean, until eventually I touched Chris's arm and we made our way back to the beach.

At the shed the bird waited for us in the dim light, its bones laid out as we had left them in clumsy imitation of its lost form. We knelt there in the dust of the floor of the hut and began to work, we handled the creature with a new care, weighing each bone with a patience that had previously escaped us, testing our patterns against a fragile image of a living form that seemed somehow to have clarified in our minds. At first we had the impression of a small advance, but the further we pushed the advance the faster we found the puzzle giving way before us, pieces of the skeleton that had lain awkwardly together all summer were dovetailing smoothly; rib, joint and socket began now to match with ease, until the coupling of bone on bone acquired an effortless momentum of its own, and the outline of a new, vital pattern began to take shape in the dust. There was no stopping us now, we were the agents of a mechanism that moved with some older and deeper logic, and which now that it had been set in motion swept aside the trivial errors and false starts of the past months . . . We were laughing and shouting as we worked, the long summer which had seemed to disintegrate around us outside the dim confines of the shed, the abandonment of our crops and our plans to build the boat, the decline and final madness of Chris's mother and now the cloud that had appeared out to sea . . . all this was a distant irrelevance when set beside the intoxicating power of the process that we had become part of, the rebirth of the great creature that had once ruled the shores of our ancient ocean.

When we had finished, we sat very quiet and very still beside our completed work. The skeleton expressed a perfection of form that reached out of the past and silenced us with its beauty. It was much more than the proud creature of my dreams reborn into the present, it was the vehicle for a form of knowledge that had previously been denied us, and which was linked to the dry wind that had sprung up outside and was rattling the windows of the distant house. Chris knelt beside the creature and gently stroked the great bone of the leg. I stood behind him, my hand on his shoulder, and felt the slow flex of muscle beneath his skin. We were very close again now, we belonged there together in the gloom with the creature, and I knew then that we would never leave the hut, we could not abandon the bird at such a time. I heard the wind rising in the apricot trees beyond the stream bed, but all sound had somehow become external to the hut, and even later, when the wind was howling up the floor of the valley from the sea and beginning to pry with steady insistence at the door to the shed, it did nothing to disturb the deep, clear silence inside.

Visitors

JOHN CRANNA

My grandfather was a large man with a strong laugh who grew pomegranates for pleasure, but for reasons that only gradually became clear to me, and certainly were not clear to him, it was felt necessary from time to time to strap him to a bed and apply electric shocks to his head.

When I saw him after his treatment he had difficulty in recognising me, so I stood at his side for a while, repeating my name until the dullness had gone from his china-blue eyes. Although I was only fifteen, I was careful to arrange my face into a mask of apologetic innocence, in fear that he would begin to link my appearance with the treatment he was receiving. When the Pale Suits had gone away he would get up slowly and go out into the garden, where he would walk for a time, occasionally stopping at one of his fruit trees to touch the skin of a pomegranate that had hung there all summer, as though extracting its smooth permanence from the wreckage that had been made of his immediate past.

My grandfather had travelled in the time when this was still possible, and had collected musical instruments from around the Pacific. They stood in the dim corners of the house, or hung on the walls, a great Javanese gamelan in the hallway, and a Chilean lute on a shelf above. In the long afternoons when our visitors worked on my grandfather in the front room, I could hear the instruments in their other lives singing to me. The gamelan I knew well; it sat on the edge of a clearing in the jungles of Java, played by smooth-faced boys, its heavy sound mingling with the trees and the soil. The sound was very clear to me; it lodged in my chest as a kind of ecstasy, and it would only fade when the surge of voices from the front of the house told me that the men had finished with my grandfather. They went then to the kitchen and spoke to my mother, although I could never hear what they said to her. I watched from a window as they walked down the drive, two men in pale suits, one of them carrying an aluminium case, which was laid carefully in the back of the waiting vehicle.

The house and the garden were too large for the three of us who lived there, we had unused rooms, some still locked and containing the possessions of members of the family whose whereabouts were no longer discussed. On one side of the long hall that ran through the house my grandfather and I had our rooms, and on the other, at the furthest end of the hall, was my mother's room, a sanctum that no one was allowed to enter. My mother was a graceful person who moved about the house without ever seeming to touch it, and who each after-noon following lunch would brush my cheek with the lightest of kisses, before retiring to her room for the remainder of the day. After she had gone the long hall held a trace of her perfume, lingering there amongst the instruments, as though the house was reluctant to con-cede her departure.

At the edge of the orchard my grandfather sat and watched his pomegranates ripen, indifferent to passing showers. In a murmur that carried across the lawn to the house, he spoke endlessly of his years travelling the Pacific in search of instruments for his collection, strug-gling to prevent the treatment he was receiving from unravelling the thread of his memory forever. I sat beside him on the grass and tried to follow the path of his reminiscences. From Java and the jungles of Indochina it would lead suddenly east to Mexico, then south to the deserts of Chile, before veering west again to the island chains of Micro-nesia. A story that began in Djakarta might end in Santiago without his being aware that the location had changed, and fragments and characters from one tale would find their way into others, so that his monologues were jigsaws of confusion that held me entranced for hours, but which I could never fully understand.

Some things, however, were clear to me. He had always stayed among the ordinary people, whether it was in the shanty towns of the great cities or in the small, poor towns of the interior. He was obvi-ously welcome in these places, and because of his enthusiasm for the music of the people, instruments would be produced and impromptu concerts arranged. He was often invited to join in the music-making and in this way he became a competent performer on dozens of the instruments he had collected. I could only dimly recall the times from my childhood when he performed for the family in the front room, but I have a clear memory of his large figure stooped forward slightly, playing a lute made from the shell of an armadillo, and holding it so carefully in his arms that he might have been cradling the shell of a massive rare egg. The lute, which was from Chile, now rested in the hallway, where it had remained untouched for many years.

One of my grandfather's remaining clear memories was of his time in Chile and he told me of the year he had spent there in the northern deserts, studying the ancient music of the Atacameno Indians. The language of their songs, he said, was so old that the performers did not understand it themselves, and he described the strange sound of the great side-blown trumpets that accompanied the performance. He had lived in the home of one of these musicians and he spoke of the stark beauty of the deserts and of the resilience of the people who had lived there since the dawn of time. One day, as we sat in the orchard, he told me with surprise in his voice that he had never been happier than when he was with the Atacameno, but when I asked him why he had left, his eyes dulled and his story slid off once more into confusion.

The men in pale suits were visiting twice a week now, and as I sat there beneath the fruit trees, I heard the quiet sound of their vehicle pulling up at the bottom of the drive. My grandfather fell silent at their footsteps on the gravel, and was suddenly very still in his chair. We could hear the Pale Suits talking with my mother, and then her breathless voice calling to us across the lawn. My grandfather got up and walked slowly towards the house, where our visitors would now be waiting for him in the front room. I waited for a while, then went into the hall and sat there in the gloom amongst the dead instruments. I concentrated very hard, until the loudest sound I could hear was the steady beat of the blood in my ears, then softly, across a great distance, I heard the strains of the lute singing in an Atacameno village, and the music grew stronger and more clear, until I was there among the scatter of low huts, listening to the lute as it cut the thin air of the desert. I saw my grandfather, dressed in the clothes of the Indians, working with them in their carefully irrigated fields on the desert's edge, and returning each night to study their ancient music in the household of a master musician. I saw him crouched by an oil lamp, taking down the music of an evening performance in his notebook, and writing out the unknown language that was used in the ritual songs of fertility and death. And then the lute began to sing of strange Indian tribes my grandfather had never mentioned, the Aymara and the Pehuenche; it sang of their languages, of their music, of the rich collection of myth that held together their pasts, and it sang of their struggle against the lethal promises of a new order that had come recently to their land. I was so absorbed by the tales of the lute that I almost missed the babble of voices from the front of the house that signalled the end of my grandfather's session, but the moment the Pale Suits opened the door into the hall, the lute fell silent again.

When the men were in the kitchen, speaking in their sing-song voices with my mother, I went in to see my grandfather. He lay on the bed, the straps loosened at his sides, staring up at the ceiling with unblinking eyes. An acrid smell hung in the room, and a circular stain lay around him on the sheet. I stood there for a while, listening as the kitchen door closed and our visitors' footsteps receded on the drive. I watched the stain spread out across the bed, and thought, They've embalmed him and the fluid is already beginning to leak out. His body seemed a long way off, as though it was withdrawing into the angles of the room, and I felt a sensation of falling. I put a hand out to the wall, and as I did so my grandfather turned his head to look at me, his face blank and his eyes empty of all life. He made a weak gesture with one hand. 'They're very kind to take so much trouble with me. I feel I should be more grateful . . .' I had never spoken to him about his treatment before, and now, hesitantly, I asked what they had decided was wrong. He frowned, as though trying to remember a complicated diagnosis that had once been fully explained, but eventually he shook his head and lay back, his eyes fixed once more on the ceiling. Behind me the door opened and my mother came into the room in a cloud of perfume. She opened the curtains with one hand while holding a hand-kerchief against her face with the other. 'What have you done, father?' she said. 'You know you really can't behave like this in front of our visitors.'

That evening, as though in protest at my grandfather's lack of discretion, she failed to appear for dinner, so the two of us ate alone. Although he had bathed and changed his clothes, a faint odour still hung about him, and when I sat down to eat I found my appetite had gone and I could not bring myself to finish my meal.

It had been six years since my sisters and my father had gone away to the mountains. I was too young to understand at the time, but soon after that the schools closed down and before long the Pale Suits called at our house for the first time. My mother would not allow me to go into the city, so the only Pale Suits I saw on foot were the pair who came to visit my grandfather. At other times I saw them passing the house in their long vehicles, and always they were on the wrong side of the road, driving very fast. When I asked my grandfather about the Pale Suits in their vehicles, he was unable to tell me anything. He was fully occupied, it seemed, with his dissolving past, and the only energy he had left for the present was expended on his orchard. There his pomegranates hung thickly on the trees, the best crop there had been in years, he told me, and the fruit were at the point of cracking from within with their own ripeness.

My grandfather spent many hours in the orchard, inspecting the bark of the trees for disease and the leaves for the first signs of summer blight. Often he would stop and stare at a ripening fruit for a time, touching it with his open palm, before moving on to the next laden tree. The longer his treatment continued, the more important the orchard became to him and sometimes he would call me over to a tree and explain his methods of soil preparation and pruning. It was important, he said, that there was someone to take over the orchard when he could no longer manage it. From the bottom of the orchard I could see the outline of the distant mountains, and I began to watch them more closely, thinking of my sisters and my father, trying to imagine them eating and sleeping somewhere among that jumble of pale shadows.

On the next occasion that the Pale Suits visited, the gamelan sang to me, and it sang from a shanty town on the edge of the great city of Djakarta, the music of its gongs shimmering and dancing in the Javanese dusk. Behind the knot of musicians the shanty town stretched away until it disappeared in the haze of cooking fires. The music of the ensemble was very solemn; it spoke of the land the people had struggled for and lost, of their flight to the city, and of the new poverty they had found there. The steady chime of the gongs reached into the corners of the furthest houses, so that it seemed in the end that the entire shanty town echoed with sadness for a time when better things had been promised, and the promises had come to nothing. As night fell, the music faded into silence, and I saw a small boy, asleep on the dirt floor of a hut, clutching in his arms a perfectly made model of the great gongs my grandfather had spoken of. Although he was fast asleep, he held the gong so tightly to his chest that it was possible to believe it was his only possession in the world. But now that the gamelan had ceased, the shanty town was slipping into shadow, and before long I was back in the gloom of the hall, waiting again for our visitors to emerge, the instruments lifeless shapes around me.

I no longer had the courage to visit my grandfather in his room, so I went out and waited for him by the orchard. Eventually he came across the lawn, moving like a blind man, groping his way to his chair beneath the trees. I watched as he tried to speak, his tongue lolling between thickened lips, and I knew then that if his treatment continued in this way it would eventually silence him altogether. I never thought of discussing any of this with my mother. For some years now she had been so detached that her presence in the house seemed almost accidental. We did not discuss the Pale Suits and my grandfather's treatment because we did not discuss anything of importance. It seemed that some part of her had become too fragile to exist in the world of the Pale Suits, so that she had retreated to the sanctuary of her bedroom, a room whose only concrete reality for me was as the source of the mysterious scents and beautiful clothes she wore.

Then something happened which changed the course of the summer. One evening I looked from my window and saw a glow on the horizon, a glow which flared gradually brighter until it lit up a great section of the central city. At one point I thought I heard the distant sound of explosions. It was nearly dawn before the glow subsided to a dull red. The next day there was increased activity on the road outside, with the long cars of the Pale Suits travelling faster and in greater numbers than I had ever seen. In mid-afternoon there was almost an accident, when a driver approached our bend too fast and had to struggle to keep his vehicle under control. I saw a momentary look of fear on the face of the Pale Suit at the wheel, a look that stayed with me for long afterwards. It had never occurred to me that Pale Suits might be able to experience fear. The activity on the road outside continued into the next day, which was a treatment day for my grandfather, and the two of us sat in the orchard and listened to the steady sound of the passing vehicles. My grandfather was slumped in his chair, watching the drive in silence. Even the most halting reminiscence now seemed beyond him. Flies from the orchard settled on his face and arms and he did not seem to have the strength to wave them away. The hot afternoon stretched out for an age, and to pass the time I counted the vehicles as they took the corner. By dusk I had counted a hundred and forty-two and yet the Pale Suits had still not arrived, so at last we went inside to eat. There was a feeling of unreality about the meal that night, I could not recall the Pale Suits having ever missed a treatment day before.

This feeling continued into the rest of the week as the Pale Suits still failed to call. Outside the vehicles came and went on the road, sometimes alone, sometimes in great convoys, but none of them pulled up in the drive, and by the end of the following week the Pale Suits had missed five treatment days in all. By now I had begun to notice small changes in my grandfather. He moved among the trees in the orchard more freely, his shoulders were straighter and he no longer trailed the faint smell of urine that once had followed him about the house. Before long his reminiscences began again, and now they were a little easier to follow. Tales that had once baffled me with their shifting locations and broken plots started to hang together, as though a fragile thread had begun to run among the scattered pieces of his memory. Some of his stories stirred in me a strange feeling of recognition, as though I had heard them before but when too young to remember or to properly understand. He spoke of his voyages among the endless atoll chains of Micronesia; he told me of the time he had contracted a rare strain of malaria in the Mariana Islands and of being paralysed by village liquor in Guam. The liquor had been drunk at a celebration to mark his mastery of the rare stomach bow after months of apprenticeship to the leading musician on the island. He had lain in a coma for ten days, and on coming to, had been presented with one of the oldest bows on the island, cut from hibiscus wood and strung with finest pineapple fibre. Through some special reasoning that was never explained to him, his coma had been taken as a sign of exceptional suitability for the instrument.

My grandfather told his stories with a new vigour now. There was no stopping him once he had begun on a tale, as though the long months of his treatment had diverted his memories into a dammed lake of the imagination, and the obstruction that had been holding them back had now been cleared away. Instruments which had lain in dusty corners of the house for years and whose origins had been a mystery to me became suddenly recognisable — I identified the stomach bow from Guam at once. The instrument hung in one of the unused rooms, a length of curved wood with a split gourd half-way down its length. My grandfather explained that the gourd was placed against the musician's stomach to amplify the vibrations of the fibre string. From his tales I also identified a shawm from Guatemala, a nose flute from Truk and a log drum from the Philippines.

We would sit in the orchard until after dusk, the trees turning to dim shapes around us, the line of distant mountains catching the last of the light, as my grandfather exercised his returning memory and the fruit flies gathered in clouds above our heads. It was very peaceful there in the orchard, the vehicles on the road outside were another world away, and I began to believe that the Pale Suits had bypassed us, that we no longer had any place in their scheme of things. We had come to a silent agreement not to discuss this, however, for fear that we might alter some delicate balance of invisible forces that was keeping them away.

My mother was unaffected by the absence of the Pale Suits. She came and went in the house in the way that she had always done, appearing in the morning and for meals and retiring to her room for the rest of the day. The house, however, had changed. The windows now let in more light, the dust on the floor did not seem so thick, and the doorways of the unused rooms no longer gaped like mouths onto the hallway. The house was breathing again. I could sense the sweeter air moving among the rooms, and although the instruments were no longer singing to me, they rested more easily in their corners and on their shelves. I fely sometimes that the instruments were beginning to replace my sisters and my father, and I thought of them as more real in some ways than those distant members of my family who had gone away to the mountains so many years before.

In the orchard my grandfather's pomegranates had reached their full maturity, and the branches of the trees bent almost to the ground with the weight of the fruit. The day had come to taste the first of the fruit and we decided to hold a small celebration to mark the occasion. We set up a table under the trees and spread it with a white cloth. My grandfather laid out two plates and a cutting board, and I hunted through the drawers until I found the sharpest knife in the kitchen. We knew which of the pomegranates we would choose; we had been watching it for weeks. It hung on a tree near the bottom of the or- chard, perfectly formed and with an unmarked skin of deep crimson. My grandfather took the fruit from the tree, placed it in the middle of the cutting board, and we sat down facing each other across the table. We had agreed that I would carve the pomegranate and he would be the first to taste its flesh. When I cut into the fruit I thought that I had never seen a brighter splash of red, and the juice ran in rivulets across the board and stained the white of the table-cloth. My grandfather lifted the pomegranate to his mouth and bit into the flesh, his hands trembling a little as they always did when he ate. I was watching the pleasure spread across his face, when a movement in the direction of the house caught my eye. At the edge of the orchard, standing very still and watching us intently, was a Pale Suit. My grandfather was so engrossed in the fruit that he did not see the expression on my face, he went on eating the pomegranate until he had finished it, while I sat there across the table from him, unable to take my eyes from the stain of the juice on the white table-cloth.

When they had gone inside with my grandfather, I dragged the table around the house and placed it under the windows of the front room. By standing on the table I could reach the level of the window, and although the curtains were drawn, I found that by positioning the ta- ble carefully I was able to see a part of the room. At first I could not pick out any details, but as my eyes began to adjust I made out my grandfather's feet on the end of the bed, shoeless and still. Beyond his feet something winked in the gloom of the room, and after a while I realised that it was the light catching the turning reels of a tape machine. I stood there, mesmerised by the reels, my face against the window, and I might still have been there when the curtains were thrown back, if a pale shape had not moved between the machine and the window and broken into my trance.

I carried the table back to the orchard, and set out the cloth and plates as we had left them. Then I went inside to where the stomach bow hung on the wall. I concentrated on the instrument, listening for the hum of its fibre string. Nothing disturbed the quiet of the room. I tried again, straining into the silence, searching for the echo of the distant atolls, and knowing now that it was more important than ever to communicate with the instruments. But the bow would not sing to me; it remained mute and still on its hook on the wall, and I realised then that in my weeks away from the instruments I had lost my old intimacy with them, and I did not know how I was going to close the gap that now separated us. I thought of the pale shapes moving in the gloom, of the turning reels of the tape machine, of the other, unseen contents of the aluminium case that our visitors always brought with them. And I thought about the change that had come over them while they had been away. The Pale Suits had been impassive before; they had come and gone without showing any sign of emotion in their work. But there was something different about them now, a new tension, as though a deep anger lay behind their bland faces. Our visitors were in the front room for longer than I could ever recall, and eventually, exhausted by the knowledge of their return and by my attempts to rouse the instruments, I fell asleep on the floor of the unused room. Much later I seemed to hear the sound of my mother calling, and because she was calling something that was strange to me I could not decide whether I was dreaming. I lay still, and after a long pause I heard her voice again and realised that I was awake and that she was calling to my grandfather in the orchard. I got up and went outside to where the evening light had begun to illuminate the back garden. When I saw the orchard I stopped. Not a single pomegranate remained on the trees. In the middle of the orchard, swaying slightly on his feet, was my grandfather, and around him in all directions lay the remains of the crop of pomegranates. In his hands he held a heavy stick, and his shoes were crusted and stained from trampling the fruit as they lay on the ground. He was squinting into the trees, inspecting each in turn to make sure that he had not missed any of the fruit, and then he threw down the stick and walked past me towards the drive. He stumbled a little, regained his balance and went off down the drive like a blind man, leaving behind him in the gravel a trail of seeds and red pulp. I saw my mother, pale and motionless, watching us from the porch. She seemed to be looking past the wreckage of the orchard to the mountains beyond, and I knew then that she was thinking of the others, but I could not tell from her face whether she believed we would ever see them again. Then she turned and went back into the house. My grandfather was nearly at the road now and I ran after him down the drive. Although the traffic had fallen off a little in recent days, the road was busy, and the great vehicles of the Pale Suits still came and went at speed. I had almost reached the bottom of the drive when my grandfather crossed the pavement and went out onto the road. A vehicle that had just rounded the corner made a wide arc to avoid him, its horn blaring and its tyres crabbing on the asphalt. My grandfather followed it with vacant eyes as it pulled to a halt further down the road. The driver looked back at us through his rear window. By now I had my grandfather by the elbow and was leading him to the pavement. I raised an arm to the driver in the hope that he would drive on. As I led my grandfather back up the drive, I heard the vehicle pulling away into the stream of traffic. Back at the house my grandfather sat in the kitchen looking into space. He did not move or speak for several hours, and eventually I had to lead him like a sleep-walker to his bed.

As though making up for lost time the Pale Suits returned the next day and on this occasion they brought their vehicle to the top of the drive. When they got out I saw why. On the back seat, in place of the usual case, there was a much larger case made of the same bright aluminium and heavy enough to need both of the men to lift it. They were too concerned with getting the case into the house to notice the condition of the orchard. They carried the case down the passage and past the gamelan to the front room, and as they did so I imagined I heard the low chime of a gong, as though the instrument had been brushed in passing. My grandfather sat in the kitchen, watching the

Pale Suits come and go, his blue eyes sharp and feverish. When the front room was ready the Pale Suits came into the kitchen and waited for my grandfather to get up. He remained in his chair, his arms limp before him on the table. The three of them seemed to be there an age, the men standing silent by the door and my grandfather motionless in his chair.

At last he got to his feet and went out into the hall, and I knew then that his resistance was over, that his last defence lay in the wreckage of the orchard and that the Pale Suits would now be able to do with him what they wished. When the door to the front room had closed behind them the house became very quiet and I tasted the stale air moving once more through the unused rooms, ebbing and flowing among the inert instruments. Then from the hallway I heard the chime of the gamelan, and as I listened it came once more, a low echo on the dead air. The instruments were waking again, and they had not waited for me to try to reach them first. The chime of the gamelan was solemn and regular now, welling up through the house like a heartbeat, until I could feel it through the soles of my feet and sense its heavy pulse in the pit of my belly. I saw again the shanty towns of Djakarta, the smoke haze low over the huts, and my grandfather sitting cross-legged in the circle of gamelan players; and then through the sound of the gamelan like a sharpened blade came the pure tone of the lute, singing from the deserts of Chile, telling of the ancient music that anchored the past of the people against the shifting sands of the desert. And now other instruments were waking and crowding in on the lute; I heard the sigh of the Guatemalan shawm and the rapid beat of the Filipino log drum. Instruments that had never sung before were breaking their years of silence, emerging from their dusty corners of the house for the first time in order to jostle for place in a chaotic rising choir. The air around me was alive with rhythms that broke in on other rhythms, with melodies that surfaced briefly before being drowned by the surge of some new voice joining the chorus, as instruments struggled to find their true voices after years of disuse. Slowly the milling sounds began to take on some order, the instruments were beginning to complement each other, as though fumbling their way towards a common voice. And then they began to sing in concert, sometimes one taking the lead, sometimes another. They sang of the howl of the typhoon in the tin roofs of the great shanty towns of the East, of the blinding rains and steaming heat; they sang of the harsh lives of the shanty town dwellers and of the peasant farmers on their meagre plots of land. I heard then of the hopes of the people for another life, of their struggle to make a new, better order from the old . . . and suddenly the music of the instruments grew dark and discordant, and the gamelan sang of blood on the grass of the teak forests of Java, the lute spoke of burning huts in the Chilean deserts, and the drum beat out the rap of midnight fists on the doors of Filipino slums.

And like shadows appearing in the cities and in the countryside, I saw men in pale clothing who emerged from the dusk, who stood on street corners and listened in market-places, who went quietly among the people with their soft, sing-song voices, watching and waiting, and who moved when they were ready with deadly swiftness to still the struggles of the poor. I knew then as the dark chords of the music swirled around me that my grandfather had been touched by these things, that his life of travel among the peoples of the Pacific, the secrets he had learnt from them, the music he loved and its sacred place at the heart of their cultures — all this had eventually led him to the dim front room of his own house, where the pale figures of our visitors attended him on a urine-soaked bed, while a lifetime's knowledge slipped through his mind like water through sand.

At that moment the chorus of instruments stopped abruptly and I heard the door of the front room burst open and the sound of feet in the hall. The Pale Suits stood in the doorway, looking about them at the silent instruments. One of the men wore gloves of pale rubber that came half-way up to his elbows. The Pale Suit with the gloves went over to the stomach bow and gently plucked its fibre string. The instrument gave out a low, dull sound, as though it had hung there untuned and unplayed for twenty years. He listened as the note faded into the corners of the room, watching me closely as he did so. 'A young musician,' he said. 'Following in the footsteps of his grandfather.' The Pale Suit walked among the instruments, sometimes running a gloved finger across a dusty body or plucking a slack string. When he had finished his inspection he stood once more in the doorway with the other man, gazing thoughtfully around the room. Then he turned and the two of them went back down the hall to the front room.

Later I sat in the chair at the edge of the ruined orchard and watched the Pale Suits load the instruments into their vehicle. First they packed the gamelan, after dismantling it into its various pieces, and then added the stomach bow, the lute, and the Filipino log drum. When they had stripped the house of the last of its instruments they climbed into the vehicle, backed slowly down the drive and moved off in the direction of the city.

I set off for the mountains that night; travelling only by darkness and avoiding the roads, I estimated that it would take me ten days to reach them. I did not know how I would find my sisters and my father when I got there, or even whether they were still alive, but I knew that I could not stay to watch the final decline of the house. I saw it then as the Pale Suits would eventually leave it, gutted and open to the weather. I saw the wind lifting the iron of the roof, the rain beating through open windows onto the floor . . . I saw my grandfather wandering through its empty rooms and I saw him going out to sit by a blackened orchard overgrown with weeds, freed at last of the intolerable burden of his memories.

This Place We Call Home

LLOYD JONES

The Maoris were at it again outside Toobey's last night. The old women were keening — it must have been close on dusk, there was little wind, and the sound of the women entered everything, like bad weather. Bruce Toobey in jeans and tramping socks came out and stood in the shop doorway. He folded his arms and bit down hard. You could see through his consternation the thought, 'Well, this is interesting, but I hope it doesn't go on too long.'

Eventually the women stopped their keening — it just dissolved of its own accord. Bruce unfolded his arms and knelt down to get the door latch at the bottom, and the one at the top; by the time he was done the women had disappeared in a white van.

Several days passed before I had cause to visit the shop. A rarity in itself, since it was only ever our forgetfulness that brought us to Toobey's. We tended to store up Saturday morning from the new mall. I wanted a bag of unpolished long grain rice which I wasn't hopeful of getting at Toobey's.

Bruce regarded me with sleepy eyes. He thought rice might be down by the biscuits, directions which however ridiculous I felt obliged to follow.

'Down that aisle,' he said, and sniffed unhealthily. He was a creature of the indoors, snuggling up to single bar heaters — despite his mountain clothing.

Grit and dust lay over the boxes of teabags, and I made a mental note to check the expiry date on anything else that might tempt me. Incredibly the rice was where he said it would be. Less surprising, Toobey's had only the polished white rice in supply.

Bruce picked the rice off the counter and wondered how much it cost. He picked up the bag of rice, stared hard and wondered. Bruce's unshaven cheeks were starting to redden when a voice sang out from the living area behind the shop.

'Dollar eighty-five, Bruce . . .'

It was Bruce's dad, Mr Toobey, and my eye travelled to the mirror I had tried all along to avoid. Anyone standing up to the counter was bounced along a line of carefully placed mirrors into the room of the bedridden Mr Toobey. The mirrors were so Mr Toobey could keep an eye on things. The rumours, the other things said of the mirrors, didn't bear thinking about.

Bruce made no reply to his father. Then Mr Toobey called out, 'Is that you, Christine Walker? Could you spare me a moment?'

Did he mean for me to go back there — to his bedroom?

Bruce nodded.

I passed around the end of the counter and followed the trail of mirrors to Mr Toobey's bedroom. Once I might have been afraid. But I wasn't afraid. I was curious, and finally vaguely disappointed. What I found was not what I had expected; but what had I expected? The smell of merchandise was as strong back here as in the shop, and it wasn't as if I had crossed any boundary at all. Beside Mr Toobey's bed was a pile of invoices — which was reassuring and possibly what I might have expected, that he wouldn't trust Bruce with the book-keeping.

'Christine,' said Mr Toobey, and I thought he was going to get up, but it was only a token gesture of movement, a slight adjustment from his cheeks onto his hip. 'Chrissie,' he then said. 'Throw the paper off the chair there and sit down. Bruce, go back to the counter, would you, please.' A small portable black and white TV was set up at his bedend. A pile of aging newspapers spilled out from under his bed. At the foot of a lampstand with a long black frill Mr Toobey's briefcase sat open. I looked around for some personal detail. I was aware Mr Toobey was watching me, but I thought, 'That's the price you pay for inviting me back here.' My wandering eye settled on a photograph of Mrs Toobey in a tennis dress and halfway into a backhand. The photo had been taken at the moment Mrs Toobey's mouth had snapped open. The colours had all but faded, but the mouth, Mrs Toobey's lips, had been retouched with a bright red colour, and for the first time I felt a little afraid, and wished Bruce was in here.

'She could hit a ball,' observed Mr Toobey. 'How old were you when it happened, Christine. Eight? Nine?'

'It' referred to Mrs Toobey's unexpected death.

'Nine,' I said.

'You were nine,' said Mr Toobey. He nodded with a thin smile, as if I had been caught out. 'You were nine because you came to Bruce's ninth birthday party. Out the back. Remember? Yes, you must have been nine. There were still cowboys and Indians back then. Did you hear the Maoris last night, Christine?'

In fact it had been two nights ago, but somehow I guessed he was aware of his mistake, because next he asked me, 'What are people saying out there?'

'I can't say it's been a talking point.'

'Christine. I've known you since you were kneehigh to a grasshopper. You used to buy Sante bars. 'The dark ones please, Mr Toobey,' you would say. The dark ones. They say this is theirs. My shop. The Maoris are saying it belongs to them.'

'The land, Mr Toobey, I think they mean.'

'Bruce wanted to shoot them. I said, 'No Bruce.' ' Mr Toobey raised his eyebrows, as if to ask, What did I think of that? Then he said, 'Will you help me, Christine?'

'I won't shoot anybody.'

'I hope not,' he said.

Questions. I did not see why Bruce could not do this thing. Why couldn't Bruce visit the Museum, and leave Mr Toobey to tend the counter? I did not understand why Mr Toobey had to languish in bed, convinced by the idea of his being a sick man. Or why Bruce wore a bush jacket when he never moved further than the shop doorway.

The question Mr Toobey wanted answered concerned the claim of the Maoris on his shop, the details of which he handed over in a letter from the Maori Trust Board.

In 1852 Walter Mantell had been employed by Governor Grey to nail down boundary lines with the local Maoris, and pave the way for settlement. The negotiations carried over to several days and nights. Mantell made his camp on a riverbank, and had reason to believe things had gone well. Although, when he had asked whose land he was camped on, the Maoris sheepishly declined an answer. The Trust's letter claimed Mantell's campsite had occupied an urupa, a sacred spot. Tribes were reluctant to inform strangers of its whereabouts for fear of desecration of their ancestors' remains. Sixty years later a river changed its course, and left Mantell's campsite stranded on the plains. Forty years on, the plain sprouted a suburb, and Toobey's Four Square, so the letter argued, had been built over the urupa.

Mr Toobey wanted to find out that it was a lie. Or, failing that, that a mistake had been made. All this history, he said.

'Christine, you're a student. You like finding out these things. But I *need* to know because the Maoris say it happened. I am being forced to know . . . What do I know other than biscuits, cheese, ice-cream. Foodstuffs. Merchandise is what I know. You know the sort of thing.' He shook his head, and it was hard to tell whether it was sadness or anger that moved him. 'How do they know, how? They say this fella Mantell camped underneath Toobey's. It's an outrage!' And as I turned at the door, to say goodbye, Mr Toobey said, 'Bruce is hopeless. Just hopeless.'

The library of the Canterbury museum is located in a small anteroom. Before then you pass by the Colonial New Zealand exhibits; the sunless bedrooms, small and intimate as a doll's house; beyond the blacksmith's and store, you head for the stairs at the bottom end of the Moa-hunters' floor. Each morning I wandered through the picture book in search of the text at the back — up the stairs — to the small library, where the minute and slanted handwriting of Walter Mantell gave me headaches.

> *Tuesday. Slept in a flax bush. Up at sunrise. Took a sketch. Ate some potatoes. Coffee.*
> *Wednesday. Fine. Bone grubbing. Fish. Went to Rakaia.*
> *Friday. Returned from Rakaia. More moa bones. Pig killed.*
> *Saturday. Clouded sunrise. Lovely day. Slept well, attacked by millions of sandflies and mosquitoes, which I smoked off. Breakfast. Potatoes and bacon. Walked. Found a few more moa bones.*

Mantell was in the area, but there was little mention so far of negotiations with the local Maoris. Walter seemed to be more interested in moa bones.

*

After two days Bruce knocked on my door, and said his father would like to see me. Once again, there was a minor struggle underneath the bedding, the promise of a special effort to get up, before Mr Toobey settled on his side and, out of breath, said, 'So what can you tell me?'

I told him it was coming along. I was still unravelling Walter's moa bone expeditions from his travels for Grey.

In fact I was becoming seriously sidetracked. The droll campsite diaries were less interesting than Walter's scrapbooks, which in his neatest handwriting contained copies of Walter's favourite essays from Montaigne, poems by Coleridge, Bryron, Shelley. These poems had been thoughtfully collected and packed away, with a compass. Included too was this snatch of music:

> *Three sailors bold from Bristol City.*
> *Three sisters from Bristol City.*
> *They took a boat and went to sea.*
> *They took a boat and went to sea.*

I can't think why Walter would have taken down this song, except for an emergency. A request from the Maoris for a song to enliven the evening, perhaps. Yet the lithograph of Walter reveals a humourless mouth and rather serious eyes, which suggests the song to be no more than insurance — a song packed for a stormy night in a stranger's camp. Over Toobey's Four Square? I was still to find out.

Last night the Maoris returned. The women set about their eerie wailing. Their men stood about in bush jackets and white gumboots. The sole light on in Toobey's came from the neon around the sausage logo. I watched from our letterbox, the bottles still in my hand, the arrival of the television crew. Otherwise the media presence went unnoticed, or perhaps the Maori women swaying and keening in front of Toobey's just thought it was unimportant to what they were doing. A young woman reporter clutching a notebook had a word with her cameraman, and ventured around the side of Toobey's looking for a door. The reporter moved in the brisk manner of a dog looking for somewhere to piss up against. Fat chance of Mr Toobey responding, but I did wonder what Bruce was doing. I couldn't imagine him away from that counter. I couldn't think what other world he might make for himself.

I made the milk bottles clatter, and the reporter looked my way. She held the notebook against her chest and watched me cross the road.

'If it's Mr Toobey you want, he's bedridden. Mr Toobey is a sick man,' I said.

'Oh?' the reporter said. 'You know Mr Toobey do you?'

'I just wanted to let you know Mr Toobey can't get out of bed.'

The reporter nodded, like she was taking note, and I felt a screw turn in my stomach in the knowledge that Mr Toobey's condition would not, on its own, be enough to warrant future consideration.

'Mr Toobey has a son, doesn't he?'

'Bruce,' I said.

'A grown up son?'

'Bruce,' I nodded. The reporter thanked me and went and hammered on the back door of the shop. From outside the shop one of the camera-hands called out, 'Hurry, Trude. We've got ten minutes.'

The hammering grew louder, more insistent, and the reporter began to call out to Mr Toobey. Could she come in? There were some questions that needed answering. 'Hello! Mr Toobey?' A crash sounded from inside the house. This was followed by some muffled shouting. A few minutes later Bruce appeared at the front of the shop. The Maori women had stopped their wailing. They made room around the doorway, which was where Bruce in his tramping socks and untidy hair now appeared. The cameraman yelled, 'Trude!' A shadow darted along the side of Toobey's, and the reporter waving her notebook overhead cut through the crowd to the doorway. The lights turned up and Bruce's uncertain and frightened figure hovered about in the bright lights. Mr Toobey was calling from the back of the shop. From his bed he was urging Bruce to do something. The reporter had turned away from Bruce to face the camera, talking as though she had a lot to say.

Bruce didn't know where to look or what to do. I could hear Mr Toobey again. Then Bruce turned and yelled inside the shop for his father to shut up.

'Excuse me, Mr Toobey,' the reporter was saying. She had hold of Bruce's sleeve.

'Bruce, tell them to leave the premises! Tell them I'm calling the police right this minute. Tell them . . .'

Bruce wheeled around in the doorway and screamed for his father to shut up. When he turned back the camera was in his face. It was difficult to tell whether he was shielding himself from the brightness, or whether he had lashed out, but in any event the reporter and crowd fell back. Somebody said, 'Hey steady on, mate.' Bruce singled out a face and swore in a particularly ugly way at the soundman. The effect was immediate. A space grew between the crowd and Bruce, and I thought how we had arrived at a moment in which there was probably nothing he wasn't capable of doing, and I was also thinking how I was glad it was him and not myself facing this situation. But somebody else was quietly telling him to take it easy, and it seemed to be working. 'Just breath through the nose,' the man was gently saying. It was something of a surprise to find a calm voice cutting through the confusion, and all that bad feeling, but that was the voice Bruce heard. It was the one that saw him nod his head and quietly retreat inside the shop.

The reporter was sitting on the pavement. She had made no effort to get up again. Up close, under the streetlight, I saw how uneasily her make-up sat on her face, and that she wasn't very old at all — maybe my age, or a year or two older. She looked back at me without saying a word, and I thought how she would smell of the very next thing she ate whenever she managed to get home later this night.

For the next few days I couldn't bear to go to Toobey's. I went along to the Museum in case Mr Toobey asked me where I had got to; then I might at least have the excuse of research. In fact I had paused from the deciphering of Walter's notebooks, and was exploring a file of father and son correspondence.

I could find no photograph of Gideon Mantell but there was an 1853 woodcut of a dinner party assembled inside a huge model of an iguanodon, one of the exhibits or 'geological islands' built on a lake adjoining London's Crystal Palace.

The names of those who have contributed to the study of fossil vertebrates are inscribed on standing placards behind the diners. Gideon's name is up there on account of his discovery of the iguanodon, the first great dinosaur known to Man. Mrs Mantell manages only a footnote, despite her having been the one to have bent down and picked up the worn fossil tooth in the iron sands of Tilgate Forest in

1822. But for this fortunate moment Gideon would have been just another 'bone man'. Instead there follows a feast of honours: degrees from Yale, election to the Royal Society of London, and the Geological Society's highest honour, the Wollaston Medal. A year later his children's classic, *Thoughts on a Pebble*, is published. The following year Gideon and Mrs Mantell separate. Two years later his oldest son Walter, just turned twenty, chooses to abandon the career in science his father had mapped out for him, to emigrate to New Zealand. In Mr Toobey's era, Gideon might be described as being beset my a mid-life crisis — desertion of wife and, now, his favourite son embarked upon a 'directionless' voyage.

Moa bones. Who would have thought salvation on such a variety of fronts might be obtained so singularly, and outlandishly, as from the remains of a flightless bird found on the other side of the world?

Two years later, from the new colony, and if anything more than ever driven by the need to please his father, the prodigal son writes, 'My dearest Father, I have just returned from my moa bone hunting expedition. Five "boys" are now staggering townwards with their scientific burdens. They might all arrive tomorrow evening and until they have arrived and the bones have been sorted and packed I shall give up all hope of completing this letter which should be of nothing but moas.'

Some of these prize bones Gideon keeps for himself, and much to the father's joy a good many London 'savants' drop by to praise the collection of bones spread out on a table in the living room.

Gideon loses no time in transcribing Walter's notes and descriptions into the language of scholarly dissertation. Darwin is there when Gideon, with the results of Walter's beachcombing, lectures to the Geological Society in 1848.

Gideon writes to Walter, 'My great desire is to make this collection a means of promoting your interest with the Governor of New Zealand. I shall do everything in my power to make your discoveries known.'

And again: 'Do not let the matter rest, but be on the *qui vive* for any new facts so as to have your name inseparably connected with the history of these marvellous relics.'

Gideon: 'I have left nothing undone to give celebrity to your illustrations; I have written, talked and lectured . . .'

Increasingly, though, Gideon's letters are full of bitterness for another bone man, his nemesis, Sir Richard Owen, the great anatomist who first postulated the existence of a great flightless bird on the evidence of a single bone.

Walter, from afar, obligingly humours his father: 'Have you seen Owen's hallux? I think it's an hallucination. I still don't believe the toes bit. I still intend to look for footprints.'

Gideon: 'Owen has a perfect foot of the largest species: he says he found with a hinde toe! I do not believe it.'

Walter: 'François, the gendarme of Akaroa, saw a moa twenty feet high fly over him one night with a sound like thunder and howling. I could give you fifty such "yarns." '

And so it goes, back and forth — Walter's beachcombing and bone grubbing, for the sake of his father's declining career and disappointments, eventually bringing him a commission from the governor. He travels south — to our neighbourhood — and one night may or may not have camped where now there stands the Toobey store, and sung:

> *Three sailors bold from Bristol City.*
> *Three sisters from Bristol City.*
> *They took a boat and went to sea.*
> *They took a boat and went to sea.*

A picket line had now formed outside Toobey's. The banners read: 'Occupied Land', 'Sacred Ground Desecrated'. Through this thicket the neon of the pig logo bravely flickered on, and Bruce (from habit or stubbornness) kept his place at the till. And I felt a glimmer of admiration. Perhaps it wasn't even as distinct as that. I probably smiled — yes — because something had registered, or whatever that something is before an idea turns to a plan of action.

But first, I had to get past a short, stocky Pakeha woman who had placed herself in the doorway.

'We are here to demonstrate our solidarity with Maori aspirations in Aotearoa,' she said.

The woman showed no sign of moving aside. It did not look very hopeful at all. I stepped back and a Maori man in a leather jacket, office collar and tie spoke to me. I thought I would try to explain that

I didn't plan to buy anything, that I had known the Toobeys most of my life. Why once I had attended Bruce's ninth birthday. We were the same age, and once, a long time ago, we had played together. Somewhere between then and now he had become marooned. But for the moment I couldn't find the words; there was no adequate way of explaining coherently the chunk of shared history which sat on top of another block of time in which Walter Mantell might or might not have made his camp here.

'Please,' I think I said.

A tug on my arm wheeled me about, and there was the stocky defiant woman.

'If you have any questions, ask me. Maoridom is too tired to answer your questions. They have endured one hundred and fifty years of white . . .'

'Frances,' the Maori man interrupted. 'I believe this young woman is a neighbour of the Toobeys.' And he gave a firm nod to indicate that I should be allowed through.

Bruce was surprised to see me. I could say he was happy, but this was never an expression easily recognised in Bruce. He raised his hand to gesture behind, to Mr Toobey's room at the back of the shop, and I shook my head, and touched my lip to shush him. Carefully I dropped onto my knees. I could see the dust, the years of lazily accumulated dust underneath the counter.

Bruce leant over the glass top and asked in a whisper, 'Do you want Dad?'

'No,' I said, impatiently, and quietly told him to lock the door.

'Bruce!' It was Mr Toobey. 'Who is in the shop?'

Bruce looked around guiltily. I wondered if this was his first venture into betrayal.

'Nobody. No one is in the shop,' he called back.

'I thought I heard another voice.'

'No, Dad.'

Bruce quietly locked the door, and I whispered to him to pull the plug on the pig logo in the window. Some of the picketers were staring in the window. Then I told Bruce to follow. We got down on our knees, found our way around the counter, and crawled along beneath Mr Toobey's mirrors. His door was half ajar and some light band music was playing on his radio.

At the end of the hall we stood up again. This was as far as I had ever been in Toobey's. Bruce took over the lead, and we tiptoed by the shelves stacked with dried and canned goods, the labels of which looked terrifically ancient, and I could well imagine Mr Toobey's justification: 'We have to look after the older clientele.'

Bruce locked the back of Toobey's and we fled across the road to my house. Once he looked back to where it was just possible to make out the edge of the picketers, and seemed to enjoy the mischief of their being there, and us here.

In my bedroom he looked around with approval.

'Books,' he said at the books piled on my desk and at my bedside.

I felt sorry for Bruce. But I wonder if there is any point in even saying that? I only knew there had not been much of a past, no glories there on which to stand tall and, despite Mr Toobey's plans of the shop promising Bruce a start, I did not see much of a future.

I expected Bruce to grope. But no. He opened me like a box of merchandise at the back of the shop: first the outer layers, then the peeling open of the inner wrappers. In Bruce's fingertips I felt the tampering excitement of discovery, of 'What's this then' and, as he pressed on, his still breath gathered, until I had to say, 'Bruce, it's all right if you breathe . . .'

Afterwards we lay side by side on the bed. We did not talk much. Thank goodness. And I was reminded of when we used to lie on the grass at the back of Toobey's, and look up at the sky, struck dumb by the uselessness of words. So it was in the failing light of my bedroom. We stared up at the ceiling. I could not look at Bruce without fighting down an impulse to fetch a razor from the bathroom and deal with the ridiculous bum fluff which he allowed to grow wild on his upper lip and chin.

It was late. The streetlights were on. I made Bruce cheese on toast. I poured him red wine which he pronounced 'Good. Very good,' even though I suspect he had never before drunk wine. There were no further clues to the hour, except it was late, when I steered Bruce across the road to the back door of Toobey's. 'Home,' he said, as if in his own mind the question had been asked.

Bruce wanted me to come inside. He was too full of wine to worry about his father. In the warehouse at the back Bruce giggled, and I had to push him from behind. Mr Toobey's door was closed, but I don't think either of us could have cared less about the mirrors, or what Mr Toobey might say or think.

We made our way to the shop counter, where Bruce switched on the overhead light. His face was flushed, but his eyes held a shiny alertness. He sniffed at the air. Then he saw something distracting, and brushed past the food aisles. I followed after him.

'Look at this . . . This crap,' he said.

The shelves had been restocked with the old merchandise from the back of the shop. I went to pick up an old yellow packet of Gregg's Jelly Crystals, and my hands slid off its sides. The same with the shelf below where I tried to examine a packet of Edmonds Custard Powder. The packets had been glued to the shelves. Further along the aisle Bruce rattled old cans of sardines with rusted lids that had been nailed to the shelf. Mr Toobey had nailed down the merchandise.

'He must have got out of bed. Dad got out of bed. He must have made two dozen trips between here and the back of the shop,' Bruce said, and I suppose the order of revelation depended on one's priorities. But up and down the aisles Mr Toobey had brought back the merchandise from my childhood.

This is how it had looked. I recognised the old labels — graphics in Indian ink, of gay mothers in sunfrocks and beaming children in sandals. And it occurred to me that it wasn't the loss of merchandise that Mr Toobey feared, but a period of time which he had understood so well.

Me, Clark and Wilder

LLOYD JONES

La Turbie is an old Roman town in the French Maritime Alps. Beside the tree-lined cafes the tour buses disgorge their passengers, and it is here the rock climbers turn off and drive to a promontory which overlooks the tiled rooftops of Monte Carlo. Cars with licence plates from Italy, the UK, Germany, huddle here.

Abutting the carpark are the wonderful limestone cliffs with names such as 'Mort au con'. There are easier climbs and with more pleasant names. 'Chausson aux pommes', for example.

Clark Griffen, the Canadian writer, turned up in sandshoes. The pastels of good clothes and shoes worn by climbers camouflage their practical aspect. Climbing shoes combine the virtues of a running shoe and a ballet shoe. The shoe is light but with a hard narrow toe able to probe a crevice or lesion.

It was a gorgeous afternoon. The spring rains had just finished, and the air was left thin, and the chalk had been washed from the rocks. I think we climbed Les Fleurs, a small easy outcrop.

The track takes you past the abandoned military quarters, and runs along the foot of the first lot of rockfaces. Far below was the toyland of Monte Carlo. But we were up here, in the lap of the gods, the sunshine, the warm rock; and the blue sea without hint of pollution spread south, east and west. The grunts of climbers could be heard, and the tinny jangle of the carabiners. Otherwise there was a concentrated quiet, except for Clark, who kept taking stock of our whereabouts. All the way to Les Fleurs, every so often Clark pulled on my arm — 'Look at this! Will you look at where we are.' He said this with the intimation of some slight wrongdoing: of our having got away with something.

Clark was also excited at finding another writer — although it had been Liz Griffen who, one morning one week ago, boldly knocked on the door of the Isola Bella. She was enrolled in a literature course at the Canadian University in Villefranche. Mansfield was on the list, which is what had brought her to Isola Bella.

Liz Griffen gazed at the bronze bust of Mansfield on the wall. With some deference she touched the old green bedspread with its moulting corrugation. The prints of old New Zealand failed to engage her and before long, regrettably, she brought her eye to bear on the bookcase with its worn detective and mystery stories that my predecessors had failed to return to the English Church library in Menton.

Clark duly appeared in the doorway. He measured the walls with his ungainly arm span. He gazed at the ceiling and scuffed the tiled floor, poked his head through the curtains. 'Bathroom out the back? Fantastic. This is fantastic.' Hands in pockets, he spied the writing material on the desk. 'Hey, teletype. You use teletype too.' He walked over to the desk and craned to read the page in the typewriter.

'Wilder, eh?' he said.

'Clark,' his wife gently admonished.

'Oh I'm sorry. There I go. Hey, listen . . . Oh God, isn't this what I always do?' He held his head in his hands.

The thing is, he told me, he was a writer too. Oh nothing much. Nothing like this. Nothing profound.

He said he wrote 'commercial stuff'.

'Clark, there's nothing wrong with what you write,' said his wife.

'I know. I know. I always feel this stupid need to apologise . . .'

'There's nothing wrong with what you do,' said his wife.

'Hey, look, we barge in here. We're holding up the poor guy from work,' Clark said. 'What about Teddy and Mouse?'

'Did you lock the doors, Clark?'

They had their kids waiting in the car — the same age as my children it turned out, so I invited them down to our house. The building site opposite our house was in full cry; Friday is concreting day, and we had to stand out the back of the house under the lemon trees to be heard.

It seems Clark had always wanted to be a writer. Other circumstances demanded he become a lawyer. He was unhappily successful.

Then one day he decided, enough.

Coincidentally, or deliberately, he never did say, he had looked up a list of birthdays for the famous and infamous, and happened to notice the centenary of Jack the Ripper approaching. In a fit of vision and giddiness he gave up his practice, bought a typewriter, learnt to type, rented a house for the writing, and inside three months had *Death Merchant* written. Then what? He was still on this high. The America's Cup was being contested in Fremantle. He got a friend to mock up a jacket, and on the strength of this dummy the book was sold to a small Chicago publishing company. Clark spent two weeks in Fremantle. Loved Australia. Raced back to Toronto and wrote *America's Cup* inside six weeks. It was duly listed in the *New York Times* book review section as one of the season's best books. But it was *Death Merchant* that had turned things around. Good reviews in Canada alerted the agents in New York. Clark chose the biggest. Next thing he was fifty thousand dollars richer, and *Death Merchant* was being 'sprayed' into supermarkets across America.

At La Turbie while I pulled on my shoes I started to explain a few things, mostly cautionary aspects, about rock climbing.

'Treat the rock like you would a narrative,' I said.

A foot placed here will have consequences further up the rockface. The idea is to trace a vague line. Don't hurry your moves but, equally, hesitation can lead to a gluey situation. Next thing your knees are shaking: the way up appears impossible, and the way down has mysteriously vanished.

'Above all,' I said, 'concentrate.'

Les Fleurs is nothing more than a warm-up exercise. The only way to fall would be to throw yourself from the face. But all too soon Clark had forgotten my cautions, and was talking about 'writing' again.

He was saying that before the success of *Death Merchant* he and Liz used to fly down to Manhattan for a weekend of hobnobbing with the rich and famous. By Saturday afternoon they were ensconced inside the Russian Tea Room.

'The first time I ever walked in there, I felt like a stiff. You know,' he said, 'like walking onstage to receive a leaving certificate. Now? Now it's no big deal.'

457

They had been in the Russian Tea Room while Woody Allen was there eating cheesecake. Norman Mailer was another regular. Warhol. Another time their table was smack up against the table of Truman Capote who was entertaining a party of people. Capote was in fine fettle. Everyone at his table was laughing. Crying their eyes out. And after a while Clark and Liz laughed too. You couldn't help yourself. Laughing with Capote that time in the Russian Tea Room.

You can virtually walk up Les Fleurs. But there is one interesting overhead hold which calls for some technique, and with the concentration it required I had tuned Clark out.

The next I heard was a rather meek request from below. I had instructed him to follow and copy my holds, but he was several metres off the line of the climb.

'Looks like I need some help here, eh.' He managed to sound calm. Understated. His chin, usually varnished with some kind of after-shave treatment, dripped sweat. As I say, his voice was composed, quite a stranger to the alarm gripping his face.

I had to drop maybe three metres, come over one, and climb up to Clark's stranded position. There is nothing heroic in what happened next. If anything I am guilty of negligence. Clark appeared secure. So I didn't hurry beyond a normal descent.

I was directly underneath Clark's foothold, such as it was, when he decided he could hold on no longer. He simply let go, and without surprise or complaint had begun to freefall down the rockface. I had a very good foothold, and smacked him against the face until he found a foothold. It had happened very quickly, in a matter of seconds.

At the bottom of Les Fleurs he walked around in a small circle. He slapped his sides and took deep breaths. I think he was mostly relieved. 'Look at me,' he said. 'Look at my arms. My legs. I'm shaking. I might never stop. I could have died. I can't believe this. I should be dead. Hey,' he said, resting his hand on my forearm. 'Hey, you know what I'm going to do . . . No, listen. No bullshit.' He was still shaking, but focused and earnest with it. 'I want you to meet Al. You have got to meet Al.'

Al was Clark's agent, a kind of literary oracle for Clark. Al says this, Al says that. Clark said, 'Al says all novels can be boiled down to a three-act play.' Or, 'Those bookshops playing Bach are bullshit. Carpet and a coffee machine and they think they can charge a higher margin. Books should be in supermarkets. Warehouses. Why should a book be any different from Heinz baked beans.'

'You have got to meet Al,' Clark said. 'Listen, I'm going over there in three weeks. I need more money. You write a synopsis of what you're writing and I'll see Al gets it. I owe you this buddy.'

It was useless protesting. I don't mind gratitude, but it was nothing, really. He had fallen maybe two feet. But Clark felt he had a debt to repay.

He shook his head. And breathed mightily. Glad to be alive.

'You have got to meet Al. Those small print runs. Hey.' He ticked his finger as if at a bad habit.

We had a beer in a cafe at La Turbie. Clark asked what I happened to be writing. 'See, I need to know, so I can present it the best way to Al.'

I told him I was writing about goats. Yes. It's surprising how bits of disconnected story choose the oddest moments to come together. I described to Clark a journey undertaken by a New South Wales doctor late last century to purchase a herd of high quality wool-bearing goats from a place in the Urals. A town meeting had been called and the doctor, no doubt with adventure in his heart, had volunteered to undertake the journey. He set out on foot from the Urals with two thousand goats and walked across what was then known as Asia Minor. In Calcutta he lost five hundred goats to disease. Elsewhere he had had to fight off hill bandits. Customs. Bureaucracy. And now he had to find a ship to take him and the goats back to Australia. It was an epic tale.

'And a true one,' I emphasised.

But Clark's disappointment was plain to see.

'You have to understand,' I said. 'It isn't really about goats but a travel story. Retracing the doctor's journey in the latter part of the twentieth century.'

'Goats, eh,' he said. 'If I introduce you to Al you have to promise me you won't mention goats. Please, you have to promise me this. No goats.'

'Well, nothing is set in print, yet. It's just an idea,' I said.

Still, the damage was done. I could see Clark was still thinking 'goats', and given to second thoughts. Goats gave way to professional pride, and I told him about Wilder, the prison artist and escaper.

Clark's eyes lit up.

'A prison escaper. Now you're talking!'

Clark's wife rang the next day. She said Clark had woken from a deep sleep about 4am. Liz said, 'He sat up in bed, shouting, "I coulda been killed!"'

Then Clark came on the phone — 'How's that synopsis coming along?'

At La Turbie I had told Clark a few facts about Wilder. He was a car thief, a prison escaper and, later, a prison artist. And, briefly, a folk hero in the sixties. Clark, of course, saw a man hurtling up creekbeds ahead of tracker dogs with thick necks straining at leashes. He saw Wilder 'sprayed' out across America. Money. A film contract. Maybe a mini-series option.

'Listen,' he said. 'We can meet in Monte Carlo. We can discuss how to deal with Al there.

Clark met me off the train. Hands in the pockets of his corduroy jacket, he stood on the platform tall and dignified above the swelling mob of backpackers. He wore the same white shoes that had failed to hold him on the rocks at La Turbie.

We walked up the hill to the old town and found a cafe opposite the lines of tourists entering the Jacques Cousteau aquarium. I ordered a *chocolat chaud*, and Clark, a small black Nescafé.

He talked about the first time he went to Al's office. An old brownstone in Greenwich Village. You walked up the stairs, and in a glass box was the first draft of Al's protégé Brad Seager's *After Dark*. All kinds of Seager memorabilia lined the staircase and reception area. Inside Al's office Clark sank up to his waist in a deep brown leather couch, and just listened to the man talk. Al might sell commercial, but he knew art. He had taught renaissance literature at Yale. But hey, now he was out in the real world. He confessed to Clark he was a little worried about Seager's form. Success had made him soft and unmotivated. In Clark's *Death Merchant* he sensed something of the young Seager. A good sense of pace. Sharp scene evocation. A bright slap of blood and violence, but by no means sodden with it.

Clark had got to meet Seager. Great guy. At Al's suggestion Seager loaned Clark some old drafts to study.

'The thing about Al, he thinks conceptually,' Clark was saying. 'You got to have this Wilder guy mapped out, so Al can slot him into the marketplace. Five . . . maybe ten minutes is all you're going to get with him. In that time you have to sell Wilder. That's all you get. Start off on the wrong note and his eyes will glaze over before your second heartbeat.'

'I don't know, Clark,' I said.

'Hey. Come on. It's not the usual bullshit about money tainting the goods?'

'No,' I said, and it wasn't.

'Listen,' he said, and reached over to clasp my forearm. He spoke very seriously, like someone who has successfully returned from a reconnaissance mission across enemy lines with crucial information.

'That first time I was in Al's office there was a pile of covering letters on his desk. Al showed me. This high,' he said, and he released my arm to paddle his hand six inches above the table. 'So, anyway, Al was called out of the office and I sneaked a look. These were quality people. Names from literary magazines and reviews. And the covering letters. Shameless. Talented, talented people, begging Al to take them aboard and save them.'

Clark settled back with his Nescafé. After a while he said, 'Hey, will you look where we are. Will you look at this!'

Monte Carlo was Clark's territory. His characters frequented casinos; were comfortable in evening dress; ran drug-boats into port from Algiers. He had until December to organise this cast into a manuscript. Al said he was 'allowed' four characters. At least one had to be a woman, but concessions could be made there. Two of the characters had to be American, and that was more or less mandatory. The storyline was some drug odyssey. Al had contacts all over the globe. Arrangements had been made for Clark to cross the Mekong into the Burmese sphere of the Golden Triangle. He had ridden horseback in the company of Thai police. In Paris, he had been taken to a vast subterranean area beneath the Charles de Gaulle airport, where dozens of North Africans caught smuggling drugs were detained. He met pregnant women who, it turned out, were not pregnant. He was shown LSD film cooked into clothing. In Clark's book the North Africans were the bad guys.

461

I saw North Africans every day on the building site across the railway line from the Isola Bella. The site was run by a short grumpy-mouthed Italian. His wife looked to be from the south, as well. On Fridays she came by with the payslips for the North African workmen, who lined rue Webb Ellis which departs rue Katherine Mansfield for Gare du Garavan. The foreman's wife would approach heavily in her flat black shoes. Her dress code was one of mourning. The payslips were in her black handbag and, as she moved down the line, in the face of each workman arose the dreadful possibility that his pay had been overlooked, or that today a mistake of some kind had been made. The foreman folded his hands behind his back while his wife dealt with complaints. The North Africans still to receive their pay grew increasingly anxious. Their arms fell quite lifeless at their sides.

Until Clark mentioned it, I hadn't thought of them as drug-runners.

'Any industry has its rank and file,' he pointed out. Then he said, 'So, what about this Wilder guy?'

I was writing about Wilder, but mostly I was writing about failed immigrants. How, in a small country, no one let go of old friends. The community was too small to permit lives to be shed. No redundancies here mate. In the event of an attempted escape old photographs were mockingly presented. Old IDs. The old life. Paroled after a decade spent in prison, Wilder attempts to launch himself on an artistic career. Within six months the old crims have looked him up. 'This isn't you, George,' they must have said; not in so many words of course. Wilder didn't see the year out before he was back in court, listening to his counsel describe him as a 'weak, impressionable man'.

One afternoon, a week before Clark was due to fly out to New York, he dropped by the Isola Bella to ask if I had a photograph of Wilder.

'Al might need something more to go on,' he said. 'Every bit helps.'

I did have a photograph of a self-portrait. Strictly speaking it isn't a self-portrait (prison artists were not allowed mirrors) but the painting is by Wilder of a 1970 news photograph of himself in handcuffs being led from the Rotorua Police Station to a waiting paddy wagon.

No embellishment of the news photograph has interested Wilder, unless a case is to be made for the eyes where he has settled for dashed off lines, the sort of brushstroke meant to signify seagulls in the high right hand corner of seascapes in cheap seafood restaurants. Elsewhere there is a fullness to his cheeks, and the pug nose as ever, tumescent as a piece of ripened fruit about to scatter its seed. The rest is simple reportage: an electrician's peaked cap, a v-neck sweater, a windcheater. The dark bristly start to a beard. But always it is the eyes that delay me, and I think they were the reason I didn't show the photo to Clark. Out of loyalty. Yes, loyalty. Look at the eyes and you ask yourself, are Wilder's eyes still undilated slashes seeking obscurity? Does he remain haunted by the prospect of the telephone ringing, the unexpected knock on his door, and the unimaginable: his life 'sprayed' out to supermarkets across America?

'Well,' Clark said with disappointment. 'A photograph always helps. It may spark off a cover idea, and with Al that can be enough. You know.'

'Gee, Clark, I'm sorry.'

'Well,' he said. 'I've come all this way. We might as well have a drink.'

We passed Clark's drug-runners on a building site, and wandered towards the old town in search of a cafe. Old photographs show a narrow beach running the length of Garavan to the old town of Menton. The newer postcards with tanned melon breasts fail to reveal the new marina and its retaining wall of large round boulders, in between, and at the base of these boulders, has formed a detritus of old rubbish, beer and wine bottles, and various plastics. A gentle swell pushes in there, gurgles and slurps out to the depths. In May the German tourists settle over these rocks. At night itinerants unravelled their soiled bedrolls over these same rocks still warm from the afternoon sun.

One week later I might have pointed out Wilder to Clark. I might have said, 'Look, over there.' Among the German sun-worshippers bathing on the rocks, the broken crock smile of Wilder. It was the older Wilder — the one I imagined leading a quiet life on the other side of the world. I recognised the cut and thrust pattern in the corners of his eyes, torn between watching the tip of his rod for bites, and scanning the horizon for nosy reporters and writers.

The night before Clark flew out he rang up for the synopsis. On the phone Clark sounded let down by my failure, so I admitted to having a photograph I had managed to dig up from the bottom of a suitcase. The photograph is a police mugshot of the young car converter. Wilder's hair is slicked back. His face is drained of colour. You can smell the free school milk on him. I showed Clark this photograph and immediately wished I hadn't. He was a little taken aback, I think. I wondered if Wilder's unsophisticated looks placed him in the false bottom suitcase era of Clark's genre. And what would Al make of it?

But, back to that afternoon I first saw Wilder on the rocks in a pair of old black stubbies. A Hawaiian shirt was open at the buttons. He didn't appear to have any other possessions.

The next time I looked I found Wilder trying to win over my children with a simple finger-play. 'Here's the church. Here's the steeple . . .'

My boys didn't take to him. They stood back warily. I didn't know whether it was relief or shame I should feel and, had Clark been here, whether I would have made the introduction.

The next night Wilder turned up in a bar along the esplanade of the old town. He had changed from his stubbies into some dreadful stovepipe black attire, otherwise he was the same. Clean-shaven for the evening. He sat at the far end of the bar. Detached, of course. I watched him in the mirror behind the bar. Every so often he looked over his shoulder, his grin unable to mask his ill ease.

Following his first prison escape, the newspapers describe a person happier to lounge outside the doors of a dance hall than risk inside, under the gaudy crepe paper, the sweaty lights falling on his 'sallow complexion, fair hair, grey eyes and boil under his left eye'.

During the week Clark was away I ran into Wilder all over town. Where didn't he turn up?

The local tabac was no surprise. It offered a noisy scrabble of drinkers, and was largely patronised by the boat mechanics from the marina. Wilder leant up against the bar with a pastis and a leery grin. He chatted with a surly mechanic who had fixed the suspension on my car. Wilder looked happier, and I suppose some of that had to do with finding his name and the mechanic's teamed up on the chalkboard for the pool table.

Evidently Wilder favoured the same fruit stand in the market. He made a big thing of inspecting the fruit he chose. But his French was appalling. Often he was so slow getting the words out that the proprietor's eye skipped on to another customer. No loss there. Wilder only bought one piece of fruit at a time. He would take it over the road to the beach, where he sat on the flat white stones, among the mattresses and bare flesh.

The other night Clark rang from New York — breathless and shoulder-slapping, even over the phone. Al liked the Wilder script. But, and here a well-controlled note of caution came over the line, 'Al wants to relocate Wilder. He feels, you know, what with the market where it is, Wilder would be better off in Texas. They got long roads for car chases. Small towns. They talk a kind of English. Al had in mind a prison farm. He drove past it one time outside El Paso. These are just ideas you understand.'

'No, Clark,' I said. 'The answer is an unequivocal no.'

Then Clark did a typically North American thing. He apologised.

A postcard arrived within the week. It was of the Russian Tea Room. He had got more money from Al.

Meanwhile, mornings vanish one after another. I imagine Wilder standing alone on a farm staring out to sea, and listening to the wind.

Visitors and well-wishers climb over the wrought-iron fence. There's no keeping them out. They knock on the door and wait. Patiently they knock again. 'Just wondered if someone was there?'

The other morning a stately Maori woman with a large greenstone pendant gave me a fright. She called through the window just as I happened to be writing a scene about Wilder — about what? — well, it doesn't matter. Would I mind if her husband photographed us together? She thought against the walls of Mansfield's Isola Bella would be appropriate.

'Is that all right?'

Is it?

Distance does not prevent one being implicated. Look at Clark and Capote in the Russian Tea Room.

Then this afternoon, from Beijing, a student's crumpled face stared from the pages of the *Herald-Tribune*. Picked out of the crowd. A random shot. His buckled trousers happened to match those of a 'counter-revolutionary scoundrel'. In the same newspaper, Rosemary Melo Nascimento — who launched a signal flare onto the field during a soccer match between Brazil and Chile — is to appear nude in next month's Brazilian edition of *Playboy*.

In a newspaper I first found Wilder.

I have become seriously worried about Clark. I wonder if he is writing about me. I wonder how a casual knock on my door has led to this unsympathetic portrait. It worries me to think what Clark will have to say of a man who goes rock climbing. And who otherwise spends all his time writing in a white-washed room about characters he will not talk about or admit into the light of day.

Barking

EMILY PERKINS

So I'm in my drama class, right? And I think like I want to be this very cool actor-type, Brando or James Dean or something — and I could have been too, you know, I really could. But the stupid dumb fuck drama class I'm taking is some idiot thing run by idiots and we spend all this time looking for our centres or relaxing or rubbing each other. It's pretty disgusting I'm telling you. But still I was sticking it out because I thought, you know, this is how people get discovered, who's going to know I've got a great face and a mean snarl if nobody ever sees it? But this day, where things really started getting rotten, I'd just about had enough. And we're in Clown class, the worst possible thing ever.

Let me tell you something about clowns — they're sick. Anyone who takes a fucking Clown class ought to be locked up. So, Mr Jones, what do you do? Oh, I'm a Clown teacher. Right, good one. And these people really think they're contributing, that's the sad thing, they really think they're doing the world a service by teaching losers like me how to Find Their Clown. Our Clown teacher, she was worse than most at that stupid Drama Centre — one of those deadly serious people who pretend they've got a really 'natural' and 'spontaneous' sense of fun, and it's all about learning how to play 'just like you did when you were a natural, happy, unafraid child'. Well, I'm so sorry for not growing up in the Waltons Family. Anyway, that's her. You can imagine the type? Wheatgerm coming out her ears, forced maniac grin on her stupid face, probably goes home at night and cries in the dark. Probably has kids with eating disorders. Lucinda the witch.

So, I'm in Lucinda's class, and today we're going to improvise with our clowns. That means we're going to put our stupid clown costumes and our stupid clown make-up on, and with everybody watching we're going to make something up. Something 'childlike' and 'spontaneous' and 'delightfully funny'. In other words, we're going to make total fuckwits of ourselves.

And sure enough, we sit through about eight people doing their little clown act, and I'm just about asleep this is so deadly. There's one girl that's quite funny but that's only because she's got this really huge arse and seeing her try and do mime with her black tights on and her big old butt bouncing all over is pretty good. She's the least graceful thing you've ever seen, tiptoeing around like one of those hippo ballerinas. Anyway, Lucinda must have guessed that my snickering is hardly out of childlike joy and wonder, because she picks me next.

— That was really special, Ginger, she says. — Thank you for letting us see that. Dog? Perhaps you'd like some playtime now?

I am serious, that's how she talks. I better explain about the names — they're our clown names. Janice or June, or whatever Hippogirl's name is, made the original choice of Ginger — she has red hair. I mean, Jesus, I thought we were supposed to be encouraging imagination here. My clown name is Dog. I know it's kind of weird but it's better than my first choice, which was Cunt. I didn't tell Lucinda that — we went through this stupid naming ceremony where we put our costume and make-up and most importantly our stupid red noses on, the red nose is fucking sacred to Lucinda, how sad is that, a ping-pong ball painted with nail polish, it's supposed to make us either 'in clown' (red nose on, breathing blocked, snot collecting in bottom of ping-pong ball) or 'out of clown' (red nose around neck on elastic, big creases across cheeks where elastic has been pulling too tight). Anyway the naming ceremony goes like this, you put all your clown stuff on, including, finally, the nose, and you're supposed to have this big spontaneous moment where suddenly your inner clown is released and bingo, you've taken on its personality and given it a name. And Bingo is about the standard of most of the names these retards picked. Bingo, Bungo, Pongo, Ginger. And I'm sitting there waiting for my turn, waiting for my clown to reveal himself and all I can think of how much I want my clown to be called Cunt. Cunt the Clown, ha ha. But I realize this would be going too far, even for me, Lucinda'll probably cark it or something, so when I get up in front of all those other bozos I just say the first word I thought of, which was Dog. So now I'm Dog the Clown. Ruff, ruff.

And I'm sitting there in my stupid clown pyjamas with my idiot clown nose on and fat Ginger's just sat down and some other moron is rubbing her back, like, oh, thank you, Ginger, that was so cool, and Lucinda the bitch picks me. I mean, I know I've got to do it, I can't get out of it, it's what this fucking course is all about, doing things you don't want to, it's like the fucking army. When are they going to give us the class in cigarette smoking for Christ's sake? Or scowling? Or swinging a mean right hook? That's all Brando and Dean ever did and thank Jesus too, none of this pussy touchy feely shit. But not me, not Barking Billy here, I've got to Discover My Clown.

So I stand up. I walk to the middle of the room in front of the class. My mind's a blank. How can I make something up? I can't think of anything. What am I supposed to do? What is my clown supposed to be? I just stand there and look out into the air and I can't think of anything. Then I remember my name is Dog and so I get down on my hands and knees and start growling. I look at the class, their eyes are on the same level as mine, and I growl at them a bit more. I give them a really good snarl, then I start snapping my teeth. Some of them are frightened, I can see it. Ginger is holding the hand of the girl next to her and shaking her head. I move towards her, slowly, growling. I think about letting out a big drool, a big slobbery drool all over Ginger's feet, and it cracks me up. I start laughing, it all seems so fucking stupid, I just start giggling really bad and I can't stop. I hear Lucinda saying,

— Keep in the moment, Dog, stay in the moment, though her voice sounds kind of quivery and I get the feeling she doesn't much like where the moment is going. It doesn't seem funny any more and I stand up. I look at her and I tell it to her straight.

— Lucinda, why do you think so many psychos dress up as clowns?

— Dog, your nose is on.

— My name's Billy and I don't care if my fucking nose is on or not. It's just a fucking ping-pong ball, Lucinda, it's not a magic wand.

— Dog, in my class, when the nose is on, the clown is on. Now if you want to take the nose off that's fine.

— No, I say. — I don't think I do want to take the nose off. Did you ever see that film with Brian Dennehy in it, Lucinda? Any of you guys?

Some of the class have taken their noses off, some of them are just sitting there nodding. They're all watching me. It feels great. The girl next to Ginger starts crying.

— He was a fucking psycho, Lucinda. He was a clown who used to fuck young boys and then kill them. How do you feel about that, Lucinda? Do you think he should have taken his nose off first? Huh?

— Billy, you are poisoning the air in my class, says Lucinda. She's shaking and her nostrils are totally white. I've never seen her like this, not even the time in the group improvisation when I made everyone kiss my feet — clowns are so gullible.

She holds the door open. — Please leave.

— I will be leaving this stupid fucking idiot class, Lucinda, you dumb cunt, I tell her with my nose still on, enjoying every minute of this, — and I will not be coming back.

Then I bow to the rest of the class, give Lucinda the finger, and walk out the door. I can hear the shocked silence behind me. I was waiting to do this for a long time.

I'm in the bathroom trying to get all the white crap off my face when the Drama Centre Administrator comes in. He tells me I've upset not only Lucinda but several of the other students as well, and it won't be possible for me to continue my term here. I don't say anything, I just keep washing my face, and when he says, Billy? Do you have anything to say? I flick water in his eyes and growl like Dog. He leaves pretty quickly. And I'm thinking that the only thing that pisses me off is, now I won't get a refund on my fee.

So I get home thinking, Fuck, now what am I going to do, I'll have to go and sign on tomorrow, and there's a message to call my mother. I call her and she tells me that my sister, my stupid dumb beautiful fuckup sister, has decided to accuse the whole family of involving her in a child molestation cult from the age of three to eleven. Which considering that I'm two years younger than she is, is pretty interesting.

I'm in a café drinking a coffee, surprise surprise, when all of a sudden I realize the two girls at the next table are talking about me. I don't know how I know, something in me just picks it up, I'm scanning the paper, not really reading it, when I hear —

— You know I see that guy around all the time.

— Which one?

— Just there.

They're talking all low and whispery. I pretend I can't hear, pretend to be engrossed in some stupid sports page, as if.

— I've seen him around so much, and you know what?

— What?

— I've never once, ever, seen him in the company of anyone else. He is always on his own.

The girls says this like it's the weirdest thing in the world. It really pisses me off. Who the fuck is she, to watch me and decide I'm some loner freak? Who does the bitch think she is? I put my paper down and look at her. She's looking at her friend, who's looking at me. Her friend says something and the girl turns and looks at me. She looks embarrassed. I hold her gaze until she looks away. I look at the friend and she looks away too. Dumb bitches, I go back to my paper. When I've finished my coffee I walk past their table on my way out. I stop by her chair, put my hand on her shoulder and smile.

— See you, I say, like we're old buddies.

She just about jumps out of her skin, then she laughs.

— See you, she says.

It wasn't what I was expecting. I don't know, I don't know anything about her. The friend looks like an idiot, but the girl who thinks I'm a freak — she looks kind of nice. Once I'm out of the café I look back through the window to see if she's looking at me.

And so now my sister's coming over. God knows what this crazy shit's about. Satanic ritual abuse? My family? Don't make me laugh. What it is, is she'll have been seeing some asshole shrink who wants to keep the money coming in for a few more sessions, and they'll have said, So, Carol, do you ever think you might have been . . . abused? And my sister's such as sucker, she's gorgeous but she's a total waster, she'll go, Yeah, hey, now that you mention it — I really think I might have been forced to eat live babies while being raped by a pig down at our local church on Thursday nights. I mean, it's hard to understand, but it's just her — she's got several screws loose. She's been anorexic since before it was fashionable and she likes sex way too much. I'm no prude,

471

but she is constantly getting herself in these really warped situations with guys who are called things like Mario and Luigi and have these horrible long fingernails. My parents are such morons, she's got them totally fooled with her 'harmless fun' act, but not me.

I fall asleep while I'm waiting for Carol and wake up freezing and sore from the floor. I dreamed that my feet were cold and I had to burn my shoes to keep warm. That was the good thing about the Drama Centre — about the only good thing — it got me out of the house in the mornings. Now I'll just sleep for hours, I know it, like before, and my dreams'll start seeming more real than my waking time. Maybe they are, anyway, who's to say. Let's face it, that Drama Centre was worse than any nightmare I could have dreamt up anyway. Fuck who needs them. I can still be an actor. I can still be anything.

— I'm a survivor, Billy, says Carol, all shaky and thin.

— Of what, Carol, I say, — Auschwitz? Because that's what you look like.

— This is real, Billy. You don't know how hard it is. I'm frightened for you.

She's chain-smoking and ashing all over the floor, it's not like I'm houseproud but she could be reasonable. She helps herself to some more Scotch. First thing she told me was, she's not pressing charges — yet. Her bitch shrink wants her to 'as part of the healing process', yeah, right, healing whose bank account? But Carol's toying with the idea of forgiveness first. Good one. Thing is, she knows there's no money to be got at anyway, something Ms Freud obviously hasn't been told.

— Then how come I don't remember any of this? I say to her. — Tell me why you have so-called flashbacks of burning crosses and purple hoods and all that blood and shit, and I don't?

— You're blocking, that's all.

— Oh, come on, Carol, you're sounding like one of my drama teachers for Jesus' sake. How can I be blocking anything that isn't there?

— Don't you think there's something creepy about Mum and Dad? Don't you get creepy vibes when you go there? To that house? She's really letting herself freak now, barely keeping her hands still enough to get the drink to her mouth.

— Of course they're creepy, I say, and I can't help laughing, — they're total shitheads, Dad's some moron asshole and Mum's a whingeing cunt, it doesn't make them the High Priest and Priestess of Beelzebub. They're just your average parental creeps, Carol, nothing more or less.

I'm getting a little bit pissed off by now, Carol's drinking all my Scotch and I'm surprised she's bothering to keep this bullshit act going for so long.

— I was abused and I know it, she says, sniffing. — Marian said people would try and deny my reality —

— Who's Marian? Your shrink?

Carol nods.

— She's a sick bitch, Carol, face it. What kind of pervert is she to put these things into your head?

— She didn't put anything in there! Carol stands up and just about screams it at me. — It's all here! Here, here, here!

She starts banging her head with her fists and crying. Holy Jesus, I wasn't prepared for this. I'm finding it a bit spooky, I've got to admit.

— I'm sorry, I say, — fuck, Carol —

— Don't say that word! she screeches, — don't say it, you don't know what it means, you're a pawn, Billy, a victim, a henchman!

I try and put my arm around her but she throws me off. She goes and slumps down in the corner, crying. I pour myself some Scotch. Fuck, I need it. This is crazy. This is just some crazy shit.

— Carol . . .

I stop. I don't say anything. We sit in silence for a while, then she gets up and straightens herself and lights her last cigarette, always a sign she's going to leave.

— God, Billy, do you have to have all those pictures of James Dean all over the place? Don't you get sick of them? Why don't you ever open a window?

I don't even answer this. About the only real fight we ever had was when she tried to tell me James Dean was a fag. Bull fucking shit.

— Could I borrow some money? I feel bad asking her, especially now, but God knows Mario or Luigi or whoever that greasy bastard is gives her enough to play with. It's not like she spends it on food. She sighs, and takes a twenty out of her pocket.

— Why don't you get a job?

— Drama Centre. No point telling her I quit. — Thanks.

— When did you last have a job, Billy?

— Don't start with me.

She comes over to me and kisses me on the lips.

— Keep your pretty head low, she says.

I start to say something but she's gone.

I am just waiting for the day when she sticks her tongue in my mouth during her goodbye kiss. I fucking dream about that day, her soft mouth and her wet tongue and her skinny legs, treating me like she used to when we were too young to know better. One day it's got to happen but it better be soon, at this rate the next place I'll be visiting Carol is the loony bin. In the meantime it's just me and my fantasies, fucking around and around in my head.

— You're tearing me apart.

That's James Dean, in *East of Eden*.

— You're tearing me apart.

I watch it all weekend.

And it's weird, I guess it's a coincidence, I'm in the same café and there's that girl again, the one who thinks I'm some strange-o lone wolf. She's on her own this time, which is kind of a neat twist. The place is packed so I've got a good excuse when I ask to share her table. She looks at me in that way like she's trying to pretend I'm just another person, she's never seen me before. But I know and she knows and she knows I know. I watch her while she's reading her book. She doesn't like this. Finally she cracks.

— Is there something wrong?

— No, I say, — you look familiar, that's all.

She's really hating this. She glances around to see if there's another table free. Bad luck, babe, you're stuck with me.

— I don't think I know you, she says slowly, then goes back to her book, really cool like she's got everything sussed, I don't faze her. But I can see her eyes and they're glued to the same words, she's not reading anything, this book thing's not going anywhere.

— My name's Billy, I say. — I do have a name.

She puts her book down and looks me in the eye. I have to say I admire her for this. I can tell she's weighing it up, talk to the freak or chicken out.

— I'm Karen.

I like a girl who can rise to a challenge. Karen, that's nice. She's not as skinny as Carol but there's a similarity there.

— Hi, Karen, I say, and smile. — Bye, Karen.

And I leave her there, keep her guessing, thinking any time I want I can go back to this café and she'll be there, it's fine, she's here for me now.

There are about eight messages from my mother. On the last three of them, she's crying. This is probably the exact response that Carol's after — she was always better at achieving it than me. I'm pissed off with my mother for taking this whole thing so seriously — can't she just get a life? Dad'll be on her back, what did you do wrong, you're a useless mother, why do your children hate you? Convenient memory loss on his part.

Then this was the week we would have started rehearsing our final production from the drama course. Fucking Lucinda. They'll be doing some horror, some crap expressionist thing with everyone in whiteface. Now *Streetcar* — if they were doing that, I'd spit. I practise in the mirror — Stella! Stella! I've got it down. I wish I was living in hot sweaty New Orleans instead of this dumb fuck cold town. Nothing's happening, nothing's happening, nothing's happening. Nothing's happening.

I have this dream where I'm in a cupboard with Carol. We're kids, just young, and we're in this cupboard together and I really like it, I feel good, you know, here I am and I've got Carol all to myself and it's kind of fun in the dark. But then I get the idea that we're stuck here, we can't get out, and I start to get scared. I start crying, like a real baby, and I'm so scared and I want whoever put us in here to let us out now, I'm fucking panicking, shit, then Carol isn't Carol any more, she's fucking Lucinda and she's laughing and laughing and she's got this big clown mouth laughing and laughing and I wake up shit scared, breathing fast, clammy, with my blankets all twisted around me. This has got to be a joke.

Darling Billy (this is what the letter says)

You've always been the only one who understands me, the only one I can trust. I love you. But I can't take you down this road with me. Some scary stuff's going to come up and the best thing is to leave you out of it. Marian says I need to do this on my own. I'm going away for a bit to work out exactly what I want to do. I don't know if everything will be all right or not. Just please take care of yourself. I can't tell you not to talk to them but it'll be better if you don't.

   I know you probably think this is part of my victim act but I'm not going to be a victim of this, Billy, I'm a survivor, I promise. Be one too.

                    love Carol.

She is such a drama queen. Who's them? She must mean Mum and Dad. This is getting ridiculous. I could kill her fucking shrink.

So, because there seems less and less to do with my days and I've got to get out of the house so I don't have to hear my mother shrieking on the answer machine for the thirty-seventh time, I go to the café. I walk up and down the street outside it first, looking in, trying to see if Karen's there. It gets too miserable to stay outside so I go in, I can't see her anywhere but I get a coffee anyway, read Carol's letter over and over, imagine Marian standing behind her while she writes it, talking that stupid shrink-speak — you can do it, Carol, this is empowering, visualize yourself in a safe environment — Carol wouldn't know a fucking safe environment if she was on a witness protection programme. Witless protection is what she needs. I hate shrinks, I hate them, especially fucking losers like Marian who can't stop messing with other people's lives. The one time I saw a shrink — my father forced me, he thought I was a fag and I didn't bother telling him otherwise — she tried to get me to talk to a chair. Fuck that shit. Pretend the chair is your father, she told me, now is there anything you want to say to him? Yeah, Dad, get off all fours, I said, which OK isn't that funny, but she got really pissed off. Don't you think you should overcome your fear of embarrassment? she said. Oh, I said, is that what I'm here to overcome? Silly me, I thought it was my fear of fucking women that we were working through here, bitch, and by the way have you got teeth up there under that tweed skirt? Bet you do. She kicked me out, of course, told me I was a very sick boy and needed help that she wasn't qualified to give. Funny how people think they can handle anything until you get them where they live. At least it got my fat fuck father off my case.

The waitress is looking at me weird. What the fuck's the matter?

It's not as if I don't have any friends anyway. I could have friends if I wanted, it's just the losers that inhabit this town aren't worth my time and effort. Carol's my friend. I mean, she is my sister, too, but it goes beyond that. Carol would be my friend even if we were raised in different families. And from everything she's saying now, it looks like that might be the way it was. It's not as if I never had a girlfriend either. I did have a girlfriend at high school, which seems to me about the only time in your life when it matters whether or not you have one. Mum and Dad didn't know about her because there was no need for them to know, they only would've wanted to meet her and that would have been a force fucking ten disaster. There wasn't anything wrong with her but they would have found something. She's not our religion, Billy, she's too young, Billy, she's got dirty eyes and a dirty mouth, Billy. She did too. That was about all we bothered with really, that and wandering through the hills behind school looking for other people's roaches to smoke. She used to hassle me, tell me I was just a mixed-up middle-class boy with nothing to do. Lucy, Lucy. Juicy Luce. Her family moved town. I got a couple of letters and then nothing. I wonder if I could find her now. She's probably fat with three kids on the dole.

Carol's first boyfriend, though — I do remember him. The first one that mattered. I was fourteen, she was sixteen. I was sick with jealousy. It wouldn't have mattered so much if I'd at least liked him — but fuck he was a pretentious cunt. Drove a VW Beetle that he thought was really cool — had some idiot name for it — and used to come round and call me pal while Carol stuck her diaphragm in in the bathroom. It was so unfair, he was such a prick, and at night I had to lie in bed listening to them get one last poke in outside Carol's bedroom window. She used to moan and carry on, not too loud in case Mum and Dad heard, but enough to make him think he was the hottest thing in baggy trousers. Sometimes she'd climb in my window — I never knew if it was by mistake, or she was drunk, or what — and I could smell her all drink and sex and cigarettes. Once I didn't pretend to stay asleep and she sat on my bed and talked. I even managed to choke my pride and asked what it was like. I could see her roll her eyes in the dimness and she said, Oh — you know, Billy — everything it's cracked up to be. But her voice was flat and hollow. And after Baggy Trousers there was Jeff and he was even worse, and after Jeff there was another and another until she met Mario or Luigi and he introduced her to all his friends and she stopped limiting herself to just one at a time.

When I get home from the café I see my mother's car parked outside my building. Shit. There's got to be a way of avoiding this. There is. I turn around, like somebody pretending they've forgotten something so it doesn't look as if they've got lost or gone the wrong way, and walk down to the river. It's the usual scene of scuzzy tramps and teenage petrol sniffers, only tonight I don't accept anyone's offer of a mouthful of brown muck. I sit on a broken concrete post, my arse getting colder as the night gets darker, and think about Marlon. How could you get so fat and gross, Marlon? How could you start wearing kaftans and that stupid pony-tail? God, he used to be so beautiful. I don't know, that better-to-burn-out stuff seems to make sense when I think about him. But then I look over at one group of kids standing right down by the river, passing a plastic bag between them and it gives me the shits. They're not going down in a blaze of glory. They're not going anywhere. They'll probably never even leave this dumbass place. Dumb. Ass.

Some days go by and I don't hear any more from Carol. I don't hear any more from my mother either, thank Christ. She's probably locked herself in her room and praying her guts out. It's only in the gap of their silence that I wonder why I haven't heard anything from my father about this. I'd have thought he'd be the first on my case, asking what this nonsense was all about, did I put Carol up to it, push me around the room a little bit, then try and hold my hand and make me ask forgiveness from the Lord for being such a little shit. When I imagine this I realize how lucky I am that he's not around hounding me. I make a decision not to pick up the phone or answer the door. But nobody rings and nobody knocks. Why isn't he calling me? It seems like a bad tactic, like an admission of something. There's no way I believe that weirdo sex-on-the-altar-candles-and-bones rubbish that Carol's claiming to remember, but maybe there was something else. Maybe there was something that just went on with her.

I'm in town standing in the street just outside the café, wondering whether or not to go in, when the door opens and she just about walks into me.

— Karen, I say. — Hi.

She looks at me blank and then I see her remember who I am.

— Hi, she says. She looks over her shoulder and I hope that idiot friend of hers isn't coming out behind her, but there's no one there. She looks at her watch. She starts walking and I walk with her.

— What are you up to? I say.

— Oh, nothing much. I'm just going to visit a friend.

She's trying to brush me off. How can I stop her? I really want to talk to her, to get to know her properly. She looks like she'd be good to talk to, like she's different from the other stupid schmucks around here, like she'd understand how things are.

— Um, Karen — She's gotten a few steps ahead of me down the street and she stops and turns round.

— Yes? and there's anger and impatience in her voice, fuck, she just thinks I'm a weirdo twister, how am I going to get through to her, how can I make her see?

— Do you want to, um . . . ?

— What, she says, and she's biting her tongue I can tell, she's thinking why is this fuckwit talking to me in the street, I don't even know him, why did I tell him my name?

Fuck, I think. Piss. — Nothing, I say, and she makes a dismissive half-wave with her hand and keeps on walking. I stand there for a while. It's after five and the street's filling up with people leaving work. I can still see her up by the movie complex and without really thinking about it I start to follow her.

*

I was careful. I sat on the same bus as her and she didn't even see me. I got off when she did and stood around the corner while she went to the dairy. I watched her come out with the paper and a carton of milk and I saw her go across the road and into her house. I know where she lives.

I'm on my way to the café again, to see if she's there — I'm not going to talk to her this time, just want to see her — and I hear someone calling my name.

— Billy! Hi!

It's the fat girl from the Drama Centre. She's running over the road towards me. She just about gets hit by a car, the fat slob idiot — and here she is, grinning at me like a maniac.

— How are you? like we're bosom buddies. I give her a look of disgust but it washes right over her fat pink face. She's so enthusiastic, what's she got to be enthusiastic about?

— Everyone's been wondering how you are, what happened to you — we had a couple of group meetings so we could all work through what you did in class that day, but I think we've all come to terms with it. Oh, it's so good to see you, what are you doing? The others will be dying to know. Have you lost weight? You look so thin!

I look at her in amazement. If she doesn't stop gushing on me I'll puke on her shoes. How can she even ask somebody else about their weight without wanting to die of embarrassment? She takes my look for something entirely different.

— Oh, Billy, you don't need to feel bad about what happened — I forgive you, I really do, and I know Lucinda has too. You felt a lot of pressure, anyone could see that, and clowning is a very big challenge.

I want to laugh. If clowning's a big challenge then standing in the street listening to this idiot rave is the biggest of them all. She's the big challenge, stupid Ginger with her fat arms and her orange hair. She's still going. I can't believe this girl.

— and then, if you're not ready to explore, it can create an almost aggressive environment, you were only reacting against that, it's obvious, and now Lucinda's got over her feelings of inadequacy that she had because she couldn't reach you — you should come back and see us, Billy, the production finishes this weekend — come and say hi, just drop in, we'd all love to know what you're up to now.

I am truly touched. Those creeps. It's taking a lot of effort not to say anything but if I do there'll be trouble, I know, and I don't want to destroy Ginge right here in the street. She squeezes my arm and I'm just about sick, then she looks deep into my eyes.

— You really have talent, Billy. I really believe that. Don't give it up.

Then — this is the worst part — she kisses my cheek. I rub it off as she squeezes me again and says, Take care. I watch her fat back and elephant legs bounce down the street in shock. She's wearing the stupid Drama Centre sweatshirt with a picture of the sad mask and the happy mask, and underneath it says, There's method in our madness! Christ. Thank God I got out of there before I turned into one of those earnest born-again type crazies. By now I'm too depressed to go into the café, too depressed to look for Karen. I just go home.

And there it all is again, my flat, the mess, the answer machine with one message — the video shop telling me *Eden* and *Rebel* are weeks late, as if I didn't know. The phone rings and I let the machine pick it up. There's a hesitation after my message, and then someone hangs up. Carol. Damn. Where the fuck is she?

I don't leave the flat for a few days, hoping she'll ring again, ordering delivery Chink food and watching Dean until I can do the whole thing myself, backwards. Natalie Wood reminds me of Karen. I think about her, too, remember her street, the bus ride over the bridge to her house, the shabby suburb she lives in, shabby but OK in a not too arty kind of way. I think about her in her house, walking around, taking a bath, talking on the phone. I wonder what she does. I wonder when I'll see her again. Then one afternoon I get up, groggy, and there's a letter under the door. The envelope says, To Billy from Carol, like it's a note on a Christmas present or something.

Billy. I've spoken to Louise and told her what I want.

It takes me a while to figure out who Louise is, then I realize she's talking about our mother.

She's agreed to come and see Marian with me. We need to talk about this as a family. The idea of even being in the same room as her scares me, but I know it's some-

thing that has to be done. The only way she will face this is if we talk about it, and I can only do that with Marian in the room. I've asked her to bring Ken but I don't know if he'll come. He's very angry with me and he's a very influential man, Billy, so be careful. These people are everywhere. You just don't know.

Her writing's all spindly and shaky. I smell the letter but it doesn't smell of Carol, just of paper.

I want you to come too, Billy. It will help you to re-member. This is the most important thing I've ever asked you to do. If you love me, I'll see you there.

And in the envelope is also a card with an address and a time on it. Tomorrow. I don't like this. I don't like it at all.

I try to write a letter to Karen but it's no good. Can't say what I feel. I end up just writing her name out, with mine, over and over and over again. We will be together, soon. It's nearly the right time. We're going to save each other from this shit-heap.

So this is as far down as it's gone — further than I could have imagined was possible — and now here I am. God, it's like I can pinpoint everything back to that damn fuck drama class, when something gave somewhere and the stench really started to seep in. I can't decide what to do. I get right up to the building where Carol's shrink works without knowing if I'm going in or not. I spent a lot of last night imagining the scene, and it always took place in a high brick building with wooden-floored offices inside. I'd stand by the window looking out, while Carol and our parents threw allegations and insults at each other. Finally I'd turn around, give Marian and Louise and Ken a withering look of disgust, take Carol by the hand and lead her out with me, into my car which is waiting to take us to some big city, where we live in freedom without any bullshit.

But now I'm here in front of it, and it's a low-slung prefab-type building, you can imagine, cork notice-boards with sad old 'does any-one want to buy some puppies', or 'youthlink — meet interesting young people' messages on them. And retards shuffling around in slippers, twitching, and women like Lucinda making cups of herbal tea and being patronizing. It makes me laugh to think of my parents stuck in there, sitting in a circle with Carol and her stupid shrink. It makes me feel sick, too. Dad'll probably have a fucking stroke. I didn't have to leave the army you know, he'll shout, again, I did it for my family, I could have been a Major — yeah, right, Dad, you already are, Major Asshole. And your lovely wife, Mrs Asshole. Oh, I'm tired of this. Standing outside this building feels familiar to me, like standing outside buildings is something I've done all my life. I smoke half a pack of cigarettes I've bought specially for the occasion, and I leave.

I feel like an asshole for ditching Carol like this, but fuck. She can't seriously expect me to go through with it. It's not even so much having to listen to all the crap Marian's going to talk, or to Carol reeling off these fantasy atrocities of hers, or my father clearing his throat and my mother crying softly. It's the thought of all the stuff they'll want to dredge up, the shit they'll want to sift through, trying to prove they were perfect parents, trying to prove their innocence. And Dad might be angry but Carol's angry too, angry and out for some revenge. I don't want to have to hear it.

I wander around for a bit, feeling as if I'm at the end of something. I don't know what it is but not going into that building feels like more than I know. I think about going back to my flat but I don't want to do that. I don't want to watch those videos again, I don't want to sleep, I don't want to think about what I'm going to do tomorrow. What am I going to do tomorrow? I can't think of anything I would want to do.

I see a bus coming and I get on it. It goes across the bridge. It's a sign. All in the timing. Karen. There's got to be a way of getting through to her. I know I could talk to her, try and explain, and she'd listen to me. I think if she got to know me she'd like me, too. I'm sure she would. Here's her stop. I get off and remember the way to her house. I'm just going to stand outside it and look at it, imagine her, maybe pretend to bump into her when she gets home. Maybe she already is home. I walk up to the door and knock, afraid she's going to answer it, afraid she's not going to answer it. I lean my head against the cold wood of the door. Nobody comes. I go around the side of the house and see what must be the bathroom window. I take the louvres out and climb in.

*

It smells nice in here, in Karen's house, clean and nice. I walk around looking at her things, posters of ethnic-looking prints, rugs, old pots and shit. She's kind of a hippy, I guess. Well, that's okay. There's not much in the fridge. Maybe she doesn't look after herself properly. I eat some leftover rice but it's cold and hard. I find her room. By her bed there's a table with photographs on it. Karen by the Taj Mahal, Karen with her arms around a dog, Karen with some idiot-looking guy. That friend of hers from the café's there too. I rip a bit out of the picture so the guy's not in it any more. That's better. I lie on the bed for a bit. Smell the pillow. Girl smell. Mustn't fall asleep. There's a scarf draped over the foot of the bed. I pick it up and run it through my fingers. Soft. Wrap it round my hand for later.

I open her wardrobe door. There's the skirt she was wearing the first day I saw her, and the coat she had on when I followed her home. They smell sort of musty like hippies' clothes smell, love oil or whatever that crap is they use. We can talk when she gets home, talk, then maybe go to a movie or something, or go to my place and watch videos. I wouldn't mind seeing them with her. And when Carol's better she can meet Karen and maybe we could all go away somewhere together. A big city, yeah, or the other side of the world even. In a car. The three of us. That'd be good.

I climb into Karen's wardrobe and shove her shoes in the corner so I can sit down on her floor. I pull the door closed so it's dark. Sometimes I wonder if I've been a fool with my life. But right now this is all I want to do, sit here in Karen's wardrobe in the dark, bits of hard rice in the side of my mouth, Karen's clothes brushing against my face.

Waiting for her to come and find me.

The Shared Experience

EMILY PERKINS

These are her options.

1. Drive away. The keys are in the ignition. He's in the back of a long queue waiting to pay for the petrol. The car's an expensive one. She could get a lot of money for it. Quietly open her door, take the petrol pump out of the car, get in the driver's side and take off with a full tank. Drive as far as you can, to the nearest port. Sell the car to someone who doesn't want to see the papers. Get on a boat. Disappear.
2. Stay in the car. Go to the hotel. Feign exhaustion. Order food up to her room, have a bath, go to bed alone.
3. Stay in the car. Go to the hotel. Cross the line that's been waiting to be crossed all day. Become the sort of woman who sleeps with her boss.

He comes back to the car, folding the receipt into his wallet. She sits politely in the passenger seat, hands crossed in her lap. Say goodbye to Option 1.

He starts the car and pulls out into the traffic. He jerks his seatbelt over his shoulder. The buckle won't do up.

— Can you?

She twists in her seat and tries to jam the buckle into the things it's supposed to jam into. His left hand moves over, as if to help. It's big and dry and covers both of her hands. She feels the flush starting at her throat and moving round to the back of her neck. She has a tendency to go blotchy when embarrassed. She hopes he doesn't notice.

The buckle finally clicks into place and he moves his hand back to the steering wheel. She turns round to face front and presses the button to unwind her window. Pushing her sunglasses up on her nose, she sneaks a look at his hands, their casual touch on the wheel. Big hands. Big hands with a big gold wedding ring on one of them. When she went to America she wore a ring on her wedding finger, a cheap imitation number she'd picked up from a street stall. Her sister told her it was bad luck, that if you wore a ring on that finger without being married, it meant you never would be. Her sister's authority on luck was questionable, as she was married at the time to a man called Dwayne who spent all his money on gambling and had no sense of humour. This seemed like a fate far worse than spinsterhood, but she didn't say so to her sister. The fake American wedding ring seems ridiculous now, a flimsy attempt to shield herself from physical or emotional danger. She laughs.

— What's funny?

She can't tell him she's thinking about wedding rings.

— Nothing.

— You're a strange one.

Why did men feel compelled to say things like that to her? Really and truly. What a horrible thing to say. You're a strange one — it's not the kind of thing you'd ever say to someone you considered an equal, is it? Well, so, he's never going to leave his wife for her. It doesn't mean Option 3 couldn't still happen.

He clears his throat. — Do you mind if I put a tape on?

— No.

This'll be it. If it's *Eric Clapton Unplugged* she's definitely not going to bed with him. In fact the list of tapes that would put her off him is potentially endless. *Yodelling Favourites. Ravel's Bolero. Twenty Big Band Hits.* Anything played by Kenny Gee.

— Do you want to find one? They're in the glove box.

Oh shit. Shit shit shit. This way it's her own taste on the line — at least, her choice of his selection. She opens the glove box and yes, it's her worst nightmare. Next to the maps and a tube of toothpaste (toothpaste?) are five or six tapes of classical music. Does it have to be this way? She knows next to nothing about classical music. It occupies the same place in her head as wine lists, or the inside of car engines. Things she can't concentrate on long enough to ever figure out. OK, don't panic, breathe. What have we got here? Mozart, Mozart, Haydn, Beethoven, Handel. Mozart's nice, isn't he? What's the difference between Haydn and Handel? Opus? What does that even mean? She pulls out a tape at random. Beethoven. The deaf guy. OK then, here we go.

Big dark booming notes bounce around the car.

— Jesus, says her boss. — That's a bit grim.

— Yeah, sorry, she says, and presses stop. The tape won't eject and she pushes and pushes the button desperately till it pops out.

— I don't know what that tape's doing there, he says. — I haven't heard it in years.

— What one do you want?

— Oh, you choose.

This is starting to feel like a challenge. She grabs one of the Mozart tapes and shoves it in the tape deck. She turns to the window again, hot with embarrassment and anger.

— That's nice, he says, and she feels a bit better. The countryside rolls past and she starts to feel much better. The tape crisis is over, and now they don't have to talk.

They arrive in the town where the meeting is going to be held just as it's getting dark. Standing at the reception desk in the hotel, she is struck by the full force of the romance of the situation. Here they are, checking into a hotel together. Sure, they're getting separate rooms and they're here on business and they're not lying to the receptionist about their last names, but still — anything could happen. She stands just behind her boss while he does the talking with the woman at the desk. He passes her a key. She turns it over and over, feeling the cool outline of its ridges warming up in her hand, the embossed 13F on the tag.

She follows him down the hall, clutching her small weekend bag, trying to take in the old wallpaper and gilt-framed paintings and thick carpets without losing her blasé expression. She could probably count the number of hotels she's stayed in on one hand. She steps into the lift. He presses the button for their floor. The silence in the lift is excruciating. Say something, say something, she tells herself. There must be something to say. The lift stops. They check their keys.

— I think, right . . . and the . . . He could be talking to himself. She pretends not to notice.

Her room is right next to his. They stand in front of their respective doors. She looks at her shoes.

— Have you got everything ready for tomorrow?

— Yes, she says, — I've just got to sort some papers together.

— Mm, yes, I've got a couple of calls I'd better make and then I thought I'd grab a bite. We may as well eat downstairs. Half an hour?

He's inside his room with the door shut before he's finished talking, before she says, OK. She puts her hand to her face and feels how hot it is. She lets herself into her room.

It's small, just a double bed next to a window looking on to the wall of the next building. There's a door leading to a shower cubicle, basin and toilet. She washes her hands and lies down on the bed. Through the wall by her head she can hear him talking. She shuts her eyes and feels a rush of tiredness, and something like nausea. She sits up and blinks, dizzy. There's not enough oxygen in here. She kicks her shoes off, enjoying the thump they make as they hit the floor. When she was a teenager she used to throw her shoes against the wall of her bedroom just to listen to the sound of it.

Should she change for dinner? The clothes she's been wearing in the car all day feel sticky and gross, but maybe changing would look like she was making too much effort. Perhaps one thing. She decides to keep her skirt and change her top. She takes the papers for tomorrow's meeting out of her bag and spreads them out on the floor. Can't be fucked sorting through them now. Her own company is making her tired. She takes a small bottle of vodka out of her bag and has a couple of mouthfuls. Drinking with inferiors again, she thinks, and laughs. She'd better be careful.

The shower's a dribbly contraption with water that runs only extremely hot or extremely cold. She shivers under it for a minute and gets out. Drying herself, she has an idea. Maybe she shouldn't wear any knickers. Wouldn't it be exciting not to, in a private and slightly scary kind of way? But it would make her even more self-conscious than she already is. She can imagine getting a kick out of it though, feeling powerful and secretive as she toys with her linguine. Though if anything happens between them later, he'll know and he might think she's overly forward. Unless he's the kind of man who likes that. Maybe she'd feel too vulnerable. And then, if nothing does happen, she'll feel like an idiot. Of course, nobody ever needs to know. Option 3, Option 3, she sings to her reflection in the steamed-up mirror. No. It's stupid. He's her boss, for goodness sake. They've got to work tomorrow. She should be preparing for this meeting instead of fantasizing about his big hands and his pin-striped suit. This is just a power displacement thing. She should want to screw him figuratively, get his job or something, not literally. That's not going to get her anywhere. Besides, he's married. How can she even be considering this? Has she got no scruples at all? She could at least pretend to have a moral dilemma about this. But the only dilemma she's having is whether or not to put on her underwear. Well. That settles it. She puts her clothes back on, including her bra and knickers, and brushes her hair.

There, a nicely presented young woman. Competent, attractive, and desperate. She must be desperate, to have fixated on her boss like this. He is good-looking, there's no doubt about that. But surely she should be looking for someone from her own peer group? Well, it's obvious why she isn't. They're all fatuous, self-obsessed, undirected, confused, emotional retards. Whereas her boss, her managing director — she loves those words! — is nothing like that. He's young for his position — he must be driven, focused. And he's interesting, isn't he, and knowledgeable? She lights a cigarette and sits back down on the bed. So what if he is, and so what if he isn't? She's fascinated by him the same way she's mesmerized in the menswear sections of department stores. She can wander around them for hours, hypnotised by the umbrellas and wallets and canes and gloves. The ties, the hats, the pipes. The smell — no, the *idea* of the smell — of tobacco and leather and shoe polish. She loves it. She loves it all, and she wants to get close to it.

She hears his door shut. Stubs out her cigarette and fans the air. There's a knock on her door. Coming, she calls. She looks in the mirror. Fuck it, she's going to take a risk. Why the fuck not? She hitches up her skirt, takes off her knickers, and throws them in the corner of the room. There. She smooths her skirt down and smiles. She's still smiling as she opens the door, looks her managing director straight in the eye, and walks with him down to the restaurant.

*

It probably started at her interview for the job, the first time she shook his hand and smiled her job-interview smile and asked herself what it was he was looking for. But the moment she knew it was there was when she read back a fax she'd typed for him arranging an appointment. Instead of 'if this suits' she'd written 'if his suits'. And as soon as she saw the words she knew they were a sign. If his suits were under her hands. If his suits were pressed against her cheek. If his suits hung in neat rows in his wardrobe. If his suits ever came off. She didn't talk to anyone about this new way she had of looking at him as he sat at his desk. Watching him on the telephone, or in meetings. Dressing for him every day. When she went drinking with other girls from work she kept her mouth shut as they speculated about his marriage, his past, his private life. Because she worked the closest with him, they accorded her a certain respect, but she could tell that her silence irritated them. She didn't care. She'd get quietly drunk and go home and get more drunk and go to bed and dream, drunkenly, about him.

— So, tell me how you find the company, he says.

Her first thought is that he means his company, here tonight, then she realizes.

— Oh, it's good, she says. — I'm enjoying it.

— Not too stuffy?

— Well, they are a bit, she says. — Not everyone, I mean. But, mm. She trails off.

— Yes, well, he says, and laughs. — Wine?

— Yes, please.

— Red all right?

— Sure. You choose, she thinks. Just don't ask me.

— Good. He orders some wine from the sullen waiter. They study the menus.

— This is on the expense account, so have whatever you like. The writing on the menu blurs in front of her eyes. Expense account. Somehow those words expose the tackiness of the situation more than anything so far, the way they conjure up images of travelling salesmen. Men with moustaches. Wife-swapping parties where the car keys get thrown in the swimming pool. The horror, the horror.

— I'll have steak, he tells the waiter, — rare.

He says the word as if it's an announcement, a declaration of his hunger. His carnivorous, bare-fanged hunger. She crosses her legs.

— I'll have the salmon, please.

— With red wine? He raises his eyebrows.

Who is this man, James Bond? — Why not?

Surely this discomfort, this nervousness, this level of tension, means there's something going on? Surely he can feel it too?

He takes off his jacket and hangs it over the back of his chair. This is really too much. She's got to stop staring at his hands, their clipped nails, the thick veins running from his knuckles back into his shirtcuffs. The thick brown leather band of his watch-strap, the thick gold band of his wedding ring.

Their wine arrives. She thanks the waiter. He doesn't. She drinks too quickly, eyes down, nearly emptying her glass.

— Cheers. He toasts vaguely in her direction. — Here's to it.

To what, to what, she wants to ask. What is this thing? What is this thing called, love? Watch it — she'll make herself laugh again. Can't have that.

— Well, I must say work's a much more pleasant place to be since you've started with us.

Did he really say that? Did she hear him right? She smiles.

— Thanks, she simpers.

— Have you ever been to America?

It's clear to her that the conversation will go wherever he leads it — it won't be appropriate for her to initiate anything. This is probably OK — it's hard to know what she could think of to say anyway.

— Once, she says, and clears her throat. Her voice is coming out funny. — I went to New York, and down to the New Orleans jazz festival. It was great.

— Yeah, it's a pretty exciting place all right. This is off the record — we're thinking of merging with another company there. In New York City actually. I'm going over next month to sound it out.

— Wow. That would be great.

God, is she reduced to this pathetic sort of platitude after everything he says? She makes herself sit up straighter.

— Yes, it could be exciting. As long as they don't swamp us.

— Is it a big company?

— I'd better not say too much. Big enough. He smiles.

She feels like a child being taught how to add with building blocks. This is the big one, see, and this one — that's smaller. Say something intelligent, she tells herself, furious.

— Would there be a staffing merge as well?

He raises his eyebrows at her. — You mean, is there a chance for free trips to the States?

She goes bright red, pulls her napkin onto her lap and twists it hard. — No, that's not —

He laughs. — I'm teasing. There may be the odd swap — I'm looking into all of that.

She feels as if she's had a sense of humour bypass. Maybe she's just too uptight to get a joke any more.

The restaurant begins to fill with other diners. Old people mostly, the odd lone businessman. What are they thinking of the two of them? What do they look like together? She hopes they look like a glamorous couple. They do suit each other, she's sure of that. She wonders what his wife looks like. She imagines blonde and gorgeous. This is daunting, but at least picture-perfect and unreal.

The salmon comes complete with bones. So unfair. She drops her fork. Did that have to happen? It's an effort to stay on her chair as she slides down to retrieve it. She's just lifting it back up to the table when the waiter brings her a new one. Red again. Blotch Girl. Lovely. Her boss eats like a guy, which is reassuring she supposes — he seems completely unselfconscious and in control. Since the fork incident the table has become an obstacle course to her — everything there only to be knocked over, or split, or hit against something else with a loud and resonant ping.

They talk about travel — he's done a lot, she very little. And opera — the same. And sailing — that too. She begins to wonder if there is a topic she knows anything about. Asks him if he likes going to the movies. It sounds like a come-on, she knows it even as she's saying it, lets her voice die away, her sentence unfinished.

— Are you all right there?

— Yes, she smiles brightly, — fine. Pull yourself together, she thinks.

At the same time she thinks it's unfair of him to draw attention to her nervousness. She's supposed to be nervous, isn't she? They both know what's in the air, on the agenda, up for grabs. Of course she's bloody nervous. Getting angry has a calming effect. She tackles her salmon again with renewed confidence. Smiles flirtatiously at the waiter when he pours her more wine. Hopes her boss notices. He doesn't. Too busy tucking into his steak. Zoltar, Ruler of the Universe. It's so easy for men.

They somehow muddle through dinner. Her most hopeful moment is when he orders a second bottle of wine. Once their plates have been cleared there is a long silence. All she can think of is touching him. She keeps her eyes down, for safety. What if she made a move? Just reached her hand over to his. She experimentally probes under the table with her foot. Nothing. His feet must be tucked under his chair. Then he leans back, stretches his legs out, and a foot collides with hers. She makes herself keep her foot there. It's a light contact but it's something. Risks a glance at him. He's looking at her. Oh boy, oh boy. She feels giddy. Drunk. Smiles. Looks away. Smiles again. Looks back. He raises his eyebrows. She's entranced by his face, his eyes, his jaw, his mouth. Wants to kiss him. Feels immobile. Opens her mouth to say something. Has no words. Closes it again.

— Didn't you do something funny at university? he asks. — Horticulture or something?

She nods, bewildered. She must have mentioned it at work. — A couple of papers.

— I should introduce you to my wife, he says. — She's a very keen gardener.

Jesus, that was out of left field. She manages a smile.— Oh really.

— Yes. We have a beautiful garden.

What is he raving about? — Excuse me a minute, she says.

She heads towards the bathroom and at the last minute veers off towards the lifts. She falls into one, back into the corner, mouth open, head throbbing. Turns to face herself in the mirrored wall. Christ. Her lipstick's all eaten off. At least she hasn't got food in her teeth. She staggers to her room, jabs at the lock with her key, gets in, retrieves her knickers from their landing place by the waste-paper basket, drags them on, falling back on her bed in the process — pulls herself up, smears more lipstick on and goes back down to the restaurant.

— Are you OK?

— Yes, thanks, she says. How long has she been gone from the table? It felt like seconds but maybe it was unnaturally long. She dabs at the corners of her mouth, hoping he'll attribute her absence to bulimia. She shifts in her chair, feeling happier now that she's fully clothed, feeling stronger.

He pours out the last of the wine. Coughs. Says, — Do you mind if I smoke?

— Not at all, she says with relief. At last she can light up herself. He's not going to pull out a cigar is he? No. Thank God. He passes her the lighter. Now is her chance. She lets her fingers brush against his. They look at each other. She can feel the pulse knocking in the base of her throat. Don't blotch, she tells herself, just don't. She lights her cigarette with trembling hands. Light-headed. Feels queasy, almost. That salmon was too rich.

— We must get you on some more interesting projects, he says. — You're a bright girl.

Oh, please, she thinks. — That'd be good.

Doesn't want to talk about work. Doesn't want to talk at all. The waiter comes over, asks if they'd like anything else.

— Cognac? he asks her.

What's the right answer? Yes, stay and have more to drink, or no, go straight to his room? They are going to his room, aren't they? This can't end in nothing. She tries to look noncommittal.

— Two cognacs, he says to the waiter.

And two become four, and four become six. Blurry. Slurring words. A lot of cigarettes. Somewhere between the second and third cognac he reaches under the table and puts his hand on her knee. She's too drunk to blush any more. Blinks slowly. Puts her hand on his hand. Moves her fingers over it, tries to ignore the fucking wedding ring. Just avoids that part of the hand, the way you avoid touching a pimple on someone's back, or a coldsore on their mouth. Watching his two faces, she has to keep herself from squinting in an attempt to bring him into focus.

The waiter hovers. He doesn't even look up.

— Could we have the bill, please.

He slides his hand out from between her hand and her knee, finds his wallet. Takes out a card, puts it on the table.

— What do you think? he says.

She smiles. — What do you think?

— I asked first.

— I think . . . She lights another cigarette, stalling. The waiter brings the receipt back and he signs it.

— I think I'm drunk. The words don't seem as gauche and uncharming to her now as they will when she remembers them later. If she remembers them.

He smiles. — So am I. Shall we go?

Standing up is a bit tricky. She follows him out through the restaurant like an air hostess, steadying herself on the backs of chairs as she passes. Things begin to fragment here. Flashes of consciousness, moments of blackness. It's as if a light somewhere is being turned on and off at random. Through the reception area. Slippery floor. Don't slip on the floor. The lift. He kisses her in the lift. She feels tired. The awkwardness of standing outside his door while he tries to find his key.

In his room. They're both in his room. It's dark. What if she throws up? He's unlacing his shoes, unbuttoning his shirt. Isn't she supposed to be doing that for him? Come here, he says, and she sits gingerly on the bed next to him. Did she fall over on the way up here? Her knee hurts. He kisses her. She can smell the aftershave smell of him, and smoke. Then they're, you know, fooling around. She feels very uncoordinated. It's kind of nice though. In a far-off sort of a way. Soon it's all happening, the clothes are off, the sheets are off, she's in an out-of-town hotel room doing it with her boss. Oh boy. Shouldn't there be a condom here somewhere? Oh. There is already. She must have missed that bit. How embarrassing. She must have blacked out because a few minutes later she has a sense of time passing and he's still there on top of her, grinding away. This is excruciating. She makes an effort to wake up and get into it. A big effort. Why is she so detached? Oh come on, come on, get it over with. This seems like it's been going on forever.

It does go on forever, and then it stops. She lies there thinking about her room, thinking she should go back to it. The energy involved in dragging herself out of bed and running to her room with her bundle of clothes seems impossible. She'll just lie here a little bit more. Just a little bit, then she'll go. Her mouth is dry. She's vaguely aware of her boss next to her in the bed, naked, hairy, snoring. How can she ever go back to work for him now? Yuck. As she falls into a stupor, the thought passes through her mind that if he brought condoms, then he must have had some idea of something.

Somewhere in her coma she hears the phone ringing. A light snaps on. Her boss sits bolt upright. He grabs the phone. Doesn't look at her.

— Yes? Hello?

She can hear a woman's voice, faintly, and a child crying, less faintly.

— All right, put her on. Darling? It's Daddy. Hello. Was it a bad dream?

This seems like an opportune moment to leave. Keeping her head down, she grabs her clothes and keys from the floor where they're all jumbled in with his. Remembers to get her earrings from the table — a mistake she's made before, losing jewellery — though she had no memory of taking these off. She shuts the door behind her, not looking back at him, feeling like shit.

Now here she is in the hallway with no clothes on. A nightmare made real. Which door is hers? Her eyes can't focus enough to read the letters. Oh bugger, these aren't her room keys. They're his fucking car keys. Oh Christ. Why her? Why? She performs a crouching half-run up and down the hall, checking for any sign of life. Shivering, she knocks lightly on his door. No answer. She can hear him still talking on the phone. Did he hear her knock? — maybe not. But it's so unbearable to have to make a noise. She takes a deep breath and knocks again, slightly louder. This is hell. People go to the theatre to laugh at things like this. A fucking farce. Why doesn't he come to the door? Why? Help me, help me. This is desperate. Her face burning more than ever before in her life, she hammers on the door. She wants to call out, Let me in, but what if someone hears? Her feet are freezing. Then to the right she hears the lift bell ding and knows she's going to be caught naked and drunk and post-sex in the hallway. It's too much. She dives from the door to the stairwell. It bangs shut behind her just in time. Through the smoked glass she sees a couple weaving down the hall, arm in arm, to their room. Kissing. Then she sees his door open and her boss looking out into the hallway. For some reason she shrinks back against the wall so he doesn't spot her. He looks bleary and tired and intensely irritated. Irritated with her. What a mess. How can she go through with it? How can she go through with the meeting tomorrow, with the drive back to the city, with the next days and weeks and months typing that bloody bastard's boring bloody memos? Never able to tell anyone. Never able to relax. She watches as he closes the door.

Shit, it's cold. Her hands are numb. She scrambles into her clothes, skin crawling with the awful itch of putting her legs back into day-old stockings, the awkward hooks of her stupid bra, the ashtray stink of her hair as it falls around her face. The taste in her mouth. Her too-tight skirt and her too-high heels. She's never going to wear anything but jeans ever again. She opens the door, wincing as it squeaks. Pushes the button for the lift, checking over her shoulder that no one's coming.

Thirteen floors down and she's felling nauseous, her head starting to throb in a sharp and painful way. She staggers out into the reception area, nearly going over on her ankle in these mindless shoes. She makes her way to the desk. They must have a spare key to her room. Presses the buzzer, hears it ringing back in the office behind the desk. Waits. So tired. Suddenly hungry. McDonald's. A big greasy hamburger oozing fat and sauce. Chips caked with salt. A Coke. Where are these people? She holds the buzzer down for a few seconds and leans forward on the desk, rests her head on it, arms hanging slackly by her sides. Feels the pulse in her temple against the marble desktop. Oh for God's sake. She thumps the buzzer again, bashes it with her fist, the tinny ringing of it making her more angry every time. What, are they all asleep? Watching the wrestling on TV? Drunk? Hello? Fuck it, she'll sleep in the car. It can't get any worse than this.

She stumbles around the car park as if it's happening to someone else. One day this might be a funny story to tell someone. Not right now, but it probably has potential. Spice up the sexy details a bit. God, she'd have to make it sound worth it. Where is his goddamn car? What she'd like to do now is take her shoe to the paintwork of every one of these big fat sleek self-satisfied automatic four-wheel drive kiddie-proof stereophonic convertible tinted-window monstrosities. She could do some pretty good damage, scrape them up, put in a couple of dents. She goes to touch one of the cars, feel just what sort of kick it is these guys get out of them, when she gets too close and its alarm goes off, shrill and angry in the darkness. She jumps back as if she's been shouted at. Hits the ground, crawls between two other cars to hide, stockings ripping on the concrete. Shit. Please no one come. Shhh, shhh. The alarm sounds as if it's coming from inside her head. Shut up, shut up. She's too scared to look out over the cars to see if anyone's heard. There must be security guys all over this place. Bangs her head back against the car behind her. Just about brains herself on the door handle. Wait a minute, this is it. His car. Fantastic. She kisses the door. Breathes out at last. Sleep, soon she will be asleep and this will be all over. She controls the shaking in her hand long enough to get the key in the door and open it. Climbs carefully into the passenger seat, locks the door after her. Safe at last. The other car has finally stopped screaming. Maybe she won't be arrested after all. Secretary Screws Boss, Smashes Up Saab. Drunken Doris Dents Daimler. Auto Attack By Tipsy Typist. With the headlines of her evening flashing up in lurid colours behind her eyes, she curls up in the front of her boss's car and falls asleep.

When she wakes up she is cold. She has a crick neck. She is unsure where she is. Oh. That's right. She laughs croakily. It is kind of funny. It's going to be one of those things, she can tell already — flashes of memory will come unbidden to her in the street, at work, in the shower — those cringey moments that make you grit your teeth or suck in your breath or rub your hand across your forehead as if to erase what's there. There are a lot of involuntary blushes stored up from this one. She shakes her head. It's getting light outside. Grey misty light. She looks up at the hotel, sees a couple of lights on. Wonders if he's awake yet. Awake, guilty, going through his stuff for the meeting. Or perhaps he's not guilty. Perhaps he's having a shower, planning to knock on her door and invite her downstairs for breakfast. Yeah, likely story. The fuck wouldn't even let her back in his room. Wanker. No, he'll be trying to pretend he hasn't got a hangover, trying not to think about last night, just get through the meeting and get back to his wife. Thinking, Yes! Probably punching the fucking air. He knows she can't afford repercussions at work. He's got away with it, the tinny bastard. A brief aberration and then everything back to his normal in-control I'm-so-powerful life. She's getting worked up now. The energy feels good. Her head's not that bad either. Could be still drunk. Starving.

Something snaps. That fuck. She's not going to go back up there, pretend nothing's happened, pour fucking coffee for the fucking meeting and take notes. Nuh. He can take his own bloody notes. She's taken enough notes to last a bloody lifetime. Shook enough hands, made enough tea, typed enough minutes. Probably sterile from spending so much time standing by a hot photocopier. Probably got sick building syndrome. Repetitive strain injury. Early Alzheimers, for all she knows. No more. Not going back. No way. What she might do instead doesn't seem to matter at this point. She'll think of something. The first thing she's got to do is get something to eat. Get out of the Godforsaken shit-heap and get a life. A hamburger as well. She rubs her face. Checks herself out in the rear-vision mirror. Not pretty. Mascara smudges under her eyes, greasy hair, waxy skin. Too bad. No more girly office eyeshadow for her. No more dress code. No more being nice to stupid jerks and stupider cows just because they're more senior than her and make more money.

Money. Damn. It's all back in her room. She's not going to risk going up there. It's not much, she can easily say goodbye to all that old junk. The office clothes she won't be needing any more. The so-called notes she's prepared for the so-called meeting she's supposed to attend, as if she's something more than a glorified secretary. Her reputation. She grins, looking around at the car. Seems like a fair swap. Shoves her hand down the back of the seat till she finds enough coins for breakfast. It's true, she thinks, remembering a conversation from last night, she really hasn't done enough travelling. What a good time to start. She slides over into the driver's seat. Can she handle one of these big cars? A breeze. The key slots into the ignition with a satisfying click. Pulling out of the car park on to the main road, she runs over her options.

Acknowledgments

The publishers are grateful to the authors and publishers concerned for their permission to reprint the stories in this collection:

Frank Sargeson, 'A Piece of Yellow Soap', 'A Great Day', 'An Affair of the Heart' and 'The Hole That Jack Dug' from *The Stories of Frank Sargeson* (Penguin Books, 1982).

Maurice Duggan, 'Along Rideout Road that Summer' and 'The Departure', from *Collected Stories* (AUP/OUP, 1981) used by permission of Barbara Duggan.

Janet Frame, 'A Sense of Proportion' and 'The Bath', from *You Are Now Entering the Human Heart*, (VUP, 1981) and 'An Incident in Mid Ocean' and 'How Can I Get in Touch with Persia?' from *The Reservoir* (George Brazillier, 1993) used by permission of Curtis Brown (Australia) Pty Ltd, Sydney.

Maurice Shadbolt, 'River, Girl and Onion', from *The New Zealanders* (David Ling, 1993).

CK Stead, 'Class, Race, Gender: A Post-Colonial Yarn', from *The Blind Blonde with Candles in Her Hair* (Penguin Books, 1998).

Russell Haley, 'Dutch Mosquito', from *The Sauna Bath Mysteries and Other Stories* (The Mandrake Root, 1978).

Vincent O'Sullivan, 'Putting Bob Down', from *Palms and Minarets* (VUP, 1992).

Patricia Grace, 'The Lamp', from *Collected Stories* (Penguin Books, 1987).

Patricia Grace, 'Journey' and 'It Used to be Green Once', from *Collected Stories* (Penguin Books, 1987) used by permission of Addison Wesley Longman.

Dame Fiona Kidman, 'Dry Rot', from *Mrs Dixon and Friend* (Random House, 1982) used by permission of Fiona Kidman and Richards Literary Agency.

Owen Marshall, 'The Paper Parcel', from *The Ace of Diamonds Gang* (McIndoe, 1993) and 'A View of Our Country' and 'The Rule of Jenny Pen' from *Tomorrow We Save the Orphans* (McIndoe, 1992) used by permission of Owen Marshall.

Sue McCauley, 'Mia Culpa', from *It Could Be You* (Random House (NZ) Ltd, 1997) used by permission of Glenys Bean.

Elizabeth Smither, 'The Mathematics of Jane Austen', from *The Mathematics of Jane Austen* (Godwit, 1997).

Michael Morrissey, 'What's in a Name?' (Listener, January 2, 1999), 'Beethoven's Ears' from *Octavia's Last Invention* (Brick Row, 1991) and 'Hitler's French Letter' (Listener, October 15, 1994).

Sheridan Keith, 'Pleasuring Mr White' from *Animal Passions* (New Women's Press, 1992) and 'Dancing in the Dark' from *Shallow are the Smiles at the Supermarket* (New Women's Press, 1991) used by permission of Sheridan Keith.

Shonagh Koea, 'The Dancing Master', from *The Woman Who Never Went Home* (Penguin Books, 1987) used by permission of Random House (NZ) Ltd.

Witi Ihimaera, 'The House with Sugarbag Windows' and 'The Kids Downstairs', from *The New Net Goes Fishing*, (Heinemann, 1977) used by permission of Reed Publishing NZ.

Peter Wells, 'Perrin and the Fallen Angel' from *Dangerous Desires* (Reed, 1991) and 'A Casual Kind of Incest' from *The Duration of a Kiss* (Reed, 1994) used by permission of Peter Wells.

John Cranna, 'Archaeology' and 'Visitors', from *Visitors* (Reed, 1989).

Lloyd Jones, 'This Place We Call Home' and 'Me, Clarke and Wilder', from *Swimming to Australia* (VUP, 1991).

Emily Perkins, 'The Shared Experience' and 'Barking', from *Not Her Real Name* (Macmillan Publishers, 1996).